TAOS

In the year 1680, the Pueblo Indians, massing their tribes, rose up against their Spanish overlords, slaughtered four hundred men, women and children, overthrew the Franciscan Missions and in a few days destroyed the administrative, religious and economic edifice created by the Spaniards over the last hundred years. Here is horror and brutality, saintliness and treachery, blind lust and tenderness, unspeakable cruelty and unsurpassed courage, for from this little known revolt has been recreated a story of epic dimensions with a grandeur as savage and contrasts as violent as the country and the period in which it is set.

The vast province of Nuevo Mexico, sparsely marked with garrisons, haciendas and missions, symbolized the declining power of the Spanish Empire. It needed but one unifying force to unite the Indian tribes, and this it found in Popé, the medicine man of sacred Taos, who commanded obedience but was incapable of seeing past the hour of victory. Against him, in the Villa Real de Santa Fe, Don Antonio Otermin, Governor and Captain General, could pit greater strategic skill, years of experience and the cold light of reason.

The struggle, characterized by the bitterness and compassion of Indian and Spaniard alike, touches a variety of sharply etched characters: the young Indian cacique in love with Manuela, daughter of an exiled grandee; Fray Julio, a Franciscan who put the fleshy comforts of a Spanish woman and the opulence of his Mission before God, until the crucifixion of a fellow brother brought him to sanctity; the mistress of Don Alonso Garcia, who killed and, in her fiercely loyal love, was herself killed; the Governor, whose ill-omened relationship with the widow Maria grew into a love out of character and breaking convention.

Pillage, rape, attack and siege: relentlessly the reader is forced to take part in terrifying massacres and, finally, the gruelling Jornada del Muerto, the long retreat where inexorably each participant reveals himself for what he is. The word 'epic' has been used —and justly so. For this is indeed a tale of men and women who, by accident of time and birth and circumstance, become superhuman in the endurance of their minds and bodies.

By the same author

BEHIND THE LINES (Editor)

TAOS

IRWIN R. BLACKER

CASSELL · LONDON

CASSELL & COMPANY LTD.
35 Red Lion Square · London WC1
and at Melbourne · Sydney · Toronto · Cape Town
Johannesburg · Auckland

Printed in Great Britain by
Lowe & Brydone (Printers) Ltd.,
London, N.W.10
F.360

For My Daughter Hope

who knows that the camino real
to understanding between peoples
begins at both ends.

ACKNOWLEDGMENTS

There are many persons to whom I owe thanks for their help in the writing of this book. Among them are the librarians and scholars of Albuquerque and Santa Fe who were helpful to a stranger; Professor Harold R. Jolliffe of Michigan State University; Dean Russell F. W. Smith of New York University; Mr. Frank DeFelitta, Mr. Harry M. Rosen, Mr. Bruce Nims, and Dr. Murray Port of New York City; Mrs. Nancy Lane of Santa Fe; Mr. Cleofas Calleros of El Paso; Professor Frank D. Reeve of the University of New Mexico who read the manuscript and made suggestions; the directors and staff of the MacDowell Colony; the staff of the World Publishing Company; and most especially to the two persons without whose help this book could not have been written—William Targ, my editor, and my wife, both of whom advised, encouraged, and were patient.

Verse by Dante Alighieri is reprinted from John Ciardi's translation of *The Inferno*, copyright 1954 by John Ciardi, published in a Mentor edition by the New American Library of Literature, Inc. The quotation on page 65 is from *Public Speech*, poems by Archibald MacLeish, copyright 1936 by Archibald MacLeish. Reprinted by permission of Rinehart & Company, Inc.

BOOK I

The time has come when, with tears in my eyes and deep sorrow in my heart, I commence to give an account of the lamentable tragedy, such as has never before happened in the world, which has occurred in this miserable kingdom and holy custodia, His divine Majesty having thus permitted it because of my grievous sins.   ANTONIO DE OTERMÍN

THE
PROVINCE
OF
NUEVO
MEXICO

✛

1680

✛

✛

ZUNI

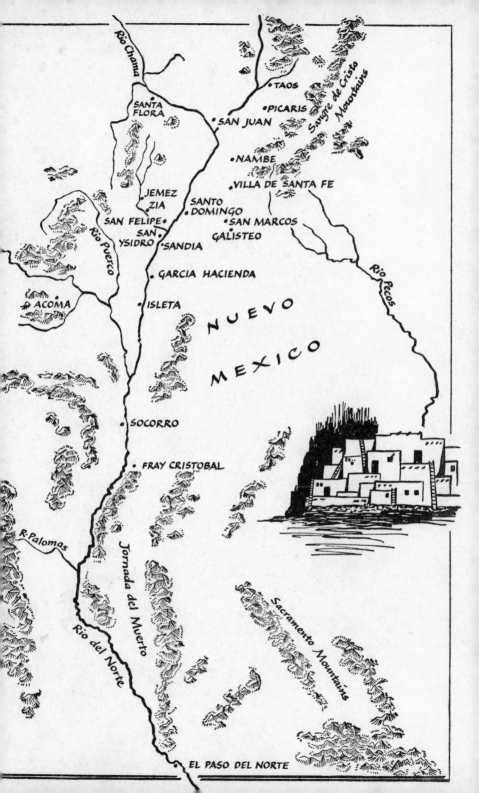

1

TWO young Indians paused at the edge of the Rio del Norte and bellied down to drink. The night sky was dark above them and there was a small ring of brightness about the moon. A breeze rubbed against the cotton-wood leaves and then there was silence. The youths rose to their feet and trotted eastward along the bed of a rock-lined arroyo. Several hundred paces farther on they heard a sound and slipped into a shadow. As four men emerged from the darkness ahead, the runners moved slowly toward them.

One of the strangers spoke first. "You are of Taos?"

The taller of the youths answered. "We have been sent by the medicine man Popé of San Juan who now lives at Taos."

The stranger who had spoken approached. He was a broad man and even in the faint light the runners could see the lines of age that marked his face.

"We have agreed to join with Popé."

The shorter of the runners slipped a rope from about his waist and held it out. "Popé has sent this to the cacique and principales of your pueblo."

The older man accepted the rope and held it up with one hand as he counted the knots in it with the fingers of the other. "Nine knots."

The taller runner explained quickly. "Untie one knot each night. When there are no longer any knots, you will destroy the Whitefaces of your pueblo. Then your warriors will march to the palacio of the Governor."

The older man wrapped the rope about his waist as he asked, "And the other pueblos?"

"It will be as the medicine man has said. You will be met by the warriors of the other pueblos at the Villa de Santa Fe of the Whitefaces."

There was silence for a time and then the old man nodded. "We will do as Popé has asked."

"We shall tell him," the youth said as he and his companion turned west and trotted back down the arroyo towards the rio from which they had come.

To the north other runners emerged small under the sky. They came up from the kiva of Taos, the dark chamber beneath the earth that was the tem-ple of the ancient gods of the puebleños when they were akin to the Sun Father, the Earth Mother, and the Corn, the winged serpent that is the thun-derbird and the masked gods. The youths scattered in pairs over the land of the Indian nations of the pueblo kingdom: they ran south to the Tewas, the Queres, and the Tiwas, and eastward to the Pecos; they turned westward to the Jemez nation and farther to the Zuñi. The young men ran from pueblo to pueblo as did their fellows who had departed earlier. They used the old trails that linked the adobe kingdom, avoiding the dusty Camino Real of their conquerors. Their lean faces were square with large noses, their hair black, tied with red bandos. Closer by certain customs to the Aztecs of Mexico than to their plains neighbours, they were the worshippers of the winged serpent and the myth of Montezuma brought north through the pass by the conquistadores. Wearing cotton loincloths or pantalones or leggings, they trotted over the burnt ground of Nuevo Mexico.

From the night sky—the province shaped like an arrowhead spreads from Taos Mountain to the pass by the Rio del Norte one hundred and fifty meandering leagues south. And between: the valleys are sparse green; the hills bare; the mountains scattered; the dunes high, topped with dust devils and old bones; the lava beds black over red clay edging to the butte's bottom, torn by arroyos smelling of past rains, pebbled, shadowed by mesas—the unfinished hills breaking the sky. And to the far west as seen from above lies the pueblo of the high rock—Acoma, built for protection from the Apache and scarred by the guns of the conquistador, and still farther west where the landscape is torn with the cañon of the Colorado while the earth between is armed with broken rock and cactus. The Rio Pecos trims the land eastward. Here, too, are Dark Cañon and the bluffs of Llano Estacado. And beyond lies the rio called Kansas where the seekers emerged northward, failed to find gold and were martyred or frightened or wearied and returned or did not return. And to the south: el jornada del muerto—the journey of death over the dry place where the scorpion lives and the snake, where the owl hunts at night and the coyote wanders. Between, flowing south, is the Rio del Norte of the Spaniards, P'osoge of the puebleños. And beside it is the Camino Real—the royal road, the king's highway of the seekers and the settlers, of the conquistadores and the missionaries who made the long trek for silver and souls before Oñate of Zacatecas came with the colonists and the cattle. He who in 1598 brought the one hundred and thirty men with their wives and their children, their arms, their ploughs, the seven thousand horses and mules, the oxen and beef cattle, the sheep and the pigs, the three miles of caravan straggling north over the deserted plains marked by scattered mountains, barren, watered only by scarce rains, few springs and fewer rios, northward across the ford at the pass of the Rio del Norte, moving slowly between the rio and the Sierra del Olvido bringing civilization and Christ into the new province, northward to the land drained by the Rio del Norte which is desert, which is forest, which is mountains. Mostly it is a gaunt land of creosote bush, popotilla, cactus, agave, bunch grass, and yucca. The prairie dog and the antelope share it with the horned toad, the bannertail rat, and the snake. The cottonwood grows by the rio as does the willow, and the pine—the piñon —in the hills. Spruce, aspen, juniper, and fir forest the north, tall against the mountains, covering the slopes and marking the sky with their tips. Above it all are the hawk, the eagle, and the butcherbird, while the horizon is always the sierra—jagged-toothed and harsh, or distant and dark.

The messengers who carried the knotted rope of Popé turned south toward the capital of their conquerors. They sped through the night. Birds flushed upward as they passed. Game avoided their trail and the dust they raised fell back unseen in the darkness.

2

IN the dark past there had been a great storm. The rain fell for many years, and the Virgin Mother of the Sun and the Moon was tossed about in the angry waters of the deluge. Finally, she came to rest on the loma where she gave birth to the twin gods of war. Here, years later, the Indians who called themselves the People built a village named Kwa-po-ge, and here a thousand years later the conquistadores decided to build the Casas Reales. The plans were approved by the Viceroy in Ciudad Mexico and the King in Madrid, and in 1610 the Villa de Santa Fe—the town of the Holy Faith—was built. The site was defensible. It was also cooler than most in the wild country above el Paso del Norte.

Seventy years passed, and the summer of 1680 was one of the driest and warmest in the memory of the People who lived as slaves in Barrio Analco —the Little-Suburb-Across-The-Water from the Villa de Santa Fe. The August night was clear, and the People sat about in front of their adobe houses trying to catch what little breeze came off the rio. They waited for the tolling of the bell from the Villa and for the runners they knew would be coming from the hills to the north where the future had been predicted in the dark kiva of Taos.

On the other side of the rio all was quiet in the plaza mayor which was the centre of this small outpost of Spanish empire. A lone soldier rested before the Governor's palacio watching a brown cat meander, as though addled by the heat of the now dead day, toward the Quarters of the Women —la casa de puta—across the dusty grey area. The guard turned his head as the bell tolled from the tower of the church of the Immaculate Conception on the left side of the plaza. He looked up at the steeple which rose above the other buildings of the small square. In another hour he would hear the bell of the chapel of San Miguel, the slaves' church across the rio, named in honour of the dragon-slaying saint. And then he would be relieved from duty to drift into the shop at the far end of the square, where, after a small bottle of freshly crushed vino, he, like the cat, would wander across the plaza to the casa de puta. He turned to the west as he heard laughter emerge from the casa where his campañeros and the women were playing, and then to the watchtower on Atalaya Hill where another sentry was stationed to look over the town. This man had a clear view of the Sangre de Cristo Mountains to the north and east and could see the farm lands stretching south to the rio itself and beyond to the forests.

The bell ceased to toll and the soldier seated himself on the portico before the palacio. The ground was still warm from the flushed sun which
had hung over the Villa de Santa Fe through the long day. He rested his
heavy harquebus against the wall and his back against a post and closed
his eyes.

Inside the palacio, Don Antonio de Otermín, the Governor and Captain
General of the province, rose from behind the board plank table where he
had been working. Wearing only a white linen shirt and black velvet pantalones, he relaxed from the hundred small paper tasks which fell upon an
administrator in the carefully organized empire of España. A short man,
solidly built for his years, he moved with the quick and unexpected agility
that came after a lifetime of military service.

He rubbed his short grey beard with the back of his hand, pinched out the
candle and strode through the palacio. He was tired. The day had been
warm and the air was close. A guard wearily pulled himself to attention
outside the Governor's office and Don Antonio paused to inspect the
man's uniform. Sloppy, wrinkled, boots dusty. For a moment the Capatin
General considered a reprimand. Then without warning, he struck the
sentry sharply across the face with the back of his hand. The gesture
was as much in anger at the disrespect he felt the man's appearance was
to him as it was a stroke in protest against the situation in which he
found himself.

"Your boots. Your uniform," he snorted in disgust. "You represent your
king. You are a Spaniard. Act like one. You are a soldado. Look like one."
And he walked away, not certain that a soldier such as this would learn
from the lesson, but at least satisfied that he himself felt better for having
given it.

With quick strides he crossed through the darkened palacio, pausing
only once to plant the mark of his boot heel in the dirt floor. This was
part of the reason for his anger and disgust and he knew it as he entered
his sleeping room, lighted a candle and looked around. He was weary
of this dirty casa real itself with its earthen floors, its adobe ceilings streaked
with rain and half a century of collected dust. Two years within these
dirty walls and they had become less walls to him than the symbols of
authority that had never been fully established.

Dropping himself down on the large four-poster bed, he started to
unlace his shirt, only to pause at a hesitant knock on the door. He cursed
softly to himself as he rose. "What is it?"

"The Indians, Excellency."

He rubbed his beard as he tried to understand what the answer was
supposed to mean. Quickly drawing the laces of the shirt together again,
he flung the door open.

"What Indians?"

It was a soldier, tunica open, one hand resting on the sash about his
heavy waist. "The Indians, Excellency, the ones that will go to the mines."

Otermín looked at the man for a moment, wondered what could possibly
be wrong with the prisoners, decided not to ask, and walked past the

sentry to the compound behind the palacio. Standing in the open area inside the walls that made up his small presidio, the Governor surveyed the sullen faces of the Indians in the dark. There were fifteen of them, eight Apaches from the west and seven puebleños from Acoma. Their chains seemed secure. There was no sound from them. Each was sprawled on the ground near the post to which he was chained. Then Don Antonio realized they were staring at something beside him. Turning, he saw the swaying figure hanging from a beam. The copper body was limp. The black hair hung loose about the twisted face. Otermín closed his eyes against the sight. When he opened them again, he saw the dark eyes in the dark faces of the Indians. He knew they were accusing him of something. In disgust at the sight of the suicide, he ordered the sentry who had followed him out into the night, "Cut him down. Bury him in the morning." Then he slowly walked back into the palacio.

The rooms were empty and he was alone as he slumped into a high-backed chair. He was tired and he wished he were asleep. Now there was another death. He would have to mention it in the records. It would be expected. His head turned from side to side. He was rejecting the whole idea of the death. He was rejecting the idea of being a captain general with ten soldiers to guard his capital, to hold an outpost of empire with only the empty titles which were his and which he knew would never turn back an enemy. And was that dead Indian swaying in the night an enemy? He was not certain. The Apaches were enemies. In recent years España had lost five pueblos to the Apaches, five pueblos without a fight, five communities where missions had been established. But that Indian dangling by his own sash was a puebleño, a Christian Indian, one of those souls he had come to protect.

He looked up to see the stocky figure of Fray Pedro Martínez before him.

"I have been in the chapel, Excellency, " the padre explained.

Otermín nodded. He knew this Brother, the assistant to the Fray Custodio, one of the more eager young missionaries.

"There is a suicide out there, Padre," the Governor informed the clergyman. "Hanged himself."

Fray Pedro made the sign of the cross. "It is cursed."

"I know," wondering how much the padre thought was really cursed. "He is from Acoma. Would not pay his tribute or work." There was silence for a moment. "I was sending him with the Apaches to the silver mines in Mexico when the supply train returned next month." And when he was done, the Governor wondered how much he had really explained.

The padre nodded. The concern of this governor for his charges interested the young man. Most of the officials in the province did not seem to care what happened to the Indians. And Fray Pedro was never quite certain if this grandee from España really cared what happened to his charges or was more concerned with the complications they created for him.

"The man will not be permitted burial in holy ground."

The Governor nodded. The padre's statement was correct. Otermín

changed the subject. "You were going to have a count of the Spanish in the
Villa?"

The shaven head bobbed in agreement as the young man started to
give his report. "There are three hundred and twenty-eight females. Thirty-
two of them from Mexico and ten soldados and . . ."

"Tears of the Virgin! How many Spanish are there, Padre?" Then the
Governor knew he should not have shown his impatience. "I am sorry.
Will you just tell me how many? Tomorrow we can list those born here—
the Creoles, and those born in España—the peninsulars. But for tonight . . ."

Fray Pedro's head bobbed again. "Five hundred, Excellency." He knew
this Governor well enough now not to add the fourteen others. Five
hundred would suffice for his concerns of the moment. The padre wondered
what those concerns were, however, and was tempted to ask. But the
Governor rose to his feet and walked off with barely a nod. The broad-
shouldered Franciscan looked after him, angry at the arrogance of it, taking
the action personally, but refraining from comment. In time he might
need the Governor's assistance. There was no sense in clashing with him
now. Instead, the padre made his way through the dark rooms to the
small chapel tower of the palacio. Here he could be alone. In the mission
church across the way there was usually someone who wanted his attention.
It was night now and he wanted to be alone.

In his sleeping quarters, Governor Otermín was mulling over the figure
the padre had given him. Five hundred. Ten under arms. For the second
time he dropped onto the large four-poster bed. He stared at the canopy
spread over him and the carved posts themselves; he wanted to laugh.
What kind of a vain man or fool woman had dragged this clumsy, ornate
bed in pieces on the backs of mules over the mountains all the way from
Ciudad Mexico, dragged it to adorn this casa real—this royal mansion
that no longer even had doors?

Don Antonio snorted. The symbols of empire were more a burden than
an asset when they were empty, and here in Nuevo Mexico the trappings
of his office were meaningless. After two years as governor and captain
general, his cynicism seemed justified and, though he was reluctant to
admit it, he was angry with himself and disgusted with what the years had left
him. Though he had never said it aloud and would never permit another
to say it, he was a failure. Sometime, somewhere, his career had collapsed,
and for hundreds of nights, lying on this bed, staring at the canopy above
him, he wondered when things had begun to go wrong. Tonight he
wondered why.

All the long tours of duty in dirty little outposts, all the long months
of fighting the English through the Isthmus of Panama, all the wearying
years of trying to maintain his honour in the corrupt cities of decaying
elegance had led to this capital held by only ten, ill-trained soldiers. This
was the failure, the absence of real authority in the face of responsibility.

He rose from the bed and crossed over to the window and stared out
into the night. His disgust for himself was almost complete. Another night
and no sleep. Another night and the loneliness. It seemed so long since

he had not been lonely. He saw the two Indian runners cross the open plaza, knew that they had run a long way and wondered why. Well, he shrugged, if it was news for him he would hear of it soon enough. It seemed that almost all the news these days was bad. He wished now that he could sleep, because then he would not be going over it and over it as he knew he would. But he could not sleep, and so, as he did almost every night, he tried to understand what was going wrong in the province and why.

And as always, he began in despair. The politics of the situation were all wrong, and there was nothing he could do about it, nothing he could say that would change anything. He was not certain the Viceroy, playing with his mistresses in Ciudad Mexico, could have changed anything even if he had wished. But he had not wished. He had abdicated his responsibilities for Nuevo Mexico and left them to the Governor to be met at a minimum of expense—as every aviso read, "*at the least possible cost.*"

Don Antonio spat through the open window and looked about his room which had become a symbol for him of what was wrong with the province. It was old. It was tired. It was dirty. It was empty. As there was nothing for him here, so there was nothing for España in this province. The old dreams of gold, of the Seven Cities of Cíbola, which had brought so many ill-fated expeditions north, so many adventurers to their unmarked graves— the old dreams—they had faded in the bright light of the braising sun. And with the dreams went any hope of the province adding an extra peso to the strongboxes of the King. There was no gold here. There was no treasure, though some fools continued to seek it until they died of fever or thirst. Otermín closed his eyes against the shabbiness of the room. The only treasure here was a little turquoise mined in the hills, and this was not sufficient even to pay for the few soldados. The Governor rested his head against the sill as he recalled how he had first checked the records and accounts of the province, and of his initial astonishment when he discovered that there was more brought into Nuevo Mexico each jornado from the south than was ever taken out of it.

He grasped the lighted candlestick and held it in his hand as he stared at himself in the polished metal mirror. His high cheekbones threw shadows across his cheeks. There was grey in his beard, but he would not admit that he was old. There were older governors in the provinces than he. But still he wondered why he was here, why this place so far from home, so far from where he had dreamed his career would end, and now he knew this was the end of it.

The candle flickered in his hand and wax ran down his fingers. He looked at them and set the taper on the sill. Thoughtfully, he gnawed the wax off his knuckles as he turned his attention once again to the empty plaza that stretched beyond the window. There was one thing he could say in his own behalf, one justification he could make: the padres knew why España held this province. Though the cost came out of the pockets of the State, the profits derived would redound to the Church. And, perhaps, he consoled himself, this was justification enough.

Anyway, it was one consolation. The province was maintained for the

Church, was maintained to permit the good Brothers to make their conversions, save the souls all agreed must be saved. This much satisfied him, but he knew it was not the whole picture and that when he was done with telling himself this fable, he would be troubled by the façade placed on the whole of it, the façade that made him, Don Antonio de Otermín, a governor and captain general.

Standing by the window, he cursed himself now for not having sought out Juan Treviño and discussed the assignment with him when it had first been offered two years before. Treviño had just returned from the Villa de Santa Fe and knew what the province was, what it meant—and, more, what it did not mean—to be Governor here, for he had held the office himself. Perhaps, after talking to Treviño, Don Antonio thought he might not have accepted the assignment. He shrugged and walked out of the low-ceilinged room. He had had no choice. Refusal would have meant retirement and being under fifty and without money, he knew he would have accepted regardless of anything Treviño might have said. There were so few illusions he could find to wrap his loneliness in.

He stepped out into the night air and stared for a moment at the dark sky and the ring of light about the moon. It was cooler here than inside and he turned to speak to the guard. The dishevelled guard was asleep under the colonnade, an harquebus leaning against the wall beside him. The Governor's face set in anger and disgust. This was the sum of all he had been thinking about. This sleeping sentry. Otermín rubbed the back of his hand against his beard as he thought how in another time and another place he would have hanged the man for sleeping thus. Then he thought of the Indian hanging in the compound behind the building, and his hand fell away.

He walked through the building again, to his office. There he lighted another candle. And as he slipped into the chair behind the plank table he wished that he could sleep. It was going to be another long night of drifting through these empty rooms alone, another night of forcing himself to face these papers stacked before him. He set a square palm down on the stack. Here were all the complicated documents which kept the province together, all the complicated details which flowed from him to the Viceroy and thence to Madrid and even to the King himself. Don Antonio understood the need for these papers. Information was the life-blood of empire, the basis of judgments, good or bad; but judgments at least made with knowledge. Perhaps the decisions would not meet his own approval, but that was not important because he knew that there were always considerations which he would know nothing about. But when decisions were made concerning his own province, they were at least made with some understanding of his position. He closed his hand and turned it over slowly so that the back of his fist rested on the papers as he realized that this small satisfaction was as much as any clerk would expect. When had he started to settle for so little?

The document on top of the stack held his attention and he took it in hand as he settled again in the high-backed chair that was another sign of his authority.

"From Don Antonio de Otermín, Governor and Captain General of Nuevo Mexico, and presidio for His Majesty, etc. . . . Whereas in virtue of our royal order, I hereby direct Maestre de Campo Pedro de Leiva to depart to el Paso del Norte accompanied by twenty-seven soldados, properly mounted and equipped to serve as escort to the Procurador Francisco de Ayeta, en route for this casa real with the supply train from Ciudad Mexico . . ."

Twenty-seven men. A token force in the event of trouble, but a symbol that the State was paying its proper respects to the Church. Suddenly, Don Antonio began to laugh. The soldier he had slapped, the soldier who had been unable to explain to him that an Indian had hanged himself, and the soldier who was now asleep beside the main entrance of the palacio—these three men constituted one third of his total force.

He dropped the document to the desk and picked up the one below it—his report on the need for further support and the inadequacy of his forces. His statement would go to the Viceroy with Fray Francisco de Ayeta. But there was no apology here. As Governor he would assume no responsibility for the failure, though he knew that the clerks of the Viceroy would add his request to the records as a mark against his administration. He wondered for a moment about the files concerning himself and those concerning this province. They both probably read as a history of failure. Too much expected and too little delivered. Somehow, for a moment, he felt an unexpected kinship to this command of his. The paper fell back on the stack and he stared at all of the documents. Another year and he would be done with them, another year and he would find the money to retire. This much he had earned for himself. But what would it be? More lonely nights. Then he knew he wanted a woman, and knew, too, that he was not seeking one. For Don Antonio had little respect for the commander who crawled into the closest bed or reached for the nearest native wench. It was difficult enough to maintain the hollow symbol of authority without adding the portrait of the decadent philanderer. And besides, the story always took on strange proportions when the wencher was the father of two and the grandfather of six.

Otermín poured himself a brandy from a decanter on the table and slowly turned the goblet in his hand. The coat of arms was there—the last symbol to remind him that his family had once held power and known office in España, that his father's father had commanded armies, and that his father had also been a captain general. He traced the family code on the worn metal: *While Life Remains.* Somehow he had the bitter feeling that it had remained too long. Maybe it would have been different if his wife had lived. Maybe they would have found their way back to España, to the small villa that had been her father's, where their daughter now lived with her cousin-husband and their children. But his wife had not survived the fevers of Cuba. In silent tribute to the woman he had married, Don Antonio rose from his seat, lifted his goblet, and drank alone. He was willing now to admit to himself that he was never going back to España. He did not know when he had made this decision, but he accepted it. Any return would mean facing his classmates who had expected so much of him and who would recognize how meaningless his career had been when they heard that he had finished it as the Governor and Captain General of Nuevo Mexico. They would know how empty titles were when associated with this tragic land. He twirled the goblet in his hand. Perhaps there would be a place for him in Ciudad Mexico, a place where he might teach the sons of some silver-digging hidalgo what it meant to be a grandee and an officer. At least there he would be near his own son who was a captain in the Viceroy's guard and near, too, to his three grandchildren who boasted about the old man who ruled all the land above el Paso del Norte.

With an angry motion Otermín pushed the papers from him and emptied his goblet. *Ruled*. He crossed the room and stood over a box, steel-strapped and carved, that rested in the corner. Here was the power. In this box were the land grants of the kings of España from Philip III to Carlos the Idiot. Here was the real power, and none of it was his. Here, in these land grants lay power, in the hands of the smaller holders—the hacendados and estancieros. Don Antonio knew his authority was like that of a medieval king whose nobles held fiefdoms. Carlos the Idiot had power: What the Crown had granted the Crown could take away. But the King was in Madrid, and only the Viceroy could act directly in his behalf.

Ruled. Otermín laughed cynically and set the goblet down on the table and pinched out the candle. He was not going to do any more work no matter how long the night became. Tomorrow he would sit with Fray Pedro and listen to him break down the list of Spaniards in the capital. It would be correct, as the young padre was always correct. He might make a good Fray Custodio. He had ambitions for the post. And as he left his office, Don Antonio smiled to himself. The good Brother confessed those ambitions on all occasions as though the confession lessened the sin of ambition. As he buttoned his tunica and slipped his baldric over his shoulder, the Governor wondered if there was not actually some method in the young man's actions. The confession served notice on all that the padre wanted promotion and even pointed to the post he sought.

The Governor shrugged. The promotions of the clergy were a Church problem and those of the State were enough for Don Antonio on a night like this. He half drew his sabre to see how easily it slipped from its scabbard as he stood for a moment at the entrance of the palacio. The sleeping sentry had shifted his position and knocked the harquebus to the ground. It had failed to fire, and the Governor knelt down and picked it up. The weapon was over-ornate, as were most of those that wandered almost useless, to the frontier posts. It was nearly a half-century old and would offer no more accuracy than a badly aimed crossbow. Don Antonio flipped the pan open, saw that it was empty, and set it down. In the morning he would deliver himself of a lecture on preparedness. The harquebus would be as unserviceable then as it was now and would be a meaningful symbol.

The night sky fascinated him as he stood with his hands on his hips and his head thrown back. He knew he was not going to sleep for a long time and he knew, too, why he had put on his tunica. Over in the officers' quarters

Ismael Pando would still be awake. Together they would have a drink and the Governor would listen to the old man's lies about Nuevo Mexico and perhaps try to understand why a man like Pando had made a career of a place like this.

Otermín crossed the deserted plaza mayor and paused as he listened to the drunken laughter of a woman coming from the casa de puta. He had heard the same laughter on three continents and knew that it always followed a soldier. It was as much a part of the life of the lonely men as the crash of sword against helmet, of harquebus, or the battle cry, "*Por Rey y Santiago.*" The casas de putas of the world had not come up for discussion in the Academia de Madrid any more than the years of loneliness to which they were related.

He entered the Officers' Quarters and walked down the clean corridor to the room of Maestre de Campo Ismael Pando. And as he passed the many doors, he realized again that there were the quarters, if not the tropas, to protect his capital.

Before the door of the old soldier, he stopped and knocked twice. Inside the room Maestre de Campo Pando was seated near the narrow window with a drink in his hand. He wore only his pantalones, and the white hair of his broad, dark chest was exposed to what little breeze there was.

At the sound of the knock the old soldier set down his drink of rum and walked over to the door in his bare feet. He came quickly to attention when he saw who his visitor was and, at the head-shake of the Governor, stood at ease. A few minutes later both of them were relaxed. The Governor was seated on the edge of the old man's bed and the Maestre de Campo had returned to his chair by the window. They each held a drink now from an amphora of rum made in the Indies.

The Governor watched his Maestre de Campo. There were those in the service of His Majesty who would have criticized his having come to the barracks. There were those who would have questioned his having come to visit a junior officer rather than sending for him. But Don Antonio had learned over the years that what he needed most on any assignment was a man he could depend upon, and this came best through the simple gestures of respect and friendship.

Ismael Pando was the man he had selected in all of the Villa. The ex-sergeant-major was the oldest soldier in the armies of His Majesty, Carlos II of España. He was certainly the oldest Maestre de Campo as well as the only man in uniform who had been born in the province and had never left its borders, had never even crossed the rio to the hills south of el Paso del Norte. The fact that there was no record of his holding a commission in His Majesty's army was unknown to him, and Don Antonio, who had made the appointment only the year before, thought this was best for all concerned.

Don Antonio realized there was a loyalty to God, King, and Country in this simple soldier that could only have been found in a colonial who had never seen the disillusioning sights of a decaying Mexico or the corruption of the great civil service that administered an empire for the gold it yielded, the moneys that flowed into the pockets of the important and the unimportant.

Only an old officer like Don Antonio could appreciate how completely uncorrupted his lieutenant was. He did not even know which troopers paid their officers for the rights to an extra furlough or the privilege of bringing an Indian wench into the enlisted quarters to keep their beds neat and warm. He did not know which of the padres kept mistresses and which of the Indians paid less than their annual vara of cloth and bushel of corn in forfeit to support the encominderos who failed so completely to protect them.

But there were things which Ismael Pando did know and which Governor Otermín and his predecessors had come to respect.

Sitting in the small room that was now the only home of the old soldier, the Governor listened as the Maestre de Campo talked. He could tell that the older man was proud to be paid this visit and that he was embroidering his tale a bit here and there to make it worth the while of the Governor who had known the faraway places of Cuba, Ecuador, Peru, and glory to God, even the homeland of España itself.

Ismael Pando had trouble remembering what he had already told his superior in the past, and so he just rambled on, spinning the usual cross between fact and legend. He paused only now and then to take a sip of rum and wish there were just a bit of breeze and that the Governor were seated on the more comfortable chair instead of the edge of the bed.

"It was not always like this," he said. "I remember when I was a boy we had good years. Crops enough and the rain to grow them. Those were the building years. My father worked on the missions and my uncles helped him."

The Governor waited. He knew what would come next. It always did with its touch of pride.

"My mother was there then. One of the first women ever to make the jornada del muerto."

Then there was silence as they both thought for a moment.

"Then something went wrong. It happened a long time ago, but it went wrong. Maybe it was the governors, begging Your Excellency's pardon. Maybe it was the padres; when they began to quarrel, everything seemed to go wrong. It was little things, accusations that the governors were encouraging the Indians to the old religion, accusations that the padres were trying to gather riches on the sweat of the Indians.

"Then there was the governor who imprisoned a fray custodio and the fray custodio who excommunicated a governor."

The old soldier paused to think about this tragedy of power. "Perhaps it should not have gone so far, but when it did, the troubles began. That was almost twenty years ago."

He stopped speaking and sipped his rum and wondered just what the reasons had been: conflict with the Church or heavenly justice for Indians wantonly killed. The Lord God was a mysterious power to Ismael Pando, who had been raised between the religion of his Catholic parents and that of his Indian compañeros.

"The Apaches—the Strangers—came. They burned the crops, leaving the pueblos hungry. Martyred three padres. Fray Jaime was an old friend of mine. We had hunted rabbits together when we were boys. He was taller than I was, but somehow I always managed to run faster. My father commanded the escort that took him to Durango with the procurador when Jaime first went to the Seminary. He came back all educated and able to write and to quote the Holy Book. He was not like the rest of us born here. And then they killed him. Tied him to the back of a wild horse and set fire to his cassock and the horse took him off into the brush and all of it caught fire."

The old man was wandering, but the Governor was patient. Each man has the right to open his own sores, know his own wounds, and treat them as he sees fit.

"We waited about three years, what with the pueblos to be relocated and the reports to be written to Durango and Ciudad Mexico. Finally, I rode south with twenty men and just above La Cruces we were joined by a hundred men from Chihuahua. We rode north. Bows, lances, harquebuses, swords ready for battle. Two abreast we made a long line past the Cuballo Mountains, and in the shadow of Pajarito Sergeant-Major Juan de la García, who commanded the hundred, and I, who commanded the twenty, found a large rancheria with Indians minding the sheep the raiders had taken."

The flavour of the old campaign replaced the rum in his mouth and he savoured it for a moment.

"The sun was hot, you know how it is on a day in August. We spread the tropas out in a great semicircle, backing the Indians against the very rocks of Pajarito itself. Then we waited until dusk, when they were lazy and tired. We killed a hundred warriors and sent a hundred and twenty-five women and children to the mines in Chihuahua. Sergeant García was one tremendous fighter, but I have wondered sometimes if we really needed to kill the old men."

It was a question the Governor decided to ignore. The evening was warm and this was not a time for a discussion of the morality of empire. There was quiet in the room as the older man picked at the scar of a whitening wound that ran over his chest. Finally he continued:

"The trouble was not just the Indians. Five years later there was the Time of Hunger. Sometimes I hear the Indians call it the Season without Rain. All the same. It was a time without food. It began twelve years ago, in 1668. There should have been growing, and the new-bred lambs and young calves, and the leaves on the cottonwood should have sprung out along the rio. But instead there was just hot sun and the plants withered under the glare. The lambs all seemed to die at birthing. The black tongue clung to the back of a cow's mouth. By summer there was starvation in the pueblos.

"I remember watching the men fight over the food and the women and children die without fighting. By September we here in the Villa de Santa Fe were without food. Some men raided the pueblos where there was even less. They fought over the maize which should have been saved for the coming crop."

Pando rose from his chair by the window, crossed the room, and tipping the jug filled his mug and his guest's. He stared down at the short, stocky man who was his Governor and Captain General and realized that he, too, was a lonely old man. And he wondered what scars he carried, what tales he could tell. Then he set the amphora down in the corner and started talking as he walked back to his seat by the window. He looked only at the window as he talked now.

"Over four hundred died from what the Indians called the 'empty sickness' and another hundred from the grains of wheat and the leather straps from the harnesses which we wrapped in the brown leaves and cooked."

He said nothing about the Indian wife and the three children who had died. But Don Antonio knew the old soldier had lost his family during this time and had returned to live in the barracks. There were certain advantages in having the records of the province within easy reach, advantages one never discussed.

The old man talked on as though he had to get beyond this part of his tale.

"After the Year of Hunger came the pestilence, and by 1675 the Apaches were back again. There are those who say they had grown hungry on the plains. I do not know the reasons for their returning, but five years ago they attacked Senecu pueblo and martyred poor old Fray Alonso Gil da Avila."

The old man crossed himself and emptied the rum in his mug.

"This time we never rode after the Apaches. If we had withdrawn a hundred tropas from the pueblos, we would have left ourselves open to attack."

"From where?" The Governor was asking the question which had been bothering him for days.

Without answering, Pando rose again, and again filled his mug from the amphora in the corner. Was the answer the Apaches or the pueblos? Had they failed to ride five years before because they feared for the safety of the pueblos or the padres themselves? The old man who had been raised in Nuevo Mexico and thought he knew every one of its dubious turnings was not certain now. He had faith in the Indians, but somewhere things were askew. The times had changed since he was a boy. The Indians were restless with the restrictions and tithes and work levied on them.

He returned to the window and stood there with his back to the Governor and felt the hot breeze creep over him. The People. He would be living with the People today if his wife had survived. He loved them and they had accepted a son of the moon; and in his case they were happy that he had married a daughter of the sun. The People, as they so humbly called themselves, came to his mind as he heard the Governor repeat the question.

"You feared attack from where?"

"I have no ready answers, Excellency," he said, turning and facing his superior. He emptied his mug and took a piece of cotton and wiped the sweat from the white hairs on his chest.

"I am sorry, Governor," he apologized because he could not tell this peninsular—this man from España that what he really was beginning to fear was the restlessness of the puebleños themselves.

Don Antonio rose, clapped a hand on his compañero's arm. "It grows late, amigo. Tomorrow I would like to talk to the guards. They are getting lax."

And he left the room with the dark eyes of the Maestre de Campo looking after him.

The plaza mayor was empty when he entered it. He looked about and saw the lights were out all over the Villa. There was even silence in the casa de puta. He looked to the hills which backed the palacio to the north and east and wondered if the trouble would come in his time. The answer Ismael Pando had not given was clear enough. If he believed trouble was going to come from the Apaches, there would have been no hesitation; and so, whether he knew it or not, this ancient soldier had a feeling about the future, a feeling he could not voice because it involved the puebleños.

Otermín felt confident about the old man. The years had taken their toll of him, but while he waited for the long rest, he would give his last efforts for the Two Majesties as they saw their need of him.

Crossing the plaza, Otermín approached the entrance of the palacio. Two shadows blending in the darkness separated at the sound of his foot-steps. A different sentry was on guard now. Smelling of native whisky, he held a jug in one hand while his other rested on the shoulder of a woman. Sheepishly, he greeted the Governor with a casual nod.

Don Antonio started at the pair of them. He had never seen the woman before, but when she laughed softly in his face he knew he had heard her only a short time ago, for hers was the laughter from the portico of the casa da puta, the laughter that made him question the wisdom of celibacy and sainthood. From the dark eyes and the darker skin he took her for a mestiza—one of those born of the conqueror and the conquered. The laces of her bodice were loose and in the light of the disappearing moon he could make out the shape of her breasts. She made no effort to cover herself as she saw that he was staring at her. The back of his right hand rose to his beard as he slowly began to rub it. When the sentry pushed the wench farther into the darkness, Otermín reached down and took the amphora from the guard's hand.

"The next time you diddle on guard I will have both of you flogged."

Then he smashed the earthen jug at the whore's feet. She stood for a moment, screamed, and ran into the night. Don Antonio looked up at the sky and the faint light of the stars and felt more lonely than he had ever felt before, and for an instant he knew fear. Then he saw the cross above the mission and he straightened his shoulders, was again the Governor and Captain General as he watched the two Indians he had seen earlier in the evening cross the plaza. They were dressed only in loincloths and seemed to be carrying nothing more than a piece of rope. They were swallowed by the night as they ran west.

Then he turned and saw someone climb the steps of the mission—Fray Pedro. It was a late hour for the padre to be walking.

He turned and stared at the rigid figure of the guard. Two buttons of his tunic were open at the collar, and his boots were covered with the dust of the plaza. The Governor shrugged. In the morning he would deliver a discurso, and tomorrow night there would still be dust on the boots of a guard like this. But the discurso would be recorded and would satisfy him that at least he was doing his duty. He entered the casa real and wished that he were not so lonely, wished he were ready for sleep, wished he could forget the laughter of the woman of the casa de puta.

3

STANDING at the door of the friary, Fray Pedro thought for a moment of the empty officers' chapel he had just left. This seemed to be one place where he could find peace and quiet away from the duties of the day. The Fray Custodio was getting older and there were so many new chores, so many new details of administration which fell on the shoulders of the thirty-five-year-old assistant, who had, fortunately, been educated at Valladolid. The few hours of the evening spent at the chapel La Hermita de Nuestra Señora were necessary for the young man, for contemplation and for evaluation of the many happenings of a crowded day.

He saw the Governor enter the palacio and then he turned and went into the friary. He walked down the barren corridor toward his own cell, paused for a moment at the door of the Fray Custodio and finally knocked.

The old man was seated at a table in his cotton pantalones, his cassock carefully hung from a hook on the wall. Fray Pedro did not need to ask the name of the book which kept the grey-haired man up so late. It would only be Duns Scotus, which was the quiet way in which the old conformist expressed his own individuality.

"You wanted something, my son?" the old man asked his junior.

For a moment, Fray Pedro was hesitant. Then he began again on the subject they had discussed only a few hours earlier.

"If we are to do something about the missions which are failing us, might it not be best if I made the inspection now, before the season turns wet and then the snows isolate us from our responsibilities?"

The Fray Custodio moved no more than his head as he stared at the younger man, his finger tips coming together just below the point of his chin.

"And if I name you visitador you will journey as inspector to each of the missions . . ." He did not finish the rest of the sentence that ran through his mind—"and they will know you to be my successor."

Fray Pedro nodded. "We have agreed it should be done."

The older man did not move a muscle as he weighed the comment. "Let us speak of it again after the procurador has brought us our supplies from Ciudad Mexico. Then, perhaps, there will be more reason."

He closed the subject as he returned to his book. Fray Pedro stood for a moment staring at the lean back which had borne so many years of lonely service for the Order across the kingdoms of the Indies. Then he closed the door quietly and continued down the corridor to his room. If he waited for the supplies and made the jornada to distribute them, his task would be that of a mensajero, a mere messenger, and not a visitador with authority. The image was not the one he wanted to create.

In his own cell, he removed his cassock and washed his face in the basin set on the low table beside his bed. It was a rugged, square face, darker now than when he had left his home and the casa of his father in the Villa de Alba de Tormes in the province of Valladolid so many years before. He thought for a moment of home and knew there was a task he had to complete before the arrival of Fray Francisco de Ayeta, the procurador from the south. He let some of the water run down his dark chest and seated himself at the table where his books, papers, and ink were kept. He sat and thought for a moment, and then, not quite ready to write, he rose and filled the ink pot partly full of water from a small pitcher. He seated himself and took the time to sharpen a quill with a small desk knife. Finally, there were no longer any excuses and he started to write with the flourish that marked him as an educated man.

La Villa de Santa Fe de San Francisco
Nuevo Mexico
Anno Domini 2 Agosto 1680

Reverend Sir and Father in Christ, Bishop of Ciudad de Valladolid of the Province of Valladolid and Councillor of our Order, the Friars Minor:

I take pen in hand to write you again as Agosto is upon us. Today is San Estevan Day and soon, our dear Lord granting him time and guidance, we expect Fray Francisco de Ayeta to arrive from Ciudad Mexico. He still makes the jornada with regularity despite his advancing years, giving both inspiration and courage to all of us who work for our God in this strange world of Nuevo Mexico. It has been a year and a half since last I was able to post a letter, and as you requested when I left the Seminary ten years ago, I will endeavour to send you as complete a personal report as is within my humble powers concerning the activities in this remote province of the Two Majesties.

I hope that our Gracious Lord in His mercy has been as good to you as he has been to us in His own mysterious way. We have been tried in our faith. Very few of us who serve Him have been found wanting. A certain measure of success has crowned our work. The Fray Custodio reports that we have brought 60,000 Indian souls to salvation. The pueblo communities now number thirty thriving missions. Though the seasons have been unusually dry and the crops poor, we have continued to grow in numbers and strengthen in faith.

Through the will of our Merciful Lord, the attacks on us by wandering nomad Indians of the east have brought consolidation of a certain few missions and a renewal of faith on the part of those puebleños who walk each year more humbly in the way of the Lord.

As the summer months are upon us and the land turns brown, I think of the years spent so happily at the Seminary and wonder how the friends of my youth and compañeros of our Order have fared, to what parts of the world their faith has taken them. Have you news of Brother Cleofas in the Orient? Brother Crystóbal in Ecuador? There are those members of our Order here who have fallen from grace and now live in concubinage. The Fray Custodio has discussed appointing me visitador so that I may inspect each of the missions next year and discover in what ways we may reorganize our parishes and remove certain of our brothers from temptation.

Greed, too, is with us as there are ever-increasing numbers who seek to enrich themselves by building their missions larger in material structures and comforts than they build them in spiritual numbers. It seems as though they seek to make permanent monuments to their own memories rather than to the Church and the God they serve.

Many of the missions have prospered with sheep and cattle—where the natives of a pueblo serve as herders and sow crops for the Brother and render faithful service for his comfort and the care of the church. This has not made for wealth in the great sense of European kingdoms, but it has knitted us into an organized community and has given the lives of the natives purpose and direction. The seven thousand cattle and sheep brought north over eighty years ago by Captain General Oñate have blessedly increased many-fold. Many of these missions are adjoined by large and well-maintained haciendas where live our co-workers for the Two Majesties, the men of Governor Otermín.

One of the largest and in many ways most successful missions is the pueblo of Santa Flora under the spiritual guidance of a most wayward member of our Order, Fray Julio Malinda. His mission has for several years been dominated by the sister of his late alcalde, a certain Beatriz Ramírez. While theirs is a tautly administered community which has brought many poor Indians to the path of Jesus, I cannot help but feel the example set by Fray Julio and this woman can only reflect in a negative manner upon all of us who wear the cloth. The woman I have not met. Fray Julio, whom I last saw several years ago, was then a quiet member of our Order, undistinguished, but certainly a man of faith.

I confess, Your Grace, that the very harshness of this strong land is a trial for those of us who dwell here and has brought out in each those qualities which most reflect the weakest part of our characters.

I often think of Fray Rafael of the pueblo of San Ysidro. A native of

Oviedo, he was educated at the Seminary at Madrid and is a licenciado of the university of that ciudad. Perhaps, taking Holy Orders was the most momentous decision he ever made for himself, as he seems wholly incapable of deciding what must be done at his mission. While none of us questions the faith of the man, his profound belief in our Order, the noble aims for which he stands, I must admit I am deeply concerned about the outcome of his seemingly unguided actions.

And for myself, I must confess an ambition I had not known myself to be capable of. I wait for the retirement of our custodio and hope for advancement. I believe the day may come when Nuevo Mexico may warrant a bishop, and I hope that I may help prepare the community for God and Jesus in such a way that this would be pleasing to our Holy Father in Rome. This is my ambition, my pride, and my sin.

It is going to require a strong hand here for the next few years as the puebleños frequently show tendencies to regress to their old ways and heresy is not unknown in this arid land where, in times of stress, faith alone can sustain us.

Maestre de Campo de Leiva of Galisteo has departed south to el Paso del Norte to meet Fray Francisco and escort him to the Villa. A number of men of this escort are criminals whom Fray Francisco brought north on his last jornada in his sincere belief that we on the outposts of this province needed additional security. These men were collected from the jails of Ciudad Mexico and have in most instances been scattered throughout the province to serve as soldiers. They have all taken Indian women as housekeepers and have quickly succumbed to the leisure of the land and the ready fatigue from the sun.

As this missive cannot be posted until Fray Francisco joins us here at the Villa, I shall not endeavour to close it until that time and shall hope to include such information as Your Grace may find of interest about our custodio.

Putting aside the pen, Fray Pedro rose and walked to the narrow window of his cell. Across the empty plaza mayor the palacio was dark. He could barely make out the figure of the sentry on guard. He looked up to the sky and crossed himself as he did every time he saw the Sangre de Cristo Mountains and thought of the Blood of God for which they had been named.

It was growing late and there were fewer lights about the Villa de Santa Fe than there had been when he had crossed the plaza only a short time before. Then he saw a candle being lighted in the window of the palacio. The Governor was still awake. He wondered about that quiet, elderly man who seemed to see so much, who knew exactly what had to be done, and whose only regret was that there was so little to do things with. Fray Pedro felt the Governor possessed a certain impatience which he assumed came from his background, position, and—yes—his age. There was also a bit of arrogance about the man, a touch of disdain because he was, after all, a grandee, a governor, and a captain general. Don Antonio de Otermín was very different from Fray Pedro and therefore a puzzle the young padre could not quite solve, and as with anything left uncertain in his very clear mind, this disturbed the padre.

In the Little-Suburb-Across-The-Water from the Villa, the Indians sat counting the knots in the rope which had been left by the runners from Taos.

4

THE Blue Lake high in the mountains is the last home of the ancient pueblo gods. Beneath its turquoise waters live the shades of all that have passed on earth, the eternal souls of those things that once were known to the People and now are merely dark shadows, glimmering beneath still waters. This is the Sacred Place, the final home of Those-Who-Speak-Between-The-People-And-The-Gods—the Katchinas.

The-Waters-Which-Make-Life flow out of the Blue Lake. They are only a thin stream in August when they trickle down the mountain's side, lap at the base of the tall spruce and the gnarled pine and flow on, pausing to feed a mountain meadow and satisfy the thirst of an angular deer, past the cottonwood bosque where the yellow tanager noisily disputes his rights with the long-tailed magpie, and on through the pebbled stream bed beside the high boulders and the yellow aspen, then sweeping around the sacred mountain and down the cañon where the red willows line the bank by the pueblo of Taos. Finally, the waters mingle with those of the Rio del Norte, and the spirit of the Sacred Place Where-Only-Truth-Is-Left is spread through the kingdom of the pueblos.

Rio Pueblo divides Taos into two parts. On one side rises Hlan-Oma, the tall block form of the five-storied pyramid which is the communal home of the Summer People, and on the other side of the rio rises its mate, Hlan-Gima, which is of the Winter People.

Near by, reaching out of the ground like a talisman toward the light is the end of the ladder that leads to the great kiva—the large temple hidden beneath the surface of the earth. In all the kingdom of the pueblos, Taos has power. Through here first flow the waters from the Blue Lake. From here is made the annual pilgrimage to the home of the katchinas. From here come sacred corn meal and sacred seeds.

There are seven kivas in Taos, for this is a holy city. On the north side of the rio are the kivas of the Earring People, Day People, and the Dripping Water People, and on the south side are the kivas of the Feather People, the Water People, and Old Axe People. The seventh kiva of Taos is a shrine.

The Big Earring Man is chief of those kivas which lie on the north side of the rio and chief of the houses, presiding at the council. He and Water Man and the cacique suggest the pueblo governor and the war chiefs to the thirty men who sing but do not dance and are the council of Taos.

Standing on top of Hlan-Gima in the darkness watching the waters flow south, was a tall man who seemed to overwhelm the very roof tops about him. His black hair hung in two long braids over his bared bronze chest. On his head rested a pair of large bull horns and about his waist was the golden pelt of a jaguar. Thrown loosely over his right shoulder was a blanket into which were woven secrets few eyes would ever unravel. He stood without moving as he watched the caciques and war chiefs of the neighbouring pueblos descend into the darkness of the kiva.

These were the leaders and war chiefs who would carry the burden of rebellion, who would co-ordinate the operations with those of the region to the south to which the knotted rope and the simple details were being carried. It was upon these men, working together for the first time, that success would depend. And so to these men must be made the final appeal, the last exhortation to success, or the world of the adobe kingdom would remain forever in tribute to the Whitefaces who did not care to understand it.

The five leaders of the northern pueblos entered the kiva and waited for their eyes to adjust to the faint light of the piñon torch. Then they settled in a semicircle about the sipapu which led down into the underworld. They said nothing. There was nothing to say. El Saca was there when they came. He was Big Earring Man of Taos and the friend of Popé of San Juan for whom they waited. The faint light caught the scar on the forehead of Luis Tupatú of Picurís. It revealed the stolid face of the old cacique of Cuyamunque and the closed eyes in the square head of Fay-yat of Tesuque. Obi of Santa Clara shifted in his place and glanced at the doubting eyes of Nicolás Bua, the young war chief of San Juan.

Knowing that he had revealed himself, Bua closed his eyes and turned toward the shadows. There were doubts in his mind. But perhaps he had come too far to reveal them now. There were those who would depend more upon him than upon the others, for he was young and knew both the ancient ways and the ways of the Whitefaces. And because he was the son-in-law of Popé.

Yet the doubts were there. Was the revolt preached by the holy Popé best for the People? Many would die in the rebellion and among them would be friends and family. The Spanish would be killed, their priesthood destroyed, and one could never be certain about a priesthood. Who could know if the shades which revealed themselves to Popé were really stronger than the Holy Jesus and the Holy Mary of the men of the kivas beneath the cross? And if the shades of Popé were not stronger, what would this mean to the People? What revenge would fall upon them? Would the Blue Lake become dry? The land know thirst? The Corn Mother fail to appear?

Nicolás Bua had doubts which ran even deeper than the questions he now asked himself. He knew Popé, knew the sudden passions of the man, as well as the long, cold anger he had built against the Spanish. And because he knew Popé as a man and a father-in-law, he was uncertain whether the shades were honest with Popé, whether Popé was honest with the caciques. Nicolás Bua was a young man and though he did not speak, he feared for the People.

There was silence. The faint light flickered. Corn meal drifted from above into the grim dark purple of the hidden, holy place. Firelight was crimson on the bloody sheep's-head drums. Then the golden jaguar and the white owl feather. Then the glistening bull horns, and he came. Popé. Popé, silent, brooding in the darkness like a shadow of the ancients and a vision of the past.

He stood for one long silent moment before the caciques and war chiefs, who had come at his bidding, and he ignored them.

He whirled his huge figure about and faced the faint fire across the sipapu which threw his shadow like a giant's over the semicircle of men behind him. He grasped a handful of the holy corn meal and scattered it before him. Slowly, he began to talk, to tell of the vision which had come to him, Popé.

"It came to pass as I journeyed back from the Blue Lake of Copala that I looked and beheld a dust devil grow from the east where the Sun Father rises. It grew to a great cloud and a fire was in it and there was the brightness of the sun about it and at its very centre was the cold blue of the turquoise and out of its centre came Caudi and Tilini and Tleume from Those Below.

"They had the likeness of a man and then of a woman and the strength to turn the Sacred Mountain about to the east where life comes warm or the west where death lies cold. Two lizards crawled away from their feet, one to the east which was burned by the brightness and one to the west which was frozen like the snows of winters to come.

"And as I beheld the shades of the ancient gods, the sky opened like turquoise and all was beautiful and there was much water flowing and many deer gathered at the Lake of Copala and the Corn Mother greeted them with golden ears and sacred meal. Then Montezuma, the father of all, and the Great Captain since the world was buried beneath the floods, spoke to me.

"And He said: 'The People are my people but they have turned to strangers.' And He whom I could not see, who was the Great Captain, dusted me with the white corn meal, and then I saw how the sky had come apart, and He towered above me like the sacred mountain and yet higher than the eagle flies.

"And again He spoke and He said, 'My people have betrayed me. And if the People would wish the rain to fall and the Corn Mother to nurture them, they must burn the false God the Strangers call the Jesus, must kill the woman the Strangers call the Mother of God who is not the Corn Mother. No sign, no symbol, no talisman must remain, and those who will not join in the destruction, those of the kingdom of the pueblos who will not return to the old ways, will know pestilence and be consumed by famine. You must destroy the crosses. You must destroy the white kivas which rest under the crosses. You must destroy the white medicine men with their gods upon the crosses which are an abomination to the sight of the Earth Mother and the Corn Mother.'

"And I, Popé, listened as He spoke and felt the fires which rose about his feet and knew the shades of the past and the cold places which are beneath the Blue Lake, and I heard the thunderbird rock the mountain and saw the plumed serpent that is the lightning shake the sky, and Montezuma said to me: 'Tell the People there must be violence against those who have turned the People from the ancient paths, and those who will not join you must know the violence along with the false priests of the false gods who would have you be good but are not good, who would have you believe what they do not believe, who would have you obey the king whom they do not obey. Those who will not move with you to destroy must be destroyed.'

"And I stood and wept for the People and He said: 'You need not shed tears, for when the black symbols are gone, the false gods slain, and the grey-cloaked priest banned from the land, then rain will fall and the sky will turn bright and the People will be as they were in the past.'

"And then He left me and I stood alone beside the stream which flows from the Blue Lake and I knew that I must come and tell what I had heard to the leaders of the People as He wanted me to tell them."

Then Popé turned to the leaders of the pueblos. They were silent, eyes glazed, the skin of their faces taut. The square jaw of Obi trembled. The caciques were completely Popé's. Then he held out his hand with the sacred corn meal. Louis Tupatú with the scar on his forehead rose and took a handful and spread it in the sipapu. He was joined by Obi of the square face and the stolid cacique of Cuyamunque and Fay-yat of Tesuque.

Only Nicolás Bua, the young war chief of San Juan, remained seated. Then slowly he rose and faced the medicine man who was his father-in-law, the holy priest with the outstretched hand, and when he found that he could move no further, he closed his eyes and was still. The other caciques and war chiefs looked at the young man for a long time. Then they ascended the ladder to the night above. Later they would return. Later they would plan each final detail of the revolt to which they had pledged themselves. But now Popé must settle with the young man who had married his only daughter.

Saca of Taos waited until he was alone with Popé and Nicolás Bua. Then he turned to the older man and asked, "Is there nothing that I can do?"

Popé shook his head slowly and looked up to the exit of the kiva. Saca understood and climbed after the others. Now the priest was alone with the war chief. The faint light of the torch reflected off the bull horns and the jaguar pelt came to life as he shook. Then he closed his right hand and stood before the younger man.

He was still for a long time. Then the jaguar pelt about his waist began to tremble. Suddenly he was the whirlwind who was driving the puebleños to the edge of rebellion. His heavy arms struck wildly as he pummelled the youth before Bua could raise his hands to protect himself. Stunned, Bua stumbled back, fell to the floor and was still while Popé, bending over, continued to strike again and again at the young man's face until there was no longer sense and then until there was no longer life. Finally he regained his composure. He drew himself up to his full height. The jaguar pelt was still. He spread the sacred corn meal over the sipapu and a handful of seeds he had gathered along the banks of the Blue Lake, and he prayed for forgiveness for what he had done: "We who must live must live even though others must die so that we may live."

Then he turned and slowly climbed the polished ladder into the night where the caciques and war chiefs waited for him. He approached Saca and spoke so that the others might hear:

"And those who will not move with you to destroy must be destroyed."

He walked away, unable to tell them how much he had feared the hold the white priests had on his son-in-law, or how much he feared what Nicolás Bua of San Juan might have already told the Spaniards.

For Popé feared the Spaniards, knew their strength and feared them. Yet he could obey them no more. He could be harassed no more. He had drawn the line beyond which he and his people could not be pushed.

And though he feared, he was confident. He had to be. He had turned about to face the enemy, face down a lie. A lie at least for the People. They could continue to bear the lash as he had borne the lash. They could have borne hunger as he had borne hunger, for if some died, others would live, but they could not, must not any longer live outside the spirit of the seasons, the Earth Mother and the Corn Mother which nurtured them. They were ill and did not know why they were ill. They were restless and did not know what disturbed them, did not know that for generations their very souls had been turned from harmony to discord, from nature and the rhythm of the seasons to foreign symbols of a foreign god. The People had lost their affinity with the stars and the creeping things.

5

THE tall, dark-eyed encomendero with the white beard stood at the gate that led to the large hacienda behind him and watched the caciques come slowly up the path along the rio from Taos. He had seen them arriving in the dusk of early evening and he was not certain of the significance of their visit. Don Jaime de Marcos had been aware of an increased activity in the pueblo ever since Popé, the medicine man, had come here from his native village of San Juan, where he had been hounded by the deputies of the governor.

Damn the pompous administrators of the province. Don Jaime wanted no part of them. And as he thought about these caciques as well as the runners he had seen departing south and west for days, he decided that as long as the puebleños completed the tasks he set for them, so long as his tribute was gathered, so long as the Indians gave him no trouble personally, he did not care to communicate with the governor and captain general in the Villa de Santa Fe to the south.

In fact, he did not know who this governor was, any more than he had ever known who his predecessors were. Don Jaime never sought their company, and if they sought his, he avoided them. In the eighteen years he had been in this heated hole which marked the end of the road of his exile, he had avoided whenever possible the seventy Spaniards who dwelled in Taos valley. He never visited their homes or permitted them to enter his. He never joined them in the mission chapel, nor would he allow one of them inside the small chapel on his hacienda where his young daughter worshiped. As far as Don Jaime was concerned, the other Spanish members of the Taos community did not exist. The soldiers reported to their officers and minded their own business. If any thought to do otherwise, they found Don Jaime's Indians and dogs blocking their trail. If any of the hacendados or their señoras became curious about the tall, handsome recluse, they too were turned away by smiling servants and growling dogs.

This was the cardinal rule by which his hacienda was governed. It brought enough wealth of the modest kind to be found in the province. The hand labours of his craftsmen were better than those of the other encomenderos, the grain was slightly more plentiful, and the cattle were just a little fatter. This made the tithes sufficient to protect Don Jaime from any official busybodies.

He wanted only his privacy. For as far as he was concerned Don Jaime de Marcos, formerly the Conde de Iteo, was dead.

He had died on the Day of San Lorenzo, eighteen years before. The final confessions had been made and the last rites granted him, and he had died. It did not matter that the young man in the black velvet tunica with the silver-handled sword at his side turned away from the padre after the rites and took the hand of the stranger, the former maid of the Queen, who was now his bride, and walked up the dock at Sevilla to board a caravel for Nueva España. Don Jaime was dead. Dead to his family. Dead to his friends. And more important, he was dead inside. The spark which had made him one of the most dashing and brilliant young men of the court of Philip IV in that ciudad of decaying elegance, Madrid, was dead.

He had walked with slow, deliberate steps aboard the ship that was to carry him into exile and he had never looked back at España. And never again if he could avoid it in the years that followed did he speak to another Spaniard—layman, padre, or even the woman he had married.

The August night was still. Taos loomed in the darkness like blocks one upon the other. The encomendero did not move.

The years had crystallized Don Jaime de Marcos to the brittle hardness of a chispa—that flint and stone used for building a fire. But there was no fire in the middle-aged grandee, only cold, hard hatred for the world of Philip IV and his son Carlos, the Bewitched, from which he had sprung and from which he had so long lived in exile: the world of jealousy, injustice, and unbridled power, of the silken garrote about the white neck and the unsheathed daga in a man's ribs after a walk in the dark, of black-haired women in soft beds gathering intelligence and baiting traps for King or Inquisition.

Don Jaime hated every memory of it, and in all the years he had wasted among the mesas, none of it had faded from the foreground of his mind.

He knew he would never forget the girl, Manuela, in the scarlet brocade dress and lace mantilla, the beautiful girl of the white skin he had met in the pink stucco villa north of Madrid. He had courted her and he had taken her in what he had believed to be one bright moment lost in passion. This was followed by wonderful weeks in the silken bed with the green satin canopy.

Then came the disillusionment. The trap was sprung. The Inocente was taken into custody and Philip had the excuse he needed. For the girl Manuela was a cousin to the king and it was not difficult for the Audiencia to reason that in bedding a member of the royal family without the royal permission, the young Conde de Iteo revealed his ambitions and was striking at the very Throne itself.

The entire affair was handled with quiet dispatch. The young grandee was stripped of his land, heritage, and titles, and the girl was sold to a visiting French nobleman who was willing to pay for the honour of breeding with a Spanish Hapsburg. The infant had a name and Philip had two fortunes. This was all the public excuse that was needed. But there were no advantages in having the former Conde about Madrid, and there might be a place for him in the more remote sections of the provinces. And so with the grant of an encomienda in his baggage and a penniless bride of the King's choosing on his arm, the embittered young Don Jaime de Marcos departed España.

It was only when he arrived at the remote and shabby capital of Durango in Mexico that he found out that his encomienda was located north of the Villa de Santa Fe de Nuevo Mexico. The representative of the Viceroy, who told him, had worn a smirk on his face when he named the young exile Alcalde Mayor of a pueblo called Taos in the province to the north.

Don Jaime had listened without saying a word. Then he turned and walked back through the dingy, unpaved street to the small adobe hacienda he had rented for himself and his bride. He sat down with a bottle of native liquor and got drunk. And drunk he remained for two months, taking time out only to curse the King and ravage the woman who shared his bed.

Finally he was notified by a supercilious courier that a caballada of mules and horses was ready to depart to the Villa de Santa Fe and that from there he could make his way to Taos.

Five months after he arrived in Taos, the hacienda he had designed was completed by the efforts of the Indians, who found him understanding, and thus different from the Spaniards who had preceded him. Three months later he was a widower and father. When the native midwife handed him the child, he sat down and penned a note to Fray Vicente of the local mission. The girl was to be named Manuela, was to be raised by an Indian nursemaid to be the daughter of Don Jaime de Marcos, formerly Conde de Iteo, and was to be educated by Fray Vicente himself, for which services certain benefits derived from the encomienda would be turned over to the mission.

Whenever possible he avoided contact with both the girl Manuela and her instructor.

The years had passed and the young grandee had become the middle-aged encomendero. The glitter which had been his when he walked as a youth gave way to a certain dignity and force of character as he built his own small empire out of the bitter countryside that was Nuevo Mexico. And with the years there came to Don Jaime a quiet understanding of the life about him.

He came to know and appreciate the gentleness of the Indians who worked his lands. From the first time he paced out the plot which was to be the hacienda, he had never used a whip, never struck a worker, never antagonized the gods of the puebleños. This did not mean he was not prepared to exact the work he desired or that his was a loosely administered part of Philip's province, but rather that the prosperous hacienda was the joint accomplishment of the Indians and the man who directed them. It was with never-diminishing awe that they accepted his knowledge of their language, for he was the first of his rank who had ever bothered to learn it. It was with warmth and appreciation that they recalled how Don Jaime had dealt with the two soldiers of the garrison who tried to sack the town and held as hostage the wives and daughters of the principales. The drunken men had reeled out of their small presidio about dusk and without hesitation had killed two of the men and taken four of their women back to their quarters to meet their needs. Fifteen minutes after the Indians appealed to Don Jaime, he walked through the narrow gates into the presidio itself, dressed only in the leather pantalones and hide tunica which had become his costume, and armed with the silver sword which had hung at his side when he departed Sevilla. Five minutes later, shepherding the women ahead of him, he walked out. The two soldiers never did. There was peace in Taos after that. When an Indian was whipped and the whipping was reported to Don Jaime, he walked to the hacienda of the offender and either struck the man openly before the puebleños, or as he twice had to do when there was resistance, he killed him. This made the former grandee unpopular with his own people, and protests went forward from the Spaniards of Taos to the governors at the Villa and even through the clergy to the Fray Custodio. However, each governor or clerical official looked at the papers which had been granted Don Jaime by the King and forgot to answer the protests, or suggested that the protestant might find a hacienda elsewhere in the kingdom of the pueblos.

Over the years many voices had been raised in anger. There were those Spaniards who said Don Jaime was a traitor to the Empire and was making control of the Indians a more difficult task. There were those padres, ignored by the man and crushed by his aloof dignity, who claimed that he was in league with the native caciques against the mother Church. There was talk of bringing the powers of the Inquisition to Taos or braving the hacienda of the alcalde mayor and bringing that very man himself to the Villa de Santa Fe to face a court of the Inquisition. After all, what Spaniard and good Christian failed to attend Mass, failed to attend confession, turned his back on the Church and those padres who represented it? But nothing was done. For an inexplicable reason, there was greater peace in Taos than at any time before the arrival of Don Jaime, and if he himself had turned his back on the Church, he had also given his only daughter, the Señorita Manuela, to the Church for instruction.

Standing now before the gate which led to the large hacienda, Don Jaime turned to look at his daughter standing on the portico above him. She had become a pretty girl, though a shy and seemingly frightened one. He did not

remember her mother too clearly, for in his drunken dreams he had gotten
the maid of the queen who had been the gift of Philip confused with the
cousin of Philip. But the girl Manuela was pretty. She took after the line
of Iteo, and in another time and under a different king she might have grown
up to be the Condesa de Iteo. Now Fray Vicente, in that small, nervous
holograph which was sent each sixth month to Don Jaime and rarely read,
informed the father that Señorita Manuela must be sent to Ciudad Mexico,
where she would meet proper young men and be introduced into the social
circle becoming her station as the daughter of the greatest encomendero in
the northern province and the Alcalde Mayor of Taos.

Don Jaime stared at his daughter and smiled to himself. The pompous
old padre really believed the titles and properties had meaning to their
holder. He had been in the province for almost twenty years, had known
Don Jaime remotely for most of that time, and actually knew less about him
than the Indians who ploughed his land and planted his fruit trees. But if the
girl had to go, so much the better. There was no need for her here in Taos.
It never crossed Don Jaime's mind to discuss the matter with Manuela herself. He had rarely found it necessary to speak to her, and her impending
departure seemed to make conversation even less important.

He turned to the Indian youth, Juan, who had grown up to be his assistant,
whom he had educated himself, and who was the only person with whom
he discussed his daily problems. Juan, tall, dark-complexioned, and alert,
had gradually assumed a position of authority in Taos beyond that which
would ordinarily have fallen to a nameless Indian waif. But there was very
little resentment of the young man, even by those who had learned to distrust the Spaniards. Popé himself had come to believe, though wrongly, that
the reason he was permitted to live in Taos without the harassment he had
known elsewhere was because of the influence of the youth, Juan. But,
though the young Indian would not have disturbed the medicine man, the
reason was actually to be found in the attitude of Don Jaime, who had not
only turned his back on España, its King, and all of its intrigues, but had
equally rejected those who might eventually be its enemies.

Juan and Don Jaime devoted the evening to a discussion of areas in the
cañon of the red willows where fruit trees could best be grown.

6

MANUELA DE MARCOS, standing on the high portico of her father's
hacienda, knew that he was looking at her; knew, too, that he had turned
away to talk to Juan. Only a year older than herself, the Indian orphan had
been raised on the large farm of her father which stretched from Taos south
along the Rio Pueblo as far as man could walk in a single day.

From where she stood, the slim girl with the soft hair could make out the black wall of trees which edged up the mountainside and the terraced town of Taos. The walls were now long destroyed which had surrounded the pueblo when Captain Barrio-Nuevo first marched through its gates a century and a half before. Only the broken outline of the adobe barricade remained as a memory of former independence.

The buildings were tawny in the evening light, and with the sun on them, the multi-storied community houses loomed as large as small mountains to the girl's eyes. She had always been a little afraid of Taos, of the mystery there and the secrecy of the world just below the surface where the native gods were hidden. The bustle of the town—the coming and going of the Indians—disturbed her. Born on her father's estate, Manuela had rarely been off it, except on special occasions to walk to the mission chapel under the protecting shadow of her tutor, Fray Vicente.

The nervous old padre from Estramadura was her protector and her educator. And though she was not fully aware of it, he was also the reason her hand shook when she set it on the rail of the balcony and the reason her thin face had lost its shy smile. She was afraid, and it was he who had created the fear within her, with his long preaching and his brimstone concepts of what the future held for girls. There was a starved quality about the padre that needed expression; and he found it in the way he plagued the young girl who had been given into his care. Fray Vicente was not an evil man. By most lights he might have been considered a good one, but he was afraid of women as men are apt to be afraid of anything they cannot understand. His fear came from ignorance, while Don Jaime's came from knowledge.

It was the character of his fears that shaped Manuela. As a child she would have liked to take off her shoes and dip her feet in the rio as she had seen the Indians girls do. She would have liked to run over the fields and throw herself down in the piles of corn shucks and roll over and over as she had watched Juan do when he was a boy. She would have liked to ride a horse over the hacienda as her father did. But the old padre told her many times there were things which girls did not do. And being Fray Vicente, he always expressed the disapproval by saying things *good* girls did not do. And with all the frustration of a man who was hungry for the wider world of Madrid or Rome or even—Heaven help him—Paris, he spread his meagre knowledge and his small hatreds before the girl. Spelling out what was wrong with all of the things he could not have, he created a world for her in which almost everything was evil. It was a world so like Dante's that in time he himself came to believe that the one in which he lived was part of the Inferno created by the old Florentine.

For himself this might not have been so harmful. He spoke with a fervour which if it did not convince the Indians at least impressed them. But for Manuela his vague details about a more vague Hell only meant confusion. And being a shy, lonely girl, the confusion expressed itself in fear. She was afraid and she did not know why she was afraid.

But at this moment of her life she feared most of all the land to which she was being sent when the caballada of Fray Francisco de Ayeta departed the Villa de Santa Fe. Fray Vicente had often described the Ciudad de Mexico to her. He had told her the tales of the great conquests when the land was being made ready for God. He had told her of the lively ladies in the beautiful mantillas and the lighthearted caballeros with the trim beards who were eager to meet a beautiful girl whose father controlled a wealthy encomienda. But in the telling he always added his own belief that there was something wrong with the lively ladies and that the lighthearted youths were seeking evil. He had the ready faculty of souring a dream.

And so Manuela was afraid of the place to which she was being sent, and because of her fear she had made up her mind, the night before, that she was going to take the veil when she went south.

She was only seventeen, and she was very young for seventeen. There were so many simple things she did not know, like the pleasure of watching an ant hill, hearing the laughter at a festival, or enjoying the conversation of another girl. Though she had been raised on a frontier, she had spent most of her life in the confines of her father's hacienda and had left it only at the side of the padre as he hurried back and forth to the mission chapel. Among the things she did not know was why she liked the lithe Indian youth whom her father had brought up as his protégé. She did not know that there was nothing wrong with a young girl finding a young boy nice to look upon and nicer still to talk to. She only knew that there was an evil involved in the relationship of a boy and a girl. And so she turned her head away from what she most enjoyed, the easy companionship of the only other young person in her life. And she and Juan had much in common: they had been children together even if the world was shown to them through different eyes.

Below, she saw the familiar face of Juan smiling up at her and the dark face of her father as he turned toward the rio where Popé, the medicine man with the long braids hanging over his shoulders like two desert serpents, approached the hacienda along the rio's bank.

7

THE tall medicine man ignored the encomendero and the youth who stood at his side. Popé was buried deep in his thoughts. He had killed, killed with his own bare hands, and he was disturbed. He had destroyed a creature of the Earth Mother's making. He had destroyed a young man whom he loved, the young man who had married his daughter and had sired his grandchildren. All the proper words had been said, all the prayers offered up, the death ceremonies completed. Everything was over except the shaking of

Popé's hands. He clutched them together and stared at them. He had killed who had never killed. It had seemed right for him to preach rebellion and organize rebellion. Someone had to do it. But Popé was disturbed. The rebellion had begun with him. The first death had been at his hands. And it was murder. And the victim was not of the Whitefaces, not of the Men of Iron or the men of the blessing words, but a man of the People, of the People. The sign was not right. The symbol was wrong. And Popé believed in signs and symbols as any person who leads must believe.

He considered how the problem of rebellion had become his own—his mission, his task—as separate from that of the others. Other pueblos had their medicine men, their holy beliefs which differed in small ways and large ones from the ways of San Juan and Taos. Why had it fallen to him?

The white bull horns weighed heavy on his head. Without thinking, he tried to fluff the pelt about his waist. When had they become the symbol of his calling? He remembered the days of his youth in San Juan, the years of learning the old ways from the cacique who had been his father. And his thoughts of the wizened old man were kindly thoughts. With his father he had journeyed to the far places in the west which were the cliff dwellings of the ancient people. Here he had fasted and prayed. Here he had known the rooms carved in the cliff walls and heard the sounds of the old pipes and the old drums. Here he had found the cottonwood drum that weighed more than a man and the high piles of dried piñon branches which had been left as fuel for fires never built. Here he had found the long-dried maize and the skeletons of men who sat in a large circle waiting for the death that had taken them. Popé had learned the familiar shape against the sky of the Old Place and in the learning he had become aware of what was happening to the People. The years that followed—years of marriage and children and preaching—had become meaningless to him. He had been a passive man in his youth. It had been his decision to live life with the Whitefaces as they prescribed it. He had preached acceptance to the others of San Juan and to the councils of the caciques who had wanted to rise and fight a decade ago. He had stood by when that small rebellion had met its inevitable end and the Spaniards had triumphed.

But the past was a dead thing, like an antelope stiffening its legs in the hot sun or a bird lying limp beside the flowing waters. The taste of it was still in his mouth though the words that he had preached in the past were long lost in the winds of winters. The past had died and the words had failed five years before when the Whiteface warriors and the Blessing Men had taken him and his fellows to the Villa de Santa Fe to stand trial for heresy. There had been forty-four of them. And each of the men chained in the long cell had stared at Popé and asked him how their familiarity with the ways of the Sun Father and the pregnant Earth Mother was a heresy and how they could deny this knowledge. He had not known. He had had no answer for them when they had sought an answer. Weeks later four of their number were hanged. And in his turn each of the others was taken into the open area of the great plaza mayor and strung up by the arms, back bared, and flogged by a weary but eager soldier. The Blessing Men had stood by to watch and approve. It was they who had cried Witch. It was because of them that the lash fell. Popé knew it now and flinched at the recollection: his face down where it had been shoved, his back bloody where it had been torn, his arms aching from the weight of his limp body. And all the while the Blessing Men had prayed for his immortal soul and the soldier chewed his green end of weed and flayed the copper body in front of him.

The People had gathered before the Governor and asked for the release of the Holy Men and it was granted, because they no longer mattered—neither the People nor the Holy Men. The others had returned to their respective pueblos. They nursed their backs and their pride and held their silence to them like a cherished thing. Only Popé had dared to face the future with equal eyes and admit his distaste for the look of it.

When the shackles dropped from his feet and the way to the Whiteface future spread before him, he had journeyed again to the place of the ancient ones he had known as a boy. Here he found that hope belonged only to those prepared to grasp its unknown offerings. Here he spent the time alone from a moon's rising to a moon's rising. And when he returned to San Juan, his path was as clear before him as the Sun Father's trail across the morning sky.

He had travelled from pueblo to pueblo. His message had been a simple one: Freedom and a return to the old ways, the right to select a crop and a mate and die facing the Sun Father. The People had listened. The caciques had agreed that the Time of Troubles and the Time of the Great Hunger had been bad times and if Popé could discover the trail back to their salvation, to the affinity with the Earth Mother and the Corn, they would follow that trail.

It was in this belief, in this promise, that they had agreed to take up their arms and destroy their oppressors. Now, if it were only done, the battle concluded, and the People again on the land! But it was only begun, and since it was begun in the wrong way, he was concerned about the path it would follow.

8

TWO of the runners of Popé who had taken the western trail from Taos ran with quick strides down the dried banks of the Rio Pueblo and on until they reached the Rio del Norte, the wandering rio that grows in the high mountains above the land of the puebleños and splits Nuevo Mexico into two parts, pushing south between hills and mountains, shaded by the twisted piñon, the chopped mesa, the abrupt butte. On the edge of that rio the runners turned south. The leagues fell behind them. Their legs gathered weight as they ran west along the Rio Chama across rock beds and hard clay.

To their left rose Pedernal and to their right they could make out the heights of Brazos Peak. They ran on until they came to the silhouette against the sky that was the pueblo of Santa Flora—the cañon to the north, the low hills to the left. In that place the runners slowed their pace and made their way carefully up the old trail until they arrived at the broad cut of a red-lined arroyo. Here they were joined by five men who disappeared into the arroyo with them.

Later the runners emerged and turned back toward the Rio del Norte, leaving the five men alone in the shelter of the dry rio bed, holding the knotted rope in their hands and the plans of Popé locked in their minds. They were the cacique, the principales, the war chief, and the medicine man of Santa Flora.

They walked slowly out of the arroyo and made their way to the cave near Pedernal which for generations had been for them the Sacred Place. They did not speak. In the long months since their cacique had made the journey to the kiva of Taos, they had known what they would do when the time came. Now the time was marked with knots in the rope they carried. They would untie a knot each night until none was left. Nothing more needed to be said. The medicine man took the old symbols from the cave— the bull horns of his authority, the wolf pelt of their clan, and the katchina doll. Then they left the cave and made their way back through the night to the compound of the mission.

The thick walls that surrounded the mission church threw dark shadows across the dark ground between the low buildings. The sheep were within the walls, and several puebleños stood guard over the cattle that remained in the fields beyond. Fires had been lighted in the cooking area, and maize cakes were steaming on flat rocks. Some of the women stood about still stretching their backs, bent with a hard day's labour. Others washed clothes in the wells by the firelight.

Beyond the compound in the darkness could be seen the shape of the multistoried buildings of the old pueblo which was little used now that the Indians had been brought inside the mission walls. Some of the older men stared silently at the tops of the white buildings which they had known since childhood. Soon they would eat, and when the meal was done they would listen to the gaunt padre with the large hands preach to them in a language they could not understand. Then they would enjoy the night sky as best they could. But until they were called to eat, they would wait.

All of the men knew that the cacique and the principales had gone off under the confusion of the end of the day's work to meet the runners from Taos. When they returned they would bring with them the plans of Popé and the rebellion to come. Staring at the silhouette of the empty pueblo beyond the walls, the old men dreamed of the time when they would walk out of the mission, its great gates hanging open never to close again. Then they would cross the ground between and return to their homes. They were patient men. They had waited a long time. They could afford to wait until the day of the uprising.

When the cacique and his companions entered the compound, the puebleños stopped what they were doing. One of the returning principales took out his small reed pipe, while another sought his sheep's-head drum. Together they began to play while the cacique hid the katchina.

Soon they were joined by the others who stood in a large circle around the music-makers. Finally the young medicine man could wait no longer for the day of freedom. He put on his bull-horn headdress, wrapped the wolf pelt about his waist, and began to dance. Slowly at first, and then as the music-makers played faster, his dance matched their pace.

9

FRAY JULIO MALINDA, seated in the small room of the mission house which he so proudly called his study, paused in his reading to listen to the wild sounds of the reed pipe. The strange music sounded like a mingling of the cry of an injured animal and the wind blowing off the mountains in winter.

There had been no music in the compound for months, and its sudden return puzzled the padre. And it disturbed him. He shoved his heavy chair back from the small table and walked to the narrow window. From here he could see his Indians gathered about the music-makers and the dancer, and he was frightened. He looked beyond the group to the high walls of the compound which resembled a prison more than a church and felt secure again. He realized after a moment that he had not seen the bull-horn headdress or the wolf pelt that dangled from the loins of the dancer since his first lonely months at Santa Flora so many years before, when he had arrived at the remote pueblo with only his faith, his frock, and the cross to protect him. These symbols had hardly seemed enough when weighed against the names of the many martyrs who had died in this country above el Paso del Norte.

The bull horns disappeared in the years that followed as part of the many changes that took place. The small misson chapel grew into a large church and the mission yard became a walled compound.

There had been many years of building, and Fray Julio was proud of them. Much had been accomplished during his pastorage, and he felt confident that history would record The Years of Fray Julio.

He rested his elbows on the window ledge and watched the dance, his lean face quiet. A tall, thin man of strength and grace, there was a surprising weakness about his face that always confused strangers when they first met him. After knowing him a time, this gave way to either revulsion or admiration, depending upon the perception and judgment of the viewer. For Fray Julio permitted himself to be used to accomplish his own ends and not those of the users.

The many mission buildings were an example of this peculiar talent. Where brother Franciscans had spent their years in deep concern with blasphemy and witchcraft or heresy, he had blinded his eyes to such and used the natives in the ways he believed would best serve the Church and God. No one would question that the crops of his mission were the tallest, the herds the best bred, the wines the finest. Why, in all the province only those wines prepared from the vineyards of his mission were selected to be sent as a present to the Viceroy so far away. And always there was the thanking letter in return. Let the men who worried about dogma criticize him. He, Fray Julio, had learned how to come to terms with the life about him. If there were deviations from the code decreed for the Order of Friars Minor, none could say his failures had not at least been successful failures.

And all because he knew how to let himself and his position be used.

Standing by the window of the study, he watched the Indians and thought of his conquest. It had begun almost ten years before when the frightened young padre from Durango opened his doors to two refugees from Ciudad Mexico, Alverez and Beatriz Ramírez. They had appeared at the small mission and offered their services, and Fray Julio had accepted them. He was lonely and aware that without help he would never succeed in his dream of building a church worthy of his memory and his efforts. The brother, Alverez, was a pleasant rogue who tried convincing the ambitious young padre that where there had been smoke for so many years, there must have been a blaze, and that somewhere in the great mountains of the country must be hidden the treasures sought by Coronado, Fray Marcos, and the Indian known as the Turk.

Fray Julio was easily convinced because he quickly learned that the help he would need to accomplish his tasks would come from the sister, the heavy, dark-haired girl with the swift movements, the nervous temper, and the great bull mastiffs she had brought with her to do her bidding. And while the brother, Alverez, disappeared for years at a time in pursuit of the dream so many had abandoned, the sister took over the direction of the mission. It was under her firm hand that it had grown to its present magnificent size.

It was she who decided what should be planted and when the sheep must be clipped. It was she who had made the decision that the compound must be enlarged to house the puebleños where she could more carefully watch them, and that the building be done when there was no planting and the idle hands could best be used.

Fray Julio watched the war dogs wander about the compound and saw the Indians shy away from them as though from the devil himself. The dogs were large and brown and stood higher than the waist of a man. Their ancestors had been raised in the Canary Islands and they had been used in Nueva España since the landing of the first conquistadores. Fray Julio had seen them hunt for a fugitive and knew there was nothing alive this side of el Paso del Norte which could move one breath faster or kill so readily on demand. The dogs were the special charge of Beatriz and had played their own part in making Santa Flora the great landmark it had become. The padre knew there were those who did not approve of the dogs, but he was not one to criticize success, and that was what the dogs and their mistress had brought him. Since her arrival, he had lost his fear. There had been no more letters from the Fray Custodio, impatient to know just what Fray Julio was doing and how he was succeeding with his charges. Since her arrival, his reports were such as a man could be proud of, and he had been left alone. Standing now and looking at his accomplishments, he thought about that future time when the Fray Custodio would resign from his post because of his years, and he hoped that he might assume the greater responsibility he had earned.

The music grew faster and the padre watched Beatriz as she stood in the portico of the rectory, her head against a square adobe pillar, her eyes closed as she swayed to the rhythm. Fray Julio knew most people would not approve of Beatriz, but she knew how to meet his needs, how to satisfy his ambitions and make him comfortable. She knew how to use him in the way he wanted to be used, and he smiled as he considered who was conqueror and who was conquered.

He knew it was not given to all to see the total revelations of God and know all His ways, but even those with only limited vision could build for Him, and so Fray Julio told himself that he and Beatriz were building for God.

He heard the loud slap of her hand against her broad thigh and shuddered as he saw the mastiffs come to their feet. Then he looked away. There are some things, he believed, which should remain unknown and, if unknown, need not bother the conscience of a man of God.

10

THE slow, measured step of the Indian as he danced back and forth at the edge of the compound sickened the heart of Beatriz Ramírez. The nervous pace of the music-maker coursed its way through her fattened limbs like green tequila. She tried not to hear the music, tried not to see the bouncing dancer with the wolf pelt around her waist and the bull horns mounted on his head, for she, Beatriz, could no longer dance.

She had not danced since that night over ten years before in the Ciudad Mexico festival when her growing weight was already upon her. Her pendulent breasts had bounced that night and her fat thighs shivered so much that the onlookers laughed. That was why her brother, Alverez, killed the Lieutenant Governor's son, and why they had joined the caballada of mules and horses on the long jornada north to Nuevo Mexico, and finally to the pueblo of Santa Flora.

They could have remained in Ciudad Mexico and tried to find passage back to Lima, but Alverez would probably have been garroted and Beatriz exiled to the Street of Women without the protection of her brother. So they took all of their property—the clothes they wore, their four dogs, and Jorge, their Negro slave—and made the jornada through el Paso del Norte. They had stopped at the pueblo of Santa Flora. While Alverez searched the surrounding hills, Beatriz raised and trained the dogs which were the source of their power and earned their living for them.

She listened to the sound of the native music and looked up to the dark silhouette of the mountains and crossed herself.

Alverez. Alverez. Alverez. She had loved him more than sister, more than wife. She had been his when he had first wanted her in the narrow confines of their father's hacienda nestled in the cragged outskirts of Lima. She had been his when she danced the zarabanda at the Rio Rimac Cabaret on the Street of Women and he had collected the silver centavos which were tossed at her small feet. She had gone with him up the tortuous route over the Andes on mule from Lima to Ciudad Mexico when the Alcalde had asked them to move on. She had worked for Alverez in Ciudad Mexico, and she had earned the price of the Negro he wanted by sleeping with the drunken padre of Vera Cruz while Alverez stole the chapel ornaments. And she had met his needs when they were without a peso to buy him the comfort of even a mestiza wench.

And all the years they had lived in Santa Flora she had rounded up Indians like cattle, taught them to plant wheat and tend the fruit trees and showed them how to clip the sheep. She had ruled the pueblo with a tyrant's hand because she had never known a gentle one herself. And through those years, as the fat clung more heavily to her broad frame and life became a mockery to the girl who had danced the wild and lustful zarabanda in her youth, Alverez had tried to track down the legend of gold, the Gran Quivera, the hidden mines behind the Sandia Mountain and in the far corners of the Magdalena Range. But he had always returned with empty hands, an empty stomach, and a desire only she could satisfy.

Her eyes shut, she stood against the wall of the small adobe rectory and swayed heavily with the constant rhythm of the sheep's-head drum pounded by strong brown hands.

Alverez had been dead two years now, and she was alone with the padre.

Maybe it was the closeness of their small quarters, maybe it was the heat or the knowledge of the Indians mating around her. Whatever the reason, it was only a matter of months after Alverez had died that she found herself in the bed of Fray Julio. He was a strong man, a quiet one. Once he would have made his penitence for sins of the flesh, but the years of succour he had found with Beatriz guiding the mission, judging the lives and deaths of his charges, had already eaten away at his resolution, at the very core of his faith, and so he accepted her.

The night was warm. The only breeze came off the desert to the west, and Beatriz began to sweat as she swayed. The flush of her full cheeks was hidden by the white corn powder on her face. The loose curls that hung over her low forehead sprang gently as did the blackened ringlets about her heavy shoulders. The two years of gathering wealth she could not spend, of sleeping with a man who could not meet her needs rose in her throat and almost choked her. One nervous hand came up and wiped the sweat from her neck and she stared at her fat, pudgy fingers in the semi-darkness. She wanted to dance, to shake off the fat and the years and be the girl who had whirled so lightly through Lima in the shadows of the peak of San Cristóbal.

The tempo of the strong brown hands built higher and higher until she was almost ready to shriek as she watched the slim, lithe Indian stepping faster and faster. She had to stop the dancer. His return to the old ways was open defiance of her power and the dance was mockery of herself. She slapped her hands to her heavy thighs and the great dogs lying beside her rose to their feet. The drummer paused, one hand half-raised above his drumhead. The piping stopped. The dancer froze. Fear crawled over the compound like a desert animal. The Negro slave, Jorge, thought he heard a distant drum. Then Beatriz pointed to the dancing Indian and clapped her hands.

"Matale!" she commanded.

The great dogs leapt forward.

The frightened Indian ran two steps before the beasts reached him. He screamed twice as one pair slashed their white teeth into his brown legs and the other pair hurled themselves at his throat. Blood splashed over the dark ground and covered the bull-horn headdress. Beatriz walked across the compound and stood over the dancer as he died. She slapped her hands again and the dogs came to heel beside her. When she looked around, only Jorge, the slave, was still to be seen, and as she turned to walk back to the mission house, the dogs followed her.

Fray Julio, brought by the shriek, stood in the doorway. The light from the room shadowed his drawn face as she approached him.

"A witch man," she said, "praying to his devils with katchinas." And she brushed past the padre into the room beyond.

11

JORGE, the Negro slave, watched the dogs heel to the call of their mistress and return with her to the mission house. He felt no emotion. The Indian was dead, torn to pieces by the angry jaws, and there was nothing Jorge could have done about it if he had wanted to. And he would not particularly have wanted to. He had seen men die before, more than he would ever be able to remember. He had seen companions killed in the hunt, seen them lose a leg to a crocodile by the big green river's banks. He had seen them trampled before the charge of a half-crazed rhino and die pierced by the assegai of an Ashanti warrior. Jorge had seen his own mother crushed to death for having lain with his father's brother, and seen his father die slowly, fevered from the bite of an insect he had failed to notice.

Death was Jorge's lone companion, the only one he could depend upon; the doctor with the sparse grey hair, skin like a toad, and face like a hyena. The doctor who danced upon the final drum signalling all to join him. Jorge knew this man. They were not strangers. They would meet again and again until it was time for Jorge to watch the dance and hear the drum and know that it was calling him.

He paused to listen for what he rarely heard. There was no place for a bird to alight and so there were very few about the mission area. And Jorge could still hear the birds of home: the loud questioning of a black owl, and the soft evening music of the dewer. He wanted to snare a bird and hold it in his hand and feel the soft down of its feathers and the shy beat of its heart before he opened his fingers and let it escape skyward to flutter excitedly in a high branch among the dark leaves and look back at him, bewildered and not quite certain if it should complain.

Jorge missed the birds at sunset, and he missed the sun as he knew it, tangled among the trees of the high forest. He recalled it as warm and friendly and not the oppressive enemy he had found it in this far place. He missed the great trees his fathers had known and the verdant undergrowth, alive with bright and crawling delicacies. He could smell the damp, sharp grass along the big green river the Spaniards called the Congo and his fathers had always called merely the River, because for them there was only one.

Walking slowly back to the friary where he slept, he wanted to turn and run, to be a man again, to find another lion like the one he had killed the year the medicine man tattooed the four white spots on his chest and everyone knew him for a man, the same lion whose fur dangled about his loins the night he took his woman into the bushes for the first time.

Jorge's hand rose and felt the twisted scar of flesh on his left shoulder where the white men had burned their mark on him the day they killed his woman. He had never fully lost his anger. She had been full with child when they captured her and because she could not make the long trek to the Big Water, the grey-bearded man covered with shiny metal drew his sword and thrust it through her and the unborn child. When Jorge recovered consciousness from the blow they had given him, the body of his woman was in the big green river with the crocodiles. He caressed the scar on his shoulder as though it were her soft brown flesh, softer than the blue velvet skirt the gross White Witch of the Big Dogs wore. He did not cry now, as he had not cried then, because he did not know how.

He paused before the cross at the edge of the compound that marked the long resting place of the White Witch's brother. This man had purchased Jorge at the banks of the Big Water when the ship first brought him to Nueva España. He had Jorge marked a second time with the burning iron and then had taken him to the great old city of whites that lay in the centre of a lake. Jorge, when he learned the language, knew the place was called Ciudad Mexico and he was called Jorge.

By the time he had learned the language, he had learned other things, too. He was a piece of property like an assegai or a lion skin or a goat, to be kept and tended and used. Then the man who was his master and the White Witch joined a caravan of mules and men and Indians and marched for almost a year.

Finally, they arrived at this place where the white medicine man in the grey frock ruled the Indians. Here they stopped. Here they built a larger house in which to worship the god of the outstretched arms who dangled on a cross branch, gathered more Indians to shepherd more sheep and break more soil. Here they had come to live many seasons ago.

The master had sought the yellow metal, while the White Witch had raised her dogs which helped her track down more and more Indians to worship the white god. Jorge was always there to meet his masters' demands, to feed them, clean for them, and carry them on his huge shoulders.

Then his master had died and he belonged to the White Witch who slept in the room of the white medicine man. Jorge slept outside their door at night, protected them, brought them water, and buried their stillborn child. They would never know the prayers he made to the gods of the sun-drenched forests of his home that the child which filled the White Witch's belly would join his own son as a slave in the world of the big green river. And when they gave him the infant body to bury, he carried it to the river a half-night's walking and dropped it in with a she-goat's fæces spread on its face and three of its father's hairs in its mouth. Then, as the body drifted downstream, Jorge bathed himself.

When he was done, he felt cleaner than he had at any time since his capture. The burial of the child had happened ten days ago. Two days afterward the White Witch came out of her room, laid the lash to his back, and took the dogs to the fields to drive the puebleños.

But something had changed. Jorge could not understand what it was. But the change was there. Only the night before, he had dropped the left ear of a rabbit into a pot with the silk of last year's corn, but it had told him nothing. There was no clear sign, and yet he knew something was wrong.

He had learned the language of the whites, and even a few words of the Indians, but there was no one for him to talk to. There was no one to explain the strange happenings of the past few nights about the compound of the mission, no one to say why the weary runners came after dark and left before dawn, and why the Indians who gave offerings to the god with the outstretched arms suddenly brought out their katchinas—those dolls and masks which interceded for them with their ancient gods.

There was no one for Jorge to talk with. The Indians would have nothing to do with him because he was of the white household and as much a foreigner as the Europeans. Jorge was lonely for the company of the woman long in the big green river.

Staring at the stars, he thought of the distance between himself and the forests of home. Then he entered the house of his mistress, knowing she would be angry at his absence and express her temper with a beating.

She did not disappoint him.

12

FRAY JULIO waited outside the rectory until the Negro slave entered. He was an understanding man and he appreciated that the sensitivities of Beatriz were greatly disturbed. In his own mind he questioned whether the katchina had been used by the Indian and then thrust the thought from him. She would know better than he what was troubling the Indians and how best to settle their problems. This was her domain, as their souls were his. In the morning they would come to Mass and in their turns they would come to confession. Each of them was accepting the faith, and this was his task, his duty, the basis for the vows he had taken and the core of the Brotherhood he had entered. The treatment of the Indians, the day-to-day understanding of them, he willingly abdicated to Beatriz.

He heard the sharp blows which he knew would be the Negro's punishment for coming late to quarters, and then he entered the large open room of the friary off which were his study and the sleeping room he shared with Beatriz. She was already standing there in her thin cotton shift. Jorge was on his knees washing her legs from a pot of water he kept for the purpose of readying her for bed. Julio watched the hem of the shift come up as the slave washed with slow deliberateness the fat legs of his mistress. Then, with a large towel, the Negro wiped her legs, calves, and thighs. She took the towel from him and swabbed at her huge breasts, knowing all the while that Fray Julio was watching her.

Finally, she turned to the padre with obvious patience and a touch of weariness.

"Aren't you getting ready for bed?"

Fray Julio nodded and began to remove the grey frock which was so warm in the August night.

When he went over to the window to put out the lamp, he saw the Indian who had been blowing on the hollow reed standing in the middle of the empty compound, staring at the friary. Then the Indian removed a rope from about his waist and carefully untied a knot in it. Puzzled, Fray Julio blew out the lamp on the table and went to join Beatriz in their broad bed.

In that part of the compound where the Indian families were housed, the cacique and principales reviewed their actions and the directions which they were to follow the morning after the last knot had been removed from the rope sent them by Popé.

13

MEANWHILE, through the night, the runners whom Governor Otermín had seen depart the Villa de Santa Fe continued southward. The mountains lay behind them. To their right as they ran were the low conical hills of long-dead volcanoes behind a wall of sheer cliff and on beyond were the vague tips of higher mountains. The numerous arroyos slowed the messengers' pace and often they ran in the soft bed of the great rio itself. The earth beneath their feet turned red, then black, then red again and the mountains to the right edged closer to the rio. They passed the flat box-cañons and moved on. Several times one or the other dropped to the ground to drink from the sluggish waters, rose and joined his companion ahead. Off in the distance the vague slopes of Sandia formed against the sky to their left. The sun rose behind them and a faint breeze shifted the tumbleweed across their rocky path.

It was daylight when they arrived at the pueblo of San Ysidro.

The small scattered communal houses of the pueblo set among the hills overlooking the rio were brown in the early light. Most of them were the simple two-storey buildings that were to be found in the kingdom from Taos south. Ladders rested against the smooth walls, and the only windows were to be seen above the second-storey terrace. San Ysidro like most of its sister pueblos had been built for defence. It was a simple matter to draw up the ladders and hurl stones down from the terraces. It would have meant more if the puebleños were a warlike people and knew how to fight. But they were planters and builders. The few attacks they had sustained had driven some of their neighbours to the high places like Acoma, while others had given their towns up to the Apaches and fled to the shelter of the Spanish haciendas, abandoning their freedom at the same time. The people of San Ysidro were no different from the other puebleños. They feared the new gods. They feared the old ones. They feared to die. They attended the religious service conducted by the Blessing Man in the mission chapel and the religious service conducted by their own priest in the kiva. They knew the hunger of long drouth. They had the vague feeling that somewhere in the years behind them something had gone wrong, that the world was disturbed, but they could not explain the trouble. They were restless and unable to understand why they were restless. Their cacique was a wise man of their own selection. He knew more than most of them about the Blessing Men and the Whiteface conquerors. He had attended the schools of the Whitefaces. But even he could not tell them what had gone wrong. And so he like the other caciques of the kingdom was waiting for the arrival of the runners of Popé.

When the two young men carrying the rope and the plan entered the narrow streets of the pueblo, only the sleepy Indian guard was to be seen. He rose to his feet and pointed out the adobe-walled court that was the kiva of San Ysidro. The runners nodded and entered. The guard brushed the sleep from his eyes, stared for a time at the hacienda on the hill overlooking the town, and wondered how long this symbol of the Spanish conquest would remain to plague his days, how long the fields would be parched, how long he would have to cross each morning to the small mission chapel to listen to the slight padre with the gentle face talk to them in a language only Ruaha, the cacique, could understand.

Inside the kiva, Ruaha, his principales, and the medicine man of San Ysidro were listening to the plans of the uprising as told by the runners. The details were few. The runners were saying the same things that had been said in Santa Flora, in the Villa de Santa Fe, and which their fellows were saying through the other twenty-seven pueblos.

When the talking was done, the runners rose and gave a piece of rope with seven knots to Ruaha, the cacique of San Ysidro. Then all filed out of the kiva. The runners looked at the sun and turned back to the great rio. Ruaha stood and watched his neighbours return to the communal houses of their women. Then he rested his back against a ladder.

He was a short man compared to his neighbours, and the white cotton shirt he wore hung loosely over his pantalones. He kicked the dust in front of him, bent down to straighten his legging and tighten the thong of his moccasin. The purple-black hair, loose from his sweated bando, dropped over his face and he brushed it back with a gnarled hand. When he stood erect again, his dark brown eyes were half-closed. The alertness about his face remained. Ruaha was not an old man but the years had been difficult for him. He had wrestled with the gods of two nations and had found little peace. He had known the parched earth and the famine that grew on it. He had known the pain of the Spanish lash and the ready forgiveness which hurt more. And in the past year he had learned more of hatred than he had known in all the years that had gone before. But like the caciques of the other pueblos, Ruaha had learned patience. He could wait until the sun no longer rose and the rios forgot to flow so long as he had reason to believe the change would come.

He stared for a time at the small white kiva with the cross above it that lay beyond the fields. In a short time the shy white medicine man in the grey cloak would expect the puebleños to gather here while he prayed to his lonesome god.

Turning, Ruaha stared at the hacienda on the hill above the mission. Here his daughter Poy-ye lived with the bearded soldier. The square-faced Indian held the knotted rope in his hand and wondered how many nights would pass before his daughter would bear the child of the soldier. He clutched the rope tightly as he remembered that the children of the soldiers and Indians were never the ruddy children of the sun, but always the bleached children of the moon. And the moon was a sure sign of destruction.

Then he looped the rope about his waist and went to join his wife, Yad-wan, so that they could go together to the white kiva with the cross above it and listen to the white medicine man in the grey cloak invoke the god who seemed to be so inadequate, so unable to bring them the rain they needed.

14

ACROSS the fields, beyond the white chapel, in a small room of the large hacienda on the hill, lay Ruaha's daughter. She was a young girl, barely fifteen summers. Her face was thin, her cheekbones high and flat. The small chin trembled under pale lips. The green turquoise jewelry on the ledge reflected the slanting light of the sun like green butterflies on the white wall. Natividad, resting on the wool colchón, felt the increasing pains in her loins and closed her eyes against the fluttering of the turquoise butterflies created by the necklace her father had given her when she had been the Indian maiden Poy-ye.

It was almost her time. Her hair lay unbraided upon the brightly coloured blanket which covered her so that there would be no restrictions against the child about to enter the light. There were no knots in her clothes. Everything she could do she had done to make the way easy for the child. But she knew that this child who waited to burst out of her womb into the light of day would have no easy time.

For this seedling there was no midwife waiting to take the afterbirth to the rio and purify it. There was no grandmother waiting to wash the child's eyes so that it would always see the sun brightly. There was no aunt to hold the child to the sun or set the two ears of corn beside it for protection until it was named. In fact, this child would have no sponsor man but the sun itself and the rising moon.

The thoughts burned through the young Indian girl's mind as she writhed from side to side, trying to avoid both the thoughts and the wrenching pains that shook her.

The rising moon for a sponsor man. The rising moon. There was something humorous in this, but Natividad had to pause for a moment to recall what it was. And then she knew. She, Natividad, had been named the Rising Moon by her own people. She was the child Poy-ye. The heel of her hand went to her mouth and here in sharp tooth-marks she buried her anguish.

Suddenly the pains of her loins grew sharper and were lost with the pain in her head and she was trying to answer a question that seemed to crawl like the brown snake of the sage through the fuzz in her brain and she did not want to answer it. What had become of Poy-ye? Where was the child Poy-ye?

Her eyes opened and the butterflies held their place on the wall. Beside them as the pain fell away she could make out the thirteen cornstalks she had gathered so the child would know the full seasons of the full year.

The child. The pain came again and Natividad crossed herself and turned to look at the brightly coloured image of the anguished Cristo on the crucifijo.

There must have been a way. There must have been a way she could have avoided finding herself on this colchón in this hacienda so far from her mother's house.

Where had they gone? Where were the privileges that passed from generation to generation from mother to daughter to daughter, and on through the seasons, as the peaks above the great rio gathered their snows in winter and shed them in summer and the abandoned cliff dwellings of the ancient ones down in the valley grew heavier with the dust? The pattern had never varied. And yet for her, somehow, it had changed. She was not lying in a room she had built with her own hands for a husband who had courted her, a room she had built beside her mother's for a man she had herself selected and desired. The pattern had changed. And then the pain returned and it was the same as it had been earlier in the morning, only it was coming more frequently now.

The pain left her shaking, but the question crawled back. And for one long moment she stared at the empty ceiling and tried to recall the child Poy-ye. The girl she remembered had been a happy girl, quick with the loom, light in the dance before the evening fires and the music of the hollowed turkey-bone flute. The child Poy-ye had learned to make her husband's clothes and tend the hard maize field with the bent stick and pound the wheat. The child Poy-ye had been a slim girl with golden skin, a daughter of the sun and the evening sky; Poy-ye the Rising Moon, with plaits as black as the back of the summer beetle.

The pain attacked her again as fiercely as had the bearded soldier who waited out on the portico for her to be done with her labours. She wanted her own people, but she knew they would not come. It was morning now and they would be going to Mass at the small adobe kiva of the slight padre of the grey cloak who talked to them of the Cristo. She wanted her people, and they might even have wanted her, but the tall, bearded soldier had let them know that she was his and they were not to go near her, not to turn her mind from him or the tasks he set for her. And so when her brother was killed, they turned away and abandoned her as the pain was leaving her now, alone and weary and weak.

Natividad lifted her head and stared at the Cristo on the wall and re-called the tales the padre had told her of the Madre de Cristo. She, too, had been alone and rejected. From this compañera the girl drew some comfort. And she wished for the padre himself, though she knew he would not come as long as the bearded soldier stood, arms crossed, at the entrance of the hacienda.

Nothing was going to come but the pain, and it did.

And she remembered now that it had begun ten months before, at the Dance of the Corn Mother in the dusk of the early summer. She and her sisters had joined the men about the large gathering of stalks to pray for the crops of the years to come and, instead, he came. Out of the shadows made by the low buildings of the pueblo the four bearded soldiers stepped forward, swords in hand. The dancers had paused. The music had ceased and the maidens with their plaits still pulled behind their ears moved to the rear of the wall made by their fathers and brothers. Then there was the loud crash as though of a cymbal and the tall man with the dark beard and the bright silver covering stepped forward. He banged his sword against his helmet to frighten the men of the pueblo, who fell away before him as he walked through them to her side and took her by the arm and led her away into the night.

She could remember clearly only a few things of that night: one was the pain of her brother, trying to rescue her, slain with a sword thrust through his belly and the blood running between his clutched fingers; and the other was the pain she herself had felt as the bearded soldier had flung her onto the colchón where she now lay, and forced her.

The pains then and the pains now. It was only that they came more often now. And then her eyes opened. The room was bright. She knew the child was coming. She wished there were someone to help her. But she knew she was going to be alone with the child and the bearing.

15

THE father of the child of Poy-ye was José Reyes, the bearded soldier, a killer by profession, a highly skilled assassin who by the time he was thirty-five had practised his craft for twenty years. The skill, he had found, was not in killing a man, for it is a simple task to remove the life from a person. The skill rather depends upon practising the art discreetly and disposing of the body in such a way as not to reflect upon one's compañeros in the profession, or the person who hired the service done.

In narrow alleys of Córdoba, where he was first apprenticed, he had been taught the tools of his craft: the daga, the longer and clumsier cuchilla, and, of course, the garrote. By the time he was twenty-two he had emptied the pockets of dozens of travellers, made numerous wives wealthy widows, for which they happily paid in pesos and favours, and had disposed of about an equal number of wives at the request either of hopeful mistresses or of ambitious or bored husbands. José Reyes became a name to remember in Córdoba, and one which even his competitors respected for his skills.

It was about this time that he made his first serious mistake. He fell in love. If the woman had been married, she could have been widowed. If her father had objected, she could have been orphaned. But it was the misfortune of José Reyes that she was a Bride of Christ. This left him only one acceptable recourse, kidnapping. And as he was an assassin, and not a kidnapper, he bungled the task. He had taken her out of the convent, had even raped her twice and was looking forward to the time when she would accept him willingly, when the law, in the form of the Inquisition, caught up with him in the back of a shop where he had hidden the Holy Wench, as he called her. He might not have been caught if the storekeeper had been paid his usual bribe for protection, but José Reyes had leaned too heavily upon his reputation and had threatened the man with a full display of his skills instead of paying him the fifty silver pesos he could easily have lifted from any convenient body. And so, for his greed, he was captured, taken off to jail, and sentenced to death.

This came hard to José Reyes. He had lost the woman. His reputation had failed to stand up to the use to which he had put it, and besides, while not actually an abductor, he had always believed kidnapping a lesser art, and to fail at it was humiliating. The more he thought about it in the narrow confines of his cell located below the level of the Guadalquivir, the more he was convinced that he had to rebuild his reputation. For after all, as he put it to himself, no one likes to die a failure, regardless of how difficult a task he has undertaken, and the task he had set for himself had only been the bedding down of a wench who had caught his eye. But to right the situation, José realized he would need time, and in prison under sentence of death this was a valuable and limited commodity. So he decided to buy more of it.

Spending all the money he had and making what promises he could for the future use of his services he bought his way out the prison and that section of España.

It was with regret that he departed the hidden alleys that he knew so well, the wenches who favoured him for the coins resting at the bottom of his never-empty purse, and the place where he had made his reputation. He did not want to leave, however, a prophet wholly without honour in his own community, and so he took time to pay his respects to the talkative storekeeper. Here José Reyes felt he had achieved the full mastery of his art. The killing had been slow, painful, quiet, and was carried off undisturbed with assurance in the full light of day. José Reyes knew this to be his masterpiece and felt that at last he had reached maturity. He made his rubric by removing an ear of the man, and departed Córdoba.

José Reyes was prepared to forget the entire circumstance which had necessitated his departure, but the Inquisition and the State lacked this broader view and followed him wherever he went. Finally, he realized his talents were not receiving their full due. Assignments were difficult to obtain because righteous men were reluctant to hire for their assassin a man who drew such eager interest from the authorities.

It was with profound regret that he took the purse as well as the life of a young banker of Sevilla and purchased passage to Mexico. Once he arrived at Vera Cruz, he was unemployed again. The Mexicans were accustomed to hiring the talents of Indians, and so, after watching the clumsy efforts of several of these primitive craftsmen, he failed to pay the bill to the innkeeper of Vera Cruz and journeyed to Ciudad Mexico. Here he found that there were men who appreciated the better things of life, and his services were soon in demand by those few able to pay for them. José believed he could learn to love this sprawling, wealthy ciudad with its pretty mestizas, its elegant ladies who spent their afternoons in their petticoats peering modestly through windows and their evenings in strange beds. There was a charm about the place, there was money and a chance to practise his art.

In a matter of months he had regained his reputation so sadly lost in Córdoba. And then he made his second mistake. He killed an Indian. Not that the killing of an Indian was a particularly serious crime. In fact, the Viceroy accepted the fact that during a normal year a certain number of his native subjects would die violently. But José Reyes made the almost unforgivable mistake of killing someone else's Indian, and a cacique besides. This was embarrassing, and both the State and José's client felt he ought to wait in jail until the assignee of the encomienda could be pacified.

Life would be made easy for him. Food could be ordered out and wenches ordered in. Every convenience was promised, and rather than embarrass a fine client who would be good for future assignments at much higher fees, José acquiesced. He found the life tolerable, the service good, and the regular, mounting fee for his time something to look forward to with pleasure, for after all, any person who knows his business believes there comes a time when one eye must be cocked toward the future and security.

However, as José was to learn, when a man thinks too much of security, he neglects details, loses a certain keenness, as well as ability to discern. And thus in prison two things came about which he had not planned. The first was the French pox. This he resented profoundly, for he had even spent time in Barcelona and been able to avoid it, and to contract the sickness in jail from a tired mestiza prostitute was more than his sensitive temperament could bear. When next the girl visited him in his cell, he waited until he was done using the wench and then strangled her. The carcelero who was responsible for the jail readily understood the sorrows involved in a crime of passion, and the incident was soon forgotten.

But no sooner was it forgotten than the second misfortune befell José. Without regard to the nature of the prisoners, their privileges, prerogatives, or special agreements with the carcelero, the Viceroy had the temerity to order forty-eight of them to Nuevo Mexico, there to serve as soldiers.

It was the tragic and unjustified misfortune of José Reyes to be so dishonoured as to be put on the Governor's rolls as a working soldado at a few pesos a month for six years' service. It was also his misfortune that there were none who appreciated his special skill. So, after taking the long journey north through el Paso del Norte with Fray Francisco, José Reyes found himself located at the hacienda at San Ysidro with three other soldiers who had likewise been unfairly treated. Their only other civilized compañero was the quiet Fray Rafael. For a time they put up with his nonsense about Mass and sacraments and leaving the Indians alone. But in a matter of weeks his preachings began to annoy them and they told him they wanted to hear and see no more of him or they would encourage the Indians to heresy.

Only once more did the padre ever call upon them, and that was the night José took the Indian girl Natividad from her people at one of their heathen dances. The pressures of the cacique and the conscience of the padre brought him to the door of the hacienda for the last time. He said his piece and prayed that the men would see their way clear to return the girl to her people. But José laughed, and while the other three men were reluctant to cross with the Church, they were more afraid of José Reyes, who lived with them. And they had reason to be. For when the winter came on and food became scarce, it seemed that unaccountable accidents began to happen to all of poor José's compañeros, until he was finally alone with the girl, Natividad.

Each day the Indians of the pueblo brought food and drink to the door of the hacienda. Otherwise they left the bearded soldier alone. And rarely did he bother the people of the pueblo. Once when the hungry sickness was on them in the middle of winter, he had gone down to the pueblo and had taken two of the young men and strangled them with his bare hands before the others of the tribe and then returned without a word to the hacienda. His actions fully explained his purpose and there was never again any delay in delivering the necessary food.

Now, however, things were different. José stood on the portico of the estancia and watched the Indians cross the dried fields in the hot sun of morning and enter the small mission as Fray Rafael stood at the entrance and smiled at them. It was different now, for José Reyes was about to become a father. In the estancia behind him, in the room they had shared since he had taken the girl from her people ten months before, Natividad lay in labour. This was a part of life to which José had never been exposed. He had never been a domesticated creature. He had never even gathered about him the amounts of money or property that went with having a permanent woman, a hacienda, and a child, and now suddenly all three were thrust upon him and he was uncomfortable. Perhaps he should have sent the wench down the hill to her people and made them turn another over to him. Yet there was something exciting about the way in which she was full with child, and something quiet about her manner which satisfied him. And so he had made up his mind to see what this child would look like. After all, it was not every day that a baby was born with José Reyes as its father.

Reyes had never been so much a part of society before, had never even been part of a family. From his childhood, the orphan youth had been a spectator. As the scrawny boy with the ugly face scavenging the alleys of Córdoba, he had tried to communicate with the world, but no one had had the time, patience, or inclination to talk to him. And so he had lived in silence, hating with increasing intensity the dumb beast—society. He had no understanding of it, and as time went on, he desired none. Now he was about to become a father and have his first link to the world he had never known.

And for a brief moment, he even envied the padre he saw standing on the mission steps waiting to perform the morning Mass.

16

THE hot August sun burned down on the small white chapel of San Ysidro and Fray Rafael Manendez, the shy, isolated padre from Oviedo, stood in the summer heat and watched the slow procession as his charges crossed the burnt hill country toward the mission.

He turned to look at the hacienda on the hill and he saw the soldado, José Reyes, standing on the portico in the early morning light. His black pantalones hung loosely about his legs, the laces untied, and his dirty shirt lay open across his bare chest. The narrow head bobbed back and forth like a carrion bird's while his lean figure stood as still as one of the pillars of the portico. To the sad-faced Franciscan with the gentle eyes, Reyes was a symbol of evil—was evil itself. He looked above the hacienda to the turquoise sky and prayed for the soul of the man. Then he prayed for the girl Natividad as he had done through the long night.

The puebleños began to mount the few steps leading to the mission chapel, and the padre smiled at an elderly Indian woman as she walked, proudly upright, through the wide doors of the adobe mission. From the fields he could see others coming. There was Ruaha, the cacique, his wife, Yad-wan, and the families of his principales. They had thrown back the blankets with which they usually covered their shoulders, and turned their browned faces upward to the sun.

Fray Rafael believed that there was an element of worship in their action. He was not a fool, and being an honest man, he wondered just how successful he had been with these leaders of the tribe. The sun was still to them the source of creation, the symbol of life and fecundity, and he knew that if they believed in any transcendence, it was in the movement of the heavens. To them the earth was still the fertile thing and the moon the sign of death. And though he was reluctant to admit it, water itself, the very water that flowed so thinly now, was for his congregation the final symbol of beneficence and destruction. And he wondered if the beliefs they had so long held might not be the best for them.

In his youth he had been a student, considered by his superior and teachers a man who might some day even be a teacher of clergymen. He had probed more deeply into the realms of theology than his colleagues, had found the doubts that come with any probing, and in time had argued them down, had rejected the doubts and moved more fully with faith than those who have never questioned.

Fray Rafael knew that he would never be able to explain the full revelation that was Christianity to the unsophisticated minds he worked with each day. He knew that what he had to teach was too much to be glimpsed all at once by any mortal man. It certainly could not be seen by those who had spent a lifetime satisfied with the simplicity of a natural religion. For them the fidelity of God was known only through the regular patterns which can be seen and felt in the daily and seasonal shifts of the universe. He knew, too, all the weaknesses which occurred when men reduced faith and belief to actions they could measure like a great clock. He knew this was how the glory of God was humbled to the corruptible equivalent of men and birds and four-footed creatures and crawling things.

Fray Rafael was a thinking priest and a sensitive one. Somehow he had to convey to these people that the earth itself was a great Bible, each object expressing in its own way a symbolic universe in which things taken in their very essence were merely so many expressions of the one God. The mysteries and wonders of the world were disclosed in fragments which he and the people could grasp only in their merest parts.

For one long moment as he watched his flock pass by him and enter into the mission for Mass, he wondered just how wrong he had been in coming to this world. It was so far from the one he could understand, and he felt ill-equipped to explain those things with which he himself struggled, to men and women unwilling to struggle with them. Perhaps, he should have remained at home and left the missionary work to those of his brethren better equipped to convert and explain and teach and even govern the daily lives of others. Given a quiet room in a monastery far from the day-to-day tasks of leading a flock, he might have made some contribution of thought and scholarship to his faith and the Church which was so completely his life. But here in Nuevo Mexico he felt inadequate and he knew that his superiors believed that better service could be rendered in this small pueblo down the rio from the Villa.

He had had notes from the Fray Custodio urging him to spread his activities, to bring more souls to salvation, to consecrate more marriages, and ensure more baptisms.

He knew that, compared to his fellows, he had been slack. But he also knew that he was having a great deal of trouble holding the members of his flock from going off and spending their nights in the dark kiva which stood only a few hundred varas from the very doors of the mission itself. This kiva was the symbol, this the opponent, with which he was wrestling. He had stood at the entrance of the small adobe mission and watched the members of his congregation gather at the native temple after they had filed out of the mission and Mass had been said. And there was nothing he could do about it.

Perhaps they did not respect him, as his own colleagues did not. He was aware that the assistant to the Fray Custodio, Fray Pedro Martínez, in the Villa de Santa Fe was standing in judgment of his failures, that there were those of the cloth who laughed at him and his feeble efforts to strengthen his flock. Yet he, too, had questions. He knew how Fray Julio lived and how the great mission at Santa Flora had been built from a chapel no larger than his own to the size of a church which almost any diocese in España would have been proud to claim. He knew the blood and energies that had gone into the building and had shied away from any such undertaking. He felt that there must be something else he could do. There must be a way to make the simple revelations come to life for his people so that they would worship in the mission they had built so crudely as though it, too, were a cathedral, which it was in its own humble way.

The puebleños had all entered the chapel now, and there was stillness inside as they awaited his coming. He looked up at the sun and across the rio. It was time for him to begin Mass. He had planned for it through the night, as he always planned for it. It had to be something particular. It had to be the spark which would capture their minds and hearts and reveal to them what he knew it to be.

He turned with a quiet prayer on his lips and entered the chapel, holding the heavy cross clutched firmly between his hands as the talisman of the God he loved.

He walked to the altar and turned to the congregation and began the Mass. And as he performed his humble services, Christ was born again, suffered again, and died again. For Him there was the eternal triumph all in one simple action, and through this action He was breathing a new impulse toward the oneness of God and good into mankind, into the immobile brown-faced parishioners who watched the padre's rapt face. He was breathing a vitality again through the vessel of mankind into all creation. Fray Rafael felt this and wanted so much to make his congregation feel it. It was all there, sacramentally and mystically, if only they would let themselves know it. But the faces were still, were impassive, and when he was done, and the men walked out with the women and children behind them, Fray Rafael wondered if any were aware of what had taken place before them.

He waited until the small chapel was empty. Then he walked slowly to his sacristy where there was a small desk on which lay his only volume other than the Bible, the *Summa Theologica* of his adored St. Thomas. He sat down and pondered again, as he turned the pages, how one inadequate padre could explain the eternal actuality, the eternal living presence of Christ, the Glorified Saviour, to the sullen-faced men who would now toil over the brown fields, burned by the sun and parched by the long absence of rain. How could he explain the Christ to men whose only interest was to make enough grain grow to feed their families in the weeks to come? How could he, Fray Rafael, the humble son of a journeyman printer, take these men who had to live in this burning land of the high forbidding hills into the new world of God? It was a world entirely different from the world of nature with which they had daily to fight to maintain their very breath.

Who was he, Fray Rafael, to cope with this task? He was even incapable of coping with a single soldier, his countryman, Reyes. He recalled the comely girl in the hacienda and he went to his knees and prayed for her. Then he rose, closed his book, and quietly walked out of the chapel and down to the fields where the Indians were watering their twisted dying stalks of maize. Without any more than the smile he had given them at the mission door, he went to the rio and filled his large broad-brimmed hat with water. Then he walked back to the first withering stalk he came to and emptied the hat at its base. He returned again to the sluggish stream, again filled his hat, and again returned to the watching Indians.

The cacique, Ruaha, stared at the padre who joined the people in the fields. He watched his feeble attempt to water the dying corn from the thin stream. It was a symbol, a gesture to show that the padre understood the problems of the people, but it was all wrong. There was no understanding of the real problem. How could this thin, Whiteface stranger know how the Corn Mother had been offended, rejected by the people who listened to the talk of a single God, who forgot the dust of their fathers and all the subtle links which tied them to the Earth Mother herself?

Ruaha saw the padre turn his head upward and look toward the hacienda, cross himself, and return again to the rio. Then he made out the figure of the tall, bearded soldier holding something in his arms and knew that this must be his daughter's child. Ruaha swung his back to the hacienda and joined his people in clearing the small irrigation ditches through which the trickle of life flowed to the Corn Mother. And he consoled himself by running his hand slowly over the rope looped at his waist.

BOOK II

AUGUST 9, 1680

Speaking alone for myself it's the steep hill and the
Toppling lift of the young men I am towards now—
Waiting for that as the wave for the next wave.
Let them go over us all I say with the thunder of
What's to be next in the world. It's we will be under it.

ARCHIBALD MACLEISH

IN THE uncertain light of the ninth dawn of August, two Indian youths from Taos ran south. Catua, the older of the two, was a lean, hard-faced young man, anxious to make his reputation as a war chief in Taos. His companion, Omtua, was recognized by the cacique and principales as the leading athlete of the pueblo. He had danced longer and had run farther at the Rites of the Snake than anyone else had. Both young men were tall and light-footed, and at times they seemed to blend with the copper clay country over which they ran.

They were carrying the rope which had been given to them the night before, the short piece with two knots which would mark the morning of the uprising. They approached the appointed place above the rio near the pueblo of San Marcos, where they waited for the cacique and the war chief. But no one joined them. Finally, they abandoned their hiding place in the arroyo and entered the pueblo itself, but no one would talk to them. The two youths stood among the adobe buildings and tried to stop the passing Indians, but none would acknowledge that they were there. In frustration and creeping shame, they hung the rope which was to be left at San Marcos over a large rock at the kiva and were about to depart when Catua, remembering his desire to be a great war chief, spoke loudly to the stones of the empty gathering place, aware that there were unseen ears to hear him.

"I am to tell you that those who do not join in our revolt will be punished, that those pueblos which will not raise their arms in protest against the Spanish deserve to be destroyed. And we will destroy them."

Having stated his warning, Catua ran out of the kiva and down the trail toward the rio with his companion.

Later in the morning they arrived at the pueblo of Tanos. Here they were greeted by four old men who listened quietly to the plan which had been created in the Sacred Place of Taos by the holy man Popé, and they heard the warning for those who would not help, and they accepted the rope which had become a symbol, and they returned to their people.

Catua and Omtua ran on. Finally, they reached the pueblo of La Cienega. Here they were invited in, fed, and listened to with great care. They ate and boasted about what would happen two days hence when the great revolt would begin and all the Spaniards would be killed like so many gabbling turkeys. And when they departed for the pueblo of Tesuque, where Fay-yat was cacique, the cacique and war chief of La Cienega sent a runner to the Villa of Governor Otermín. This young man trotted to the rio and turned north, and as he ran, he was joined by another runner from the pueblo of Tanos, and together as they made their way up-river, they overtook the runner from the pueblo of San Marcos, where no one had come forth to speak to the messengers from Taos.

2

THAT same hot morning in the pueblo of Santa Flora, Fray Julio completed his Mass before dawn so the puebleños might leave early for their work and not disrupt the schedule of activities which Beatriz Ramírez prepared with care. By the time the Mass was over and Fray Julio had returned to the friary, she was dressed and waiting for him. Jorge, the Negro slave, had already prepared their breakfast of eggs and corn bread and salt pork.

The full sleeves of Fray Julio's grey cassock were rolled back and he ate slowly. This morning he was going on a jornada, and though he wanted to discuss the details with Beatriz again, he had learned over the years that she was not to be disturbed while she ate, so when he had finished, he set down his knife and waited for her. Finally, she looked up at him and nodded to Jorge, who handed her the padre's plate which she dumped on the floor for the dogs who sat beside her.

"You will make a list at each of the visitas," she reminded the padre, who nodded as she spoke. "We will need the supplies here, so do not forget anything. Later I will add what I want."

He nodded again.

She looked at him a moment and then shook her head sadly. "You should not have waited so long. Fray Francisco will be at the Villa within weeks." She paused to taste the idea of the jornadas from Ciudad Mexico and wished she could travel back through the years. "If they had had your list earlier, they would have known by now how much we need. Now when they receive it, it will be a list among lists. Be careful to write down the full tragic state of each of the smaller pueblos you visit. Be careful to make the report read as though this were one you prepared each time you visited."

Fray Julio nodded.

Finally, Beatriz rose. Jorge removed the chair from behind her and she walked around the table to stand over the seated padre. She took his face in her hands. "*Infante, Infante.* Do not trouble yourself about it. You can read me the reports before the runner takes them to the Villa." Then she bent over and kissed him tenderly. He held her in his arms for a moment, drawing security from her nearness. Backing away from her feet, the dogs growled softly.

Twenty minutes later the sedan chair was resting on the ground before the rectory and the four Indian bearers stood quietly at their posts as Fray Julio climbed in. He was proud of his sedan chair, confident there was not another in the province. He had seen one once as a youth in Mexico and it had become for him a symbol of success, of achievement. He knew his fellows rode mules or walked. He was proud that he did not.

He waved to Beatriz as she stood in the shade of the portico. She nodded and called to the Indians, who shouldered their burden and trotted down the walk to the gate of the compound and out onto the trail that led south. As they disappeared in the hot morning brightness, Beatriz turned to Jorge. He was dressed in tattered cotton pantalones, his huge brown chest bared to the sun.

"Agua," was all she said, and he disappeared to return a minute later with a mug of cool well water. She drank it slowly as she watched the Indians in the fields across the compound and beyond the gates. They were carrying water in large skin bags and dropping it into the narrow ditch which ran between the rows of corn and the sections of wheat. There were women among the men, and children. Far out at the edge of the fields dozens of the large dogs stood, more like sheep dogs herding a flock than sentinels.

Beatriz was satisfied that the Indians were working. She did not care about the sun or the near-futility of the work. For they were not people to her, but copper bipeds suited to certain tasks, as were dogs and horses. Their value was below the value of a dog or a horse or a cow and above that of sheep. They were plentiful, easily replaced, and not difficult to control when one realized just what their value was.

Lowering the mug from which she drank, she let two of the dogs which followed her finish the cool water. Then she handed the mug to Jorge and walked from the portico into the sun. The Negro rushed back into the house to replace the mug and then out into the compound to follow his mistress at the respectful two paces which she had taught him. They crossed the red clay compound, and as they passed the sparkle of blue and yellow flowers which two Indians tended in the garden of their mistress, Beatriz pointed to three golden flowers and Jorge knelt and plucked them for her. She pinned them in her hair and walked on. The two Indians returned to their endless task of watering the flowers.

Beatriz moved with her entourage of slave and dogs through the fields where the Indians laboured. She pointed to the ground at the base of a stalk of wheat and Jorge gave her a handful of dark earth. She squeezed it between her fat fingers and was satisfied that the Indians were keeping the crop irrigated. Then she walked on. As she passed, each puebleño bowed his head. When she had passed the cacique who carried the rope about his waist and had untied the knot the night the dancer had been killed by the dogs, he turned and watched her. In an instant two dogs bounded over to him and stood growling at his feet, their bared fangs white and ready. Beatriz turned back and looked into the face of the Indian, who stood staring at her. She signalled for him to approach. The dogs moved aside to let him take the four steps which closed the distance between them. When he neared her, she struck him sharply across his face with her open hand time and again, until he looked toward the ground at her feet. Then she turned and walked on.

When she came to the bank of the Rio del Norte, she walked downstream until she reached a large pool in the rio, overhung and shaded by a cluster of cottonwood trees. Jorge seated himself nearby as she pulled the bright blue blouse over her head, kicked off her slippers, unlaced her skirt, and let it slip to her feet. For a long moment she stretched her arms above her head and then walked to the water's edge and entered the stream wearing only a cotton shift.

The waters of the rio, rolling slowly down from the distant mountains that marked the horizon enveloped her and she felt cool and light and agile, and for a brief illusory moment she was no longer the fattened exile, living away from her people who understood and appreciated her art. Here she could be young again. Here in the waters, the weight she bore fell away from her and she could dance again.

Jorge tried not to watch his mistress. He had seen her cavorting in the water hundreds of times and, while he was less than a horse to her and only a biped like the Indians, still she disturbed him. The disturbance was not to his manhood, but to his fears. He was terrified by her, and he did not want to see the white ugliness.

He watched the large brown mastiffs rise and walk to the stream and drink. The White Witch approached them and playfully splashed water over their faces. They backed off and settled themselves to await her next command.

Jorge knew the terror he felt was interwoven of the White Witch and her dogs: together they created a special fear. Though Jorge had known terror and fear before in his life, this was different. He had stumbled once during an elephant hunt, had lost his footing another time crossing a gorge, had known the red-bright branding iron eat into his own flesh, and had seen his woman killed. But those terrors had been only of a moment. The dogs and the White Witch were different: they built and maintained a fear that crept over a man and remained like a rash of the Bad Grass or the fatal green spread of an old festering wound.

Beatriz rose from the stream before him, large and white. Her huge thighs dripped as the water ran down her stomach. She began to bend backward, farther and farther, as though she were going to turn into one great white ball of flesh. Her pudgy hands grasped the back of her legs and she dipped her head into the water. Finally, she stood upright and looked at the Negro before she whirled away again and swept into the depths of the water and her fantasy.

Jorge watched her and did not know the dream she tried to recapture in the lightness of the blue waters. But he did know a secret that kept creeping into the back of his brown head. It was something he had learned only two nights before when he placed the right eye of a she-goat together with the nail parings of the White Witch in a small pot with steaming water—the things which made a sure sign. And they had told him, had whispered the dark secret to him; for that very night as he watched, he saw the Indians gather their arms—bows and arrows and knives and lances and macana—and hide them at the edge of the field near the compound. He knew now what the many runners meant. He knew that the Indians were going to rise and kill the white medicine man and the White Witch of the Big Dogs. But he did not know what he himself would do. He was not of the copper people and he was not of the white. He was the lonely man between and there was none for him to talk to about his part in what would happen. There was no one to tell him when the blows would fall and if he would fall with them.

Beatriz began to tire of the dancing which she knew was not dancing, of the flights she knew were not flights, of the pirouettes which were not pirouettes, and began to feel the shame that always crept over her when she awakened to the fact that she was no longer young, was no longer lithe, and was, most tragically of all, no longer a dancer. She stepped to the water's edge and made one desperate effort to convince herself that she was still Beatriz Ramírez who had danced when she was only fourteen through a whole drunken night for her brother Alverez and his friends. She swung one foot high and tried to spin on the other. Instead, she fell back into the water splashing Jorge on the bank. For one embarrassing moment she thrashed about until she could regain her balance. Then she stepped sadly onto the bank. The dogs held back and Jorge, who had risen, tried to brush the water from his face. When she looked at his palm, rubbing his eyes, she saw all of her humiliation, and lumbered, in her dripping shift, to where he stood. She struck him across the face again and again with her hands, her fists, and tore at his black face with her nails, leaving streaks of red and then blood. Once he stood his full height and faced her only to see the dogs inch forward, and his arms went over his head as he protected himself as best he could. Eventually she wearied and walked back to the pile of bright clothes and slowly began to dress over her wet undergarment. The water of the rio and her own tears streaked the white corn-flour on her face, and the charcoal blacking on her hair ran down her shoulders and breasts in dark rivulets.

Jorge shook. His flesh was torn and the pain was like a loosed animal in his head. He opened his eyes and saw the dogs, slack-jawed, glaring at him. He did not move for a long time. Then he walked to the rio and splashed water over his face. He waited for her to finish dressing, and when she was ready, she called the dogs to heel and started back to the mission compound. Jorge walked behind her, pausing only to pick the nettles from cacti to put with the dinner he would have to prepare for the dogs when they returned. They were sharp nettles that would tear into the vitals of the great beasts. And all the way back to the mission he stepped to the tune of a distant drum beaten by the doctor with the sparse grey hair, skin like a toad, and face like a hyena.

3

THE three youths running north from the reluctant pueblos arrived at the Villa de Santa Fe and entered the empty plaza mayor. They approached with some hesitation and much fear the colonnade where a Spanish sentry in a burnished breastplate and heavy iron helmet stood rigidly at guard. He remembered the lecture he had received only days before from the Governor himself. And when the Indians in their sweat and loincloths came near, he stepped smartly before the door, held his pike at the ready, and blocked their entrance.

For some time the four of them stood, unable to understand each other, quarrelling about whether the Indian couriers should be permitted to disturb the Governor. In disgust, the young man from San Marcos turned and walked away. He would find a cool drink in the rio, and when the sun went down he would make his way home. No one would blame him. He had tried. His two companions were not so easily turned from their task, partly because they found the stupidity of the guard too baffling to accept, and partly because the caciques of their pueblos had spoken to the emissaries of Taos and were more concerned about the dangers. But the guard was firm as he tried to explain in bad Castilian that the Governor only a few nights before had taken away his harquebus, and the guard was to be alert. The Governor was not to be disturbed.

However, his was that common ignorance which believes that explaining something in a loud voice overcomes the barrier of language, and so Governor Otermín, whom he was trying so hard to protect, was awakened from his nap. He listened to the noisy guard for a few minutes, and then walked over and looked out of the window. It was just past the noon hour. With great weariness, Don Antonio drew on his pantalones, buttoned his tunica, and walked out to the front entrance of the palacio. The guard came to immediate attention and the two Indian youths started to edge away, but the Governor called them to him, dispatched the guard for Maestre de Campo Pando, and ushered the surprised Indians into his study, past the ornate furniture, the heavily brocaded tapestries, and the gilt-painted table on which rested feathered fans, the whim of the wife of an earlier governor who had eventually found the energy required to switch the fan greater than the heat it disbursed.

Waving the two young men to chairs into which they slipped with some hesitation, Don Antonio seated himself behind his writing table and stared at them while waiting for Pando. No one spoke.

Half an hour later, the Maestre de Campo had arrived and completed the questioning. Don Antonio rose from his chair and stood facing the narrow slit of a window. Off in the distance he saw the haze above a mountain top. He hoped it might rain but knew it would not. Behind him, erect and formal, his uniform properly cleaned and his boots polished, the elderly officer waited for the Governor's reaction to his report. Otermín did not want to face the situation. He wished he could mount his horse with the silver-ornamented saddle he had won from an English captain in Jamaica and ride south. This was not his country. This was not his problem. With great effort he turned and faced Pando and the two Indian youths.

"Two couriers went from Taos to both Tanos and La Cienega. They carried a plan for an organized revolt that will take place the morning after tomorrow, Sunday, the eleventh. Their talisman is a short rope with two knots." Each sentence was punctuated by a nod from Pando. The Indians did not understand what was being said. Even the names of their home pueblos meant nothing to them, as the Spanish names were not the ones which the People used.

Otermín was not satisfied. There were too many unknown factors. He knew a governor or a commander who acted on small information had small results, and that more intelligence was needed. Which pueblos? The nature of the revolt? The leadership? Too many questions. He bit his lower lip and felt the bristle of his greying beard between his teeth.

"You have the names of the two runners?"

Pando nodded.

"And you know where they are?"

"They said they would go from La Cienega to Tesuque."

Otermín walked over to the map on the wall beside his desk. It was a fine map with many colours; the names of the pueblos were splashed carelessly down the rio line; the direction North was lost in a compass rose in the lower right-hand corner while the mapmaker's rubric flourished in large clear letters across the opposite side. The Captain General stared at the chart for a moment and finally abandoned the pretence of gaining information from it.

"How far away is Tesuque?"

Pando began to explain, "It is, if one travels along the rio, only . . ."

"How far away is Tesuque?"

"Two leagues to the north, sir."

Otermín's decision was made for him. "Take three men, good horses, and ride there as fast as you can. Formally arrest the pair and bring them back. Do not harm them. I want information from them."

The Maestre de Campo saluted and prepared to depart.

"Don't forget these two," Otermín delayed him. "See that they get fed in the inner compound and that they are here when you get back. I might want to put them face to face with the other pair."

Ismael Pando nodded. He was impressed with his Governor. At his signal, the two Indian youths followed him out into the compound. Five minutes later Don Antonio saw his lieutenant ride away, followed by three soldiers. That left him only seven soldiers in the Villa de Santa Fe. He thrust the figure from his mind and consoled himself with the hope that the hacendados would be prepared to fight for their lives should the occasion arise.

4

FIFTY leagues south of the Villa between the pueblos of Sandia and Isleta was the hacienda of Don Alonso García, Lieutenant Governor and Lieutenant General of Nuevo Mexico. From his large casa, Don Alonso ruled the Rio Abajo jurisdiction in the name of the Governor.

Don Alonso was an unusual man and one of the last persons in all of Nueva España whom anyone might have expected to find serving out his years as a lieutenant governor. But there was no one more pleased and surprised by this than the old soldado himself. Seated in the loggia of his hacienda, sheltered from the fevered August sun, a pewter mug of tequila in one hand, and Nita, his mestiza mistress, on his lap he viewed the rio twisting below and drank to the fortune that had made him a man of authority.

In his youth in Mexico he had been known as the Waif of Zacatecas. His father had been the farmer of Zacatecas whose soil never seemed quite rich enough, who never had quite enough rain, and finally found it best to forget these small problems in a bottle of cheap tequila. Some said the woman who bore Alonso was a pure-blooded Spanish dame direct from the Islands, while others snorted and smiled and said that such legends always gathered about the pretty mestizas who died young. For himself, Don Alonso was inclined to believe the first tale. It made him happier.

But whatever his background and however dubious his antecedents, Don Alonso had literally fought his way to his present position. For over twenty of his fifty-four years he had been a common soldier fighting Indians in Peru, fighting rebellion against the Throne in Chile, fighting English marauders in the Caribbean. He had fought well. In fact, as promotions came slowly to those without the prestige of parentage, he had to fight brilliantly to make himself known to his superiors. He had learned how to ambush, harass, infiltrate, and destroy. He had followed the lesson of the terrain and had learned how to fight the small war over bad ground—swamp and hills and desert and jungle—under heat that sought to fry a man's brains. Then came recognition. First the promotion to sergeant. Then the commission and the post of maestre de campo at Durango, and finally the position of hacendado and lieutenant governor at Isleta.

In the hot August afternoon, Don Alonso sat in his cotton pantalones, sweat pouring down his aquiline face as he thought about the fate which had made a don of him. He was proud of his success. He had done what he had done by his own hands and his own brains. It had not been easy for him to learn to read at thirty or to keep records and accounts at forty. But he had done it.

Nita rose from his lap, filled his mug, and wiped the sweat from his scarred face. She was also proud of him. In the thirty years she had been with him, he had always been good to her and their children, and now the boys would have property—a hacienda and land of which they could be proud. If she had lacked a name and Alonso had been born with little more than she, at least their four sons would have something they could point to and say was theirs, made for them by the ageing man who was now, the saints be praised, a lieutenant governor.

Don Alonso ran his broad palm down Nita's thigh and she stood still. The years that had passed between them had not always been so good. They had known hunger and insecurity and the poor food and bad pay that is the lot of a colonial soldier. But they had shared it together as they had shared their bed since that night he had first found her, cold and alone outside the burning hacienda above Concepción in Chile where her Indian mother worked as a kitchen wench and bed companion to a rebel Spanish hidalgo.

"I hear that Don Jaime of Taos is sending his daughter to Ciudad Mexico," she told him.

He nodded and thought a moment about the grandee of Taos whom he had never met, but whose name had become a legend in the province. He did not ask where she had heard, because he had learned long ago that there was little she did not know about the world in which they lived.

"It will be a fine hacienda for someone," she added. "I have never seen it, but I am told he builds well and is liked by the Indians."

Tippling from the large mug, he looked over its brim and smiled at her. "Like still water, I see through you. Don Jaime is no older than I, and our boys will have enough."

He waited for an argument which did not come. "You never wanted until you had, Nita. Be happy that we have," and he pulled her slight figure to him and was kissing her when his wife joined them in the loggia.

Doña Josefa García stood for a moment with her eyes closed and then walked over to the edge of the portico where she could watch the rio beneath. She had been married to Don Alonso for eight years, and yet she was never comfortable finding him with Nita in his arms. For Doña Josefa was a lady, at least she was all Spanish and, as far as anyone knew, her tale that she had been born in Madre España itself was probably true.

She was properly dressed, and the heat welled up beneath her heavy brocade gown and petticoats and shook her as she stood. For a moment she felt faint and wanted to retreat to the cool, dark interior of the hacienda where she could relieve herself of her stays and outer garments and be as comfortable as Nita or her husband, but she turned to find them separated, and held her ground.

Nita poured the master of the house another large drink and his flushed face revealed to his wife how many he had already had.

"Join us, my dear," he invited, as he rubbed the sweat pouring down his scarred chest with an open hand. He looked at his palm and cursed.

"Heat I knew as a boy in the narrow streets without wind or air. In the jungle in Panama it was all heat, wet heat. In the mountains in Peru it was all fevered and dry. Here it is wet one day, dry the next. No fit place for a man to grow old. Yet here are the things I have. Here we will hold."

Doña Josefa nodded. She had heard this before. He was getting drunk and almost ready to start boasting. He was a modest man when he was sober, but the pride came out with the hot sweat and the burning tequila.

He rose to his feet and his large, browned legs showed the strength which had made him. With great care he took Nita's mug from the table beside him and filled it with tequila and handed it to Doña Josefa, ignoring Nita as though she were no longer with him.

He held the mug for a long time, waiting for his wife to take it, clearly knowing she did not want the harsh liquor and that the heat of it bothered her, dressed as a lady. But he waited until she took the drink and held it in her own hand. Then he grasped his own mug and lifting it up to her, he toasted, "My beautiful wife, Doña Josefa." And there was no irony in his words. He was proud of her as he was proud of his hacienda and the sons which were his and Nita's and the titles he had gathered for himself.

And she knew she had to drink because she was trapped. He meant the toast. As she tipped the mug back to sip at the warm liquid, she looked at Nita, dark and slim and cool, wearing nothing beneath the sheer cotton dress which clung to her.

Doña Josefa knew she was trapped. She always had been. From the time she was a small girl and her father had lost everything but his tawdry elegance to the gambling table and sold her off as the mistress of a ship's captain bound for Nueva España. Her freedom had come in captivity, when an English privateer had taken the galleon and its women passengers to Jamaica. Here she had been briefly happy in the dignity she wrapped about her so firmly that her captors left her alone, as they speculated on the ransom she would bring. And she was alone when the tropas of Captain Alonso García had raided the island and he had taken her to Cuba, where he had married her, for she was the chief prize of an otherwise uneventful foray.

Now they were here and the house was filled with the boys that were his and Nita's, for she had had no children. He reached over and tipped her mug so that she would drink the tequila, and she could see that he was very drunk.

With effort she swallowed and almost choked as she watched Nita, standing beside his chair and laughing at her with her dark eyes. She wanted to rise up and strike the mestiza, but she knew she would not because she lacked the courage to force him to make a choice between them.

Nita lifted the amphora and filled Doña Josefa's mug without a word before the mistress of the house could protest. Then she walked over and filled Don Alonso's, standing between the two with her back to the Spanish lady. Don Alonso held out his mug and when she spilled part of the tequila playfully down his broad chest, he reached out and swung her across his lap and shoved his hand down the front of her dress before she could set down the jug, which tumbled to the floor and spilled across the feet of Doña Josefa.

Without a word, Doña Josefa rose and started to leave the loggia. But her husband rose with her, dropping the surprised Nita into the pool of tequila at his feet. He stepped over her, took his wife by the arms and turned her about.

"Have you never learned," he said, "white women are for marriage? Mestizas and Indians are for play and for bed."

She shook his calloused hands from her fine brocaded sleeves. "And marriage is only a ceremony. I was better off with the English. They were gentlemen to a lady."

Don Alonso laughed loudly. "The English!" he said, taking her arms again and holding them firmly. "Would they have been gentlemen when they found there was not going to be a ransom? I have land for you and a hacienda and servants and clothes, and I have given of myself." He thought for a moment as his strong hands dug into her arms. "The wealthy men of Mexico, where I was a boy, do not have so much now. The mines are running dry. Where there was gold to be shipped back to España, there is now only silver and less and less of that each year, leaving nothing for those of us who sweated and fought, knew the green copper water and the sickness of the thin air and high mountains without names where we sought out the gold that was no more and killed 'Por Rey y Santiago' for pesos and wine. Remember what we have, woman: good, rich dirt and great estates, and I have sons to keep it going forever."

She looked at his scarred, burned chest with the droplets of water running down it, the sweated cotton pantalones, and the wench on the floor who attended him in the day and warmed him at night. "You are right, Alonso. You have just dirt. Dirt."

For a moment she thought he would strike her. Then she realized he was sober again as he dropped his hands and smiled at her. "My Doña Josefa. You see me as I am. The dirt of Zacatecas."

He turned back to Nita and picked up the nearly empty jug from the floor beside the mestiza, raised it to his lips and tilted it. Then he looked at the two women who shared him. "But the dirt, the land I have, is forever."

However, of all the secrets of the country which found their way to Nita's ears, one had been held back. No one had told her of the runners of Taos.

5

THE small horse tropa of Maestre de Campo Ismael Pando clattered over the round pebbles at the rio's edge and the broken stones which had fallen from the collapsed wall of the eroded cañon. The sun still cast short shadows from the cottonwood clusters when the four riders whirled like a host into the small pueblo of Tesuque.

The Maestre de Campo's horse reared as he drew it to a sudden halt and raised his hand to those who followed him. Standing in one place, he spun his horse about in a complete circle, taking in at a glance the situation in the nearly deserted plaza area in front of the dirty pink buildings. An old woman with a worn red blanket covering her shoulders scurried to escape the stallion's hooves.

He spoke quickly in her own tongue, "Tell your cacique the Maestre de Campo Pando seeks him. Hurry, woman."

His compañeros took their positions behind him, each horse's head facing a different compass point, each soldier with one hand loosely on the reins and one firmly on his sabre hilt.

Five minutes passed. The plaza was deserted. Finally, the short, squat man whom Pando recognized as Fay-yat, the cacique, walked out of one of the buildings, nodded to the Spaniard, and stood firm some distance away.

Each recognized the other. At a different time they would have been smiling, would have clasped hand on shoulder and reminded each other of the deer they had run down in their youth or the time Pando had stumbled and fallen in the Cebolleta Mountains trying to search out an eagle's nest. But the days of the past were dead days; and if a line were to be drawn, they would find themselves on different sides looking across it as they now stood staring at each other across the empty plaza.

Pando shook the boyhood from his mind, pushed the hot helmet back on his grey head and remembered Don Antonio's "Haste. Haste."

"I seek Catua and Omtua of Taos," he said.

There was silence for a time. Finally, "This is not Taos," the cacique answered.

The sabre of the Spanish officer flashed in the sun as it sprang from his side and landed flat against his horse's rump. The startled beast bolted toward the Indian who did not move. With great skill the horseman avoided the collision and sat staring directly down at Fay-yat, who wrapped himself in impassive dignity.

"Do not play me, old friend," Pando ordered. "The runners of Taos or twenty of your own young men." Time had rolled back a century and more, and the conquistador emerged as the two men faced each other across years, culture, and near-forgotten friendship.

To the other soldiers, who could not understand the exchange, the pause was long. Then the Indian turned back into the communal house.

No sound was heard across the pueblo. Even the flies seemed to be avoiding the visitors and the hot sun reflected off the adobe walls. Pando turned his head and the light bouncing off his helmet flashed through the dark entrances of the communal houses, revealing anxious copper faces in the sheltering shadows. He pointed his sabre at two of the soldiers. "Reatas," he said, and a moment later each had a loose rope dangling from his saddle.

Pando nodded approval and turned again to the dark entrance which had swallowed up the cacique. The old man stepped out into the light with two tall Taoans, whom the Spaniard recognized from the description he had received at the Villa.

Softly, and in their own tongue so that they would understand, Pando spoke, "We do not mean you harm. But in the name of Don Antonio de Otermín, Governor and Captain General for Carlos II of España in the Province of Nuevo Mexico, I hearby arrest you."

His sabre was still light in his hand as he nodded to the horsemen who had moved to his side. In an instant they dropped their loose reatas over the heads of the young Taoans and paced their horses backward to draw the nooses tight about the captives' waists.

Pando raised his sabre in salute to the cacique and put it back into its scabbard. "Let us not forget the bright days of our youth," he said.

But as he whirled his stallion and trotted back toward the Villa, his soldados dragging the trotting Indians behind, both the old Nuevos Mexicanos knew the days of their youth were no longer bright.

The cacique of Tesuque waited until the dust raised by the horses was no longer visible. His old friend Ismael Pando, the three soldiers, and the two prisoners were well along the camino to the Villa when he walked back to the middle of the empty plaza, and life returned to the pueblo as men and women came from the dark interiors of the communal houses, paused a moment when first struck by the sun, and then crossed the plaza to join the cacique. Even the flies rose to hover again, gathering about the droppings of one of the departed stallions.

Spaniards had been in Tesuque before. There were several haciendas near by, and the shaven-headed padre visited weekly. Tesuque paid its taxes to the King and tithe to the Church and tribute to the encomendero, as did its neighbours. Now, looking down the trail which had brought his old companion and trouble to him, the cacique hoped the Spaniards would never come again. But he remembered that his predecessor had stood on this same spot only six years before and plotted an uprising which had failed, and that the failure cost the lives of many. Holding the rope with the two knots in his hand, the old man knew he must fare better. If the People were to survive, Popé's plot must not fail. The men who had been meeting for months in the dark kiva of Taos must not have plotted in vain. The death of Nicolás Bua of San Juan only the week before must have meaning, and it must not be that the youths who had carried the plans from pueblo to pueblo had run so far only to die.

He looked at the two knots in the rope and the faces of the principales and the others who stood about him and he wished that Popé were with him, that there were time to meet with the tall medicine man. But Popé was in Taos, and there was no time for consultation. Two knots. One to be untied that night. One the next. Two dawns distant. Then the square-faced cacique reached under the cotton shirt which covered him to the waist and drew out his knife with the steel blade which had been given him long ago by his old friend Maestre de Campo Ismael Pando. With great care he cut the rope between the knots and held it up. Those standing about him were confused as he handed one knotted piece to a principale and one to his war chief.

"Send runners to the People—all the People. The Spaniards know much, and what they do not know they will learn by dark, no matter how brave the war chief and the dancer of Taos, for I have seen the Spaniards when they sought gold or a secret. Tell the People come tomorrow's dawn, for the Old Gods and the Old Ways, we begin the plan. We cannot wait for the untying of two knots. Tomorrow this time let there be no Whitefaces in the lands of the People, no gods on crosses or shaven-headed men. The vision and plans of Popé must be revealed to the brightness of the Sun Father when next he comes."

Those around him understood. The principales quietly selected runners to go north to Taos and across the rio and south to all the pueblos above the mountain pass which lies far down the great rio to the edge of the land which once was Montezuma's.

The war chief waited until the runners departed, took the remainder of the men to the kiva surrounded by layers of stone wall where they reviewed the plan of action for the last time. The cacique raised a prayer.

> O Sun, our Father
> Sun Man
> Sun Commander
> Father, on the road stand ready,
> Father, take your way,
> Father, arrive,
> Father, come in.

Then they distributed their arms and waited for darkness and the dawn which would follow it.

6

SEVERAL leagues south of the Villa de Sante Fe and the Cañon of the Strangers is Galisteo, where the August sun flickers off the waters of the small rio after which the pueblo was named. Dorotea de Leiva sat on the banks of the rio in the shade of the spruce trees and waited. She had been waiting for days, and she marked each of them with a small pebble beside the pool into which she dipped her bare feet. Twenty days had passed since her father, the Maestre de Campo Don Pedro de Leiva, had gone south to escort Fray Francisco to the Villa. How many more pebbles before he came home again? How many more pebbles before she met the young hidalgo from Potosí to whom she was betrothed and whom she had never seen.

Señorita Dorotea was a pretty girl, tall, with black hair. She had lived in Nuevo Mexico ever since her father had purchased the hacienda fifteen years before. Now she was twenty, and eager to be wed. Her sisters had wed, and both of her brothers. They were older than she: her brother Juan had a daughter almost her own age who had been married a year before to a tall soldier only a few weeks after her grandfather heard she was going to have a child.

Now it was Dorotea's time, and she knew the young man riding north to marry her must be handsome and tall with a fine silky black beard and startling dark eyes. She knew because she had been dreaming about him for almost three years, ever since Fray Francisco had first told her father about the young man, and the two had agreed that he would be satisfactory for Dorotea and that he would share in the encomienda.

The young girl watched the small ripples of the stream and picked up a white pebble and held it against her hand as though it were a ring, a sign that she was a woman and someone wanted her. Then, with a smile, she put the stone aside and decided that this would be the stone she added to the small pile when she returned to the cool waters of the rio the next afternoon. She rose to her feet and looked about. There was no one in sight except Askon, her father's stableboy, a slim young Indian almost her own age, one she had known since she had first come to this wonderful world of varied colours.

Askon was standing some distance away and staring at her as he had done so many times since they were children. A long time ago, when they were very young, Askon, his sister, Concepción, and she played together by the rio. But as she grew older, her father thought it best that she maintain her place as the Spanish lady and that the two Indians remember theirs. In the years which followed, they continued to be friends. It was she who had comforted Askon the night his sister was raped and killed by the soldiers. And it was she who had angered her father when she protested that he should do something to the man who had slit the throat of the pretty Indian girl. Her father had nodded and listened patiently, and finally he struck his daughter across the mouth to remind her that he was her father. Then he finished his tequila and forgot all about the affair, for there were other things more important in directing an hacienda than an Indian girl who was foolish enough to let three Spaniards get under her skirts.

Askon had changed after that. He did everything he was told to do, but he had removed himself from the midst of the family. He no longer stayed at the hacienda at night and had even taken to making jornadas to Taos and other places without permission. She regretted that her father had had to flog him. Her brothers thought her attitude disrespectful and had not hesitated to let her know their feelings. When she argued with them, her father shut her up in her room for a week. Dorotea found it difficult being the only unmarried daughter in a family and even more difficult to understand the place of a woman in the house.

She waved to Askon and walked up the pebbled path to the house. It was almost evening and she would have to see that the meal was prepared, that the table was set to satisfy her brothers and their wives and even her niece who was married to the soldier.

As she neared the white adobe hacienda which sprawled so beautifully across the landscape, she remembered that Askon had not waved back to her, had disappeared instead into a thicket. Well, she would have a talk with him later. There were things an Indian had to learn, and one of them was respect. This much her father and brothers had instilled in her, respect and the ever-continuing need for it.

The slim, dark-faced Indian girl who was her maid met Dorotea as she climbed up the steps to the patio. She saw that the girl was frightened and wondered which of her brothers had been annoying her. Juan had been eyeing the girl for weeks, and Juan had an easy way with Indian wenches. His father encouraged it as a sign of the manhood which never seemed to have emerged in any other way in this youth who dressed like a grandee and acted like a child with all but native women. His father had married him off when he was young to the daughter of the maestre de campo of one of the western pueblos, but it had not made any difference. Juan had been afraid of the white girl and would not sleep with her. In fact, as far as Dorotea knew, he never did. It had often puzzled her who was the father of the two boys who now ran yelling across the open loggia. She was certain it was not Juan.

Dorotea started to enter the kitchen when her maid, half-afraid, tugged at her sleeve. She turned and cuffed the wench for touching her, and asked, "What do you want?"

Then she saw that the girl, holding her cheek where she had just been struck, was too frightened to talk. So Dorotea put both hands on the girl's shoulders, swung her about, and shoved her into her own sleeping room. She knew she was going to have to hear the story about how one of her brothers or the soldier had abused the girl, lifted her skirt and tumbled her on some cold floor or comfortable bed. Dorotea sighed. This had happened so often to the Indian wenches she had trained as maids that she was becoming angry with her brothers. This time, at least, she knew it was not her father, because he was away and only one girl had ever dared tell the encomendero's daughter when Don Pedro had flattened her. The whipping the girl received put an end to such tales. She had been sent away to another pueblo to have her child, and that was the end of the incident.

Dorotea waited impatiently for the maid to get over her fears and start talking. Finally, she reached out and slapped the girl across the cheek. The shy face came up to hers, startled.

"You have something to say?"

The Indian maid nodded.

"Say it." Dorotea released the girl and stood back. Her patience was clearly gone.

"They are going to kill Her," the girl stammered.

Dorotea sighed. "Who?"

"The Holy Mother." The girl winced as she said the words.

Dorotea, puzzled, began to grow angry. "What are you talking about?"

"The men. On the dawn which follows tomorrow. They will kill the white medicine men and the white strangers. Then they will kill God and Jesus and the Holy Mother." The words spilled loosely now.

With great effort Dorotea controlled herself and took the girl by the shoulders and set her down on the bed under the blue canopy, then sat beside her and asked again, "Who is going to kill the padres and us and the Lord Jesus and the Holy Mother?"

The girl was crying now. She had betrayed her people and she was afraid, not as afraid as she was of the hell of the medicine men with the shaven heads or the anger of the limp god of the outstretched arms or the horror of any-one trying to kill the Holy Mary. But she was afraid of the story she had to tell.

Dorotea listened and asked questions until she was certain the girl knew no more than she had related. The pueblo would rise in arms on what would be the eleventh of August, and the Indians of Galisteo would be joined by the Indians of all the other pueblos at the same time. This was all the girl knew and she was frightened because she was not supposed to have heard this much. But she had heard it as she lay in her bed at night in her mother's room in the communal house. Her brother had been talking with her father, and so she had heard.

Leaving the girl, Dorotea made her way across the loggia to the patio where her brothers Juan and Esteban and two of their friends were seated with Fray Domingo. She stood at the door for a moment and listened.

The small group of hacendados seated comfortably about the still waters of the tiled pool in the centre of the loggia were smiling at the tale her oldest brother was telling, while his pretty, dark-haired mestiza mistress passed among them filling their polished pewter mugs with fresh tequila and the last of the rum from Jamaica.

Esteban de Leiva, dressed properly as a host in his best black brocade clothes and soft leather boots, grinned as he recalled the incident he was re-lating.

"The old padre had been talking to the Indian for some time," he said, "and the Indian wanted to work on the mission farm, and so the padre asked him how many gods there were. The Indian paused and finally said, 'Two.' The poor padre shook his head. 'Three,' the puzzled Indian offered. This did not suit the padre either, and as the Indian piled number on number, the padre's, face clouded over and he threw the ignorant savage out. On the steps of the mission the bewildered Indian met a friend. 'How many gods are you going in there to tell him there are?' 'One,' the newcomer answered. 'Don't be a fool,' the other one said. 'I offered him fifty and he would not accept them. Why should he take your one god?'"

Not all the men standing on the loggia laughed at their host's tale, but as his sister entered all of them turned and compared her to the mestiza wench. Dorotea paused beside the ageing padre, aware that she was not supposed to be present when there were visitors. She had been told often that it was not proper for a girl to be seen by other men than those of her own family. And at another time she might have thought about the lecture she would get from Juan and the punishment the two older brothers would find for her. But at this moment she did not care. She knew that when she was finished with her tale, her intrusion would be forgotten. And so, carrying her boldness as far as she knew she might, she filled a crystal glass of wine and drank it before the startled faces of the men.

Then she turned to Fray Domingo and told him in detail what she had just heard. No one spoke until she was finished.

One of the guests, a middle-aged man from a neighbouring hacienda, burst out laughing when she was done. Her brothers looked at each other, puzzled, and wished their father were not now on his way south to el Paso del Norte. Fray Domingo seemed to be shaken.

No one spoke until the old padre had had time to think his own thoughts. "It might very well be true, my dear." Then he turned to the men. "We have tomorrow to prepare ourselves. But now I believe one of you should ride to the Villa. I would like to send a message to the Fray Custodio. Perhaps we should tell Governor Otermín what we have learned. By tomorrow we could have his opinion and know just how serious this actually is."

Juan brushed his hair back from his face and tugged at his thin, straggling beard. For a moment he had a vision of himself as a hero, saving all of Nuevo Mexico, being sent to Ciudad Mexico to be honoured by the viceroy himself and then, who knows, even—a man can dream about Madre España.

"I will go," he volunteered. "I will go at once." And without waiting for further instructions or the message of Fray Domingo he dashed from the room. A moment later the others saw him running down the steps, fully booted, his helmet bright in the fading sun, a sabre at his side. Then they saw him galloping out of the courtyard north toward the capital.

What they did not see was the slight figure of an Indian emerge some distance away from the estancia, raise a bow and fire an arrow into the back of Don Juan de Leiva. Nor, when Juan dropped to the ground, did they see the Indian approach him cautiously, kneel down, and slit his throat before he dragged the body into a thicket and led the horse to a small barranca near by.

When he was done with the bloody work of the evening, Askon put down his bow, set his knife beside it, and went to Mass. He knew that here he would meet an Indian girl who had betrayed her people and would have to die.

7

TO the north in the Villa de Santa Fe which Don Juan de Leiva never reached, the shadows were lengthening outside the window of the palacio and the Governor stood watching the people as they kept to the overhang of the buildings to avoid the heat of the open plaza major. He was quietly waiting for the answers of his inquisitors. Maestre de Campo Pando had questioned the two young runners of Taos for an hour, but he could offer no more information than they had had earlier in the day from the young men of Tanos and La Cienega who had given them their first warning.

Now Pando rested in a large chair. His helmet was on his lap. His right hand inside his tunica scratched the itching scar on his chest as he stared at the stiff back of Don Antonio and regretted turning the youths of Taos over to the three soldiers for further questioning. He did not doubt the necessity of the Governor's decision, but the circumstances disturbed the old man. He had been friendly with the people of Taos all his life. He had known the secret pueblo of the coloured stones and recalled the time over fifty years before when he had first ridden there with his father. The walls were still intact then, the Indians more restless, the Church influence more remote, and the face of the Spaniard more respected. For a time after that things seemed to go wrong for the Taoans. It was almost as if they had lost their hard, firm character, almost as if the adobe and sandstone with which they built and which seemed to cover their lives had hidden them. But now they were ready to emerge again. Ismael Pando, staring at the carved timbers which roofed the casa real and the ornate furniture which filled it, felt a world away from Taos and the people of his youth.

The ride from Tesuque had been hot and dusty, and he wished Don Antonio would offer him a drink, wished he were back in his quarters, sprawled out on his bed with his boots and tunica off. But he sat erect and waited for his superior to turn around. Finally, he began to wonder if the Governor would move at all until the soldiers reported their success or failure.

The day was fading and the concern of Don Antonio was growing. There was going to be trouble. Was it the famines? The hard years of the past? Or was it something more? He was older now than when he had first faced rebellion against the King. That had been in another country thirty years before, and then the youthful captain Otermín had found the explanations simple. Now he was not as certain. Men had more faces for him. And revolt was like a fish with its nose out of the water. There was not only more underneath, but what was there shimmered and was vague, difficult to see, more difficult yet to capture and hold.

He was aware of Pando seated behind him; aware, too, that the moment the soldiers returned, he would have to make a number of decisions. This did not bother him. He had been trained for it. Yet, as he grew older, he realized that he could only do his best with the information at hand, which was always too little and always coloured by other eyes. He had been fortunate in his decisions. When he had made the wrong ones, circumstances had shifted and he had won despite his errors. And many times he had made the right decisions and victory had been his only because of factors he had not known.

Now it was growing late, and the soldiers had had enough time. He turned to the Maestre de Campo, who pulled his hand out of his tunica and came to his feet.

"Fetch the Indians," was all the Governor said. After Pando had left, he walked over to his desk, took his pen in hand, dipped it, and quickly made out a list of names of the Cabildo—that town council that would delay matters even more if not consulted: the Fray Custodio; Fray Pedro; the alcaldes mayores of the smaller jurisdicciones, and Lieutenant Governor Alonso García.

As he was finishing the list, Pando returned with the three soldiers and the two Indians, Omtua and Catua. The faces of both youths were bruised and the war chief of Taos was holding his chest. But this seemed to be all, and Don Antonio was thankful if . . .

"Have they spoken?"

Pando answered. "They confirmed what we knew and gave us the date, which is dawn of the eleventh."

The Governor thought for a moment. "The day after tomorrow. How broad is the plot?"

"All the pueblos."

There was a long silence as Don Antonio rose from his chair and walked around the desk. He stood for a moment staring at the two Indians.

"I do not believe it," he finally said. "There would have to be a leader, and one who is capable of uniting these people."

"There is a heretic from San Juan. An apostate. He has been preaching."

"From San Juan?"

"The Alcalde Mayor of La Cañada—Luis Quintana—tried to stop his work two years ago. He moved on to Taos."

Don Antonio sighed, walked over to a chair and sat down so that the soldiers and Indians would have to turn to see him. He had done it so many times before, this action of pivoting persons being interviewed was done now without thinking.

He knew Luis Quintana—too literal, too precise, too eager, and to finish the list, too damned much the fool. He had driven the medicine man to Taos where control was more difficult, had harassed him and thus set him apart from his fellows. He had given him a certain status and added further reason for hatred. But there was more to the story, and this more, this unknown factor and all of its implications, were what troubled the Governor.

"Take those two," he directed the soldiers, "to the compound behind the palacio and tie them up."

When they had departed, he turned to Pando: "Hand me that list on the desk." Then with the list in hand, he spilled his orders, quickly and clearly.

"Everyone on the list is to be notified at once. Send a special messenger to Galisteo to warn the family of Maestre de Campo de Leiva who is riding with the escort to el Paso del Norte. Horsemen are to leave within minutes. All Spanish men, women, and children must be warned. Christian Indians who want to join us will be notified if there is time. Plan the route and move the couriers out at once."

The Maestre de Campo absorbed the order, inwardly shuddered at its implications, saluted, and departed at once.

Don Antonio rose, filled a crystal glass with wine, and stood waiting for the Fray Custodio to arrive with his assistant, Fray Pedro. They would request his help in notifying their missionaries as he had planned for them to do in order to show them their dependence upon the Throne. The members of the Cabildo would also come quickly to protest their not having been consulted earlier, and he would throw them the task of readying the Villa de Santa Fe for siege, because he needed their supplies, arms, and manpower, for which he could only give them status and responsibility in payment. This would suffice if they were as vain and ambitious as he believed them to be.

His chief concern was his lieutenant governor. He regretted profoundly that he barely knew this old mestizo who believed himself a Creole and assumed the title Don. Most of the Spaniards lived in the Rio Abajo area and would be forced to depend upon the judgments of García. Don Antonio had lived too long to give a damn about the tales whispered in his ears about the women of García and how his sons were not the children of his wife. He had been in the Indies too long to care much about anything in a moment of crisis except the ability of the man upon whom he had to depend. With all his uncertainties he had fewer qualms about an old professional like García than he would have had about a fool like Quintana. The first thing a real soldier learned was that any bold attack could succeed, that there was no wrong way if the men in command knew how to function with speed and courage.

He regretted that he could not be in closer contact with Don Alonso García, but as that was not possible, he finally decided to write him at Isleta. The carta would serve two functions: give advice and encouragement to García who might need them, and impress his own expected visitors with the fact that he was busy when actually the most he could do until he knew there was going to be a revolt was wait and discover its character, then face the problems it presented.

8

AND the complications of revolt were beginning far to the south. The sun was already lost behind the mountain rim and the first shift in the breeze could be felt at the pueblo San Ysidro. Ruaha, the cacique, stood before the large white communal house and stared at the small white kiva of the cross, less certain now than he had been a week ago when the two runners arrived from Taos, less certain than when he had met months before with Popé to discuss the allying of his people with those of the other pueblos. He did not know why his heart had begun to hesitate. There was no word from the hacienda on the hill where the bearded soldier lived with Poy-ye. There were no changes in the innocent demands of the foolish white medicine man. Time alone had its way with Ruaha, and his first enthusiasm for blood had cooled.

He fingered the single knot of the rope about his waist and turned to his wife, Yad-wan. They had been married in the old way, with the simple acceptance of each other, and then they had satisfied the demands of the cassocked padre to marry before his god, where he could proclaim them man and wife. The mixing of old ways and new confused Ruaha. Perhaps there was something in the message of Fray Rafael he had not understood. Yet he was not a foolish man, Popé was not a foolish man, and many of the others felt the same dissatisfactions they had felt for years. If only he and the puebleños had been left alone, undisturbed—but they had not been.

He watched his wife grind the corn meal on the hollowed stone metate and began to sing softly.

> Now bring the corn, our Mother,
> And all the common corn;
> In all our thoughts and ways
> Let us be all as one.

She looked up at him and smiled and the long stone in her hand rolled to the rhythm of his song. They had made their dinner together ever since that first night twenty years before when she had cooked the corn bread for him and let him know that he was acceptable to her. Now her hands were harder, the veins showed clearly, the fingers were no longer supple. And her mind wandered as she worked to things she did not want to remember. Once there had been a son and once there had been a daughter.

> Now! Now!
> Our Mother, Corn Mother!
> Her Sun is coming up!
> Our Mother, Corn Mother!

The words of the song came to an end as she mixed the powdered meal with water and poured the batter over a hot stone before the entrance of the house where they both sat to catch the faint drift of summer air.

When they had finished their dinner, she carefully swept the stone with a small brush of slender branches and rose to her feet. Ruaha looked at his woman and without a word went into the room of the communal dwelling which was theirs. Several minutes later he emerged with her father's macana in his hand. Flint had broken away from the edge of the wooden sabre. It was an unimpressive weapon. But there was determination in his face even if there was none in his heart. He knew he must not falter. Younger men might falter, women could doubt, and boys be forgiven, but he was the cacique, and upon him rested the decision. He had listened to the advice of the principales and jointly they had come to their decision, and he had to live as though it were the only one.

"I shall try to fix the flint," was his explanation as he disappeared in the dark toward the kiva where the other men had already gathered.

Yad-wan looked after him. Her face expressed neither doubt nor belief. It had come. Finally, it had come. Her people were turning again to the old ways and under the spell of Popé they had laid their plans. Most women did not know this. It had been forbidden to tell the women. It was not woman business. And besides, it had to be kept a secret. But Yad-wan knew. There had been nothing in twenty years Ruaha had not told her, and in twenty years she had never betrayed his trust. But as she watched him disappear into the darkness and stood looking up at the moon she knew this was the night she would betray him.

Yad-wan was no different from the other women of the pueblo. She had grown up within the confines of the communal house within the rooms of her mother; and when she had married Ruaha, she had made a new room for them to live in. She had learned to weave and make the clothes she and her husband wore and prepare the food they ate, and when she was pregnant she scraped the dust from the penis-shaped stone, mixed it with water and drank it while praying for the son which would make Ruaha a man. The son came and they were happy. Then the daughter came and the house was full. Ruaha was elected by the pueblo to be the cacique and they were both proud. They had learned to bear with the intrusions and demands of their conquerors as best they could. Life flowed with the seasons. Yet the men were no longer as happy as they had been. The old gods seemed to have departed. Underlying their lives was a growing discomfort in the pueblo which disturbed all of them, but it was nothing they could tell the old gods about. They had lost the gift of communion with the old gods. Then the bearded soldier and his compañeros came to live in the hacienda on the hill behind the kiva of the cross. At first the Spaniards kept their distance, only asking for food and supplies. They had kept their distance until the night of the last Dance for the Corn Mother. And when they departed, Ruaha and Yad-wan no longer had a family.

The old woman thought of all this as she walked slowly to the door of the mission of the padre in the grey cassock. She stopped on the steps and looked about her at the quiet night. There was smoke rising from many of the rooms of the communal house, and she could make out the slow drift of grey smoke wandering skyward above the kiva where Ruaha was preparing with the others for the action two dawns hence. This place was her home, the only one she knew. Her world lay within the rim of mountains that encircled the horizon. She was aware that the rio flowed down from the Blue Lake above Taos, but she had never seen the lake and had never seen Taos.

She turned her back to the pueblo and entered the mission. Fray Rafael stood before the altar. He heard her enter, crossed himself, and joined her at the back of the church. His knowledge of the Tewan language was slight and she knew no Spanish. So she confessed her sins to the patient man who did not fully comprehend them, approached the altar, crossed herself, and backed out of the kiva beneath the cross.

After she left, the shy padre thought for a long time of what she had told him. There was something in it about going to see her daughter and something about a revolt at some future time when there were no longer any knots. But none of it made sense to him. Then he recalled who the woman was, recalled that this was the mother of the girl Natividad. He crossed himself and went into the small room he used to prepare his sermons. He would have to talk about revolt, about apostasy, when they met for Mass in the morning. He would have to prepare a sermon which would reach the puebleños. Pleased that he had a task to do, he quickly set about it.

Yad-wan made her way from the mission up the hill toward the hacienda. She had never been here before for fear of her own life and that of her child, for she remembered well the night Poy-ye was taken, and the death of her son. But now she had made her confession, now she was clear with Him of the bleeding hands, and she had to warn Poy-ye.

Darkness hung over the barranca. She saw the lights of torches about the hacienda and the smoke meander above its beamed roof. The path was narrow and there were many stones. With great difficulty she approached the house. She was almost at the portico when she tripped on the cord that was carefully hidden in the dark. It caught her foot and she fell forward on her face. Then the boulders rolled down the side of the trail and two of them struck her as she tried to rise to her feet. She felt the weight of them as her chest was crushed, and then there was her scream, faint and startled, hanging with the darkness in the night.

The sharp slaps against her face brought her eyes open into the blinding light of the torch held by the bearded soldier. For one long minute the old woman of the pueblo stared into the dark eyes of José Reyes. Then he pulled her to her feet. And as he shoved her back down the trail, she heard the cry of an infant from the hacienda, and she tried to tell the bearded soldier that she wanted to talk to Poy-ye, to Poy-ye. She had to talk to her daughter, tell her to be far away from the hacienda two mornings hence. She kept repeating the name of the girl who was her daughter over and over, but it meant nothing to José Reyes, who had never heard the name before, and he pushed her away and drew his sword and held it before him.

José Reyes did not know the old fool of a woman who had disturbed him. He only knew that when morning came he would have to set the trap again, and he was tempted to kill her for this. For a brief moment as she stood, breast forward against his sword, he weighed the wisdom of keeping her alive to do the job for him. In the torchlight, however, he saw the blood running out of the corner of her mouth and with the knowledge of an expert he knew she would never live until morning. So he laid the flat of his blade against her side and drove her away as he would have a cow that had wandered into a garden.

He stood watching her stumble back down the trail and shook his head. He was wondering if there was any connection between this visit and the runner he had seen enter the pueblo earlier. He wondered what was to take place. Then he heard the cries of the infant behind him and turned back to the hacienda. Natividad would be waiting with his drink and a warm meal.

Yad-wan stumbled from the base of the hill to the communal house where she had been born. As she passed the kiva beneath the cross, she was glad she had made her confession, for she knew that it was not good to offend any god when one is dying. She walked with failing steps to the room where Ruaha was waiting for her. When she saw him, all she could think to say before she collapsed on the floor was, "There is a child in the hacienda. I heard it cry, and I think it is a boy-child." She wanted Ruaha to be proud of her daughter.

Then she died.

For a long time the old man looked at the body that had been his wife. Slowly he began to cry. He turned to the hills over which morning would come and prayed. When he was done, the doubts were all gone. He knew what he had to do when the knot in his hand was untied. He stumbled out into the darkness holding the carved wooden handle of the macana in his clenched fist. He listened to the soft sound of the rio and knew that he, Ruaha, had turned about to face the Spaniards and that there would be no turning back.

9

THE couriers of Don Antonio made their separate ways across the dark countryside. The fevered sky had retreated and night had fallen over the twisted land. The soldier riding south to the hacienda of Don Alonso García saw no need for haste. To his simple mind the Indians were unlikely to rise against him, and if they did, he almost enjoyed the prospect of killing them.

Seated *a la gineta,* legs forward in the high remnant of the Moorish-type saddle with the short shoe stirrups, the rider felt confidence against the tens of Indians and, should the need arise, against the hundreds. It was true that he had never fought them. Nor had most of his compañeros, but there was that assurance which his hand resting on the hilt of his cold blue sabre gave him, that belief he had that the leather jacket he wore would turn an arrow, that the dark chestnut horse he rode with its short back, low-slung belly, and firmly jointed legs could outdistance any Indian, should that doubtful need arise.

And so when he came to the great rio, he reined his horse and swung out of the saddle to the ground. He led the broad-breasted stallion to the water's edge. There he removed his helmet and threw himself prone on the bank. With quick splashing motions, he bathed his face and soaked his full, dark beard. Beside him, the horse quietly drank its fill.

When he was refreshed, the soldier rolled over on his back and stared at the star-washed sky, brushed to the north by wisps of clouds hanging over the sierra. He stretched out his arms, relaxed, and was comfortable. He lacked only wine and a woman to be happy. And as for the wine, he rose and removed the small jug dangling from his saddle, pulled the wooden stopper and drank deeply before he slipped a second time to the ground to rest.

He winked at the sky and thought of a certain mestiza wench with cool hands. He grasped a long strand of green weed and chewed the tip of it. Only governors, maestres de campo, and dying old men like the Fray Custodio had to concern themselves with haste. For him there were going to be long years, any number of pretty mestizas and full jugs. Then maybe sometime when he was older he would find an estancia and a Spanish woman, the

way the old soldier García had. But there was time enough for that as there
was time enough now. He closed his eyes and listened to the chestnut horse
chomp on the fresh grass.

Soon he fell asleep.

He did not hear the tawny runner of Tesuque in his moccasined feet
come down the trail. He did not see him pass on and disappear to the south
toward Isleta and San Ysidro.

10

WELL into the night the wordy speculations in the palacio continued, and
Don Antonio de Otermín was weary. The members of the Cabildo of the
Villa de Sante Fe had met shortly after the evening meal and with lengthy
discussion agreed that his warnings were the only steps which should be
taken without more information. There was no military force with which
to meet a unified uprising, they were not prepared to enjoin one, and the
Governor's plan to consolidate the Spanish population in the north under
his command in the Villa and in the south at Isleta under the command of
the lieutenant governor seemed reasonable but only, of course, if there was
actually trouble.

Then the Cabildo adjourned, leaving only the Fray Custodio, Fray Pedro
Martínez, and Maestre de Campo Pando with the Governor. The wizened,
aged padre had said very little during the evening's discussion. When his
assistant spoke on behalf of the Church, he barely nodded his assent. The
old man's mind had left the details of the defence early and was weighing,
as it had so many times before, how the Order of Friars Minor—the Franciscans—had come to this point in its history.

A failure. A failure. The words wandered through the corridors of his
mind like a lost child looking for another answer. But there was none. And
he felt the failure was his. Had he pressed too quickly? Converted where
there was little understanding and less faith? Or, perhaps, a stronger hand
might have been the wiser course. The Throne—the State—could have
been forced to support the Church with more than thieves, orders stating "at
the least possible cost" and men almost as old as himself. If more had been
invested. . . But this was a fruitless path to wander down at this late hour.
The soul of an Indian convert has limited commercial value and the King's
money was always destined to support the King's follies. And there were so
many of these. The old padre, who had spent his adult years away from the
homeland of his youth, wondered what it would be like living in España
with an imbecile king on the throne. Men became accustomed to corruption
as a way of life, learned to exist within its warped framework as they had
for centuries. But an imbecile king, uneducated and uneducatable, a Carlos
El Hechizado, "The Bewitched". . .

He turned his shaven head to watch the Governor and Captain General nodding to the suggestions of the youthful Fray Pedro and did not hear them. It was Don Antonio who interested him. The Captain General was probably ten years his junior. The soldier's career had paralleled his own in many ways. If he had not taken his vows, he would probably be sitting in a governor's chair in some remote corner of the imbecile King's world waiting for the dawn two days hence and fearing what it might bring. And he knew the Governor was intelligent enough to have his fears even if he was not voicing them. Destiny. He snorted, and when the other turned to look at him, he coughed to cover his thoughts. Destiny. His would have brought him here whether he had carried a cross or a sword.

Ismael Pando was talking now about another uprising and the words were confusing to the old padre for a moment.

"Came with the corn dance. Treviño, governor then, worked to keep it down. Dance and the mission. Would not accept the two as part of the country."

The Fray Custodio nodded. Treviño. A young Otermín with more fire and less judgment. Maybe if this quiet Governor had more fire, more energies, and . . . but a man is no more than he is.

"And they rose up. A few pueblos. Late in the year. The snow was early. There were some deaths and the medicine men preached," the Maestre de Campo talked on.

The old man, almost lost in his cassock, was not listening. He was thinking instead of the thirty-two padres in the province and Fray Francisco riding north from Mexico with supplies for the Brotherhood. He was thinking of the place of the Order in the province and why the Brotherhood was there. For the Order, the Indians were reason enough. For the individual padres, well, each had his own motives, and the old man never sought the personal motives of his fellows though each in time revealed his own in his own way. But for the Order, it was the Indians. Sixty thousand or sixteen thousand. Here was a world for God.

"Martyred three padres. Lit fires under them or stretched them on the church door. Then danced to the corn. The dance done . . . then we came. Forty soldados, mounted, with harquebuses."

What brought a frightened Fray Rafael to a frightening mission? The old man thought of the disputation they had held over their evening meal the year before: Scotus versus St. Thomas, and the old arguments rolling back to quiet country monasteries centuries dead and civilizations away. Now that shy little Fray Rafael was almost alone in the pueblo of San Ysidro. The cacique Ruaha was there and the Fray Custodio remembered him as a reasonable man. Perhaps. . . .

"The fighting. Brief. Quick. Some blood on the snow. A wounded horse. Two soldados dead and it was quelled." The officer poured himself a drink and talked on.

The same visita which had taken the Fray Custodio to San Ysidro Pueblo had taken him to see Fray Julio. Fray Julio. Fray Julio. All the failures welled up in the old man and he wished he were younger so he might have years before him in which to grow, or older so that he might no longer be responsible. Then he knew he was in flight again and from himself. He should have done something about Fray Julio and his concubine. He should have been strong enough to salvage the man, but he was not. Perhaps, when his time came, Fray Pedro might. Hope and postponement.

"Then the winter. Cold. A hard journey of it to the Villa again. The prisoners starving. Families scattered. Praying to God or gods. And our not knowing which. The burials then. The martyred. The two soldados, lances in their guts. And the clay graves."

The Fray Custodio rose to his feet and excused himself. He wanted to spend some time in the chapel before retiring. There was much he must discuss with God. Fray Pedro rose to leave with him, but the old man shook his head, waved his assistant back to his seat, and departed.

Pando watched him as he left. The soldier was fond of the ageing Fray Custodio. He found this padre a complex man. He was deceptively simple, and the grey-thatched Nuevo Mexicano knew there was more behind the dark, cold eyes than devotion. Maybe the complexity lay in the way the padre understood people. Maybe it was in the rigid manner he had created to cover a quiet gentility. Ismael Pando admitted his own limitations, and not understanding the Spanish-born padre was one of them.

Fray Pedro raised his chunky figure out of the chair on which he sat. "Tomorrow will be an important day," he prophesied, and the obviousness of the remark brought Otermín up sharply. He was not certain if the man was serious. Then he remembered that the young padre from Valladolid was always serious—obvious and serious.

Then the padre was gone, and the two old soldiers sat staring into their wineglasses.

"Do you know Don Alonso?" the Governor asked casually.

The glass in the big, browned hand of Ismael Pando turned slowly around and around. "I have been to the hacienda at Isleta."

The Governor had long ago learned there were certain values in patience. Though he felt at times it was too highly valued a virtue. Now he was patient.

"Several times," the Maestre de Campo added.

And there was another silence.

"As you know, Don Alonso soldiered in many places."

The Governor nodded.

"He has sons. They will fight."

The crystal glass reflected the light of the candle and streaked brightly across the wall as it turned in his hand.

"His woman, fine stock. And the Señora, she is from España."

The Governor now had heard almost everything he already knew about Don Alonso. He knew, too, that he should not be asking a junior officer about the Lieutenant Governor. But the large gilt clock with the Roman numerals poorly painted on burnished silver told him that time was closing in on the Spaniards of Nuevo Mexico. He knew what he could do, knew what his own abilities were, and how to protect his command from his own weaknesses. But Don Alonso García was an enigma. The government and the army of Carlos II were clumsily managed, and fools frequently found their way into high office. But in class-structured Nueva España these men were usually Creoles or home-country hidalgos with money or influence or a properly placed mistress. Don Alonso appeared to have none of the usual advantages. It was just possible, Don Antonio conceded to himself, that his Lieutenant Governor possessed ability. If so, he might need every bit of it.

Pando finished his drink and filled the glass again. "Many soldados are two men, and as I have never fought beside Don Alonso, I know only one."

The Governor nodded and walked to the window. If he was fortunate, his riders would be able to alert the near-by haciendas and ranchos in time for the people to move into the Villa in the event of an uprising, and the soldier riding south would arrive at the hacienda at Isleta in time for Don Alonso to warn the people of the Rio Abajo jurisdiction.

The hour was late and the plaza mayor was empty. There was only silence, and for a time it bothered the grey-bearded Governor standing rigidly by the window. He saw Fray Pedro emerge from the chapel and walk over to his quarters. He watched him for a moment, and then he turned back to Pando, lifted his glass, half-defiantly and half-amused at himself: *"Por Rey y Santiago."* The ageing lieutenant rose to his feet and joined his superior in the toast, but firm resolution was the only note the Governor detected in his voice, and he was comforted by it.

Fray Pedro walked down the corridor to his cell in the friary. The day had been difficult. The hour was late. Inside his small room he removed his cassock, folded it neatly and set it on a shelf. Then he sat down on the straight chair at his writing table and stared into the darkness.

His well-organized mind weighed the accomplishments of almost a century against what appeared to be the failures. And he found that he could not bring the pieces into focus. He struck a light in the dark, encouraged its growth, and lit a candle. One square hand rested flat on the table while the other toyed with the feathered tip of a quill. Then he slowly began to write, as much to organize as explain.

In Continuance   9 Agosto 1680

As I wrote only a week ago, I shall add to this letra such news as may be of interest to Your Grace. Today we have reached a crisis in the history of our Order in Nuevo Mexico, and I feel we must inventory our deeds in relationship to our accomplishments. We have laboured for the honour of God and the propagation of our faith with as much fervour as our brothers in far Tartary or Abyssinia, and yet only today we have learned that our converts plan to reject God and return to their heathen ways. This truly has been a brutal disappointment to all of us.

The padre chewed the feather of his quill as he considered what he had written. Well, there was the truth and the only thing he could do was set it down and look at it himself.

We have converted and baptized these people. We have given them a common language, metal, cattle, sheep, pigs, as well as new ways to plant their fields. Fray Arteaga many years ago gave them grapes, and now they have wine as well as the new fruit trees we have brought into the land. We have worked hard to show them the way of God and give them resolution to discard their pagan ways which are an abomination in the sight of the Lord.

I am aware that it has been said against us by those who do not know the circumstances under which we live that we have enslaved our charges. This is not true. The Indians knew slavery of enemies before the first Spaniard ever entered this land. We have enslaved only the rebel against the Crown and the heretic who practices witchcraft.

We have designed the economy of the province for the good of the Indian as well as the Spaniard. Here as elsewhere rancheros and others may draw upon native help to labour for them depending upon the common need. For this service the Indian is paid a real a day as has been directed by the Viceroy himself. We of the Brotherhood have sought to keep this system free of abuses. To relieve the burden of expence it has been necessary to require the Indians to furnish their own food and travel without pay to the place at which they must work. Yet the Indian has not always been co-operative and in some instances the rancheros have had to resort to flogging and even taking away their blankets to prevent desertion from appointed tasks.

As I sit at this moment of evaluation and write you this carta, all of the manifold measures which have been directed for the good of the Indians come to mind. The Brotherhood has brought all violations of the system to the attention of the authorities. Women are not supposed to be given for personal service. The carrying of heavy loads is forbidden. And His Majesty's own officials are not permitted the unpaid services of the Indians.

Only the Holy Church possesses the right to conscript labour for construction, and it is believed the Indians have built the large, magnificent mission churches and friaries out of their eagerness to serve and honour God.

The padre read over the case he had prepared for the Order though he was not yet ready in his own mind to admit that he had prepared an apologia. He was, however, willing to admit to himself that he could not understand what had disturbed the Indians.

The pen came up again and he closed his note for the evening.

As I write Your Grace, I am encouraged in the belief that we have accomplished much that is good. I feel confident, too, that we shall find a means of conveying our understanding to the converts who waver in their faith so that they may remain humble to Our Lord and know His goodness. In this belief I shall end my writing this night and pray for His help and Your Grace's good health. I kneel and kiss Your Grace's hand.

After carefully setting the quill in its holder, he knelt in prayer.

RUNNING north, the messenger of Fay-yat of Tesuque reached the Rio Pueblo and turned toward Taos. Darkness had already fallen and silence covered the land. Only the distant and protesting voice of the coyote was heard. The youth who had been selected by the principales to carry the news to Taos and Popé passed the high gates of the hacienda of the Silent Spaniard, reviewing the story he must tell, and made his way quickly to the entrance of the kiva of Taos. Here he stopped as a guard stepped out of the shadow of a building with a Spanish sword in his hand.

"I am sent by Fay-yat of Tesuque to Popé of San Juan." The shadow of the guard moved aside and the youth descended into the dark world below. His eyes came to focus after a moment and he saw the torch set in the wall, the flame of the sipapu, and the shadowed faces of the men of Taos.

He repeated his credentials to no one in particular and was received in silence. Finally, a lean, wiry man rose to his feet and identified himself. "I am El Saca of Taos."

The runner nodded. The name was familiar.

"There was something you were sent to tell us."

And the story was told of the coming of the white Maestre de Campo who was born in the kingdom of the pueblos but was not of it, of the threat to Tesuque if the war chief and the dancer of Taos were not made known to the bearded soldiers with the shining sabres, of the departure of the Spaniards with the messengers of Popé, of the decision of Fay-yat to cut the rope, and of the other runners now making their way south to tell of the lone knot and the action to follow when the Sun Father was seen again. Then the youth was silent.

A large figure of a man with bull horns on his head and a jaguar pelt about his waist rose from the shadows behind El Saca and stepped forward. His back was to the light and his face was vague in the darkness of the kiva.

"Fay-yat of Tesuque is a wise friend. We must prepare for the coming of the Sun Father. We must wash ourselves in the waters with the amole root and cleanse ourselves of the rites of the Holy Mary and the Jesus with which we profaned the Earth Mother and the Corn Mother. Then we must gather our arms and seek the intercession of the katchinas so that we may be acceptable to the twin gods of war, to Monster Slayer and Born-to-Water." As he spoke he stepped back and drew a long pole from the rear of the kiva and set it in the ground with a mighty thrust so that it stood upright between the men seated in a semicircle. This was the scalp pole of Taos.

The principales nodded, and in their turn took the sacred white meal held out by the holy man and scattered it over the sipapu. Then they climbed out of the kiva, one at a time, to seek the waters of the Blue Lake flowing south, to cleanse themselves of the heresy against the old gods and then blacken their faces, gather their women, and briefly dance the war dance about the scalp pole before the Sun Father brightened the earth, for a wise man appeases the ghosts of those to be slain.

When all of the men had departed except Popé and the runner, the large man of the shadows placed his hands on the arms of the youth and said, "Speak for me to Fay-yat of Tesuque and tell him that we shall meet before the Villa of the Whitefaces when we have destroyed those who would live on our land and by our labours and on the death of our gods."

And he sprinkled the sacred white meal as he pledged himself to the cacique of Tesuque.

The youth disappeared up the ladder and into the darkness southward. Popé stood alone in the kiva beneath the ground. He turned to the direction from which the Sun Father would come and spoke to the katchinas of the kiva.

"There can be no other path. For if we fail, we have lost no more than the help of the old gods, and they have not been with us while the hearts of the People have been in the kivas of the blessing men. We must liberate ourselves from the green waters in which we have rested and move like a spring torrent toward the ways which were our fathers'. We must return to that which was ours, hold holy our own, or by not holding it holy in our eyes deny it and fail. There can be no other path though it lead to our own blood."

His hands came to his face for a moment as he listened for a sound which did not come and which he knew would never come. He had lived so long in silences that he could no longer accept them as answers. For he had learned that the worst silence that existed for him was the one created by the medicine men with the shaven heads and the crosses in their hands, the silence of rejection, the silence he could not breach because they could not hear what he had to say or what his people felt, the terrible silence which prevailed because men would not listen.

He climbed out of the kiva to find himself alone and he looked at the stars splashed across the sky, felt the silence which reached through the night, and knew now it would only be broken by the splash of blood and then there would no longer be silence to breach as there would be no master to turn his head from the slave.

12

AMONG the men who had climbed out of the kiva of Taos was Juan, the assistant and protégé of Don Jaime de Marcos. The tall, lithe youth was standing in the shadows when Popé emerged and stood looking at the stars. The Indian boy felt compassion for the medicine man from San Juan. What

Don Jaime de Marcos had given Juan, Popé had never received—acceptance and beyond, friendship.

Yet, these too had their toll, for Juan was troubled, torn between the Spanish encomendero who had taught him to read and write, taught him what was valuable and what was dross, the mockery that was the love of a woman for a man, the dust-devil instability of position and titles, the ridiculous pursuit of the tumbleweed of wealth. Juan owed much to Don Jaime, but the former Conde de Iteo had a white face. The man was the symbol and his encomienda was the fact of what was happening to the People. Even a friendly, compassionate despot was still a despot. Don Jaime himself had taught the Indian youth this much from the books he had brought from the peninsula which neighboured his own so far away, the tightly wrought words of Pico, Fecini, and Bruno—the Renaissance philosophers of man.

Juan watched the tall figure of Popé disappear into the darkness and then walked out of the pueblo along the banks of the rio where he heard the Taoans splashing in the waters. He could never cleanse away what he had never accepted, any more than he could accept the old gods in whom he could never believe, and so he was left with compassion for the people who were his people and with friendship for the man who was not of his people.

Juan stood for a time in the darkness, staring at the fires of the pueblo as he tried to remember when it had ceased to be his home, tried to recall that first time so long ago when Don Jaime had taken his hand and walked with him to the farmhouse. Juan had been a thin, wild boy of eight then. His father had died two years earlier in an accident at the turquoise mines in the Cerrillos Mountains. His mother had caught the eye of a Spanish soldier and died a year later in childbirth. The baby had died, the soldier had ridden south, and Juan had been left alone.

The Indian youth turned away from the pueblo and started once more down the path that led to Don Jaime's home. He was pondering the same question that had troubled him for years, the question he knew even the encomendero could not answer: why had de Marcos adopted the orphan? Why had he taken the boy into his home, made him a part of his household, raised him as a son? Juan knelt down and picked up a handful of pebbles and threw them at distant trees as he walked. He was taller than most puebleños; thinner, too. And though he dressed like a Spaniard even to his heavy bucket boots, he retained a lightness to his step and a grace of movement that anyone watching him would have associated with the People.

The silhouette of the casa rose before him in the darkness and he entered the gates knowing the world in which he had lived would no longer exist when the morning sun burned the sky. He crossed the courtyard and climbed the familiar steps to the patio. Don Jaime rose from a chair where he had been sitting alone, watching in silence the spray of stars that fell on the Eve of San Lorenzo. The bearded grandee looked at the tall figure of the Indian youth coming toward him and smiled. He had chosen well when he had adopted this waif.

The boy spoke Castilian better than many of the Creoles, could read and write with greater ease than most of the clergy. But more important, he had learned how to think, to plan, to organize. Don Jaime did not know how he would accomplish it, but he would find a way to leave the hacienda, perhaps even the encomienda, to Juan. The papers which were signed by the imbecile King's father granted the "authority unto the third generation." But España was far away, and the justice of a king is a fiction spun of frailty, deceit, and avarice.

There was also, of course, the problem of the girl, Manuela.

Both the middle-aged Spaniard and the young Indian were thinking of her when they settled down to a pipe and a drink before bed.

Don Jaime knew he could send her to España. She would find cousins there and maybe a marriage. She was pretty enough, though he doubted if she would know her way around a man. The notes he received from Fray Vicente were vapid and meaningless. "The girl has learned her catechism." "The girl has been taught to read." "The girl has been taught the history of Holy Church." "The girl reads Dante faithfully." This last note puzzled Don Jaime. He could not imagine of what earthly or heavenly use Dante could be to his daughter.

But she would be leaving soon for Ciudad Mexico with sufficient money for a dowry and travel. His obligation to the drunken orgy in Durango which had begotten her would be fulfilled. And as he sat on the patio staring at the stars, he thought for the first time in many years of the woman buried under the white cross in the cemetery of the Taos mission. He wondered who she had been, what flotsam to be tossed so casually by the ruthless Philip into the wake of the Conde de Iteo's destruction, to wash up on the shores beside the Rio Pueblo, drop this girl-child, and die alone and frightened.

Juan was also thinking of Manuela. But his thoughts ran down a different stream of the past. He thought of the child wandering lonely through the rooms of the large casa, studying by day on the open loggia away from the prying faces of the curious white neighbours, and ascending at night to her room to eat alone.

"The girl," Don Jaime broke the silence. "You'll take her to the Villa de Santa Fe in a few days. She will go south from there."

"The caballada will arrive soon?" And as he asked his question, Juan thought he saw a flaw in the plan of Popé, for he knew the caballada would never arrive, and the supplies—the food, the horses, the arms and munitions —would be lost forever.

"Fray Vicente informs me it will arrive within the month. The girl will make the jornada back with it."

Juan nodded, thinking his own thoughts. Popé might have feared the escort, the additional troops, the added weapons. And then he fell to thinking about his patrón's daughter. He wanted to rise from his chair and walk over to his friend and stand before him. He wanted to tell him of what he knew was to come in the morning. He did not care about the other seventy White-faced men and women and children. He did not care about the padres with the shaven heads and the heavy cassocks, the Blessing Men who brought only a curse to the People. But he did care about his friend and the girl Manuela who had been mentioned between them now for the first time.

Juan himself had seldom spoken to the girl, though he had attended several study sessions with Fray Vicente until the padre's temper revealed his anger at being asked to tutor an Indian. The girl had accepted Juan's presence, had even smiled at him on occasion. And when she was younger, she had turned to him several times when frightened or hurt. The Spaniard, the señorita, and the People. The youth found he was already caught up in the torrent of revolt flowing angrily down a narrow arroyo. But he did not rise and warn his friend. Instead, he thought of the jornada he must make to the Villa, so different from the one planned by Don Jaime.

When he could bear the silence no longer, he stood up and crossed over to the table and poured himself a drink from the jug and stared down at the silhouette of the grandee. For a moment he thought of what he must do in the morning. His hand shook and he dropped the amphora to the stone floor where it splashed a pattern of red wine on the stucco wall.

Seated at the window above the patio where she spent her evenings striving to hear the voices of her father and Juan in the night, Manuela sprang to her feet, startled. Then she heard her father laugh and his soft voice, "How much have you poured tonight?"

And she knew what had dropped and who had dropped it. She had spent most of the evenings of her life alone at this window trying to make out the quiet conversation beneath her and had learned by innuendo, tone, and imagination to create the setting. So many evenings as a child she had fallen asleep on the window ledge to the hum of voices she could not separate into words or ideas. But with practice and age she learned much by eavesdropping. She knew the philosophers and poets of whom her father spoke, had a portrait of España which matched the hells of the Italian poet for corruption, carnal vice, avarice, and heresy. The girl Manuela had been taught much more about the world by her father than that cynical exile would ever know.

But this night was different from the others. It was the first time she had ever heard him mention her, the first time that he ever acknowledged in any way that she even existed. She ate alone and lived alone except for the ancient who cleaned for her and the ageing Fray Vicente who preached at her. She never knew what she had done to her father or why he had rejected her. But whatever her sin, she knew it must be great, for she could only see Don Jaime as a good and virtuous man. She knew also that before she left she had to talk to him, had to ask him what her sin had been so that she could understand it and do proper penance.

She remembered with quiet pain the hundreds of times as a child when she had run up to him—laughing, talking, or crying—only to have him pick her up and turn her around before he walked silently away. Finally she had learned to keep her distance. Now, however, she was too big for him to pick her up and turn her away. Now he was going to have to face her and tell her. If she was to save herself, he had to tell her what she had done.

The girl walked to the table where the candle burned low and stared at her thin face in the mirror on the wall. She wondered for a moment who the woman was she looked like. Then she buttoned the front of her dress and pulled the skirt straight about her slender hips. She wet the tips of her fingers and pinched out the flickering light of the candle. Standing in the dark, she could barely hear the voices below. Brushing the tears away from her dark eyes with the back of her hand, she walked slowly out of her room and down the broad staircase which led to the patio. For a moment she stood inside the archway and listened to her father as he planned.

"The sheep. Better have them move the second flock across the rio to the high ground beyond the second hill. The grazing . . ."

And she heard him stop as she stepped out into the night before him.

"Don Jaime, Father. I wanted to ask you . . . I wanted to . . ." she blurted the words out before he could speak, but she paused, frightened, pathetically gasping for breath.

And in that pause the greying grandee rose to his feet in the dark. He placed both of his hands on her arms and held her away from him. His face was tense, firm. Manuela was terrified. Juan, watching the pair, did not know if the father was going to shout or cry. Then, with what sounded almost like the wail of an injured beast, Don Jaime set his daughter aside and strode quickly into the hacienda. The slim, shaking figure of the girl turned to watch him as he disappeared. After a time she looked into the sympathetic face of the Indian youth, half-hidden in the shadows. He did not know she did not see him.

She began to sob. Her face crumpled to her hands as she went stiff and then limp. Juan stepped up to her and placed a hand on her shoulder to comfort her. But she flung her arms outward, brushing him away, and stumbled down the stairs, across the courtyard, and into the darkness toward the edge of the stream.

Juan started to follow her. Instead, he stopped and listened to her footsteps as they grew faint in the distance. He looked up at the stars, aware of the silence as he had never known it before, and he wondered what tomorrow was going to be like when dawn came for him, Juan, the newly elected war chief of Taos. Then he turned back, toward the pueblo where Popé and the others were waiting for him.

BOOK III

AUGUST 10, 1680

When hopes are loose in the streets, it is well for the timid to lock doors, shutter windows and lie low until the wrath has passed. For there is often a monstrous incongruity between the hopes, however noble and tender, and the action which follows them. It is as if ivied maidens and garlanded youths were to herald the four horsemen of the apocalypse.   ERIC HOFFER

1

THE dull green leaves of the small apple trees were still. The four Indian youths, standing on the high ground above the orchard, watched the sun crawl over a distant butte and then walked down to the rio's edge. They knelt and drank slowly from the clear stream. One of them pointed to a large fish, half-hidden by a frond. Another drew an arrow from his quiver and set it in his bow while his companions settled back to watch. The arrow struck the water, deflected, and when the ripples faded outward, the youths saw the impaled fish thrashing on the bottom. The bucks yelled loudly and jumped to their feet. Each one wanted to shoot a fish, and though they waited for a time, there were no more to be seen. Finally, the archer waded into the stream, retrieved his arrow and carried it ashore with the fish still on it.

He stuck the arrow in the ground while the impaled fish continued flapping. The youths stood over the catch and then turned to look at the Sun Father. It was morning.

Without a word, they walked upstream to the small shed where the ollas for watering the orchard were stored. Each picked up a club as he entered and began to lay about him vigorously. In minutes all the ollas—the large clay water jugs—were smashed, and the brightly coloured pieces were strewn across the ground. Then they tossed their clubs away and walked out into the sunlight.

They paused for a moment before they walked over to the small orchard where the fallen apples spotted the ground with red and green. The young men gathered about the first tree they reached and systematically tore the branches from the twisted trunk. The stripped tree looked like a child's drawing—a few wild lines of black. Then they went on to the next tree and the next. It took them most of the morning to destroy the orchard of the hacienda, to rid the countryside of the foreign trees.

As each branch bent, broke, and fell away, the youths recalled the days spent under the fevered sky hauling the heavy jugs from the stream, emptying them in tribute to the hidden roots of the now disfigured trees and returning to refill and carry and empty. And as they rent their enemy, leafy limb for leafy limb, they stamped on the apples falling underfoot until the ground was a slippery mash.

Only when the last apple branch lay on the ground and they were certain that the last tree was dead did they feel their rebellion complete. The archer picked up his arrow with the fish on it and they walked back to the pueblo together.

2

THE Eve of San Lorenzo had been a long and unhappy one for Beatriz Ramírez. One of her great dogs had died, and the other three which remained in the house with her were ill. She did not know what had happened to them. Nor did she know what had happened to Jorge, her Negro slave, whom she had sent for water and who had not returned. As she sat waiting for him, she thought of the punishment she would have to mete out for such flagrant disobedience. It seemed to her that everything was going wrong at once. In the many years she and her brother Alverez had owned Jorge, they had found him faithful and useful, and now when her brother was gone, when Fray Julio was away, and her dogs were ill, the Negro had left her alone in the mission.

Seated in her straight chair by the table, she turned the pasteboard cards over and over, playing a game of Patience with herself, and knowing that her own patience was slowly disappearing. She could scarcely bear the whimpering of the dogs on the floor beside her, and when she looked down at them, she saw the corpse of the youngest. He had been one of the finest, quickest, and most vicious she had ever owned. He was the culmination of her art as a breeder and trainer of fine dogs. And he was dead. It hurt her to see the stiff legs and the open jaws with the blood gathered in the corners of its mouth. It hurt her more to hear the whimpering of the other beasts. For they too, were a part of her, her strength, her protection, and now that the Negro was gone in the darkness, her only real possessions. And she felt she had done well with what little she had. Beatriz took pride in the mission she had built. She would share no credit for her work with the strange padre with whom she shared her bed. He was there. It was nominally his mission, but he knew and she knew who had created it, who controlled it, and made it fruitful. Seated in the chair, holding the fading queen of spades in her hand, Beatriz Ramírez felt proud of her accomplishments. There were very few women in the world who had ever raised such an edifice. There was none in the whole of Nueva España who could claim such a monument to her own efforts.

She set the pasteboard queen down and wished she were not alone. She regretted the loss of the padre's child which had been given to the Negro to bury so many weeks before.

She turned a jack of clubs and smiled. In her youth she would have been superstitious, but her youth was behind her now and she had learned the only way things happen is when one makes them happen. Fate was a word and nothing more. It was an excuse for the weak and a label for those things which the strong accomplished. And Beatriz believed herself among the strong.

She set the card on top of the queen and looked at the pair and thought of Alverez. Alverez. How often he came to mind. How often since his death she felt that there was no longer a purpose for what she did. If the child had lived, perhaps there might have been a future for her, but now there was only the fattening of her limbs and long lonely years ahead. And as she thought of this, she set down the cards and pulled her robe more closely about her. She listened for a moment to the whine of one of the dogs and wondered again at the pain they bore, wondered what was the cause and if she would be able to survive their loss, survive her own need for the strength and courage and company they gave her.

With a shake of her gross head, she dispelled the thoughts from her mind, picked up the cards again and returned to the game. It made no difference if she won or lost for there was no one she could tell about the feat. In fact, as she sat and played, she realized what her problem really was: she was alone. It was a loneliness the padre would never dispel. It was the loneliness of knowing that there never would be anyone else. She knew that when the caballada came north through el Paso del Norte there would be a ball at the governor's palacio, that all of the men in the jurisdiction would gather to drink their wine, and the women would exchange small talk of dresses and new dance steps and the gossip of babies and lovers. She knew, too, that no one was going to invite her. If she had been the mestiza mistress of a hacendado, it would have been different. But it had been her decision to remain at the mission of the pueblo on the upper rio, her decision to cast her lot with the clergyman who pawed her in his clumsy, insufficient passion, her decision to build here rather than enter the community of the matrons of the Villa.

She might have her regrets now, but she knew that too much time had elapsed. Too many tales about her had been told. And worse, the padre had woven her into his life so completely that neither of them alone could break the bonds of ambition that held them.

Ambition. The word rolled through her mind with the clumsy motion of a tumbleweed in the autumn wind. Ambition. That was what had taken Alverez into the best homes of Lima and had brought both of them to rejection by their neighbours, had taken them to Ciudad Mexico, to Vera Cruz, to the damnation which both of them faced when they turned their tracks northward. Ambition. She weighed the word with another: greed. And then she rejected the idea. It was more of a dream they had both carried. There was a place on the peninsula from which their forefathers had sailed so many decades before, a place with a fine white villa surrounded by beautiful vineyards and filled with the best wines poured by the finest servants who would wait on the beautiful dancer and her handsome brother through their last years. It was a dream they had only talked about at night and to each other. It was the dream that drove Alverez into the cold mountains in search of gold and silver at first and later to anything which he might turn into the trunkful of pesos which would permit them to sail to the far peninsula and the wonderful villa.

But Alverez was dead, and the beautiful dancer was a corpulent woman sleeping in a bed of the damned, protected by great dogs, and even those dogs were dying. With an angry sweep of her hand, she pushed the cards from her and turned to the mastiff who had come, feebly, to rest his large head on her lap. She brushed back the short hairs of his scalp and felt him shiver. One of the other dogs was silent now and she knew that it was dead.

She petted the sad-eyed beast who had come to her for comfort and lifted its weary head so that she could look into its eyes. He tried to lick her palm and something scratched her hand. Very slowly, she slipped to her knees beside the beast who she felt was the only creature in the world who loved her, and held its brown head against her soft mounds of breast. The animal was still. She took its head in her hands and felt it cringe from pain as she touched its mouth. With great tenderness, she opened the large mouth and stared into it. Then she saw what had killed her dogs. There was a nettle—white and green. The beast shuddered and flinched as she put her hand in its bleeding mouth and pulled one out. Standing in the middle of the room, she stared at the bristle of plant and wondered how many the dogs had eaten, how they had got them. And then she knew. There was only one person other than herself who could ever feed the beasts and that was the absent Negro, who had gone out almost an hour before for water. She squeezed her hand in anger and anticipation until the nettle was buried in her palm and the blood ran. The damned black had killed her dogs, and for this she would have his hide. She would strip it and pierce it with the very same nettles. She would kill the ungrateful animal.

She thought of the advantages she had given Jorge, of the food he had eaten from her own table, of the clothes she had bought to cover his naked blackness and of the opportunity she had presented to him to save his soul.

Then she looked at her fat hand and felt the place where the nettle had pierced it and she cursed. She would kill him. She had to kill him. Hurriedly, she ran about the mission until she calmed enough to remember where the sabre of Alverez was stored in her wardrobe. Throwing the clothes aside, she grasped the tarnished sword by the hilt and swung it viciously about her, cutting great arcs in the empty air and believing for the moment that each was filled with the black form of the slave Jorge.

Then she ran to the door, drew the wooden bar, and flung the door open. "Jorge. Jorge. Jorge."

She stood facing the empty darkness calling his name and cursing him as she called. But there was no answer.

Running into the open court alone, she tried to find the field dogs which guarded the gates of the compound. The Negro could never have got past them. They most surely would have stopped him. And when she reached the gates, she saw the hounds, great brown dead bulks of rigid flesh, and she went down on her knees to them and caressed each in turn, saying its name over and over and over as she kissed it and set its head back in the dirt. When she rose, her anger was greater than before, her fury more blind. She wanted the Negro. She had to have him. He belonged to her. He was her piece of property and she alone had the right to destroy him as she would destroy an Indian or a ragged dress or an empty wine jug.

"Jorge. Jorge. Jorge."

But the words echoed off the walls of the compound and there was no other answer.

Then she tried to control herself, and with great effort she stood up full height. With tense, deliberate steps she walked across the compound to the communal quarters of the Indians. The door should have been barred, but it was not. The puebleños should have been on the pads, asleep, but they were not. In anger she called them, having trouble remembering the names or faces of any, as a person has trouble remembering all the cattle of a great herd or the people in a crowd.

And as she stood alone in the darkness of the rooms, she was aware of her loneliness. The sabre in her hand clattered to the floor and frightened her. And when she looked at her hands and found them empty, she slapped her palms together. One dog. There must be one dog who would answer her call. She waited for a long moment, and when she bent down to pick up the sabre in the dark of the entrance to the empty quarters, she heard the one dog. Turning in anticipation, she saw it, crawling slowly toward her on its belly. Beatriz stared at the painful movement of the large hound, and its name clearly flashed through her mind—Tigre. And she shortened the distance between them, bent down to pet the dying beast, which rolled over for her affection. Then with a sudden sweep of the sabre, she slashed its throat, ending its misery and pain.

Alone in the empty courtyard, she stared up at the sky. Flashes of white streaked it and she knew morning was almost upon her.

Alverez. Alverez. Alverez.

She stared at the dark mountains and crossed herself as she always did when she looked at them. If only he were beside her, but he was not. There was no one beside her. She was alone except for the figures of the Indians she knew were looking at her and whom she could not see in the dark.

Clutching the ornate handle of the sabre Alverez had taken from the body of a wayside traveller so many years before, she crossed the compound again and entered the mission. Once inside, she closed the door and set in place the large timber which served as a lock and seated herself in the straight chair with the padded leather seat and stared at the door. The candle she had lit so many hours before was faltering, but it made no difference as morning was almost here, and with the morning would come the light. And she knew that with the light would come the Indians. They never had come before in her memory. But she knew they would come this morning. She set the sabre on the table at her side and reached for the comb which she carried in her pocket and started to comb her hair. She was going to look her best. She was going to look the way she had dreamed she would look when she had lain beside Alverez and they had talked of the villa so far away that would be theirs. She was going to make Alverez proud of his little sister. Proud as he had been proud when she had danced for his friends in Lima, when she had danced for them in Mexico, proud when she had seduced the drunken padre in Vera Cruz—and all for Alverez. He would remember her even if Fray Julio would not. Alverez would remember her.

Outside the streaks of light grew brighter and the cacique with the sullen face emerged from the shelter of the shadows and the puebleños followed him. They had seen the Negro depart hours before and they had not stopped him. They had seen the dogs die and they knew who had killed them. They had watched the White Witch seek them in the open compound and in their dark quarters and had not disturbed her. They had patience. They could wait until morning or whenever the time was bright enough for her to see them face to face when they captured her. The cacique, touching the bruises where she had struck him, held the katchina doll he had hidden with such care days before when the young medicine man had paid for his rashness to the great dogs, and he stuck the long pole he held in his other hand into the ground. And the war dance began in the open courtyard beneath the sun where the White Witch could see it through the small slit of window and feel the throbbing of drums she could never stop. The cacique and his people were patient. They could wait until she decided to join them.

3

SOUTH of the pueblo, running with easy strides, Jorge felt the heft of the captain's lance in his hand and knew it lacked the weight and accuracy of a well-made assegai. But he knew, too, that it would do for a hunt. The very prospect of a hunt thrilled him. It had been so many years since he had taken the trail after an animal, had measured its skill and speed against his own, and known the sure thrust of success.

It was still dark. There were stars in the sky and every so often as he stared at the blackness spread above him he was aware of the sprinkling of falling lights. These he knew must be a sign, but he could not read the sign and he was troubled. Twice when the sudden splash of white brightened the night, he paused and turned about three times and rubbed his hand on the underside of a stone, but there was no revelation.

In his own mind he felt it had something to do with the action he had taken, with the death of the dogs and his departure from the mission. But he could not be certain whether it was a sign of success or a warning.

The light, silver-trimmed lance rested easily in his hand and the steel-bladed knife bounced gently against his hip. He trotted south along the rio's edge, and while he ran, he thought about the dark shadow of the mission falling farther and farther behind him. Here he had spent so many planting seasons, had seen Indian children growing up, his master's unaccountable search for the golden metal, and the violence of the White Witch. But she was behind him, as the dogs were behind him and unable to follow.

It had been an easy task to stick the hard nettles of the cactus into the chunks of meat. The dogs had died slowly, but they had died. When their mistress became aware that something was wrong, she had awakened Jorge with a sharp slap and had sent him out for cold water for the dry-nosed beasts. Once outside, he had picked up the lance and the knife of his dead master which he had hidden during the day in an eave over the door of the mission. Then he knew he had to be his own man again.

There were no Indians in the compound, and as he approached the large, closed gates, he heard the soft and distant drumming of the hyena-faced man. He saw the field dogs lying across the entrance they were staked out to protect and knew they were dead and that he had killed them.

The drumming grew louder in his ears and for a moment he feared the figures he could not make out in the darkness and the shadows. He knew he was being watched. He had been born of the dark and the jungle and had a sense which told him that there was danger behind the edge of light cast by the sky. And so he turned to the dark and the shadows and spoke loudly.

"The White Witch of the Big Dogs is alone. The dogs here are dead. The dogs inside are dying, and she will be a witch without power. She does not know how to use her gods. She does not know which are the sure signs of death or under which cloud hides the man with the hyena face."

His language was partly that of his own people and partly that of his white captors. But there was a tone of assurance about it and a matter-of-factness which made itself known to the ears of his watchers. When he turned, opened the gate and walked out, no one troubled him. Only after he began his long run beside the rio did the Indians come out of the shadows and look after him. He had known this, and it was this he thought about as he saw the sky above him sprinkled with whiteness.

It was a strange night and he was alone in it. And as he ran, he became aware that there was no place for him to go. The edge of the Big Blue Water was far away; should he find it, he knew no man could cross it alone; and so he was forever cut off from the land of the big green river and the jungles of his youth.

Jorge heard a noise behind him and turned off the trail to hide in a clump of small brush. After several moments, two lean Indian youths trotted down the trail and disappeared into the distance. Jorge knew them for the runners he had seen visiting the pueblo and quickly forgot them as he emerged from his hiding place and continued south. Twice he had to leave the rio's edge and climb down the sharp banks of a dried arroyo and once he had to wade through a small stream which joined the great rio. He took his time about crossing the cool water, bathed himself, and cleaned both of his new weapons. The knife fascinated him for never before had he owned anything with quite so keen a blade. Standing in the water, he sliced a small frond to gauge the edge of the knife and was happy with the clean slices that fell away.

On the trail again, his legs aching now, his breath coming short as he felt his years of confinement. The night sky was flushed away and the sun rose. He paused several times to drink and gather berries from some bushes beside the stream. When the sun was high above him he began to consider where he was going and why he was running thus. But the fear of the White Witch stayed with him and he knew that he must get far away from the mission, must place many paces between him and the slavery he had known, before he could feel free and be his own man again.

The old gnawing gathered at his stomach and for the first time since he had come to this strange world, he knew it was not fear, but his older friend, hunger. And he was quietly pleased that they were together again. Now he would take the time to hunt, to select his own game and make his own meal. He stopped along the bank and was preparing to search out his food, when he heard a noise behind him. Looking about, he found the ground too bare for hiding and dived into the stream. The ripples ebbed away and his head came out of the water in time to see a white soldier on horseback being chased by a small group of Indians. When the distance between them began to grow, one of the Indians halted and fired an arrow from his bow. The white soldier rose high in his saddle, slumped forward, and then tumbled to the ground. The bewildered horse continued to race along the rio. In an instant the Indians pounced on the Spaniard, stripped him of his weapons, tore off his clothes, and shoved his body into the stream. Then they trotted back in the direction from which they had come. For a long time Jorge settled himself in the water. This was not his fight. As far as he was concerned, it could have been two lions attacking each other. Neither was of his people and neither would have hesitated to kill the black-skinned man.

Finally, he rose from the water and made his way back to the bank. The naked body of the white man held no interest for him, and without looking at it, he clenched his silver-decorated lance and started down the rio again. He had run only a few hundred paces when he saw the antelope drinking in the shade of a large clump of cottonwood trees. The giant Negro suddenly became alert. He paused and felt the small shift of breeze across his face and approved the direction of the scent. He noted the high ground just behind the antelope and quietly, with the softness of a night beast, made his way toward it. Should the angular pronghorn break from sudden fear, he could only whirl away from the stream and the cottonwood trees toward Jorge. When he had placed himself with care, the black hunter bent over and picked up a small pebble. It was white and smooth from the shifting bottom. Twice he placed the pebble on the back of his hand and twice he raised that hand to retest the wind. The signs were favourable. Holding his lance in his right hand and the pebble in his left, he easily lofted the stone so that it fell in the water just in front of the fawn. Startled, the antelope whirled and ran toward Jorge. His arm came back, and as the beast hurled itself, unseeing, toward him, he drove the point of the lance through its neck. The animal shied, tried to shake itself free and then tumbled to the hunter's feet, thrashed a moment and lay still.

Jorge pulled the lance from the antelope and rubbed both of his palms over the newly bloodied point. This was success. This was the fine luck and the good sign. This was what he had not found through the night though he had questioned the bottom sides of the stones after the falling lights.

He rose to his feet and looked about him and listened. There were no drums. There was no fear. He was free. He was again the youth who had killed the young lion and given its pelt to a woman. He was part of the wild land again and all the years of the whites fell away from him.

4

THE *old man with the gnarled hands sat on the bank of the rio at dawn and watched the sun coming over the mesa and the small white boy swimming in the quiet water. For almost eighty years he had watched the Sun Father arrive over the sierra and for almost eight he had tended the boy of the hacienda. There was very little else in his life now. The years of working in the fields had left him permanently stooped, and there was no longer a woman to knead his aching muscles, for his wife had died the year before the patrón had taken him out of the field and given him the care of the child. He had returned to live in the room of his mother which was now the room of his sister's daughter, and he rose in the morning and dressed the boy and took him to the rio for his swim or to the stables where his father taught him to ride the white mare with the short legs.*

The old man often wondered what it would be like to ride a horse. He never had. It had been forbidden the People. The one long journey he had made in his life, he had trotted on foot beside a tropa of soldiers to meet the Apaches—the strangers. This had been his only battle, the only time he had ever killed a man. It disturbed him yet to recall that he had killed, because this was not the way of the Earth Mother who granted a place for all—from the ant to the eagle. But he had killed as the Spanish soldiers had expected him to kill, and he knew afterward that he would always be troubled.

The sky was brighter now, and the old man knew he could wait no longer. He rose to his feet, slipped out of his moccasins, crossed himself, and waded into the stream. The naked boy, browned by the sun, waved at his guardian and splashed confidently toward him. As the boy approached, the ancient crossed himself again, stretched out his hands and grasping the boy by the hair, held his head a rigid arm's length under water. At first there was splashing and writhing. Then the pool was still except for an occasional bubble breaking the surface. How long before the boy was limp, how long he stood with his hands beneath the surface, the old man did not know. His eyes were upon a black hawk, cutting smaller and smaller circles in the distant sky. When it disappeared behind the mesa, he relaxed and opened his hands. The small body floated to the top of the water, and the aged Indian gently turned its head to the east. He took the sacred corn meal from a pouch at his waist and scattered it over the boy. "We who must live must live even though others must die so that we may live. Forgive us."

Then he released the body and waded ashore. After he slipped into his moccasins again, he turned to see the slight white figure drifting face downward toward the centre of the stream.

He crossed himself again and walked back toward the estancia. His revolt was complete. No one would mutilate the boy now. No one would hurt him. And as for himself, the ancient one was pleased that he was old and would not have many more years to be troubled about the role he had played on this day.

5

SPARKS sprang toward the night sky. Large fires flared over the dancing Taoans and katchina masks bounced in the shifting shadows to the rhythm of the sheep's-head drums and the shrill flute tones of the turkey-bone pipes. Frenzied women whirled in the great outer circle, chanting ancient songs beyond the blazing torches. While the young men waited for the coming of the sun, the black-painted youths and the golden-faced women swung a frantic arc about the scalp pole of Taos.

The Monster Slayer's temple, the house of ghosts to come, was clothed in black. From here the haunts fly northward. From here no man returns. From here the dead know rest.

Deer-hoof rattles backed the rhythm of the dance. Dried gourds shook. Bare shoulders swayed and black hair tossed. The serpent staff flashed in the bright, burning spruce. Fox pelts dangled and turkey feathers crested the warriors whirling, swirling, bouncing through the shadows.

Then came the old men and all was still. They marched about the scalp pole and squatted on the ground. The black-painted youths charged toward the fire. Corn meal swirled and all was still.

Then the belly drum throbbed and the golden jaguar shook. White owl feathers burst across the darkness. Bull horns glistened and he came. Popé standing high. Popé looking down.

He raised a copper palm and there was silence. He turned to the east and his voice broke loud across the stillness of the plaza.

"There was a great darkness and from this darkness stepped Montezuma, the Great Captain. And there was light all about him and he spread his hands before him and he told a story of the People who were his people. And he asked me to tell his story and I shall tell his story.

"'A long time ago Men of Metal marched into the land, men who could not hear the People and could not feel for them. These men mounted the People and rode them. And they drove them with whips. And the Blessing Men followed the Men of Metal and baptized the People in the name of a foreign god. Their praise became infamy. Their censure, praise. And they stood away from the People and hid behind a god who was not the god of the People.'

"And the Great Captain wept as he told his story. 'The People,' he said, 'the People once were free. And the visions I have seen tell me the People must free themselves again. Tell them that Montezuma has said this to them. Tell them.' And he was gone and there was darkness then as there is darkness now.

"And I have come to tell you as he told it unto me. Once we were free. If we do not shed our masters, we deserve to be slaves. If we do not look upward to our own, we deserve to be the lesser beasts which they have made of us. We did not seek their blessings. We did not seek to be saved as they would save us. What can their god mean to the People if the People mean nothing? What can their single, lonely god mean to the People who have known the Sun Father and the Corn Mother?

"Their War Captains burn our holy places. They would destroy our katchinas who intercede with the old gods in our behalf. And so they would leave us dumb before our gods. They have taken our women. They have scattered our seed. They have turned us down strange paths where we have wandered in darkness.

"But there is hope for the People, as Montezuma said there would be hope for the People. When the People free themselves, he will return and there will be light.

"The ancient gods have burned a trail. They have dried the earth. They have cleared the land of growing things and have given us a sign as clear as the waters of Copala. The way is clean and there is no place for the Men of Metal and the Blessing Men to hide. They have weapons, but we have the People. They have their single god, limp and bleeding, and we have the Sun Father and the Corn Mother and the Great Captain.

"The pain will last only a little while longer. The stain they have brought to the People will be washed away with the blood of their holy men and their warriors.

"They have not listened. They have not cared. And they will fall. There will be no Whiteface in the land north of the great pass where the blue waters flow to the south. There will be no kivas for the limp god. There will be death, and then there will be only the People."

His palm turned down and the puebleños watched as he drew an arrow from the ground beside him and dipped it into the flames and shot the arrow across the sky where it disappeared into the darkness. Then his hand was filled with the holy corn meal which he scattered into the fire. Then he handed the bow to Juan, the young war chief of Taos. "The People would rid the land of the Whitefaces."

And the shouts rose behind his words and the men gathered about the youthful war chief as the sun rose.

Popé watched the puebleños stream out of the plaza toward the Spanish settlement. The uprising had begun. All the years of planning had borne this bloody fruit. Hate, despair, and loneliness took on the face of murder. He stood quietly in the light of the dying fire and the early morning and raised his arms to the Sun Father. "We only kill to live. We only destroy so that we may not be destroyed." It was not forgiveness or even strength that he sought. He wanted for one brief moment to have again an affinity with the universe about him, to be able to explain and know he was heard, to feel that somewhere there were gods who cared what happened to the People.

Popé had loosed rebellion on the land and was prepared for the havoc that must follow. He would remain in Taos until the white settlement was gone, and then he would go south to the Villa de Santa Fe where the governor and his soldiers lived, and when they were destroyed, he would have to journey to San Juan. Here he would meet with his daughter. She was only a woman, but he wanted to tell her why he had killed Nicolás Bua. He wanted her to understand that he had loved the young man.

The tall Indian priest removed his bull-horn headdress and, holding it in his arms, settled down on the ground to wait for the destruction of the enemy. When he saw the smoke burst upward, he knew the haciendas were aflame. Then he looked in the direction of the mission of Fray Vicente. Smoke rose in a thin black streak. It was done. Popé stood up, replaced his heavy headdress and walked slowly toward the mission building. The warriors had already departed and as he stood watching them, he knew they were now heading for the manor house of Don Jaime de Marcos, the silent Spaniard. Then Popé turned and walked up the steps of the burning mission. The aged Fray Vicente lay sprawled across the entrance. His cassock spread over the stones, and his open eyes stared forever at the rising sun.

This was the enemy. This frail man with the shaven head and the thin face was the enemy. And as he stood looking down at him, the native priest remembered all the tales of the Spaniard's hell as young Juan had heard and described them, and he wished he might have disputed the nature of hell with the old man. He would like to have talked to the Blessing Man and been understood. It had never happened. It never would. The small pool of blood gathering at the base of the steps separated them now as their gods had separated them before.

Popé wanted to turn this man to the east, spread the holy corn meal over him, and know the victory was his. But he did not, for the victory belonged only to death.

6

DON JAIME slept little the Eve of San Lorenzo's Day. The intrusion of Manuela into his thoughts had disturbed him greatly. And when he was finally prepared to retire for the night, he realized the girl had not returned to the hacienda. At first he thought of searching for her. He walked down to the gate and looked out into the darkness, but he knew there was no finding anyone in the wild countryside before morning. He wondered what had happened to her as he walked slowly back to the patio where he spent the night in his chair waiting for her return. Twice he dozed off and twice his dreams awakened him.

There was little breeze in the night and what there was, was warm. There were few noises beyond the lonesome cry of a coyote somewhere off in the distance. Several times as his head fell back in his chair, Don Jaime saw the meteorites that mark the Eve of San Lorenzo streaking across the sky. Their faint trails disappeared in seconds, and the sky was dark again except for the scattered stars.

The girl kept crowding her way into his thoughts and he was annoyed. For all the years he had lived here, he had never permitted this to happen. It should not have happened now. But it had. Well, he would send the padre a note and request that he talk to the girl. She must keep her distance so long as she remained in the hacienda. She would be leaving soon enough. He wondered several times if he should talk to the girl herself. But each time he rejected the idea. He had lived well enough without a Spanish voice and this was not occasion enough to warrant changing now. Sometime before the dawn, he rose from his chair and walked out into the courtyard. Nothing stirred. There were no signs of life, no sounds other than his own footsteps as he swung open the gate and walked to the edge of the stream which flowed near by.

Standing alone in the darkness, Don Jaime de Marcos wondered for the first time in almost two decades what had happened to him. How had he come here? How had he let fate and a woman make such a fool of him that this twisted empty land should become his grave, that these mountains rising about him should become the sepulchre of the youth who had been the Conde de Iteo.

For the first time in years he felt lonely. He wondered what it would be like to sit across from a woman and talk to her, hold her in his arms, as he stared at the darkness from his bed. He shook his head. It was the girl. She had intruded herself too far into the shell he had constructed with two decades of building. She was his daughter, but she was also a daughter of España. He had learned a long time ago that Spanish women could destroy a man.

Don Jaime knelt down and let the cool water of the Rio Pueblo run against his hand. It should be morning soon. Then he would have to mount his horse and go in search of her. He did not want to, but he knew that this much he owed to her and to the woman who slept beneath the cross in Fray Vicente's cemetery. He turned and looked toward the mission and saw the thin black streak of smoke edging its way upwards, and beyond he saw the larger clouds hanging over the haciendas. He rose to his feet. It had begun. Maybe it was just as well the girl was lost for the moment.

Don Jaime did not hurry as he walked back through the gate, across the courtyard and up the stone steps. Nothing was going to happen to him that had not happened years before. He walked into the large room where he kept his harquebus, took the weapon in his hand and saw that the pan had been removed. He had almost expected this. He reached up on the shelf for his helmet. It was there, crested and polished, but the lining straps were slashed and he would not be able to wear it. His breastplate, too, was polished and the crest of Iteo showed gilt against steel, but the straps were gone. He did not need to remove his scabbard to see that his sword was missing.

With quick steps, he walked across the room and opened a heavy wooden wardrobe. Throwing the clothes which filled it aside, he found three daggs, ivory-butted and fully loaded. What was there about his relationship to man which had placed a final doubt so correctly in his mind that he had never displayed this weapon to the boy Juan as he had displayed the others? There was no question in Don Jaime's mind who had stolen the sword and had destroyed the helmet, the breastplate, and the harquebus. It was the youth whom only that very evening he had considered making his heir.

The Castilian laughed to himself. The doubts had never fully left his mind or he would have shown the boy the small hand guns. He shoved one into his belt as he thought of the consistency of man: given the opportunity he was always corrupt, faithless, untrustworthy. He heard the noise outside the gate, swung to the door of the manor house and slammed it closed. Outside in the courtyard he heard the clamour of the Indians as they worked up their courage to attack the first householder who had been warned of their coming.

Don Jaime wanted only a few minutes longer and they unwittingly gave them to him. He walked up the stairs to his sleeping room, pulled out the large wardrobe which had been under his bed since the house was built and removed the two boxes of gunpowder he had brought from Mexico so many years before. Once there had been four boxes, but with his hunting and teaching Juan to use an harquebus, there was less powder now. He carried the two boxes into Manuela's room where the portico overlooked the courtyard. He set the boxes down, removed from the table the candle which she had extinguished only hours before, and lit it with a chispa lying there. As he held the candle in his hand, he saw himself in the mirror. His face came almost as a surprise. It was bright and smiling. The black beard was edged in grey, but the high cheekbones stood firm as they had in his youth. He nodded and winked to himself. It was going to be over soon. Too bad Philip was dead. Too bad Carlos was an idiot. He wondered for a moment about the girl who so long ago had been married off to a French gentleman for cash and a name for a child. Was she dead, too? Or was she flat on her back putting horns on the Frenchman and making a fool of some other man giddy with dreams of romance? Inferno for her. She deserved to be old.

He was starting to walk out onto the balcony overlooking the courtyard when he realized there was silence below. Through the window he could see the Indians hiding behind the walls which surrounded the courtyard, and off in the distance he made out two Spanish horsemen. For one long moment, Don Jaime debated whether he should go out onto the balcony and signal the Spanish soldados for help. But he was an honest man to the end. Instead, he carried the two boxes of powder out onto the balcony, set them down with great care, and as an Indian whirled and pointed a bow at him, he pulled his dagg and fired. The black-faced young warrior collapsed at the feet of Juan. The Castilian recognized the youth who had been as his son and nodded to him while he emptied one of the powder boxes onto the floor at his feet and dropped the other to break on the flagstones below. Juan stared at him puzzled for a moment and then he spun about and ran through the gate as Don Jaime, grinning after him, knelt, lit a trail of the powder at his feet and tossed the candle into the broken box below.

An instant later the hacienda exploded with a roar which shook the walls of Red Willow Cañon. The Indians crowding the courtyard were killed. And the Castilian grandee who had been given the last rites on the dock of Sevilla twenty years before died with them.

The two soldados who had given up finding anyone alive in Taos paused, watched the smoke rise, and then rode on. There was nothing they could do at the hacienda of Don Jaime.

7

MANUELA DE MARCOS did not know how far she had run in her flight from her father's house in Taos. She did not know what trails she had passed, what cañons she had wandered through, what streams she had blindly crossed as she hurled herself beyond the cradled world of her father's hacienda and out into the dark and foreign night.

Her thin satin slippers, torn by the sharp edge of the rocks, gave way about her feet and she abandoned them in the muddy bottom of a stream. Her robe, hanging open, flapped behind her like the frail and fluttering wings of a woods harpy. The silken hem of her nightdress was caught and frayed by the brambles of a thicket. She ran on.

The pain which had driven her from Don Jaime's hacienda gradually turned to fear as the shapes of the night about her began to take on meaning. She forgot why she was running. The pain which had propelled her remained, but the reasons were lost in the fear. And she ran on.

She had lost her way. A barren path of large stones loomed before her in the darkness. The high walls of a narrow barranca pressed in upon her. And she was lost. Forever, irretrievably lost. Dark clusters of cottonwood trees seemed to whirl about the horizon like dancing demons. All the Dantean lore she had learned from Fray Vicente pushed forward in her mind. Suddenly, she stopped with a shriek. The way was blocked. There was no path ahead. The rock-lined wall of a butte rose before her. Her hands went to her face as she ran full length into the rise. She stumbled back. Her face was scratched and bleeding. Her hands were torn. Above her was the black sky rimmed by the walls of the barranca and the butte, and she crouched down in the darkness against a large rock and stared at a distant heaven. She felt she had fallen into the pit that only led downward.

Tears streaked her dirtied face. What had she done? What had she done? She had listened at night to her father. She had tried to talk to him. She had dreamed of going to Cuidad Mexico.

Then she heard the noise. It was distant and plaintive. It was like sounds she had heard before, but it took on meaning now, because she heard it with a different ear in a different context. The coyote crying the moon became all the sinners who had ever wailed for surcease, wailed for relief where there was no relief.

And Manuela hid her face from the black sky and covered her ears with her bleeding hands. The sounds were still there. The crying was still there. And she could not shut it out. She could not make it stop and she knew she had to flee.

She staggered to her feet and felt the walls of the barranca until she came to a small cut in its sandy side. Stumbling, she climbed, holding onto weeds and branches and slimy things. Finally, she pulled herself to the top of the rise and looked about her. Off to the left and away from the crying in the night she saw a small murky stream meandering through the darkness. Barefooted now, her hair a dirty straggle about her face, she started for the stream. If she could cross it. If she could get away. If . . .

Her feet were cut and they were bleeding when she tripped and fell headlong into the brambles that lined the bank of the stream. And then she lay still for a long time. There was darkness before her and darkness above and she believed that finally it was all over, that the end and relief had come. But there were pains in her feet that would not cease, and she rolled out of the brambles and sat up.

Her robe was torn into strips. Her sleeping gown was dirty. With great effort she took her feet in her hands and saw the thorns which pierced them and she shrieked, for she knew they were poisoned. They must be poisoned. There was nothing clean in all this hell she was wandering through. One by one she plucked the thorns from her bleeding feet until she found no more. Then she rose and made her way to the stream, no longer running because she no longer had the strength, no longer terrified because she was no longer able to feel the fear which had consumed her.

When she reached the other side, she started to pull herself over the bank and the clay gave way in her hand and she slipped back into the water. She had difficulty finding her footing again; and when she did, she stared at the red clay in her hands and screamed. The red. The rio of blood.

Then she looked at the bank before her and she saw the beast, yellowish-brown, sleek, and large, staring at her over the edge of the rio and she backed down the stream away from the curious mountain lion which had been attracted by her screams.

Numb and dazed, the girl made her way backward out of the water where she had entered it and stumbled onto the bank. As she did, the mountain lion across the stream growled a frustrated complaint and disappeared into the night. Manuela fell back into a small cluster of marsh bushes, and heard the cries of the distant coyote summing up all protests of living things against the demons which haunt their souls. She closed her eyes as the first light of morning reflected off the waters at her feet.

8

THE *old Indian woman carefully dusted the altar of the white adobe mission. Soon the padre would be stirring and the people would arrive for Mass. And after Mass she would prepare the padre's breakfast and then go down to the rio and wash his clothes, sit in the sun while they dried and listen to the women.*

Now it was quiet. The candles near the altar flickered and threw strange shadows across the white walls. The largest shadow was of the figure of the Cristo cast by a wooden bulto, carved crudely and painted brightly, which rested beside the altar. The old woman stared at it and crossed herself as she had every morning since her husband died and she had been given the chores of the mission.

She was happy and as she worked, she sang to herself:

> *The Corn Mother is entering!*
> *She is the One who gives us the road.*
> *Her Sun is entering.*
> *The Mother Mary is the One who makes the road.*

This was her church. This was the place where she was important, the place where she had something to do and someone to do it for. There never had been such a place for her in the kiva, for her or any of the other women. She had tried to explain this to the cacique, but he did not understand.

Her dusting done, she stepped away from the altar, genuflected, crossed herself and went to her seat to wait for the People who were her people.

The tired eyes in her seamed copper face closed and her head fell back in quiet repose. She sat for twenty minutes in that hushed area on the edge of sleep. It was the doors swinging open that awakened her, brought her to her feet in horror as she saw the war paint on the young men who were carrying torches and clubs and macanas. They paused on the threshold, hesitating for a moment. Then they entered the church and she screamed for the padre. He must come out and talk to the young men. He must tell them about respect for God and the Holy Mary and Her Son and . . .

She stumbled into the aisle and stood blocking the way. The young men paused and she began to tell them, "Go back. Go. Leave. You are not dressed for the Mass. You are not . . ." Her words faltered and she looked about for the padre to help her explain, and as she did so, two of the young men took her gently by the arms and set her carefully on a bench.

Then, screaming for courage, they ran up to the altar where the candles flickered and the shadow of the brightly painted bulto sprang so large upon the wall. One of the young men in a white loincloth with a scar down his leg and a ring of dead skin left by an ankle iron raised his club and smashed the bulto. His companions tipped over the altar, stood upon its side and, reaching up, tore the crucifijo from the wall. It tumbled with a crash.

There was a long silence as the Indians stared at the crucifijo, waiting to see what would happen, not believing, but afraid to disbelieve. Those with torches tried to burn the altar and the benches, but the large planks would not burn and the intruders became frightened. At another time, they would have understood, would have realized that heavy planks do not spring quickly into flames. But now they were not thinking. They were feeling and they were afraid. They hurled the torches into the corner where they faltered and went dark.

Now there was only silence and the candles on the wall beside the tumbled altar.

The Indian warriors stood looking at the crucifijo for a long time. Then they quietly walked out of the mission and closed the door behind them.

Only then did their courage return, and they ran screaming toward the nearest hacienda, several hundred varas away. When their noise disappeared in the distance, the sobs of the frightened old woman sitting in the dark could be heard.

9

THE four Indians who carried the sedan chair of Fray Julio Malindez had been clumsy about it. The ride they gave the tall padre had had a peculiar ending, resulting in an accident which at the time it occurred seemed most unfortunate. Later Fray Julio was not quite so certain about this.

The group had left the pueblo of Santa Flora on the morning of August 9 and had arrived in the late afternoon at the first of the pueblos which made up the visitas of Fray Julio. They paused here while the padre conducted services for the Indians, married those couples who had begun living together since last he saw them, baptized the children born since his previous visit, and performed the other duties of his office. At the same time, he made a full list of supplies needed at the small chapel, as well as a survey of the state of the community, so his report would be complete.

And strange as it might have appeared to his mistress, Beatriz Ramírez, Fray Julio knew exactly what to do. He was an amazingly competent person who paid great attention to details. It was this care which made him one of the best administrators in all of the province. But care and a sense of administration had been obscured over the years by the other and more predominant qualities of the tall padre. Ease and ambition tended to conceal the strengths of the man. It was almost as if he himself had abandoned his better qualities for the worse ones.

It was late in the afternoon when the padre's work was completed at the pueblo, and as he stood blessing the puebleños, he made the decision to depart at once for the next visita.

His bearers lifted the sedan chair, he waved his parting blessing to his charges, and rode his swaying journey down the trail toward the Rio del Norte. His bearers jogged on into the evening. They were aware of the plans of Popé. They knew of the uprising that was going to take place. But in their absence from their homes, they were not aware that the date of the revolt had been changed by Fay-yat of Tesuque. The four men who bore the weight of the padre were prepared to do so for another day. They were patient. They had waited this long. They could wait. With each step they took, their anger built within them. But they could wait. They had so much to remember: the jugs of water carried day after day under the watchful eyes of the great dogs, a browned leaf and the whippings that followed, the sudden death of the young medicine man only days before, the huge timbers carried for leagues to build the mission chapel. There were so many things to remember that the Indians who jogged with the carrying pole of the sedan chair on their shoulders knew they need not rush the day of the revolt. Their cacique had warned them before they departed that any premature act might warn the other Whitefaces, the Men of Metal as well as the other Blessing Men. And so they jogged on until they came to the Rio del Norte and dusk overtook them.

They wanted to pause for the night, but Fray Julio envisioned himself sleeping in a bed within a few hours and so he signalled them to run on. That was what caused the accident which seemed so unfortunate at the time. The bearers had just trotted up a small hill on the west of the rio and were descending the other side when one of the runners stumbled, dropped his corner of the sedan chair, and fell forward. The chair itself crashed to the ground, spilling the tall padre out onto his face. He rose in fury and turned to the culprit who had been responsible for the accident. But that poor Indian was unable to rise. He had twisted his ankle so badly that he could not walk a step. Fray Julio stood over him a long time while the others awaited his decision. At last, in disgust, he threw up his hands. There was nothing they could do. It was dark. The three men would not be able to carry the large sedan chair with the padre through the darkness. It was all most unfortunate. And as annoying as anything else to the self-satisfied padre was the prospect of an evening without a meal. He was furious, but there was very little he could do about it. He waved one of the bearers on with orders to make his way to the next pueblo from where he must bring back a replacement and food as quickly as possible. It was already late, and Fray Julio directed the other Indians to make a bed for him of the pads which were part of the sedan chair. When they had done this, he excused them to get a night's rest, as the next morning was the Day of San Lorenzo and he wanted to complete his visitas and return to the pueblo of Santa Flora, to the ministrations and the bed of Beatriz Ramírez.

The Indians slept through the night on the open ground beside the rio. But the pads were not sufficiently comfortable for Fray Julio, and he was up before dawn. The runner he had sent ahead had not yet returned, and so he saw no reason for disturbing the sleeping Indians. He rose and walked along the rio's bank until he found a place which edged off into a gentle slope where he could make his way easily to the water. Here he knelt down and was washing his face when he saw the red colouring the water. At first, believing he saw a reflection, he looked up at the streaks of dawn. But this did not explain it. He held his hand in the water. There was no question that the water passing over his open palm was red. He crossed himself and rose to his feet. Fray Julio was not a superstitious man. He had seen too much of life to believe readily in miracles. He was convinced as he stood looking down at the water that there must be some simple explanation. He walked a few varas up the bank before he saw the body. Fully dressed, helmet still on his head, face down in the water lay a Spanish soldier. Fray Julio knelt down and flipped the body over. Then he saw the cluster of arrows which pierced the bleeding chest and he knew he had the explanation of the red water. But the Indian arrows bothered him. He had lived too long in this country not to recognize them as belonging to the People. He had seen too many antelopes brought down, too many hawks shot on the wing, not to recognize the arrows. These were not of strangers; these were not Apaches.

Fray Julio started to pull the body out of the water when he saw the small leather dispatch case in the soldier's belt. He dropped the body back and flipped the pouch open. Quickly he read the document from Governor Otermín to the alcalde mayors warning them of the possible uprising. Fray Julio rose to his feet and stood looking down at the body. It had already been stripped of its sword and daga. Heaven alone knew where the horse was. For a moment he thought of returning to his charges and rushing back to the pueblo of Santa Flora with them. Then he dropped the paper and watched it catch in a whirl of water and disappear downstream. There was no going back to Santa Flora. Only a fool would attempt anything like that. Beatriz. Beatriz. Her name flooded his thoughts and he forcefully shoved it back. If there was trouble, there was nothing he could do about it, nothing he could do to help her that her own dogs could not do better. If there was no trouble, then she would not need him immediately. But if there was trouble. . . He thought of the puebleños sleeping by the sedan chair, and then he remembered the one he had sent ahead to bring back more Indians.

Fray Julio shook his head. There was nothing to be gained by remaining here. The Villa de Santa Fe lay twenty leagues to the south. He would risk the discomfort, would make his way there. And if he found there had been no trouble, he could easily borrow a horse and return to his tasks. Why, if there was no trouble, he could finish his report of needed supplies, invent from imagination the remainder of his visits, and make a personal appearance before the Fray Custodio. Beatriz would respect this decision. It would bring him directly to the attention of the Fray Custodio.

And so, without waiting longer, half in fear and half in anticipation, the tall Creole padre crossed the rio and struck out across country, making every effort to lose his trail behind him.

10

THE *old señora sat upright, her twisted hands clutching the arm of the Savonarola chair; she moved only to reach up and spring a loose, white curl into place. Her face was set and still. Her aged back was rigid, her hands trembled, and beneath her spreading skirts her knees shook. She was waiting for Don Luis, the patrón, her husband, to return from his explorations to the northern plains. She had been waiting each morning as dawn came off a jagged peak for over twenty-seven years. And as far as she knew, she would be waiting thus at dawn on San Lorenzo's Day a year hence. She was a patient woman who loved passionately. Hope rested before her dimming eyes like the mist off the Rio Chama on a clear morning.*

It was with such hope than Don Luis had kissed her before he rode off many years before in search of the Seven Cities of Cibola. It had been with such hope that they had sailed on their honeymoon from Barcelona for Manila and with equal dreams that they had embarked from Manila for Nuevo Mexico five years later with their son and daughter. The large dream which made for empire, fortunes, futures had sustained them in their early years. The dreams had sustained them because both knew that over the mountains to the north lay the kingdom of gold that Coronado—a man of little faith—had failed to find.

The señora had not abandoned her hope or her dreams when the carta arrived informing that her son had been killed in a skirmish with the English pirate, Morgan. Nor had she abandoned them when her daughter died in childbirth and the common soldier who had seduced her assumed control of Don Luis' encomienda. For she knew Don Luis would return and punish this insolent peasant who wandered about their estancia nightly in his pantalones with a drink of green native liquor in his hand.

Seated on the portico, looking at the sun edge over a distant, blue-shadowed range, she watched the soldier as he prepared to mount his stallion, angry that his Indian groom had failed to appear. The seducer of her daughter was a fat, middle-aged soldier, uncouth, unpolished, and unhappy in the assignment given him by the Governor. Somewhere other men found beautiful wives, fine assignments with the booty and glory of battle, but he had been given the duties of an overseer with an old crone to frown at him.

Mounted, his feet resting in the crudely carved wooden shoe stirrups, the soldier caracoled his stallion past the portico and started for the gate.

Suddenly it crashed open and hundreds of Indians, black-faced and stripped to their loincloths, burst into the courtyard, swarmed over the surprised soldier, dragged him from his saddle, and pulped his head like a gourd for the mash.

Then they turned their attention to the wife of Don Luis. She had watched their entrance, heard their cries, and continued to sit impassively. She had seen death before. She was an old woman and quite prepared to die. With a slow, deliberate movement of her stiff arms she crossed herself and was praying quietly when the Indians clambered up the stone steps, held her tightly and lashed her feet and arms to the chair where they had seen her sitting while their own women served her for over a quarter-century. The señora did not whine, did not move a muscle while they bound her firmly into place. Nor did she turn her head when they lifted the Savonarola chair, which fitted about her like a carved cross, and carried it through the house.

In the large family room, the Indians carefully smashed the vargueño with the red velvet facing and the hammered copper fittings which had served Don Luis as a desk. They paused before the enamel-faced clock with the E-flat chimes and the gilt cherubs and watched the pendulum swing back and forth several times before one of them struck it with a cottonwood club, still shiny with the soldier's blood. They climbed onto the carved wardrobe to cut up two oil paintings of the Madonna and threw the canvas onto the table and chests they were piling in the centre of the floor. They opened the chests to shatter the goblets and strew the linens about. Then they carried the chair with the old woman to her sleeping room where they tore down the pink canopy and piled it on the bed with her clothes and those of her dead daughter.

They paused before the jade Buddha the señora had brought with her from the Philippines and wondered who this secret green god was and if she worshipped it. Fearing what they did not understand, they shied away from the carved figure and went on with their labours.

And so they carried the old woman in state from room to room that she might see the care with which they were preparing the manor house; and preparing it they were, for as they lifted her for the last time, one of the young men ran through the rooms with a torch, lighting each pile of her belongings. And while the fire grew, the Indians carried the old woman in the chair out of its reach onto the flagstone portico and set her down facing the gate as she had faced it through the memory of most of them.

Then they filed into the courtyard, turned to look back at their handiwork —the old woman facing them and the yellow and red tongues of flame licking out of the open windows. Finally, they departed and closed the gate after themselves, never to return.

For a long time the wife of Don Luis sat immobile, but as life began to leave her, the ageing body relaxed and sagged forward. The white curls hung freely while the unblinking eyes continued to stare at the gate through which Don Luis might yet return.

11

ASKON, the Indian youth of Galisteo who had been raised in the manor house of Don Pedro de Leiva, sat on the ground outside the high walls of the hacienda. He was surrounded by fifty Indian youths. Each had cleaned his weapons and had said the proper prayers for victory and survival. Now there was only the waiting.

Askon looked at the light which still flickered from the window of Señorita Dorotea and wondered what had disturbed her sleep. Was it the maid who had failed to appear after Mass? Was it the wild tale the maid must have told? Or was it the dreams of a girl waiting for her father and the man who was going to marry her? Askon had often sat in this very same spot at night and stared at the window of his childhood playmate. But when he sat there, his thoughts were usually of Concepción, his sister, now three years dead, still unavenged, and whom he always recalled by the name the Blessing Man had given her.

The light flickering in the window of the manor house disappeared and Askon looked up at the sky. There had been falling stars all through the long night's waiting. There were none now. The sky was black as it often is just before the first dawn streaks through. The youths were getting restless. One of them suggested they wait no longer, but Askon shook his head and the large burnished helmet of Juan de Leiva bobbed.

"There must be no warning; and if we attacked now, the noise of a single harquebus would warn the mission and the other hacendados before our people were ready."

Askon was no soldier. None of the others was. But there were certain things he had learned in his years of living with the Whiteface intruders. Among them was the belief in organization and a plan. His knowledge of just what these things meant was slight, but he was not a fool, and he respected Don Pedro for what he knew and what he could do. And Don Pedro always believed that there should be a plan. He spent weeks each planting season deciding what seeds should be sown, what ground should be cultivated. Why, Don Pedro had even planned for three years who would be the young man of Señorita Dorotea. This simple fact made a great impression on Askon, whose people rarely remembered to save their seed from season to season and who doubted if there were a white girl worthy of three years' planning.

The Indian youth removed the polished lobster-tail helmet from his head and rubbed his hand over the smooth metal. This should save a man from any harm. It was strong and was of the Whitefaces. But looking at the helmet, Askon failed to remember how simple it had been for him to kill Juan de Leiva and obtain it.

The sky was already streaked when Askon finally rose to his feet. By now the other men of the pueblo must be waiting before the walls of each estancia, each rancho, and the mission. All the roads leading out of the valley would be blocked, and there was no longer any reason for waiting. Besides, the patience of the youth had come to an end. As he entered the open courtyard of the hacienda, the others followed him. They fanned out quietly, keeping to the shadows. Without sound enough to disturb a bird sleeping under the eaves of the broad colonnade which surrounded the manor, they made their way into the main entrance and paused.

With his fingers up to show the number he wanted, Askon led small groups to the various doors, and taking the rest of the men, he went himself to the door of the soldado who slept with the granddaughter of the absent encomendero. All the young men were tense. They grasped their clubs, macanas, and machetes nervously. Askon alone among them had ever killed, and he only Juan de Leiva and Dorotea's maid, the day before.

The other youths turned to their young war chief as they stood in the corridor of the sleeping quarters and watched for his signal. It came suddenly and in the form of a loud yell he had once heard the Spaniards use as they practised their battle tactics against some captive Apaches, a cry he understood meant attack, but whose specific meaning was fuzzy to him. *"Por Rey y Santiago!"*

The Indian warriors picked up the yell and hurled themselves into their respective rooms, killing the Spaniards as they lay in their beds. When they were done, they dragged the corpses out and scattered them about the patio and the courtyard beyond. Then they counted the bodies to be certain all were there. Only Señorita Dorotea was missing, and this was as Askon had planned. The youth who stood outside her door had not entered the room. Instead, he had hurled the girl back when she ran out to discover what was taking place.

Askon walked into her room and closed the door behind him. The others waited for a long time, but when no sound came, they pillaged the hacienda and departed for the plaza where they knew Askon would join them for the march north.

Once inside the sleeping room of Dorotea, Askon closed the door and stood against it. When he entered, the girl stepped away and stared at him. There was no doubt that the helmet he wore had belonged to her brother Juan and that the sword hanging at his side was also Juan's. There was no question in her mind that her brother was dead, and as she stood in her thin nightdress, her black hair tumbled about her head, Dorotea slowly realized that Askon would only have entered her room if there were no one to stop him.

"Don Esteban? Doña Lucia?"

The tall Indian youth shook his head. There was no need for him to explain anything, as she seemed to understand.

"All of them," he said. "All of them."

For a moment each tried to avoid the other's eyes. There was no shame in Askon for what had just happened on the patio. Nor was there any lingering hate. The girl was frightened and her mind wandered over the collection of stones by the rio where she had marked the day of her father's return and the arrival of the young man from Potosí. Her thoughts stumbled over the fact that her father would not return, the young man would not arrive. Dorotea would never be wed as her niece had been wed or as her brothers had been. And then as Askon walked across the room and took her arm, she realized for the first time why he had come to her and she stepped back.

Not Askon. He was an Indian, and white women and Indians . . . the thought trailed off as she recalled her father's "Respect. Respect. Respect. Make them respect you." Her hand lashed out and she struck him across the face. For a moment he did not move. Then he dropped his hand from her arm and stood quietly before her.

"How was it different with Concepción?"

The slim figure of the girl trembled and she turned and knelt before the small crucifijo with the candela beside it and started to pray.

Askon watched her for a moment, and then he reached out, took the figure of the Cristo in his hand and smashed it against the wall. The head fell away and the cross shattered, leaving him with only the wood body in his hand. She stared at him, frightened.

The Indian youth felt the fear in her eyes, and opening his hand, looked in astonishment at the broken figure. Suddenly he had to drop it as though it were something alive. It fell to the floor beside her knees. Neither moved for a long time. Then Dorotea reached out, and picking up the body of the Cristo, held it tightly to her breasts as she began to weep.

The sunlight edged its way into the room and crawled across the floor. Bound for the moment by the sobs of the girl and the torpor that followed the violent action of the morning, Askon slipped to his knees beside her. His head went down on his chest and the helmet fell off. Neither of them seemed to hear it clatter on the stone floor. His arm went about her shoulder to comfort her, and she relaxed and leaned against his bared, copper breast.

When she could cry no longer, Dorotea looked up at him and pushed herself away. She rose, falteringly, to her feet and with great care set the body of the Cristo back in the niche on the wall, crossed herself, and turned to the Indian. He had risen and was going through her wardrobe. Finally, he found a simple black dress that suited him and he held it out to her.

"You'll have to dress. We must go to the pueblo. The others, I must join them. We go to the Villa where the Governor lives."

She took the dress in her hand and tried to understand what he was telling her.

"And you'll kill the Governor as you killed my mother and my brothers and my . . ."

Askon grasped both her arms and shook her. "Dress. Or you will go as you are. The People are waiting."

When he realized she had no intention of doing as he asked, he pulled the dress from her hand, found a robe among her clothes, threw it over her shoulders, and shoved her out the door. The bodies on the patio were undisturbed and the sight of them shocked the girl, who tried to run back to her room. But the Indian pushed her past them and into the courtyard where the other bodies lay in the brightening sun. Before she could pause, he shoved her on. Only when they were outside of the gate and on the path leading to the pueblo did Askon stop, only then did he realize that she was wearing no shoes. He knelt down and slipped his own moccasins onto her bare feet and drew her away from the hacienda, explaining as they went: "You will remain in the rooms of my mother. And you will be as Concepción, or the People will punish you. And when I return from the Villa, we will build a room of our own near my mother's or we can go back to your house if that is what you want."

At first she did not seem to hear him. Then she brushed her hair away from her dulled face and looked at him puzzled as he pulled her along. Suddenly she started to laugh, broke loose from his grasp, and fled down the trail. He watched her as she ran away from him. When she tripped and stumbled, he walked over to her, picked her up and carried her toward the pueblo where the other men were waiting for him.

12

THE *señora abandoned the search about the estancia for the child's nurse and carried the infant into the sleeping quarters herself. As she changed the little boy's clothes, washed his face with cool water, and prepared him for his morning nap, she thought of the punishment she would order for the nurse. The Indian wench had not been whipped for months and apparently the time had come again.*

In the three years since her husband had been granted the encomienda for services he had pleasantly rendered in the Viceroy's bed, the señora had learned that the savages must be taught with an open palm and a ready lash. This was regrettable, as the señora abhorred violence. But, as her husband had so carefully explained, the Indians had thick hides and dull minds. It took effort to get through both.

She leaned over, kissed the boy who looked so much like the Viceroy, drew the white canopy about the bed to keep away the flies and, rising, brushed back a lock of black hair. When she walked into her own room, she found her maid missing. For a moment, she was angry. But as she laced the front of her bodice before the mirror, she became calm. There were certain things a lady had to bear with when using native servants. Back home in Aragon one could depend on a peasant wench. There was an appreciation of their masters which was lacking in the Indians.

Then she heard the yelling in the courtyard and knew she would have to put a stop to it. The savages would disturb the child. She fluffed her overskirt with care and swished out of the room, across the loggia, and out onto the placita.

Here she stopped, for the courtyard was filled with screaming naked savages whirling about with pikes, wooden sabres, and bows. Their faces were streaked with black soot and their hands were blood-red. Then she saw they were taking turns dipping their hands into a pool of blood gathering on the flagstones. Both her maid and the nurse were in the courtyard. The señora was about to call to them when it slowly came to her that the blood flowed into the pool from a corpse suspended from a cottonwood tree, and that the corpse was her husband.

Then she screamed, and again as her palm covered her face. The Indians were quiet as they turned toward the señora. She saw that one of them carried her husband's sword hanging from a black-embroidered baldrick over a naked chest. Her maid wore his white silk sash loosely over her bare brown shoulders. Slowly they began to edge up to the placita where the white lady in the white gown stood frozen.

The señora wanted to talk to them, but she could not. Then one of the older men, carrying a flaming spruce limb, climbed the steps. Standing tall and erect as her hands came away from her face, she stretched her arms across the doorway to block his entrance.

Suddenly the square-faced Indian hurled the burning brand at her. She watched its flight, fascinated, as it struck the hem of her gown. The white satin caught fire and her shriek was the only sound to be heard as she ran out into the courtyard. The crowd separated as the torch she had become ran through it.

The señora almost reached the gate before she fell down and rolled over and over.

The Indians watched silently as the flames consumed her. Then they climbed the steps and entered the estancia where the little boy who resembled the Viceroy drowsed under a white silk canopy to protect him from the flies.

13

FAR to the south in the pueblo of San Ysidro, Ruaha watched the young runner disappear into the darkness, and then joined the other men who had already gathered their weapons—almost two hundred of them standing together in the small open plaza wearing only their pantalones or loincloths and moccasins. One of the young men was carefully scraping the charcoal from a burnt limb into a small flat pot. And as he added water, the men took turns streaking their faces with the black wash. Ruaha alone did not join them. His war was not only against the gods of his enemies. He was fighting now to revenge himself, and he felt ill as he thought of this. Revenge was not a motive which impressed the old man. He had never much respected the Spanish youths who felt they had been insulted and must step forth to fight for their names or alleged dignity. He had been repelled by the wasteful duels he had watched in his younger days when he had attended the mission school at the Villa, and revenge for him had always worn a tragic face, a pose without dignity.

Ruaha watched as some of the young men scoured the communal houses for the small bultos of the saints. These brightly coloured statues of carved wood had replaced the katchinas for almost a century, and now they were in their turn going to the fire. A young man holding a San Ysidro hesitated before he hurled the wooden figure into the flame. The small patron saint of the farmers stood on a platform behind a group of oxen figurines and held one hand to his ear so that he might hear those who would pray to him. A small pine angel painted blue and white stood beside him. Ruaha recognized the bulto as having rested on the house altar of Yad-wan, and when the youth who held it turned to throw the carved figure into the fire, the old Indian wanted to stand forward and tell him of how this bulto came into being, of the time he had carved it. He wanted to tell the youth of the nights he had spent talking with the ageing Fray Custodio when both of them were younger, seated on the steps of the mission of Santo Domingo. But Ruaha did not step forward, he did not speak, and the bright collection of figurines crashed into the fire and the ageing cacique watched the flames eat away the blue and the white, and then. . .

He turned away and stared at the sky. It was time. Their rebellion would begin now. It would be a small rebellion in numbers as they had only the slight padre with the cowl that never quite fitted him and a soldier with a black beard and an angry eye to destroy and then they would be done with the Spanish. Ruaha did not know when, if ever, they would be done with the gods the Spanish had brought with them. Inwardly the old man smiled at himself. Their gods. Their gods. The gods of the Blessing Men. He recalled the long disputation with the Fray Custodio the year before when they had discussed the nature of the white god who had a holy family and how this was different from the many gods of the People. The lean, hardened Fray Custodio had talked beautifully for a time. Then his assistant, the young Fray Pedro, had permitted his anger to grow on him and they found they could no longer talk to each other. The apostate. The heretic. The foolish savage. All the old names had spilled too readily from the younger man, and Ruaha had risen, looked at the Fray Custodio, and shrugged. They had never been able to talk again. Now the Fray Custodio would take his place with the other padres and be killed for it. Ruaha raised his hand, and those about him became silent.

"I will make no speeches. We do this which we must. And we kill only so that we may live. It is best not to kill those who have been made by the Earth Mother without asking her forgiveness for killing that which she permitted to be born."

And for a quiet moment he prayed to the Earth Mother of all living things, the womb of the gods from which blessings flowed.

When he was done, he started to walk across the fields toward the kiva with the cross on top of it. The other men fell in behind him. There were no women because he had decided days before that this was not for the women. Religion belonged to the men, and if the men rejected the old ways, the men must return to them, and what the men did the women would also do.

Several times youths started to scream to build up their courage. And each time Ruaha turned to look at them until there was silence. Then he went on again. He did not mind the loud boasts he heard behind him, because it is the nature of young men to talk in vast wishes. But the screaming disturbed him. What they were about to do was a religious act. It meant the changing of gods, a return to a way of life which had been known along the rio for generations and generations. It was not something which should be done without dignity and thought and feeling. This was not a great game constructed around the tumbling of weeds or the racing of relays for a fine blanket. This was the most important thing that any of them would do in their lives, and Ruaha wanted them to know it. For if the Spaniards left and the rains came, they would have done well, but if no rain came, if there were no gods to hear them . . . Ruaha was frightened.

The puebleños approached the mission, and standing on the steps, Fray Rafael watched them cross the fields. He was surprised at their coming so early. However, he was prepared in his way to meet them. He had spent the night planning a text which would, he hoped, lead the Indians from their doubts and possible apostasy. He had thought often of the old woman who was the wife of the cacique and wished that he had better understood her. It was the language. The Indians would have to learn Spanish. There was no further doubt in his mind about it. He would speak to the cacique, the man Ruaha whom the Fray Custodio seemed to believe had so much understanding, and he would explain to him that for the sake of their souls they would have to learn the language of the Spaniard and that he would be willing to teach Latin, the language of God, to the young men so that they might better understand what was meant by the Mass and the holy days, so they could more truly appreciate the beauty of that for which Christ died.

Fray Rafael was making resolutions now, decisions on what must be done and he knew that these were things he could do and so he felt relieved. He could teach Spanish and he could teach Latin. He held a degree from his university and had been an honoured student in the Holy Language. It was altogether proper that he approach his problem in the way he best understood it.

The Day of San Lorenzo was going to warm. The sky clear. He wished for the sake of the Indians that there might be some rain, but he knew there was not going to be any.

As the puebleños crossed the fields, he heard some random shouts and was bewildered. This was not the way they had been taught to come to Mass, but the noise ceased, and as the group approached, he saw that there were only the men. And as he stared at them, he slowly began to understand what the old woman had told him. His ignorance of her language had been the trouble; he blamed himself for not having known that this was the day.

The Indians, copper faces streaked with black, were carrying their weapons. There were macanas as well as machetes which had been issued or stolen or borrowed over the years from the Spanish conquerors. Several of the men carried long lances with stone tips and one had a Spanish lance with a steel tip of the type used over a hundred years before by the cavalry of Coronado. One man swung a brightly shining steel sabre at his side which someone must have taken from a soldier of Governor Oñate's entourage two generations before. The puebleños were ready for war, pathetically, tragically, and seriously ready. They had come to fight and kill even though they had never done so before. The only lessons they had ever learned about war and murder had been taught to them by the Apache strangers to the north and the white Spanish conquerors from the south.

Fray Rafael walked down the steps of the mission and stood waiting for Ruaha, the cacique. When the Indian approached him, he raised his hand and spoke in Spanish, which he knew this Indian would understand.

"Weapons and hatred cannot be taken in unto the house of the Lord." The words were spoken softly and Ruaha understood them. The old cacique started to walk past the slight figure of the padre, but Fray Rafael stood his ground. "If there is something you would do out here, then you must. But if you plan to enter the house of the Lord, you must leave your weapons out here."

The few men standing behind Ruaha started to push forward, but the Indian spread out his arms and they dropped back.

"You would prevent us from entering your kiva?" Ruaha was patient and curious.

The word kiva to describe the mission angered Fray Rafael, though he had always known this was the term the Indians used for it.

"I will prevent you from entering a holy place armed and with hatred in your hearts." Then seeing the firm faces staring at him in the bright light of the early morning, Fray Rafael amended his words. "I shall endeavour to prevent your entry."

One young man, who had worked for a time as an interpreter on a distant rancho, laughed loudly. But he paused and looked puzzled when Ruaha turned to stare at him.

The cacique was fascinated and impressed with the courage of the Blessing Man who had come such a great distance to save the souls of the People. For the moment it was not important that this foreign medicine man did not understand the People or what he was doing to them and how the old gods had absented themselves from the land between the mesas. What was important was that this Spanish padre believed, had faith, and drew courage from this faith.

There was silence as the men of the pueblo waited for Ruaha to act. The principales knew him and were certain of his wisdom. The younger men respected the old man whose wife had died only the night before, and one of the young men who had hoped to marry the daughter of the cacique held up his hand to hear what the cacique would say.

It was the shy Spanish padre who spoke first. "Will you not leave your weapons and come in for the Mass?"

Ruaha stood for a long time, then set his macana against the wall and entered the church. The padre followed him and the startled men of the pueblo were confused. Then one by one the principales stepped forward and rested their weapons beside the wooden sabre of Ruaha. Finally, the others followed. The men took their usual places in the church, sat as rigidly upright as mountain spruce and waited.

Slowly, with great care, with every emphasis he could bring to bear and every bit of knowledge he had, the padre began the service.

"*Confessio et pulchritudo in conspectu ejus; sanctis et magnificentia in santificatione ejus.* Praise and beauty go before Him; holiness and majesty are in His sanctuary. Sing to the Lord a new canticle; sing to the Lord, all the earth. . . ."

And the Franciscan raised his head in prayer: "O Almighty God, strengthen us so that we may extinguish in ourselves the flames of sin as Lorenzo was able to withstand his fiery torments. Through our Lord."

Then the padre opened the Book in front of him, but before he read, he told the puebleños the tale of San Lorenzo. He regretted that he could not tell it to them in their own tongue. But he hoped that they would understand in part and that perhaps later at another time and in another place they would understand it fully. He wanted to reach out to them to let them know that he was a friend and a shepherd. He wanted them to know the nobility of love and the strength that came with faith.

"When Sextius II was Bishop of Rome he had for a young archdeacon a pious padre named Lorenzo who was a Spaniard of Oscia in the Kingdom of Aragon. Unto his care Sextius gave the humble treasures of the Church, and on being condemned to death, the Bishop of Rome commanded Lorenzo to take all the treasures of the Church and distribute them among the poor, the sick, the naked, and the hungry. And Lorenzo did as he was bade until he was arrested and brought before the prefect and asked where he had hidden the riches, and Lorenzo gathered those to whom he had given the alms and said unto the prefect: Behold the treasures of His Church. The prefect fell into a terrible rage and ordered that Lorenzo should be stretched on a bed of iron and a fire lighted beneath it which would gradually consume his body to ashes. In the midst of his tortures, Lorenzo said: 'Seest thou not, O foolish man, that I am already roasted on one side and that if thou wouldst have me well cooked, it is time to turn me on the other.' Thus was San Lorenzo of Oscia in the Kingdom of Aragon on the tenth day of August."

The sombre eyes of the cacique looked up in admiration as they met those of the padre who was preaching what might be his last sermon in both humility and defiance. Then the Franciscan read the Gospel of the day's service:

"*Verily I say unto you, except a corn of wheat fall unto the ground and die, it abideth alone: but if it die, it bringeth much fruit. He that loveth his life shall lose it . . ."*

Fray Rafael was certain for the first time that Ruaha understood the service and as he looked about at the other faces, he was convinced that the old cacique was the only one.

"If any man serve me, let him follow me; and where I am, there shall my servant be, him will my Father honour."

There was silence in the chapel as the padre approached the end of his service. His voice was a plea as he tried for the last time to reach his charges.

"O come, let us worship and bow down; let us kneel before the Lord, our Maker."

The small figure in the grey cassock crossed over to the large figure of the Master upon the wall, and kneeling, prayed silently to himself.

"O Lord, accept the gifts which we offer with honour to You. May we be aided by the meritorious prayer of your blessed martyr Lorenzo, that these offerings may help us toward our salvation. Through the Lord."

And Fray Rafael was done. There was nothing further he could say. The set face of the cacique showed no emotion, revealed nothing. There was quiet in the small church. Finally, Ruaha rose to his feet and motioned for his companions to depart. There were those among them who were bewildered. But as the principales opened the broad doors and walked out into the sunlight, the others followed. At last, only Ruaha and Fray Rafael remained in the mission. Turning back to the padre, Ruaha beckoned to him.

"You will have to come with us," he said.

The padre nodded, knelt, crossed himself and prayed quietly for a time. Then he rose and walked to the door of the mission and Ruaha followed him. They stepped out into the sunlight where the People were waiting for them. Ruaha turned and carefully closed the doors of the chapel behind him and then called the young man who had once wanted to marry the child Poy-Ye. "You will see that no one enters this place, no one disturbs it; nothing is to be profaned. There will be no offence against the gods of this man. We are not the Spaniards and we will not destroy their kiva as they have destroyed ours."

Then, standing on the steps of the church, he addressed his people. "We have promised our allies in the kingdom of the pueblos that there will be no shaven heads in our land. We have promised our allies and pledged our gods to rid the land of them. This promise we will keep. But let us wait to decide if we kill this medicine man or drive him south." He nodded to two of the more eager youths. "You will see that he is locked in that room behind the mission in which he sleeps. We will not harm him now."

There were some angry looks and a group of the younger men stepped forward to protest. They had pledged the gods, they had put on the paint, they were ready for more than the closing of a door.

Ruaha listened. They did not know how much courage it took to close some doors, and so he said nothing. Only a little of what was being discussed was understood by Fray Rafael, who wished now that he had learned the language of his parishioners.

The voices of the young men rose and one of the principales stepped forward. "What of the bearded soldado?"

Ruaha nodded and walked slowly down the steps to the place where his macana rested, grasped it in his hand and started to walk up the hill toward the hacienda where the bearded soldier lived with his woman and the child who was Ruaha's grandson. The other men raised their weapons above their heads and their voices to a shout and followed him. This time Ruaha did not turn about to silence them. His voice joined theirs as he looked forward to his meeting with the Whiteface man to whom he owed so much.

Fray Rafael, standing on the steps of the mission and watching the Indians depart, suddenly started to run after them. Perhaps he could talk to them. Perhaps he could explain there were vengeances which were the Lord's; that good Christians did not kill. But the two young men who had been set to guard him grabbed his arms, swung him about and marched him to the rear of the mission where they hurled him to the floor of the small room which served as his sleeping quarters. Then they closed the door after him.

The men of the pueblo of San Ysidro followed Ruaha up the hill toward the hacienda of the bearded soldier. They made their way around the boulders which half blocked the rocky pass, and twice they paused to clear their route of traps. When they came to the steps which led to the placita, Ruaha pressed forward. Then two of the younger men placed their hands on his shoulders, and shook their heads slowly. He nodded and the two went into the large manor house which had been built by their ancestors for a Spanish lord almost a century before. Ruaha waited with the principales and the young warriors soon appeared at the door and beckoned for their companions to join them.

Ruaha entered and stopped. Lying in a pool of blood, face down on the floor, was an Indian youth. The old cacique knelt and turned the body over. It was the runner of Tesuque who had departed the pueblo only a few hours earlier. His face was battered. He was missing several fingers of his left hand and his right ear had been sliced from his head. But most of the blood on the floor came from the slash across his throat. The cacique turned to the two young warriors with a question on his face.

"There is no one. The bearded soldado has fled."

Ruaha did not move for a moment. He prayed briefly over the body of the youth from Tesuque. Then he rose to his feet and walked through the house. He paused in one of the sleeping rooms and looked at the thirteen ears of corn gathered there, and as he was about to leave the room, he saw the shape of a turquoise butterfly on the wall. He looked about and then crossed over to the window where he picked up a small necklace that was reflecting the morning light. It was the one he had given the girl Poy-ye several years before. He closed his fist over it and stood staring at the thirteen ears of corn.

After a moment he shook his head slowly and made his way back to the main room where the others were waiting. The young men gathered about to hear his decision. It came quickly.

"Find the trail of the bearded soldado, the Whiteface killer and profaner. When you have found it, return and all of us will join to follow."

Several of the young men started for the door.

Ruaha raised his hand and they paused. "Remember, he cannot be far, for there is a woman with him and a child."

The youths nodded and departed. The old man walked out onto the patio and watched them as they scattered in ever greater circles seeking the signs which would tell them where the bearded soldier had fled. Ruaha looked at the sky. It was mid-morning now. He was patient. He could wait.

14

THE early sun burned the bare flesh of Natividad as she clambered over the rocks ahead of José Reyes. The baby in her arms was quiet for the first time in almost an hour. She hoped it merely slept. Her hips ached where the bearded soldier struck her with the flat of his sword every time she paused to catch her breath or insure her footing. Reyes was in a hurry. He had no intension of being trapped. Only a fool was trapped and only a fool would let himself be killed by ignorant savages.

Once the girl had paused when the sole tore loose from her moccasin; and when she bent over to see if it could be repaired, he struck her with his clenched fist, knelt down, removed the worn footgear, and then shoved her on to walk with a bare foot. Now it was torn, the track was bloody. But he would not pause again.

José Reyes was frightened. For the first time in his life he knew fear. It came with the dawn and grew with the sun climbing above him. It had been a simple thing for a man of his skills to follow the runner of Tesuque whom he had seen enter the pueblo, and bring him to the hacienda. It had been simpler still to make the reluctant Indian youth talk about the uprising—the schedule, the plans, and the hopes of the Indians. It had also been simple to kill him. But when dawn came, Reyes knew he had to be far from the hacienda. He realized now, as he made his way up the rio's bank northward, that he should have travelled alone. There was little to be gained by bringing the wench. But without her he would not have his son with him, and for some reason, not quite clear in his own twisted mind, José Reyes wanted his son. The boy was the sign, the symbol that there was a man named José Reyes who would live forever despite what happened in the world of the pueblos. In its own feeble way the killer's mind sought immortality. José knew that for a generation the members of his craft in

Córdoba would remember the mark of Reyes, the dead body without an ear. But it was the years that would follow that bothered him, and so he journeyed now with his son.

He thought of the boy with pride. His son. The son of José Reyes. It mattered not that there seemed to be something wrong with the flat bridge of the infant's nose, which a physician might have recognized as the brand of the French pox, or that his eyes had trouble focusing. What mattered was that he was a Reyes and that he would live to know his father and be trained by his father in all of the skills that artist had learned from the masters of Córdoba. This great knowledge would be the heritage of Reyes, what the father wanted to pass on to his child.

The heat of the morning burned savagely on the black chestplate and polished helmet of the soldier. The sabre in his hand was heavy and his feet were weary. Waves of hot air seemed to billow back at him from the rocks which lined the banks of the rio, and he wanted to take off his armour, but feared to do it; wanted to pause and walk into the rio to cool himself, and feared to do it.

The Indians were not fools. They knew their own country. They would pick up the trail and be after him. He climbed a small hillock and looked south. There was nothing in sight but the winding rio and clouds of heat breaking a clear view.

The girl Natividad slipped to her knees, set the infant on the ground, and stretched herself out to take some water from the rio in her cupped hands. She washed the child's face, flushed from the heat and the illness it had had ever since it was born. Then she turned back to drink from the stream, but Reyes was already down from the hillock and standing over her. The flat of his sabre smashed across her buttock before he reached down and picked her up by the hair. The terrified girl waited for him to strike. Instead, he picked up his son, fondling the child in his hands for a moment, then passed the bundle to its mother. He pointed upstream and she turned and started walking again.

The sun had climbed to the top of the sky when Reyes came to the white-rocked arroyo which crossed the stream. He placed his arm on the girl's shoulder and shoved her into the rio ahead of him. With uncertain footing, they made their way through water up to their waists, out onto the other side and up the dry bed of the pebbled arroyo. Half an hour later they rounded a bend and found themselves facing the closed end of a barranca.

When the height rose in front of him, Reyes almost panicked. He felt trapped, caught in a place without exit, and the fear that grew inside him pressed against his gut and he became ill. He stumbled against the wall of the barranca, dropped his sabre, and stared at the sun until he was almost blind.

The heat and the sudden stopping woke the baby and it began to cry again. Natividad tried to calm it with rocking motions in her arms as she stared at the soldier and tried to comprehend what had happened to him. Then he removed his helmet, wiped his face with the back of his arm, and glared back at her. She avoided his eyes as he lifted himself away from the wall and looked about. There was a small ledge part way up the side of the ravine, sheltered and out of the sun. He knelt down, recovered his sabre, poked the girl to gain her attention, and pointed to the ledge. She nodded and started the difficult climb up the stone wall. Reyes followed.

Ten minutes later they had gained the shelter of the ledge. The soldier stood for a moment looking back down the ravine, then he took off his helmet again and wiping his face, motioned for the girl to remove his heavy bucket boots. Waiting until he settled himself against a rock, she set the infant on the ground beside him and pulled off the boots. Suddenly conscious of the heat of his bare feet, Reyes stretched them and rested. When he motioned for the girl to feed his son, she relaxed and opened the front of her dress and tried to satisfy the child.

15

THE *Indians had tired of their destruction of the white estancia and wandered out into the courtyard where the body of the patrón and his women lay sprawled in the growing pools of blood. The flies of summer had begun to gather and a small dog nuzzled about the corpse of a young girl.*

One Indian stood in the courtyard and stared at the body of his master. The bucket boots he had polished for the Castilian were marked with dust and spots of blood. With care, almost with tenderness, the Indian rolled the body over on its back. He looked into the open eyes and thought of the years he had known this man who had never been his friend, of the years they had spent growing up on this hacienda, the almost forty plantings of gold wheat. And he thought of the seeds which the Castilians had brought with them, seeds of the golden sheaves which symbolized the illness they had which could never be cured by anything other than gold. Then the Indian knelt down and started to remove the black boots from the stiffening legs. But the open eyes disturbed him, and he had to roll the body over again before he could bring himself to do it.

Seated on the ground beside the bloody pool, he fondly caressed the soft leather as he pulled the boots up to his bare thigh. Then he rose and admired himself, standing naked except for the loincloth and this symbol of the Castilian. His companions watched him, each trying on the buff jerkin or pantelones or pikeman's pot helmet or skirt he had taken from the rooms of the hacendado and his señora.

To the Indian the boots were more than leather, more than something to wear on his feet, even more than the symbol of his fallen master. The boots were what a man wore, a whole man, one who had a certain privilege which the Indian had coveted all his life. With long, uncertain steps, he walked around the courtyard to the back of the manor house and into the stable where the horses which had belonged to the patrón were lodged. He knew every inch of this stable, every inch of the floor which he had cleaned for over twenty-five years, every one of the horses which he had curried since they were foaled. And he knew just the horse he wanted—the great black stallion which was the patrón's, the broad horse with the nervous gait. He opened the stall and led the beast out into the courtyard and tied it to the small hitching post, as he had done almost every morning for the past five years. Then he went back into the stable and carried out the saddle with the silver ornaments and the caparisoned seat. On his shoulder he carried the blue blanket which he had washed only the night before in anticipation. The horse shied away as it always did when he dropped the blanket over its back, but seemed to accept the saddle without protest. Finally the horse was ready for riding. The Indian stepped back and looked at the animal. It was awesome and might have frightened a lesser man. But the Indian was determined. He had never ridden a horse, had never been astride the broad back, crossing over the countryside. Puebleños rarely did. The laws were firm on this matter, and even the most indulgent patrón—and there were so few of these—knew that much of his power lay in the ability he had to rise above the natives and look down upon them from the back of a horse. The first conquistador himself had said, "After God we owed the victory to horses."

And so, for the Indian, to mount a horse was more than just to ride; it was the ultimate freedom, the final symbol that he was equal to any man. With deliberate care and his fears well hidden behind his straight face, the Indian in the bucket boots approached the stallion, untied him, placed his foot in the large shoe stirrup and swung himself on to the back of a horse for the first time.

Startled, the black stallion rose on his hind legs and whirled about as though to see who was on his back. Barely set in the saddle and unfamiliar with the jerking motion, the Indian tumbled to the ground. He lay still for a moment and looked up at the horse which had come to a halt and was staring down at him. Both were bewildered. Then the Indian rose, grasped the reins hanging loose, and with a swift, strong motion drove the small daga he carried into the throat of the beast. In a sudden, surprised burst of pain, the huge stallion backed away, broke loose, ran out of the courtyard and across the fields until it suddenly crumpled onto its forepaws and then its face. The Indian watched it die and hoped that he would not have to keep on killing the Castilian to be free of him.

16

DON ALONSO GARCÍA sat on the patio of his hacienda south of Sandia and watched his wife, Doña Josefa, eat breakfast. The old warrior had finished his own breakfast with Nita hours before, when the sun first reflected off the rio. They had risen early all their lives, and the luxury of position could not change either of them. Nita was in the house now seeing that the Indian maids straightened the rooms with care and that the kitchen had its menus for the day. This was a task Doña Josefa envied her, but as it involved work it was not one she would quarrel about.

She smiled at her husband, who was surprised and pleased. Things had not gone well between them of late. Nuevo Mexico had not brought the Señora all the pleasures she had expected would come her way with rank and position. For after all, since his marriage to her, Don Alonso had taken on a certain prestige, and for this she was prepared to accept her share of credit. Whatever manners the old soldier had, she had taught him. Whatever ambition had goaded him on, she believed herself the force behind it. And the fact that he had achieved a measure of success was, she felt, wholly to her credit. It was not important that he had worked hard and fought hard for these things. Nor was it important that he had an almost childish passion to gather property for his sons, who were not her sons. What was important was that this mestizo—call himself what he would—had married a woman of España. But the promotions had meant less for her than she had hoped. There was very little satisfaction in being the wife of a lieutenant governor of a province as large as España itself if there were none to whom she could show off these honours. They did not entertain. They did not hold court. They did not even live with the people clustered about the convent at Isleta to the south. No, her husband had elected to live on an isolated hacienda, because there was work for him here. Work. She looked across the table at him, white shirt, black pantalones, and bucket boots. What work had he done since he had arrived in this place? Overseen the planting of some crops. Held trials for dirty Indians. Taken visitas like an inspector general from pueblo to pueblo. This she did not consider work, not the work at least of a lieutenant governor. He should be holding court, having the important holders of ranchos, haciendas, estancias coming to him, listening to him as he told them what to do and how to do it. The work of a lieutenant governor, she was convinced, was to govern, and that meant to rule. She could not understand the man who came home at nights from the fields where the irrigation ditches were being cut, his hands muddy and calloused. She could not approve of the days spent with the caciques and other Indians trying to solve the petty problems of supply in a barren season. No, Doña Josefa did not comprehend or approve of her husband.

Don Alonso sat quietly waiting for her to finish her breakfast. This was the Day of San Lorenzo, and he had promised himself that he would not work, but would remain at the manor and keep Josefa company and spend some time with Nita, visiting the small estancia of their son half a league to the south. He reached out and placed his hand on his wife's.

"Perhaps you would like to walk by the rio?" He wanted to be closer to this woman who he knew disapproved of him, yet shared his bed when he was not with Nita. He was proud of her. She was his wife and she was a lady and he never forgot that he was the Waif of Zacatecas.

Doña Josefa nodded. She wanted to walk out into the sunlight, though she dreaded the blaze of it across her face. Her breakfast finished, she wiped her hands across the front of her white blouse and rose to her feet. Don Alonso rose with her and as they walked down the steps toward the rio, he realized again how small she was compared to his towering bulk. She put her arm through his and they descended to the rio in time to see the horseman racing toward them from the north. The Lieutenant Governor paused and waited. In a flurry of dust a large white stallion bore down on them, pivoted, and came to a halt. Doña Josefa brushed the dust from her face and turned to her husband expecting him to do something about the manners of the soldier who dismounted with a leap before them. But her husband said nothing as he waited.

The youth came to attention before his commander. "I am from Jemez, sir."

Don Alonso nodded. The young man was obviously upset.

"At Jemez, sir. We heard yesterday. That is, the Alcalde Mayor heard. The Alcalde Mayor and Captain General of Jemez and Queres heard."

"Yes?"

"Pardon, sir, but he heard . . ."

"What?"

The youth took a deep breath and held the bridle rein tightly as he finally brought out the words. "The Indians will rise up against us. They plan to kill all of the whites and the padres." The horror of what he said frightened him and he looked away as he finished speaking.

The voice of Don Alonso was soft and almost inaudible. "From whom did he hear this?"

It took the young soldier a moment to return from his fear to the problem that created it. "From an Indian, sir. One the Alcalde Mayor feels he can trust."

Don Alonso nodded. Something stirred inside him and he recalled the feeling. Years had passed since he had known it. Years behind him and old campaigns, but it was there—the churn of blood that preceded action. Only it was different now. Now he had something to lose if the tale the boy brought was true.

He looked at his wife and from her to the large hacienda with its white walls and planted patio.

It could not be true. In all of his travels through the countryside, in all of his meetings with the caciques—the puebleños—he had felt no sign of it, no awareness, no single overt action which would lead him to believe this tale had foundation in other than the night-spinning of legend by an Indian who might want no more than to draw attention and perhaps favour for himself.

The young soldier and Doña Josefa watched the Lieutenant Governor as he tried in his own mind to deny the news he had just received. It was unacceptable news. And besides, it was not the kind of news he would ever hear. His responsibilities never came down to those of defence of a community. He was merely an old soldier who had worked hard and was being paid in favours and position for his years of campaigning. He was not a man to assume the prerogatives of command. But as he argued with himself, he knew that in assuming the position and the title, and in accepting the hacienda and all that went with it, he had incurred an obligation. The word that went through his mind was duty. It kept rushing forward while he tried to think of all the arguments against it. But he smiled to himself as he realized how well conditioned he had become with all the years in the field. If he heard a drumbeat or the cry, *"Por Rey y Santiago,"* he knew he would get off his deathbed and go charging empty-handed against the black angels of Hell.

The two watching him were surprised at the smile that crossed his face, completely unaware of the fierce humour behind it. Don Alonso shrugged and turned to the young soldier, "Go and get a fresh horse from my stable. Tell the five soldados who are probably still flat on their backsides in the small building behind the hacienda that I want to see them at once, fully equipped to ride."

Doña Josefa's fingers tightened on his sleeve and he placed a large palm on top of her hand to reassure her. The youth walked up the path leading to the stable, and as he reached the top of it, Don Alonso called after him, "The large roan with the broad chest, bring it with you, and all of you be here in five minutes."

Then he turned to his wife. The blood turned warm within him and he felt an acceleration he had not known for years and had never expected to feel again. "I must ask your forgiveness. There is something I must do before I leave." He leaned over and took her hand, squeezed it, and then walked rapidly up the stone steps, across the patio, and disappeared into the house.

Doña Josefa watched him go, stood still for a moment, and then decided that the parting which was taking place within the house was one she would prefer to miss. She brushed the back of her hands across her eyes and walked slowly down along the stream.

Inside the hacienda, Don Alonso called loudly for the two sons who were living with him and without pause went directly to his sleeping room. The boys joined him there as he started to drag his gear out of an ornately carved wardrobe. They were silent as they watched. The older was eighteen and had been born when his father was campaigning in the Caribbean. His brother, four years younger, was born in Ciudad Mexico when his father was on furlough. Both youths were tall, much slighter than their father, and had the dark colouring of their mother. Neither had ever seen the old warrior prepare his military equipment before, and they watched fascinated. With a quick flip of his wrist, Don Alonso bent his Toledo blade almost double and let it snap back into place with a whine and a quiver. He was proud of this sword. It had cost him a good part of a year's pay and plunder when he was younger, but he had never regretted the purchase. Swiftly he settled the halberd over his shoulder and set the blade in place. Then he removed his pikeman's pot helmet from the wardrobe, walked over to a lighted candle and carefully held the shiny steel headpiece over it until the soot gathered and the shine disappeared. Then he adjusted the leather straps inside and thrust the helmet on his head.

He turned to his sons and saw that Nita was standing beside them.

"You will gather food in the hacienda. Keep any of the Indian men out. Be friendly but firm about it. Clean your own weapons and see that the water jugs are filled."

He was opening the harness on his breastplate when Nita took it out of his hands. She had done this many times before and never thought she would have to do it again. As she reached around him to place the shining steel breastplate in place, he continued to talk to his sons.

"You are men now only because you have ruffled the skirts of some Indian wenches and a mestiza or two. You may be men tomorrow because you have killed to stay alive. I expect you to take care of Doña Josefa and your mother."

Nita pulled the straps of the harness tight and then walked over to the cold fireplace, removed some charcoal, mixed it with the wax of the candle and started to rub it over the shining metal. Don Alonso looked down at her and smiled. It had been a long time. It had been over a quarter of a century since he had first taught her how to prepare his gear so that it would not shine in the sun. He thought for a moment of the days in Chile when he had found her, and he reached down, put his hand on her head, tipped it up and kissed her firmly on the mouth.

"There is word from Jemez. It might be a fool's fancy, but if it is not, there will be apostasy and war with the Indians. I will know better when I return."

Don Alonso looked at the two youths and saw anticipation in their faces. He wanted to tell them this was not the same as riding down an antelope or bear-chasing. These animals would chase back and there were more of them than of Spaniards. There were almost three thousand Indians in Sandia only two leagues to the north. Two untried boys without guidance might have little opportunity to learn the meaning of battle, let alone be able to protect the two women he was entrusting to them. But this was all better unstated. He would be back. He would have to ride to Jemez and return, if possible before dark. That left him so little time to find out if the Alcalde Mayor who called himself a war captain actually understood what he had heard.

He held out his hands as Nita slipped on the large gauntlets with the chain mail which spread over the backs of his hands. Twice he clenched his fist. Then he reached down and took up the small daga which he had once taken from the body of an Englishman, the daga with the blue blade, keen-edged and black-handled. This he shoved into his boot. Then he drew out of the wardrobe the two heavy daggs, the short pistols with the ivory butts, quickly poured powder from a leather bag down the bell-nosed barrels, dropped a lead ball in each and shoved the daggs into his belt.

Nita stood back and looked at him. He closed his eyes for a moment while he prayed as he always did when he was finally dressed for a battle, crossed himself, and reached for the short steel lance she held out to him. He weighed it in his hand for a moment and smiled. It felt comfortable there.

"Remember," he told his sons, "Doña Josefa and your mother are your responsibility until I return."

He struck both of the boys on the shoulder with his open palm. "You will be safe. Should anything happen, look to your mother for advice. She has seen more campaigns than any man in the province."

He turned and pulled her to him, his heavy gauntlets pressed into her back. The feeling was familiar to her. The brusque manner which always came over him when he was ready for battle was known to her. His lips brushed her hair. "Take care, woman. Take care," was his only instruction, and she knew what he meant. She would be held responsible for everything that was his, including his Spanish wife. He held her for a moment and then strode out of the room, across the courtyard, and down to where his men were waiting for him with his horse. They were already mounted and had already heard the tale from Jemez.

These men were troopers. Two of them had campaigned with the old man in earlier years. Two were almost strangers, that breed of criminal regurgitated from the jails of Mexico to serve His Majesty in the province. The Lieutenant Governor stood looking at them for a moment as he made up his mind.

"You two," pointing to the strangers, "ride to Isleta and tell the padre at the friary as well as Maestre de Campo Mendoza that there may be trouble from the Indians. He is to bring as many people together as he can. And ride fast. Do not take time out to tip any jugs or women."

And he stood looking at them until they understood that he meant his words. Then they put their spurs to the rumps of their horses and plunged southward.

Don Alonso watched them for a time and then swung himself up onto his horse. "We ride to Jemez."

The young soldier did not seem to understand.

"You are able to ride with men?"

The youth felt goaded, and as the captain turned his horse northward with his two older companions, the saddle-weary soldier spurred his horse after them. Don Alonso smiled. He could still lead. He was almost convinced he could still fight if the occasion arose. But for the first time in his life, he prayed that it would not arise.

RIDING north along the rio toward Jemez, Don Alonso García felt the heat of the sun as it burned through the morning sky. The old warrior would not give his horsemen leave to pause, to refresh their horses or themselves. Twice his old campañeros suggested they rest and twice he shrugged off the idea. To hell with the horses. To hell with anything that might deter his return to his own hacienda should there actually be trouble. And as he rode, he wondered why there should be any. The Spaniards had had as difficult a time as the Indians. The bad seasons struck one as hard as the other. The Apaches encroaching from the east and west struck one as viciously as the other. Why rebellion?

It felt good to the old warrior to have his spurs in a horse again, his hand on a bridle with a lance resting on his shoe stirrup as he rode. But for the first time in many years he felt fear, and this troubled him. He wondered if it was because he was older and therefore more cautious. Or was it because of Doña Josefa? There would be no one to take care of her should anything happen to him. With Nita, well, with Nita it was different. She was a woman who could take care of herself; and besides, there were the boys for Nita. But it was not any of these things, and always as bluntly honest with himself as with a stranger, Don Alonso knew it was because for the first time in his life he had something to lose. It was one thing for a man to die with a sabre in his hand in a swamp in Guatemala when he had nothing to live for except the next jug of cheap wine and the dubious charms of a whore in some casa de puta. It was something quite different for the lieutenant governor of a great province, greater than all of Zacatecas and Guatemala together, to die beside some rio's bank when he had a Spanish wife and a hacienda. Yes, the old warrior admitted to himself that he had changed.

The three men who rode with the Lieutenant Governor wanted to swing off their horses, remove their helmets, and wash their faces in the stream. There was no Spanish woman drawing them back, no title or duty or property. They swung wide to avoid the pueblos of Zia and Santa Ana. They rode for a time through low hills and for a time they trotted over the loose pebbles of a dry arroyo which took them back towards the rio. They had reached the water's edge and turned north again when they heard the shouting.

Don Alonso's hand went up, his horse rose on its hind legs and came to a halt. The men behind him reined in and waited for his commands. With slow and quiet deliberateness Don Alonso led the group away from the rio to a large clump of cottonwood trees just off the trail. A moment later three mounted Spanish soldiers and a padre topped a rise, running south.

They were followed closely by a mass of howling Indians, faces painted black and hands brandishing macanas, wooden lances, and bows and arrows. An Indian was holding firmly to the bridle of the padre's horse and stumbling along with it as he tried to strike the rider from the saddle. Several Indians paused to fire their arrows in a scattered shower over the riders and their own companions. The leading Spaniard whirled his horse about to knock the Indian away from the padre and was himself instantly surrounded by natives thrusting lances upward, trying to drop him to the ground.

"Por Rey y Santiago!" The old war cry shattered the sky and drew the attention of the struggling group as García waving his three followers forward, attacked in the heart of the fight. His lance struck a startled Indian in the chest, was pulled back and smashed across the side of another's head as the native tried to cross lances with the old warrior. Then the lance was drawn back and hurled into the back of the Indian who was pulling the padre from his saddle. Swinging his sabre from its sheath, the old warrior continued his battle cry as he laid about him. In a few minutes there were half a dozen Indians lying on the ground. One youth sat up puzzled at the way the blood poured out of the place where his arm had been. Another tried sliding over the ground away from the horses' hooves while a lance poking through his body waved back and forth. Don Alonso rode over, jerked the lance free, and the Indian collapsed.

The remaining puebleños fled from the unexpected attack. Several turned to stare at the Spaniards who had so suddenly appeared, but when Don Alonso swung his horse toward them, they continued their flight to a safe distance. Then two of them paused, took their bows in hand, carefully knelt and shot their arrows. The feathered shafts fell about the horses, and Don Alonso waved his own men as well as the rescued party south.

Half a league down the rio, he raised his hand, dismounted, and removed his helmet. The others were about to follow his action, when he pointed to one of his campañeros, "That rise. Ride over and watch. I would like to drink in safety and peace."

The soldier saluted with one gauntleted hand, half-cupped, whirled and mounted guard on a small knoll overlooking the trail to both the north and south.

Paying no attention to the others with him, Don Alonso strode down to the rio, watered his horse and then, kneeling, dipped his helmet into the stream. When it was full, he emptied it over his bowed head so as to keep his equipment dry. All of the old manners and gestures of the field had come back to him on this ride. He was a soldier again. He knew it and was proud of the efficiency with which the old skills returned.

He removed one of the leather gauntlets with the mailed back and wiped his face with his bare palm. Then he turned to the others who were watering their horses beside him. The short, lean Alcalde Mayor of Jemez stood several varas away drinking from his cupped hand. Don Alonso shook his head. This was no soldier, and he wondered who had named this incompetent a war captain over the Queres and Jemez pueblos. Graft or a wench. It certainly was not the man's looks or ability. The small man's name kept escaping him.

"Luis de Granillo?" he tentatively called.

The fugitive turned and approached him. "We thank you, Don Alonso. We might have been killed had we not had your magnificent swordsmanship on our behalf."

The Lieutenant Governor snorted. A talker. He was never fond of the breed.

"What took place at San Diego de Jemez?" He was formal now. He wanted a report, and he wanted it quickly. He had to return to his hacienda. He had to secure the safety of all the haciendas, estancias, and ranchos in his jurisdiction. He calculated the number of Spaniards and knew it was over fifteen hundred, closer to seventeen hundred, including the padres.

"Well?"

The Alcalde Mayor had difficulty shedding his own importance and reporting to one who was clearly in his eyes a common soldier—the lowest social bracket in the class-conscious Spanish Empire.

"He came about midday, and. . ."

"Who came?"

"An Indian riding on horseback, called himself an ambassador of the northern pueblos, and . . . "

"On horseback and you did not kill him?"

The small man was intimidated by the angry bulk of the Lieutenant Governor. "The news he brought made one hestitate."

García snorted. "The news?"

"He rode through the pueblo on his horse singing a victory song and telling the Indians that the Governor and all of the Spanish as well as the padres from Taos to Santo Domingo were dead and their homes robbed and that the Spaniards of the south were the only ones left to be killed."

Don Alonso closed his eyes for a minute as he tried to realize just what the Indian ambassador's message really meant. And as he thought, he hid behind a question. "And you let him say it?"

"He urged the people to take arms and destroy us, and before we could stop them, they took arms and began to chase us. They had followed us two full leagues when you so fortuitously saved us."

"Madre María. We ride through a sweltering morning because you feared you might be attacked and our meeting is fortuitous." He slammed his fist into his side. "If you had killed the prattling fool who was rousing the Indians or captured him, then we might know what has really happened to the north. You might even have stopped the uprising with one bold stroke."

"But, Your Excellency, if we had tried to stop the . . ."

With a wave of his hand, Don Alonso cut him off and motioned to the others to mount. "We ride south to Zia and see what has happened. From there to Santa Ana."

Don Alonso led his small band southeast along the bank of the Rio Jemez toward the Rio del Norte. There were eight of them now. The youth who had first brought the warning was making the journey for the third time without pause, and weariness showed on his tense face. Don Alonso, with one eye on the youth and one on the trail, did not fear for the boy. He was young and there was nothing a young soldier could not do. The padre was well mounted, and despite the girth of the man, which seemed to fill out his broad cassock, he rode easily. He had no concern for the others. His own men were soldiers and those who had fled with the fool Granillo would have to take care of themselves or fall by the wayside. No handful of men meant very much to him at this moment. There was half a province to save and the prestige of an empire at stake.

García's hand went up. They were nearing Zia and he could hear noise and shouting in the distance. Then he stopped. Two loud explosions were heard. Harquebuses. There were Spaniards fighting there. He could not yet credit the natives with having firearms. He swept his hand forward and rode headlong down the trail. Without pause, he hurled his small tropa into the open plaza of the pueblo. He saw where the Indians, bare to the waist, faces streaked with black, were trying to force their way into the white adobe mission. His lance went up and he rode into the assembled mass of Indians.

"Por Rey y Santiago!" The cry broke across the square with the suddenness of his attack. The lance brought one Indian to the ground and was twisted out of his hand. As another jumped at him, from a small wall, he drew one of the bell-nosed daggs and fired point-blank into the face of his assailant. The Indian's head was shattered. The body struck the side of García's horse and fell limply away.

The eight Spanish horses rose and trampled and rose again as the sabres of the horsemen slashed a clearing to the entrance of the besieged mission. Once he reached the door, Don Alonso swung to his feet.

"Keep them back," he shouted loudly, and yelled to the occupants, "Open it." He banged with the butt of his empty dagg until he heard the bar shift and saw the door open a crack. Without hesitating, he forced his way in and shut the door behind him. A frightened old padre and three Spaniards with harquebuses in hand stared at his bloody clothes. The mission was crowded with cattle and sheep. In the darkness of the room, Don Alonso made out the figures of several horses.

No face was clearly visible and he had no time for arguments. "I am Don Alonso de García, Lieutenant Governor of Nuevo Mexico. Mount those horses and get them to the door. Padre," he said, placing a hand on the old man's shoulder, "you will have to take whatever you think you must of the holy equipment."

He urged the Spaniards to hurry and mount. "To the inferno with a saddle. Mount up. Leave those harquebuses here. They are good for only a single firing and useless when you ride."

As he spoke, he dropped the empty dagg in his hand and was thankful that one remained in his belt. Finally, even the padre, carrying a small bag in his arms, was mounted. Don Alonso yelled loudly so that his compañeros outside could hear him. "I will open the door and you will ride, ride fast and south. My men will join you as you go."

Then the door swung outward and the light poured in. The cattle began to move toward it, and Don Alonso drew his sabre and with the flat of it cleared the way for the three Spaniards and the padre who rode out into the plaza ringed by hesitant but shouting Indians. Clubs were thrown and rocks. Several arrows hit their gear and fell away as they broke for the open country-side to the south. García mounted his horse and followed his own men out of the plaza. The Indians started to press in to bar his escape, but the sabre swinging lightly in his hand deterred them. One youth picked up a macana and charged the old warrior, who swung his horse neatly to one side and bent down to meet the attack. The blades met and the Lieutenant Governor's rose a second time to split the youth's skull. Then he rode out, slowly and calmly. He had to retreat but he would not run from the face of treason. His only regret was that he had lost his lance somewhere in the bodies scattered about the square. He caught up with his small band of refugees a quarter-league down the trail leading to Santa Ana.

Behind them they heard the church bells begin to toll. The Indians had taken the church and for the moment it was in their hands. Don Alonso rode beside the old padre with the holy objects resting in a bag before him, and he put his hand out to comfort the man. The ageing peninsular had devoted his life to that small mission whose bells were now tolling behind him. He turned and looked at the Lieutenant Governor and the soldier could see the tears coursing down his cheeks. But he crossed himself and rode on.

They rode rapidly. There was no need for a pause now. Less need for ques-tions. What Don Alonso needed to know, these people could not tell him. How widespread was the revolt? What was the condition of Governor Oter-mín and his followers? What was happening at Sandia? At Isleta? At his own hacienda?

Don Alonso assumed the lead of the tropa and rode south along the rio. His old compañeros did not speak to him as they took their positions at the rear of the growing band. There were twelve of them now. García had to see that twelve reached safety, for these men could bear arms and he did not know how many others there were who could.

Granillo spurred his horse and drew up beside the Lieutenant Governor. "Would it not be wise, Your Excellency, to avoid Santa Ana? There may be trouble there."

García did not turn his head. "How would you feel now if we had avoided San Diego de Jemez?"

Granillo dropped back. Riding southeast with the Rio Jemez at its left, the group braced itself and entered the small open plaza of the pueblo of Santa Ana. There were no men in sight. A few women, gathered about the en-trances of the communal houses, stared at them.

Don Alonso addressed the women, "Where are your men?"

There was a moment's silence as the Indian women conferred among themselves. Finally, a tall young woman stepped forward. "They have gone out to kill Spaniards," she answered in hesitant Castilian.

The Spanish horses were restless and tense in the restricted space. A wall rose to the right and the left, and many eyes watched from the slits of windows and the roofs.

"May they find the Spaniards," Don Alonso said quietly. "It will save the Spaniards time hunting them." The young woman smiled as she nodded and stepped back among the others.

The Lieutenant Governor raised his hand and waved his tropa on through the gap where a gate had once stood, and out into the countryside. The laughter of the women followed him. He turned to the see the young soldier starting to rein his horse and turn back. "Stay, fool," he said, and the youth nodded and joined his commander. The group rode swiftly south. Don Alonso did not stop when he came to the Rio del Norte, but plunged his horse into the stream and forded it. On the other side, he waited only until the last man rode out, dripping. Then he whirled and rode on to his own hacienda. Only at the gates of his own manor house did he finally swing out of the saddle. Before the others could join him, he raised his hand.

"Granillo, you, you, you," he pointed to his old compañeros and the youth. "Dismount and stay with me. The rest of you ride to the friary at Isleta." He turned to the two padres. "Tell the Alcalde Mayor Mendoza there that I will try to make contact with Governor Otermín, God willing, and he lives. No one is to ride south of Isleta without my permission. We will make our stand there. See that all of our people are gathered and ready for a defence. As soon as I receive orders from the Governor at the Villa de Santa Fe, I will join you. If I can, I shall hold the line here."

Without another word, he tossed the reins of his horse to one of his compañeros and climbed the stone steps he had descended only hours before with Doña Josefa. He was tired and the years he had so often denied were having their way with him.

18

IT was shortly before the sun reached its zenith that the trackers of the pueblo of San Ysidro returned to the hacienda where Ruaha and the others waited. They had found a trail which led to the north. Ruaha followed them down to the stream and slowly trotted up the rio with them. Soon they found the place where the bearded soldier had removed the moccasin of the girl Poy-ye. And they trotted on. Several leagues to the north they saw the track of blood left by the bared foot and the place where the girl had bathed the face of the infant. And they trotted on.

Finally they came to the dry arroyo with the white pebbles. For a long time they tried to read the tracks that disappeared into the rio. Two young men ran up each side to locate the place where the Spaniard and the Indian girl had emerged, but they could not find a single sign. The waters of the stream had washed away the blood from the girl's foot and there was no longer a trail.

Ruaha waited by the arroyo and when the runners returned, he stared at the dry stream bed and knew there would be no trace over the white pebbles. But still he must search. Selecting several of the youths to accompany him and sending the others to seek out any sign they might find, he turned east and walked carefully up the arroyo. The thousands of pebbles washed down into the dried bed by centuries of sudden floods revealed not a trace. Almost an hour later they paused before the closed end of the ravine: there was no exit here.

Sprawled on the ledge overlooking the arroyo below, José Reyes heard the approach of the Indian warriors and drew back into the shadow. With a sweep of his arm, he knocked Natividad flat, placed one hand firmly over the face of the infant on the ground, and with the other thrust his daga under the chin of the girl. His dark and frightened eyes were a hand's breadth from hers, and though she knew the meaning of the sounds and the calls of the Indians below, she was silent. Reyes' fear distorted his face and his beard trembled under his tense jaw. The girl looked away and tried to see the child beside her, but as she started to shift her head, the point of the blade pricked her throat and she lay still.

Moments passed and though the day was dry, beads of sweat gathered on the Spaniard's browned forehead and dropped onto the face of the girl lying beneath him. His weight and his fear pressed upon her and she wanted to move, but the steel point dug into her flesh and she was still.

How long Reyes sprawled with his blade at her throat and his hand on the face of the child, he did not know. But he had learned in his youth that safety came with time, with the patience to wait until an enemy has abandoned his search, and wait even longer until there was no chance that that enemy would change his mind and take another look. The sounds of the Indians below had long disappeared into the distance and the girl's throat trickled a small pool of blood down the valley between her full breasts before Reyes finally relaxed. He sheathed his daga, removed his hand from the child's face, and soundlessly peered over the brink of the ledge. There was no one below, and he rose to his feet. For the moment he was safe. He would wait until dark, make his way over the top of the ravine, and strike north again by the light of the moon.

He turned to the girl on the ground, her brown eyes marking his every move. He motioned for her to sit up and she did so. He knelt down and handed her the child from the ground. She stared at it for a moment as the slight streak of blood still coursed its way down her dress. Then she held the child out to its father. Reyes looked at her, puzzled, and shook his head. But she continued to hold out the infant. Finally, he took it from her and stared at its blackened face. He held its small chest up to his ear. He held his palm over its small mouth. Then he handed the child back to her.

"He is not dead. You nurse him and he will be all right." He paused, could not comprehend, and said again, "He can not be dead," as he thrust the infant back into her arms and with a sweep of his hand tore open the front of her dress, motioning for her to feed the child.

Slowly, the girl Poy-ye began to rock back and forth, holding the smothered baby to her breast, and the moan that fell from her lips was the only dirge the child would know.

19

Declaration of Pedro Hidalgo, Soldado

The Villa,
10 Agosto, 1680.

In the Villa de Santa Fe, on the said day, month, and year, his lordship caused to be brought before him Pedro Hidalgo, soldier, a resident of this villa, from whom he received the oath in true legal form before God, our Lord, and a sign of the Cross, under charge of which he promised to tell the truth concerning what he might know and as he might be questioned. Having been told to state and declare what happened to him, what he saw, and what he learned as regards himself and the father preacher, Fray Juan Pio, and the Teguas Indians of Tesuque, he said that what happened is that, this witness having set out from this villa at dawn this morning in company with the father preacher, Fray Juan Pio, for the pueblo of Tesuque, they reached it by daylight and found the said pueblo empty of people and of the few cattle which the Indians had; and that this witness said the said padre passing on in search of the people of the pueblo, because said padre was going to say Mass for them, they came up to the people about a quarter of a league from the said pueblo, where they found many Indians wearing war paint, with their bows, arrows, lances, and shields. The said padre went up to them saying, "What is this, children: Are you mad? Do not disturb yourselves; I will help you and die a thousand deaths for you." The said padre and this witness with him went on to summon and detain the mass of people who were going toward the sierra, so that they would go back to the pueblo where he could say Mass for them. The said padre went on to one side toward a ravine, telling this witness to go by the ridge to intercept the people. In a little while he saw an Indian named El Obi come out of the ravine with the shield the said padre had been carrying, and he saw also a second Indian of the pueblo named Pandro, painted with clay and splattered with blood. These Indians and others assailed the witness, grasping the reins of the horse he was riding; they surrounded him, taking away his sword and hat, whereupon he grasped his harquebus, and making good his escape, spurred his horse down the hill, dragging along those who had hold of him. He broke away from them and descended to the plain, where they followed him, discharging many arrows, none of which reached or harmed him, and he escaped safely. Seeing that the said preacher, Fray Juan Pio, did not again appear, he judged him to be dead, whereupon he came to this villa as quickly as possible to give the news. What he said is the truth, and what happened and what he saw; under charge of his oath he affirms and certifies his statement, it being read to him. He claims he is about thirty years of age, and signs with the señor governor and captain general, ANTONIO DE OTERMÍN, PEDRO HIDALGO. Before me, ISMAEL PANDO, Maestre de Campo.

Governor Otermín held the paper in his hand and looked at it without seeing the words. It was only seven in the morning and he had known the contents of the document for an hour, yet they still had little meaning for him.

When the soldier had reported in, Don Antonio had been awakened. He had dressed in a hurry and walked into his office where Pando and several of his War Council were already waiting for him. He had listened, ordered the report made formal, and then rechecked the plans he had dictated the day before. He had done all that could have been done then. But this would not satisfy the Viceroy's clerks. The records would show that a padre had been killed during his administration, that there had been an uprising of Indians while he was governor, and all the years of work that built reputation and respect would mean nothing. He shook his head as though to clear it. The voluminous records of His Majesty's service would reveal only the facts—no understanding, no interpretation, no concept of terrain and circumstance.

He rose from behind his desk and walked back to his sleeping quarters. Here he stood a few minutes staring at himself in the mirror. His face was dark from years of sun and lean from years in the field. At least he had not gone soft or bulky with age. The beard was grey and the hair on his head was thinning. He smiled at his own vanity and slipped into his tunica. Buttoning it with care, he made up his mind.

There were not going to be any thoughts of retirement for a time; that had to be forgotten—he had work to do. There was responsibility here. His titles were empty but he would stand for no man questioning him in time of emergency or conflict. Now he was going to assume command: he was going to put the Villa on a war footing.

He walked out of the room wondering about his Lieutenant Governor, wondered whether help would come if he needed it, whether the carta he had sent the day before had reached the south, wondered too, if he was correct in assuming that the alcalde mayors, once warned, as he had warned them only the day before would be able to meet the situations which would face them in the event of an uprising. He straightened his shoulders. These men were Spaniards and descendants of Spaniards, part of the generations that had grown up since España had built its empire—generations of fools and knaves, but they were still Spaniards, tough and courageous. This he did not doubt.

Walking to the main entrance of the casa real, he nodded to the guard standing there and sent a runner across the way for Maestre de Campo Pando. There were details which must be attended to.

Don Antonio stared at the bright sky. Across the rio he could hear the loud bell of the chapel of San Miguel. He stepped out into the empty plaza and turned to look at the Sangre de Cristo Mountains. It was almost as if he were trying to see the trouble that lay beyond them.

There was a sound behind him. He did not turn as Ismael Pando stepped to his side and followed his gaze.

"This is a beautiful land, Governor," the old warrior commented.

The peninsular nodded, wondering how a man who has seen no other could be so certain.

"You sent for me, sir?"

Don Antonio nodded again. "There is much to be done." And he walked back into the palacio. The Maestre de Campo followed without a word. When they reached the Governor's reception room, Otermín seated himself at his desk.

For a long time, he said nothing and Pando wondered if he was going to get caught up in his thoughts as he seemed to be so often. There was a contemplative quality about the Governor which the old warrior, born in Nuevo Mexico and exposed only to the duties which were assigned to him, never quite felt comfortable about. Soldiers talked, drank, acted. Padres thought. Then he realized the Governor and Captain General was studying him.

Don Antonio finally said, "I want everyone in the immediate jurisdiction moved into the casas reales. These buildings make for a compact unit. We can defend them if we have to. We can move out of them for attack with some security. Bring in every man—servant, planter, tradesman. Post sentinels around the Villa itself so that we will know of any approaching Indians. Detail a squad of armed men to the church. We must protect the Holy Sacraments and all things of divine cult."

He paused and waited for a reaction.

His lieutenant said nothing. He was trying to total the number of men who would come under arms at this order, the numbers of people who would be brought to the casas reales. A thousand refugees and fewer than a hundred able to bear arms. And that hundred, he would wager, would include the Governor and himself. He waited for what he knew would follow.

The Captain General looked at him and sighed. "When you depart, send in a scribe. I will prepare the formal report for the Viceroy and authorization to the hacendados."

Pando saluted and walked to the door. As he reached it, Don Antonio spoke again: "Remember, amigo, we are Spaniards, we are Christians. They are only natives, heretics, and fools."

The old soldado turned to his commander. "Once, Governor, they were my friends." And he departed.

Don Antonio sat looking after him. It was only an accident of birth that kept this Maestre de Campo from being on the other side of the line which had been drawn. He did not know Madre España, her hills, her fields, her cathedrals wedded to the sky. Her traditions were only words to him. Yet the Governor felt confident that the promotion he had given this man was one of the wisest actions he had taken since his appointment.

There was a knock on the door. "Enter," he said, expecting his scribe. Instead, the Fray Custodio walked into the room and closed the door behind him. Don Antonio rose to his feet out of respect for the ageing priest.

"You wanted to see me, Padre?"

The rigid body of the old man bent slightly in acknowledgment. "I came to inform you that I am leaving the Villa for Santo Domingo."

Don Antonio decided to be patient with the old man. "It might be dangerous. I would not recommend it."

The Fray Custodio nodded. "Santo Domingo was once my curacy. It is the centre of our order in the province and where I should be. I know the people there. They know me. I would like to talk to them. I must endeavour to prevent any apostasy among them."

The Governor slipped back into his chair, stared at the erect cassocked figure before him. It was men like the Fray Custodio as well as the conquistadores who had made the Empire. This religio was a peninsular. He knew España. He knew the Church. And above all, he knew his own mind.

"I have no intelligence concerning the situation to the south of us. Perhaps the pueblo of Santo Domingo has risen against us as the others have. I would not recommend your going just yet."

The Padre nodded. "Nor would you prevent my going. If they have risen against us, I shall talk to them and see if it is possible to bring them again to the path of God. If they have not turned from the path, my being with them will encourage them not to leave it."

Don Antonio was silent.

"Fray Pedro shall remain, should you need his help. He is young, but he is able."

"I can spare only a few soldados to accompany you."

The old Padre shook his head. "I will go alone. The presence of more soldados may upset the Indians."

The Governor rose and walked to the door with the clergyman. "I will respect your wishes," and he knelt while the older man blessed him. Then he rose to his feet, opened the door, "We will meet again soon."

The Fray Custodio smiled at him. "I am certain of it, my son." And he departed, his slim back erect, his manner confident.

Don Antonio watched him as he walked down the corridor. Then he turned to his waiting scribe. "Draft an order that all men able to bear arms will be issued them from the royal stores."

IT was already late in the morning when Ismael Pando rode back to the Villa with the small tropa. He rode with the same soldiers who had accompanied him to Tesuque the day before. They had ridden hard. They had spread out and notified each of the landholders in the jurisdiction of the Villa that the Governor was ordering them to the casas reales as quickly as they could come. Some few argued that they wanted to remain, that they trusted their Indians, that they could not leave their land, that they were unable to travel with their women or their aged. But when Pando and his men stated the Governor's order clearly, and related the tragic martyrdom of Fray Juan Pio as reported by the soldier Pedro Hidalgo, all of the arguments faded away.

As he approached the Villa from the north, Pando could see many of the families already making their way into the small town. Some rode horseback. Others were in wagons or carts. Some few families had bothered to pack their furniture high in the wagons, while others appeared to have taken the road to the Villa with only the clothes they wore and what few weapons they possessed.

Pando raised his hand and the tropa reined its horses to a halt behind him. Turning to face the three men, he ordered them back to the Villa as fast as they could ride. Then he turned south and rode on alone. He knew he had other duties to perform. He had heard of the order to distribute arms before he had departed. But there was something else he had to do, and he was certain that he had the time to do it and that the Governor would understand.

Riding through the hills leading to the east, he crossed an arroyo. It would be filled soon. He wondered if he would be there to see the water running through it. This dry ditch would not mean very much to others, but to him it meant a great deal. A few hundred varas to the east was the solid adobe and stone house his father had built almost a century before. Here Ismael Pando had been born. Here he had grown up, taken his wife, watched his own children born, his parents die, his wife, his children.

He approached the old house, tethered his horse to a cottonwood tree before the patio, and mounted the steps. The door was open, the rooms empty. He listened to the echoes of his boots as they struck the stone floor.

A sentimental old fool who ought to be busy doing more important things. He knew this was the type of thing a padre might do or even the Governor; it was not the act of a fighting man. But here he was. His long sabre swung at his side, and he shifted it across his lap as he sat on the stairs.

Pando took his heavy helmet from his head, set it on his lap and looked about the broad sitting room which had been his mother's and his wife's.

There was dust on the floors now. He saw a large spider web framing a window. This had always been a peaceful home. Now violence was coming. He did not know where it had grown. He could not understand who had taught it to the People.

He slipped the helmet back onto his head and rose to his feet. Crossing the room, he paused at the window and with a sweep of his hand gathered the spider web into his palm. His mother would never have approved its being there, though his wife might have hesitated to disturb a crawling thing.

He had no more time to waste upon his dreams. Without turning around to look at the rooms which were so clearly recorded in his memory, he walked out the door and closed it with care behind him. Beside the house was a well which the Indians had dug long ago for his father. Here he paused to drink. When he was done, he filled his helmet and walked back to the cottonwood tree where his horse was tethered. While the horse emptied the helmet, Ismael Pando tried to solve the problem which was troubling him. The violence—where had it come from? How had the People learned it?

When the horse was finished, the old man put his helmet back on his head, mounted and rode back to the Villa where he would report to the Governor and distribute the weapons from the arsenal of His Majesty, Carlos II, who was very far away from all that was happening to his province.

21

THE Indian boy had never handled a macana before, and he swung it from side to side with the assurance of youth and inexperience. The hardwood was highly polished. The flint chips formed a fine cutting edge. The older man standing by his side near the wall surrounding the estancia nervously drew his bowstring and released it, and drew it and released it, as the tension grew within him. He was almost forty and he had never killed a man. Does a man die like a deer, cleanly shot—a few stumbling steps and then collapse? Or does he turn on his slayer like a mountain lion and die shortening the distance between in one final, vicious effort to kill? His muscles tightened as he thought of his lash-scarred back and drew the bowstring again.

The boy was not thinking of death. The black paint on his face was streaked with the sweat of the dance, and he was more eager than tense. No Castilian had ever laid a lash to his back. No woman of his family had ever been stretched on the grass by a white soldier. He had been raised to shepherd a flock of Basque sheep, to shear them and deliver the wool. No one had ever taught him to fight or to kill. But now he was going to do battle, and when he was done, the sheep he tended would belong to him and the wool that he clipped would belong to the People. He shifted the macana from his right hand to his left as his companion set an arrow in the string and drew the flexible bow again. The boy was glad he carried the wooden sabre, for he

*would close with the hacendado, meet him face to face, and the Spaniard
would know who killed him.*

*There was a noise now in the hacienda. A woman shrieked and was silent.
A child shrieked and was silent. But the yell of the People echoed off the
butte and fell back again across the fields.*

*The boy clutched the weapon in his right hand and moved to block the
arch of the open gateway and saw the Spaniard coming toward him, chased
by three black-faced warriors in loincloths. The hacendado whirled about
and slashed the air with his broad steel sabre, driving his pursuers back. Then
he dashed again toward the open gate only to find the Indian youth standing,
feet apart, waiting for him.*

*For an instant they faced each other—the copper shepherd boy in his loin-
cloth and moccasined feet and the white Creole from Quito in the high bucket
boots, pantalones, and oiled buff jerkin. Then each raised his weapon and
struck savagely at the other.*

*There was a crash and then silence. The Indian boy stared at the splintered
wooden hilt in his hand. Ten paces away lay the shattered blade of the
macana.*

*The pursuers began to close in from behind. And without hesitation the
Spaniard drove his sharp blade into the bare belly of the youth. There was a
soft gasp as the Indian stared with a question in his eyes at his red belly as
the blade was withdrawn and the white man ran past him toward the open
fields beyond the courtyard. The boy took three steps and then curled up on
the ground and shut his eyes as though he were going to take a nap in the
morning sun. The fleeing Spaniard ran almost twenty varas into the field
before the Indian bowman stepped out of the shadow of the wall, drew his
finger tips back to his ear and let his arrow fly. He knew then that a man died
like a deer—a few stumbling steps and then collapse.*

22

IT was late afternoon when the full impact of the revolt reached the Villa
de Santa Fe. It arrived in the form of long lines of refugees. There were those
who had been rounded up and urged on by Maestre de Campo Pando and
there were the others: those who had already felt the impact of the uprising
and carried with them the scars and stories of its violence.

There were the families of the wealthy hacendados, the marginal rancheros,
the servants carrying their masters' only possessions in their arms, the rancheros, horseless, who had walked for half a day while they mourned their
dead wives, and the widows who had fled with their children leaving their
husbands lying dead in some field. There were the orphan children who had
hidden in a lonely clump of trees and watched their parents struck down,
and then wandered, barefooted, toward the Villa. There were the old women

and the old men who had made their way across country with only the garments they wore. And there were the soldiers who had fought their way out of encirclement and fled toward the only security they knew.

Each brought a tale of destruction and murder, desecration and blasphemy. And each wanted to tell his story to the Governor and Captain General as though the fault were his, as though they expected that he could do something for them, bring back their dead, their burned-out estancias, their horses, the trampled crops and the stripped trees.

And as each of them talked, he revealed a piece of the pattern of destruction. The Tewa pueblos which covered that area to the north and west to the junctions of the Rio del Norte and the Rio Chama appeared to be in revolt. The pueblos of Santa Clara, San Ildefonso, and San Juan had already joined them.

The last reported uprising came from an old man and woman from Nambé pueblo. They had fled their home with their young son. The youth had dropped off their wagon to fight a delaying action against some Indians. He had never caught up with his parents. They stood before the Captain General's table and related their story as though they were waiting for him to do something.

Don Antonio merely nodded when their story was told. There was nothing he could say. He rose to his feet, looked at the old man and old woman standing before his desk and walked over to the window. They had to turn to watch him. Outside he could see guards walking the plaza mayor now. He could see the stunned looks of the men and women who squatted on the colonnade and just stared into the distance. Off to one end of the plaza Don Antonio made out the shape of one of his cannon—one of two. He was at this moment governor of nothing more than this small villa.

But this could not be correct. The unforeseen happened, situations collapsed, empires had lost provinces in the past and would lose them again. But it did not happen this way: not this abruptly, not with natives, not with leaderless, passive people. He did not believe it.

Swinging about, he faced Maestre de Campo Pando who had sat listening for hours in his chair. "Take four soldados and completely reconnoitre all the pueblos of the Tewa and the jurisdiction of La Cañada. Find out how many are already dead, what damage has been done, what we can do. Ride as far afield as you wish. I will expect your return tomorrow. Your orders will be written by the time you are prepared to leave. Any questions?"

Ismael Pando looked at his superior and shook his head. He had no questions. Certainly, there were others who could make this jornada through the inferno of the north, but none knew the country any better than he, and as he shook his head he recalled his father's philosophy: the old sargento had always asked his son, "And why not you?"

"And if we should need armour and fresh horses, Excellency?"

Don Antonio smiled. "Today we are being generous with the royal commissary. Issue anything your men need." Then, satisfied that the two old people who had been listening knew that at least he was doing something, he smiled at them. "I hope you will find a place that is comfortable for you

F

in the casas reales." He watched them nod, uncertain what they were supposed to do, and then they departed with the giant old Maestre de Campo. As Pando was about to close the door behind him, Don Antonio called him again, "I regret that I can only spare you four men."

"I understand, Excellency. Though the Villa is crowded, it is unfortunately not crowded with soldados."

23

THE squad of armed men gathered on the steps of the mission in the Villa de Santa Fe. There were six of them under the direction of a middle-aged settler who had arrived only hours before from his rancho to the west. None of them had ever used arms for other than hunting before, and they stood proudly holding their swords and shields which had just been issued to them. Their leader swung his sabre from side to side to become accustomed to the feel of it. The weapon was heavier than a sickle and longer than he had imagined it would be.

The squad awkwardly came to attention when they saw the Governor leave the colonnade of the casa real across the plaza. Don Antonio was dressed in his best black cotton suit. His highly polished breastplate glistened in the sun, and the sabre at his side swung freely. The amateur soldiers moved back from the doorway as he approached them, and the settler from the west attempted a clumsy salute. The Captain General smiled at him and walked down the flagstone path to the friary. He entered the door of the small building and disappeared inside. The squad on the steps of the mission relaxed.

Don Antonio knocked politely at the door of the cell of Fray Pedro.

"Enter," the padre from Valladolid invited.

The Governor opened the door and waited for the Brother to come to his feet.

"You might have sent for me, Don Antonio."

The weary soldier blinked as he tried to focus in the darkness of the small cell. "There are some things we must discuss, Padre, which I would rather discuss away from other ears."

"The Fray Custodio has departed." This was gratuitous information from the younger man. It also served notice to the layman that he was talking to the proper person.

"For Santo Domingo. I know." The Governor wished the missionary had a sense of humour, knew how to relax. It would make working with him less difficult.

Fray Pedro looked at the Castilian and wondered by what route the man had come to the Villa. He understood there were children: a son in Mexico, a daughter in España. "If there is anything which I might do in the absence of the Fray Custodio, please ask it. It is why I am here, Excellency."

The Excellency rolled lightly off his tongue. Don Antonio entered the room and decided that he would work with the pompous young man until he found this did not meet his needs. His needs? He wondered when in his career as a soldier he had ever thought of his own needs?

"From everything we now know, I believe we will come under attack within the next few days. At present I have less than a hundred men under arms. I have sent two Indians and one soldado south to Lieutenant Governor García. They carry orders for him to remain in Isleta, should we be forced to withdraw."

He saw the surprise on the young padre's face.

"This is a possibility I do not overlook."

The short, heavy-set cleric paced the floor before the Governor. It was one thing to replace the Fray Custodio in his absence and direct the activities of one's fellow padres, perhaps even accomplish the distribution of supplies according to one's own judgment when the procurador arrived from Ciudad Mexico, but it was another thing to abandon the missions, the church itself rising above the plaza and casting its long shadow over the friary. There are certain things no padre could be expected to do.

The doubts showed in his broad, dark face, and Don Antonio felt relieved. The man was not all self-praise. He was quite human, and if ever he recognized the fact himself, perhaps this padre from Valladolid might make a great missionary. He had the energy and the intelligence. Well, Don Antonio thought, he might get the opportunity.

"If we have to abandon the province, Your Excellency, the missions, what of the missions?" This could not happen. The disbelief was clear.

Don Antonio rose and stood facing the younger man in the small confines of the cell. "Abandon? We will not abandon. We may have to withdraw for a period. But we will not abandon." As he spoke, he realized that he was shaking. The concept of failure was new to him. He was uncomfortable with it.

A touch of the irony of the padre returned: "What of the missions in the event of your deciding to withdraw for a period? Is the Church's position any different should you withdraw and not abandon?"

The Governor's right hand trembled and he grasped the welt of leather rimming the top of his bucket boots. "Should the need arise for us to withdraw, I shall notify you. If I feel that we will not be able to protect the church buildings in this jurisdiction, I will notify you, and you will join me in the casa real. Should that occasion arise, I will expect you to consume the holy sacrament and collect the images, sacred vessels, and other things and bring them with you. The people at the casa reales will need the ministrations of a clergyman." This was no longer discussion. The facts and fears had been stated, and Fray Pedro knew they did not come easily.

"I shall be prepared to do as you direct, Your Excellency." And Fray Pedro realized he was feeling sorry for the Governor, pitying the man the circumstance.

"My men, Padre, they may be fighting tomorrow. And the others who will fight with us, the refugees."

The broad shoulders bent forward in recognition of the request. "I will hear their confessions."

"I thank you," and Don Antonio walked down the corridor past the open door of the Fray Custodio's empty cell. He wondered about that ageing man and how he was faring. Then he stepped into the light, watched the small squad of would-be soldiers come to attention, and walked over to them. One of the men, a farm youth from an estancia to the north, was holding an harquebus muzzle down in the dirt and leaning on it. He came to attention when the Governor approached him.

"Should you get dirt or a stone in that weapon," the Governor informed him, "you might easily kill two persons: possibly the one you are firing at and most certainly yourself when the barrel explodes." Then the Captain General took the heavy weapon in his hand, turned it over and returned it to the youth. "You must take good care of it. It is like an old man. It fires once and it takes a long time before it can fire again."

And the Governor walked away with the pleasant laughter of the soldiers behind him. Maybe they would be a little less nervous. He wished he were.

With the Governor gone, the young padre became increasingly anxious. He had not expected the departure of the Fray Custodio. There had been no warning that the old man would mount his donkey and ride south alone. Fray Pedro would have liked to believe the ageing missionary had deserted him, but he knew better. That small, thin ancient might well have ridden to his death. Death. Fray Pedro pondered the prospect. He did not fear it, but he did not want to die now, not here, not under these conditions. The prospect of martyrdom did not appeal to him. He knew there were Brothers in the Order who would look at this with a different view, but he had his ambitions and they were not yet fulfilled.

At this moment in his career he had a status and a power he had never known at any other time. A governor had come to his cell, had discussed the problems of the province with him, had bared his soul and his fears as one man to another. Yet there was something missing. He tried to identify it. As he wiped his hand over his warm face and the top of his shaven head, his square, almost chunky features seemed to be accentuated by the tight muscles of his flat cheeks and large jaw. He tried to relax. There was almost no light in the room now. Evening was slowly spreading over the Villa. It would be followed by darkness and tomorrow. Fray Pedro had never questioned tomorrow before in his life, but now there were questions in his mind. He shrugged them off. A man could only believe that his ways were wise, and there could only be faith in what would come. With a quick gesture he crossed himself and walked to the window.

The six soldiers who had been assigned to guard the church had relaxed and were seated on the stone steps waiting for their relief. One of them held an harquebus gingerly, as though he did not know what he was supposed to do with it. The others were talking rapidly among themselves.

Fray Pedro thought of all that had happened to these men in such a brief time: the homes left behind, the crops standing unwatered, the possessions abandoned. Tomorrow he would rise early and walk among them and try to comfort them. That was what he would do. Suddenly he realized that he had always believed the responsibilities of the Fray Custodio were administrative. Now he saw the situation required a pastoral padre—a man to comfort and understand. He had never been adept at this and he knew it. But then, was it really important?

He turned back to his cell. In the dark corner set in the wall was a bulto which had been carved for him a year before by an Indian craftsman, and beside this lay his Bible. He dropped to his knees before the niche and prayed. The talents he had, had always sufficed. He could organize, he could plan, he could attend to details, he could study, and he knew all the complex turnings of his theology. There were routes he could walk. God would appreciate his path and not set him upon a strange one.

Finally, he crossed himself, rose to his feet and with care lighted a candle on the small table which served him as a desk. The carta to the Bishop remained unfinished. Perhaps it would never be delivered. But Fray Pedro wanted to talk to that stern man who had been his mentor in his youth. He pushed back the large sleeves of his cassock, seated himself, and picked up his pen.

24

THE Fray Custodio had ridden south through the early afternoon. His small grey burro stumbled along the road as though its master's slight weight were a burden. Both of them were older now than when they first travelled to Santo Domingo, and they had spent a long time together. The Franciscan did not want to count the years any more than he wanted to count the failures which had mounted up through those years.

Instead as the grey burro and its grey-cassocked rider made their way along the Camino Real, the padre thought of the years he had known as a missionary. He recalled the early battles against ignorance and the later ones against apostasy. That last battle was being fought again. And he knew enough of the world to know that it would be fought again and again. He knew enough of the world to see it as an eternal battleground between the ideal of the spirit and the weakness of human nature.

He was a wanderer on earth and the wide world was his cloister. He had accepted this fact when he was young, and the only treasure he had sought was poverty, because poverty would bring him and the Order to the kingdom of God. And the old man believed in the Order almost as much as he believed in the kingdom. He knew that the Order was not that of a select society of saints, but rather a federation of mere mortals with a saint here and there. He wondered as the little burro paused to nose a rainbow flower just who among his brothers had been the saints. He did not know. How can a man tell a saint from a mortal? There were answers but he was not as certain of them as he once had been.

He only wanted to love his brothers, hoped they loved him with as much affection, was concerned about the weaknesses of some and the strengths of others, but he was not always clear in his mind what was weakness and what was strength. Perhaps that very uncertainty was the reason why the history of the Order was its own drama—sometimes comedy, sometimes tragedy, but always alive and vital.

Even now in his last years, in what might be his own last act, he was moving to face the end as the Franciscan Brotherhood had laid down the Rule so long ago. He tried to recall the dates of the Order that had been taught him when he was younger, could not quite remember, realized just how old he had become, and urged his burro to hurry on.

Then he smiled to himself. *The Rule of 1223.* Four and a half centuries and more ago. And here he was wandering south to meet his fate as the Rule prescribed: as a pilgrim and a stranger in this world, serving the Lord in poverty and lowliness.

Ahead he could make out the sweep of land leading to the mission that was the centre of the province. It was not a very large centre or a very impressive one. But it did not matter that the mission was not imposing. *Neither house nor land nor anything at all ... and this humbly as becomes servants of God and followers of most holy poverty.*

The Fray Custodio slipped off his weary beast, took its lead rope and slowly walked before it. As he walked, his back became erect. His narrow shoulders seemed to fill out the loose cassock. His head went higher under the bright sun. And the canticle of St. Francis came to mind.

> Praise be to Thee my Lord with all Thy creatures
> Chiefest of all, Sir Brother Sun
> Who is our day, through whom Thou givest light. . . .
> Praise be to Thee My Lord for Brother Wind, and for the air, and for
> the cloud, for clear skies and all weathers,
> By which Thou givest nourishment to all Thy creatures . . . .
> Praise be to Thee, My Lord, for our Sister, Mother Earth,
> The which sustains and keeps us:
> O creatures all! Praise and bless my Lord and grateful be,
> And serve Him with deep humility.

The old warrior of God finished the canticle aloud and came to a halt. There were birds in the distance over the pueblo. At his feet he could see a small stream of black ants crossing the trail. The burro looked with sad eyes at its master and waited while the padre brushed his hand over his face and thought about the words of the canticle and how he had never been able to bring the light of its meaning to the puebleños. How close they were in thought and how eternally far apart. His hand came to rest on the crucifijo that hung about his neck. He bowed his head in prayer as he recalled again the Rule of the Order: *no jewels, nothing but a plated crucifijo and a mean chalice.*

All he needed in addition was his faith and this he had. His head went up again as he strode with his burro toward the pueblo where his charges waited for him.

BOOK IV

AUGUST 11-20, 1680

Oh! what a fight and what a fierce battle it was that took place; it was a memorable thing to see us all streaming with blood and covered with wounds and others slain.   BERNAL DIAZ DEL CASTILLO

1

DON ALONSO GARCÍA walked about the grounds of his hacienda north of Isleta with his oldest son at his side and his two compañeros behind him. The old warrior was tired. The morning ride which had revealed the uprising, as well as the long afternoon of work, had shown him that his years could not be overlooked. Ever since his return he had been driving those about him. When he found that the Indian women who worked the hacienda were absent, he turned the kitchen over to Nita and the household work to Doña Josefa. There was food to be prepared for himself and the few men who were stationed at the house. There was food to be readied in the event of a siege or withdrawal to Isleta. As for the house itself, Don Alonso knew that in the event of abandoning the place, he would do it under duress, and therefore they would be able to carry little with them. Doña Josefa had been given the task of packing their clothes and personal belongings and stripping the few small wardrobes to the barest essentials.

For himself, Don Alonso had spent the hours clearing the area about the hacienda for a siege. The brush which edged close to the building was burnt away. The few trees which had provided shade were either stripped or dropped to the ground. He laid the land bare for almost a hundred paces in every direction. There was no place to hide, no cover to protect anyone who might want to kill the occupants or burn the hacienda. It was all open ground, and around it all the wool and cotton cord that both Nita and Doña Josefa possessed was strung several hands off the ground with dried gourds hanging loose to rattle a warning if anyone approached in the dark.

Now Don Alonso was checking his defences a last time. There were four soldiers, two of his sons, the fool Alcalde of Jemez, and himself to defend the hacienda and two women. There were weapons enough for the men and munitions enough for the harquebuses. As for the women, Doña Josefa had orders to remain within the confines of her room in the event of an attack. Nita would help with the weapons. She could load an harquebus as fast as any of the men and knew how to tie off a wound or remove an arrow more readily than anyone else in the group. As he walked the perimeter of his defence, Don Alonso felt proud of his mistress. She was a woman the equal of any. And as he looked at the two youths at his side, and thought of the two others with their wives to the south of Isleta, he swelled. Nita was a woman. Doña Josefa was a lady. What more could an old warrior want in time of peace or war than one woman to fight beside him and another to fight for?

169

Dusk was gathering and a soft mist rose off the Rio del Norte. He turned to those with him.

"I intend to ride north to Sandia. I doubt if we shall be able to get into the pueblo. Then we will swing west and south making contact with all of the isolated estancias. I want every landholder to move into Isleta under the cover of darkness."

"May I ride with you, sir?" It was his older son who asked. The young man had shown a sense of eagerness through the day which disturbed his father. Soldiers are never eager for a fight. They do not lose their energies in anticipation. And a man who has fought would just as soon avoid a battle if he is not certain he will win it.

Don Alonso shook his head. "You and your brother will remain here. There may be an answer to the messages I have sent to Governor Otermín. There may be none. But should there be orders, I will want someone here who can read them." He was pleased that his sons could read. Very few of the young men of the province could do more than make out their own names or the slips listing debts incurred at the gambling tables in the Villa de Santa Fe.

The Lieutenant Governor squared his broad shoulders. "My horse and your own," he said to the two soldiers who walked with him. "We will take the fool Alcalde Mayor. In ten minutes by the rio." As they disappeared around the rear of the courtyard, he reminded his sons: "Remember. No Indian men within the line we have drawn. Consult your mother on any decisions which must be made. She will know what to do."

Leaving them, he went into the hacienda. Doña Josefa was kneeling over a brass-bound chest packing a pile of dresses. He stood looking at her from the doorway, wondering how she had dragged the heavy trunk into the entrance hall and what she thought could be done with anything as useless as the silks and satins she was so carefully folding. He shook his head and, crossing the room, slipped into a chair beside her.

"I am riding out now. Nita and the boys will care for the house should there be trouble."

She looked up and stared at him. Her pretty face was drawn. For a moment she considered arguing with the old Creole who was her husband. She was mistress of the hacienda. It was her house which would be coming under attack. If there was any decision to be made in his absence, she wanted the right to make it. Not Nita. Not the old mestiza with her brood of boys. After all, she herself was a peninsular, she was a lady, she had the right to command. And she was his wife. But before she could speak, García shook his leonine head slowly.

"Nita has known war. She will know what to do."

Doña Josefa rose to her feet and stood before her husband, wondering if this was the time to make her stand. Then in the light of a torch set in the wall at his side, she saw that his face was tense, his hands were moving nervously back and forth over the arms of the Savonarola chair in which he sat. Don Alonso was much older than she, but only at rare times was she aware of this, for there was animal vigour about him which never seemed to abate. But now as he was about to take up his equipment and ride out into the night, she could see his age.

"I will finish packing," was all she finally said.

Don Alonso smiled. "Do not bother. We could never carry all that. If we leave here, we will ride out with our horses and a pack animal or two."

"But these clothes from Madrid, you bought them yourself, and . . ."

"No," he explained, rising. "We will not be burdened with anything but our lives. And should we abandon Isleta with the fifteen hundred people there, I shall want them to travel light. My wife will set the example." He reached out a large hand, cupped the back of her head and kissed her firmly on the lips. His other hand passed over her body and as she tried to brush it away, he resolutely kissed her again, and returned his hand. Then without a word he stepped back, looked at her with a weary smile and walked across the loggia to his sleeping room. Doña Josefa stared after him. She was certain she would never understand this bear of a man she had married, but she was also certain he was a man few would equal.

Then she saw Nita cross the loggia and enter his sleeping room. She though of joining them, but discarded the idea and stood looking down at the dresses she might have to leave behind. She wondered which she would wear if they had to ride south.

Don Alonso García was putting his equipment on again with the help of his mistress. The ritual was the same as it had been early that morning. When they were done, he took her hand and held it for a moment and repeated his charge: "The boys and the Señora. You will look after them." Then he pulled her to him and the hard metal of his breastplate pressed into her as he kissed her.

"I do not want to lose everything," he said as he walked out of the house and joined his compañeros for the ride to Sandia.

The small tropa paused several hundred varas from that pueblo. From where they sat on their horses, they could make out the silhouettes of the gutted haciendas. García chewed the finger of his leather gauntlet as he thought about the messengers he had sent north to Governor Otermín. If Santo Domingo had fallen, as the Indians claimed it had, and Sandia was in flames, then there were fifty leagues of Indian-held territory separating him and the capital of the province. And he had no reason to believe that the Governor or anyone else to the north was alive. His half-cupped hand went to his helmet in salute to the dead whites of Sandia, and he whirled his horse about and rode southwest. There were isolated haciendas in this region. There might be something he could do for these.

Darkness now claimed the land. The moon was slight. The air was still. García and his small tropa passed hacienda after hacienda where they saw no need to pause: the flames or the gutted buildings told them they were too late. But there were other houses farther south and Don Alonso still hoped. He saw the house of one of his neighbours in the distance. There was silence and no sign of fire. He raised his hand and the horsemen who followed him slowed to his pace. They moved forward with caution, their weapons at the ready, their hopes rising as they saw no signs of trouble. Just outside the courtyard Don Alonso reined in his horse and sat staring at the high wall, the strong gate, and the dark adobe building behind. He knew someone was going to have to brave the darkness, to reconnoitre the courtyard and the buildings, because he had no intention of committing his small force to an uncertainty.

He swung about in the saddle and beckoned one of his old compañeros to join him. Seated stirrup to stirrup, he explained his problem. Someone had to move forward, knock at the gate, enter the courtyard and see if it was safe, see if any Indians were waiting in ambush, and whether the owners were dead, dying, or prepared to move out.

The soldier listened to his commander and nodded. He understood. He had done as much a hundred times in his life in different provinces in different terrains. The picture was the same. The circumstances remained unchanged. Only now the commander was an old amigo who had himself done all this as often as the men he ordered. This gave a strange and new kind of confidence to the soldier who had come to respect and not envy the Lieutenant Governor. Tossing the reins of his stallion to one of the troopers, the scout stepped lightly to the ground and waited while Don Alonso positioned the two men who were carrying harquebuses. Then he drew his sabre, better at close fighting than the lance which he thrust into the ground beside his stallion, and watched his compañero toss his reins over it.

When everything was ready, the scout moved with cautious steps toward the gate. Approaching from one side, he kept out of the direct line of the small port above the gatebolt. Then with the hilt of his sabre he broke the night's silence with two loud knocks. He waited. García and the others waited, ready to charge forward to protect him should he require such help, ready to back him up with fire should this be necessary.

After a time he knocked again. Something was wrong. If the Indians were inside, they would have attacked so small a party. If Spanish, they would have acknowledged help. Then the soldier stepped away. He could hear the port of the gate being opened. In the darkness he made out the face of a frightened woman. A closer look showed her to be an Indian wench. The scout's sabre went up as he prepared to thrust it.

"My mistress. She is ill."

García heard the plaintive voice laid over with fear of the armed men.

"And your master?" he called.

For a time the woman did not speak. "He has not returned from his journey to the south."

This could be true. It could be false. García was not prepared to trust the woman.

"Slip the bar of the gate and throw it open. Then come outside. I am Don Alonso García, the Lieutenant Governor of his majesty's province of Nuevo Mexico."

The men waited. The horses felt the tension and had to be held with a strong hand. The harquebuses were poised to break a charge of Indians.

Then the scout heard the bolt slip. The broad gate swung open. An

Indian woman, half crippled with age and huddled by fear, stepped out into the night. García waved the scout inside the courtyard. It was empty. The soldier held his sabre above his head with both hands and waved it in a small circle. He was going on. García signalled the men about him to hold their places as he walked his horse into the open courtyard to cover the soldier who was now entering the dark house.

The wait was a long one. Don Alonso had almost made up his mind to dismount and enter when the scout appeared in the doorway.

"There are four women here and nine children," he called to his commander.

"And no men?"

"None. They rode south earlier in the day when they heard about the uprising from her," pointing to the Indian woman.

Don Alonso was puzzled. He swung off his horse and entered the house. Two boys, both under ten, stood at the door to meet him. They were armed with small clubs and prepared to defend their home. He rubbed a gauntleted palm over their black hair to assure them and walked through the house until he found the sitting room. Here he could make out a huddled group of figures.

Calling to his compañero, "Light a fire, damn it," he waited. Minutes later a torch blazed in the wall and several candles had been lighted. Don Alonso stared at the four women, two of them middle-aged, two about twenty.

"Where are your men?"

One of the older women stood up from where she had been crouching to protect the children. "Don José and his two brothers have gone to Mexico. They told us they would return when the troubles were over."

For a moment Don Alonso found this difficult to believe. Then he reached out and removed the torch from its niche on the wall and walked over to the women, holding the flame near their faces so that he could see them more clearly. Indians and mestizas. So, the damned peninsular had fled and forsaken his women.

One of the younger pair, a sad-faced girl with long lashes, spoke up. "They said the Indians would not disturb us and that you would protect us. We have nothing to fear."

García looked at the women for a moment. A pretty enough wench. The kind who always had something to fear in the middle of a war, a rebellion, or any other action where law depended on circumstance. He wondered what sort of a fool mestiza ever believed she was safe. But he wondered more about the three men who would ride out and abandon their women and children.

"Are there any horses left?"

The old woman shook her head.

The Lieutenant Governor removed his helmet and scratched the top of his greying scalp. How in inferno to move them?

"Take your clothes and any valuables you can carry and come outside at once."

He turned to his compañero who had been at his side.

"Hurry them."

With those words, he walked out onto the patio trying very carefully to control his temper. He would like to meet Don José. There were things he would do to the man and his brothers. Well, one thing was certain. This hacienda would have to be reassigned. No man should have the right to hold it who would not defend the Crown's property, who fled before the word of an attack without waiting for the attack itself.

Jamming his heavy helmet on his head, Don Alonso stood waiting. Shortly, the scout came, pushing the women and children before him. The women were loaded down with bundles and the two smallest children. Passing in front of the group as though he were inspecting a column of soldiers, García went from one to the other. They were all wearing shoes. The women carried too much. He reached out and asked if there were any jewelry or money in the bundles as he took them. Each woman shook her head.

"Don José said the jewelry would be safer with him."

García nodded. "Drop the bundles. There is nothing in them worth your lives." Then he called for his small tropa to join him. Four mounted men, the scout, and himself.

He turned to the scout. "They are your package. Take three of the men and start for my hacienda. Let the older women and the younger children ride when possible. Avoid any pueblo. Tell Nita these are her charges."

Standing by his horse, he watched the refugees disappear into the distance. Then he turned to his lone compañero. "Imagine a Spaniard deserting his family. So they are mestizos and Indians. They were still family." He was angry, and his anger showed. He could not imagine himself ever abandoning Nita or their sons. It was incomprehensible to him. He mounted up and headed south again. As the soldier followed, he thought of the young wench with the long lashes and the sad face.

2

JOSÉ REYES pulled himself over the edge of the barranca thrusting Natividad before him. It was night now and the sliver of moon barely lighted the ravine behind him as he turned to look at it. Without the rio to guide him northward, he paused a moment to select his direction. He considered turning back toward the stream and following it to the hacienda of Lieutenant Governor García, but Reyes was a cautious man and knew the rio trail would be busy with Indians and refugees. If only he were certain that he was going in the right direction. Having always known his way about the back alleys of old Córdoba and been able to locate himself with ease in any dark city street, he was annoyed at being lost in open country. Any fool farmer or peasant could make his way across country. But Reyes was not certain he could. The Indian girl standing at his side with the quiet baby in her arms waited patiently for him to make up his mind. Finally, he pushed her and started toward what he believed was the north. The girl stumbled on. Her feet were still bare, and the hard, broken surface of the rocky ledge they travelled over cut into her soles and left a track of red, unseen in the darkness.

Reyes, thirsty now, regretted that he had abandoned the rio and without pausing to drink since morning. The day had been hot, and he had been frightened. It was a strange feeling and a new one and he was troubled that such a thing could happen to him. The very thought of it brought a choking resentment.

The girl topped a small rise, paused, and turned to see if he was following. The resentment within him spilled over and he struck her with the flat of his sabre across the ribs. She stumbled to one knee. Reyes grabbed at her hair, pulled her to her feet and shoved her on. Bowed with the bundle she clutched in her arms, faltering as she walked on her torn feet, she became a symbol to Reyes of his weakness and failure. How had he come to this point? What had brought him—José Reyes, craftsman and artist—into this strange land, into flight and fear? He knew only, for the moment, that he was entangled with this wench, this smelling, copper-coloured sow. The humiliation of the situation crawled over him like a scorpion and bit into his small and twisted mind. She was it, she was the reason, she had done this to him. He was thirsty. He was hungry. The damned breastplate weighed on his chest and the helmet pressed down on his head. The sabre he carried dragged at his side. The lithe cat had been turned into a beast of burden. The freedom had departed. And she was the reason for it.

He caught up with the girl, threw his arms about her and hurled her to the ground. The bundle she carried rolled out of her hands and down a small slope. Reyes dashed after it and returned to her side, where he set it on the ground. This too, was her fault. A child, and she did not know how to take care of it, how to appreciate the son of José Reyes.

Standing astride the frightened girl, who was completely bewildered by what was happening, he kicked her ribs with his bucket boot. At first she moaned with anguish, and as she raised her arms to protect herself, Reyes saw the small bag she had been carrying. He had forgotten this in his blurred fury. Kneeling down, he tore the leather strap loose with a jerk. Here was food—good meat and tortillas. He ripped the bag open and stared at it. He forgot that she had carried it at his insistence, as he knelt beside her and struck her across the face time after time. She had been hiding the food from him. She had been planning to eat and let him starve. When he was exhausted, he squatted down on the ground and cut the cold lamb into small pieces with his daga and ate them from the tip of it. The girl watched him, silently.

Pausing a moment to relish the juices of the meat, he saw her staring at him. His palm lashed out. Then he pointed to the child. With effort, she sat up and looked at the covered corpse of the infant.

"Take him. Feed him. He is the son of Reyes."

And as she tried to understand what he was saying, he reached out with his daga, plunged it into her dress and ripped downward. Only his extreme skill with his weapon kept him from tearing the girl herself open. He poked at her bosom with the needle tip of his daga, and then pointed to the still bundle beside her.

Natividad wanted to rise and scream out to him that the child was dead, that his heavy palm had killed the child, and that she could not feed it now as she had not been able to feed it earlier, but instead she reached over and picked the bundle up and held it to her bosom. Reyes, ignoring her now, returned to his dinner. He failed to notice that she did not even spread the blanket which hid the child's black face.

The food bag emptied, Reyes rose to his feet and looked about him. The straggling landscape pressed inward: the broken edge of rock hills, looming like dragons' teeth across the horizon, the macabre piñons like drunken dancers against the sky, the bosomed roll of white sands. He was lost and he knew it. Though there was no way of being certain, he believed that he had been drifting northward. But what he did not know was how far he had journeyed from the rio itself. The possibility of missing Isleta or the García hacienda frightened him. He would have to turn west and try again to find the rio. There were dangers there, but there, also, lay security.

He reached down to lift the girl by the hair when he saw that she had set the bundle beside her and was trying to close the torn front of her dress. He knelt and ran his hands over her bosom and the softness excited him. For the moment his fears departed and he was willing to forget that she was the cause of his problems, for the moment he knew only that he wanted her, wanted a conquest no matter how unimportant or how simple to achieve. His hand closed over one copper breast and he forced her backward until she collapsed under the pressure onto her back. Then he flipped up the bottom of her dress and ran his hands over her lean thighs.

When his need was satisfied, he sat up and looked down at her, her eyes closed, her fingers clutching at the short, burned grass. The girl was only a girl. He had known better, prettier, and in comfortable beds with soft mattresses and sheets. He had left his finger marks on softer buttocks and had brought smiles to prettier mouths. And Natividad became again the sign, the symbol of what had happened to José Reyes. He slapped at her bosom with his open palm and she opened her eyes and looked at him. He motioned for her to rise, and as she did, he reached out for the bundle which lay beside her. Natividad rose falteringly to her feet and looked down at Reyes. The blanket which covered the dead infant had come open. He was staring at the black face. With one slim finger he tried to open the child's eyes, and when they remained open, he covered them with his palm. He shook the child as though to hear it rattle, make some sound that would inform him that it was alive. But there was no sound. There was no sign of life. He held the infant at arm's length and slowly accepted that which he had not been able to accept. Then, in an instant of panic, he hurled the bundle away. The child was himself. The child was Reyes, was his warped dream of the shining future, and it was dead.

Natividad watched without a sound. She would have liked to slip into the darkness and disappear, find the great rio and cry by its waters. But even though Reyes was silent, was distant and dazed, she did not trust herself. The bare blade of the daga lying at his side captured the light of the moon above her and she wondered if she dared to reach for it, dared to destroy the bearded soldier who had killed so many. Then she saw his hand cover the hilt of the daga as he started to rise to his feet. His face was twisted, his eyes half closed. For one moment she swayed in the moonlight. Then they both were still. There was a sound behind the hillock. It was strange to her ears and it took Reyes a moment to recognize it. He swiped at the girl with the clean blade of the daga and started running toward the sound. He yelled as he ran, making no particular words, only a loud halloo.

The two horsemen on the other side of the hillock reined in, poised their lances and sabres, and waited for the figure which burst out of the darkness toward them. When they recognized the stranger as a Spaniard, they relaxed. One of them paced his horse forward to meet the man who grasped at his stirruped foot and hugged it.

"Easy, soldado. Where are you from?" The tall figure with the soot-covered breastplate and the Toledo blade in his great hand looked down at Reyes. "Where are you from? Do any others live?"

It took Reyes time to adjust to the situation. "I am trying to find Lieutenant Governor García. The Indians at San Ysidro have risen against us."

The grey-bearded giant seated unbending in his saddle looked down at Reyes. "I am García. Do any live at San Ysidro?"

Reyes thought for an instant. He did not know about the padre, nor did he want to waste time finding out. "No," he said, "I am the only one who survived."

The Lieutenant Governor shook his head wearily, signalled the man behind him to move forward. "The two of you mount up together. We will ride toward the rio and north again."

When Reyes was mounted, they disappeared into the darkness.

From where she had dragged herself on the ground, Natividad watched them go. One hand clutched her side where the daga had sliced into her flesh. The warm blood ran through her fingers, but she knew she would live. Suddenly she felt stronger than she had felt for a long time, more assured than she had been since that night almost a year before when the bearded soldado and his compañeros had appeared at the Festival of the Corn Mother. She knew she was rid of him at last, and she lay back and stared at the sky and the rising moon and remembered she was Poy-ye, the Rising Moon, born in the darkness and waiting for light.

WHEN he had eaten his fill of the fresh antelope meat and satisfied himself that the knife he carried was excellent for skinning the beast, the Negro fugitive Jorge found a clump of bushes and went to sleep. He wanted to avoid the heat of the day as well as any movement along the rio.

It was evening when the noise of the wolves fighting over the remains of the antelope carcass awakened him. He shifted slightly to bring his silver-mounted lance with the long steel point into position. He did not want to fight these beasts, but he believed they might attack. With apprehension he backed out of the bushes into the night and made his way quietly down rio, avoiding any sound which might arouse them from their feast. But the wolves ignored him, and several minutes later, beyond a small hill and after passing a clump of trees, he measured his stride and again took up his long trot southward. There was still no direction in his flight, only the desire to place distance between himself and the pueblo of the White Witch.

The moon inched its way up the sky as he ran. Hours later he saw the silhouette of a hacienda before him. He slowed his pace. There were birds over the courtyard of the house, and he suddenly realized that he had seen birds several times during the day. There had been very few in the sky during the years he spent with the White Witch. She had had powers which he had never believed existed. Jorge drove the lance into the ground to quiver briefly as he took his knife in hand and carefully opened his thumb with the point. A man who knows, washes the powers of a witch away with blood. Very thoughtfully, he wiped his thumb across his forehead. Then he set the knife back in his belt and clapped his hands together twice. He felt secure. If any power of the White Witch remained, it would not follow him now. A jerk of his hand brought the lance out of the ground as he stood staring at the birds slowly circling the sky.

Born of the forests, of the dark places where small things crawl and lightning etches the sky, Jorge was familiar with the signs, and these birds were signs. His hand went to his ear and he heard the distant drumming of the hyena-faced man. Here were carrion birds. And here was death. The Negro was not afraid. The drum was not signalling for him. Stepping softly over the ground, Jorge approached the hacienda. The courtyard was open. There was no life to be seen as he peered in from the cover of a large rock. Then he saw the bodies strewn across the open ground. There were several men, and from the billow of clothes he knew there were several women. The only movement in the night was the circling of birds overhead. The only light was the moon's.

A flutter of wings near by. He whirled and saw carrion birds flush toward the sky from the corpse of a large black stallion, already stiff-legged. Jorge, lance poised, walked slowly into the courtyard. Three Spanish men were lying there. One, face down and barelegged. Two white women, their skirts thrown back and their hair spread in a large circle about their heads, stared wide-eyed and unseeing at the moon. The fugitive slave looked at the whites and was unmoved by the violence of the Indians. He wandered about the courtyard looking for anything which might be of value to him. Finding nothing, he entered the house. The heat of the fire which had gutted it clung to the walls, and charred furniture lay scattered about. Abandoning all hope of recovering anything he might use, he turned and walked back into the night. The birds rose and cut their circles over the courtyard as he departed.

Jorge walked slowly for a time, thinking of the wreckage that lay behind him. He did not judge, because it was not in him to have an opinion on the whites or the Indians. Neither would have cared about Jorge. When he saw the moon reflecting off the rio, he entered the stream and waded across it. By the time he reached the east bank, he was no longer thinking of the hacienda or what had happened there. He shook himself dry and began his steady trot southward once more.

Sometime later he felt hungry and knew he would have to hunt again. He slowed his pace at the sight of the first clump of trees he came to and approached it quietly. In this shelter a deer would drink. In the cover of these trees he would find his night meal if he were patient. With upraised hand he tested the wind and found there was none. The night air lay as still as the unmoving leaves of the cottonwood trees. Jorge stood a moment and selected his place, a small hillock near the stream overlooking what he believed was an animal trail. There was not quite enough light for him to check the trail for tracks. He slowly moved to the hillock and settled down to wait in the light of the climbing moon.

Half an hour later he slipped down onto his belly as he heard the beast coming toward him in the darkness. His lance was loose in his hand, his knife ready in his belt. The pebbles near the stream moved, and he rose to his feet to hurl his lance. Then he hesitated. The beast whirled toward him—a mountain lion. Gold even in the night. Fire-eyed and furious at being disturbed, the creature cried out its annoyance and closed the ground between them with two huge bounds. Jorge set his lance butt down on the ground, point forward, and held it firm. The streak of lion gold hurled itself through the air at the intruder. The lance shook in Jorge's hand. The surprised cries of the impaled beast rose over the cottonwood trees. The deadly claws unsheathed from their pads swiped the empty air reaching for the Negro; then the lance was dead weight. The night was quiet again, and Jorge dropped his weapon and stood staring at his kill.

He did not know how long he stood and travelled back in time to the kill of a different lion in a different land when he was younger. Before he had worn the golden pelt. Before the medicine man had put the four white dots of manhood on his chest. Before he had tumbled the girl in the bushes by the big green river and given the golden pelt to her.

Finally, when he made the journey back to the mountain lion at his feet, he knelt down and pulled out the silver-ornamented lance. He placed his

hand in the blood of the lion and covered each of the white spots on his
chest with red. Then he pulled his knife out of his belt and skinned the
beast. He paused only to eat the raw heart of the lion, because this was a
good thing.

When he was done, he washed the bloody golden pelt and threw it over
his shoulder. His lance was again in his hand. Jorge forgot his hunger as
he walked back to the stream and drank his fill.

Then he turned and ran south again.

It was almost midnight when he swung away from the rio eastward to
avoid a pueblo he saw in the distance lighted by the flames which consumed
a small mission. He had seen no Indians or whites for hours and he had
covered several leagues from the place where he had killed the mountain
lion whose pelt bounded on his shoulder with each easy step. Jorge was beginning to feel confident. He believed he was beyond the reach of the White
Witch, and if he were fortunate, he was beyond the reach of any of the whites.
But the Indians troubled him. There were more of them. They knew the
country. And he was a strange figure in their world.

The white sand slowed his pace and he headed toward small hills in the
distance. Several times he watched birds rise toward the moon now high
above the horizon. Once he watched a rabbit break across his trail, and another
time he paused to watch a doe.

Only when he heard the sound of a moan in the distance did his lance come
up again. He stopped and tried to locate the noise, and as he listened he knew
that it was a human sound and to his left. With the stalking step of the
hunter, he closed the distance in the dark. When he thought he was close
enough to the sound, he sprang forward, his lance arm back, ready to hurl
the silver-layered weapon.

Then he saw the girl lying on the ground, clutching her side and staring
at the moon. A few feet away from her was a small bundle, partly wrapped
in a blanket. Jorge was uncertain what type of wraith this was, or what
signs a man made under these conditions. The girl cried again. He dropped
his lance by her side and bent over her. The small copper face of the Indian
girl turned. She stared at him. Her eyes opened wider, surprised, frightened.
She had never seen a black man before, never knew that such existed. Had
he come from the bottom of the sipapu, where the lower world emptied out
its horrors? Had she died and failed to find the holy place? Had she offended
the gods of the People or the god of the limp hands? Was it Natividad, or
Poy-ye, who was in Hell?

The black giant reached out and opened the hand which clutched her
bleeding side, felt the dampness there and listened. There was no sound.
There was no drummer against the night. Jorge looked at the girl and did
not know what he could do. Then he remembered that the lion was strong
medicine. He pulled the still green pelt from his shoulder and spread it
over the Indian girl. The raw hide scratched her bared breasts where Reyes
had sliced open her dress, and the gold skin of the beast frightened her. She
tried to roll away from the black figure that knelt over her, tried to strike

at him and drive him away like a bad dream or an unhappy ghost. But his strong hands tightened on her sides and she was limp.

"I will not hurt you," he said in the Indian he knew, but the language was strange to her. He repeated the words over and over, but they meant nothing. Jorge, who had only known the Indians of Santa Flora, did not understand his failure. Finally, he tried Spanish, "I will not hurt you," and the girl's face lighted. In her year with Reyes she had learned some of these words, though she had never heard this sentence from the bearded soldier.

Seeing this slight reaction, Jorge repeated the words again and again as he tucked the lion skin about her and lifted her up in his arms. She was a light bundle, almost a child against his broad black chest with the four blood-covered dots on it. Then he knelt down and retrieved his lance. This he might need. The fears of the girl increased as he started to walk westward with her. She screamed and pointed to the bundle which lay on the ground near by. Without bending down, Jorge toed the bundle to discover that it was a dead child. He saw no value in this and continued to carry the sobbing girl away from the hillock.

Eventually Poy-ye was exhausted. There were no more tears, merely an acceptance that this was the way things ended. A black man came out of the black night and wrapped a girl up in a golden lion skin and carried her off toward the great rio through which tumbled the waters of the Lake of Copala. This was the way the journey concluded, the story closed. There was no fighting the way of the Earth Mother or the Corn Mother.

Jorge felt her blood running down his arms and he was angry. There were things a man did to an enemy: he killed him, destroyed his home, assumed and used his women, killed his offspring, but no man who ever lived by the big green river ever stabbed a girl and left her to bleed. He looked down at the accepting face of the girl he carried and realized that she was young and pretty, and he remembered the girl with child whom the whites had sliced up and thrown into the river. And he held the Indian girl more closely to his breast as he began to run, smoothly and swiftly, without jarring her.

Poy-ye closed her eyes against the waning moon. This was a part of dying no one had ever explained to her, but it was not bad. It did not hurt so much as the days and nights with the bearded soldier had hurt.

As he approached the rio from which he had turned away hours before, Jorge crossed the stream without pause. He knew there was a pueblo only a short distance to the north, and he desired to avoid the copper people. He had seen the violence of them and did not want to face it now.

When he found the shelter of some small piñons, he set his bundle on the ground and the girl opened her eyes again and looked at him. With gentleness he pulled back the golden pelt which was a sign of strength and tore away her dress from the place where the blood continued to ooze. He splashed water over the wound, and mixing some of the water with the soft black earth of the rio's edge, he spread the mud over the wound. The girl looked at him with frightened eyes, but did not move. The Negro rose, stripped the leaves from the branches of a near-by cottonwood and carefully spread them over the mud pack. Then he wrapped the silent girl again in the lion skin, picked her up in his arms and walked away from the rio toward the place where the sun sets in the evening.

4

RUAHA, the cacique of San Ysidro, spent the night with his young warriors and principales at thát junction where the dry arroyo with the white-pebbled bottom had obliterated the trail of the bearded soldier and the girl who walked ahead of him. They had searched through the afternoon without finding a trace, a sign, a scratched pebble which would indicate where the bearded soldier had disappeared. One of the principales believed the man and woman and child had been taken away to the other place by Montezuma, the great war captain who had pledged his aid to the People. Ruaha was not so certain. He would wait until morning and search again. He did not doubt that there were gods and that they played their games of hiding with men, but it was themselves they hid—behind clouds, in the midst of a swirling pool, when the lightning scratched the sky. He had never known them to hide men. He saw no purpose here, and he always believed they had a purpose, an intent, a direction. He would wait until dawn and search again.

It had been a difficult two days for the cacique. His woman was dead. His child was missing. The world of the limp god and the Whitefaces in which he had grown up was overturned.

It was morning now and the young men were out again in search of the lost trail. The wooden macana lay beside Ruaha and with it his regret that he had not had an opportunity to use it as he had planned. There was the sound of running steps and he rose to his feet with the men about him as a young warrior appeared running down rio.

"I have found a trail," he called. And as he approached Ruaha, he pointed toward the path they had taken the day before, up the white-pebbled arroyo leading east.

"I found where they spent the day," the youth explained, "and where they went in the night."

He turned and trotted up the white path. The others took their weapons and followed. The blank wall of the closed barranca rose before them and they halted in the same place as they had the afternoon before. Standing beside the old cacique, the young guide pointed to the ledge which had protected Reyes.

"I found their footprints at the top. They turned northward from there."

Ruaha nodded and the men followed him as he made his way up the steep walls of the barranca. They paused at the place where Reyes had watched their approach and saw the marks on the ground which indicated that the man, woman, and child had been there. When they reached the top, the signs were clear. There were the torn plants which Reyes had used to pull himself upward, the bare footprints of the girl, and the sharp heel marks of the soldado. The trail was an easy one to follow as it led through the brush and into the sandy place and finally to the hillock. Here, signs were plentiful. The first thing the young men saw was the body of the infant. Ruaha stood a long time over his grandchild with the blackened face, the soft nose and the open eyes, and wondered how the baby had died. Then he took out the sacred corn meal and spread it over the small body. When he was done with his prayers, one of his companions took the child and walked over the brink of a hill and buried it. Meanwhile, the youths found the place where Reyes had run to join the horsemen and the direction from which the strange, large footprints appeared. These puzzled the young men, and Ruaha had no ready answer for them. Several of the warriors placed their moccasined feet into the barefoot marks in the sand and saw how small their own feet were by comparison and they were frightened. Whoever it was that had approached the girl Poy-ye was a giant. Ruaha knelt down and felt the bloody sand and wondered whose blood he touched. Then he looked down the clear trail where the large footprints turned alone toward the rio. There was no sign of Poy-ye. The girl herself was gone and she had left no tracks. The young men tried to decide if the impressions left by the giant were deeper, which might indicate that he was carrying something, but the footprint was so large and broad, there was no gauging this. When the old companion of Ruaha returned from his task beyond the hill, they all turned in wonder and followed the tracks of the giant.

Eventually they came to the place where he had crossed the rio, found where he had scooped up mud and where he had stripped leaves from the cottonwood tree. They discovered also the place where the giant had turned toward the sun and walked west. But there was no sign of the girl Poy-ye. They all gathered about Ruaha and awaited his decision.

The old man looked into their faces and knew they felt cheated. He knew they had set their hearts on revenge, for themselves, for the People, and even for his own daughter now lost. He had little choice. He had to give them what they wanted.

"We will return to our homes, and tomorrow we will destroy the medicine man with the shaven head."

There was approval on the faces of those about him and as they started to trot down rio toward their homes and women, he joined them. But he did not do this willingly or because he believed he had any choice.

THE Day of San Lorenzo had been the longest in the life of Juan, the young war captain of Taos. He had led the people against the intruders and all of the Whitefaces were dead. He had seen the ironic smile on the face of Don Jaime just before he dropped the candela into the powder, and he knew the eyes of the Spaniard revealed his final truth to the waif he had taken into his home. No man was to be trusted. No woman.

Juan remembered his own frightened flight from the courtyard when he realized what Don Jaime planned and knew that in his flight he had admitted the superiority of the Spaniard. This humiliation did not bother him. Other things did: his own betrayal of the man, the fact that Don Jaime had never quite trusted him enough to reveal the secret of the daggs—the small hand guns which had been hidden in the house, and most of all, the continuing absence of Manuela.

After the house had been destroyed and the fires started by the explosion had cooled, Juan walked through the smashed ruin, room by room, trying to find some clue to the girl's disappearance. It was almost evening now and he had found nothing. He could only believe that she had never returned from her flight into the darkness the night before. And he feared for her safety.

Should Manuela return to the hacienda of her father, the People would kill her as they had killed all of the other Whiteface women. Should she meet the warriors of another pueblo, they too would not hesitate to destroy the young girl. And if she had not returned, what had happened to her? Juan sat quietly on the roof of the communal house of his people and stared at the fading sun. What was he to do? In the morning he was expected to call the men of the pueblo together and lead them south to the Villa de Santa Fe. It might be a week before he returned. He might never return. And if the girl lived, what of her? There was no one other than himself in all the province above el Paso del Norte who knew about the girl or cared. And as he sat holding her father's sabre in his hand, he knew he cared. Sometime in the past—some meeting of theirs, some gesture, some words they had said or failed to say, had brought them together. He was conscious of this now. He hoped she was. He was aware also of why he had thought her flight the night before perhaps better than her remaining. It gave possibility to her being alive.

And so many people were dead already. Given the knowledge of battle he had received from Don Jaime, it had been a simple task for Juan to lead the massacre of the other Whitefaces in the area.

Juan watched a small gathering of men in the open plaza below him and barely heard their boasts as he wondered why Don Jaime had selected the violent death that was so different from that which any of the People would have chosen. Juan wondered why a man would kill himself, and then he recalled the restraints against suicide so needlessly preached by the volatile Fray Vicente. To take a life is a sin. To take one's own life is another sin. So the old padre had preached. If this were true, then Don Jaime had sinned and would live forever as a wood's harpy.

> Their wings are wide, their feet clawed, their huge bellies
> Covered with feathers, their necks and faces human.
> They croak eternally on the unnatural trees.

The lines of Dante that the Spanish priest had taught him ran incongruously through his mind. But Juan did not know what a wood's harpy was, or what was wrong with being one. And if a man cannot take his own life while killing his enemies, then what of the medicine man with the magic hair Fray Vicente had told him about—the blind man standing between two pillars who had killed both his enemies and himself? It was all confusing to Juan, who wished that he were done with it. There was so much trouble in the world of god and gods, Juan wanted no more of it.

But the girl Manuela. The thought of her troubled him. He rose from his perch on the roof of the communal house, looked up toward Hlan-Gima the house of the Winter People, where Popé stood staring at the sun, and made up his mind.

The rebellion Popé had preached would be good for the People. It might be the only way in which the puebleños would ever know the pattern of the seasons again. But Juan doubted that it was necessary to kill all the Whitefaces.

He climbed down the ladder and walked across the plaza of Taos. His companions of the day smiled after him. They were proud to have as their war chief someone who had been trained by the very Whitefaces they killed. They were proud to have a person who knew the white language and the white way of attacking and defending, who knew how to use the white weapons and white armour. The People of Taos were pleased with how much he brought them of the enemy's knowledge. But they were proud of the wrong things, and this annoyed Juan. The good he had learned through years of living with Don Jaime meant nothing to them. This knowledge was worthless knowledge. There was no need to read the white books or write the white language. There was no need to discuss the philosophy of man or know how a map is drawn. There was no need for so much that Juan had learned that he felt as dead in his own way as the former Conde de Iteo had in his.

Juan began to see the irony of the situation as his townsfolk asked him when they would travel south to the Villa and kill the Governor and all of the others who were part of the Whiteface government.

Juan pointed to the fading sun. "When next it comes, we will be on the trail to the Villa de Santa Fe."

And he continued his walk, out of the pueblo, down the rio's bank to the stable that had been Don Jaime's. The horses here had not been disturbed. After the great explosion had shaken the valley of the red willows, the

People had fallen away from the hacienda and shunned it as they would shun a sacred place. Juan knew what had happened, and the fears he felt were not for the hacienda, but for a girl, small and dark-haired, with frightened eyes.

Inside the stable behind the collapsed walls of the hacienda, Juan threw a saddle over one of the black stallions—broad-chested, short-legged, and nervous. The beast looked at him with questioning eyes and then turned away to ignore him. Setting the bit in the sensitive mouth, Juan held it firmly as he guided the animal out of the stable. Once in the courtyard and the brighter light of the almost dead day, he swung himself into the saddle, jammed his feet into the shoe stirrups and settled himself, knees up and back erect. While he had never ridden across country before, he had practiced in the courtyard many times. Only a day earlier the chances of an Indian rider being brought down by a lance or harquebus had been great. Now the world was new, and the order of things altered. Indians rode and white men died. The horse shied for an instant, but firm hands on its reins, and knees dug into its sides, steadied it.

Juan felt confident he could ride the horse. There never had been much doubt in his mind. His heel came into its side and his arms relaxed. He had to find Manuela, find her before morning, before he rode south to battle.

He caught sight of a piece of white cloth snagged on a thorn bush. Swinging off the horse to the ground, he picked up the white cotton. From her gown? From that of another woman? The pantalone of a man? The tracks on the rocks were not clear. He took the reins in his hand and walked in front of the stallion. A hundred varas farther on he found more white cloth, and beyond that a muddy slipper. He was following Manuela. So had the mountain lion whose paw prints were pressed so clearly in the mud. Then the animal tracks seemed to wander to the rio and away, but the girl's straggled on.

Juan passed the entrance of a small cañon and walked on across the beds of two dried arroyos and on to the muddy bank of the rio. There were many tracks here, and he was not as certain now as he had been before. Then he saw the girl's robe, torn and muddy, lying near the water. He dropped the horse's reins and ran to it. Kneeling down, he took the ragged cloth in his hand and tried to read some direction from it. Why had she abandoned it? Where had she gone?

For several minutes Juan looked from the cloth in his hand to the rio's edge and wondered if she had shed the robe and entered the stream. He knew the fears of the girl as well as the reasons for fear in the wild night. His horse began to wander away and it was a moment before he realized this. It took time to corner the beast against a cañon wall and mount it again. He still carried the remnant of robe. It was almost dark now. He had to find her, but finding her was going to be difficult. He was tempted to call her name but hesitated. Should there be any puebleños in the area, they, too would be looking for her, and there would be no explaining why they should not kill her.

He rode a short distance down the rio's bank looking for another sign of her, but the night made tracking almost impossible. After a time, Juan swung to the ground, looped the reins over a small piñon and with some effort made a torch.

It seemed to unsteady the stallion, but Juan held the reins firmly as he mounted again and rode south. At the entrance of a high-walled barranca he paused, decided she could have gone little beyond this point, and rode into the ravine. He would have to ride up every ravine between the hacienda and this point through the night until he found her.

Manuela was not there. The high black walls loomed before him and with difficulty he turned his horse about and made his way back to the rio. The next ravine was only slightly wider at its entrance, and as he entered he heard the frightened scream and the sobs. In an instant he was off his horse and walking toward the sounds. Then he saw her, gown shredded, feet torn, clutching the base of a rock beneath an overhang. Her hair was straggled and terror marked her small face. Juan set the torch in a crevice just above her head.

"It is only Juan, Manuela. It is Juan. You remember Juan."

But there was no response from the hysterical girl who clutched the rock and would not turn her eyes away from its hard security. Gently, the Indian youth took her by the shoulders and tried to hold her, but she was stiff and would not release her grasp. Her torn nightdress had fallen away from her shoulders and her bosom was pressed against the rock.

"I will not hurt you, girl. I would not hurt you, Manuela. It is all right. I have come to take care of you."

But she did not seem to hear him. At last he reached up and took her hands and loosened them from the rock. Her arms remained stiff and outstretched as he turned her toward him. Her eyes did not meet his and the loose hair fell over her tense, tear-streaked face. He pulled the hair behind her ears the way maidens of the tribe wore theirs as a sign they were still unwed. Then he took her face between his hands and looked into her eyes. They were looking back, but he knew she did not see him. After a moment, she collapsed and went limp. He sat on the ground and held her to his breast and rocked her back and forth slowly as he tried to comfort her.

"It is over now. There will be no more trouble. No one will hurt you. Juan is here and he will take care of you. He will take care of you now, and he will take care of you always."

His own words surprised him, but he knew this was what he had come for

Then her body stiffened in his arms and he heard her say, "I did not mean to hurt Don Jaime. He was my father, and I did not mean to sin against him. I never wanted to sin against him. I never wanted to wander in this place I did not mean to sin against Don Jaime."

She tried to rise and run, but Juan held her. Taking her by the shoulders and holding her at arms' length, he tried to decide if she were talking to him and what she meant. Who had hurt Don Jaime? Who had betrayed Don Jaime? What was she talking about? What did she know? Was Manuela what they had whispered of her in Taos, a white witch trained by the old padre to do the bidding of the Dark Ones? What was she talking about, and where had she learned of his betrayal of her father?

Then the Indian youth realized that for the first time she was actually looking at him.

"I wandered," she said, "through the Dark Place all night. And everything was as Fray Vicente and Dante said it would be, and when morning came I could not find my way back and I fell asleep. And I am hungry."

He looked down at her bared breasts, pulled her to him, and clutched her tightly. She was not a witch; she was bewitched. She had gone simple. Her wits had been lost in the night's wandering. His lips brushed the top of her head and he rocked her as he had before and she lay still and started to sing, but he could not understand her.

Juan did not know how late it was or where his horse had disappeared to in the darkness when the torch flickered out. He rose to his feet and pulled the girl up beside him. She stood no higher than his shoulder, though only a year separated their ages. There was much he had to do before morning, and he did not know what to do. Where would he take her? Where would she be fed? Where would she be safe?

Then she turned to look at him in the dark and said, "Let me ask Don Jaime what I did that was wrong. Perhaps he will tell me."

Juan appealed upward to the stars. She did not know what had taken place at the hacienda or that Don Jaime was dead. There was no way she could have known, and now he would have to tell her. With his hands on her shoulders, he stood and talked about Popé, the visions he had had, about the troubles of the People and their will to rise again, and about her father who had disappeared in one great smashing sound that would have put the Infernos of Fray Vicente to shame, and about Fray Vicente. And when he had finished talking, he knew he need not have troubled himself, for all she said was, "I will have to ask Don Jaime what it was that I did that I should not have done."

And the Indian youth, looking up, found even the stars had no answer for either of them. He placed his arm about her waist and walked with her between the high walls of the barranca and down to the edge of the water. Here he sat her down and tenderly washed her torn feet and her tear-streaked face. Then, as he knelt beside her, he leaned over and clutched her to him, his hand passing over her soft breasts and his lips pressing against her hair. She did not protest. She did not seem to notice. She said nothing, even when he released her and placed his leather jerkin about her shoulders and pulled her to her feet again.

A hundred varas upstream, he found his horse and, letting go of Manuela's hand, he caught the stallion and brought it back to where she stood staring at him. Juan put his hands about her waist, and lifted her into her father's saddle. Then he swung up behind her, clasped one arm about her, and pointed the horse toward the destroyed hacienda that had been her home. When they arrived there, Juan slipped from the horse's back to the ground and tied the reins to a near-by cottonwood just outside the courtyard. Manuela started to dismount and he shook his head and held up one hand.

"Wait, Manuela, I will only be a minute. Everything will be all right."

And she said nothing, though he saw that she was disturbed. When he returned with one of her dresses over his arm, her shoes in his hand, some blankets, and a large bag of food he had taken from the storehouse, she said, "Don Jaime did not want to see me?"

There was no answering this and the Indian youth did not try. He lifted her out of the saddle, handed her one of the dresses and the shoes, set down the bag of food and the blankets and disappeared a second time into the courtyard. This time when he returned she was buttoning the bodice of the dress, and she looked up at him.

"He might at least have given me a petticoat."

Juan realized his oversight, but decided to ignore it. The second horse he led was older than the one he had ridden out earlier and, he believed, more gentle. He took the girl in his arms for a moment and then swung her into the saddle. Throwing the bag of food across his own horse, he mounted and rode off into the night, leading Manuela's mount behind him. The girl was silent at first, and then she began to recite aloud:

> By that foul water, black from its very source,
> We found a nightmare path among the rocks
> And followed the dark stream along its course.

Hours later they came to the Sacred Place in the mountains which Juan believed no one would visit and where he hoped she would be safe until his return from the battle at the Villa. And he knew he had to return because the girl would never survive alone, and because should any of the puebleños find her here among the sacred caves, they would kill her. And if they learned he had brought her here, he doubted that even a war chief would be permitted to live.

After he had settled her belongings in one of the small caves, spread out the blankets for her bed and handed her one of the tortillas from the food bag, he walked to the entrance of the cave and looked down the long valley that stretched as far as he could see. To the south lay Taos. And the sun was beginning to streak the edge of darkness to the east.

Juan felt uncomfortable in the Sacred Place. He had believed that all religion was behind him, that the conflict of the gods was no longer his concern, but standing here in the darkness, he doubted only himself. After a time he turned back to the cave where the girl sat on the blankets near the entrance, eating the flat maize bread. There was no doubt in her eyes. There were no questions. He wished there were as he knelt down beside her to explain.

"I shall go away for a time. But you will be safe here. No one will bother you. There is a small stream just there," he said, pointing to a thin cascade tumbling over the edge of the rocks. "I will be back. Believe me: I will be back to take care of you."

He did not want to go. He wanted to lie down and rest. He felt the fatigue, two nights without sleep, two days of tension. And tomorrow, the journey south to the Villa. He just wanted to sleep for a time.

Manuela smiled at him solemnly and nodded. "Is Don Jaime coming today?"

And he knew she did not understand. His hand went to her cheek and he stroked it. He wanted to turn and run down the path to the foot of the mountain where the horses were tethered and beyond to where he would never hear this question again. But he held his ground. The hard training of the dead grandee governed the youth more completely than he knew. There was never any turning back. And as he looked into the innocent face of the girl, Juan knew he would never want to turn back, knew he had to go to fight at the Villa and return to Manuela because it was the only thing he wanted to do.

His hand brushed her hair behind her ears again. "Wait here," he said, as he took the path down the mountain toward Taos and the Villa. He was as trapped by his decision to live for this girl as her father had been trapped by his decision to die for another.

6

THE people of Santa Flora had finished their dance, buried the war dogs of Beatriz Ramírez, and gathered about the mission. They had been patient through the day. They had not disturbed their former mistress. In fact, except for the two young men stationed at the door to welcome her should she desire to come out, they ignored her completely. In the afternoon they took care to tear down sections of the walls of the compound which had been their prison since she had directed its construction years before. They had also destroyed the holy objects of the church which had been built with such loving care and ambition by Fray Julio Malindez.

Everything was being done which could be done to remove the stain of the Whitefaces from the land. The cacique with the welted face, whom Beatriz had beaten only the day before, was finding it difficult to hold the people back now that night had fallen again. As they all sat about the compound, lighted by the large fires made of the pew seats of the church, the piper was blowing his wild music on the reed pipe and the drummer was matching the rhythm with his sheep's-head drum. Several of the youths had brought out the old katchina masks and were dancing as they had not danced in almost a generation.

The tones were wild and climbed through the night toward the streak of moon. The horn headdress bobbed in the shadows as the delight-maker whirled about the crowd which stamped its feet to the hurried beat and the shrill pipe.

The sounds shook Beatriz Ramírez as she sat in her straight-back chair inside the mission and watched the mad shadows cavorting about the white walls of the room. She was alone as she had never before been alone in her life. She was frightened as she never before had had need to be frightened, though there was no question in her mind as she sat rocking to the noise outside in the compound that she had known fear before. She remembered when her father and his friends had found her in the bed of her brother Alverez, when the Inquisition accused her and Alverez of the theft of the church properties at Vera Cruz, when she had crossed the mountains with only Alverez, the dogs, and the black. She slammed her fist down on the arm of the chair. Damn the black. May his soul twist in Hell. May he know all the pains of loneliness and miseries of loss. May he feel the anguish she felt now that she saw the magnificent creation of the finest mission in all of Nuevo Mexico crumble before her eyes. May he feel the loss of a person who meant as much to him as Alverez meant to her.

Alverez. Alverez. Alverez. The time was almost here when they would meet again. She listened to the shrill temper of the piper and watched the leaping shadows and dreamed of Alverez. She and Alverez and the villa near Madrid where they would be waited on by the arrogant peninsulars, where hidalgos would seek to hold her hand and watch her dance, where beautiful ladies of the court would vie for the favours of Alverez and he would turn away and smile at her. Alverez. Alverez.

And all because of a black slave, an animal who could not feel, who could not know, who would never know what it meant to love. Her hand smashed down again on the arm of her chair and she rose to her feet. Her vast bulk filled the blue velvet dress she wore and as she walked to the window to look at the Indians, she smoothed out the broad skirt with one hand while the other seemed to be moving like a small dancer to the beat of the drum which backed the reed pipe. The wild scene in the burning courtyard silhouetting the frenzy of the copper animals beyond the window brought her back to reality. She could not step out there. They did not like her. They had feared her and because of this they hated her. She would have to wait. Fray Julio would come and with him would come soldados and they would punish the Indians. It was not her task. Not now. She would have to wait.

Her face showed large and white in the window and the dancers behind the katchina masks saw it clearly. Then the drummer saw it and then the piper. The music seemed to race faster and faster and the dancing youths matched its pace. Each circle spreading farther from the fires brought the young men closer to her door. The cacique seated on the ground knew that he would be able to hold them no longer. They would have their way. He rose to his feet, pointed to the door, and yelled loudly over the music. Church benches yet unfed to the fire were swept up in the charge across the compound as the puebleños hurled themselves in fury at the door. They fell back and hurled themselves again. Then again. The heavy door splintered and the people were in the room and dragging Beatriz Ramírez out into the courtyard where all could see her.

Then the cacique raised his hand and there was silence. Beatriz, held firmly by half a dozen youths, stared at him. She saw the streaks of raw flesh on his face and wished she could reach him again. But she could not. She wished she could strike her hands together and know the dogs would come. But she could not.

Then the cacique walked out of the courtyard of the mission and the people followed him dragging Beatriz Ramírez with them. They walked down to the edge of the great rio where they staked her out in the shadow of a cottonwood tree and they tore her clothes off her. And the young men used her.

There was no jubilation, no celebration, because to the Indians of Santa Flora the subjugation of Beatriz Ramírez was a solemn ceremony that involved the exorcising of evil by humiliation. Days later they set her on her feet and fed her, forced her to water flowers by day and dance by night. Their final rites would be performed only after a long time, and they knew just how long it was going to take.

7

FRAY JULIO MALINDEZ had hidden himself during most of the day in a small grove of trees near the rio. He had sat with his back against the trunk of a white fir and drowsed as the day became warm. Once he had walked with caution to the rio for a drink, but at the sound of approaching noises took cover again. From where he had lain stretched out on the ground, peering through a thicket, he had been able to see a mob of Indians hurrying south. He did not move for a long time after they had disappeared into the distance. Then he sat up against the tree trunk again and tried to plan a course of action. His decision of the morning to make his way to the Villa de Santa Fe was not going to be as easily fulfilled as he had thought it would be.

If there were Indians going south from this point, they might be gathering from other directions. The padre was frightened. After a time he could not understand why he should be, and he became calm again. He would by-pass the Villa, go overland, avoiding the rio trails, and come out to the south near one of the other missions. Because there was trouble in the north was no reason to believe there would be trouble south of the Villa.

Darkness claimed the land now, and though he was hungry and wished he had been able to sleep better during the day, Fray Julio rose to his feet, stared at the sky, prayed quietly for a moment, his hands saying his beads. Then he walked out of the cluster of small piñons and bushes, heading south and away from the rio. The journey was difficult for him. He had not exercised for years, had walked almost nowhere. He did not know the country he was in, and his youth in Mexico was so far behind him that he was having trouble locating the stars by which he had hoped to travel. After an hour, he sat down on a rock and wondered if the Indians would really attack a padre, a man of the cloth, one who had come to help them, had worked to save their souls. But what if he were mistaken? What if the revolt was against the soldiers and not the Order of the Friars Minor? He would look foolish, and Beatriz would laugh at him. And yet he had seen the dead soldier and he had seen the savages with war paint. He weighed his alternatives with what reason he could wearily muster.

Then he started walking again. There was moonlight enough to see the broken ground before him. Several hours later he paused a second time. He was hungry and tired and frightened. Twice he had seen rabbits break from high grass and cross his path in bounding steps. Once a hawk had swooped down a distance away and then risen shrieking victory to the sky with a field mouse locked in its talons. The tall, thin padre crossed himself and walked on. But now he was becoming increasingly conscious of his hunger. He stopped by a flat rock and seated himself, an incongruous silhouette against the Nuevo Mexicano night.

He had crossed country before, known the night trails, hunted, and survived. Raised on a small farm in Mexico, there had been little outdoors that he had not been able to accomplish. He tried to remember what he would have done in his younger years. But he had raised too many barriers against his past in his efforts to forget it, to build the mission which lay behind him now. He had trouble climbing the barricades of time and recovering the years between his youth and the present.

Once he could have snared a rabbit. Now he did not have the time. Once he would have constructed a bow and arrow and brought down game, but now he did not even have a knife. Once he would have run down a deer, now he knew he had let himself grow clumsy. The youth was gone and in its place was a stiff and spoiled padre used to being cared for. Now he did not have the comforts of a fine mission, war dogs, and Beatriz to protect him, and above all, he was alone. Alone with God. The words came to mind and he crossed himself.

Solitary and weary, seated on a rock in open country with mountains far to the west and the ridge of a butte to the east, Fray Julio for the first time in a decade had no one to look to but himself, no one to turn to, no one to blame. All of a sudden he felt ill. He wanted to fall to his knees and pray, but he knew it was not in him to pray now, or for himself. Aware that the view he had of the world about him was undulating and hazy, he could not bring himself to recount the ten years through which he had just passed. Not now. Not while he still had breath and hope and some little faith that those powers which had protected and shaped life to meet the needs of Fray Julio might only be resting from their labours and would soon be ready to take up the task of righting his domain.

He struggled to his feet and pressed on to the south. Once he stopped by a small tree, and stripping away the branches made a staff for himself. He did not waste much time in the task as he felt the need to hurry. He had a rendezvous at some distant place and he had no intention of being late. The future was shaped to serve him, and he was willing to let himself be used, as he always had before. And so, though he could not have explained his pace, it quickened and grew almost frenetic as he crossed open fields, the beds of small rios, and climbed the few hills which blocked his path to the place where God would organize the world to match the desires of the fleeing padre.

Whatever it was that had suddenly given the padre's flight direction and purpose drove him on through the night. He paused to drink from a small rivulet before he waded across it. He hesitated long enough to eat from a berry-laden thicket. He was hurrying on almost blindly when he climbed the small hill and started to descend its southern slope. There were no stars now. The sky was brightening in the east. The heavy fatigue he had known earlier was gone and he was staring at the sky when he tripped over a root and plummeted down the side of the hill. First, on his feet as he tried to keep them under him and failed. Then, sprawling face down, he slid and finally rolled to the bottom, his arms flailing, his legs askew. The dust-covered grey cassock settled over him and he lay still. It was several minutes before his eyes were able to focus on the hills in the distance and know the earth from the sky. Then pain wracked his body and he did not move as he tried to locate it. He reached out his arms to bring himself into a sitting position and found that only one of them responded. Surprised, he rolled over and looked at his left arm, limp and aching. Without moving his body he felt the length of the arm carefully with the other hand. It was broken, splintered. Bones had torn through the skin and his cassock sleeve was dampening with his blood. A crazy picture of himself seated opposite Beatriz at breakfast with the loose sleeve rolled back to keep it clean ran through his pain, and he thought for a moment of how he would clean the sleeve again. Then he realized this was not important. The broken arm was.

Slowly, he raised himself into a sitting position. With his right arm outstretched he felt about the ground near him for his staff and, when he did not find it, forced himself to open his eyes again. The staff was nowhere about, and so with his single arm he braced himself against the ground and rose to his feet. The splintered bones grated together and he shuddered. He wanted to scream, but no sound came from his lips. His tall, lean figure bent forward as he grasped his broken arm and pulled as hard as he could to separate the shattered bones. He dizzied and almost fell. His unguided feet shuffled under him and held him erect. Then he stood bolt upright and continued his walk.

He had lost time with his fall and feeling impelled to make up for the loss he hurried on. There was a meeting he had to attend, something unfinished he had to finish. Once he paused to try to recall what it was, but he could not. He was puzzled, because he felt the shock of the fall had driven the reason for haste from his mind. But he staggered on, a lean, dusty figure crossing the hills and open country west of the Rio del Norte on a mission just beyond his memory, to keep a rendezvous beyond his understanding.

8

MAESTRE DE CAMPO Ismael Pando had ridden through the night of August 10 and into the next morning. And everywhere he had ridden devastation scarred the land: pillaged haciendas, burnt crops, dead horses, and desecrated missions. Several times he had brought his small tropa to a halt, swung off his horse and paused long enough to bury a padre or a settler or his woman or a child. In all he could account for thirty dead. How many more had died in the vast area which stretched from the Pecos Pueblo in the east to the city in the sky called Acoma, he did not know. There were over eighty leagues between, and every Spanish stronghold he passed had fallen.

The soldiers who rode behind him were saddle-weary and anxious to return to the Villa de Santa Fe. So far as they were concerned, the message they had to bring the Governor was complete. But the Maestre de Campo galloped on. He approached Galisteo from the east, hoping to find some sign that the pueblo still held, but less than a league's distance away he saw a grey mound stretched out in a meadow. Again his hand went up, again two horsemen rode out a short distance to mount guard, and Pando dismounted. He rolled the gray figure over and recognized the face of Fray Fernando de Velasco, the padre of Pecos. There were four arrows in the young martyr's chest. Pando crossed himself and wondered how the body had come this far from Pecos, knew he would never find the answer, and as he remounted his horse he ordered two of the soldiers to bury the body.

Seated on his tired stallion, Pando slipped his hand inside his tunica and scratched at the itching scar. It was mid-afternoon now. The sun was high. The helmet seemed to be baking his brains. His aching body pleaded for rest.

When the padre was buried and a small cross of branches erected over the mound of loose earth, the soldiers knelt and prayed briefly. Then they turned to the officer who was staring at the sky to the west as though he expected to see something come out of it. The soldiers shifted their feet nervously, mounted their horses and waited for the old man to return to them. One of the tropa believed the old Nuevo Mexicano with the grey hair and silver beard was losing his wits. Only a fool would remain in this territory. Only a fool would continue to ride from pueblo to pueblo as though he were expecting to be greeted by a friendly face. The soldier would never have understood that it was exactly this which drove Pando on, this and the implications it held for him alone. Any other officer would have accepted the signs for what they were, but for Pando they were more than the signs of a rebellion. This was the world his father had journeyed to, this the world into which his mother had made the jornada del muerto—the journey of death across the arid lands of the south. For him and his it had always been hospitable. He was having difficulty understanding just what had taken place, just why the land and the People of his youth had risen up against him. And he felt they had risen against him—Ismael Pando. It was at him they had struck. What he had come to stand for and believe in had come under murderous attack. Looking down from his almost sagging horse, Pando did not feel that the Indians had committed treason, because treason is against a state. Instead, they had betrayed his love and friendship. And this to him at the moment was much worse. It was personal and not political. It was not the heresy and apostasy which crushed him, but the fact that they had rejected him.

Finally, one of the soldiers swung his horse up beside the Maestre de Campo. "We return to the palacio?"

Pando shook his head slowly, less in disagreement than to clear away his thoughts. He did not answer for a moment.

"To the Villa?" The soldier was more insistent.

This brought Pando to the present. "We ride to Tesuque," and he galloped off, expecting the others to follow him.

The soldier who doubted his officer raised his hand and shook his head. "That way is madness," he told his compañeros.

The others rode off behind Pando, the sceptic following.

Darkness overtook them before they reached the pueblo out of which they had ridden so assuredly only two days before. The blowing horses showed their fatigue and several times the men paused to walk and water them. At last, still some distance from their goal, Pando swung to the ground with a signal to the three who rode with him.

"You," he said, pointing to one, "will stand guard until midnight." He selected another. "And then you, until morning." Moments later, his helmet and his bucket boots beside him, Pando lay down on the ground under the blanket of his horse, tethered within reach, and went to sleep.

Shortly before dawn, Ismael Pando rolled over and looked at the sky. His back ached. He wished he were in his bed in the barracks with a pillow under his head. His tunica was rumpled and open and with the back of his left hand he rubbed his bulbous nose while scratching his chest with his right. He was an old man. Any more rides like these of the past week and he would have to resign from the army. Then he remembered why he was sleeping in the field and all of the scenes of tragedy which he had been viewing for days slipped by one by one and even closing his eyes did not stop the pattern. There was no resigning now. Probably never. There was war, and he was an old man who wondered whether he would live to see the end of it and what would happen to the province when it was done.

For Ismael Pando, this earth he slept upon was home. He sat up and took a handful of dirt in his fist and stared at it as it sifted through his fingers. Once, in his youth, he remembered his father saying that a man could feel the growing if the land were his own. Now the season was dry. The rains had been fugitive. What passed through his fingers was almost dust; there was no growing here. In disgust, he turned his palm over and watched the earth which remained blow away in the faint morning breeze.

The soldier who stood guard stared at the hoary officer, wondered briefly what was passing through his mind, wondered, too, what they were going to be able to do in Tesuque. But his curiosity vanished with the first rustle of grass near by and he turned to watch a rabbit bound through the field and away.

An hour later the detachment, mounted, tunicas properly buttoned, lances at the ready, found the Camino Real and galloped toward Tesuque. The small pueblo lay less than half a league distant and they were almost upon it when the shower of arrows scattered them. Pando waved the soldiers behind him to the cover of a small clump of trees and rode on. Arrows fell about him, shying his horse, bouncing off his helmet and breastplate. Still he rode on, until he came within calling distance of the plaza. Then he reined in his horse, raised one hand to his mouth and bellowed loudly, "I would speak with Fay-yat."

The arrows ceased falling. There was only silence. A hundred paces from where the horse stood were the remains of the low wall which once had surrounded the pueblo. The near-dry bed of Tesuque Creek ran south at Pando's left. Behind the wall and the stream he could see the communal houses. Not a person was in sight. Yet he knew he was being watched, knew, too, that a hundred bowmen were taking aim at his head.

From somewhere before him a strange voice asked: "What do you wish of the cacique?"

"I would speak with Fay-yat."

Silence again. Then Ismael Pando saw a horse swing out from behind one of the communal houses, trot through the opening in the wall, and approach him. The rider was Fay-yat. He wore a Spanish helmet, a sabre at his side, and a red altar cloth wrapped about his waist. The lance in Pando's hand came up slowly and then went down again. He had sought the parley. He could not break what might be understood as a truce. But the red of the altar cloth blinded him, and his left hand went to his face and he wiped it. Tension and anger squared his large jaw. An altar cloth for a sash. There was really no longer any need for a parley. No need to ask where the compañero of his youth had placed himself in the rebellion, no need to ask what had happened to the small mission building erected with such loving care by Pando's uncle only a generation before. Only one question needed asking now, and Pando knew that he was only asking it for himself.

Swaying from side to side in the unfamiliar saddle which betokened equality, Fay-yat approached the Spaniard. He knew that his own warriors were behind him and that the small tropa of Pando had taken cover in the clump of trees. He half feared that one of them might be carrying an harquebus, but he did not remember seeing it as they approached.

The two men faced each other now. Neither seemed to have anything to say, as each waited for the other to speak first.

"Why, old friend? Why?" Pando asked the only question that disturbed him, the only one he felt needed answering.

"Should I tell lies? Should I say it was the plot of others? Should I relate all of the ills which have befallen the People? If these things I must do, then you would not understand. You were born among us, but you were never of us. You rode a horse when a cacique would have been killed for riding a horse. You were only a soldado, but you gave orders to a cacique and his principales. You do not understand how the People feel about the rising of the moon or the death of a snake. I could not tell you why we have done what we have done, except that we had to do this thing."

The two ancient Nuevos Mexicanos, both darkened by the sun and whitened by age, faced each other across their own years and regretted that they had ever been friends, because now it was more difficult to be enemies.

"Should we meet again, amigo mio, I will kill you," Pando said. "I will kill you because you wear an altar cloth about your waist and because it is forbidden the People to ride a horse."

And as the Indian turned his stallion toward the pueblo, Ismael Pando spoke again, "But most of all, I shall kill you for what you have done to the province."

Fay-yat halted his horse, turned his head, "And I shall kill you for what your people have done to it."

Then each rode away thinking of what the other had said.

Ismael Pando and his tropa travelled the three leagues from Tesuque to the Villa de Santa Fe in less than an hour. As they approached the isolated capital, they raced their horses past the scattered Indian groups which were beginning to drift into the area.

Coming to a halt at the entrance of the casa real, the Maestre de Campo turned his horse's reins over to one of the sentries and walked down the corridor to the reception room of the Governor. Several civilians were lounging about, waiting for an audience. Pando nodded to them, knocked at the door of the Governor's office and entered without waiting for an answer.

Don Antonio was alone, seated behind the large writing table. His lined face revealed his fatigue and his cheeks were unshaven. He had not taken off his clothes for three days, three days of waiting. His lean hands were spread flat on a map he had been drawing up of the environs of his capital. The change which had come over him was apparent to his junior officer. Pando saluted and stood silent.

"Is there any area of the north now in our hands?"

"No, Excellency."

Otermín nodded. "Is there anything else I need to know now?"

Pando thought for a moment. The devastation, the bodies buried, the conversation with Fay-yat—these were all details. Suddenly they seemed unimportant because they no longer had relevance to the situation at the Villa itself.

"There is nothing else, Excellency."

Don Antonio stood up and walked to the side of the dark-faced Nuevo Mexicano, rested his back to the table and seemed to relax. The formality of his questions disappeared.

"Get yourself some rest, amigo. Dictate your report, and then come and have your noon meal with me. There is much we will have to do." He placed his hand on the older man's arm and turned to look up at his face. He saw the years and the disillusionment. "If I drive you hard, amigo, it is because I have great need of you. Madre España has great need of your years and your knowing."

The old man smiled. The ache in his back did not bother him as much as it had on the ride homeward. The pains of his legs were less important now. He drew himself upright. "Have we any word of Isleta, the Rio Abajo jurisdiction, the whole area south?"

"We wait. I have asked for support from Don Alonso García. So far we have not been answered."

Pando saluted and walked out of the office leaving the Governor with his problems.

Otermín watched the broad back disappear, the door close, and stood wondering for a moment if he should listen to the complaints. He knew of the half-dozen refugees who wanted to know why they had been asked to come to the Villa and abandon their haciendas before they were attacked, wanted to know what plans he had to protect them, wanted to know why they and their families had not been given better quarters in the casas reales, wanted to know what Don Antonio was going to do about punishing the Indians, wanted to know. . . The questions and complaints would stuff a full file of documents. Don Antonio knew it would be wise to record them so that each could be dealt with in its turn, and so that the small details would not take on greater proportions should the situation worsen and the report go forward that he had not even bothered to listen. So listen he must, for there would be no understanding of his problems in Ciudad Mexico. No clerk sitting behind a desk would realize just how unimportant all these questions and complaints really were in time of crisis. And no one was going to be sympathetic to the position of a governor and captain general who lost a province that was bigger than Madre España herself. Don Antonio braced himself and, walking to the door, flung it open.

"Gentlemen, you wanted to see me?"

Later, his hearings finished, he retired to his own sleeping room. He looked at his unshaven face and untrimmed beard. He should have known better. He should have remembered the signs and symbols of office. No commander should let himself forget details. There were extenuating circumstances, but he recalled the number of times he had denied these very words to subordinates, recalled his own discurso to the soldiers only a few weeks before. A few weeks? The meeting in the barracks seemed longer ago than that. How many of those men had died trying to carry his messages to the hacendados and Don Alonso? At the moment this was something he could not remember.

He unbuttoned his tunica and threw it on the bed behind him. His room had not been cleaned for several days. The decision to find other work, outside the palacio, for the Indian servants who tended his needs had been made for reasons of safety. He wished they were here now. The tunica needed to be pressed, his shirt needed washing, and there was the dirty linen on the bed. He stood for a moment looking at the bed, wanting to stretch out for a moment to relax.

It was almost time for the noon meal and there were plans to be made now. The Alcalde Mayors of La Cañada and Nambé would be joining him, along with Pando. He had called the meeting. He thought for a moment. Fray Pedro might as well know the situation. He crossed the room and opened the door to the corridor. A sentry stood at attention near the entrance of the building.

"Soldado, ask Fray Pedro Martínez to join us for the noon meal. Wait." He hesitated for a moment. "Tell him the Governor would appreciate it if he could join us."

That was better. He closed the door and stood with his back against it. He had to relax. The strain of the days and nights was no worse than he had faced before. He could remember. . . . He paused. He had to stop remembering. He was not that old yet, and if he was so old he could not think ahead but only behind, he should resign his command to someone else. This was a pleasant thought. He smiled to himself as he rejected it. Now that the luxuries of dreaming were over, he had things to do. He walked over to the small table that held his washbasin and found the pitcher beside it full. Someone was thinking of him. Fifteen minutes later he had completed his toilet, trimmed his beard, and dressed as smartly as he was able to. He was again the Governor and Captain General of Nuevo Mexico and not a tired old man.

He approved of what he saw in the mirror and joined the others in the dining room. When he entered, the two Alcaldes Mayores and the Maestre de Campo rose. He waved them back to their places. The meal was being served by the wives of several of the settlers. He smiled at them and took his seat at the head of the table. As he was sitting down, Fray Pedro hurried into the room.

"You sent for me, Governor?" The curt, efficient tone, confirming what was already known.

"I did, Padre. We must talk, and I think you should know the situation as I understand it."

The padre nodded his shaven head, pulled back a chair, and leaned forward at the table, ready to be informed. His quick, inquisitive eyes darted about to evaluate those the Governor had selected to meet with him.

The others waited until the Governor sliced his cold mutton, and then they proceeded to eat. Don Antonio set his knife down; the padre was staring at him. After a moment, the other three paused, and then Fray Pedro said grace.

Otermín listened patiently. There was no criticism, because the man was right. But did he always have to be so coldly correct? Perhaps he did. Maybe that was the same as his own holding of the soldiers in check.

When the others resumed eating, Don Antonio started to speak. "Do not let me interrupt you, gentlemen. I just want to have this opportunity to discuss our plight when we can do it without everyone in the Villa being aware that a meeting is taking place."

Luis Quintana, the eager Alcalde Mayor of La Cañada, looked up and grinned, showing several black teeth and a split lip. "I knew it was something important when you invited me, Your Excellency. Why, I told my wife, Don Antonio is a busy man, and if he wants to see me . . ." His voice trailed off as he saw the Governor was not listening but only waiting for him to be quiet.

There was a pause and Don Antonio became again the officer trained at the Academia de Madrid. "Gentlemen, our situation is almost impossible. We must defend the ground we are on, but it is not very defensible."

"We have cannon." The hopeful note was from the youthful, blond Alcalde Mayor of Nambé.

Don Antonio was patient. "Two fieldpieces almost a century old. They take a long time to load and can only strike a line about eight centimetres wide. Should an attack begin, we will be entirely encircled by thousands of Indians."

The young man pressed his point. "Not to question Your Excellency's opinion, but why were they brought here if not to be used?"

Holding back a sigh, the Governor answered him. "They are good weapons, if we have to take a fortification or break a siege wall. But we will be the besieged. The Indians will be attacking."

"But the cannon will kill? Is that not important?"

The little knowledge misused, and the Captain General waved it aside. He had not planned a debate or a lesson. "The enemy will be able to afford losses. We have at last count almost one thousand people here, but only a hundred able to bear arms, including four of us sitting here. With so small a fighting force, we should have facility of movement, but we have not. We are harnessed to the other nine hundred whom we must protect—your wives, friends, children."

Luis Quintana grinned. He believed he had a solution. "We could break out, attack. I say we could attack."

The Governor nodded. "I always approve of a bold stroke. Out of a hundred, how many would you commit to leave the cover of the buildings, and how many hold in reserve as some small protection for those not fighting, should your attack fail? Fifty? Ten? Would you want to leave ten, or attack with only fifty? And should we succeed, what would be the success? Break a part of the perimeter. If we followed up our attack and rolled back a portion of their line that will be tied about our necks like a copper noose, will the rest of them not swing back, close the line with their thousand to our tens and leave the attackers stranded outside the defence line?"

Quintana nodded. He approved the wisdom of the man who would lead them. But where was the answer? "We have horses?"

Otermín nodded. This, too, was important. "But now they have horses also. We must remember this. It will be important. Important, too, is the fact that we will be fighting in and about these buildings with little room to deploy, less to charge."

He looked about him. All of the men had stopped eating. Pando had said nothing. He was waiting. The Captain General knew this. And he knew, too, that he was going to disappoint the man who would expect a miracle of him.

"What is our goal?" Don Antonio finally asked, and answered the question himself. "We cannot conquer the Indians or destroy them in our present state. We have not the food for a long campaign and what we have will be drained off because for every fighting man we feed we need more rations for those not fighting. And the enemy will have no supplies we can capture. He does not think in those terms. This much I need not tell you."

"We cannot conquer. We cannot destroy the enemy in our present state." Pando repeated the verdict. It came with difficulty, because it left no room for miracles.

The Governor looked into the dark brown eyes set in the leathern face of the old warrior and nodded.

"Survival will be victory for us. We will do the best we can. Few men are born brave. We will have to believe that those with us have been so blessed. Novelty and surprise are almost our only weapons, God and courage our protection."

Then he faced the silent padre. "We will need your full support. Those not fighting will require all of the strength you can give them, and we must remember that for them the task will be the more difficult because their courage will not have the support and excitement of action which ours will have. They will need you, Padre."

Fray Pedro nodded, thinking as he listened of how he could best organize the women and children to help the soldiers—those who would be wounded, those who would need to be fed, those who would tend the animals. He nodded.

"There is much to be done." But he and the Governor were thinking of different things.

Don Antonio pushed his chair back and rose, stood over the others and smiled. "I wanted to be certain you knew the situation. I do not believe it is hopeless. How can it be? We are Spaniards." He raised his cup: *"Por Rey y Santiago."*

The others stood and joined him. When they were done drinking, he turned and looked at Luis Quintana. "What we have discussed must be kept between us. Even from Señora Isabella Quintana."

He smiled at the Alcalde Mayor of La Cañada, who grinned back.

As the others departed, Don Antonio took Ismael Pando by the arm. "Would you see that a complete inventory of food is made this afternoon?"

There were civilians present. The Maestre de Campo saluted. "Yes, sir."

Fray Pedro turned back. "Let me help you."

And as the padre walked out with Pando, Don Antonio could not resist a smile. This task the padre from Valladolid would accomplish better than any other person.

As he went down the corridor to his own office, the Governor recalled the words of Flavius Vegetius Renatus he had learned in his youth: "The good commander consults many and communicates with few."

So far none knew what he might do, what hopes he still held.

In his office an Indian stood waiting for him. Otermín stared at the man until he recognized him. This was one of the messengers he had sent out the day before to a quarter from which he believed he would receive some aid. "You have information?"

The Indian hesitated, then spoke. "The Tanos of San Marcos and La Cienega have revolted, Excellency."

Don Antonio stared at the man, who nodded as though to confirm his report. Smiling tightly, the Governor thanked him and closed the door behind him. He could believe him. His wife and children were in the Villa as hostages; he would not lie. Otermín walked to the window and stared into the plaza without seeing.

He had not communicated what hopes he still held. What hopes he still held. Only days before these very pueblos had warned him of the plot, and now they were in rebellion.

What hopes. What hopes.

Don Antonio picked up a piece of wax that lay on the window sill and warmed it between his palms as he realized that his only advantage now lay in the fact that he knew just how weak his position really was.

9

IT was August 12 and two days had passed since Lieutenant Governor Don Alonso García had returned to his home three leagues north of Isleta. They had been two days of waiting, waiting for word from Governor Otermín, waiting for an attack from the Indians. Warriors frequently passed within sight of the hacienda's defence, but they never tried to breach it. Several times, the small tropa had called to the Indians to engage them in parley, but each time, the black-faced men had either taken to the hills without a word or had merely moved away and settled down to watch the hacienda.

Don Alonso did not know whether he was actually besieged or not. His messengers were able to get through to Isleta to the south and return. But those sent to the north seemed to have disappeared. It was almost evening now and, seated on the portico of his manor, he tried drawing up a list of the soldiers whom he had with him and whom he knew would be available should he move to Isleta. The list was appallingly short.

There was no mug of liquor or brandy before him now. Despite the heat of the day, he was fully dressed in his uniform. A change had come over the Lieutenant Governor which surprised those who did not know him. Among those with him, Doña Josefa was probably the most confused by his manner. For he no longer drank or lounged half-dressed about the hacienda. He remained up late to check the small perimeter guard and rose early to apportion the food supplies. He regularly inspected the arms of the soldiers and their uniforms. He would permit no slovenliness and demanded an attention to details and a respect which only an old sargento would know.

Doña Josefa, seated near by watching the Rio del Norte flow thinly past, turned to stare at her husband. The pen he held seemed small in his huge hand, and the scratches of the point, already dulled, were the only sound. She thought of him as she had seen him the first time, a bandana about his forehead under a black helmet, bared to the waist, a bloody sabre in his hand, leaping over the wall of the Jamaican manor house where the English held her prisoner. He had paused to wave those behind him on; and when one young man had hesitated, Don Alonso had smashed him across the side of his head with the flat of the sabre, leaving the wet blood streaked on the youth's cheek. Then Don Alonso had laughed and pushed the youth before him into the fire of the English blunderbuses. Two men had fallen in the foray, but she never learned if the youth had been one of these. Over the years the question had often come to her mind. The grimy soldier she met that night had slaughtered the English landlord and his companions and allowed his men to rape the English women before he withdrew with her and his men to the small boat which had landed them. The soldier did not match the picture she saw before her of a serious and firm-handed commander.

Looking up from his papers, Don Alonso saw that his wife was staring at him, and he nodded to her. Then he cocked his head to one side as though he were listening. There was a noise from somewhere, but Doña Josefa could not identify it. After a moment García rose to his feet. "Some fool is getting drunk in the barracks."

And she wondered how he could tell what was taking place in the small adobe building behind the hacienda.

"That kind of laughter only draws arrows," he commented, as he strode off the portico toward the rear of the casa. Bewildered by his comment, she decided to follow him. She had always before avoided the barracks where his old compañeros slept and where he had bedded down Luis Granillo, the talkative Alcalde Mayor of Jemez, and the soldier named Reyes whom he had rescued two nights before.

As she walked behind her husband, Doña Josefa admitted to herself that she was interested in the peninsular, Reyes. In many ways he was different from the other soldiers whom she had met in Nuevo Mexico. Only the previous night, when Don Alonso had placed the man on guard in front of the hacienda, she had talked to him. The memories he had brightened of España remained with her. Reyes had known Córdoba and Sevilla and Barcelona and all of the places of Madre España that were important. And his contempt for Nuevo Mexico was as complete as her own. Granting the man was no hidalgo, he still came from a world she had known and a world she dreamed of returning to when this trouble with the Indians was settled.

Approaching the door of the barracks, Doña Josefa realized for the first time that she had made the decision to return to España. The bulking Lieutenant Governor who stood before her, his hands on his hips, was almost as old as her own father, and she knew no love for him. He had sought this when he first took her into his bed after the padre of Vera Cruz had married them, but as her disinterest made itself apparent, he had withdrawn from any regular relationship with her.

She came to his side now and stared into the darkness of the barracks building. This was the first time she had ever seen the inside of it. She knew that, only the week before, her husband had drunk himself unconscious here and that Nita and two of the soldiers had carried him back to his sleeping quarters in the hacienda. There were bunks along the walls of the room and a table in the centre. Reyes was seated here with a mug in front of him, and one of Don Alonso's old compañeros was standing beside the table, tippling from an earthen jug.

The Lieutenant Governor did not seem to notice his wife beside him as he looked about. Reyes saw him and raised his mug in a half-mocking toast while the other soldier set his jug down without a word. The room was quiet and Reyes failed to understand what was happening as he bent his head back to finish his drink.

With two long strides, Don Alonso crossed to the centre of the room and grabbed the skinny Córdoban by the collar and raised him off his seat to dangle before him like a doll. The copper mug clattered to the ground and Reyes started to curse. No one who knew who he was had ever dared lay a hand on him since his boyhood. He reached for his daga, and the open palm of Don Alonso smashed across his head so fiercely that the weapon fell to the floor. Then, while the Córdoban was still dizzy from the blow, Don Alonso carried him over to the wall where the clothes of the tropa were hanging from large pegs. He held Reyes with one hand while he hooked his collar over one of the pegs. His feet dangled several hands from the ground.

Then Don Alonso crossed back to the table, took the jug in his hand and hurled it against the wall above Reyes' head so that the liquor and shards spilled over him. To his old compañero, he only said, "Amigo. Amigo. Amigo. I have said we remain sober. We are in the midst of death. Many depend upon me, and I must depend upon you." Then he turned to Reyes, who was struggling to reach the floor. "I could have your life for reaching for that weapon. You are no soldado. But you will act like one when you fight under my command, or I will kill you the next time."

Pinned like a bug to the wall, Reyes' struggles looked ludicrous, and suddenly there was the stifled laughter of a woman in the room. Don Alonso turned to the doorway where Doña Josefa, startled, stood watching him. It was not she who had laughed. He stared from bunk to bunk. Finally, he walked over to one that was shaking and jerked the blanket off, exposing a naked girl. One hand grasping her hair and the other throwing the loose blanket over her shoulders, he hauled her to the window for a better look. She was the young wench with the long lashes and sad eyes to whom he had spoken two days before in the hacienda abandoned by his neighbour; one of the four women and nine children whom he had ordered taken to Isleta. Still holding onto her hair, he dragged her over to the table.

"Who brought her here?"

There was silence. Don Alonso turned to the girl. "I will turn you over to the Indians if you do not speak up."

The frightened girl pointed to the old soldier and Don Alonso hurled her at him. Crashing together, they fell to the floor, and looked up at him. Then the girl tried crawling away to hide under a bunk. García, planting a booted foot on her bare bottom, pinned her to the ground. Then he ignored her while he spoke to the soldier.

"From this dirt on the wall I can expect insubordination. He is an animal, but you, amigo, are a soldado. Dress this wench and send her to the kitchen, and should you want her after we have settled with the Indians, that is your business. But there will be no more drinking or wenching until we know if we live or die here. I must be able to depend on you, amigo."

Then he took his foot off the girl and turned toward the door. As he was about to depart, he looked back at Reyes and the other soldado. "Both of you will be on guard through the night. And remember well that I will check each post."

He walked past his wife and out into the fading sunlight. His temper was cooler now, and the only thing that bothered him was the idea that a soldier would reach for a daga when an officer corrected him. This was almost inconceivable. It was certainly something of which he would have to be watchful.

He paused and waited for Doña Josefa to catch up with him. When he had left the small barracks building, she had stood there for a moment until Reyes had struggled loose, reached the ground, recovered his daga, and stared cursing at the doorway through which his commander had disappeared. Doña Josefa did not blame him.

Reaching her husband's side, she did not say a word, and they returned to the portico. Only when they settled down again did he speak.

"The barracks is no place for a lady."

He would have said more, but a horseman rode up to the steps and dismounted.

Don Alonso left the portico to meet him. "From the Villa?" he asked.

"No, Your Excellency, from Isleta." García recognized the youth of Jemez who had brought him the first warning of the uprising, the same youth who had ridden with him on San Lorenzo's Day.

Taking the dispatch the young soldier handed him, Don Alonso suggested, "Change horses and return. You can wait until you reach Isleta to eat."

The youth saluted and walked his horse toward the stable, while García mounted the stone steps to the portico. There he lit a candela and sat down to read the carta. At last he looked up to Doña Josefa who waited for him to make some comment.

"From my son in Isleta. Will you fetch Nita?" And he turned back to the paper he held. Doña Josefa hesitated, remembered the lack of patience he had shown in the barracks, and disappeared into the house. When she returned with his mistress, García was folding the carta and looking out towards the rio northward.

Nita approached him, her hands still wet from the kitchen, her light dress clinging to her slim figure.

"There is word from the north?" she asked, as she saw the parchment in his hand.

García shook his head. She knew what was important. "From Miguel, your eldest. They are almost out of rations and there is much discontent in Isleta. He does not know if he will be able to hold them longer."

"Hold them?" It was Doña Josefa asking.

Don Alonso looked at her. "Hold them," he repeated. "Maestre de Campo Mendoza is inciting the refugees. They believe their safety lies in Mexico. They forget the Manso Indians to the south of them. They forget it will require many days' rations to travel that distance. And when they arrive at el Paso del Norte, they will remain a long distance from help."

"There is Fray Franciso Ayeta coming north with supplies."

He smiled at Nita. She would have made a fine commander. "If he is not delayed, if he does not turn back believing none of us remain alive."

"A rider should be sent south to alert him." Nita again.

García nodded and ran his hand through his greying hair. "In time. When we hear from the north."

"And if we do not?" The warning was from Doña Josefa.

It disturbed Don Alonso to be discussing such matters with her. Nita understood the problems, and after years of thinking aloud with his mistress, he was comfortable doing it. But Doña Josefa was different. She was a white woman, Spanish, and ignorant of the way to fight a war or rule a province.

"And if we do not hear from the north?" she asked the question again, and he turned upon her angrily.

"That is a decision. I will make it when I believe I should make it."

He rose to his feet and walked to the edge of the long stone stairway leading to the rio. If he withdrew to Isleta and the Governor attempted to reach him here, found the hacienda burnt out and believed him dead? If he withdrew and the hacienda were burned out, what of all his years of work? What of his dreams for his children, his and Nita's? When does a man abandon his life's achievements?

He stared at the rio while he spoke to the two women standing behind him. "We will wait until morning in hope that our people in the north still live and that they will contact us. In the morning I will decide."

But he had already decided.

10

THREE days had passed since Juan, war chief of Taos, had departed the area of the sacred caves about Arroyo Seco, and Manuela was still alone. She had found the first day restful. Sleep had come easily in the high cave where there were no animals to disturb her and only the sun looked down in the day and the stars and moon in the night. The food Juan had brought from the hacienda had been simple for her to eat even though she had never prepared a meal for herself. She did not know how to light a fire, and she had nothing to light one with. Juan had known this when he left her. A fire would send its mark against the sky, and the People would be curious to know who was in the Sacred Place when all the warriors were south at the Villa. But Manuela had survived without a fire.

When the light of the third day began to fade behind the distant hills, she felt the loneliness she had known the night she had fled her father's hacienda, and though Manuela had known loneliness all her life, this feeling was strange. In the past, there had at least been people about her. There had been Fray Vicente and the Indian women who worked at the hacienda, and there had been Juan. Now there was no one.

The girl sat on a rock beside the small stream falling off the mountain's side and stared at the distant valley. There was no life that she could see from her remote perch. There was no life in the sky, no birds leaving their faint tracks across the scattered clouds, nothing at all for her, and she wondered if Purgatory was always a lonely place. For Manuela did not know where she was. If she had journeyed through Hell, and in her own mind she was convinced that she had, then where she was now was different, and therefore Purgatory. It was not Heaven, because Heaven was a particular place where girls spent long evenings talking to their fathers, where Fray Vicente told people just how good young girls were, and where Juan came and sat with her. This was not Heaven and it was not Hell.

She took a small pebble and tossed it into the stream and watched it tumble over and over in the smooth bed of rock until it was forced off the mountain's side and fell without a sound into the gully below. She threw a second and a third. This was the only diversion she had found in three days, the only movement she had seen other than the water's, and it fascinated her. In the retreat from the world she had made inside her mind, this satisfied her for a long time, and it was dark before she stopped throwing the pebbles and watching them tumble. She rose and climbed to the cave where she had spent the two nights alone in the darkness, and as she stood in the entrance, darker than the night about her, darker than all the places of her old fears, she realized suddenly that the fears were gone. She did not know what she had done to Don Jaime, and she doubted if she would ever know. The punishment was here and now. It consisted of banishment to a high dark place; if it was to be no worse than this, she felt she would survive it forever and forever. She did not remember that her food was limited and that the nights grow cold. She only remembered the horrors of the Hell she had travelled and the fact that she had emerged to a different place, had found the punishment that fitted her sin. She failed to remember that Juan had found her and brought her here, that he had told her he would return. The hysteria she had known then had fallen away and left only a young girl numb to the world about her.

IT was now the fifteenth of August and for five days Don Antonio had waited in the casa real at the Villa de Santa Fe. No word came from Isleta. No word came from any place to the north which would lead him to believe that the Indians planned anything other than a direct attack upon his capital. Seated in his office in the palacio, he stared for the hundredth time at the small map he had drawn of the area about the Villa and recalled that each time he had sent someone out to reconnoitre the terrain, that person returned with the same report. Indians were gathered for almost a league in every direction, not in large groups, not in any military formation. Just Indian warriors, equipped and waiting, as he was waiting. Eventually they would weary of it.

Don Antonio did not fool himself with the belief that they had satisfied their desire for blood, for violence, and for desecration of the Church they had risen against. Once a people has taken to murder and rebellion, it must continue until it has torn down all of the standards against which it has rebelled, or those standards will eventually defeat them. Don Antonio did not believe the Indians were stupid. Wrong, yes, but not stupid. And so he believed they were aware that should they pause in their effort to eliminate him, he would have to turn on them and attempt to restore the power of España and the glory of the Church. He was committed to it. He had no alternative. And this left them none.

He reached for the list of supplies which had been left with him by Fray Pedro and Pando. It was complete in so far as it stated what was available to them, but it was not a very long list. He did not believe he had enough food for a week to meet the needs of the thousand men, women, and children filling the few small buildings of the palacio. There was little feed for the few cattle they had crowded into the buildings with them and even less for the horses on which so much might depend. Gunpowder was also in low supply.

And as he thought about it, Don Antonio realized just how wisely his opponent had planned the uprising. There were trained soldiers with Maestre de Campo Pedro Leiva, probably now at el Paso del Norte. There were probably arms and ammunition enough there, too, with which to crush a rebellion. But they were over one hundred leagues to the south, unwarned and probably unable to cross the country already in the hands of the Indians.

This Popé of San Juan had planned well. There was no doubt that he had taken these factors of supply and reserve troops into account. If he had struck earlier, Leiva would not yet have left the villa with the military escort. If he had waited to strike, Leiva would have returned with the supplies and the soldiers. Now twenty-seven men were too far away and too few to be a threat. It was all of a piece and neatly joined.

Don Antonio wondered about the medicine man. What was he like? What were his motives? What did he actually believe he or his people would gain? In Don Antonio's mind they were not necessarily the same thing. He thought, too, of Quintana who was reported to have driven Popé to Taos. And he cursed those who acted stupidly in his name. But his thoughts drifted back to Popé. Thirty years in the Indies, and Don Antonio had never met the Indian capable of organizing thirty scattered pueblos, winning their support, dealing with something as simple and yet as complex as the different languages which separated the Indian tribes of the region. He had never met such a man, and he would never have believed such a man would arise.

Popé's task of uniting the puebleños was, in Don Antonio's opinion, more difficult than Captain General Oñate's had been a century before when he had subdued the pueblos and taken the land by force with the blessing of the Church. It had been possible for Oñate to conquer the adobe towns one at a time with all the centralized strength of the army that he had moved north. Popé had created his weapon of small pieces and kept it dispersed while functioning as a single striking force. This impressed the soldado in Otermín. He was professional enough to appreciate the complex task. Popé had had to organize successfully under the very surveillance of the Spanish.

He tried to think into the mind of the native leader who had brought ruin to his career as soldado, administrator, and civil servant. But he could not tear away the years and cultures which separated them. He could not see the face of the man, let alone the the forces which drove him. And as Don Antonio tried and failed, he was aware of a sense of defeat, for at this moment Popé seemed to know more about him than he knew about Popé. Damn the fools who had brought this situation about. Damn the bumbling incompetence that had placed España in such a position. Then he turned on himself and wondered wherein he had failed.

Should he have travelled about the province more? Met the Popés? Listened to their complaints and let them work off their angers in words? He had never done this in any of his other posts. He knew no predecessor who had bothered to undertake such a means of administering this province or any other. It had been the custom to rule with a firm hand, with boldness and without regrets, since the time the first conquistador had set the banner of Isabel and Ferdinand into the sand of the first beach of the Indies.

There had been uprisings before. There had been guerrilla wars in the mountains of the lower America and the jungles of the central one. España had always been victorious in the final clash, and he knew she would be again. But in the interim, he was exposed on a defenceless frontier of an almost worthless land with a thousand lives in a few small adobe buildings and with insufficient food.

Don Antonio cursed his Lieutenant Governor for his slowness in responding to an appeal for help. Appeal? No, a direct command. He cursed himself, too, for failing to know this man better. What was going on in the south that they were not in touch with each other? What was happening in the pueblos below Galisteo? What had happened to the Fray Custodio? For the first time in days the lean face of the old padre came to mind. And Don Antonio wondered if his faith had served him as well as he had served it. He recalled how he had knelt and been blessed by the padre the last time they met, and he felt better for it.

The Fray Custodio and his assistant were very different men. The gaunt ancient was a symbol of the past, of the years of a growing empire and conquering for God, while his aide was nothing more than the efficent and passionless machine that had become the empire of both Church and State. And as he sat at his desk watching the room grow lighter, Don Antonio realized what it was about the young padre from Valladolid that annoyed him. While it might not be a fair judgment, the padre was cast in the same form as all the civil servants who had come to organize the empire of the Indies and Peru, to make it function more properly—the young men without hearts and almost wholly without daring or imagination.

Feeling uncomfortable in the realization that in labelling the padre's generation for what it was, he was at the same time placing himself with the obsolete, the builders, Don Antonio rose and snuffed the candle.

It was day and he had slept little through the night. Three times he had toured the guard which was mounted on the roofs of the houses, in the entrenchments which had been built in the past several days, and the fortifications he had directed made, literally, of the walls of abandoned buildings. The night had been quiet. He had no idea what the day would bring, but if Popé were as intelligent as everything seemed to indicate, then Don Antonio should not have much longer to wait, unless the waiting meant the depletion of his supplies. This idea had been with him through much of the night, and it worried him.

Well, it was time to check the guard again, change it, and rest as many of his soldiers as possible. Fewer men would be required during the daylight hours and more would be able to sleep. He shook his head to clear his blurring eyes, rose and poured himself some water from a pitcher on the table. He dipped his hand into the cup and splashed some water over his forehead and lids. Then he buttoned his tunica, slipped his baldrick over his shoulder, half pulled his sabre from its sheath to assure himself that it was readily available, and walked out into the morning.

It was quiet. There was very little breeze to stir the dust of the empty square. A few dozen persons could be seen sleeping under the long roof that overhung the front of the palacio. They were mostly younger women with their children, seeking what air there was. The few buildings were crowded with families and cattle, even some hogs and sheep. He did not blame the refugees for avoiding the crush and the smell of the casas reales as long as they safely could. One younger woman looked up at him and smiled. She was lying on the ground, a young girl asleep on her arm. A brightly woven Indian blanket from one of the western pueblos covered them. The Governor smiled back at the woman. He recognized her as one whom Fray Pedro had assigned the task of serving meals in the palacio. There were few idle hands in the Villa and Fray Pedro worked long hours to ensure that there were none.

The young woman brushed back her dark hair and Don Antonio noticed a series of scratches across her forehead. An eager soldier? He nodded to her again and strode into the centre of the plaza mayor. The casa de puta had been evacuated, and all the women who worked there had come under the watchful eye of Fray Pedro. They now slept in the stable where they worked at caring for the horses and crushing the corn into flour. If these same women had been peninsulars, Don Antonio wondered what tasks the padre would have found for them; then realized he was being unfair and rejected the thought.

Soldiers could be seen surveying the horizon from every roof. The old watchtower had been abandoned several days before as being too ready a trap for anyone using it. Otermín walked quickly to the first building in which he had hidden a cannon. Two sleepy refugees opened their eyes and looked up at him from where they drowsed on the floor against the wheels of the fieldpiece. Without a word the Captain General crossed the plaza mayor to where the other gun was sticking its ornate barrel out of the doorway of a low building. Here the civilian soldiers did not even bother to open their eyes when he approached. Don Antonio stared at them. Finally, shrugging, he walked back to the centre of the plaza. Should the occasion arise, they would awaken and man their guns. He was not as disappointed as he might have been under other circumstances, because he did not respect these cannon as defensive weapons. He was certain they had come off a galleon over a century ago. The ornamentation was naval—fishes and bare-bosomed mermaids, and from the history of the colony he had every reason to believe they had been dragged north by Oñate himself.

The women and children sleeping under the colonnade of the palacio and on the steps of the mission church across the way were beginning to fold their blankets and bicker with each other over who would use the water from the small ditch which carried it into the square and the buildings, and who would prepare the morning meal. Doors and windows were being opened in the few buildings into which others had crowded. One young boy led a horse out into the plaza, and Don Antonio could see that the beast needed exercising. He knew this was true of the other horses also. A pig broke from an open doorway and was chased through the dust by two young girls and the young woman who had smiled at the governor earlier. She won the race with a dive that ripped open the front of her dress. But she held tightly to the squealing swine until the two girls grabbed its ears. Then she stood up, brushed off the front of her skirt, wiped her hands and walked back into the house from which she had run, ignoring the torn bodice and the soldiers who were admiring her breasts.

The Governor saw the expressions on the faces of the men staring down from the walls and smiled to himself. Those who were not soldiers at least had some of the necessary attributes. Now if they had others. . . The idea trailed off in his mind as Pando approached him from the officers' quarters.

The broad shoulders of the man shifted back and forth as he seemed to be scratching something inside his tunica. Otermín laughed at the familiar gesture as he looked at the man from his polished bucket boots to his sooted helmet. This was a soldier. He might not have the vision of some or the imagination of others, but a commander could depend upon him. Maybe this in the final judgment was what one wanted from a man in a uniform. All of the rest of the qualifications, he thought, could be dispensed with in a crisis.

He returned the Maestre de Campo's salute and waited for him to speak.

"Your Excellency, the Indians we have captured—the two from Taos that we brought in on the ninth. I have been wondering. . . ."

Don Antonio watched the man rub his nose with the back of a broad hand as he spoke. The two Indians. They seemed unimportant now. "We will hold them. Maybe we will be able to trade later for some of our own people. Maybe there will be something we will want to know from them."

Pando looked into the dust at his commander's feet for a moment. "Begging Your Excellency's pardon, but no Indian would let himself be traded off as a prisoner. It would be a disgrace. And there is really nothing more they can tell us. The knowledge they had two days ago, we have now."

Otermín knew what he should say, knew that there was no reason for keeping the men, wasting guards watching them, or for that matter, the two runners who had first brought the warning. Now that their pueblos had joined the rebellion, releasing them would only mean strengthening the enemy. There was very little choice in the matter. Before he could make his decision, the sargento who had been placed in charge of the line to the south of the Villa approached with two Indian runners.

"The two you dispatched for the Tanos and Queros jurisdiction yesterday," Pando identified the messengers.

The Governor sighed as he nodded. It had been a desperate chance, but he had hoped that there might be one Spaniard left alive somewhere in that vast area.

The Indians came forward with the sargento. "Question them," Don Antonio directed Pando. Then he waved the sargento back to his post. And as he listened to Pando interrogating the Indians, the statement he had made at lunch three days before ran through his head: *Survival would be victory.*

Finally Pando was done and waiting for his commander to listen. Otermín looked up.

"They have a report?"

The officer nodded.

"Bad news?"

"Yes, Your Excellency."

The Governor stared at the two Indians and saw both fatigue and concern on their faces. "Do we need these two men any longer?"

"I do not think so, Governor."

"Thank them. Tell them to get some food and rest. We may need them again before the day is over. We will discuss what you have learned in my office."

He smiled at the Indians and turned to walk across the plaza to the casa real, when he saw that all of the men on the roofs were watching him intently. Suddenly, smiling broadly, as though pleased about something, he swung back toward his aide. "Direct the Indians to smile and tell no one what they have learned."

With those words, he departed. The sentry standing guard at the door of the palacio came to attention, and the Captain General was pleased to see that his tunica was buttoned. Discipline and morale are made up of so many little things.

Five minutes later as he settled down at the table in his office, Pando entered the room and closed the door behind him. The Governor looked up expectantly.

"Five hundred Indians. The pueblos of Los Pecos, San Cristóbal, San Lázaro, San Marcos, Galisteo, and La Ciénega. Now less than a league south of us. They said they were coming to attack this Villa, destroy the Governor and all the Spaniards so that the whole kingdom will be theirs and that they might profit at our expense."

Don Antonio was silent.

"They say that God and Santa María are dead, that we were the only ones that worshipped them, and that their own gods never died."

Both men crossed themselves.

"They are led by a young man from Galisteo—Askon. They plan to meet with the people of Teguas, Taos, and Picurís. They believe they can sack the Villa, kill Your Excellency, the religiosos, and all the other Spanish."

The pendulum of the clock on the table clicked each time it reached the end of its arc. Don Antonio caught himself listening for the faint metallic snap and knew that he was pushing back the thoughts which were crowding in upon him. There was a small dripping of wax from a candle on the table, and picking it up between his fingers, he slowly rolled it back and forth.

Looking at the berry wax in his hand, Don Antonio started to speak. "They can cover a league at any pace they select. We may face them today, or they may wait upon their allies. See that every man is armed and ready to fight from this moment on. Kill the prisoners. Place the guards in the entrenchments. Clear the plaza of anyone not fighting. I want to see no women or children on the roofs or even in the areas between the buildings. Move as many of them in here as can be crowded in. Jam them in. Make them leave their belongings outside, but get them in here."

He stood up and fatigue swelled over him like a wave of tropic air. "Keep me informed of any problem. Assign a runner to be with me at all times and keep one with you." His face set into a smile as he flicked the berry wax across the room.

"We fight, amigo. They will soon learn whether they have killed God and Santa María. They will know what it is to face a Christian and a Spaniard. We will teach them, amigo."

He squeezed the arm of the old man affectionately. "Smile, amigo. If there is to be a miracle, it will be our miracle. Take care of relieving the guards and gathering the families. I must speak to Fray Pedro about abandoning the church."

He closed his eyes for a brief moment to comprehend all that that meant.

Then his shoulders settled back, and he walked out of the palacio and strode across the plaza mayor to the church.

When Don Antonio left the church, Fray Pedro preceded him with two refugee women carrying the holy objects. Looking about the plaza mayor, Don Antonio's professional eyes evaluated the situation. A few women were to be seen scurrying to the palacio. Several soldiers were resting on the roof, their harquebuses leaning against their knees. Two boys stood flicking stones through the dust, raising small white clouds as reward for their efforts. Otherwise, there was quiet and waiting. A moment later the boys ran into the palacio. When Don Anotonio turned back to the padre and his assistants, they had already disappeared.

"Excellency. Excellency." The call broke, worried and loud, across the plaza, and Don Antonio looked up to the roof of the casa real where three guards stood pointing to the south. Turning about, the Governor saw nothing.

He looked back to the sentries for an explanation.

"Indians. Hundreds of Indians, Excellency."

Don Antonio quickly climbed the ladder and joined the men on the roof. To the south of the capital he could see a small army of Indians crossing the maize fields of San Miguel. Some were carrying harquebuses. Others, bows and arrows. Among the disorganized horde were several Indian horsemen with Spanish sabres. On the outer edges of the plain of Las Milpas de San Miguel, Don Antonio saw the Indians lighting torches. The oncoming enemy paused only to pillage the empty houses that stood in their path and set the torch to them.

Making a quick estimate of the strength of the horde, Don Antonio called for Pando. The Nuevo Mexicano was located trying to calm the fears of an old Spanish woman who stood on a near-by roof watching the house in which she had borne her children flare up in a large orange flame toward the early morning sky. By the time Pando finally reached his side, Otermín had made his decisions.

"There are five hundred—more or less—out there. Take twenty-five mounted men and feel them out. See if we can talk to their leader. Perhaps he will parley. I want to talk to him. In any event, keep them talking until I can organize an assault team here." He spoke with forced calm and firmness. "Move, amigo."

Pando looked for a moment out into the field, knew the Indians coming from the south had already passed the home that had been his own, crossed himself without thinking, saluted his commander, and disappeared down the ladder. In less than ten minutes Don Antonio saw the horses brought out of the stables and houses in which they had been lodged, saw them saddled and mounted by the small company selected by Pando. He looked over the tropa from his vantage point and nodded his approval. Pando had selected the alcaldes mayores of half a dozen pueblos for support in his conference. He had also taken only half of the professional soldiers with him, completing his numbers from the armed civilians.

Twenty-five men riding out to parley with five hundred. These odds did not disturb the Governor. Spaniards had faced worse. What kept coming into his mind was the picture of a second column of Indians making their way south from Taos.

"Notify me at once if anything happens out there—any fighting, any change in the strength of the Indians."

With those words he climbed down the ladder and went into the palacio, ignoring the guard at the door. An instant later he came out again.

"Soldado, bring in all the sargentos from the entrenchments, from the roofs."

As the man was about to set his heavy harquebus down, Otermín shook his head. "Men have died because they were unarmed in a fight." And he watched the soldier place his weapon on his shoulder and depart.

The time was now. Don Antonio felt more relaxed than he had through the night or even in the days just passed. Now he had something to do. Now there were decisions to be made which he knew he would make as wisely as any man in the Indies.

He re-entered the palacio and had to push his way through the mass of women and children who filled every room. Some few were crying from fear while others sat calmly with their backs against the dusty walls, fanning the flies away. Two infants were weeping hysterically in the strange surroundings. One stolid-faced mother was nursing an infant from a full breast.

Don Antonio, wishing he could say something to comfort them, stood for a moment looking for Fray Pedro, then went into his office. A squinty-eyed soldier was seated in his Savonarola chair. On his lap was the young woman Don Antonio had seen chasing a pig earlier. The front of her torn dress was pinned together now, and the soldier was trying clumsily to remove the pin. He focused with difficulty on his commander. Stumbling up from the chair, he pushed the woman away from him.

The pressures against the walls of Otermín's head broke as he lashed out an open palm and struck the squint-eyed trooper across the face. The instant he did this, he regretted it. An officer punishes a man, but he does not strike him. That privilege is reserved for sargentos. The young woman slipped out of the room unnoticed as the two men stood facing each other.

"Get to the stables. Saddle up twenty-five more horses as quickly as you can. Tell the men stationed there I said it is to be done at once and without wasting time, without diddling any more women."

The soldier rubbed his cheek, cocked his head as though to see more clearly as he saluted, and walked out. As he was about to leave the room, the Captain General called to him:

"Soldado. The next time you are found with one of the women who have come here seeking protection, I shall hang you."

"Yes, Excellency." Again the salute and then flight.

Despite his disapproval of his own loss of self-control, Don Antonio felt better for it.

The tropa of Maestre de Campo Pando rode quietly out of the plaza mayor. Each man assumed his position in a file behind the broad-shouldered officer, except for the two sargentos whom Pando had selected to ride about twenty varas to the right and left of the column. Once they reached the open fields to the south, Pando's hand went up and the riders stretched out in a double line. The sargentos moved out almost fifty varas from their commander. They rode directly toward the Indians on the plain of maize. Pando was able to make out the black-streaked faces and the Spanish clothes worn by many of the marauders. He could see that a large number of the Indians had abandoned macanas and obsidian swords for steel-bladed machetes and Spanish sabres. Several armed with harquebuses pointed them at the approaching tropa. The Maestre de Campo smiled inwardly at the surprise these untrained men would get should they attempt to fire the weapons from their hands. There were more firearms, however, than he had expected; and he waved his men to spread out to allow more room between horses and remove the ready target of a close formation.

As the Spaniards approached the horde, three Indians on horseback rode to the front of the milling natives and raised their hands. One of them, apparently the leader, carried an harquebus resting on his stirrup, a long sword swinging from his waist, and a daga with a silver handle stuck in a red taffeta sash. A heavy leather tunica covered his otherwise bare shoulders. Pando crossed himself as he recognized the sash as being from the missal of the convent of Galisteo.

A distance of fifty varas separated the two leaders as they reined their horses to a halt.

Remembering how his Captain General would act, the old soldier raised his arm. The men behind him halted. Then he waited. Let the Indian speak first. Let him have his say and then know where the rebel stands. Otermín's orders were to keep them talking. Let them talk.

He did not have long to wait. The young war chief turned to his companions who dropped behind as he slowly paced his animal forward. Then he addressed the Maestre de Campo.

"We have killed all the Blessing Men and the Spanish in our land. Now we have come to destroy you."

He spoke in Spanish, almost out of condescension.

Ismael Pando raised his helmet from his head and scratched his white hair in complete disdain. Then he answered the Tanoan in his own tongue to show that he understood the man better than he thought.

"Who is boasting so loudly about killings?"

The Indian sat upright in his saddle. His shoulders quivered, and for one instant his horse shied and almost threw him. All of the youth's uncertainty displayed itself before it could be covered again.

"I am Askon of Galisteo. And we do not boast. We do not fear the White-faces or their gods any longer, for we have killed their gods and many of the Whitefaces, and we have come to kill the rest."

The words tumbled forth in Tanoan like a ritual. What we have done and what we will do. Pando had been part of too many war parties in his years not to recognize the pattern.

"You sit there on a horse which you have trouble riding and tell me you are not afraid?"

Askon laughed softly. "The old Spaniard with a face like red clay wants to fight me?"

The elderly Nuevo Mexicano weighed this possibility and then rejected it. Even if he won, there were too many men behind the Indian, as well as too many people behind himself who depended upon the Governor's hope for a parley.

"If Askon of Galisteo is not a coward, he will come to the Villa and talk to the Señor Governor and tell him what he has just told me and let the Governor tell him what he is prepared to do with those of the people who have risen against the King and God."

One of the warriors behind Askon carefully levelled his bow at Pando's chest. Without turning his head the Spaniard directed the men behind him: "Rest easy. Do not take to your weapons unless they strike."

Then he looked at the bowman while he spoke. "Askon may be afraid or he may not be, but his people are afraid for him."

The war chief whirled about, spoke quickly to the man with the bow, and then rode forward.

"I will talk with your Governor. But while I talk with him, three of your men will wait for my return."

The Maestre de Campo selected the three closest to him.

"You will wait."

The others he waved back with him as he turned to the Villa. The Indian, Askon, rode beside him, his unsaddled horse capering under the strange hand that held it in check.

Shortly afterward, the cavalcade of twenty-two mounted Spaniards and their Indian enemy rode into the plaza. Pando saw harquebuses aimed from the roof tops, noted the manned cannon through the shadowed doorways, and the twenty-five freshly mounted soldiers waiting in a line. The Captain General stood beside the colonnade of the palacio, fully armed with his ornamented breastplate, helmet, and lance. Two short daggs were thrust in the sash at his waist. He watched his reconnaissance party approach and walk out into the plaza to meet them. The Indian looked down at him until Pando signalled for him to dismount. Askon looked about the plaza. He missed much of what the Maestre de Campo had seen, but he was aware that there were almost fifty armed Spanish horsemen about him and so he, too, swung to the ground.

The other riders remained in their saddles as the Governor led the way into his office. For the sake of display he had cleared the passageway of women and children as soon as he had been notified by the guards on the roof that Pando was returning. Once inside the office, he seated himself at his large table and sat staring at the Indian youth. The red taffeta sash inflamed the old Christian, but he held his temper and his words for the moment.

It was the uncomfortable Indian who finally asked, "Your man said you wanted to speak with me."

Otermín listened carefully. This youth spoke Spanish better than most. "You come from . . . ?"

"Galisteo."

Don Antonio tried feeling the young man out. "And you know the family of Don Pedro de Leiva, the Maestre de Campo?"

Askon's hand went to the sabre at his side and he rubbed his palm over the floral-patterned hilt. "I have known the family of Don Pedro a long time."

"And he never hurt you or your people?"

The Indian started to smile. There were things he would like to tell this man who sat behind the large desk, things about a girl named Concepción and a soldado who had married Don Pedro's niece, and about another girl named Dorotea who was of the family of Don Pedro.

"That matters for nothing now. As I told him," pointing toward Pando, "we have killed all the other Spaniards and the men of the shaven heads and the women and the little ones even at their mothers' breasts. The People will destroy the Villa and those we are waiting for will join us in destroying it, unless you leave."

It was a long speech and he paused for time. Don Antonio knew nothing more than when they had begun, but they were talking. This he felt was important.

Then the young Indian reached inside his red sash and threw two small crosses on the table before the Governor. One of the crosses was red and one of them was white.

"Select the white cross and let us know that you will abandon the kingdom of the pueblos, will go south and not return. Select the blood cross and we will destroy you and the soldados with you and the padres with you and the women and the children, and we will tear down your buildings and burn the kivas of Jesus and Mary."

The two small crosses covered a portion of the map of the environs of the capital which Don Antonio had drawn with such care only days before. He stared for a long time at them. Then he pushed both of them back across the table.

"This is all very foolish. We do not want to fight a war. We would win, but we do not want to fight. We did not seek a war. Nor will we turn from one that is thrust upon us. Better your people go home quietly and your allies return on the path they have taken. I promise you that there will be a pardon for the crimes, the deaths, and the atrocities you have committed, even for the acts against God and Santa María, who can never die for they are forever. For you are baptized Christians and you cannot forsake obedience to God and to His Majesty who rules over the province of Nuevo Mexico."

Otermín rose to his feet, acting as though his suggestion had been accepted. "Let us drink to forgiveness as good friends."

The palm of Askon was almost torn as it rubbed back and forth over the rough hilt of the sabre. "I will go back to my people," was all he said as he turned and walked out of the room.

"And my proposal?" Otermín asked.

There was no answer other than the heavy tread of the bucket boots the Indian wore over his bare legs.

The Governor looked at his aide.

"Escort your three men back. No Indian is worth three Spaniards."

"What do you think the answer will be, Excellency?"

Don Antonio sighed, flicked another piece of berry wax off his table top and stared at the two crosses which rested before him. "I do not know."

Shortly afterward, standing on the roof of the building, he received his answer. Pando, making his way back with the three hostages, heard it too. There were loud shouts and trumpets blowing in the Indian camp. Then the bells of the hermitage of San Miguel in the Little-Suburb-Across-The-Water which had been the residence of the Villa Indians began to peal loudly. Turning in his saddle, the Nuevo Mexicano saw the first flames of that district reach for the sky, and then a bright flash of red covered the hermitage itself. From his position on the roof of the palacio, Don Antonia saw that the Indians were readying themselves for attack.

The Captain General closed his eyes for a moment. There was no alternative to the decision he had to make. The sargentos had been briefed. Pando and the alcaldes mayores knew their responsibilities. Vegetius, the old Roman tactician, came to mind again, as he always did when the campaigner in Otermín came forth. Vegetius said and Vegetius said. *Do Not Fight unless Your Soldiers Have Been Tried.*

Don Antonio opened his eyes and looked at the small band of fifty mounted horsemen staring up at him from the plaza mayor. Their horses were rested, their equipment the best he could find in the royal stores. Pando had now rejoined them with the three hostages. There was no reason to wait. But for an instant Don Antonio wanted to climb down from the roof on which he was standing, mount his own chestnut stallion and lead the attack. But Vegetius again—and common sense: *Good Officers Never Engage in General Actions unless Induced by Opportunity or Obliged by Necessity.*

"Officers, sargentos, soldados," he called loudly and drew the attention of the fifty mounted men. "You will attack at once and dislodge the rebels from San Miguel. We must act now before their allies join them. We can defeat them. We must defeat them. We will defeat them. Now. *Por Rey y Santiago.*"

Lances and sabres slashed the bright air of the morning as the cry was picked up and carried across the plaza over the Villa and down toward the small stream which separated the Spaniards from their enemies.

Por Rey y Santiago!

Horses trembled and burst forward under the guidance of skilled riders. They raised a cloud of dust down el Camino de San Francisco and poured onto the open ground to the south.

Stunned by the cry and the sight of the horses in attack, the Indians hesitated momentarily, and then, urged on by their leaders, they flung themselves toward the onrushing tropa. The two bodies of men, the copper-skinned Indians, breech-clothed and partially armed with pilfered weapons, and the Spaniards, mostly civilians armed for the first time, met on the plain of maize. They came together in a crush of bodies. Sabres, machetes swinging. Lances thrust and drawn and thrust again. Helmets ringing with the clash of steel on steel. Screams of anger and yells of pain. Call of exhortation in Tanoan. Cries *Por Rey y Santiago* in Castilian. Sudden stifled gasps and sabre-splintered heads. Slashed bellies open to the sun and flies. Frightened squeals of horses. And the soft sighs of dying men, chests pierced with silver-mounted lances. The sudden and frightening explosion of a Spanish dagg blowing open the chest of a startled youth in a white breech-cloth, head wrapped with the red velvet of an altar piece. The sick belch of a rebel trampled under the iron hooves of a cavorting stallion. Battle, sudden, violent, and without quarter.

A lance jerked back and blood flowed. A blind swing and blood spouted from a sabre-severed arm. The Indians were battered, bruised, and dying, but the Spanish stumbled back and back again. Pando felt his horse shoved almost to the ground, heaved his lance at a bare copper back, and drew his sword. His dented breastplate took a blow from a war club and he thought his ribs were shattered. Still he yelled above the battle sounds, encouraged his men and knew he was killing blindly, almost stupidly, unaware where his blows were falling, unaware what lives he was taking or if his horse would stand in the press about it. It had come to this. It had come to this. It had come to this. Each time the thought ran amok through his wearying brain, he slashed upward and down and sideways, rarely aiming his stroke, always hitting something, withdrawing and slashing again.

He did not hear himself scream as a sabre struck at his face and he twisted sideways to avoid it, bringing his sword hand up. The Indian sabre clattered over his legs, still clutched by an armless hand. His pantalones were soaked and slippery with blood. Twice his horse went to its knees and twice he forced it upward with a strong hand on the bridle. He was tiring. It was more than age and violence. His very body was repulsed by the sickening stench rising from the field of whirling bodies. The pain in his chest crept down to his loins and through his huge, heaving shoulders, and he retched across his saddle into the face of an Indian attempting to pull him to the ground. The startled painted warrior hesitated and was dead from the forward thrust of a bloodied sabre.

Still the Indian line held and would not break. The horde was one amorphous beast, no head to sever, no single part sending its pain and anguish to a central nervous system, and so it pushed on and forced the Spanish back.

The Governor saw his faltering tropa, saw the ferocity of the Indians, and told his messenger to sound the trumpet. There were only fifty more Spaniards under arms, only fifty more to commit and if they were lost, it was over, finished and done. But better to die here with some opportunity of success than wait for the reserves of the enemy to gather and throw themselves into the battle. Don Antonio swung himself down from the roof as he saw the Indians were capturing the houses closest to the Villa, moving into the protection of them and the entrenchments he had hoped to defend.

His chestnut stallion waited beside the soldiers already mounted. Without waiting for amenities, he swung himself into his saddle, took the lance which was proffered him, pointed to a pock-faced sargento.

"Take nine men on the left of the column. Stand back and defend the palacio to the last of your breath. Wives and children are in there."

He turned to the men about him. "You are fighting for your own, for Madre España and for God. Remember that you are Spaniards, as Cortés was a Spaniard, as Pizarro and Alvarado were Spaniards." Then he raised his lance with one hand, lowered his helmet to cover his forehead and shouted, *"Por Rey y Santiago!"* and led the small charge out of the plaza.

Vegetius again and again: *Good Officers Never Engage in General Actions unless... Obliged by Necessity.*

The first impact of their charge hurled the Indians back for a short space, but the strength of their numbers recoiled, and for the next hour the battle swayed back and forth. Several times Don Antonio thought he had broken the enemy horde, believed it would turn, but each time it finally held and pushed him back again. The sun rose high and the heat of the day pressed down on both the rebels and the defenders.

Askon, astride the large sorrel that had been Don Juan de Leiva's, stood back from the fight and drove his men on. A straggler fell by the way from sheer fatigue, and the Indian youth, riding up, trampled the man, to show those under his command the result of failure. But for all of his exhortation and all of his sudden appearances in those parts of his disorganized line that were about to crumble, Askon felt the victory was ebbing away from him.

Then the rain came.

It burst forth from an almost clear sky and showered down on the whirling, driving horsemen and the barefooted rebels. It slithered off the sun-hot helmets and pelted the steel breastplates. It streaked the charcoal paint on the faces of the Indians and blinded the horses and riders. It sogged the ground, made footing unsteady, and softened the earth beneath the heavy horses' hooves. It splashed over the maize, flattened by hundreds of fighting men and struggling horses, turned the entire battleground into a churned mass of slippery stalks and mud. It mixed with the blood and the hacked limbs on the burning ground and rose back into the nostrils of the Spanish soldiers and Indian warriors like the stench of Hades. Men retched, swallowed their vomit or got rid of it, and fought on in the rain.

But the rain made a difference.

The caciques who stood at Askon's side pointed to the sky and wept. The Sun Father had remembered the People—the Earth Mother and the Corn Mother had not forgotten them. The People had not been deserted. They were not abandoned. Their rejection of the false gods did not mean they stood alone and godless. The old strengths and the old ways would return with rain for the maize and the green springing fresh from the land.

Askon called to his warriors, and shouting above the crash of steel and obsidian sword told them the meaning of the rain and smiled, because he believed.

Don Antonio, horse's shoulder to horse's shoulder with his aide's, drove hard to hold his ground and overwhelm the copper enemy. To him the rain came only as relief from the heat of the sun. The sabre in his hand became heavier, the breastplate clumsier, and he wanted to reach up and shove the steel helmet back so the cool waters could drench his face and hair. But he knew better, knew he could not afford the time to catch his short breath, wished he were younger, and admired the incessant drive of the older man at his side, who swung and swung again with his reddened blade, almost in madness, certainly without knowing any longer what he was doing.

The day became a blur in the eyes of the Captain General; twice he fell back out of the fray, found the rebels pressing him each time, was aware that he was their target, and returned to the safety of the numbers about him. He wanted to think, but was no longer able to do more than swing his sabre, guide his horse, and pray meaninglessly under his breath.

It was late in the afternoon when Askon pulled half his warriors back in an attempted ruse. He would stand his bowmen apart and scatter the Spanish with arrows. The battle was not going in his favour, nor was it going against him, but the losses that were sustained were his losses. His people lay scattered on the ground, trampled underfoot, bleeding, gored, and dying. By the grace of their armour, their superior arms, and the boldness of their efforts, the Spanish still fought without loss. Several of the Whitefaces were now on foot, others were without helmets, others nursed wounds which should have felled them, but they fought on. The Indians were forced out of the few houses into which they had entered and were again in the open field.

Askon had to make his attempt. It was too simple.

And it failed.

The instant the weight of numbers was withdrawn from the battle so that the bowmen could take their positions, the Spanish surged forward, split the group that remained to face them into small units and chopped them to pieces with sabre and lance. Seeing what was happening to their comrades, the bowmen started to fall back, fearing a cavalry attack, fearing to take the stand for which they had been selected, and in that brief instant, Don Antonio charged, waved his bloody sword over his head, and urged his men forward.

He was no longer thinking in terms of maxims. Vegetius said . . . and fuzzily it staggered about in his head—it was something to do with opportunity being more important than courage. But a battle required everything for only one end—total destruction of the enemy. His horse stumbled over a body. He pulled it up from its knees and plunged on toward the copper backs which were turned to him.

Then he heard the cannon in the Villa behind him.

He reined his horse and whirled it about as his command poured past him after the Indians. The cannon again and the sound of an harquebus.

Standing high in his shoe stirrups, Don Antonio de Otermín scanned the Villa. A thousand Indians were swarming down the hills from the north. For one brief instant he swayed in his saddle as though he were going to collapse. Then he raised his voice to a loud yell:

"Spaniards, to the palacio. To the palacio. To the palacio."

Waiting only to see that the unhorsed men mounted behind their compañeros, Don Antonio led the way back to the Villa. He was followed by the others who abandoned the pursuit of the broken Indian column.

The Indians of the south held back and watched the attack on the Villa by their allies from the north. The men taking their positions on the hillside behind the palacio were fresh and unbloodied. The command of Juan of Taos would have to bear this part of the attack, while Askon of Galisteo regrouped his men.

Only the Spanish would have to fight without rest and reorganization. Don Antonio was conscious of the effect this would have upon his small command. He did not pause as he led them, still mounted, directly into the casas reales, jammed against the women and children who withdrew to other rooms while the soldiers took their positions at the narrow windows and prepared to repel a siege.

The cannon fired alternately at the Indians on the hill who fired back into the compound of the palacio with captured harquebuses. Arrows whirred through the slits of the buildings and pierced the legs of a boy who had exposed himself, lodged in the arm of a young woman scurrying to push a cow out of window range, and bounced off the bare walls when they found no flesh.

12

INSIDE the palacio the few candles which lighted the sparsely furnished rooms flickered and almost went out. Most of the furniture had been removed during the day to make room for the refugees who crowded the building. In the narrow corridor between the rooms some of the soldiers were resting from the day-long battle. They slept with their weapons beside them. Others dozed on the roof of the building where they had been stationed for the night. The wounded covered the floor of Don Antonio's sleeping room. Several of the women refugees moved among them, brought them water, fed them, and changed their bloodied bandages.

Standing in the doorway, Governor Otermín counted fourteen men who would be useless to him in the battles to come. One bald-headed soldier looked up at the Captain General from where he lay propped in the corner of the room and smiled over his beard. It took Don Antonio several minutes to realize that the edges of the man's lips had been sliced away, which gave him all the appearance of an idiot grinning. One young refugee, a farmer from La Cañada, rolled back and forth on his stomach as the pains of a wound in his buttock wracked his body. A young woman knelt on the floor beside him and held his hand in hers as she whispered to him.

Don Antonio turned and walked down the corridor, trying to avoid stepping on the sleeping soldiers and the women who were sprawled there. Most of the children had been gathered in the large dining room, away from the harquebus fire in the exposed rear of the building.

An old woman sat up suddenly from where she rested on the floor. "I always wanted to visit the casa real," she told Don Antonio, who wondered for a moment if she were serious. He saw that she was.

"It is my pleasure to have you as a guest, Señora."

He stepped around her and walked on. It was almost time to inspect the guard. But he was so weary. His legs barely held him. The foul air of the room dizzied him, and he envied the sleeping men and women.

The guard. He came back to the idea of inspection. It was a formality because he knew that the men who had fought through the day would be too tired to remain awake, and the ten who had remained behind had no choice but to remain awake. The windows of the buildings had been covered for the night to avoid making targets of them, and so the only defence of the palacio was the guard on the roof. Then Don Antonio laughed softly to himself. At what time in history did the fact that a soldier had no choice but remain awake ever insure the fact that he would? No, the guard must be inspected.

First he had to pull on his boots. Then he had to find his helmet and sabre. In the mad dash which had brought him back only hours before from the battlefield, he had set them down somewhere. He could not remember. It was not like him to be careless, but the fatigue which dragged his body slowed his mind. He made his way into his office. Fray Pedro, with whom he had agreed to share the room, was nowhere to be seen. Instead, the young woman whom Don Antonio had noticed several times during the day was curled up in a corner with her daughter's head on her arm. The woman opened her eyes, watched Don Antonio sit down behind his desk to pull his bucket boots on and rise to look for his sabre.

"Your sword is on the chair over there, Excellency." She gestured with her head. Her voice was soft. The child did not stir as the woman slipped a blanket under her head and stood up. She threw her shoulders back, stretched herself, and handed Don Antonio his sabre and helmet. Over the light of the candle he saw again the scratches on her forehead, the place where her bodice was pinned together, and remembered the shape of her bared breasts as she had walked across the plaza that morning.

"The air in the other rooms," she explained her presence.

Holding his helmet in his hand, the Governor nodded. "It is all right, Señora. I shall try not to disturb you when I return."

"She is going to be saved, is she not, Excellency?" The woman was looking at her daughter. The child was no more than eight years old. Her face was relaxed, her black hair askew as though she had just been playing. One bare leg stuck out of the Indian blanket that covered her.

He wanted to make some encouraging statement to comfort and assure the woman, but he was having difficulty seeing beyond the tour of the guards that confronted him.

"We are Christians, Señora. We shall do the most we are able to do, and for the rest, pray, Señora, pray."

At the entrance of the palacio, Don Antonio carefully stepped over the sprawled and sleeping body of Pando. The giant figure of the old man

H

showed the scars of the day's fighting. There were bandages on his wrist. His tunica was torn in several places and his bucket boot had been ripped open. Loud snores testified that he slept soundly, and his commander looked at him with affection. This man had helped hold the line against odds which would have made any Spaniard proud.

Once outside in the darkness, Don Antonio found the guard alert. For a moment they talked of the campfires which could be seen in great numbers to the south. Then returning the guard's salute, the Governor climbed to the roof of the building. There were five men stationed about the roofs and he could see all of them clearly. One shook his head as though to awaken and peered off to the north. The others were awake. More than this the commander could not ask.

The young, pocked sargento who had remained behind during the day approached the Captain General and saluted.

"The fires to the north, Excellency. There are many of them."

Don Antonio walked over to that portion of the roof where he could look out at the splashes of campfires scattered over the whole area occupied by the Taos warriors and their allies. Somewhere among this group was Popé. He would like to meet the man, know what he was, try to understand him, because this would solve his own problems. The thoughts inside of this heretic's head evaded Don Antonio. Unable to understand the man's actions, he did not know how he could destroy him. Flavius Vegetius Renatus again: *Novelty and Surprise Throw an Enemy into Consternation. Common Incidents Have No Effect.*

But now the surprises were all coming from the Indians, because there were no common incidents.

Staring into the campfires of his enemy, Don Antonio forgot the sargento at his side, forgot the guard he had come to inspect. Instead, his thoughts wandered back to the old Romans of the fourth century. Had they, too, felt the edge of their empire falling away from them? Were they conscious then that Rome's star was waning, as España's was now? How did the Roman legions on the fringe of empire feel with the Visigoths pressing in on them? Were the mistakes the same? Had they pressed too far? Did they know what their mistakes were? The Governor of Nuevo Mexico was certain he did not know what his had been. No question, the whole province had been operated too penuriously. No doubt too little attention had been paid to its defence. But how had it reached the place where it needed defending? What had slipped the keystone and loosed the avalanche that tumbled about them now?

The Romans had held to tradition, never broken the line of it, and by this means had held their world together.

The tradition of España, the conquistador, the empire of the Indies and the East had to hold now, and for him, Don Antonio de Otermín, Governor and Captain General.

"I shall sleep now, Sargento. You are to awaken me should there be any signs of activity among the Indians."

The sargento saluted and watched the Governor disappear down the ladder into the darkness below. As he turned back to watch the campfires of the enemy, he wondered if it would have been easier to fight through the day than watch through the night. The sargento was a very young man.

Entering the palacio again, Don Antonio saw that Pando had awakened.

"I would have checked the guard, Excellency," he apologized.

"No, amigo. I need you rested tomorrow."

"We fight again." It was not a question. His bandaged hand rested inside his torn tunica. "I hope I have an easier place to reach with my next wound, Excellency. This becomes a nuisance."

Both men laughed softly. Standing together, they scanned the sleeping faces of the women and children crowded about them.

"Will we have to withdraw, Excellency?" The words were barely audible. They demanded a particular answer, and Don Antonio did not know if he could give it. It was a long time before he answered. For Ismael Pando, Nuevo Mexico was home, the only one he had ever known, it was the place of his father and the end of his mother's bold jornada. For him to ride out of this Villa and abandon the province would mean little less than death. "I do not know, amigo. I only know I do not plan to."

And Otermín, stepping over the sleeping figure of an old woman, did not look at his aide again. At the door of his office, he stopped. The short, squint-eyed soldier with the thick neck was coming out of the room, holding his bleeding arm.

For a moment the two men stood looking at each other. The Captain General's hand went to his helmet. With a sweep, he swung it off his head and smashed it into the startled face of the man. Before he could move, Don Antonio closed with him, forcing him against the wall with one hand over the man's torn mouth.

"Not a sound. You will awaken no one or I will hang you now without waiting for morning."

Gasping for breath, his head cocked to one side as he tried to focus, the shocked soldier did not move. They stood for a long time. When Don Antonio let his hand fall away from the man's mouth, he saw that the bleeding arm had marked his own tunica.

Twice. Twice in one day his temper had run loose. He had difficulty facing the man before him because he knew what had caused his anger.

"Is she your woman?"

"No, Excellency. She is of Acoma Pueblo. Her husband had a rancho there."

"Did she encourage you?"

There was a pause. "Not exactly, Excellency."

"Can you think of a reason why I should not hang you, soldado?"

The man rubbed his thick neck with a bloody hand. "I fight, Excellency. I have been of His Majesty's army many years, and I fight well."

Under other circumstances, Don Antonio knew he would have smiled. The accent, heavy on the man's words, reminded him of a thousand other boasting veterans, reminded him, too, that most of them lived up to their words. "I shall see how well you fight. Then we will discuss hanging."

The squint eyes came into focus as the man saluted and walked out of the reception room.

Holding his helmet in his hand, Otermín looked at it. The woman. He had struck one of his command because of a woman. It was not good. It certainly was not correct. Entering the room, he closed the door behind him. The woman of Acoma lay as she had earlier in the evening. The child was cuddled close to her. A daga rested at her finger tips. The edge of it was red. Her eyes were closed, though from her heavy breathing Don Antonio doubted that she slept.

Setting his sabre and helmet on the table, he seated himself in a straight-backed chair and pulled his heavy boots off. In the corner opposite the woman and the child, someone had spread out several blankets. In the faint light of the candle, he recognized the blankets from his own bed, now occupied by a wounded refugee. This then was meant for him. He unbuttoned his tunica, wet his finger tips and pinched out the candle. Then he crossed the room and stretched out on the blankets. The battle of the day rose before him in the dark, and he jerked his head toward the wall beside him. He was conscious of the heavy breathing of the woman as he fell asleep.

It was late when Fray Pedro picked up a candle, left the tower chapel, and made his way to Governor Otermín's office. The crowded reception room was quiet. A ranchero lifted his head to see who was passing through and went to sleep again. Standing at the door of the Governor's office, the padre turned back to look again at the reception room. If the people had selected their space with greater care, there would have been less waste, and every vara was needed now. He considered for a time how he could best apportion space. Well, that was a task for tomorrow. Weary and ready to sleep, he quietly entered Don Antonio's office.

The candle in his hand flickered and burned on. A hot wax dripping ran over his knuckles and hardened there as he stood staring at the figure of the Governor in one corner and the figure of the widow of Acoma in the other. Don Antonio's face was turned toward the wall as he rested his head on his folded tunica.

After a time, the padre saw that the woman was looking at him. He wondered why people tended to make life complex, and leaving the room, sought the shelter of his chapel tower again. Here alone in the small room beside the chapel, he removed his cassock and sought a place on the floor where he could sleep. There was a wooden floor in the tower and even a small rug. The design held his attention as he tried to recall the tales he had heard about the Indians weaving religious themes into rugs such as these. There was nothing here that made any sense to him so he crossed himself, stretched out and drew his cassock over him. The candle threw a faint circle of light on the ceiling.

Fray Pedro closed his eyes and thought of the days behind and the days ahead. He was thankful it was he and not others he knew who were here at this time. A mestizo padre raised by an ignorant Indian mother or a Creole who had never known España—these men were not for the present. He wondered if they belonged in the Church at all, and remembered his first disappointed reaction when he read the *Rule of 1618* on arriving in Nueva España—a Creole to be permitted to serve the Order for each peninsular. As if they were of equal value. A Fray Julio and a Fray Custodio. Perhaps the present conflict was the result of too many concessions and the wrong values. This much he believed he shared with the Governor—the inseparable union of the Altar and the Throne. Only a peninsular would appreciate this. The Church supported the divine rights of the King and the King supported the religious authority of Mother Church. Such concepts were not for Creoles or mestizos. The Creole padres and the Creole cabildos—two ends of the same stick.

He realized that he was not sleeping and decided to put the time to use and, rising, sat down at a small table where he began to write again the carta to the Bishop. After all, had not an account of the province by Fray Benavides helped that Brother to a bishopric?

He stared at the candle beside him and then started to write.

In continuance

I am certain that the Reverend Father will understand my fears at a moment of crisis when I say that I believe the organization of the lay community of the province will eventually deteriorate into conflict. Our Cabildo consists primarily of Creoles—those colonists with the narrow perspective of town government and not España. These men already begin to chaff at the Governor General's disregard or ready modification of their suggestions, and while at present there is little they can do, I have concern for the future.

His head went down into his arms as he rested. He was much too weary to continue. Perhaps, if the room were dark, he might sleep.

13

DARKNESS covered the plain to the south, the eminence to the north, and the Villa de Santa Fe itself. Seated on a rock looking down on the rear of the palacio, Juan, the young war chief of Taos, inspected the terrain over which he would have to fight to kill or dislodge the Governor and his people. All of the patient hours which Don Jaime de Marcos had spent in educating his protégé came into focus. Juan, too, had studied the old Roman strategist, Vegetius, as well as the Italian, Machiavelli, who had worked so hard to modernize the military works of Livy.

Juan tried to call to mind the words of the old Roman and his descendant, but thoughts of Manuela pushed the words away. He wondered how she was faring, if she had enough food, if she was cold, if he would ever return to help her down from the high and sacred place where the spirits were supposed to dwell. He put one hand down on the rock, felt the dampness left by the rain which had just ceased falling, and wondered how much credit Popé would take for the rain, and how much credit for relief from heat for man and plants belonged to the old gods. The sceptic who had educated Juan had overlooked little. And where there were claims of men, there were doubts about those claims, and where there were claims for this god or that one, there were doubts about the interpretations by men. The lean Indian war chief brought the wet hand up to the side of his face, felt the coolness of it, and wondered if there was any advantage to which he might put the rain. Water, he had been taught, was an important part of any battle, and in a siege . . . the thought ran quickly to the answer. Staring at the Villa below, he knew there was much he would have to learn about this Spanish capital.

He shrugged and rose to his feet. Several of those about him noticed the gesture which Juan had developed of suddenly looking up. They failed to associate it with the morning in the courtyard of Don Jaime de Marcos' hacienda when the old Castilian had killed himself and those who had attacked his home.

Juan looked about for Popé, did not see him, and called to a young runner. "Fetch the war chief of Galisteo. Tell him it is time we met and planned our actions together."

His own feeling of futility crept into his voice and he turned to smile at the warriors about him. "Those of the south lost many men this day. If they had not been impatient and we had attacked together, we might have finished what we have come here to do without the losses and the wasted opportunity of surprise."

He walked into the darkness away from the fires which were springing up over the camp grounds. The Spaniards in their buildings below would see these, would worry, and it was meant that they should. The idea of worrying the enemy appealed to Juan. When he returned, he would have to send some men down to light fires closer to the casas reales. Possibly this would draw the Spanish out. In any event, they would be forced to increase their guard and that would mean fewer of them would be able to rest.

Away from the others, Juan edged closer to the buildings. The ground was mostly level. The rain had settled the dust and, from the look of the sky, it would rain again. Perhaps, in the morning. That meant no dust to stir up should he desire to use it to cover an assault. He kept to the shadows, avoided making a silhouette of himself against the campfires of his people, and paced off the distance from the eminence to the walls of the casas reales. It was open country and difficult to cross under the fire of the Spanish cannon and the harquebusier who knew how to use his weapon. The firing of the weapon by his own people that Juan had watched during the afternoon had almost convinced him that firearms were wasted without proper training, and he did not have the time or the inclination to start teaching warfare. He wanted to be done and away.

A noise behind him. . . . His sabre was out as he faded into a shadow. An Indian youth, helmeted and armed with a sabre and daga, stood looking about. Juan waited. An ally or a Christian Indian? Puzzled, the stranger started to walk back to the campfires.

"Down, fool!" Juan called from the darkness, and the stranger whirled about.

"Down! They will see you against the campfire."

It took an instant for the idea to reach the stranger. Then he approached the shadows that covered Juan, sabre in hand.

"I am looking for the war chief of Taos."

"You have found him."

"I am Askon of Galisteo. It was my people who fought the Whitefaces this day."

Juan heard the boast in the youth's voice and shook his head. Now the problems began. Now all of the work which Popé had done to bring the nations of the pueblo kingdom to this point would require redoing every moment so that none would be offended, so that he might have his way and defeat the enemy without the waste of lives that would come with another pitched battle.

"We had best plan tomorrow's fighting together," Juan offered.

The war chief of Taos was speaking Castilian, and the Tanoan answered him in the same language. Juan realized they had learned this much in common from their enemy.

Plan. The idea appealed to Askon, who marvelled at the ability to plan that he had seen among the Spanish, admired it with envy, coveted it with passion. It was the difference, he was convinced, between a savage and a civilized man. He did not tell himself that in some instances it was the difference between the Whitefaces and the Copper. But just how one went about this mysterious process usually eluded the youth from Galisteo. He had courage and he was not a fool. It was merely that he lacked a pattern of thought which involved thinking ahead, laying out a mode of action which would meet a situation not yet arisen and follow the design to its inevitable conclusion. This whole process was confusing.

Juan watched his counterpart from the southern pueblos as they sat together in the dark staring at the casas reales. There seemed to be no lights within the buildings. This puzzled Juan, because there should have been lights. The Spanish had to eat and tend their wounded. He wondered how many were within, how many bore arms. "In the battle of today, how many Whitefaces were there?"

Askon thought for a moment. To admit there were few meant that his people had been easily beaten. To say there were many would perhaps be dangerous in planning.

"It seemed like many. They fought like men from the underworld."

Juan nodded. He understood, and had expected, this type of answer.

"I believe that we must make them hunger, make them thirst."

The idea appealed to Askon, but it involved more time than he wanted to spend at the Villa. His mind ran back the trail to Galisteo and Dorotea. She was waiting for him. And he wanted her. He had wanted her for a long time, but only recently had he been willing to admit this to himself. It had been a simple task to carry her to the communal rooms of his mother, to tell the others that she was his and that she was to be kept for his return. It was increasingly difficult to remain away from her.

"How long would that require?"

Juan was pleased with the question. Here was an Indian who could think in terms of time. Most did not. Don Jaime had pointed this fact out to him long ago. Of course, Juan was curious why the youth of Galisteo wanted to know how long it would take. So few of the People had what would be considered time business, something that could not be done tomorrow as well as today. It was the nature of the land and the people. The pueblo kingdom was the land of slow time.

"How soon could we burn them out enough to destroy their food? And after a man loses his water and food, how long does it take him to come out fighting or die in the hole he has chosen for himself?"

Askon smiled. The war chief of Taos sounded like a Whiteface. He broke everything down into its parts and then looked at the parts as if they did not make a whole. He wondered if this Taoan would understand how he felt about Dorotea and why he was anxious to return. But this was not something one discussed with a stranger, and certainly not something one discussed with one of the Taoans, because the men of the north seemed to be so violent in their feelings about the Whitefaces that there would be no sympathy for Askon's desire. And desire was what was beginning to govern his actions. Desire followed his revenge and gave his actions a new and different drive.

"In your fighting today, did you kill many horses?"

The Taoan had changed the subject. Askon did not know what he was moving toward and so he moved away.

"I do not know. Some of the Spanish rode back doubled up on their horses."

Juan had decided to be patient. He needed this man of Galisteo, and more —he needed his people. "I believe when we fight these people who wear armour we should kill their horses. Strike at their legs, drive the men to the ground where they are made clumsy and awkward by the very armour that seems to make them strong when mounted."

Askon wished he had remembered to give this order in the day's fighting. He would do so upon returning to his own camp. But this again was something he would not tell the northern war chief. But his silence on the subject explained much to Juan.

"You now hold low ground," Juan commented casually. "I do not think you have much choice. But knowing the weakness of the terrain is an advantage. Should the Spanish attack you, we will move in on their rear. Victory depends much on the nature of the field of battle. We will try to make them fight where we choose." He was speaking the old maxims now. He recognized them, doubted if the Galisteon did, knew the Governor would.

Seated in the darkness, Juan looked away. His hands went over his face as though he were trying to hide it, and for an instant his head seemed to jerk upward, looking for something, seeing it and turning back, embarrassed. He was confused. The char night whirled in circles about his head. He was in the wrong place, saying the right things to the wrong people. If he were seated inside the palacio, seated on a straight-backed chair, his feet under a table, a drink of brandy in his hand, the Governor at his side discussing a military operation, then the days and nights to come would have meaning. Now they were only parts of a jumbled dream that seemed to fall apart each time he looked at it closely.

"Tomorrow when the light comes, let us meet again. Let us plan our diversion, decide what will bring the Spanish out or permit us to destroy them." He rose and nodded to the Galisteon. "Remember, friend, whatever disposition we take must be kept from the Spanish. Or they will counteract our measures and defeat our plans." This, he felt, was almost pompous enough to impress the stranger. Juan's Castilian was excellent, and he knew that in the dark he could even pass for a Spaniard. This, too, made an impression on those who believed they had to destroy every vestige of the enemy and at the same time admired every one of his accomplishments.

Without another word to the youth who was his counterpart among the southern pueblos, Juan slowly walked back to the campfires.

Askon watched him disappear, thought for a moment about mounting his horse and riding through the night to Galisteo and Dorotea, realized it was too late, and that should he be absent in the morning, someone would be selected to replace him as war chief. And so he sat for a time, felt the weariness of the day's fighting overwhelm his slim copper body and knew fatigue as an enemy he would have to cope with before he returned to his mother's home and Dorotea. He wondered if it would not have been better to have walked to the Villa de Santa Fe with his neighbours and not have ridden as their war chief, not have known the matters of decision, not have felt the strange tightening of the stomach when a friend dies, knowing that he dies because his leader may have made an error in judgment.

The fires on the far side of the Villa burned tall against the night. Askon stood up and looked about. Skirting the casas reales, he made his way back to his own people. There was an evening meal to eat, there was rest to be had, there was another meeting tomorrow with the war chief of Taos. This strange, almost Spanish Indian puzzled Askon. He knew things which the People had never bothered to know—the Spanish things, the foreign ones, strange and almost forbidding, yet useful.

Moving among the campfires of the People of the northern pueblos, Juan paused to help a youth from Tesuque string his bow, knelt to show a man from Cochití how to load his harquebus, stopped to inspect the food being prepared at the fires of one clan, suggested the men use fewer herbs, as tomorrow would be warm and water scarce if the fighting followed the pattern of this day's.

Then Juan saw Popé seated, alone, staring at the palacio of the Spanish governor. No one dared bother the giant medicine man with the yellow eyes and the bull-horn headdress. Without saying anything, Juan tried to read the face of the man, wondered what was behind the wrinkled forehead, what the pattern of his future was. How would it affect the puebleños? And how would it affect Juan?

There was no question in his mind that the medicine man of San Juan had become the symbol of all that the People believed, that he alone had made possible the freedom they were fighting for. And because of this, Juan respected and admired him.

Popé saw the lights of the campfires and was proud of the People. They had become one, a force to be counted, a people prepared to rise and fight. He felt happy that the rebellion for which he had worked so long had come to this point. Tomorrow or the day after it would be over. The Whitefaces and the Blessing Men would die or depart and the People would be left to live their own lives for good or bad, worship their own gods as men should.

He was proud for he was a patriot. In many ways, this giant of a man with yellow eyes who sat rigidly on the rock looking down at his enemy was the first patriot his people had ever known. He thought beyond clan, beyond pueblo, beyond the language barriers which separated the nations of the adobe kingdom.

Aware that Juan was watching him, reluctant to relax before the youth who must keep the image of the leader intact, Popé finally rose to his feet and looked into the dark eyes of the war chief he had selected to lead the northern pueblos.

"We have come a long distance since the yoke fell away. The woman clouds bore rain. The soft woman winds of the south blow victory within our grasp."

The younger man smiled. There had been times within the recent days before the uprising when he had been prepared to turn his back upon it, upon the People and the old ways, prepared to join the Spanish as one of them. But now all that had been done—the killing and betrayal—had been worth the doing. Popé was pleased, therefore he was pleased. He had not been conscious of this before, but now he knew that the holy man from San Juan meant a great deal to him as a person and as a leader. He had been what the People needed. For Juan, like Popé, had felt the discomfort that troubled the puebleños, the lack of affinity with the world in which they had always lived. Juan had felt this, but would never have been able to place his feelings before the People, as Popé had done. For what the priest had done, Juan was grateful. He had accepted the challenge of leadership which had been set before him like a holy commitment. And it had been worth the effort.

"I have talked to the war chief of Galisteo," he informed the older man.

The patience which comes with age and knowing when to be silent was a lesson long learned by Popé. Juan had not spoken without reason.

"I believe he is a man of courage," Juan continued, "but I fear that he is rash and untrained. There is much that he has done wrong already, and I fear that he may do more."

Popé listened. This was not envy. This lean, hardened young man who seemed so different from his companions had his own type of understanding. Popé might have called it the understanding of the Whitefaces, but he did not believe that was a quality they possessed. Yet, what Juan knew, he had learned from the silent Spaniard.

"There is something you want me to do?"

Juan thought for a moment. "The people of Taos and the north know Popé, know what he believes and what they must do. In the battle of tomorrow and the days which might follow before she of the south winds bears our victory, would Popé stand at the side of the southern pueblos? They will need his guidance more than we whom he has taught. They will need the strength Popé can give them and the wisdom not to move in haste or die in rashness. The patience of Popé stands as our shield. We hope we have learned his lesson. We cannot be certain that the people of the south have learned as much."

It was said. All of the doubts concerning the abilities of Askon were laid out now like a blanket.

"You have a design for the defeat of the Spanish?"

"I believe I have."

Popé was prepared to listen. The details of battle were not his concern. He had become the symbol of victory and freedom. But fighting was not expected of him and not desired.

"Have you told the plan to the war chief of Galisteo?"

"I have told him we might have to take more time than he desires. I have told him we should not strike directly at a fortress which adds the strength of many to our enemy. We must feel out his ground, must discover his weakness, and then wield it like a macana."

"Juan of Taos has a vision of this weakness?"

Juan realized there was little possibility of hiding his thoughts from the older man.

"I . . . I . . ." The word came through. The humility that was not there; instead, the belief that he could do what his fellow Indians could not do. He regretted exposing himself in this way. Then he explained his strategy to the older man.

Popé nodded his approval. The youth was not of the People though he would try, but he was important to them for what he knew of the enemy's ways. Perhaps, he would feel about the land as the others felt, but Popé did not glitter his beliefs with dreams about individuals.

"I will stand at the side of the war chief of Galisteo and see that he does as our people of the north."

With those words the yellow-eyed medicine man reached into his pouch and drew out the holy corn meal, spread some on four points of his palm and then laid the palm on the bared breast of Juan. Of the north, of the south, of the east, and of the west. He had given the young man his blessing.

The youth was silent as he watched the medicine man disappear into the darkness away from the fires. He looked down at the four spots of white on his copper chest. Then with a finger he drew a line from the north to the south and from the east to the west. He did not draw it for himself, but for the girl whom he had left in the Sacred Place and for her father who had been his friend.

14

FOR days Ruaha, the cacique of San Ysidro, listened to the arguments of the young men of the pueblo. For days they had been at him for permission to kill the slight padre imprisoned in the mission. Finally, as they all sat together in the kiva pleading with him to fulfil the promise to Popé of San Juan and the other puebleños who were now fighting about Isleta and the Villa, he yielded.

The skin was drawn tightly over his high, flat cheekbones as he rocked his small body back and forth on his haunches, nodding his final approval of their plan. It was beyond him now. He no longer had the power to dissuade them, and with the disappointment they had faced in their pursuit of the bearded soldado, there was a justice in their arguments he could not deny. The young men had been promised that the conquerors would be driven from the land. And there was no argument left that could justify this single padre remaining alive.

Ruaha looked at the eager faces of those around him and wondered if this single death would satisfy them. One death had never satisfied the Spaniards. He rose to his feet, scattered the holy corn meal into the sipapu and stood looking down at the young men. The older principales had refrained from argument, though they had expressed their desires to him personally days before when they captured the padre with the distant look about him.

"If we must kill him," Ruaha agreed, "we must kill him soon. We will not torture the man by waiting or give him more hope than we have by taking so long to act."

No one answered.

"He will be killed tonight."

The young men rose and came to Ruaha's side. "Then we will be done with it."

They were trying to make it clear that this was the end of the killing for them, that they did not want to oppose his judgment. One of the youths who had been a hunting companion of Ruaha's son and another who had hoped to marry Poy-ye held their hands out as though offering him their strength. He was an old man now and they saw it. He had not been an old man the night Yad-wan had died, but that was many days gone. Ruaha took the two outstretched hands and squeezed them for an instant, then let them drop.

All of the men watched him as he walked out of the kiva to the one beneath the cross where in a small rear room the frail padre was imprisoned. Ruaha's step was slow, his head down. At the door of the mission he spoke briefly to the youth who had been assigned the task of watching over the white Blessing Man. He would have said more, but he heard the voice through the piñon door and held up his hand to silence the guard.

The padre was praying. For a long time the cacique held his silence. Then he knew the praying would continue into the night. Very quietly he opened the door and peered in.

His cassock hood thrown back and his shaven head bowed, Fray Rafael knelt before a large cross which he had drawn in the packed dirt of the floor. Between his hands he clutched a small silver cross which he did not appear to see as he rocked back and forth slowly repeating his Ave María.

The cacique ran one hand down the leg of his own cotton pantalone to brush off the holy corn meal that clung there and closed the door behind him. The only sound was the padre's quiet prayers. At last he crossed himself and looked up to acknowledge the presence of the cacique.

"I hope that you have found your daughter and that she is well."

Ruaha did not answer. He closed his eyes and wished himself elsewhere. The padre had reached into his soul and knew what troubled him. Then to build a wall between them which the other could not scale and to preserve his own dignity, Ruaha began to answer the padre in Tewan. After a moment, he knew that what he had to say would have to be understood by the other, if only for his own sake, and so he stopped talking.

"I have told you before," the padre was saying, "that the sin of the soldado was a great sin and that the Lord in his own way would punish the man. This He will do and the blood of the sinner should not be on your hands or the hands of your young men."

"There will be blood," Ruaha blurted out. Then he looked away as he pleaded with the past.

"Why did you try to take our gods away? Why could not Jesus and Christ have shared the world, brought rain and goodness and even the love you speak of without having turned the People against their own?" He was not saying it well; he knew none could. But he had to make the effort.

"We might have accepted your lonely god—and Mary and Jesus. There is much good in what you have said."

Then Ruaha stopped his pleading for what was no longer possible. He looked directly into the face of the thin padre, almost lost in his large cassock, as the two of them stood separated by the large cross drawn on the floor.

"Tonight you will be taken from this place and killed." Before Fray Rafael could speak, Ruaha's hand went up. "There is nothing I can do. Nothing I would do. Your people came with blood. You may depart with it."

Fray Rafael crossed himself. "There was a night before you came to the mission that your woman appeared and told me what you planned."

For a moment Ruaha could not believe him. Then he knew how the bearded soldado had learned enough to lie in wait for the messenger. Yad-wan. Yad-wan. Had she betrayed him or tried to save him? Him? Or Poy-ye? It had been the girl Poy-ye. Now he understood many things that had troubled him. And in his understanding, he was proud of his wife. Then he realized the padre was talking.

"Castilian. You knew Castilian. Now you speak to me, when before . . ." The frail body was shaking as he tried to comprehend.

"I went to your schools, but I am no different from my people. If you could not make them understand, you cannot make me."

Then the padre was pleading; and it was only after a time that Ruaha realized it was not for himself.

"Your young men should not kill. It is against God's law for a man to take the life of another. They do not have the right, and for this they would be punished. Do not let them become the image of the man Reyes who killed and destroyed his own soul. Do not let your young men drag themselves into the depths of the infernos, because there is no escape if they kill and know they are killing."

Ruaha placed his gnarled dark hands on the shoulder of the small man before him, felt the very bones of the padre as he closed his strong fingers into the loose cassock.

"I would have preferred another way for the young men. Not for your sake, but for the sake of the men who will kill you and with whom I must stand. But there is no other way, Padre."

Fray Rafael wanted to dispute the point with him, but he had never been a man who could argue a point, because there is a quality in argument that is more than the seeking of truth. It is an element of conflict, and even for the sake of others Fray Rafael was incapable of conflict.

The two men stared at each other for a long time. The guard outside became restless in the silence which followed a conversation he had failed to understand. Slowly the fingers of the cacique relaxed. His arms fell away to his side.

He wondered for an instant how just he had been to this earnest stranger, recalled the jutting jaw of the bearded soldier and the lost trail of Poy-ye. He finally said, "The young man will come for you when the Sun Father has left us. I am sorry. I wish there could have been another way."

Then he walked out of the small cell and closed the door behind him. As he stood silently beside the guard and watched the sun snag on a far mountain peak, he knew he had spoken Castilian for the last time and the words coming through the door behind him as the padre prayed, troubled him.

The words swept him up in their course and he wanted to walk away from them. But he held his ground for he knew it was the man, and not the creed he espoused, that was the final measure. Ruaha knew, too, that such knowledge came with age and the warriors of San Ysidro were young men and for Fray Rafael there was not time enough for the young to learn this truth.

For days and nights Fray Julio had crossed the barren country that led him south to keep his rendezvous. One night he had collapsed for a few refreshing hours under the cover of a clump of piñon trees. One afternoon he had been brought to his knees by fatigue and had finally fallen asleep beside a small, thin stream lazily moving westward. His hunger had been satisfied by berries, his thirst by the puddles of almost dry arroyos. His cassock was now almost wholly white from the dust and alkali in which he had slept. His shoes had long since been lost. For a time his feet had hurt him. But now they were so numb that he no longer felt the aches that coursed upward. His arm had stopped bleeding, but each movement of his body, each southward step, jarred the broken bones. He had cried once when he stumbled and the jagged break ripped the skin afresh, but he had not paused. His hand was caked with dried blood. His face was covered with a straggle of beard. A gauntness as of death had taken over his aquiline features and the leanness gave his head the appearance of a skull. His eyes had sunken into their hollows and between the dust and the brightness of the sun, he had difficulty seeing the distant hills or the clumps of bunch grass at his feet. But yet he hurried south, impelled—driven.

Then in the distance he saw the roof tops of a pueblo. The smoke curled over them like a beacon against the evening sky where the sun was settling lazily below a far rise. The padre quickened his pace. His drawn nostrils sniffed the cooling air. He approached with unreasoned caution. Vaguely, behind his burning eyes, he recalled that there was some reason why he should fear the Indians. He could not remember what the reason was.

Moving softly toward the edge of the open square of adobe buildings, he slipped to his knees behind a clump of cottonwood trees. A brown toad moved hurriedly away from his feet. The smoke drifting across the sky smelled of fresh green pine. The shadows cast by the large fires being lighted by the Indian warriors looked to the blurred eyes of the padre like a battleground of Hell. He crossed himself with his good arm and felt for the cross which had hung about his neck. Somewhere in his wanderings he had lost it. And as he fumbled for it with his fingers over the front of his torn cassock, fear crept over him. He did not look down. He did not take his eyes away from the spectacle of the Indians before him. Several of the nearly naked young men were lashing together the trunks of two large trees in the form of a giant cross. Near by, their companions were digging a hole in the ground, while still others collected clumps of dried bunch grass, pine branches, and browned cactus.

Fray Julio stared entranced as the Indian youths, taking their direction from a short man with a lined and worried face, slowly raised the cross and set it into the hole in the ground so that it towered over the small plaza. Flames grew from the fires and hurled themselves against the base of the cross. Indian women, copper skins reflecting the shifting lights, stood together in a large circle and swayed back and forth as they chanted an ancient song.

Then the man with the old face who was their leader raised his hand and everyone was silent. The red bando about the cacique's head was the colour of dried blood. His black hair above it fell as he raised his head to stare at the sky and the fading sun. It was almost night.

Then the cacique selected four of the young warriors and walked out of the silent plaza across the fields. In the distance the burning eyes of the padre of Santa Flora could see the silhouette of a small adobe mission. Above it against the darkened sky, he saw a large cross. He bowed his head as his good hand still fumbled for the missing silver cross that had hung about his neck. In the plaza there was a strange expectant silence.

In the darkness of the room that had been his prison for three days, Fray Rafael knelt in prayer. Before him stretched the cross he had drawn with loving care upon the dirt floor. His eyes were closed. His frail body relaxed.

"He let us swear the oath of allegiance to Him, and gave us the opportunity to enrol under His standard. He opens to us the way of life; He brings us back to paradise; He leads us on to the kingdom of heaven."

Outside his cell he heard the Indians approaching. Fear fell away from him. He was silent for a moment as he recalled the years of his youth, of his studies, and regretted that he had never had the opportunity to write the books he had dreamed of writing when he was younger. He regretted, too, that he had been able to do so little for those who had known him, and most of all he regretted his failure in San Ysidro.

When the door opened and the night moved in about him, Fray Rafael crossed himself and rose to his feet to face Ruaha and the four young warriors. They moved forward as he prayed aloud.

"I take up arms of devotion and enter into the divine camp which is His."

Ruaha threw his arms wide against the bared chests of his companions. None was to touch the small padre who moved out and ahead of them into the night. His head held high, he continued his prayers, the small cross which hung about his neck clasped firmly between his closed palms.

"Let us arm ourselves with all our strength and prepare ourselves for the contest with an incorruptible mind, with a steadfast faith and a dauntless courage. Let the humble of God march out for the battle."

Ruaha and the youths took their places beside the small figure of the padre as he himself led the way through the open fields toward the plaza where the fire brightened the sky.

"Let the Supreme Commander who is the Christ become my example of valour and let my fear be only of God."

Once the slight figure ceased praying and looked down to the dark earth. Two of the youths moved forward, but again Ruaha motioned for them to hold their places. The padre knelt and took a handful of the soft earth in his hand, felt of the moistness and, turning to Ruaha, handed it to him. "I am happy for you and your people that the rains have come."

Ruaha accepted the rich dark earth in his open palm and nodded. The padre again turned his head to the sky and continued to lead the procession to the crowded plaza of the pueblo which had been his mission.

"He supports me and strengthens me and gains the victory with me for I shall be a co-heir with Christ. This is an examination and a sifting of my sins and God wills me to be tested and proved as He has always tested His servants."

The procession approached the plaza. Fray Rafael looked about him and felt the anguish of his failure. He had never reached these people. He had failed in his trust. This was his great sin. The circle of women fell away, leaving a path for the Blessing Man who had lived a stranger among them for almost a decade. There was no love on their faces. Neither was their hatred. They only wanted to be free of the turmoil of which he had become the symbol.

Smiling gently into the faces of the women and the warriors who came forward to take his arms, the padre prayed.

"As gold in a furnace, He hath tried them and accepted them as a sacrifice."

The tall Indian youth who had desired Poy-ye for his woman stepped up to the padre and opened the palms closed about the small iron cross. With a strong jerk the Indian tore the cord which held the cross, stared at it for a moment, and then flung it away from him into the fire.

"For your hatred I will repay you with kindness and for the torments and penalties that are inflicted upon me, I point out to you the ways of salvation. Believe and live and you who persecute me will rejoice with me for eternity."

Ruaha heard the words and understood them and closed his eyes as though this would black them out. His head slumped to his chest as he took his place beside the large piñon cross that cast its shadow over the open ground and stood out against the shadows of the fires.

Fray Rafael stared for a moment at the large cross before him. His finger tips came together beneath his chin and his head dropped. He was being honoured beyond his worth and he would not betray that honour.

Fray Julio, hidden in the bushes, recognized the figure among the Indians as a Brother, but knew there was nothing he could do for him. He heard the words and they seared through the fog which had been gathering in his mind for days.

The Indian youth who had been the friend of Ruaha's son stepped beside the one who had removed the cross and reaching out both hands tore away the cassock from the shoulders of the slight padre, leaving the thin white chest bare to the firelight. With a quick downward thrust of his hands, the young Indian pulled the padre's arms free and left the grey cassock hanging loose about his waist. The shaven head came up and the quiet blue eyes looked with kindness into the Indian's.

"I accept with complete resignation the will of God and His Son and I banish all thoughts of vengeance."

The Indian youth did not know what the Blessing Man was saying, but the tone and the expression frightened and awed him. He stepped back as the four who had walked the full distance from the chapel stepped forward and took the padre by the arms and raised him up against the piñon cross. As they stretched his arms outright on the cross, Fray Rafael stared down at the women and the men who were silent now.

"He has preferred nothing to us. We cling to His love. We take our position on His cross. His name and His honour are contested and we shall do nothing to shame them."

The young men held the thin arms still while their companions drove the Spanish knives through the padre's open palms and into the soft wood.

Ruaha tried to turn away to avoid seeing the blood on the open palms, but he was drawn to the man on the cross, and the words of the Franciscan roared through his brain as painfully as they seared the mind of the large padre hidden in the darkness not twenty varas away. The words he had learned in his youth and forgotten in his maturity flooded his mind.

To exhibit in trial that courage with which we fight and in death that patience with which we are crowned. Christ suffers in them and with them and they are invincible.

The Indians put a torch to the bunch grass and cactus and then fell away from the small figure on the cross. The bright eyes of the man stared down on the People as he prayed for them; and though most could not understand his words, they were ashamed and wanted to run away. Two warriors turned to edge into the darkness only to find Ruaha blocking their path, and they turned back to watch and listen. The witnesses beheld with wonderment the heavenly contest for God and the spiritual combat for Christ that His servant was waging, unhampered in speech and unbroken in mind and with divine courage, armed with the weapons of His faith.

And the martyr interceded for the sinners. The Indians heard and the padre in the darkness heard the soft voice which was the only sound other than the crackling of the flames.

"It is an old adversary and an ancient enemy whom we fight. But He has taught us through the practice of many years that the martyrs designati are but blood witnesses for the eternal actuality of Christ, that the Christian who suffers death for the faith has already received his reward of a crown in heaven. He shall rest under the altar of God. I have been offered no alternative. I have sought none. Your folly and your wickedness and your worship of idols must be abandoned. Only when this is done will you know the adoration and the reverence which belongs wholly to God. Only when this is done will you be able to join me in the heavenly mansion."

There were two loud cries of pain. And then the voice again, faltering now and barely audible.

"Nothing is asked of you that is impossible. As nothing has been asked of me that is impossible. The Master Himself knew the ways of pain but was most hurt by the ways of those who lived in the darkness of ignorance and turned away from His love."

The voice failed as the flames consumed the body of the man and the smoke billowed up and choked him. Ruaha closed his eyes. Tears dampened his cheeks. He opened his eyes again, stared at the stunned faces of his people. He knew that they would never forget what they had done. He knew, also, that only in time could they understand it. He wondered if this had been good for them, because now they would never know the ancient way of peace they had sought and would have difficulty finding again the white man's way from which they had turned.

In the dark place where he knelt, Fray Julio heard clearly the last words of his brother on the cross and knew that he had been brought to witness this martyrdom, had been brought through the hot days and the cold nights so that he would know again the faith from which he had turned so many years before. And as the smoke billowed up and hid the figure of Fray Rafael, his words came once more across the fires which brought him the highest award for the highest contribution he could make for his faith.

"Let the lapsed equip themselves in order to regain what they have lost. May the uninjured be spurred on into the battle by honour. Let us bear the shield of our faith manfully. May you all be led into the light."

The voice was still and there was silence.

Then the Indians heard a cry as though from an injured man, and they turned and saw the gaunt figure of a Blessing Man emerge from the darkness. His cloak was the whiteness of the moon and his arms dangled at his sides. One bloody palm was half-curled and pointing to them. The dark, deep-set eyes burned through the night which separated them. As he approached, they stepped back. For one brief instant a warrior started toward him; then he, too, fell back.

The huge priest with the straggling beard stopped before the fire which had taken the life of his brother. Then he walked into the dying embers, and reaching up with one arm, he withdrew the Spanish knives which held the martyr upon his cross. With great care and gentleness, he clasped the body to him. There was silence in the crowded plaza as the white-cloaked padre turned back to face the apostates. He held with one arm the body of Fray Rafael and with the other he held up a palm covered with fresh blood that flowed down from the rent skin where the broken bones pierced it.

"He has forgiven you and Christ has forgiven you. May you in time forgive yourselves." He spoke in the language of the People and they understood him. No one moved as he walked through their midst holding his holy brother to his breast and disappeared into the darkness.

A smell of pine smoke and flesh filled the night air.

The People were still. They looked at Ruaha, but he did not meet their eyes. Instead he stared at the cross which still cast its shadow over the plaza and the People. Eventually all of them turned and looked at the piñon cross. After a while they drifted back to their communal houses. For a long time they would avoid talking of what had taken place this night. Then someone would mention it and the others would remember it. They would speak softly about it among themselves and their children would hear them and remember and tell their children.

15

FRAY JULIO walked away from the pueblo of San Ysidro carrying the body of his martyred brother clutched to his breast. Darkness enfolded him. The only sound in the night was the wind against the leaves. He reached the bank of the rio and turned toward Isleta. His slow and measured steps flushed a shrike that shrilly mounted the blackness above. The cowl of his cassock was thrown back. His lean, bare head tilted upward as he stared unseeing at the sky. He prayed with every step he took. He prayed for forgiveness and understanding and redemption. He prayed for the opportunity to live under the shadow of his martyred brother. His good arm became numb with the weight it bore. His broken left arm hung unfeeling at his side.

He did not know the noise of the night, the soft movement of the Rio del Norte he walked beside, or the midnight sky. He did not know how long he walked nor how far. And he did not care. Once he stumbled and almost fell to the ground. Another time he sloshed unaware through a rivulet that emptied into the rio. His feet had become torn with his long days of walking. His cassock was stiff with dirt.

A bright slash of light cut the blackness above him. A timpani of thunder followed the lightning and echoed distantly from the far hills. Soon the first drops splashed across his bearded cheeks and his upraised brow. Then the rain began to fall steadily. His cassock grew heavy with water. The ground grew slithery under his feet.

Fray Julio walked on.

Thunder filled the sky. A raccoon leapt out of the padre's path and hid beneath the ragged, stiff leaves of a chamisa shrub.

Fray Julio paused, listened to the soft cough of the animal barely audible beneath the thunder, and looked about him. He was aware that he still held the body of his brother; aware, too, of what he had seen. He still heard the words of the man on the cross and knew they were meant for him as much as for the Indians who had crucified their pastor.

His name and His honour are contested and we shall do nothing to shame them.

Tears came to the eyes of the tall padre of Santa Flora as he knelt down and laid out the body which he had carried so far. With his one good arm and a sharp rock, he began to scrape a grave in the soft earth beside the great rio.

Let the lapsed equip themselves in order to regain what they have lost.

The soft dirt gave way to firmer earth and still the padre scraped and dug. He lost a nail and his hand was bleeding where he had torn it on a stone, un·een in the darkness.

Let us arm ourselves with all our strength and prepare ourselves for the contest with an incorruptible mind.

Finally the grave was dug. The padre rose to his feet and stared up at the sky etched broadly with the bold streaks of lightning and resounding from winds that hammered against the gates of heaven, to turn rejected toward the lesser hills. Rain splashed his face as he prayed and ran down his head when he bowed it and knelt beside the corpse. Finally he gently laid the body in the grave, scattered a handful of earth over it, prayed again, and then filled the grave. When the small mound was patted smooth, he looked about for a juniper tree. With difficulty he removed two branches and tied them together with the sleeve of his cassock in the form of the cross upon which the padre had died. This he set firmly in the ground as a headpiece. Then he stood back and marked his anguish on the back of his hand with his teeth as the tears flowed down his face and mingled with the rain that clung there.

When he was ready to move on, he did not know where he was, assumed he was far south of the Villa, and decided to seek Isleta. The rain had ceased and the morning light was already falling brightly on the small mound.

16

IT was almost dawn and José Reyes, seated on the roof of the hacienda of Don Alonso García, began to nod slowly. His gaunt bearded head bobbed up sharply as he thought he heard a footstep behind him. He wanted to sleep. He was ready to sleep. The night had been long and lonely and dark. But he feared the loud, brusque Lieutenant Governor who had appeared suddenly behind him several times during the night, watched him silently and then slipped into the darkness below. Reyes hated the man with the hot passion that was always simmering beneath the outward calm which he affected as part of his trade. Reyes feared García, but as always with him, there was that element of safety and precaution which held his hand. Each time the older man had appeared, Reyes considered killing him. Disposing of the body would not have been simple, yet the death could possibly be laid to the Indians. However, the years had taught Reyes a certain type of professional patience, as well as the importance of self-preservation. He knew he needed Don Alonso García, the mestizo from Zacatecas. In the few days he had spent in the barracks with the other soldiers, the Córdoban had heard all the tales of the Lieutenant Governor's phenomenal rise to power and all the legends of his prowess as a soldier. He had heard, too, of the conquest of Doña Josefa and the strength of the old mistress the men referred to affectionately as Nita. The compañeros of García's youth were proud of their commander, proud that he had sprung from their own ranks and that he had the two women. They were proud, too, to be serving under the man they believed the best campaigner in the whole empire of Nueva España. And it was this last boast which gave pause to Reyes' hatred. If he was to live, if he was to escape the fury of the Indians and complete his own conquest of Doña Josefa, he needed García and all of his fighting wiles. And so Reyes turned his temper inward, held the lid of it down, and made the difficult decision to wait until they were safe before he killed García.

As his head started to bob back and forth again, he rose to his feet and walked about the roof. Below he could see the soldier who had been drinking with him earlier in the day when García had burst in upon them. This leather-faced campaigner sat on the open portico of the hacienda with a bow and arrow in his lap and a pot of fat beside him. The strategy had been the commander's: in the event of an attack the large piles of brush stacked just beyond the outer perimeter of the grounds were to be lighted. This would give them clear silhouettes for targets as the rebels crossed the scorched earth between. Reyes was impressed with the plan. It convinced him that García knew what he was about and that he was correct in permitting the man to live.

The morning light reached the hacienda and Reyes still waited for his relief. He heard someone climbing the stairs and he crossed over and waited. His sabre rested in his hand. Finally Doña Josefa emerged from the room below. Reyes smiled thinly. He had hoped to see her earlier in the evening. In fact, much of the long night had been spent in anticipation. He had not forgotten her kindness when he first arrived at the hacienda, her long talk with him two nights later when he had his tour of guard duty.

The broad white skirt of her gown spread wide and the stiff beaded bosom swelled sufficiently to make Reyes nervous. She handed him a small basket of fruit with the simple comment, "Don Alonso expects you to remain here until he has met with the others to discuss his plans."

For a moment Reyes was puzzled. Then he realized that she, too, had been exiled from the meeting that was taking place below. There was a peevish anger turning her small lips. After a while she became conscious that he was staring at her, and she looked off into the distance, giving him the better side of her face and every opportunity to appreciate her.

The high forehead and bright gold hair made her startlingly different from most of the women of the provinces, and she was proud of the difference. Her eyes were a faint blue under brows so pale they were hardly discernible. Her cheeks, full and rounded, had a slight touch of rouge to set off the whiteness of her skin.

Reyes measured her with care and appreciation and wondered how she found the bed of that great bull of a man who was her husband. Her nose was almost pointed, but it was small, and for an instant he was tempted to touch it. He dropped his eyes and they fell to the level of her bosom. Doña Josefa was no longer a girl, but she was the kind of woman he had known only a few times in his life, fleetingly, unsatisfactorily, but with a profound hope of pleasure. He had dumped a young condesa on her bed after killing her husband for a price she had been willing to pay. He had forced the wife of a police official when she had paid him to destroy her husband's mistress. These and similar bonuses had come his way from those of station. They had never been lasting and he had never had the desire for more than the briefest passion. But something had been aroused in him, something akin to anger and ambition. It was related to that Indian wench with whom he had spent a most disappointing year. She had given him a child and a future and his own immortality. Then she had failed him completely. The child had died and there was no doubt that the fault was hers.

But because of the Indian girl, Reyes looked at Doña Josefa García in a different way than he might have at another time in his life. She could be his passport to the future he sought. There was never a question of money in his mind. This was a commodity he had always been able to take or earn with little effort. But Doña Josefa meant respectability—the quality he had never known, the quality that had never appeared to him before as even desirable. But with Natividad and the birth of his own child there was born in Reyes desire for status and acceptance and the respectability his uneducated mind equated with being married to a white woman whose father had been bred in a proper bed.

José Reyes knew he wanted Doña Josefa, knew in his own mind that he would have her and on any terms she was willing to set. He had made agreements before in his life. Some, circumstance had forced him to keep; others, well, time and distance and power or influence determined his final attitude. It would be the same with this woman who stood before him, her head high, staring off into the distance with measured disinterest in her eyes. Hers was an unsuccessful attempt to make him believe she did not know that he was evaluating her every line from the high forehead to the tightly corseted buttocks.

"What are they deciding down there?" he asked quietly. If she knew, she might tell him. If she did not, then she would feel they were sharing a mutual and sympathetic exile.

She shook her head slowly. "I think this is an ugly country. Do you remember the hills soft and green with grapes near Sevilla?"

In a single sentence she had excluded him from her private problems here and invited him into a world they already shared.

Reyes took a bite from a red plum and the juice ran down the edges of his mouth and into his beard. He had never been aware of the countryside before, either in Nuevo Mexico or España. That was for women, but if she wanted to talk about the countryside . . .

"I remember when I was a boy. Great grapes, green ones and purple in clusters as big as a gouted foot. Hills of them. Great shelves off the hills." He lied with ease as he thought about the grey-rubbled room in which he had known his boyhood and the dark and dirty streets into which he had been placed at night when his mother needed the bed for her customers. He had seen grapes, though, when he fled Córdoba. He remembered them because they were all that he had had to eat the first night of his escape when he hid from the Inquisition. He smiled as he thought that everything had a purpose, even a flight from the executioner.

Neither of them spoke for a time. Then she confided in him what she had not yet told her husband: "I am going back to España."

Reyes evaluated the comment in the scales of his own plans for her.

"That takes a great deal of money, Señora."

She snorted and turned for the first time to face him. "Don Alonso is a Lieutenant Governor and he has property."

"He is going back with you?" He bit again into the plum and she thought he reminded her of someone she knew.

Shaking her head, she said, "I'm going to make the jornada alone. Don Alonso will want to remain here in this heat and dirt and with his . . ." She ate the last words as she looked away, regretting her sudden impulse to talk.

Reyes did not need any more. He flipped his garbage over the edge of the roof, wiped his mouth with the sleeve of his tunica and placed his two hands gently but firmly on her arms and turned her so that they faced each other.

If she was ever going to resist him, she would do it now, and his crime in her eyes and even in Don Alonso's would be small. She stiffened and he became frightened. Then she relaxed and her head came down as she looked at his dusty boots.

"I will help you return to España, Señora. I have some money. I can find more. I will see that you get back to España, and if you will it, I will see that you travel escorted as a lady should be." He was proud of the last part of his offer. It left everything to her. And yet he would see that she had no alternative.

Doña Josefa raised her head and looked into the close-set eyes that reminded her of an unblinking bird. There was much about him that was repulsive to her but now that she planned to leave García, she knew she needed help. The old warrior never gave up anything he owned.

Reyes dropped his hands to his side and crossed the roof with the basket again in his hands as he heard the heavy tread of Don Alonso on the steps. As he walked away, Doña Josefa said softly, "I shall accept your offer of help."

Reyes swelled inside. He had baited his future with a promise and it was accepted. The whole affair could be simpler to achieve than he had first thought.

They were staring off in different directions when Don Alonso emerged on the roof. He wore only his open tunica and a pair of pantalones, untied and hanging loose down the calves of his legs. He looked from one to the other as he stood, head high, breathing in the fresh morning air. The lines about his eyes told the tale of his fatigue. But his voice was strong when he spoke to them. "We will evacuate this place for Isleta within an hour. If you will join me below, Josefa." Then, as she came to his side, "Reyes, you came with nothing more than you wear, and so while the others are packing, you will remain on guard until we depart."

Reyes felt he could afford to be generous for the moment. "I understand, Excellency." He did not turn to face the Commander, and only as he disappeared below did García acknowledge that he was aware of this.

"Should an Indian cross that line out there, I will feed you to him."

The soldier whirled about in anger, but the Commander was already gone. He stood for a time in his fury, but eventually his mind wandered back to the Commander's wife and he started to laugh.

17

DON ANTONIO DE OTERMÍN opened his eyes in the darkness of his office. From the small streaks of light searching their way into the room from the blacked-out windows, he realized it was morning. For several minutes he lay still listening to the click of the clock pendulum as it swung back and forth. It was the sixteenth day of August. Seven days since he had received the first warning of the rebellion. Six days since the uprising in the pueblos. One day of fighting at the Villa de Santa Fe. And today would be another. The firing of an harquebus brought him to his feet on the dirt floor. He crossed over to the window and ripped away the dark cloth which had shielded the candle.

The sky was overcast. There were puddles in the plaza mayor. Water flowed freely through the ditch which served the palacio. There was no movement outside. Not an Indian to be seen anywhere.

The crack of another harquebus.

Then the return fire from the roof above him.

As he was pulling on his boots, he noticed that the room was empty. The blankets the young woman and her daughter had slept upon were folded in the corner. On the table beside his papers and maps was a pitcher of water and the pewter basin from his own sleeping room. He paused to wash his face before he slipped his baldric over his shoulder, checked his sabre to see that it came easily into his hand, and set his helmet on his head.

The firing continued as though to punctuate each move he made. Don Antonio listened. It came from the north. There was no activity as yet to the south. He stared down into the basin of water. As soon as he checked the situation, he would have to shave. The symbols and traditions. The discipline of himself before he demanded as much of others. His command was a part of the army of España. He would not permit it to become a rabble. His dark eyes seemed set farther back in his face than he remembered them. The grey hair on his head, falling back in a large wave, was still darker than his beard. He was not old yet, though he was approaching it—the being old. There was an alertness about his body he had not felt in a long time. It had come back with yesterday's action. It brought an efficiency to his movements while at the same time he felt relaxed. It was as though he had just finished too many apple brandies or mugs of Cuban rum. There was the feeling of being a man again which he knew was related to wearing his equipment for a purpose. The exhilaration pleased him as well as his acceptance of the fact that he was still capable of responding to the excitement. He was not old. He was not old. He abandoned thoughts of retiring. He was a governor and captain general and he was going to hold onto this province. He was not going to lose to some ignorant savages who did not believe in God or España.

The harquebuses kept breaking the stillness, interrupting his thoughts. Shoulders set, he walked to the door with a springing step and flung it open. Then he stopped. There were still as many women and children lying on the dirt floor as there had been the night before. Some of them stared up at him. There were questions in their eyes, questions to which he had no answers. Smiling at them, he made his way among the blankets and bodies down the corridor to his own sleeping room. Here the wounded lay staring at him as he entered the room. The young refugee who rolled back and forth from the pain in his buttocks, the soldier grinning through sliced lips which could not be bandaged and from which blood oozed out over his beard as though he had just eaten a live beast. And the women who had spent the night beside their men, waiting to see if they would die, or would live and want something from them as simple and important as a drink of water, or a pillow fluffed to ease the pain in a smashed arm or a slashed chest.

There were questions in all the eyes.

And the years piled up on Don Antonio again. Without a word he slowly walked to the main entrance. Pando was gone. In his place by the door stood the young woman whose husband had been a ranchero at Acoma. She said nothing as she held the Captain General's breastplate out to him.

"It would be difficult if we should lose the Commander." Her voice was soft even though there were none sleeping about the doorway.

"Thank you, Señora," he acknowledged both the armour and the compliment. "Have you seen Maestre de Campo Pondo? He is the tall, old giant of a man."

"He asked me to tell you that he would be up on the roof."

He contemplated her face for a moment. She was no more than thirty. Her cheekbones were high, her skin browned by the sun, her eyes pale blue, her hair char black. She did not look away, though his staring made her nervous enough to push back the hair from her forehead, and as he followed her gesture, he again saw the scratches there. They were black now as though they might be infected. Don Antonio had seen too many wounds not to recognize the symptoms.

Without a word he took her head between his hands and brought it close to him, his hands flat on her cheeks, her loose hair tumbling over them. He was the one who trembled as he spoke.

"Those marks on your forehead, Señora. Scrub them hard until they bleed again, and then cover them."

His hands fell to his side and he walked past her, out of the palacio, and up the ladder to the roof above. Only when the sun edging through the overcast struck him across the eyes did he see something other than the face of the woman from Acoma.

Pando crossed over to him and spoke for a moment before Don Antonio realized he was there. Then he shoved the face of the woman away from him, made up his mind to move her out of his office, and tried to listen to Pando.

"Excellency. The high ground. They are able to fire down upon us. The soldados are exposed. The women will not be able to pass a window."

Sighing because the questions were upon him again, the Captain General looked across the open space to the north where the Indians had gathered. He estimated thousands now. He would not be able to check any attack made with courage.

"The windows must remain clear. Station men at each. Harquebuses to cover as many as possible. If need be, lances to turn back any attempt to enter."

A piece of adobe shattered near his head. The Indian who had fired that harquebus knew how to handle a weapon. Twice more stones flew. Then one of the guards on the far corner of the roof slipped to his knees, holding tightly to his thigh.

"Get him off the roof. Replace him with someone else. We must keep this vantage point or we are caught in a hole down there."

As Pando helped a soldier to take the wounded man below, Don Antonio stared at the ground between the Indians and himself. The terrain permitted him to attack. If he did it quickly, the open ground could be covered with few losses. He did not believe that he would have another day without a death. He had been more fortunate yesterday than he had had the right to expect. Besides, there were more Indians now and fewer Spaniards able to bear arms. Stones flew again as the firing continued. Don Antonio knew he could kneel on the roof all morning, and come to the same conclusion.

"Sargento," he called loudly. The man who had spent the night on the roof bent low and ran over to his commander as two more slugs buried themselves in the adobe.

"Get below. Tell Maestre de Campo Pando to select fifty men able to bear arms who were not on guard last night. We attack as soon as he can assemble. You will remain here with the others. Your orders are the same as yesterday. Should we not return, you will die fighting."

The youthful sargento smiled at him and climbed down from the roof while Otermín still knelt staring at the open ground. He was trying to pick a route which would permit him to break into the clearing with a maximum of surprise. He needed every small advantage he could create. He listened to the firing for a moment. Then he, too, climbed down from the roof as adobe broke over him.

Going directly to his office without speaking to anyone, Don Antonio found the two daggs he had carried the day before. As he stood with his back against the table, listening to the loud cracks of the Indian firearms and the shattering adobe, he poured gunpowder from a small cylinder into both weapons, dropped steel balls down the barrels and locked the weapons for firing. Finished, he shoved one into his belt. He was still holding the other when Fray Pedro opened the door.

The stocky padre's grey cassock was neatly flowing, his face shaven. He might have been entering any office in Valladolid from his appearance and manner.

"I hope you found shelter last night," Don Antonio commented.

"The chapel." He stared without comment at the folded blankets in the corner. Otermín knew then that he had come to this room to sleep.

"We are going to attack again."

Fray Pedro nodded. He was not prepared to judge the wisdom of this. From the discussion he had heard at lunch, days before, he believed that Don Antonio knew his profession.

"If we leave them up there behind us," gesturing to the north with the dagg in his hand, "we will suffer losses on the roofs which we cannot afford. The Indians' vantage point limits our mobility."

The explanation was unnecessary. The Commander was reviewing his reasons for his own purpose.

"The refugee from La Cañada. The boy with the buttock cut away."

Don Antonio nodded.

"He just died," the padre explained.

Striking his boot with the weapon in his hand, Otermín closed his eyes. He had lost men before. He would lose them again. In this case it had been because of a horse. When the ranchero's horse stumbled, he had leapt clear, only to be struck from behind as he had tried to gain his footing. The cause of death did not really matter. It might have been another cause or another person. That was the nature of battle.

"That woman holding his hand last night was his wife?" the Governor was asking now.

"Yes. They had no children."

Otermín grunted. "If we have the time and still hold the cemetery, we will bury him there tonight."

He put his helmet back on his forehead as Ismael Pando appeared in the doorway. "Prepared, amigo?"

The Nuevo Mexicano spoke hesitantly. "May I suggest Your Excellency remain here?"

Otermín shook his head, tossed the second dagg to his aide. "You may need this." Turning to Fray Pedro, "We will be back shortly," and he departed.

Standing by the colonnade facing the empty plaza, Pando pointed to two of the smaller buildings beside the palacio.

"I have had the men assemble there. We will be able to bring the horses out when we are ready to mount."

The Captain General stared at the sky. It was clearing now. There would be no rain in the morning. "We will mount the men inside the buildings and come out riding. We will emerge in the cover of the buildings, cross this walk unseen by the Indians behind the palacio and then charge them from that side, leaving in file and swinging into a line as we clear the building. Our objective is simple: force the Indians off that high ground behind us. Instruct the men accordingly. As you ride out, bring my horse."

Pando saluted with a bandaged hand and vanished into a building. Don Antonio thought for a moment and then clambered up the ladder to the roof. The guards saluted. They were forced to keep cover by the irregular firing of the captured harquebuses. Kneeling, the Captain General scanned the area to the south. The puebleños were still there. There seemed to be no activity. He wondered if the Galisteon still commanded after his near defeat. Swinging around, he saw that the Indians of the north had stretched out in a long line. He was not certain if they planned to attack or merely harass him with their fire.

Below, he heard the horses emerging from the stables. Quickly dropping to the ground, he swung up onto his stallion, led by a hacendado from one of the northern pueblos. They rode quickly through the colonnade and out onto the field behind the building. The leading horseman swung wide and the others followed. On a command from Pando, they turned their horses toward the Indian line, quickened their pace as they rode, began to gallop when the Captain General cried, *"Por Rey y Santiago."* And then they charged.

To Otermín's surprise, the Indians moved toward them without hesitating.

The two lines crashed with a shock. The Indians, extending farther in both directions, swung their flanks around to enfold the Spaniards. Otermín found himself in the middle of the great circle. His horsemen plunged in every direction attempting to break the enemy line, but as they attacked in one place the enemy fell on them from behind in another. This was not the mass muddle of the previous day. This was not the meeting, weapon to weapon, force against force. This was a tactic, sharp and clean. Otermín recognized it for what it was. Yelling loudly, he tried to bunch his men together so that there would be no rear for the Indians to fall upon. Then he saw that something else was happening. Horse after horse stumbled and fell writhing to the ground, throwing its rider or rolling over upon him. The Indians were charging in singly to hack at the legs of the poor beasts, slashing their tendons or breaking the bones. In minutes, Don Antonio saw almost half of his men on foot surrounded by hundreds of Indian warriors.

His attack had collapsed so rapidly that he barely had time to call to the horsemen to help their compañeros and retreat. Lance in hand, he faced the Indians swarming about him as his men fought their way back toward the casas reales. Then he, too, spun his horse about and dashed for the protection of the presidio. The Indians followed and as the Spanish, riding tandem, arrived before the palacio, one of them dropped to the ground to hold the Indians back, while the other led the horse inside the building. When the last horseman had secured his cover, Don Antonio called for the others to seek the safety of the palacio.

From the roof above him, the reserve force fired their harquebuses into the Indian swarm, and as the enemy jammed together in the plaza mayor, the cannoneers began to fire directly into their midst. Some of the screaming Indians withdrew to their high ground behind the buildings, while others took cover in the abandoned houses along the south side of the plaza and in the church.

18

AS the Spanish retreated into the safety of the palacio and the buildings adjoining it, Juan of Taos rode slowly down the small hill from which he had directed his defence. Except for the few government buildings behind the wall, the Villa de Santa Fe belonged to the People.

With complete disdain for the enemy besieged in their own capital, Juan rode his horse up to the steps of the church of the Immaculate Conception. Here he dismounted and stood looking across the empty plaza at the casas reales. From the south, the warriors under the direction of Askon of Galisteo were beginning to infiltrate the edges of the town, and Juan turned to watch them. The young war chief with whom he had consulted the night before rode up beside him, weighted down in Spanish armour. A moment later Popé joined them. They stood together as Juan directed his people to keep the open area of the plaza clear. He had no desire to draw further attention from the Governor's cannoneers or offer ready targets for the Spanish guards whom he saw on the roofs.

Following his own advice, he turned to Popé and Askon: "The holy place of the Spanish will serve us," and he led the way up the broad stone steps to the large tawny building. Juan wore nothing but a pair of cotton pantalones, a bando about his forehead, and boots on his feet. He was armed with a sabre and daga, both of which had once belonged to Don Jaime. As those with him entered the church, Juan turned back to the palacio where the Spanish were entrapped. He cocked his head and looked up. Anyone watching might have thought he was scanning the roof tops. But he looked down dissatisfied. Don Jaime would have approved his tactics of the morning. And he wished he had that approval. What others thought of him as a commander would never mean as much.

Slowly he turned and walked into the church. Standing in the doorway, he could see that the holy objects had been removed. As far as the Spaniards were concerned this was no longer a religious building. Someone had already lighted torches and set them about the large room. The People all crowded back about the entrance. Juan could see that they still feared the building and the God who had been worshiped there. Popé alone walked down the aisle between the pews, his bull-horn headdress and his jaguar pelt incongruous in this setting. The broad shoulders of the man were thrown back. His head was erect as he strode up to the altar and turned to face the warriors who were staring at him. Many of the men of the southern pueblos had never seen Popé before. For them, he was a legend. The torch fires cast strange shadows over his high, flat cheekbones and large nose. He drew himself tall and scanned the empty pews.

Juan thought for a moment that he might speak from the altar of his enemies. But there was silence. No one in the large church made a sound. Outside, the occasional firing of an harquebus could be heard. Someone yelled in the distance. A horse's hooves clattered over some stones. But no one spoke.

Popé stood in the place of the Blessing Men and knew the silence. It was his oldest companion. He spread his large hands flat on the altar before him as though to brace himself.

The padres were gone. For him it was completed, all the years of work and dreams and hope. The work had been difficult, but it had been reckoned years before when he had walked out of the Villa, his back striped with the whip marks of the Spanish lash, his friends hanged, and his religion forbidden. Five years had passed since the Whitefaces had released him as unimportant, had treated him like a cow or a dog or worse, like a criminal one punishes and frees, assured that he will not again commit his crime. The crime of Popé. He recalled the words of the Alcalde Mayor Quintana when he had berated him years before in San Juan, harassed and threatened him. Well, the criminal was now the judge. The conquered, the conqueror. The heretic, the priest.

There was a battle to be fought before the Whitefaces either died or departed the kingdom of the pueblos. But that was only a detail and one that no longer concerned him. He stood in the place of the Blessing Men who had scorned the gods of the People. He, Popé, had turned the copper faces toward the old ways. This part of his work was done. The fighting belonged to the young. The seasons which stretched ahead were his seasons, and he would guide the People as he felt they should be guided. He would lead them down the ways he selected, teach them what he believed they should know, give them what he decided they should have. The choices would be his choices, and not those of the shaven-headed men or the White-face soldiers.

He turned his large hands over and stared at the open palms. The victory was here. Reaching into the small leather pouch which hung at his side, he drew forth a handful of the holy corn meal. With a flourish, he scattered it about the altar of the foreign God, across the niche in the wall that once had held the image of the Mother of the manger and the Child she had borne.

Juan watched, fascinated. Then he saw that all of the others in the church were staring at Popé. The significance of his act was complete. There was no question that Popé believed he was the victor. All Juan had to do was dispose of the remnant of the enemy forces and the people would again be the People.

Suddenly there was laughter, and the young war chief looked back at the altar. Popé, head thrown back, was staring at the ceiling and shaking with laughter.

Juan was startled. This was all too soon. There was so much to be done before the People celebrated the day of freedom. Juan had read the account of Bernal Díaz in the library of Don Jaime. He had read Zárate's *Conquest of Peru* and the diary of the Italian Pigafetta concerning the voyage around the world, and he knew the peninsulars of España were not to be treated with scorn or taken for granted. They had fought through worse positions and more perilous times than those faced by the Governor besieged in the palacio across the way.

Without saying anything to the men about him, Juan quietly slipped out of the church and walked over to the small friary that stood beside it. Warriors were swarming out of it, arms filled with the petty loot of grey cloaks which they would wear in mockery, books they would destroy in ignorance, and furniture they would abandon in fatigue. The flat roof of this building was low and the front wall rose sufficiently above it to furnish protection. Juan looked across the plaza at the casas reales, listened to the firearms of his own men whom he had left behind to harass the palacio from the rear, and walked to the back of the friary. A footstep behind him and he whirled. It was the war chief of Galisteo. Together they climbed to the protected roof of the building and surveyed the empty plaza with safety. Juan pointed out to Askon where the two cannon were located and explained how far they would traverse. His respect for them was limited so long as the puebleños did not gather in a large group where the cannoneers could reach them.

In a soft wooden beam that held the roof, Juan traced with his daga the layout of the palacio and its adjacent buildings.

The concept of a map confused Askon, but he tried not to reveal his ignorance as he rose to his feet to see the casas reales more clearly. From his place of shelter, Juan watched one of the Spanish harquebusiers on the roof of the building on the north side of the plaza shift his weapon. Having no time to consider the dignity of the war chief of the Galisteons, Juan rolled over, knocking the feet out from under his ally. With a clatter of armour Askon tumbled sprawling. An instant later a lead pellet passed over their heads and the young Indians stared at each other.

Juan was embarrassed at his ally's ignorance and at the position in which he had put the man. "I was about to rise to your side when I slipped. I am sorry."

Lying on his back, his white pantalones dirty from the roof, Juan ignored his companion and closed his eyes to the bright sun. He had to do something that would divert the attention of the Spanish, something which would allow him time to carry out his plan. He did not know what it was. His thoughts were interrupted by Askon.

"I believe we should attack at once. Your victory this morning and our tiring them yesterday should give us every advantage."

Juan did not bother to open his eyes.

"Last night I talked to men who have been inside those buildings in the past. I am told the walls are as thick as a man's arm is long. To attack now would mean the death of many and not assure us that we could cross the open areas, break through the walls and doors to reach the enemy. While the war chief of Galisteo and the men of the southern pueblos are bold, I must admit that I fear for the warriors of Taos and their allies."

There was yelling below and Juan, kneeling, looked over the edge of the roof. Warriors were streaming out of the church of the Immaculate Conception holding the lighted torches in their hands. Popé walked before them as they turned off the plaza to the south where the southern Indians had encamped. A moment later large clouds of smoke billowed up from below through the windows and doorway of the church. Popé had destroyed the enemy gods and the People were rejoicing. Juan looked at the burning church for a moment and then at Askon.

"Perhaps," he said, "perhaps Popé has found the way. The Señor Governor and his people may come out of their hiding place to protect their church or revenge it. We should be prepared for them."

He dropped off the edge of the roof to the ground below. Askon, hampered by his heavy helmet and silver-ornamented breastplate, followed. They stood listening to the sound of the harquebuses. The Spanish were firing more frequently now.

"They may be clearing the way for an attack, or they may merely hold their position and express their anger." He explained the alternatives to Askon.

"If they attack, we will destroy them."

Juan nodded. With this he could agree. "And if they hold their position?" Askon said nothing.

"Should they offer us no opportunity, let them use up some of their food this day and we will meet tonight to decide our course of action."

The war chief of Galisteo agreed, walked over to where his horse was held by one of his men, mounted and rode back to his encampment. Juan watched him disappear, shrugged, and decided to remain where he was behind the friary for the time being. It would serve him if the Spaniards attacked and he needed to direct his men.

19

IN the palacio across the plaza from the friary behind which Juan of Taos stood watching the fire consume the church of the Immaculate Conception, Don Antonio de Otermín considered another attack on the Indians. The disaster of the morning had shaken him, his small force, and the refugees housed in the casas reales. Another such catastrophe and the Spaniards would be finished. Don Antonio quietly rubbed his numbed arm where a war club had glanced off it earlier, and stared at the burning church. He believed the torch had been set to the holy place to draw him out, and he was tempted to accept the challenge.

Behind the Governor, Ismael Pando was seated in a chair scratching the scar on his chest with a bandaged hand. His wounds of the morning had been slight, though the abruptness of the defeat had startled him. The unbelievable swiftness with which the small tropa had been forced to retreat was still incomprehensible. He was more dazed than his commander by the tragedy. Perhaps, the difference was one of sophistication. Otermín was aware of the fallibilities even of Spaniards, and Pando, to whom España was more a myth than a reality, was a complete innocent.

Pando stared at the erect back of the Captain General as the peninsular watched the smoke drifting over the Villa from the church and the houses. The anger that Otermín felt was hidden behind his squared jaw and deep-set eyes. The temptation to emerge from the palacio and fight again was great. But he shrugged as he turned and looked at the Maestre de Campo.

"Should they attack, we will meet them. Should they wait, we will decide our course of action." The Governor had given all the orders he needed to face the situation.

Pando slowly pulled himself out of the chair. "I will inspect the guard."

Don Antonio smiled. "Gracias, amigo." He measured the strength left in the man before him. The years of Pando were visible now. It did not seem possible that he could have aged so greatly in six days, but his beard seemed whiter, his hair thinner, his hand less steady as he saluted.

Don Antonio crossed the room, took the bandaged hand as it fell back to

I

the old soldier's side, and turning it over, inspected the bandage. "It hurts, amigo?"

Pando nodded as he closed his fist tightly and then relaxed it. "But it will serve to crush a heretic should I grasp one." The white hairs on the back of his hand were shaved back to his wrist where some unwashed blood clotted about the sleeve of his tunica. Neither spoke for a moment as they stared at the blood. "I shall clean it off, Excellency. My boots as well. They will expect me to set them an example." Then he left the room.

Looking after him, the Governor shook his head slowly. The few discussions they had had on the responsibilities of an officer as separate from a soldado had been understood. He wondered for a moment what course Pando's life would have taken had it been he who had been educated at the Academia de Madrid. This was fruitless. Don Antonio rubbed his bruised arm. There were so many things he should be doing, but as he stood in the centre of his office, he could not recall what they were. Rations? What could he do about rations? They would use what they had with care and when there were none left, they would do without and when they could no longer do without. . . The tropa? What could he do about the tropa? The men were stationed where they could quickly take up positions for defence, or they were actually on guard duty waiting to be relieved. There were so few of them now. The young man who had died in the Governor's sleeping room while his wife held his hand. The two men who had never returned from the galling disaster. The fifteen who lay sprawled across the Governor's bed or the floor, watching the blood and the life flow easily from them. What could he do about the tropa? The refugees? What could he do for them? Deliver them a discurso, a lengthy speech filled with many lies to put their minds at rest when they knew there was little hope and less time? Or give them a short and stirring speech, reminding them of God and Jesus and the fact that they were Spaniards? At the end of either speech the situation would be unchanged, for all one needed to do was look out of the slit of window and see the church fire darkening the sky, and the homes gutted. There were things he should be doing, but he did not know what they were.

He slumped in his chair behind his table and picked up a piece of berry wax from a candle and pressed it flat between his palms. Then as he thought of the hours ahead, waiting for he knew not what, he unthinkingly shaped the wax into a small sabre. When he was done, he stared at the useless weapon, folded it between his fingers, and saw the pile of clothes someone had set on the table in his absence. Here was a fresh tunica, pressed pantalones, a white shirt, and, most important of all, soft, clean stockings. He came to his feet, slipped out of his crumpled tunica with the torn sleeve, and started to shave. When he was done, he began to change his clothes. He removed his pantalones and stood naked, surveying the bruises he had received only hours before. The length of his right arm was turning black and stiff. There were two small cuts on his left leg where he had been fortunate enough to turn aside the enemy lances. His whole body ached as he stood erect. The greying hair of his well-muscled chest and flat stomach reminded him that, while younger than Pando, he was no longer a young man. His white skin reminded him, too, how long it had been since he had bared his chest to the hot sun. That had been the way of youth. Now he was wrapped in age and the dignity which required him always to appear as though he were attending a formal reception. He sat down on a chair and drew on the clean stockings. Then he reached for the freshly pressed pantalones. He was stepping into these when the door of his office opened and the young woman from Acoma entered. Embarrassed, the Governor held his pantalones before him.

"Señora."

"I thought I might help His Excellency."

It was difficult to maintain dignity now, bare-bottomed, with a pair of cotton pantalones in his hand.

"Señora, I am not a child."

The young woman did not smile. Her blue eyes stared at the dark bruises on his arm and two cuts on his leg where the blood had already hardened. She wore a strip of cotton across her forehead, and he thought for a moment how much it resembled the bando of the Indian warriors. However, her black hair tumbling about the white skin of her face convinced him she was Creole. Her dress was a different one than she had worn the previous day. It was dark brown with a floral pattern of red and white on the bodice. He again remembered the shape of her breasts as she had crossed the square the morning before and his face reddened.

"Señora, if you will please leave me."

She ignored his request as she crossed the room to his side and put her fingers on the two bloodied cuts. Then she turned, and dipping his old shirt into the washbasin, she scrubbed away the clots until the blood flowed clean again. With two quick jerks of her hand, she tore the sleeves off his old shirt and carefully wrapped the wounds. Perplexed at what he should do, the Governor and Captain General decided to do nothing except wait until she was done. As she bent over to tie the bandages about his naked legs, he could see the swell of her bosom inside her loose blouse. It was only with great effort that he restrained his desire.

At last she stood up and looked at him. "All of us were concerned when His Excellency returned and walked in here limping."

He did not know that he had limped. "I appreciate your concern, Señora. I even appreciate your assistance. Now, if you will leave me."

He was not a tall man and she was able to look at him with equal eyes. "I do not think there is anything I can do about His Excellency's arm."

He was happy about this and agreed readily. She gathered up the remainder of his dirty clothes. "You would not want to be disturbed," she explained, closing the door behind her.

Don Antonio laughed to himself as he finished dressing. He stopped laughing when he heard the firing of the cannon which had been silent for almost an hour. Dashing to the window, he saw that several Indians stationed on the roof of the friary on the east side of the plaza were trying to drive his own men down from their guard posts above the casas reales with bows, arrows, and harquebuses. It was at these the cannoneers were firing. The loud explosions continued to break across the plaza, and he could see the holes opening just below the roof line of the friary. Then he saw the corner of the weakened building collapse and two half-naked Indians jump clear only to be brought down by the fire of his harquebusiers. The enemy holding the high ground behind the palacio off which he had been driven joined in the firing, and from the sudden silence above, Otermín knew his men had been forced to take cover.

Soon all was silent again. There were no Indians to be seen and his own soldiers were behind the walls of the buildings or the barricade he had ordered them to throw up on the roof above him. The sun was high now. He was hungry, restless, and angry with himself because there was nothing, he could think of that needed doing.

As he walked back to his table, Fray Pedro entered the room, his stolid face set and grim. Don Antonio braced himself for more of the news which this expression always meant and which the padre always seemed to bring with him.

The casual manner the young padre assumed as he lowered his heavy body into a chair warned the Governor further. There was little subtlety about the man.

Don Antonio decided to wait for the other to speak. It did not take long. There was an impatience about the chunky Franciscan almost lost in his large cassock which had to out.

"I have been asked, Your Excellency, if you plan to send a messenger to Isleta."

How simple to ask the question. How simple to let him decide if another man was to die and who it should be.

"The jornada to Isleta has removed three men from the Villa I could ill afford to lose. Should I gamble a fourth, Padre?"

The angry impatience in his own voice came through and Otermín was suddenly conscious of the fact that he had been irascible for days except in those few instances when he had been faced with the personal misery of Pando.

"The men of the Cabildo hoped that you could spare another soldado."

The blame was shifted. But why were the members of the town council too frightened of their own suggestion to face him with it? Then he realized why Fray Pedro had brought the idea to him. He might have ordered any other man to carry the message himself.

"It is my understanding, Padre, that as Captain General I—and I alone—command here, that I am required to heed the advice of the Cabildo when I seek it, and that I am to be present at its meetings."

Fray Pedro attempted to reassure him. "There was nothing formal, Excellency. The men were just talking and wondered . . ."

"Do not continue, Padre. Do not make the situation any worse. I shall not ask why you of the Church are here. I shall not ask who spoke to you. If I asked, I would learn who was not pleased with what is happening.

Then I would have two choices: appoint that person Governor and Captain General in my stead or hang him for mutiny."

Otermín was surprised at the bitterness of his own voice. It all came from the defeat of the morning and the week that had passed before it. To lose a province, the years of building his own career, and his good name. The bitterness of these truths choked him. He could not listen to criticism now. Not now. Not when there was so much ahead for him to do if any of them were to come out alive.

"I shall do my best, Padre," he offered. "If it is not enough, I regret it. At this moment, I do not think the man is here who can do better, and so long as the Viceroy and His Majesty saw fit to make the responsibility mine, there is nothing I can do but assume it. Therefore, you may tell the Cabildo that I shall seek their aid and advice when I feel it is necessary. Until then, they will have to bide with my decisions."

He brought his arm gently to rest on the table. The pains reached from his finger tips to his shoulder now, and he could no longer bear the weight of it. For a moment he closed his eyes. When he opened them again, he saw that Fray Pedro was about to depart.

"Padre," he called, and the missionary turned back to him. Suddenly the pains reached toward his chest and he swayed for an instant. His teeth set firmly to swallow the pain. He gulped, thought he was going to collapse, saw through half-shut eyes that the padre was turning away again, knew that he was being misunderstood.

"Padre." He called more loudly this time, and the strident tone in his voice brought Fray Pedro back to the table. With what seemed like his last energies, Otermín stared into the face of the man. "I shall consider the suggestion of a messenger. It may be a very good suggestion."

He had made his peace with the padre, but he had left no doubt concerning his position. This, too, was necessary.

"I understand, Don Antonio. Believe me, I understand the difficulties you have."

The Governor gazed into the dark brown eyes of the man, bewildered. All of the right things always neatly stated as though they had been read directly from a book on the care of parishioners. Never the warmth. Never the feeling. Never the compassion which denoted any of the understanding which meant that the padre's heart felt the pain which burned another's. Never the profound sympathy that the old Fray Custodio made one feel with a simple gesture. But there was nothing he could say other than, "I appreciate your feelings. And, Padre . . ."

"Yes?"

"The young widow whose husband was a ranchero at Acoma. I do not know her name."

Fray Pedro believed he was asked it. "Señora María Valdivia." Then he started to walk away.

"Fray Pedro." The man was trying the Governor's patience. "Fray Pedro, I would appreciate it if you would suggest to the Señora that she and her child sleep somewhere else and that I do not need her solicitations or seek her help. It is difficult enough without having a strange woman to contend with at this time."

The tanned face of the padre bobbed back and forth. "Your Excellency, I only thought that if she could help you there would be fewer small things for you to concern yourself with."

Don Antonio rubbed his right arm with his left hand. "You thought . . . ?"

Fray Pedro nodded. He was obviously pleased that he had overlooked nothing in his ordering of the life within the palacio.

"Padre, I am an old man. I am completely capable of caring for myself. Please do not organize my life. Should I need your aid, I promise you I will ask for it."

The young man of Valladolid seemed satisfied. "I shall tell her, Excellency."

When he was gone, Don Antonio sat quietly for a moment. He wished Pando would return. He did not want to sit alone until the Indians decided to attack. He did not want to make the decision again that his small force should sally forth to face numbers now probably more than twenty-five to one. He did not want to be alone to listen to the intermittent firing of the harquebuses above his head and off to the right where the Indians looked down on his capital. He did not want to wait until something happened, all the while knowing it had to happen. The Indians would not permit him to sit here forever, even if he had the food to do so. With difficulty he rose, crossed the room, and poured himself a large crystal of brandy. The firing started up again and then ceased. He wondered as he drank just how long his ammunition would last at this rate.

20

DUSK settled over the Villa de Santa Fe and as the shadows about the buildings began to blend with the darkness, the campfires of the Indians could be seen about the town. The fires which had been set to several of the houses were burning out now and the flames which had gutted the church of the Immaculate Conception were only a bright glow in the warm evening. The pock-faced young sargento of the guards stationed on the roof above the palacio could see from his post that the enemy ring had edged in more closely than the night before. The Indians to the south of the town had taken control of more houses in that area and those to the north had spread more boldly toward the rear of the casas reales.

The sargento rested his head against his harquebus set between his knees and closed his eyes. There was little possibility that he would fall asleep. The rebels had not stopped their intermittent firing, and their hysterical yells continued to break across the shadows.

He regretted not being a part of the two days' fighting. He needed to strike at the Indians, to destroy the familiar copper faces that kept gathering behind his closed eyes, the faces of those who had been his friends, of those who might know what had happened to his wife, visiting in the south.

An harquebus located on the high ground slammed a shot into the adobe wall near his leg. Dust and dried mud splattered over his feet. His eyes came open and he was about to set his own weapon down on a rest to fire it when he recalled the warning of the Captain General concerning the impending shortage of gunpowder. He shrugged and decided to fire anyway. Sprawling out flat on the roof, he took careful aim at a silhouette before a fire only a few dozen varas off.

The explosion of the harquebus on the roof brought the Captain General to his feet in the office below. He waited for signs of an attack, heard nothing further and relaxed. The Cabildo had just left Don Antonio's office after three hours of discussion. Nothing was determined that would in any way affect them. He had agreed that a messenger should be sent to rouse support from García. He held little hope for this operation. But there was almost nothing else left to consider. The wounded had been gathered in his sleeping room and the small dining room. Someone was with them at all times. Nothing more could be done for them. Even less could be done for the two who had died during the afternoon.

Fray Pedro, seated in a chair near the Governor, watched his alert face, saw the fatigue which lined it, and the crow's-feet about his eyes which had deepened in the past week. The high cheekbones of Otermín were accentuated by the sunken eyes, more hawk-like than when he had first arrived at the Villa. The padre watched the Governor limp back to his chair where he sniffed at a goblet of brandy, sipped it slowly and stared back at the missionary over the crystal rim.

"How many years since home, Padre?" There was warmth in his voice and an effort toward friendship.

The younger man chewed a thick lip for a time as he thought of the years "since home."

"A decade since the Seminary. Eight years in Mexico and here." After a moment he added, "I have not seen my father's house in almost twenty years, what with school and the Seminary at Valladolid."

"And what was home?"

The padre looked at the wineglass in his hand. "Grapes. Vineyards over the hillsides and shelved terraces stretching back and away from our house. My grandfather's house and his grandfather's house. War had torn the fields, bespoiled the vines, but they always came again. They were full green in my years. Heavy with grapes. My mother was a poor hidalgo's daughter. My father an arborer. We ate, were clothed, knew the seasons, our catechism. My brothers found women, my sisters men. But the land . . ."

He was silent for a moment as he slowly rubbed one finger about the rim of his glass.

"The land can only be shared by those who can eat of it. More and there is hunger. Families grow with the years, vineyards do not. I walked the long leagues to Valladolid. My mother's father had a friend. I was accepted at the Seminary."

The years had been long, and the story said nothing of so many things.

Don Antonio settled back in his chair. He had an idea how much was left out of the tale. The gnarled hands said something. So did the nervous manner, the frenetic energies, and the desire for the order which is security.

"And where is home, Don Antonio?" the padre was asking now.

"Madrid. Two leagues west of Madrid is the home of my father. My brother lives there now. My daughter, too. My grandchildren. My mother lived near by when she was a girl. The Otermíns have always been of the armies. My father fought in his wars and my grandfather in his. We have buried our dead in the Netherlands and among the Ottomans outside Vien. My youngest brother is buried in the Philippines. My sister's husband in China."

Fray Pedro nodded. He knew the history of España well enough to recognize it. He was about to ask the Governor about his son when the little girl walked into the office.

Don Antonio remembered her as the Valdivia child. She was about eight years old. Her night-black hair was drawn back, leaving the white skin of her face in sharp contrast. The bright pink dress she wore was crumpled and spotted, and as she stood before the two men, she showed that she was conscious of this for she kept her two small hands flat against her legs to cover as much of the skirt as possible.

"Are you looking for someone, child?"

The girl stared at her bare feet and then brought her head up to look into his eyes. "It is my mother, Your Worship."

The Governor smiled faintly at the courtesy.

"Your mother is not here, Inez." The padre and the obvious answer. Don Antonio tried not to smile this time.

Without looking away from the Governor, the girl spoke to the padre. "I know, Padre; but she is not anywhere where I can find her." And now she was talking directly to Otermín. "I have looked, Your Worship. I have looked almost everywhere."

Don Antonio set his glass aside, rose to his feet, and as he took her hand, "If you will excuse me for a few minutes, Padre . . ."

Fray Pedro was about to offer his assistance when Don Antonio's hand went up to silence him. "No. We will find her mother together."

The squared shoulders of the Captain General did not seem to move as he walked, dressed without a tunica, but armed as he had ordered all of the men to be. His right arm throbbed as he made his way through the crowded reception room. The young widow was not there. In the corridor leading to the main entrance, he released the hand of the little girl at his side so that he could tighten the drape over the window. He took her hand again. The harquebuses on the high ground began to fire. There was silence from the roof and so Don Antonio continued his search. Through five rooms, through the small dining room where the newly wounded lay in rows against the walls. Here the Governor and the child stopped for a time as the Commander spoke briefly to the old woman who was tending the casualties.

"They will live, Excellency. I have prayed for them and the padre has prayed with them, and they will live."

Don Antonio nodded. As he scanned the ashen faces and the bloodied bandages about the room, he was not so confident.

"You have seen the widow Valdivia?"

The old woman was hesitant. "She is not with Your Excellency? I would think she would be with Your Excellency."

Snorting, Otermín turned away. How small the lives about him were and how quick to believe. With him. He realized now the implications of having permitted the woman to remain in his office the night before. She was not with the wounded in his sleeping room and here he decided not to make his search known to all its possible misinterpretations.

The small hand within his was limp as they turned down the inner corridor which led to the kitchen. He squeezed it as he looked down at her. She was like others he had known. A daughter, a grandchild who was not quite as old.

The kitchen was dark and, standing in the doorway, they saw no one. Only as they turned away did Don Antonio hear the sound of heavy breathing. He stood undecided. Then he walked through the crowded corridor to the small chapel where Pando had gone an hour before. Here they met the old man coming toward them.

"You were seeking me, Excellency?"

Otermín nodded. "The messenger must be sent to Isleta at once."

"You have selected the man?" Pando was slow in asking.

"You know the soldado with the eyes that look in two directions? I understand from his own mouth that he is an old warrior. Fearless." There was an almost uncontrolled anger in his words and the Maestre de Campo was puzzled.

"I know the man. Sancho de Hoz."

"Find him and send him to me at my office. Should you see this girl's mother, tell her we sought her and that the child will be with me."

His hand ran through the child's dark hair, and as she reached for his right hand when they turned about, he felt the pain of even her slight hold on his fingers. Pando saw him close his eyes and lean against the wall in anguish.

"Excellency, may I . . ."

The Commander shook his head. There was difficulty for a time bringing his eyes into focus and he seemed to be rocking.

"Sancho de Hoz. The child's mother." It was an order and Pando left the Governor standing with his back against the wall and the puzzled girl staring up at him.

When Pando found them again in the Governor's office, Don Antonio had removed his shirt and was wiping a wet cloth over his almost black arm. The little girl was sitting in the chair behind the desk holding a piece of berry wax over the flame and watching it melt down.

Both turned to look at the giant in the well-pressed tunica as he entered the room, his white-bearded head thrust forward as he pulled the squint-eyed soldier after him by the collar. With what amounted to a flourish, he whirled the small man before the Governor. The half-cocked head of the man bobbed for an instant as he almost went to his knees.

"You wanted this, Excellency," Pando said softly. The soldier looked up at him, frightened at the tone.

Don Antonio continued to rub his arm in a futile effort to ease the pain. "And the girl's mother?"

Pando realized now why the Governor had given him both tasks. The peninsular had known what he would find. "She will be with you as soon as you have finished with this," pointing to Hoz, who stood quietly listening.

"Take the child to her. She is the one who seeks her mother, not I."

He waited until Pando took the girl's hand and left with her. Then he looked at the soldier. The man wore his tunica, but it was not buttoned. His boots were dirty, his hair uncombed. His pantalones hung sloppily over the tops of his boots. Staring the man's eyes down as he spoke, the Captain General held his temper.

"You told me you were a fighter. Perhaps you will have your opportunity. I, for one, hope not. But there is a message I would like you to deliver." He walked over to his table, and taking his pen in his left hand, he began to write a carta. Just as he set quill to parchment, the firing outside began again. There was no answer from the roof. Without hesitating, Otermín began to write.

The squint-eyed Hoz watched him. He knew to whom the message was to be carried. Everyone in the palacio knew that the Cabildo had discussed another attempt to reach Isleta. It was thirty leagues and more and all through territory held by the Indians. And then, if a man got through to the pueblo, who knew if the Lieutenant Governor and his people were still there?

"Excellency. The woman. I knew her before."

The Captain General did not look up.

An harquebus crashed.

The soldier stared at the ceiling as he tried to continue. "Before. In Mexico. We came north together."

The Governor did not answer.

"I knew her before her husband met her, Excellency."

There was the splatter of adobe across the roof above.

The quill scratched on.

"Isleta is far away, and someone else could carry the message better." There was a whine in the voice.

Another harquebus was heard.

"Excellency. Please hear me. If you want the woman, Excellency, I will stay free of her."

The scratches continued.

"I do not want her. Isleta is far away. Maybe the Indians have it now."

The frightened man approached the writing table and set his hands on it.

He was sweating now. "Listen to me, Excellency. You can not do this. You . . ."

Without looking up, the Captain General swept his pen hand wide and knocked the man's hands off the edge of the table.

"You are at attention, soldado."

The scratching continued as the squint eyes tried to focus on the carta. The man could not read and his fear grew over him like a wild plant.

An harquebus crashed on the hill to the north, and adobe fell away in the far corner of the room.

"She is not a good woman, Excellency. You will not want her. I do not want her." A pause. "Isleta is so far away."

At last the Governor was finished. With his good hand he folded the parchment carefully, held the candle over the fold and pressed his large ring down firmly on the soft berry wax. Only then did he look up into the frightened face of Sancho de Hoz.

"You will deliver this message to Don Alonso García at his hacienda or the pueblo at Isleta three leagues to the south of that hacienda. If it is not delivered, we will assume that you have died trying."

He held the parchment out to the man. Hoz had difficulty seeing it through the blur that covered his off-centre eyes.

Seeing that the man was not taking the carta, Otermín rose tall from behind the table and walked around it, whirled the man about to face him and placed the carta in a shaking hand.

"The woman, Excellency. I do not want the woman." Hoz was babbling now. "Please take her. Isleta. I could not find Isleta."

Two harquebus shots in quick succession. Adobe falling across the roof above.

The squint eyes turned upwards and the Captain General's hand snaked out as he struck the man across the face. The head bobbed back and the eyes came to focus on the grey beard of the Governor.

"Excellency." It was a wail now.

"You are a soldado. You are going to Isleta. You will find it or die on the way. Maestre de Campo Pando will direct you concerning the trail. You will leave at once."

Otermín walked back across the room to peek out of the draped window at the rear to see what had aroused the Indians.

Fear finally engulfed the small soldier. He ran and grabbed the Captain General's arm and tugged at it in an effort to turn him back.

"I do not want her, Excellency. I do not want her."

The pains of the blackened bruises ran up to the Governor's shoulder and down through his chest as he stumbled forward to place his good hand on the wall and brace himself. An instant later he swung about and smashed between the squint eyes with his closed fist. Hoz stumbled back, leaving the Governor's wounded arm free.

"No one has said anything about a woman. No one wants your woman." Then he stopped. His anger was taking him beyond his control. He walked over to the door, swung it open, and found Pando waiting outside.

"Maestre de Campo. This coward is carrying a message to Isleta. He is leaving here in the next five minutes or hanging in the next ten. Should he open his mouth to discuss anything else, hang him."

He saw the widow Valdivia standing behind the broad figure of the old man. The child was at her side.

"Should you want to talk to Hoz, you have my permission, Señora. But he leaves in five minutes." He stood back from the door and all the eyes in the reception room that were staring at him, bare-chested, his bruised arm black from finger tips to shoulder. The angry energies of the Commander startled everyone watching. Pando saluted, walked past his Captain General and took Hoz by the collar from the corner to which he had retreated after Otermín had struck him.

"Attention, soldado."

The native harquebusiers again.

The small head with the bad eyes bobbed upward and then straight ahead as the man gathered himself together and tried to fulfil the simple order. It took his last efforts at control to propel himself past the Governor and the refugees in the reception room and down the corridor toward the main entrance. Pando moved close behind him. Once the man turned to say something. Pando's hand went up to caution him. "I will explain the way to Isleta when we stand on the roof above."

An harquebus ball reached the wall behind them.

The small man hesitated and Pando reached out a stiff arm and pushed him on.

Don Antonio watched them disappear. He rocked back and forth for a moment. Only when he walked back into the office and closed the door behind him did he let himself know the pain. His left fist clenched and opened. His eyes teared, and he leaned over his piñon-plank writing table, shaking his head as though to ward off the harshness of the agony. He heard the door open and he could not turn to see who was standing there. Then he heard the door close.

"Who is it?" Tenseness backed his simple question.

"Fray Pedro, Governor."

"Is there something you want?" curtly.

"Your arm pains you?"

Otermín forced himself to face the man who stood by the closed door. He nodded.

"Only your arm, Excellency?"

Otermín's left hand grasped the back of his own neck as he tried to hold still.

"Your meaning, Padre?"

The shaven head came forward. The candelas about the room shadowed it. "The Hittite, Governor. Do you know the tale of Uriah and David, Excellency?"

It took Don Antonio a moment to realize what was meant. Then his whole frame began to shake as the laughter burst forth loudly.

"Padre. Padre. Padre. I do not want the woman. Only today I asked you to send her away from me. But I will have discipline or this palacio is certain to fall and all within it die. Die, Padre. Die. And with them España's province."

The cleric nodded slowly. "I hope your reason is as you say." Then he opened the door and left.

Rubbing his right arm with the palm of his left, Otermín wondered himself. He was no David and Señora Valdivia was no Bathsheba. But for the first time he did not know how honest his answer to the padre had been.

A few minutes later the youthful sargento on the roof saw the small figure of a man emerge from the colonnade of the palacio, slip into a shadow, and disappear southward. He crossed himself and hoped that he was the only person who saw the courier. Then he turned his attention to the campfires beyond the plaza mayor. The crash of an harquebus and he swung back to the north whence all the firing was coming. The Indians were intent on seeing he did not sleep. The night was black about him now. The ring of fires created their own wild circle of light and, above, a disinterested moon arched over both the besieged and the besiegers.

21

JUAN of Taos watched a small white cloud meander across the morning sky over the Jemez Mountains to the west. The day was bright and the wind was still. There had been no attacks from the Spaniards besieged in the casas reales below. He had waited patiently for them to erupt from the small, walled presidio. But as yet they had not dared. There were no signs of life anywhere behind the walls, on the roofs, or in the two small towers that marked the ends of the palacio.

Juan had spent the evening before with the Indians who knew the enemy fortress from the inside, who had dwelled there as servants, had been imprisoned there, or merely had entered to carry a message. From them Juan had learned that the tower to the east was a chapel and the tower to the west a powder magazine. It was the second that held his attention now as Askon of Galisteo proposed they make this the focal point of an attack. The two young war chiefs made very little pretence any longer of liking each other, but they had to fight together. This was possible only because Askon respected Juan, and indeed was even a little in awe of his way of thinking, and Juan knew he needed Askon because of the men who stood behind him.

"If we made a direct attack on that tower, where they keep the cannon powder," Askon was explaining, "we could throw a torch in there and they would lose their walls. Then we could walk in."

The men about him nodded. They were prepared for the bold move. Most of them had been fighting now for a week and they were eager to return to their wives and their pueblos. The only solution would be one that ended the fighting quickly.

Askon himself was only thinking of the girl who waited for him in the dwelling of his mother, the white girl with the delicate hands who had slapped him and cried on his chest. He was anxious to return to Galisteo.

And Juan of Taos had his reasons for wanting the fighting done. But as he stared at the tower, he saw flaws in the plan. "We could destroy the tower. But they may have removed the powder to a place where it would be safer. And should we fail to destroy the tower, the walls would still remain standing and the Spanish behind them. Should we succeed, they would have their buildings to fight behind, and they add the strength of many."

The southern Indians were almost angry. Their war chief's proposal was being rejected, its logic questioned.

"The war chief of Taos has a suggestion?"

Nodding slowly, Juan began to sketch out his proposal in a broad pictograph of dust. He talked briefly and then he looked up at the small cloud which was moving leisurely eastward. He ignored the discussion about him because he knew that he had offered a victory with the least number of deaths, and there were few who wanted to die to accomplish their end. It was not that they feared, but rather that they delighted in life.

Shortly the argument was settled. The southern Indians, swinging wide around the cluster of buildings and the low wall that marked the area under siege, returned to their companions.

The war chiefs of the northern pueblos walked back to their own people and explained the plan of Juan of Taos and all approved. When the small cloud reached the far horizon, the men began to move forward.

From the flat roof of the palacio, Don Antonio watched the Indians closing in from both directions. He had not expected a full assault upon his position. The advantage was his, and whoever had directed the fighting of the previous morning had not appeared the fool. And yet a direct assault was a fool's tactic. Calling to the soldiers and refugees who were still able to fight, he ordered all the men to take their positions. Then he saw the Indians swinging toward the powder magazine. Clambering down to the ground, he gathered his men to meet them, leaving only a few guards on the eastern wall. The firing of harquebuses increased on both sides as the forces began to group and present better targets.

Arrows rose and curved into the open ground behind the walls. The Indians charged the west corner of the compound, yelling as they came. Otermín, puzzled, ordered his men to fire directly into their midst. The cannon fired and fired again. Both of the fieldpieces were already swung into position when he heard the yell go up from his own men stationed along the eastern wall. As he whirled to see what was happening there, he saw the Indians were not following through with their attack in the west, but were already retreating to the high ground and out of range of his weapons. He had difficulty believing the two small fieldpieces and the several shots of the harquebuses had routed them so easily, and when he arrived at the eastern tower, he realized what had happened. Piñon torches had been hurled through the chapel windows, and flames were already reaching out toward the sky. In fury, he directed the men on the eastern wall to put out the fire which he feared might spread. The Indians who had thrown the torches had fallen back and were watching the confusion within the palacio. Otermín withdrew some of his men from the west wall to cover the east and ordered all of the women to help the men who were collecting jugs and buckets of water. A bucket brigade was quickly formed, and only when the fire was finally subdued and the small chapel saved did one of the women approach Don Antonio.

He had never seen her before, and standing in the middle of the open area watching the chain of refugees and soldiers passing bucket and jug from hand to hand, he tried to ignore her.

When she had spoken the third time, he realized what she had said.

"The ditch is going empty. We have no more water. We have no more water."

Dazed and unbelieving, the Captain General glared at her. When she nodded to confirm her news, he scrambled up to the roof of the palacio. She was correct. The small ditch which carried their water from the rio was blocked. Two dead horses filled a portion of its route, and in the scramble and confusion of the simulated attack on the west, the Indians had filled the rest of the ditch with rocks and dirt. They had even forced him to use the surplus that remained inside the walls of the casas reales to put out the fire.

He had been fooled, completely fooled. Whoever had planned the morning's diversion had succeeded. Otermín watched the chain of buckets break up as the besieged men and women began to gather in small groups to stand and stare at him. They wanted their miracle. They felt they had the right to one. Their cause was good. Their faith had not wavered. And they had expected it of him because he was their Governor, he was the peninsular selected by the Viceroy and the King to create the miracle.

He looked about for his aide. "Clear the area. Everyone must remain within the cover of the buildings."

Then he appealed to the faces now filling with doubts.

"All water will have to be rationed with the food. No one will wash. No one will drink unless under supervision."

He wanted to encourage them, tell them they need not fear, but he knew there was little to be gained by this. These people knew as well as he just how desperate their situation had suddenly become. He stared at the sky, saw the last of a small cloud as it disappeared over the eastern horizon leaving the vastness bright and empty of all but a blazing sun.

Holding his right arm with his left hand, he walked unseeing into the palacio. A few minutes later there was not a Spaniard to be seen anywhere. The few guards on the roof tops crouched down behind their barricade and began to anticipate their thirst. Inside the men and women were asking each other just what water the Governor thought he would have to ration. Their thirst grew as soon as they knew it could not be satisfied.

Maestre de Campo Pando and two soldiers went from room to room emptying the water from the washbasins and pitchers into four large jugs so that there would be some control. Twice they had to take the water forcibly from the women. And once a refugee ranchero stood up to face Pando. "My estancia, my cattle, my wife, and now not even a jug of water. Tell your Governor he will have to fight me for it."

Pando looked at the man, saw his hands, gnarled from years of work, clutching the small jug and nodded to the two soldiers with him. Almost compassionately they took the man's hands and opened them up. After they had emptied his jug into the common supply, they handed it back to him. He had not fought, but he was sobbing as he tried not to see the expression in the eyes of his small son who stared up at him.

When Pando reached the door of the Governor's office, he hesitated a moment and then noticed that Don Antonio was standing there waiting to hand him the remainder of the palacio's supply of rum, brandy, and wine. Neither spoke as the old soldier took the amphoras and gave them to the two men accompanying him. Then the old man ordered the soldiers to take all of the jugs to the kitchen and stand guard over them.

"And if you so much as wet your lips, I will see that you are flogged."

When they had departed, Ismael Pando and his commander were silent again. The Captain General stepped aside and motioned for his subordinate to join him. With the door of the office closed, Don Antonio made his way back to the chair behind his writing table. He was still holding his right arm. His tunica was hung over the back of a straight chair, his boots on the floor beside it. The front of his shirt was open at the ruffled collar, and he sat with his left hand inside his shirt, slowly rubbing his right shoulder. His lean face was tense, and his eyes had almost disappeared into his head. The high, bronzed cheekbones were flushed with fever. After a time, the greying head dropped back against the chair as though he were no longer able to hold it up. His eyes closed and only the movement of his left hand signified that he was not asleep.

Ismael Pando wondered what had happened to his commander. The occasional crack of an harquebus broke the silence. The windows were uncovered now and a wedge of light spread across the dirt floor casting small shadows inside each boot print.

"They decided what would happen and how it would happen. And we let them." Otermín was talking as much to himself as to his aide. "When did we lose the initiative? When did we decide to die, to let them select the time and the place and the circumstance? When did we decide we were ready to die?" He did not open his eyes. His mouth quivered as though he were in pain. Then slowly, as if rejecting something, he began to shake his head from side to side.

"You cannot die, Excellency. I might die, and that would be all right. Maybe it is time that an old man died. The land is dying. The Years of the Troubles have been many years. They may end with me. But you cannot die, Excellency." His voice was soft. It seemed to be coming from a far and lonely place.

"The right to die must be earned, Excellency. My father told me that when I was a young man. To die when the time calls for a man to live is a bad thing. You have to live, Excellency."

Otermín did not answer. His mind was on a sad jornada. He was passing all of the years before Nuevo Mexico and thinking of what route he had taken to arrive here. The old captain general who was his father. The years of study and marching and learning how to fight a small skirmish and a large battle. The years of his wife and the children. And the young grandchildren who boasted to Ciudad Mexico that their father's father ruled all of the land above el Paso del Norte. And the early battles. The ones he had lost. The ones he had won. And the others—the ones he had never been certain about having won or lost. His head continued to shake, continued to reject the prospect of dying here under a grey shadow that would never permit his name to find the light again, a shadow that would cover that name for his son and his children and his daughter and her children.

The Governor was not listening to the old man who sat opposite him talking about the years. . . .

"I remember when I was a boy we had good years. My mother was there then. One of the first women ever to make the jornada del muerto. There were the years of building. Then the Apache came. And the Time of Hunger."

After a while he saw that the Governor had not heard him. He rose to his feet and started to leave the room. At the door he turned back and said, "You have not the right to die, Excellency. Not now."

He waited to see if his commander had heard him, saw the shaking head become still, the deep-set eyes open and stare at him. They were dark and dry.

"We shall not die, amigo. Your father was right. There is too much left to be done." The eyes closed for a moment and the old man thought the Governor had left him as he had so many times in the past. But as he turned back to the door, he heard him say, "Will you ask Fray Pedro to take charge of the water? No one will question his honesty, and he will know just what should be done with it."

The old man felt better as he saluted, smiled, and left.

Why? Don Antonio kept asking himself. Why? España was become like an old loaf of bread, dried and lifeless and falling away. The centre had gone bad under the once gold crust. And the rot was beginning to cover it like jungle mould. God had turned his face away from España and the century soured the memories of those who had lived in it. Gone the glory. Gone the gold. Gone the great vague dream of a world that knew only España and Christ. The Castilian conquistador was become a hated man and no longer feared, and Christ was cursed by apostates who no longer believed.

What could Popé give them? What could the Indian promise them that was more than God and Heaven? Yes, and España, too. The Indian dabbled in the black arts. Only the Devil could be guiding the heretic. Otermín rose to his feet in anger. He would not concede another yard. He would not lose again. He dare not for the sake of all those who depended on him. It was one thing for a man or a woman or a child to be killed. But it was quite another to lose to the forces of the damned inferno, to the very Devil himself. His shoulders settled back. His face relaxed. The old Nuevo Mexicano's father had told his son the truth: there are those who do not have the right to die. And he had every intention of living.

He was standing over his desk trying to find an answer to his problems when the door opened and the widow of Acoma entered. She was alone. She closed the door behind her. For a time she stood with her back against it watching the Governor whom she did not believe had heard her. After a while he looked up and smiled.

"There is something you want, Señora?"

Her voice was deep in her throat as she nodded and said, "My daughter told me that you helped her search for me last night. I wanted to thank you."

Don Antonio focused on her face. The bando over her forehead was gone. The scratches were barely visible against the white skin. Her black hair spilled loosely about her bare shoulders. As she spoke, he was thinking of how she had cared for his wounds the day before and the line of her breasts as she had bent over them.

"Thank me, Señora? There is nothing to thank me for."

She looked directly at him as she explained, "I want to thank you for not finding me while my daughter was with you."

She crossed the room and stood before him, her shoulders thrown back, her head up as though she had not just told him about herself. "Your wound, Excellency. It is better?" She was looking at his legs where she had bandaged them.

He nodded slowly as she knelt before him and placed her hand on the outside of his thigh. "You have removed the bandage," she said, as her hand fell away and she looked up at him.

Reaching down, he took her by the shoulder with his left hand and pulled her to her feet.

"I am sorry I sent your friend away, Señora." He was holding her bare arm now just below the short sleeve. She was soft and warm. It had been a long time since he had even touched a woman, and all the years since his wife had died seemed like lifetimes.

She looked at his hand, the small, square knuckles, and felt the firmness of his grasp. "I knew the man a long time ago, Excellency. We both were younger. Before Inez. Before my husband. It was fitting that you send Sancho, for though he is a coward and a teller of great tales concerning himself, he knows the woods and the darkness. He was a hunter in Chiapas, in the south of Mexico. That was where we were young. He may be able to carry your message."

"And you do not care that he may be killed?"

She shook her head. "No more than I care that any other be killed. I was alone and we met here after a long time of not knowing each other. Then I was not alone. But now that he is gone, the only thing that has happened is that I am alone again."

There was no objection when Don Antonio ran his hand over the front of her dress, paused at her breasts, and then placed his good arm behind her and drew her to him. "There is much I must do today. But should you sleep here tonight, there is no one who would disturb the Governor."

Her fingers touched his limp right arm. "I will rub the Governor's arm with grease tonight. That will help."

Then she stepped back as he released her. Neither of them was smiling when she departed.

For a few moments, Don Antonio tried with difficulty to concentrate on his charts. Then he gave up the pretence and threw down the quill. If he could not die, then at least he was going to live.

22

FAR to the north of the besieged capital the rains began to fall in the early afternoon. Soon the small stream cascading over the high rocks beside the cave where Manuela de Marcos rested, swelled into a broad torrent and crashed hundreds of varas below. The waters struck the dry arroyos, flooded them and flowed on past the red-rocked buttes over white pebbles and lime dust gathered through the summer from the overhanging cliffs. The low, soft splash became a roar as the rio disputed its passage with the rocks. The echo resounded across the hills and carried down the valleys, filled barrancas, and disappeared into the far distance.

Lying on her back in the shelter of the cave, Manuela watched the rain dripping off the stone portal above her head. She counted the drops until the task became boring. She rolled over on her blankets, propped her head up on her arms and stared off into the grey-clouded sky beyond. For a week she had done nothing but sleep and awaken to stare at the turbulent land stretching below. She rose only to throw pebbles into the stream and watch them fall away. The large bag of food which Juan had left her was not yet empty, and the thought of it becoming so had not yet penetrated the mist which enveloped her mind. She was only thinking about the stream and the pebbles when she saw a bird, broad-winged and black with a red neck and sullen look, alight on the rock at the cave's mouth. Manuela did not move as the bird waddled into the shelter to evade the torrents which filled the world outside.

The sunken eyes of the creature scanned the sanctuary suspiciously. The small figure of the girl was still. She was fascinated by the first living thing she had seen in days. The dripping of the rain and the crash of the stream were the only sounds. The large buzzard finally realized it was not alone, and pausing only an arm's length from the girl, and at eye level with her, stared boldly into her eyes. Its broad wings fluttered blackly for a moment, its back arched, and the sharp talons of one foot raked the dirt of the cave floor, leaving scratches to mark its resentment. Beside Manuela lay a piece of pork which Juan had packed for her and which she had been eating for several days. The strong odour attracted the bird of prey, still hesitant and doubtful about the unmoving figure before it. Suddenly the bird grew bold. A flash of its wings, its bright beak, and it flew a hand's height over the ground, grabbed the meat and retreated toward the lighted entrance of the cave.

Manuela only moved to follow its flight. She did not mind. If the bird was hungry, she would feed it. For a time she watched the ugly creature ravenously devour the strong meat.

Then, very slowly so as not to frighten her guest, she reached inside the food bag, found another ham and tossed it to the buzzard. There was a flutter of wings as the scavenger pressed back, poised for flight. For an instant, Manuela thought she had alarmed the creature. Then the bird eyed the gift, picked it up in its beak, and whirling, flew out into the rain.

The girl began to cry. She was alone again, and for the first time since Juan had brought her to the cave, she was afraid to be alone. She clambered to her feet and ran after the bird. But by the time she reached the entrance of the cave, the sky was only empty grey and rain. She settled down on a wet rock. The falling water soaked her dress and the puddle at her feet filled her shoes. She began to sway back and forth to the erratic tune of the waterfall as her tears mingled with the rain on her face.

She sat for a long time before she saw the buzzard again. First it was a black spot in the distance. Soon it grew to be a body with wings slowly circling above her. Then it landed on a rocky ledge several varas away. Again they stared at each other.

He had returned. He had come back to be with her. She wanted to thank him, to pet him, but when she rose, the bird shied back and lifted its wings. She knew that if she moved another step toward it, she would be alone again. Very slowly, she stepped back and back into the cave. Then the buzzard swooped down to where she had been sitting and looked up at her. He was still perched on the rock when she appeared at the mouth of the cave with the last ham from the food bag. Holding it in front of her so that the smell would intrigue her visitor, she inched toward him. An arm's length away the buzzard hurled himself at her. She stumbled back, dropping the ham, and sat in a puddle of water gathered from the dripping rocks above. There was a flash of black and a whirl of wings and the carnivore flew off with the meat.

Manuela was lonely and now she was without food. But she had not yet begun to realize this fact.

All night she had sat up beside the entrance of the cave in the mountains and waited for the large black bird to return and keep her company. She was lonely and she was hungry. For two days she had not eaten. When she first felt hungry, she had entered the cave and opened the food bag. Now it was empty. She shrugged and went out into the rain again to wait for the bird. It was nowhere in the sky, and so she turned her attention to the waterfall, but somehow by comparing it to the movement of the bird, she had lost all the pleasure she had once had in throwing pebbles into the stream and watching them tumble off the edge into the distance below. Now she was lonely and bored. After a while she rose and walked back into the cave and looked into the food bag a second time. There was nothing more there than there had been before.

Disappointed, Manuela went out and waited. All through the remainder of that day and the next she had waited for the bird to appear, but there was no sign of it. The ground was still wet, though the rains had ceased. The rock on which she sat looking off to the distance was damp. Her dress was wrinkled now and shapeless. There were tears where she had snagged it on the rocks around the entrance of the cave. Her shoes were off and set together on the ground beside her bare feet. She looked down at her toes and wriggled them, crossed one leg at a time as she rubbed the toes warm. The pains in her stomach were beginning to annoy her more as the sky brightened in the east and the first edge of sun topped the far horizon. She found herself trapped between the loneliness and the hunger. And without knowing just why, she began to recite the only lines she remembered of all the studying she had done with the martyred padre whom she was no longer able to recall:

> And I to my guide: "Detain him a bit longer
> And ask what crime it was that sent him here;
> I knew him as a man of blood and anger;
> And ask what crime it was that sent him here."

She was still repeating the lines over and over to herself, meaninglessly, emptily, when the bird appeared in the sky. It hovered a moment and dropped swiftly to her side. She reached out to touch it and it whirled off with one of her shoes in its mouth. Her dulled eyes followed its course as it traced black circles about the morning sky. Swinging her thin body to the motion above her, head back, watching, Manuela saw the bird drop her shoe into the valley and return to her side. She did not move when it grabbed her other shoe in its shiny beak and flew away. Manuela watched the bird as it became smaller and smaller. Then there was stillness again. After a time she rose from the rock, stared at the place where the bird had disappeared, and went inside the cave to see if there was any food in the bag. She was surprised again to find there was none. She sat on the edge of her blanket and held the empty bag in her hand. Her bare feet were cold and damp. She felt a chill shake her body, and then she felt warm all over. It took most of her failing energies to wipe her feet dry and wrap the bag about them. Finally, she slipped back on the blanket and fell asleep.

How long she slept, she had no way of knowing, but she awakened as the large black bird swooped into the cave and landed beside her head. Her eyes came open and she stared up into the sullen face of the creature. The red-rimmed eyes set in the ugly narrow head looked blankly at her. Without warning, the creature attacked. Its beak darted directly at Manuela's face, and only her own fears jolted her body out of it path as the knife-like weapon slashed open the side of her cheek, barely missing its target—her eyes. The hideous head drew back and struck again. Manuela's arm rose to protect her face and the creature snapped at it. Then the sharp, dirty talons closed on her side and chest, lacerating her shoulders, tearing her dress away and ripping at her bared breasts. Manuela, shrieking, grabbed at the neck of the creature, caught its head in her hands and tried to shake the sharp beak loose. She rolled over and over on the dirt floor, clutching the head of the black horror as its filthy, feathered wings beat about her face and its razored talons tore at her shoulders and breasts. She continued to scream and shake the creature long after it had gone limp in her hands. Finally, she stopped and stared at it, dazed, yet victorious. The neck of the bird was broken. Blood flowed freely from her many wounds. When she was able to rise to her feet, she looked down at her dress, ripped away to the waist, at her arms, the whole upper part of her body raked in even lines where the talons had struck.

She shook her head slowly and tried to remember where she was, why she felt hungry, what had happened to her, and why her father or Fray Vicente was nowhere about. She raised her head and called their names. But they did not answer. She called for Juan, who was always about the hacienda, but he did not appear. Then she looked around the cave, bewildered. The dead bird no longer held any meaning for her as she walked out into the sunlight. She saw the whole vast area as though for the first time, heard the waterfall she believed she had never known before, and walked over to wash the dirt and blood from her body. After all, this was no way for the daughter of Don Jaime de Marcos to appear. She was going to Ciudad Mexico when Fray Francisco Ayeta departed the Villa de Santa Fe. She stood as the water of the falls splashed over her and considered how far she had wandered since the night before when she had fled her father's house and whether he would be angry when she returned.

Emerging from the water, she slipped her dress off and spread it on a rock to dry in the high sun. She wondered where her shoes had disappeared to and why she was wearing this dress rather than the robe and gown in which she had run down the steps of the hacienda and into the night. It was all very confusing. Then she remembered the blanket inside the cave, and returned to fetch it because she was cold. She saw the dead bird on the floor of the cave and wondered what had happened to it and how it had arrived there. Then she threw the brightly designed blanket over her shoulders and emerged again into the sunlight.

She fastened the blanket under her left arm with a pin from her dress. In the fashion of a native vestido, it hung just short of her knees. She looked about for a way to climb down from the high place. It was the first time in a week that she had had the idea. After a time she made out the trail up which she must have travelled and began the long descent to the valley below, where she knew she would be able at least to find berries to still the hunger within her before she tried to discover her way back to the hacienda.

23

POPÉ wandered lonely through the camp. He was weary. His foot was sore where a moccasin thong had rubbed it raw. He had a chill. The nights of sleeping on the ground near the rio had taken their price of his energy. His white breechcloth was dirty. His jaguar pelt had lost its sheen in the dust and the dampness. The bull horns rested heavy on his head. And victory was not yet achieved.

He sought a quiet place beyond the celebrations of the camp as he listened to the loud jubilation of the People, and realized it disturbed him. One large copper hand went to his head and removed the bull horns. They looked less formidable on his lap. Unconsciously, he polished them with an open palm while staring into the darkness to the south.

It was not supposed to have happened this way. It was all planned for a great burst of violence and then settling back to long years of peace. It was all supposed to be glory and a coming back along the way they had travelled. Now something was happening he had not planned. The killings were taking time and their toll of the People. The brief bright flash of freedom had become a smouldering fire waiting to break forth. But it had not yet consumed the enemy. The imposing bulk of the priest slumped forward as he felt the weight of the campaign, the responsibilities that were his for having taken the People down this unmarked trail.

For an instant he was bitter when he thought of the length of the siege. He blamed young Juan of Taos, considered removing the youth from his command, then changed his mind. The People were fighting Spaniards, and though none of the others was aware of it as yet, this youth was thinking like a Spaniard. The Whitefaces were woven through his mind. The ideas which emerged were the ideas that might have sprung from the silent aristocrat who had died so boldly and with such a dramatic crash. Popé's thoughts drifted towards the silent Spaniard and grudgingly admitted the magnificence of the man's death. This was character. This was true symbolism. This was the way Popé would like to die, should he have to die. There had been no long whine, no appeal for mercy or understanding. There had only been the cold certainty that comes of the confidence of knowing destiny.

A beetle crawled over his feet, and the priest did not move for fear of disturbing it. In the dark distance of the night a coyote argued with the moon. The black beetle chirped on the moccasin with the twisted thong. Then it silently made its way to the ground and disappeared in the grass, leaving silences between.

Two Galisteon warriors broke through the darkness as they charged the empty night, threw themselves on the ground in jubilation, rolled over and over and over until they came to a halt on their backs beside the feet of the medicine man. They were young. They were happy with themselves. And Popé, watching them, knew they were drunk from the wines of some hacienda they had plundered. Both became still when they saw they were disturbing the holy Popé. Sheepishly, one of them raised himself to his knees and stared into the face of his leader.

"We will win your battle. We will fight as well as the men of Taos." He was boasting now and trying very hard to show that he understood why he waited through the night before the Spanish presidio.

Popé held firm, acting as though the man had never appeared and as though he were still alone in the night. Then the other warrior pulled himself up, using the shoulders of his fellow as a prop. Teetering back and forth, the second youth put one hand on his chest and tore away a cord that hung there. From his trembling hand a crucifijo dangled beside a small ear of corn and a well-wrought turquoise serpent with the wings of the thunderbird.

"I am not going to offend anybody's god. I will love them all as loud as I can and curse them as silently as I can. I will owe my life to all of them and own it only myself."

He wavered in his drunkenness. Then pulling his companion to his feet, he staggered off again into the dark.

The old priest still saw the symbols dangling before him. They seemed inseparable now and this was the trouble of Taos as the mind of Juan was the trouble of Taos. The People had been immersed too long in the foreign pattern, had been bent too far ever to stand erect again. Never wholly Indian and never wholly white. His great hands rose up like a bulwark in front of him as though he were pushing something away. It was a trap and he had helped spring it. The People were lost between the world of the ancients and the world of the Whitefaces. They might dance the old dances. They might chant the known songs. They might in summer go to the lake of the pilgrimage. But behind their thoughts would always hang the fears that there were gods somewhere they might have offended. There were gods waiting for them to waver and so be consumed. Can a man wash off the waters of the white god? Can a man who has been married under the image of a foreign god say now that god had no power? Could a man whose father was buried beside the white kiva under a white cross to the chant of the foreign tongue say that the god who had been asked for his blessing was a god without power? At what point does a man free himself of the ills of the past and know that the gods to whom he once knelt no longer reign? When the hunt fails and the crops wither, when the birds find another sky and the old die and the young seek new ways—is this the time that a man changes gods? Popé did not expect the world to brighten suddenly and the skies to fill with new plumage, the corn to grow larger and the grass a deeper green because he had turned the People away from him of the limp hands. What he had expected was a rest of soul, a fresh affinity with the black beetle and the fragile antelope, the turquoise sky and the red waters of the Rio Chama. Instead, he saw dangling before him the twin talisman of the cross and the corn. Well, he was not done yet. There was so much that he had to bring back to the

People. If only they were again the People, instead of the drunken cavorting celebrants cheering a victory which was not yet a victory.

The medicine man recalled the frown that had gathered on the face of Juan of Taos when he, Popé had stood at the altar of the white kiva of the Immaculate Conception days before. He was forced to agree with Juan that this was not yet the time to celebrate the defeat of an enemy who was not yet ready to concede it.

Juan of Taos. The young man troubled the thoughts of the medicine man. The time would come when they would stand face to face across the gap that separated them and he believed they would never be able to breach it. For Popé knew what the others of Taos did not know. He knew of the young man's long ride into the darkness for the daughter of the Silent Spaniard. He knew, too, of the journey to the Sacred Cave in search of a sanctuary. He had told no others because he had accepted the compromise which came from his need. And he needed Juan of Taos as did all of the People. Needed him because there was no one else among the People so well equipped to think inside the mind of the stocky figure in the leather tunica with the heavy silver cross about his neck who was the Governor and Captain General. How long would he have to accept the strength of his enemies to defeat his enemies? That long he would need Juan of Taos. If he had ever doubted the youth's value, those doubts were dispelled in the days of the siege when all the fine skills and knowledge of Spanish strategy had been brought against the Spaniards themselves. Popé had thrilled at the first sharp victory when the Governor and his soldados had lost their advantage and dropped back into the palacio as prisoners on their own ground. Popé had been elated with the others when the water sluice had dried up and with it the hopes of the enemy for eventual victory. Time was burning out like a dried mesquite bush. Now their time was almost a dead thing. With it too the time of Juan of Taos's ascendency over the People. The ascendency which seemed to carry with it a strange and quiet acceptance of the People as inferior and a contempt for their ignorance of the Spanish way of life.

There was a tumult near the edge of the camp, and Popé rose to his feet as he saw Juan and the war chief of Galisteo approaching him through the darkness. Askon of Galisteo had convinced Popé of the importance of Juan and the need for him. He had shown how little the People knew of the enemy and, more important, of war itself. But in the days which the old priest had spent with the ambitious youth, he had also been shown by the Galisteon the qualities he had desired for the People. Simplicity. Lack of deviousness. Naïveté that was linked to the daily things about him without seeking meanings beyond their proportion. Askon had reminded him that it was still possible for a puebleño to look at his fate as though it were a friend and something he would never doubt. This much he had learned, and this much in the learning had been against the continued power of Juan of Taos. But for the moment it was Juan. It had to be. The problems demanded it. Tomorrow there would be other problems; and these, Popé knew, he would rather face with youths like Askon beside him.

And it was another problem which had brought the two young men in search of him.

Askon explained the need directly without greeting or waiting for all the formalities of rank and age. "It is the Apaches. They have been seen moving south and are preparing to attack the pueblos to the north and west."

Popé waited for Juan to comment. After a moment the tall youth whose head seemed to be cocked to one side said, "It has been a difficult summer. Hot. Little rain. Game scarce. They want the crops."

Popé nodded. He might have expected this eventuality. He knew the Apaches, knew them better, probably, than any other Indians of the high plateau. Within the last year he had journeyed north to meet with them. There had been two long days of talk. He had not won the Apaches as allies then. Now he knew he had to win them or the past weeks would have been meaningless.

Askon put it into words without being asked. "If the People know their homes will be attacked, they will leave here, and the Whitefaces will be free to regain their power."

"This we cannot keep from the People. We must find the advantage in it." Juan was seeking again in the foreign way.

Popé was still. Very slowly he rose to his full height, set the bull horns back on his head. "The young war chief of Taos has a plan?"

Juan thought before nodding. "The Apaches—strangers—know Popé. They have heard what he has done for the People. They will fear his medicine and the words he can talk to the old gods." He paused for the effect as he knew Popé would pause, thinking as he did so how different his mentors had been. "Popé should meet with the Apaches, bring them to the Villa, let them see how the People can fight when they are united and let them help us destroy the Whitefaces."

Slowly the design emerged. "They will learn to respect us while helping us finish what we have not yet been able to do alone," Popé explained for the benefit of Askon.

"And," Juan continued his thinking, "it will give them an object for their plunder, satisfy the need they have to kill and destroy. Let this hunger know the Spanish for its game and not the pueblos."

Neither was waiting for Askon's approval now. Popé moved the next pawn. "We will tell the warriors that we have gone to bring them new allies. This will strengthen their courage and will teach them that when they can stand beside the Apaches as an ally, they may be able to stand opposite him in time as an enemy."

Juan bowed his head. This was his complete hope, the most he felt they would be able to gain from the problem.

"Then Popé will go?" he asked.

The large medicine man flung his head back as though seeking an answer from the blankness above.

"I will go and Juan of Taos will go," he said at last. "Someone must tell them how we have fought, the meanings of our strategies so that they will be impressed with the armies of the People."

Askon turned from them to look at the palacio silhouetted in the darkness. If he were fortunate, he might be able to complete the victory in the absence of the war chief of Taos and the holy Popé. This would make him a greater war chief than the People had ever known, would make his name ring through the long nights when the People danced and sang of the great ones.

Juan of Taos interrupted his dreams. "I will go if Popé wishes. Before I leave I would like to ask Fay-yat of Tesuque to stand in my stead and at the side of the war chief of Galisteo. Fay-yat knows much and the Spanish are among the things that he knows."

Popé saw what had been done: the shift of power to a man Askon could not question. "We had better leave at once. The Apache moves fast and the Spaniard nears the end of his thirst. Something is certain to happen."

He drew the holy corn meal from the pouch in his belt, scattered it about as he prayed for Askon and Juan and their separate missions.

Then Juan went down the small hill to seek Fay-yat and ask him to stand at the side of the youth of Galisteo and hold firm against any plan for an Indian attack.

24

THE noises of the Indian celebration rolled over the empty plaza mayor to the far hills behind the Villa de Santa Fe. The cavorting figures whirling, dancing, hailing the Earth Mother and the Sun Father, were frenzied silhouettes against the stark and shifting campfires. Seated on the roof of the palacio with his sargentos, the alcaldes mayores, and his aide, Don Antonio heard the crazed cries, the rash boasts. "God, the father of the Spaniards, and Santa María, their mother, are dead."

The men about the Governor awaited his decision. It had been three days since the water supply had been cut off, two days and a night since they had had anything to drink. It was almost midnight on the nineteenth of August. Twice in the past two days Don Antonio had risked the lives of the entire group to water the horses at the rio itself. This had meant taking every available man from the compound to guard the beasts, leaving the casas reales completely unprotected, ready to fall at the slightest attack. But as Otermín had explained, their lives might yet depend upon the horses. And with the slow dying of the cattle from thirst and lack of food, there was little question that they would soon be without rations themselves.

The condition of the refugees who were crowded within the confines of the government buildings and the palacio was becoming desperate. They had not been as fortunate as the horses. For them there was no succour from the thirst that tore at their throats. If the Governor was going to act, he would have to act soon. They could wait no longer. Another day and none would be able to act. And the day after that. . .

But Otermín did not speak out, did not give them any orders. The night sky was black now and he was thankful for relief from the oppressive sun which had hung over them through the long, sear day.

Pando listened to the Indians in the distance, watched their celebration, and thought of his last meeting with Fay-yat. Despite the days between and the darkness about him, the old man angered at the thought of the bright red altar cloth about the Indian's waist and all that that sacrilege symbolized. He remembered, too, the words of his old friend, the cacique of the small pueblo by the Rio Tesuque: "We had to do this thing."

Why could they not have talked? Once they might have, once, long ago, before the Time of Troubles. Once they had been friends. Compañero. Amigo. *Amigo.* The word leapt forward in his mind as he recalled the square face of the cacique.

Pando turned to see the Governor stretch out his left arm and saw that the right still hung almost limp. All of the men on the roof were waiting for their orders as Otermín moved to the edge of the roof and crawled down the ladder. When he reached the ground below, he looked up at the faces staring down from above.

"Maestre de Campo, I shall be in the chapel shortly. Please await me there." And without leaving time for an answer, he disappeared into the palacio.

The guard at the entrance saluted as the Commander entered. Otermín paused to check the condition of the man's weapon. The harquebus was cleaned and ready for use. There was rust on his sabre blade and caked blood on the hilt. But Don Antonio merely smiled as he handed it back. There was nothing to wash it off with.

A dozen women and children were sleeping on the floor of the narrow corridor. Several had found mattresses. Others had folded coats or blankets under them. An old man rose on one elbow to face the Governor.

"We will not lose, Excellency. We will be saved." Then his voice cracked as the fear creeped through. "We must be saved. I do not want to die." And he turned his face to the wall.

Otermín walked on toward his own sleeping room which had been turned into a hospital. There were fifteen men here now and two women. The women shared his high four-poster bed with the silken canopy over it. Someone had ripped part of the canopy away and he saw the blue silk wrapped around the leg of a refugee from one of the northern pueblos. He could not recall the man's name, as he could not recall even the faces staring at him through the faint light of the two candles set on a small table near the doorway. The straight-backed chair with the faded green brocade padding had been torn apart and a man with a floral bandage made from a skirt sat propped up with his back against it. The symbols dragged so far from Ciudad Mexico had failed to sustain them.

Don Antonio knew that in part the failure lay in the lack of dignity. The Spaniard had always lived with the dignity of greatness. But here he was humbled to thirst and the small frazzled ends of poverty. Here he was without the pride that had flashed like the pan of an harquebus, powder-quick and powder-bright. Here Spaniards were grovelling and waiting.

The two women lying in the bed had been hurt earlier in the day when they had exposed themselves to the harquebus fire of the Indians while trying to cross the open compound between the buildings. One of the women had lost a leg and the blood, stanched by a hot iron in the hands of an old blacksmith, still filled the room with an overwhelming stench. The other woman had been blinded by a sudden spew of adobe dust in her eyes. Her bandaged face jerked awkwardly about on her shoulders as she seemed to be seeking the light.

The smell of the sick flesh, the green gangrenous wounds which crawled up the legs of two of the men, the sweet odour of blood and the acrid stench of rot mingled within the small room that was already laden with the foul and heavy stink of excrement. The humiliation and the weeping. The vomit and the moans. The darkness and the horror and the thirst and the dirt.

Otermín's hand went to his nose as he closed his eyes and tried not to see or smell, wishing that there was also a way in which he could shut his ears to the sounds. But there was no avoiding the shame of it. And shame was what he felt. His stomach knotted within him. He knew his thirst like a lance in his innards. This he could survive, but the shame and humiliation and lack of dignity was what he could not withstand.

With quick strides he crossed the crowded rooms, mounted the steps to the chapel tower and walked in. His head was bare. Tears flushed his eyes despite his efforts to hold them back, despite his thirst. Several men and women were kneeling and praying. Their words were a low mumble to his ears. The fire tips of the candles moved imperceptibly in the still air of the small, closed room. Fray Pedro stood with his back to the door as he faced the altar. He crossed himself and turned to see the Governor bend his knees and cross himself. The padre was aware of a determination he had not seen for days on the face of the Commander. There was almost a brightness about his eyes, as though he knew what he was about to do though no one else had any concept of action. The padre waited until the Governor rose and stood with his back against the wall just beside the doorway. From a shadow near by Ismael Pando emerged to join his commander. Both of them stood facing the altar with the crucifijo above it. This was their purpose. This their final symbol. Fray Pedro nodded to several who looked up at him, blessed them, and joined the Governor.

"Your Excellency has come for succour. I am pleased."

Don Antonio did not know if this was meant to be a criticism of earlier remissness or merely the padre's usual statement of the obvious.

Speaking softly so as not to be heard and not to disturb the others, "Would you join us outside, Padre? There is a course of action I would like to discuss." And Otermín opened the door and stepped out, leaving the others to follow him. Protocol was a series of symbols which he intended to maintain.

In the darkness of the narrow staircase, he turned to the young padre and the old warrior. "Tomorrow we will attack. Every man who is able to stand will move out of the main entrance of these beleaguered buildings and fight. We may die. We may succeed to victory. But this is no longer as important as our selecting the ground and the time and the circumstances in which

men who fight for Christ and España will meet death, face it on their feet,
with weapons in their hands. We will move out at dawn and attack. Maestre
de Campo, we will meet an hour before the dawn to discuss our strategy.
Have the sargentos tell everyone fit to join us. And, Padre . . ."

"Yes, Excellency." There was approval and even eagerness.

"Should we fail to return, and well we might, will you look to those who
will remain behind?"

There was a long silence, for the favour asked was not a favour nor any
kind of request.

In the darkness, Captain General Don Antonio de Otermín knelt before
the padre and bowed his head while the other prayed. When he came to
his feet, he clasped his one good hand on the shoulder of the old soldier.

"I wish you at my side in the morning, amigo."

Then he departed. The older man and the young one looked after him.
Then the giant with the great broad shoulders slipped to his knee and waited
for the padre's blessing.

Tomorrow. Tomorrow. The thoughts of all it meant. The single cast with
the lone die. The final opportunity not for life or death but dignity. Don
Antonio stepped more lightly through the crowded rooms. The weight of
humiliation no longer bore heavily upon him.

When he arrived at the closed door of his office, he swung it open. By the
time he closed it behind him, María was at his side.

Don Antonio rolled over on his blanket, felt the weight of María Valdivia's
head on his arm, and opened his eyes. The office was still dark. No light had
yet found its way through the small openings between the draperies. The
Indian harquebuses on the high ground overlooking the compound had
broken his sleep. His throat was dry, and as he tried licking his cracked lips,
he found that his tongue was also dry. Carefully, he set a rolled blanket under
María's head and, groping in the dark for the support of a chair, pulled
himself to his feet. His right arm throbbed for the first time in days, and he
thought this sign of life encouraging.

Feeling about in the darkness, he located his writing table, the candle and
chispa. Two quick strokes and he had a light to dress by. In silence he pulled
on his pantalones, slipped into his shirt and his leather tunica. His baldric
in place, he shoved his dagg into his belt, took his helmet in hand and
pinched out the candle.

Crossing the room in the darkness, he was about to open the door when
María said, "I shall pray for Your Excellency."

They had not discussed the coming attack. It was not something Don
Antonio had ever talked over with women. They had their place in his life,
but it did not include war or politics or administration. In his mind women
were of a different world, made up of clothes and good wine and soft talk
and a warm bed.

"I would appreciate your prayers, Señora," he said as he walked over and
knelt down beside her. With his good arm he sought her in the darkness.
His hand behind her head, he raised it to kiss her warmly. Closing her arms

about his neck, she drew him down to her. Don Antonio passed his hand gently over her body, kissed her again and left the room.

A moment later he was outside in the darkness. Pando stood beside him and one after the other they climbed the ladder to the roof above.

There was no activity in the Indian camp, among the houses they controlled about the Villa, or the distant fields where many of them had been seen the night before. Their celebrations had tired them. Their victory had seemed complete and they slept assured. Otermín turned to one of the sargentos who knelt on the roof near him.

"I know the harquebusiers on the ground to the north are awake. Would you try to find your way toward the rio and return. Should they attack you, return at once. I only want to see how alert they are. I do not want to rouse them or ready them in any way."

The young sargento nodded his understanding, saluted, and descended to the ground. Otermín and the others watched him pause, take a deep breath, and slip into a shadow. A moment later he emerged from the blackness of it about twenty varas farther on. Then he was lost to their sight in the darkness. They waited for the Indians to react, heads cocked to one side for the sudden crack of the harquebus. Each man clutched the weapon he held as well as his breath. Then there was a slight scuffle in the dirt below and they saw the sargento had returned. On the roof again, he reported his mission.

"Nothing, Excellency. Nothing. Three of them with black paint all over their faces sleeping about a stone's throw from where I emerged by the rio. Nothing else."

Otermín nodded his approval, clapped the man on the shoulder with his good hand. "I shall remember your courage." Then he turned to Pando and the sargentos and began spilling his orders.

"Dawn soon. We move when I signal. First we infiltrate the north with most of the men. Sixty. The others wait for us to reach our positions and then they charge the houses to the south. Take them one at a time. Kill, kill, and kill. We will throw them into a panic before they can find the courage to defend themselves and dig in. Grab what prisoners you find and any cattle for food and then return. However, should they break, try to bolt and flee, chase them as far as the planted fields and no farther. We cannot hold more ground than we stand upon this moment. But if we can demoralize them and chase them back, we will do it."

He turned directly to Luis Quintana, the Alcalde Mayor of La Cañada. "I shall command the northern attack. Will you command the southern?" It was an order, and the eager Creole smiled. His split lip curling back revealed his black teeth as he spoke. "An honour, Excellency. I and my wife Isabella will always cherish the honour."

Don Antonio did not laugh as he looked away toward the darkness that lay to the south. It sounded almost as though Luis Quintana planned to take his corpulent wife out into the assault with him.

"Let us hope you live to remember it a long time." There was a soft chuckle among the men on the roof. "Pando, you will divide the men and have them ready to move out at once. Remember: no firing, no noise, no warning.

Just death for the rebels. Honour and dignity for Christ." Then softly, "Compañeros, the mothers of España have borne soldados." The Captain General saluted the others and, rising, walked away from them to the northern edge of the roof where he stood alone in the darkness. Pando waved the others down the ladders as they prepared to instruct their small detachments.

As the first light of morning crept over the hills to the east, the Spaniards mounted their horses. They sat quietly waiting for the order to move out of the shelter of the adobe walls. Their lances were set on their stirrups. Sabres were loose in their sheaths. Some few had their harquebuses ready for firing. Helmets were pulled low over their foreheads. Breastplates caught the early light and flashed it about the open yard. Each man was watching Don Antonio as he checked the cinchas on his saddle. He had not mounted yet. His lance was still held by his aide. He seemed to be smiling, but the crows'-feet about his hawk eyes were deceptive, and it was difficult for the men to tell just what the Commander was thinking. He tried moving his injured arm without success and abandoned the effort. The eyes of the women and children filled the high narrow windows as they watched the preparations.

Finally, the Captain General walked over to Luis Quintana. He spoke loudly for all to hear him.

"We will leave the mark of our heel on them, the edge of our blade in their bellies. Then we will return as one man, head high and proud of having fought bravely."

Quintana saluted. The torn lips squared over the dark teeth. But there was no smile.

Otermín mounted his horse, set his feet firmly in the metal shoe stirrups, brought his knees up high, his back erect and signalled with his lance to the two men who stood by the gate. Slowly it swung open, and the horsemen trooped out in two columns. One drew up in a long line in front of the palacio while the other spread out to the west and then swung north. Maestre de Campo Pando headed the column of sixty. The Captain General rode at his side, his stiff arm controlling his stallion, while in his left, he held the short lance with the steel head and the hardwood shaft. There was no sign that the Indians knew they were coming. Otermín spurred his horse and began to gallop faster. The line moved to meet his pace. His lance went high, and he shouted loudly over the clatter of horses' hooves, *"Por Santa María."*

The men about him picked up the cry and the horses hurled themselves into the mass of sleeping Indians around the remains of their campfires. Copper heads rolled over and stared upward as the lances, flashing from above, plunged into their stomachs, their throats, staking them to the ground like hides for the drying. Blood mingled with dust and ashes. Faces, black-streaked on copper, rose and fell. Startled cries of anguish and surprise and pain tore the morning. Indian horses unmounted and unsaddled fell bitten by lance heads. The ground was a writhing copper blanket as the rebels tried and failed to gain their feet. Warrior after warrior found himself caught and crushed to earth in the tide of stallion hooves. The Spanish whirled and dashed back and forth over their enemy. The slaughter was quick and simple and frightening even to the attackers. Within minutes there were none who could rise to face the Spanish. Those Indians who had gained their footing were without weapons or courage. They spurned the battle which had become a massacre and fled the field to the woods and hills beyond.

Warm with the victory, the Captain General ordered a half-dozen men to take prisoners, gather the abandoned harquebuses, and fall back to the casas reales. The others gathered about him as he listened to the clash of battle below and to the south where Luis Quintana had surprised the force of the southern pueblos. Otermín's arm went up as he led his men in support of the other column. They rode down into the empty plaza and beyond to the houses where Quintana's men had dismounted and were fighting to dislodge the enemy. Waving his men on, the Captain General plunged his stallion directly through an open door, pinned two defending Indians to the wall beyond with the point of his lance and the battering side of his horse. Jerking his lance back, he looked about the room. Now he was the only one alive. Swinging off the stallion, he thrust his lance into the dirt floor, drew his saber and rushed into the room beyond. Here two Indians were holding back Quintana's men with arrows fired from a window slit. Startled, they turned to face their assailant. But one was cut down before he had fully turned, and the other, only a bow in hand to defend himself, fell forward into the dirt floor on his face an instant later, a sabre slash opening his belly from groin to ribs. Stumbling across the bloodied floor, Don Antonio returned to his horse, grabbed his lance, and rode out into the fray.

The Indians were beginning to fall back, to yield up the houses in which they had barricaded themselves. Pando rode up to join his commander and together they plunged into the press of the battle. A face came up before Pando, and as he drew back his lance to thrust it forward, he recognized Fay-yat of Tesuque. In the moment of hesitation the old cacique disappeared in the melee. Pando spun his horse about trying to avoid the man who had been his friend, trying not to remember his threat when they had last met. Then he plunged his lance into the back of a tall warrior who was trying to unseat the Governor. The lean Indian stood upright. His hands went out as though stretching to hold the world, then he collapsed, pulling Pando's spear to the ground with him. A wave of bodies and horses washed over the corpse, and Pando was reaching for his sabre when he saw that Otermín was pressed by two Indians desperately trying to unseat him. One, swinging a Spanish sabre from a Spanish horse, was hacking at the Governor's limp arm. Otermín's horse felt the rein come loose and rose high as though seeking a way to avoid the fighting, screaming pain about it. The other Indian, standing firmly on the ground, swung his war club against the leg of the Commander. Otermín slumped forward. His lance slipped out of his hand as he groped for the reins and control of his stallion. The Indian swooped down, grabbed for the steel lance and thrust it through Don Antonio's leather jacket into his chest. The other Indian slashed at the Commander's face with his sabre, catching the edge of his cheek and laying the bone bare. Pando, pushing through the men about him to reach his commander, saw that he would be late, dropped his sabre, drew his dagg and fired it directly into the back of the Indian's head. At the same instant, Otermín fired his own dagg into the face of the man who had claimed his lance. The mounted Indian drooped over his horse. His helmet slipped away and he fell to the ground, face up, blank eyes scanning an empty sky. Don Antonio closed his bleeding cheek with the palm of his hand and recognized the face on the ground as that of Askon of Galisteo, the Indian with whom he had tried to parley days before. Then he felt the warm blood covering his tunica, flowing down his leg and into his boot. Eyes blurred, his head came up as he looked into the face of Pando.

The ancient Nuevo Mexicano's helmet was gone. Pando's hoary head jutted forward as he stared into the eyes of an old Indian who held the other end of the spear that was thrust through the Maestre de Campo's side. Both the cacique of the pueblo of Tesuque and the officer of the army of España held for a moment without moving. Then the Indian drew his lance back, dropped it, and caught the Spaniard in his arms and carefully lowered him from his horse to the ground. The bulk of the white man was limp except for his neck and head set rigidly on his shoulders. Otermín moved forward unarmed, but as he approached, he saw Pando shaking his head and warning him back. A cluster of fighting Indians and Spaniards carried the battle between them, and when Otermín could see the pair again, the old Indian was spreading corn meal over the dead figure of Ismael Pando.

Then a cry rose up from the Indians as they broke for the distant fields to the south from which they had emerged five days before. Now their war chief was dead and their allies from the north had fled, and alone they could not face the Spaniards.

Otermín, holding his torn face, watched them depart. Luis Quintana rode up beside him.

"Shall we follow?"

The Captain General shook his head slowly. "Assemble our men and the cattle they left. Take what prisoners you can find and let us return to the casas reales." When he swung back to the body of his friend, he saw the old Indian rising from the ground. They stared at each other across the body. Then the Indian turned his back on his enemy and boldly walked away. A young Spaniard raised his lance to hurl it, but Don Antonio shook his head.

"He has courage, he is an old man, and he is alone."

Then he wondered whom he was describing, as he turned his horse and slowly led his tropa back to the open gate in the distance. The enemy had been dispersed. Victory was his. Blood oozed out of the cut on his cheek as well as the one in his chest, and he felt very weak, very lonely, and very old.

When he had crossed the open plaza mayor, he motioned for Quintana to join him. "Take some men and clear away the ditch so that we will have water again. Have them clean the smell away before the water flows through."

Then he rode back through the gate which had opened before him only hours earlier. The other soldiers followed him and at his signal dismounted. Otermín was too badly wounded and too weary to drag himself off his horse and walk all the way through the palacio to his office. The face of a young sargento rose before him. "Will you try to recover my sabre and lance. They must be near the body of the Maestre de Campo." He thought for a moment. "We will bury him in the patio of the casa real."

And the face went away and was replaced by Fray Pedro's and María's. Otermín began to tremble from weakness and disbelief as he informed them of what they already knew. "The Virgin Mary has protected us and we have had a victory."

The padre and the widow of Acoma caught him as he slumped forward in his saddle.

The Spanish attack was a success. There were no rebels left in the Villa itself and few could be seen in the fields beyond. Eighty head of cattle and twelve harquebuses were recaptured. Over three hundred Indians lay dead about the Villa and forty-seven were prisoners. In addition, over fifteen hundred rebels were in full flight.

25

FAY-YAT of Tesuque watched the burial of the youthful war chief of Galisteo, saw the warriors wrap the body in a blanket and lower it into a grave. Beside it they placed the Spanish weapons and armour Askon had removed so recently from the corpse of Don Juan de Leiva.

Small holes had been torn in the Indian youth's clothes so that the life of these might escape and go forward with him. His body within the blanket had been huddled together as when it first grew in his mother's womb. Cooked corn was placed in the grave and water from the Rio del Norte so that he would not hunger and he would not thirst upon his journey.

And the words were spoken, the admission and the acceptance: "He has journeyed to Sipapu."

The warriors filled in the grave and began to prepare the next body for burial. The journey of Askon of Galisteo was beyond them, for he was now one with the gods and the remainder of the death ceremony would have to be completed by his mother, his woman, and the others of his family. For this four days must elapse.

Fay-yat stood for a long time beside the mound that held the empty body of the war chief. There were many things he should be doing. The morning had been a catastrophe. The People had been slaughtered in greater number than at any time he could recall in their history. The runners had already been sent to notify Popé and the war chief of Taos who had ridden north to meet with the Apaches. There was no purpose in bringing the plains enemy here to show them how strong the puebleños had become, for there was only evidence of massacre and defeat in every direction that Fay-yat could turn. He had held his ground with the southern war chief as Juan of Taos and

Popé had asked of him, but this had meant very little in the outcome of the battle.

Now the southern war chief lay beneath the earth at his feet. Now the sun dipped in the west and the day of Fay-yat's decision was recorded in the memory of those who knew him. The old cacique was aware that he might live another ten years, but the decision he had made that hot afternoon when his old compañero, Pando, had ridden away from Tesuque with the runners of Taos trotting behind his horses, the decision to cut the rope-of-two-knots and move the day of rebellion ahead by the single passing of the sun, had been his decision. He would always have to bear the knowledge that those who had died had died because of this. Popé had his responsibilities and would bear them. But he, Fay-yat, could never deny his share of the blood of the People that lay across the fields to the north and the south of the Villa de Santa Fe.

In a final gesture to his thoughts and the ones he would not think about now, he carefully spread a handful of the holy corn meal over the grave and turned to two of the youths who stood beside him. "See that runners are sent to each of the pueblos with the names of those who have died. I shall be with my own people to the north of the buildings of the enemy."

The two runners watched the short, heavy figure of the cacique as the old man walked across the fields. They saw that he no longer carried a weapon and wondered what had become of it. Then as he disappeared they set about their task.

Fay-yat felt the heat of the day that had been stored in the warm earth well up about his feet and perspiration gather on the red bando tied about his forehead. His arms were heavy. His legs were tired. The days of his youth. The days of his youth. The bright days in the bright sun. The days of the loping chase after the antelope and the mule deer. The days of the feathered shaft hurled against the sky to bring down the carrion bird. The days of his youth were gone. They had not died with the drouth or the Years of the Troubles. They had not died when his woman died. They had died that very afternoon not a hundred paces away when he had finally severed himself from them with the quick thrust of his lance into the bowels of the giant with the big hands and the gentle manner who had been his friend.

In each day's fighting he had recalled his promise to kill Ismael. In each day's fighting he had seen the great figure with the bright helmet in the midst of the battle and had avoided him as he knew he in his turn had been avoided. There are so many men to kill in a battle there is no need to seek out a man. But the Old Gods had had their way. There was no denying his promise in that final, futile moment when the People were being defeated and the war chief of Galisteo fell to the loud explosion of Pando's dagg. Fay-yat had killed his friend in his own anger and his own defeat. But he had killed him, and with the death of Pando, all the days of his youth had turned sour in his memory for he would never be able to recall them without the great figure with the smiling white face. And so he must reject the days of his youth and lose that final refuge which is the right of every old man.

In the distance ahead of him he saw the warriors assembled again on the high ground behind the Governor's palacio. As he approached, he saw the tall figure of Popé. Now he would have to tell the holy man what had happened as he had seen it. His bronzed and gnarled hand brushed back a strand of black hair that had fallen free of his bando. He would have to tell Popé and Juan of Taos that the Spaniards had defeated them, that the days of the siege had been meaningless and the deaths had been for nothing. They would have to begin again: the Spaniards within their walls, provisioned again, and the People moving up and surrounding those walls. It was like the cycle of the sun. It followed and it followed.

Fay-yat wondered what Popé would do now about the Apaches who were raiding from the north and realized that for the moment he did not care. As he approached the group, he saw the head of the Taoan war chief cocked to one side as though he were looking at something above him. The warriors fell away and Fay-yat stood beside Popé and Juan of Taos. Only then did he realize that the bodies scattered over the ground told the morning's tragedy more eloquently than he ever could. He felt the broad hand of Popé rest on his shoulder to comfort him as he closed his eyes against the strewn corpses. No one would understand that he wished he were able to attend the burial that was taking place within the walls of the enemy camp below.

26

IT was not until noon that the Captain General, his wounds fully bandaged, regained consciousness. He opened his eyes and stared at the dirty ceiling of his office and tried to recall the morning. The details slowly gathered about the new facts. His left hand sought his cheek, felt the clotted blood, and came away damp. His movements were restricted by the heavy wrapping sheet about his bared chest. Without raising his head to see the bandages, he wondered how serious the lance thrust was, knew that he lived, and was satisfied. He opened his mouth to call for his Maestre de Campo and then closed it again. Pando was dead. He saw again the startled face and the lance, the old Indian and the look that had passed between the two Nuevos Mexicanos, wondered if they had ever met, then admitted to himself that Pando had spent his lone shot to save his commander.

I might die and maybe it is all right that an old man die. You have not the right to die, Excellency, not now.

Otermín rolled his head to one side, saw that he was lying on the writing table in his own study. María was there, and as he reached out his left hand to take hers, Luis Quintana entered the room. The energetic Alcalde Mayor had abandoned his weapons and armour. His shirt was open and his bronzed chest rippled with muscles as he swayed back and forth in front of the Governor with his report.

"The guards are all in place, Excellency. The prisoners are being interrogated. The water flows in the sluice. Eighty head of cattle will feed us a long time."

Don Antonio squeezed María's hand as he swung his feet over the side of the table and pulled himself up to a sitting position. His chest ached, and he blinked without realizing it. He dropped María's hand and waited until she left the room before speaking.

When he finally spoke, he shook his head slowly. "We should not talk before the women. We must not give them false hopes or the chance to spread tales behind the backs of their hands."

Quintana bubbled his apology. "I regret, Excellency, but I thought she was . . ."

"Was what?" Otermín cut him short.

"I am sorry, Excellency." Quintana's face went white with embarrassment. He was like a little whipped puppy.

To change the subject as well as re-inflate the man, Otermín said, "The fighting this morning was well led. I congratulate you upon your success. Where are they interrogating the prisoners?"

"In the compound, Excellency." Then, to make it clear that he had not overlooked the praise, "My wife, Señora Isabella, will be happy that you were pleased, Excellency."

The Governor slipped off the table, stood for a moment with his back braced against it. He was still booted. Nodding his head towards a chair where his jacket had been thrown, "Will you help me with my tunica?"

Luis Quintana held the blue jacket up as Don Antonio slipped into it.

"I would like to hear the interrogation," he explained, as he started for the door.

"But, Your Excellency. Your wounds. They must . . ."

Otermín smiled, wondered what course the interrogation was taking, and walked out into the reception room. There were fewer persons there now, and as he passed from room to room, he realized that many had gone outdoors for the first time in days to feel the warm sun on their faces and know the sky again.

María Valdivia stood just beside the main entrance of the palacio, watching Inez as the child held up the sweated red bando she had removed from an Indian corpse lying a couple of varas from the colonnade. There were several hundred women and children in the immediate vicinity of the buildings, and Otermín watched them as they relaxed, enjoying their freedom.

His left hand, seeking the slash on his cheek, held there for a moment. "Quintana, these women, these children. They had better be kept close to the buildings."

María had turned to watch him as he left the shade of the palacio and entered the open plaza. Without acknowledging anyone, he slowly walked the length of the sluice, saw that it was cleared, the water fresh. Then he was alone with Quintana, who had followed several paces behind him.

The sky was bright and cloudless. The spruce in the distance barely moved with the faint breeze. The small rio noisily swept along its narrow channel.

Standing facing the capital of his province, Governor Otermín made out the black lines and splashes of soot left on the houses and other buildings by the flames. He saw the charred roof timbers that lay strewn in front of the church of the Immaculate Conception and the Indian symbols which had already been crudely painted on the tawny stucco walls of the holy place. The feathered serpent with the cloud for a body, wrestling with the great man-of-war bird which the Indians believed was the thunder and the rain. The crooked cross of their heresy and the arched line that was the sun.

He saw, too, the desecration of the crosses of the small Christian cemetery. He considered ordering a work crew out to repair the damage. Then he changed his mind. Victory was not certain, and there might be more that he could do for the living.

Quintana, an ever-active man, was annoyed by the silence of the Commander. He himself did not see any of the things which the Governor saw. To him the sluice was a ditch with needed water, the church a burned building, the cemetery a place that would be filled with the dead by nightfall. All of the symbols of authority and time passed him by. Only those which bore upon his own immediate life came through to him and then only as blunt facts. The Alcalde Mayor of La Cañada was a literal man of limited imagination, and not one who would ever know what really affected his welfare beyond hunger and thirst and a woman.

Otermín saw this as an advantage as he put his one good hand on the small man's shoulder. "We have lost a compañero who served God and his King with all his soul. We shall miss him. Yet, there is much to be done, and we must not mourn now or here. Not, at least, until we know more about the safety of these people." His hand left Quintana's shoulder and included the entire plaza in its sweep. "In the fighting four days ago my right arm was injured. Today I lost the other with the death of Ismael Pando. Would you be my arms, serve as my war captain until we have victory here or defeat, until I can make contact with Don Alonso García?"

The Creole suddenly felt proud, more pleased with life than he ever had been before. This was important. This was opportunity and the best way to see that Isabella, his wife, was well fed and cared for. "An honour, Excellency, an honour."

Together they walked back to the palacio, through the building to the compound behind. Here the Indian prisoners were trussed up in groups of three. Some few were strung by their wrists from overhanging beams. One of the soldiers crossed over and saluted the Governor. The sullen copper faces twisted towards him. Their only expressions were disinterest or pain. The black streaks across their high, flat cheeks were blotted now. Their stolen armour, torn from their bodies, lay in a heap. One Indian was being dragged across the open yard. The soldier held out his palm to the Governor. There was a broken crucifijo lying in it. The Governor picked up the cord and saw that it had been strung in such a way that the cross hung suspended upside down—a sure sign of blasphemy and allegiance with evil.

"That one was wearing it, Excellency." The soldier pointed to the wriggling form of the prisoner being dragged.

Otermín nodded. "Bring him here."

Then, as the man called to his fellows, the Captain General asked Quintana, "Does anyone here speak the language?"

"I have lived here a long time, Excellency," Quintana answered by way of apology for knowing it.

The two men holding the Indian flung him at Don Antonio's feet. Then they stepped back, weapons ready.

Otermín looked down at the man. He was close to the Governor's own age. His black hair was beginning to grey slightly. His hairless chest was hollow and his shoulders fell forward as he came to his knees, hands tied behind him, and tried to rise. With a boot on the bare chest, Don Antonio slowly pressed the man to the ground. They glared at each other, the conquered and the conqueror, the Governor in the pale blue tunica and the Indian haltered and naked like an animal. There was no quarter here. Both knew it. Otermín made no pretence as he drew his leg back, tempted to kick the face of the man, kick the dark eyes closed. He desisted. There were other Indians watching. In fact, everyone about the compound had ceased his activities to watch the Governor and the captive.

"If we were to untie you and let you go, would you then promise to live in peace?"

Don Antonio did not know if his words were understood, and so he was patient for a moment.

The Indian spat. "I will not surrender again to the gods we have killed. Popé and the People will return and they will bring the Apaches and they will destroy the Whitefaces and the Blessing Men as they have destroyed the gods of the Blessing Men."

The Spaniards edged closer to the captive. One of the soldados started to prod him with the tip of a sabre, but Otermín shook his head.

"You think Popé of San Juan will free you. Today he fled." Otermín knew where he had to take this interrogation.

The Indian tried to rise again to his knees. The Governor watched him and made no attempt to stop him.

Quintana whispered in Otermín's ear, "I recognize the man. An overseer from Pecos." This explained his knowing Castilian.

"Your Popé is a coward who fled this morning." Otermín dropped the comment with scorn. He was playing a game now that he knew well.

Again the Indian spat. "He was not with us this morning. He and Juan of Taos have gone to meet the Apaches and together they will come and kill you."

"Do you believe that lie? Popé left you to face us. He will not return." Don Antonio would like to have delved into the name Juan of Taos, but was closer to something more important.

"He will be back tomorrow. He promised the People, and he will have the Apaches when he returns. He promised the People freedom and they have freedom. From Taos to Isleta the People are free."

Otermín recorded the details in his mind, decided to weigh them with greater care. "And you would not live in peace if we let you go free."

"The Whitefaces cannot give me freedom. Rather than live with your dead gods, I would die."

The Governor looked at his prisoner and then over his head to the eager soldado with the sabre. "Accommodate him."

With those words he turned away and walked back into the building. Quintana was at his side when he reached the doorway.

"Remain, if you will. Try to find out if any other prisoner will speak of the Apaches and the situation at Isleta."

The Alcalde Mayor nodded. "This is important, Excellency."

Don Antonio smiled. "We would have enough difficulty with the Christian Indians, but the heathen Apaches. . . "

And as he entered the building he was thinking of the wild Plains Indians from the east who had attacked and harassed the province for the past several decades. Blind fighting marauders. Pirates of the plateau, plundering crop and pueblo and moving on to return again the next year or the next. No remnant of a hundred would ever be able to withstand them.

The victory of the morning soured in his mouth.

Two hours later Luis Quintana reported to the Captain General that there was no longer any doubt concerning the news. Each of the tortured Indians had confirmed the fact—the Apaches were expected and Isleta besieged. Don Antonio listened to his report with patience, and when he had heard the verbatim confession of the seventh captive, he put up his palm, "Enough."

Quintana hesitated. Then, "The Cabildo has a proposal, Excellency."

Otermín sighed. He had to hear them out. "Assemble them."

And to show his disapproval at their having met without him, he turned away and stared out of the window. He knew the Alcalde Mayor waited a moment before he departed. Then Don Antonio knew that María had entered the room. He wished she had not. This was no time for a woman, and as he watched the children playing near the entrance of the palacio for the first time in days, he wondered how wise he had been in involving himself with this woman, how wise he would have been at this or any other time bedding down a wench in his own capital—and at his age. He touched his cheek and found it difficult to believe that the battle had only ended that very morning, that he had only known María for three nights. Known her? He wondered about that. He knew the shape of her breasts and the softness of her stomach and the extent of her desires. He could call her by name and describe the colour of her hair when it caught the shifting light of a candle. He knew that she had been married and had lain on a kitchen floor in heat with a little man with squinty eyes. He wondered about Sancho de Hoz. Had the small soldado found his way through the enemy lines to Isleta where Alonso García was besieged? Or were the blank eyes staring askew at the blank blue sky, the throat of the man slit or a feathered arrow buried between the blades of the narrow back?

María. María. María. He knew she was standing beside him, wanting his attention, wanting the recognition before the others that he had not given her.

He reached out his left arm and drew her to him in the light of the early afternoon sun that filled the high and narrow window. He wanted to hold her close, but the pain in his chest shook him, made his body tremble and fogged his eyes. He closed them without looking at her and pushed her away from him.

"The Cabildo will be here in a moment. Afterward I will want to talk to you." He heard the catch in her breath as she walked away. He was still standing by the window when the men of the Cabildo entered the office. He swung about to face them.

On the ninth of August he had met with twelve men to explain what his plans were and seek their support. Two of those had died. Two others were waiting to die in the room which had once been his sleeping room and was now the hospital. The remainder all had dirty beards, unshaven cheeks, torn clothes, and weary faces with red eyes. Two of them had difficulty standing, and one old man, a merchant, slipped into a chair. Otermín smiled at him and nodded his head in approval.

"Compañeros, you have a proposal?"

Quintana interrupted. "Excellency."

The Captain General half closed his eyes. For a moment the others in the room thought he would lose his temper. Then he seemed to control himself with effort.

"Excellency," Quintana continued, "we understand your concern and your responsibilities. The others have asked me to speak for them."

Otermín nodded. His left hand pressed against his chest where the bandage was drawn tightly about it. Then he relaxed and rubbed his right arm slowly as Quintana talked.

"We do not mean to offend or disagree, Excellency, but we have talked about the situation. The infidel Apaches are coming. The whole land is devastated from Taos to Isleta. From what we have heard from the Indians I have questioned, Don Alonso García and his people are besieged in Isleta. We are cut off from the world. We will again be surrounded."

"There is very little food, Excellency." It was the young Alcalde Mayor of Nambé.

"And we may again lose our water supply." A hacendado of La Cañada.

"And we are weary, Excellency. We are very weary," the old merchant concluded.

Otermín sucked in his breath as he held to his silence.

"We want to withdraw, Excellency," Quintana pleaded. "We would like to take our families and leave Nuevo Mexico."

Looking from one to the other, Don Antonio waited until each in his turn nodded agreement. He did not smile. He did not show his pleasure that the demand came from them and not from himself. He had been thinking since he had first heard from the impassioned captive that the Apaches were coming to the support of the pueblos that he had no choice except to withdraw, but he had not wanted the suggestion to be his. He had not wanted it said in history that Don Antonio de Otermín had given up a province of the King's. Other things would be said. This he knew. But retreat, withdrawal, abandonment of a whole world larger than great kingdoms of Europe, this would not be laid to his door now. If he had been forced to make the suggestion on his own and forced to drag the others south with him to save their lives, this he would have done and damned the consequences. But now, now he was free of it and he was happy.

"This is your firm recommendation and I will have to agree with what you have suggested." He paused a moment. "In that event, let us leave before the Indians regroup and before we have even less food than is now in our stores."

The others waited for his decision.

"We will leave in the morning. All men, women, and children will depart at dawn. We must be prepared for a battle, should the Indians have returned by then, but if you want to go, we must do it then."

He turned back to the window and stood as he had before they had joined him.

The Cabildo slowly filed out of the room to tell the others. As Quintana reached the door, Otermín spoke without turning around. "Quintana, will you see that a document is drafted stating the position of the Cabildo on this issue and signed by all of those who were present."

"Yes, Excellency," and the lips drew back, showing the dark teeth in an unsmiling face. "I regret the decision, Excellency."

The Governor did not answer and the small man left the room, head bowed.

It was done. All the fighting, all the bloodshed and the deaths, had been to this end.

Don Antonio's head bent forward and rested against the adobe window sill. His eyes stared unseeing at the dust that lay there. All to end in retreat. He could not die because he had to live in retreat.

Grandfather rules all of the land above el Paso del Norte.

When María entered the room again, she could tell by the way his body shook that the Governor and Captain General was sobbing. She wondered why, for he had won a great victory that morning.

BOOK V

AUGUST 21—OCTOBER 1, 1680

Speech is civilization itself.
The word, even the most contradictory
word, preserves contact—it is silence
which isolates.   THOMAS MANN

THE Spanish evacuated the Villa de Santa Fe in the early morning of the twenty-first of August, 1680.

They flung open the gates of the casas reales and walked out blinking into the first light of the day. At their head were forty soldiers, fully armed and prepared to force a passage if necessary. To the amazement of all, however, the Indians merely held their positions and watched the retreat.

After the soldiers came the women and children, the aged and wounded. They rode double where there were horses available, but even so only two hundred were mounted and almost eight hundred began the long trek on foot. The cattle followed the civilians, eighty-nine head, lean and balky. Another forty soldiers brought up the rear of the long column. Most of these were afoot. Riding up and down the length of the straggling file, Governor and Captain General Don Antonio de Otermín attempted to hold some semblance of order,

He directed Luis Quintana who rode at the head of the column to set the pace and directed the sargentos in the rear to keep the ranks closed. But there was no way to prevent the slow line from stretching out. It made its way into the open plaza and crossed southwest toward the rio. Not once did Don Antonio look back at his capital. Not once did he pause in his efforts to force the women and soldiers to abandon their excess baggage.

Twice he stopped a farmer to explain that the plough he carried would become a burden as the leagues stretched behind and before them. To no avail. Twice he explained to the old woman from La Cañada that the small table she was pulling on a cart would delay all of them. When it did, he finally directed two soldiers to destroy it. No attempt was made to tell the señora who carried the crystal goblets that they would not survive the jornada. This she would learn in time.

In the bag behind the saddle of his grey donkey, bounced the religious objects Fray Pedro had collected. There were those saved from the church of the Immaculate Conception and those from the chapel of La Hermita de Nuestre Señora. Holding the lead rope of the small beast, the padre walked alone.

The heavy Señora Isabella Quintana waddled beside her husband, but before the column had travelled a hundred varas, she mounted behind him with the aid of several soldiers. The short-legged horse with the low-slung belly sagged beneath the weight and soon it was the Alcalde Mayor who was walking. His breastplate and arms hung from the saddle at his wife's side.

Don Antonio had dressed for the warmth of the day. He wore only a light leather jerkin, pantalones, and boots. His greying head was bared to the bright sun. His weapons and armour hung from his saddle, except for the sword at his side and the pistola jammed in the sash at his waist. His horse, a dappled grey, was the best he had been able to cull from the small collection of mounts available, and because he knew that he would be riding back and forth the length of the moving column he had not hesitated to claim the finest mount for his own needs. Each time he rode down the column he paused briefly at the side of María as she trudged, her hand firmly clutching Inez. Over her shoulder were two pairs of shoes she had scrounged and a small bag of food she had pilfered from the stores the night before in the pretence that it was for Don Antonio. He never knew how completely the others accepted her as his mistress, nor did he know that she used the fact for her own comforts as well as his own.

María was not a sophisticated young woman, but she understood the brittle, hot honour of the grandee, governor, and captain general with whom she slept. As far as she was concerned, he did not need to know that two of the four pack animals carried his clothes and his bedding as well as the collection of papers he had insisted on packing. María was only a farm girl, but the man she had sought as a lover and protector was better served than he knew. She accepted the utter contempt he felt for their relationship and made no pretence at understanding any of the ideals of duty and honour which Otermín polished with such intensity.

The column had marched without pause for over an hour when Don Antonio raised his arm and signalled for Quintana to draw his lead tropa to a halt. The men slipped off their horses and sought the shade of the nearest trees. All of the civilians dropped their baggage and sank to the ground beside it. Otermín watched the long caterpillar of a column come to a broken halt. Then he rode to the head to confer with Quintana. Moments later, several of the soldiers mounted again and took positions well to the front and sides of the column as out-guards. Don Antonio feared an attack with every moment that passed. He could not believe the Indians would let him escape in the open country without any attempt to destroy him.

He knew that if he were in Popé's position he would attack, and from what little he had been able to discern of the mind directing the Indian opposition, he knew it to be aggressive and angry. And he could see no reason why the Indians should change at this moment. He planned to make his retreat south, but make it with every precaution, prepared to fling down his meagre supplies and fight it out at any point along the way.

Once the guards had taken their posts, Don Antonio returned to his position at the rear of the column. Here he drew out the large parchment map of the province he had copied so carefully for himself days before. The route along the rio was the one that would yield the most protection, water, and possibly further supplies from any pueblos they might have to attack. But the route was certainly not a direct one, for the great rio meandered through a shifting bed. And it passed through many pueblos which it might be prudent to avoid. But as Otermín stared at the map and the alternative routes directly across country he knew he had no choice. There were the women and children, aged and wounded. Folding the map again into neat accordion pleats so that he could see just those sections he desired, he wondered if he was basing too much of his judgment on the protection of the refugees. What would the conquistadores have done in his position? What would a Cortés, a Sarmiento, have cared about the women and children? These men would have taken the quickest possible route, wasting not one compassionate thought on the consequences. If he erred, he knew he erred in favour of the civilians with him. And as he stood beside his horse and watched the scattered groups spread out for several hundred varas, their last meagre possessions with them, the children lying face down in the shade of their mother's sheltering bosoms, he knew he was thinking as a governor and not as a captain general. Somehow he had got the two offices confused in his mind. He would never be able to extricate himself from this dilemma. He was not certain that he should. Shrugging his shoulders, he put both hands over the saddle of his horse and pulled himself up.

He began the jornada south with the wounds of a week's hard fighting. He had bandages down his legs. One cheek lay open. His right arm was so weak and bruised he had difficulty holding a knife at mealtime. He had begun the jornada defeated, and out of this defeat, out of the retreat, he had to recoup some success for España and, yes, some last fragment of respect for himself. It was no longer important to Don Antonio that he had lost his capital, had been made a fool by the fates. The defeat was part of life, and he was a soldier, trained and hardened in the scorching forges of too many battles, to hold his regrets before him as a talisman of failure. What mattered now, what counted in this last effort to move a thousand ill-equipped, poorly shod, and hungry persons across enemy country in the heat of a desert summer, was his own faith in himself as well as in the God to whom he prayed. Don Antonio de Otermín for all of his years and all of his battles and all of his fortunes—for good and ill—was a religious man. He warmed to the thought of the prayer said over him by the Fray Custodio. He curdled at the memory of the red altar cloth about the waist of the war chief of Galisteo. So for God and himself, as well as the crown he served, Don Antonio knew he had to drag this weary rabble of refugees, soldiers, clergy, and wounded a long way down the length of the great rio until he could find the place to pause, regroup, and plan his return. He was not beaten. He would not be beaten. Not *While Life Remains:* a finger of his left hand traced the family creed embossed on the helmet hanging from his saddle as he pressed spur to horse and trotted to the three small wagons that held the wounded.

There were thirteen men in the two-wheeled wooden carretas. Fray Pedro had arranged for a canopy to be raised against the sun, but the heavy draperies only captured and held the heat. Most of the men were stripped to the waist and already covered with red dust. There were four women in the wagons. One of them was blind, another had lost a leg, a third was expecting a child, and the fourth—a whore—was dying of the French pox.

Don Antonio swung off his horse and stood beside the first carreta. The

bed was padded against the jolting rocks with the mattress from his own
four-poster back at the abandoned palacio. Running his hand over the crudely
made wooden wheel, he doubted if it would survive the long jornada.

Four dust-covered faces stared at him over the side. Pain was there as well
as despair. Otermín smiled at them. "We will get you to safety," was all
he said as he turned away. There was nothing else he could do here.

The women were in the second cart. They lay with their feet sticking
out of the open end, heads resting on bundles of dresses and draperies he
recognized as having been pilfered from the casa real. One of the women
raised herself on her elbow and stared at him. Her reddish hair hung loosely
over her bare shoulders. The rouge on her face was almost lost in the flush
of heat and fever. She ran a hand over her small dried dugs as she grinned
at the Governor. "When you get bored with that farm sow, I will still be
lying here, Excellency."

Otermín's stomach tightened. He walked by as though he had not heard
her. He did hear her, however, as he heard the crying of the young widow
lying beside her, waiting for her child. For a moment he thought of his own
wife and daughter, was thankful they were not here, and without moving on
to the next carreta, he pulled himself up onto his horse and raised one hand.

The break had been long enough. It was too early in the day to bog down
here where the Indians were still so close. He heard the loud voice of
Quintana and saw the refugees and soldados struggle to their feet and
straggle on.

Seated on his horse, Otermín remained where he was and let the column
move past him. Too many were without shoes. Too many of the men wore
boots that would not last ten leagues of walking. Too many of the women
began the jornada wearing fancy shoes. The Captain General watched the
high wooden heels sink into the sand and red clay and drag back their legs.
He saw the brocade covering of fine shoes from Madrid or Sevilla or Ciudad
Mexico and recognized the folly. He recognized, too, the impossibility of
talking these women into throwing the shoes into the closest clump of bunch
grass and forgetting them. They had a long way to walk. They would learn
for themselves with sore calves and blistered feet what was the best means
of walking across the torn and ragged countryside.

His knees high in front of him as he nodded his head at each passing
group, Otermín realized how much these refugees reminded him of the
tropas of young soldados he had first met in his early years in Nueva España.
They were the eager boys who always carried too much equipment and
always attempted to haul away too much plunder from the raided English
port. The route of any long march was always marked with excess baggage
and the fineries of English homes. A smile came to his bearded lips as he
watched a tall woman who held a young boy by one hand and a large clock
in the other, pause to adjust the clock's weight. She turned a blonde head
toward him and smiled. He nodded in recognition. Some soldier's wife or
hacendado's widow.

The three carretas of wounded were dragged past by three old horses. Don
Antonio tried not to see them. He had known wounds and wounded all his

adult life. He had seen the dead and lived among the dying. He had buried his share of compañeros from one end of empire to the other, but he did not want to see the gat-toothed leer of the dying whore who had invited him to share her pallet when he wearied of María. He had never been able to equate his own life and his own needs with those of the patrons of the casas de putas of the world, but he knew the needs were the same and the loneliness cut as deeply.

Riding slowly across the broken landscape that was the scene of his failure, Otermín wondered about Flavius Vegetius Renatus. What had Vegetius, the old Roman, written of defeat? This was the portion of the maxims no one had bothered to teach him at the Academia. When Vegetius wrote in the fourth century, Rome's retreat was already a rout. But where were the maxims of defeat? Or did the old strategist fear to send these on to his Emperor as Otermín feared to tell his own Viceroy and King of the catastrophe?

Who regards defeat? Who makes maxims of it?

Did Vegetius know defeat? Did the old Roman lie to himself and forget to record the holocaust that was Adrianople? Could he ignore the Goths sweeping Rome back and back?

De Re Militari. The Rules of Warfare. Do they include failure?

It is essential to know the character of the enemy and of their principle officers, whether they be rash or cautious, enterprising or timid, whether they fight from careful plan or from chance.

Otermín watched the dust rise about the long column stretching too long again, and wondered if he knew even this much about himself.

Rash or cautious? Enterprising or timid? Careful calculation or chance?

He had won battles and lost them. Made his desperate attacks from desperate necessity. And then with the back of the routed enemy before him, he had withdrawn of his own choice, pulled down his own flag, abandoned his own capital.

How does a man judge circumstances? Is survival victory enough? Should he have held his ground, let his flag fly until the Indians overwhelmed him and desecrated it? Gone down with his sword in his hand, an arrow in his stomach, dragging with him a thousand men and women and children? At what cost does one polish his own honour? With whose blood?

2

ONE of the mounted soldiers riding out at the head of the column whirled his horse about and rode back to the small knoll where the Captain General paused to watch the weary line pass him by. The soldier saluted, then spoke softly. No one heard the conversation which passed between the two men. A moment later Don Antonio galloped to the head of the long column where, beside a small thicket, he joined Luis Quintana. Without a word, the Alcalde Mayor pointed to an object in the bushes. Don Antonio tossed his horse's reins to a soldier and entered the scrub bushes. Quintana followed.

Face down in the dirt sprawled a Spaniard. His helmet lay in the sand several paces away. His weapons were missing. Two brightly feathered arrows stuck out of his back. The dried blood about the top of his head marked the line where his scalp had been removed. A small toad crawled out of his left boot, looked blindly at the sun, and disappeared under a rock. Several ants scurried away as Don Antonio knelt beside the body and slowly turned it over. He did not need to see the face to know who the man was. He knew. The blank, squinty eyes stared up at him. A small vinegarroon, disturbed by the Governor, arched its tail and slapped it about, emitting its foul odour as it struck. Then it backed away under some leaves. The ants had already got to the face of Sancho de Hoz as had the carrion birds. One cheek was torn away. So was his neck. But the off-centre eyes held their fear.

Don Antonio crossed himself as he knelt. The pouch of papers the courier had carried was missing. Nothing more could be done for Hoz, the hunter of Chiapas. Otermín rose to his feet and looked about him. Quintana was standing a dozen varas away, waving the column on so that none would see the body.

Fray Pedro separated from the others and crossed over to stand beside the Captain General. Neither of them spoke. Then when María left her place in the passing line to see what had caught the Governor's attention, Fray Pedro expressed his doubts.

"I wonder," he said flatly, "I wonder if Uriah the Hittite was a frightened man." Then, ignoring the Captain General, the padre called to two of the soldados, "We will need a grave."

Don Antonio merely opened his hands and closed them.

It was María who wrote the small man's epitaph in the warm morning air. "He was not a good man, but he knew the woods and the fields. He should not have died." Then without waiting for the burial or the final service that was to be read by the padre from Valladolid, she ran to take her place in the column again.

Otermín combed his fingers through his greying hair, scratched his head where some dirt had gathered, and looked at the padre. "Someone had to die carrying a message between the Villa and Isleta. Why not this man instead of another?" He walked back to his horse, mounted and rode on without turning to look back at the burial detail.

An hour later the long line drew abreast the first series of arroyos. The jagged scars cut the earth deep enough to hide a man. Some few arroyos necessitated scrambling down the sharp sides. Others could be spanned by a careful jump. The ditches zigzagging across the countryside like small crude canyons blocked the retreat. The refugees grouped together and stared across these cuts which scored the earth for several hundred varas.

Otermín rode his horse to the east and then westward until he reached the rio's bank. There was no choice. He signalled for Quintana to join him. And as the small Alcalde Mayor rode up, Otermín shrugged.

"We cross them, amigo. We go over those we can go over. Down and up those we must."

Quintana, wearing his steel helmet, partly for the added height it gave him, partly because his wife thought he looked handsome in it, nodded. "It will be difficult, Excellency."

Don Antonio grinned. "Everything always is, Luis. Start them over." And he rode off.

The little Creole swelled. This was the first time the Governor had called him "Luis." He would have liked to take more time to enjoy the feeling. Later he would tell Isabella about it. But now he trotted to the head of the column and began to direct the crossing.

Otermín watched the soldiers help the first woman over the water-ripped ditches. He saw them toss the bundles of clothing, silver, and useless baggage after their owners. Then he rode to the place in the line where María patiently waited her turn to cross. He sat looking down at her. The sun struck her face. As she threw her head back, her eyes caught the brightness of the morning. At her side Inez stood quietly watching the crossing. Otermín followed the girl's stare. The carretas now. They had been drawn up to the edge. Several soldiers had scrambled down into the first arroyo and were preparing to help lift the small, but heavy, carts across. The horses had been unharnessed, and jumped. The men and women standing near by pushed the first carreta to the edge and then over it as the weight was picked up by the soldiers beneath and moved onto the south brink of the ditch. Here it was grabbed and dragged onto solid ground.

Otermín leaned over in his saddle and pulled the small girl up in front of him. At first she hesitated, surprised and bewildered, as she looked at her mother. María nodded approval and the child leaned back and rested against the Governor's chest. Steadying her with his stiff right arm, he trotted over to the point of crossing.

Hundreds of heads followed him as he swung off his saddle, leaving the child holding the reins. The carreta with the women was being pushed into position. Their thin faces were strained and frightened. The loud and vulgar curses of the dying whore filled the morning air, and Otermín was embarrassed for those who stood waiting their turn to cross. The tall blonde woman with the young boy and the clock tried to hide a grin as she heard the whore scream at Don Antonio, "You got to find me a softer bed than this, if you want me, Excellency."

"Move it up," he directed, trying to ignore the gaunt face with the gat-toothed grin. "Move it up." The men and women put their shoulders to the carreta and wheeled it to the brink. The distance across was little more than the span of the cart itself. The men in the ditch below braced them-selves to bear the weight. Those on the brink beyond reached for the tongue of the carreta.

"Over it goes," Quintana yelled as he put his own lean shoulder to the back board. There was silence as the men reached up for the wheels and tried to pass the carreta on. Then the whore rose to her knees to see what was happening. The carreta tilted. There were screams from the pregnant woman and the blind one. For an instant the wagon seemed to hang in the air. Then it toppled over as the weight of the women shifted. Their screams were lost as the carreta crashed against the steep side and fell to the bottom of the ditch, pinning the leg of one of the soldiers beneath it. The wheels splintered, and the women tumbled out into the red dirt and rocks that lined the arroyo.

Otermín and Quintana leapt into the ditch, heaved the carreta aside, and with the aid of others dragged it off the leg of the soldier. Then they turned their attention to the women. The whore was dragging herself to a sitting position. The entire front of her dress as well as her bare skin was red with clay and blood where her wrinkled neck and breasts had been ripped by the rocks. But she brushed her red hair back and closed her eyes against the pain. She was not crying. The pregnant widow lay still where she had fallen on her stomach. Don Antonio knelt beside her and turned her head slowly so that he could see her face. She was unconscious, her breath coming in small gasps. A scratch above her nose extended to her right ear, and blood trickled from it slowly. But she lived. Otermín stood up and stared at the faces peering down at him over the edge.

"A blanket," was all he said as he turned his attention to the other woman. Somehow the blind woman had pulled herself to her feet by holding onto some rocks that jutted out of the steep embankment. Otermín saw that her hands bled where she had ripped them. But her face was unscarred as her eyes seemed to be seeking the light of the bright sun above them. He put his hand out and drew her to him.

"Everything will be all right," he comforted her. "We will get you back up and everything will be all right."

She seemed to understand though she did not speak. The blank expression on the otherwise pretty face disturbed him and he took both of her hands in his and held them for a moment, then put them in Quintana's.

"Help her up. She will ride in the first wagon for a time. I think she will feel better if she walks part of each day."

Quintana nodded. "The other woman, Excellency?"

Otermín turned his attention to the middle-aged farm wife who lay on her back staring up at him. He recognized her as the widow who had lost a leg earlier in the week. Now he saw the blood spurting from beneath her dress. The wound had opened again and was soaking the red clay floor of the arroyo. He saw her face drained and knew she was becoming weaker. He closed his eyes for a moment as he accepted the scene in his mind with hundreds of others he had known. This woman was dying. Then he heard the soft voice of Fray Pedro and he opened his eyes again. The stocky padre in the neat cassock was kneeling beside the woman, holding his cross to her lips and praying.

Otermín turned away from the accusing eyes that stared at him over the cross. The men were lifting the pregnant widow up in a blanket. She was conscious now. Her hand reached down and touched his shoulder as though to comfort him, and then the men passed her over the brink. Two of them were helping the crippled whore up the side of the cut while Quintana was helping the blind woman.

Finally, Otermín climbed out of the arroyo and looked about him.

"We've got to go on," was all he said to the expectant faces. He had no miracles for them and could offer no surcease to their miseries. He remounted his horse after the third carreta was successfully lifted over the ditch, and watched as María was helped across it. Then he turned his attention to the padre who now climbed out to stand beside his small donkey.

"Is she dead, Padre?"

Fray Pedro nodded. The two men looked at each other. There was neither compassion nor understanding between them.

"If you will cross now, Padre," Otermín suggested.

The padre nodded. A moment later the little donkey was prodded into a successful jump and Otermín stood with Quintana.

"We have no time for a funeral," Otermín explained. "The sun is high and we have a long way to travel. The padre has held his service."

Quintana nodded. "But the birds, Excellency." His arm swept the sky above them where large circles were being etched by black-winged vultures.

Don Antonio rubbed the back of his hand over his small beard. "Get two men to collapse the side of the arroyo over the body. That will cover it. Then get them to set up a marker from the broken tongue of the carreta."

Quintana started to turn away.

"And for yourself, amigo," Otermín called him back. "For yourself, get them started crossing the next one before we stop for a midday meal."

Quintana's small back stiffened. Then he assented with some understanding as he saw the drawn lines across the Governor's forehead.

A moment later Don Antonio jumped his horse over the arroyo and joined the Alcalde Mayor of La Cañada in urging the crossing of the next ditch.

The short padre stood watching the Governor and his assistant as they organized the next crossing. He thought of the ways in which it might be done more easily. Several soldiers could be sent to find trees tall enough to span the gaps. But he admitted the weakness of this plan to himself. They needed every soldier at hand. Besides, they were much too close to the Villa to waste hours in search of trees. All of the arguments Otermín would muster were already in his mind. His shaven head tipped back and he stared at the sun. The day was clear and bright—brighter by far than any day he could remember at home. It was the nature of this country. Maybe it was nearer to God. Maybe the air was clearer, the plateau higher. One gnarled hand passed over his face as he felt the leathern quality of his skin: like hide now and darker; darker even than when he had been a sun-baked boy in his father's fields.

For a moment as he watched the carretas being manœuvred over the next arroyo, he thought about those fields at home. A quiet resentment remained with him as he recalled the night he had let down the barrier behind which he had hidden his past. The Governor's words so soft and effortless—

suddenly he found himself talking about home. The smell of the poverty remained with him. The empty vineyards and the thin gruel. The wasted years of his mother and the bent back of his father. These were part of the barrier, and it was not his practice to yield an inch of his past to strangers. For Fray Pedro Martínez the world was composed of strangers. He had no friends, none to whom he could talk through the long night as he knew Otermín had talked to Pando and even the aged Fray Custodio.

In the brief instant before the woman died in the arroyo behind him, Fray Pedro saw that Governor Otermín was aware of his padre's weakness, knew the flaw of the man better than he knew it himself. Fray Pedro did not know when he had become aware of the flaw that was his tragic weakness as a padre. In his ten years out of the Seminary and his eight in Mexico and the Villa de Santa Fe, he had always been assigned the task of a secretary or administrative aide-de-camp. He had gravitated to those duties which had given him his freedom from people, which had taken him out of the world of strangers and permitted him to use his own special talents. He had a sense of organization. He knew that details were important, that protocol had purpose, that records must be maintained, that supplies should flow in proper quantities and to the proper places, that so many Indians required so many padres, that it cost so much to build a chapel and so much to equip it, that so many months or years were necessary to educate an Indian, build a building, or defray a loan from the state. There was method in the mind of the intense and nervous young padre, method and no understanding of people. This was the lesson he had learned about himself since the Fray Custodio had ridden south on the back of the grey donkey only ten days before. It seemed to Fray Pedro that the lean, stiff-backed old man had known what would happen to his assistant and that this was either a punishment for the sin of pride or ambition, or a way of showing him how inadequate he really was. Inadequate—a word he had never related to himself. There was nothing he could not do, organize, arrange. He was not one of the ineffectual Brothers, as was Rafael of San Ysidro. He was not one of the moral cowards, as was the giant Julio of Santa Flora. He was a man who could accomplish any task set before him. *Set before him.* The words shook his brain, and he fumbled for the beads at his waist. Softly he prayed for himself as only moments before he had prayed for the woman who lay buried beneath the ditch behind him. The tasks had to be set before him.

Tears started to fill his dark eyes and he quickly brushed them away. There were things he could not do and there were things he could. God had not meant him for a saint, only a servant, and he was prepared to serve. It was not his fault that he was unable to sit beside a dying woman through a long night, listen to the garrulous tales of a windy old man and make that poor soul believe that his failure was success, take the hand of a child who had fallen and lift her up to walk beside him and stare at the hot sun. There were things he could not do. But there were other ways in which he could serve. It was heart that he lacked, and he was finally aware of it now. It was his sin. It was also a strength, for it permitted him to see the order of things without the soft compassion through which others viewed the world. He had to live with what he had become. And he could not make himself believe that he had become a bad thing. Let others hold the hands of the ill, let others care for the poor, let others tend the fallen. He, Fray Pedro, had his place as a servant of God, if only . . . if only God had not given him this task of tending the needs of a thousand hungry and frightened refugees. This was the final cruelty, the last irony.

Fray Pedro saw that the others were already across two arroyos and that the eager Alcade Mayor of La Cañada was calling his name. He took the lead rope of his donkey and leapt across, forcing the beast to follow. He had a long distance to travel, and God had chosen a strange route for him.

The white-necked vulture sat on the edge of the grey rock butte and looked down at the ménage of humans straggling through the broad valley. A dead prairie dog hung limply from its outsized bill. The large eyes, seeking carnage, followed the movement below.

Two women saw the silhouette of the black bird against the turquoise sky and crossed themselves. A vulture is evil. A vulture is the devil's messenger. A vulture carries the souls of the damned. A vulture is the omen of trouble to come.

The green-purple black of its wings glistened in the sun. The wedge tail spread. The broad wings fluttered. Black feet raked grey rock. The great bird soared softly over the column, alighted several hundred varas ahead and waited hopefully for the line of man-beasts to pass it again.

Rocinante on the road again. And the last and lonely knight, wandering down the countryside of a gaunt and hungry land.

It was midday on the hour. Only the boots crunching, only the sad cattle bawling.

> *One footstep in the stirrup*
> *The other in the grave.*
> *The agony of death upon me.*

The words of the ancient ballad broke sadly across the valley. Women raised their heads and listened. Children tugged and queried. The lean soldado, helmet back, head sunward, sang so softly,
One footstep in the stirrup. . . .
Rocinante on the road again. The lean knight wandering.

Two hours had passed and a long, level stretch of ground lay before them. Only then did Otermín stop the column for its first meal. There had been grumbling in the long file. He decided not to hear the low voices which commented on the pace he was setting, for there were still the Indians behind and the omnipresent fear of an attack. If it came now, there would no longer be the thick walls of the casas reales for protection. They were in the open now, exposed to the sun, the elements, and the enemy. He could afford to ignore the complaints. When María had voiced them to him, not as her own, but rather as the general feeling of all those about her, he had looked up at the sky and pointed out the large birds that wheeled back and forth across it as though seeking something to pounce upon.

However, he had finally called the halt. The cattle were bunched together, the guards were out, the horses grazing on the small clumps of grass which grew thinly over the broken land. Bundles were piled and small groups of men and women settled down in circles to eat the cold food they carried. In some instances it was a piece of pork and bread. In others it was cold mutton from sheep that had been killed the night before when they knew they were going to abandon the Villa. The meat had not spoiled yet, and there were still the live cattle to sustain them. Now the meal was cold. There was no time to light a fire and less inclination as the sun scorched the very earth they sat upon. Some of the men drifted down toward the rio to fetch water for their groups. Others drank from the water bags they carried. The water was warm and smelled of the skins and bladders, but it met their needs. Some of the women removed their shoes and sat rubbing their feet with one hand while they ate with the other. Several of the men pulled off their boots and stretched out on the warm earth covering their faces with their helmets or tunicas. The children ran from group to group playing games, throwing rocks into the arroyos behind them and raising the red dust.

Don Antonio had tied his horse to a small rock and seated himself near a cluster of bunch grass and several almost leafless piñons. Quintana joined him there and Señora Isabella. Several minutes later María threw down her small bundle of extra shoes and handed Otermín some bread and a piece of smoked meat she had removed from one of the pack animals. He acknowledged the food and never noticed where it came from.

They ate in silence. Though they had only travelled a short distance, they were all tired. Don Antonio felt the pains in his legs where he had been injured. The wound on his chest burned hotly. Without being aware of his action, several times his hand went to the place on his cheek which had been laid open only the morning before. María watched him, knew that it bothered him, and after a time she rose and left the group, to return with a small piece of mutton fat with which she rubbed the cut cheek, leaving a thick coating of grease over the wound.

"The sun will not help it," she said. Then she settled down again to finish her meal.

Otermín looked at her, nodded his thanks, and wondered how she was taking the heat. Better, he was certain, than Isabella Quintana with her heavy dress, underskirts, and corsets. He wondered where the infernos these women thought they were going, to dress as they did. María was different. This much he admitted to himself. There was clearly nothing under the light cotton dress which showed every line of her body. The way the material clung to her he could see the dark circle that marked her nipples and had to restrain himself from reaching out to touch them. Curse the woman. She had done something to him, and at his age. It was different when a man was twenty-five, even thirty-five. Those years were behind him. Yet as he watched her eating, the fat of the meat glistening on her chin and the water of the bladder bag slopping down the front of her dress, finding its course over her bosom to leave a dark circle of wet on her stomach, he knew that she had become involved in his life.

She looked at him curiously as he rose to his feet and deliberately turned his back upon her while he spoke to Quintana.

"Give them another few minutes and then we must move on."

He ran his hand over the head of the girl who sat beside her mother, seriously pondering the relationships of men and women. Otermín looked over the group. There were at least a thousand. Eighty, at most, able to bear arms. Fifty whom he knew would never be able to walk the full distance to Isleta, where they would join with García.

García. García. The name kept finding its way through his weary brain as though he were thinking of a saviour, realizing all the while this was merely another soldado, probably no better a commander than himself, if as good. He did not know the man. Yet the name García had taken on special meanings—food, support, a second-in-command, protection, and, hopefully, assistance on the route back, the long return to the Villa, self-respect, and the clearance of his own name.

García. The people here. These had become the horizons of his world.

His family, his friends in presidios all over Nueva España, no longer had meaning at this moment. Only the present counted. And the present was like the words of the old man who lay buried in the compound behind the palacio, "Some of us have not the right to die, Excellency."

Pando had been correct. Thinking of García and the refugees, Otermín was not certain if he even had the right to divert himself with this woman who sat only an arm's distance away waiting for him to look at her. What was she to him? A ranchero's wife who was now a ranchero's widow. Penniless. A child at her side. None of the manner or sophistication of the women in his life. None of the culture or understanding that a grandee had the right to expect from the women with whom he associated. Associated? Infernos, slept. What was María to him? A body. Comfort. A servant to take care of the small corners of his life. Clean stockings. A pressed tunica. Food at mealtime. He thought of the comments from the knowing widows and the smiling wives, of the suggestions and leers from the dying whore. What had he exposed himself to? How much had he hurt his command? These were the things which absorbed him as he stood staring at the people who were now looking at him. Slowly, he turned back to Quintana, who was rising to his feet.

"It is about time that we moved on."

Quintana said, "I will start them walking, Excellency."

And he took his wife's hand and helped her to her feet. María rose beside them and wandered silently back to her place in the line. She had seen the looks on Otermín's face, and she was beginning to understand the man. A realist, there were parts of his problem she had days ago shrugged off as more his concern than her own.

THE lance which rested on the boot of the sargento became hot to the touch under the bright sky. Its silver tip reflected the distant mesas in one small curve. The lance had been cleaned and polished and polished again since yesterday's fighting at the Villa. The sargento was proud of the weapon. It had been issued to him by Governor Treviño more than five years before and had become his talisman. He carried it with him wherever he travelled in this cruel land above el Paso. The years had worn the sharp distinction from the two salamander tails which had been so carefully moulded into the first palm's length of the silver tip. The Latin inscription was no longer legible, but this did not matter, for the sargento could no more read Latin than he could read Castilian. Once he had asked a padre to read the inscription to him, but after fumbling for the words, the clergyman concluded that they had nothing to do with God, crossed himself, and forgot the request. This had not disturbed the sargento. The weapon was comfortable in his hand, hefted easily for the thrust, and the hard wood shaft had never broken or splintered in years of hunting animals and men. Reaching down, he ran his rough palm over its warm length. The weapon gave him confidence, the way the pikeman's pot helmet assured Quintana. Each man needs something he can take in his hand and hold, and know that it is his protection. The sargento wondered what the Captain General would reach out for and hold, and in the wondering he believed that perhaps this was the weakness of the surly man who gave his orders as though his answers were the only ones to the questions that would arise. The sargento was a sargento partly because he was not capable of understanding that the Captain General would reach out for his years of experience and hold on firmly to the training he had received and developed since his youth; these, and a concept known as dignity, were the lances which he carried.

The young woman polished the bone icon as she walked. With her bare hands she brushed away the road dust as it gathered and rubbed the faded colours to a brighter hue. Her feet were wrapped in a piece of green cowhide. Her dress was torn by brambles and cactus. But the icon her father had carried north half a century before in his saddlebag was undamaged. It was the only item she had rescued from her father's estancia when she saw him cut down at the gate. Without hesitation she had reached into the niche in the wall, taken the small figure, and climbed out of the rear window.

An hour later a neighbour, fleeing to the Villa had found her wandering through the fields with the bone Cristos clutched tightly in her hand. She was walking in a blurred and foggy world then as she walked in one now. Now she did not see the woman beside her and she was not aware of the

young soldier with the thin beard who smiled at the brown skin exposed by
the holes in her dress. She only knew the icon had to be kept polished and
dusted and undamaged until she could walk back to her father's estancia
and set the Cristos again in the niche of the wall. Then everything would
be as it had always been, her feet would not hurt, her skin would not burn,
and her stomach gnaw. Everything would be as it had been, once she
set the icon back in the niche again.

The column had covered almost a league since the midday meal. Otermín
had permitted three halts, and now the sun was slanting and the shadows
growing long. The bundles which had seemed light in the morning were
heavy now. The cattle were more balky, the children more quarrelsome, and
Otermín, riding behind the several rancheros who had been assigned as
drovers, noted the leanness of the cows. They had not been well fed in almost
two weeks. They had not been given an opportunity to graze, and the ribs
of most of them could easily be counted through their loose hides. He wondered how long they would last, how many would have to be killed each
evening to satisfy the hunger of a thousand people.

There was grass in the distance, and he rode ahead to look at it. As he
passed the front of the column, Quintana borrowed a horse and followed.
Señora Quintana had not relinquished the saddle into which she had settled
earlier in the day.

Stirrup to stirrup, the two men covered the several hundred varas that
lay between them and the possible pasturage. The Captain General dismounted and knelt down to feel the grass between his fingers. It was dry,
but he had been cavalryman enough of his life to know this would satisfy
the horses. The cattle would be able to fend for themselves. Tossing the
reins of his grey stallion to Quintana, Don Antonio walked down to the bank
of the rio. It sloped gently enough. Turning about he saw that a small
cluster of twisted trees grew near by. A low cut of a dried rio bed lay in the
east. This would suffice for a latrine. Dropping to his knees, he scooped up
a handful of the cool water and drank it slowly. Better by far than the rank
contents of a sheep's bladder. Twice he splashed water from the slow-moving
rio over his face to cut the dust that had gathered in the long day's riding.
He touched his cheek where María had rubbed the mutton grease. It was
sore, but no worse than the other wounds that brought fever to his forehead.

Finally, he rose and smiled up at the waiting Alcalde Mayor. "We camp
here tonight. The cattle there to the left with four men sleeping in a square
around them, the horses tied down after dark, two guards on that ditch over
there to see that the women have privacy. The men can take a walk. After
the evening meal anyone can bathe in the water, but no one goes more than
a few feet into the stream."

He waved to the bank opposite. "We may just find we have company
following us over there, and I will not send a rescue squad after anyone
who disobeys orders."

He was done. Without waiting for an answer from Quintana, he took the
reins of his own horse and walked the weary beast to the rio's edge where

he watched it drink. After a moment, his second-in-command whirled and rode back to lead the column to its resting place.

Half an hour later the bank of the rio was lined with men and women kneeling for a drink of fresh water. Guards were already stationed and the cattle area designated. Two women gathered wood for a fire and Otermín watched María select an isolated spot almost a hundred paces from where the others had thrown down their belongings. She had found a small rise that overlooked the camp and was sheltered by a cluster of trees.

Calling a soldado, Otermín told the youth to rub down his horse and hobble it for the night.

"Your equipment, Excellency?"

"There," Don Antonio pointed to the small rise that María had selected. The young man nodded, unsaddled the horse and carried the equipment off, leading the horse as he walked. María was nowhere to be seen and Otermín realized that the women were thinning out, taking advantage of the arroyo he had selected for their toilet.

He called a sargento to him, and as the man approached, he recognized the pocked face of the youth who had been responsible for the protection of the palacio roof. The young man had done well and the Captain General would have to tell him so. But not now. He returned the salute.

"Select four men, cut out four of those cattle and drive them near the bank of the rio. Kill them and get them on spits, pronto. These people are going to be hungry once they have rested for a few minutes."

The sargento saluted, called to four compañeros, and set about his task. Slowly, Otermín walked up the rise to where his own gear was lying on the ground beside María's extra shoes and the bundle of food she carried. There he sank down on the ground and watched the camp take shape.

Quintana was no soldier, but he seemed to have enough sense of organization to keep the group together. He paced off several hundred steps and then allotted areas to different people. This would prevent crowding and quarrels. It would also keep them in a single, closely packed location where they could be watched and protected. There were some protests as one woman wanted to bed down next to a man she had met during the day's march and another saw a clump of bunch grass she thought would make a comfortable bed. But there was a minimum of confusion, and soon everyone was watching the sargento bring his four head of cattle down to the rio's edge. Here he quickly slit the throats of each in turn, watched it start to run, stumble and collapse only steps away. Then the soldiers took out their knives and peeled the hide away from the corpses. Four men working quickly soon had the carcasses spitted on tree trunks. The fires were lit and everyone rested on the grass or the soft earth at the edge of the stream waiting to eat, waiting for the last sun to disappear and leave them alone in the darkness.

Carrying several blankets and flat pewter dishes she had rescued from the casa real, María joined Otermín. She set the platters on the ground between them and began pulling grass from the small scattered clumps. Pile after pile was spread on the knoll, and finally she laid their blankets over the soft grass, settled down, and turned to him.

Her long face was tense. The skin was drawn tightly over her high cheek-bones. She closed her eyes against the failing sun which lay just over his shoulder. "They are not all going to reach Isleta, Excellency?"

Otermín stared at the group resting below. Some of the men had removed their shirts. Almost no one was wearing shoes now. Several children stood in the rio to their knees, the cool water swirling about them. Inez was there with the others. One soldier slowly turned each of the large spits and the fat falling back into the fire of piñon and mesquite spat softly in the quiet of the early evening. The four hides lay in a heap, and as he stared at them, Otermín realized their worth. He rose to his feet and called to a ranchero, who was sprawled on the ground near by.

"Amigo, those hides, will you pin them out for the night and see that they ride on someone's horse tomorrow. They are the shoes we will need before we are done."

The ranchero, no younger than the Governor himself, sullenly drew himself up and stared past the fat, sow-like face of his woman. "Fine work for one of your soldados, or a certain widow."

Then he lay back again, staring at the reddening sky. The insolence as well as the independence angered Otermín. He was used to being obeyed. He had been giving orders all of his adult years and they had been obeyed or someone had been punished. Very quietly he closed the distance between the ranchero and himself. When the man turned his head, he saw the Governor standing over him.

"She set you to this?" The man's insolence as well as the inference were boldly stated.

Don Antonio drew his heavy boot back and kicked hard at the man's neck. There was a sharp gasp. The ranchero's hands went to his throat as he choked for air. His woman raised her huge bulk from the ground, stood bare-footed before Otermín and started to curse him loudly.

His firm tone sliced through her strident voice which was attracting the attention of the camp. "If you do not keep quiet, I will wrap the pair of you in those green hides and leave them to shrink and dry."

The woman's jaw dropped as she realized he meant the threat and, even more important, that he was in a position to fulfil it.

When she was quiet again, the Governor toed the choking man with his foot. "You will take care of the hides as I suggested."

It was not a question, but the man answered, "Yes, Excellency."

Otermín turned away and walked down to the rio where so many were gathering to wash away the dust of the march. Several women, their skirts pulled up to their knees, were standing in the water. They moved aside and left an open space for him. He knelt on the bank and washed his hands with the mud he found there.

María again. María and the talk. María and the weakness of his command. The place where he had left himself open to public scorn and public comment when what he needed more than ever before was dignity, dignity and respect. Without these no one was going to get through. The retreat would become a rout. The column would dissolve into a panic-stricken horde running and stumbling and getting itself killed. He had to keep his head. He had to hold his temper. He had to maintain his control. The man with the squinty eyes stared up at him from the shallow bottom of the rio. Twice inside of two weeks he had lost his head. Twice he had struck when he should have ordered punishment dealt by another hand. Now he was not only a wencher but a brawler. This would sound fine in a formal report in the hands of some wizened clerk in the office of the Viceroy. This would be the making of the end. He was on that road, on the Camino Real to his own destruction, but his hopes to salvage something, these hopes, these gnawing needs, he could not abandon.

Yet, back there was María, sitting on their blankets with his dinner on one of the pewter platters. María waiting for him to walk back up that hill, past the fat farm wife with the sow's face. María waiting for him, and he knew he was going to take a walk out into the darkness. He was going to be alone. He might return to join her, but he would have to make his mind up to the problems it would mean. It was not something he would do lightly now.

He walked away from the rio. People were staring at him, soft voices whispering, and he drew his daga, sliced off a piece of the spitted beef, grinned at the soldado who was preparing to carve the carcass, and then walked out into the early dusk gnawing at the charred meat.

4

MARÍA VALDIVIA sat for a long time on the knoll looking after Governor Otermín. She had heard the comments of the ranchero, had seen the sudden burst of Don Antonio's temper, and she recalled the time he had struck Sancho de Hoz. She did not think of the little man with regret or pity. She had said Hoz meant nothing to her, and it was true. In María Valdivia there was very little room for lies, for pretence. She was no more than the Captain General believed her to be—the daughter of a small ranchero in southern Mexico, who had known poverty all her life. She had worked in the fields during those brief periods when the laws preventing her father from abusing the Indians were enforced. She had torn her hands, created calluses, for just enough to eat. Once her ancestors had worked small farms for the grandees of Aragon. Then one of them dreamed of riches and position in Nueva España and had departed with a sword in hand to join Alvarado in Guatemala. But for him the pattern never changed. He finished his life with an Indian wench, working someone else's rancho on a different continent. For María's father life was the same. Only the rebellion of the pueblos had changed hers. Her husband had been a small ranchero whom she had met one hot summer afternoon in Ciudad Mexico. She had made the long jornada there with her father to raise some money on the rancho that was not theirs. Hernando Valdivia was a tall, well-built young man with borrowed pesos in his pockets and a charming smile on his face. He had no difficulty impressing the country girl with his importance and the breadth of his father's holdings in the country that lay north of el Paso del Norte.

Nor did he have any trouble avoiding the drunken eyes of her father when he took María to bed with him.

Weeks later when he had spent all of his borrowed money and was preparing to return to his father's hacienda in Nuevo Mexico, María informed him that she was going to have a baby. They prayed together in the small chapel near the inn where María was staying, and when they were done, they agreed that they should marry. María's father appreciated the delicacy of the situation, gave the pair his blessing, and pointed his donkey south while his daughter and her new-found husband took the Camino Real that led to the land above el Paso.

Life had been simple for them. Hernando's father had accepted the young girl into the family, had prided himself on his granddaughter's charms and made the most of María's ability to serve as an extra pair of hands in an otherwise overworked household. While it lasted the arrangement was satisfactory for all. But when the Indians rebelled and the Valdivia men were killed, María made her way to the Villa de Santa Fe with her daughter, arriving there with little more than the clothes she wore and a strength of character formed in the rough mould of a rugged countryside and a difficult life.

The idea of attaching herself to the Governor and Captain General had not been hers. Once His Excellency's Indian servants had fled the Villa, the suggestion that she take on the household tasks of the Governor came from the stocky young padre. It had not been María's intention that a liaison be formed between them. When she had found Hoz among the refugees, she had quickly assumed the easy relationship they had had since childhood. Hoz had been among the first explorers of her young body to see how it differed from a boy's. Their new relationship was to be expected. But its end was not very significant to María. She was surprised when Governor Otermín lost his temper and struck Hoz. She was surprised when he singled out the squint-eyed soldier to bear the message to Isleta. But her reaction was more from a lack of regard for Hoz than anything else. To the country wife any act of officialdom was impressive, be it the simple writing of a document for the records or the hasty dispatch of a message. There was for her a certain magic about government, about the finer elements of its functioning, which were as foreign as the fine Latin words to which she bowed her head when the padre prayed. To find herself serving His Excellency the Governor—the Captain General—was awesome. Finding him in her bed at night, lonesome, weary, and as needful of a woman as Hoz or Hernando, removed that awe. It made Don Antonio a man. She could understand a man. For María his greedy hand caressing her naked body was as natural as the evening dusk.

What she did not understand and what she could not bring herself to accept was the attitude of those about her, the other refugees and the soldados. Here were men and women no different from herself. There was an easy morality in the provinces. Mistresses were as numerous as wives, and yet these people resented her. She believed it was because they feared her that they moved quickly as though her suggestions and requests were commands. It had taken several days for María to become fully aware of the power she held, a power Otermín did not himself realize existed and one he would have crushed. But once María was aware of the strength she possessed, she decided to use it to the only end she knew. She sought food and comfort for herself and her child and, in the process, for His Excellency, the Governor.

In the several days since Don Antonio had first pulled her to him and said he would expect her to join him at night, they had said very little to each other. He never discussed his affairs with her. She never pried. Their companionship was a matter of quick passion on his part and ready service on hers. She was aware that she met his needs as a woman, equally aware that those needs included caring for his clothes and meals. The companionship that she saw between the fat Señora Isabella Quintana and her nervous little husband—a companionship of long talks and ready discussion on every subject from the loud curses of the whore of the casa de puta to the colour of the sky in the early morning, from the way Quintana looked with his helmet pressed down on his head to how her heavy buttocks hurt after a long day in the saddle—was a different thing. In the early years of her marriage to Hernando, she had known such a relationship. It had made her feel important. And when they abandoned it after he took the Indian wench into his bed, she missed the easy talk and the ready confidence. For reasons she could not explain to herself, she wanted the same thing from this Governor. At first she had been willing to accept him because of the security his position brought Inez, but she wanted more now. Inez would be cared for so long as Don Antonio was able to care for the child, regardless of what happened to their relationship. And this was important to her, because Inez was the only daughter she had, the only one, she now knew, she would ever have, and despite her ready shrugging off of the padre's admonitions concerning her sins, she did blame herself for her loss of fertility.

María had no illusions about Don Antonio's marrying her. There were the years between them, and the frightened señoras of the column let her know that he was not only a governor and captain general, but also a grandee with grandchildren. María was hardened enough by life to waste little time in dreaming. Yet she was a woman and she found herself thinking unexpected thoughts. Not the least among them was her growing fear that she was beginning to love the man. And with this fear grew the desire to become a part of his world—of his daily thoughts and actions. She was ignorant. She was awed. But she was also a woman and willing to learn. Though companionship was not the pattern for María and Don Antonio, she had known it before and she wanted it again.

Now as she sat on the small hillock with Inez and stared at the pewter plate of food she had set out for Don Antonio, she knew he was not going to come back to claim it, knew too that he was troubled about their relationship. This was simple to perceive, because he was always uncertain, hesitant, with her, when he was confident with everyone else. One moment he was solicitous, the next forgetful. One moment he was passionate and warm and the next he looked at her with his deep-set eyes as though he had never seen her before and wished he did not have to see her now. She was one of his problems, and he had so many. Never once had he expressed any feeling or even fondness for her. Instead, when he relaxed and showed his affection, it was for Inez.

María ran her hand through the soft hair of her daughter and drew her close. She loved the child possessively, knowing that life was going to be difficult for an orphan whose mother had nothing more than the clothes they wore and the two pairs of shoes which lay on the ground beside them.

Inez traced a small finger over the blankets and asked her mother to tell her a story. The light of the fires below seemed brighter as the day disappeared. There were few noises from the small encampment. Everyone was weary. Each knew tomorrow was going to be a long and difficult day. It would be like their first day of retreat with the added problem that it would follow the fatigue of the first day.

In a soft tone María began to tell a story about grandees and beautiful women.

5

OUT in the darkness beyond a twist of the rio, Otermín sat on a rock and stared at the night sky. There were stars. A few lazy clouds seemed to be moving nowhere in particular. He opened his tunica and slowly rubbed his sore arm. Feeling was returning to it. He was aware of pain where there had been numbness before. With effort he could bend his arm back and forth. He tried picking up some sand with his fingers, and though the effort was clumsy, he was able to close his hand and let it sift through.

Off in the distance he heard the soft complaint of a bird. After a time the low howl of a coyote. His left hand went to his waist. The daga was there. For a long while he sat and listened to the night sounds: the crickets, the water brushing against the banks of the stream. He removed his tunica and bared his chest to the cool air of the night. The wounds of yesterday were with him now that he tried to relax. His face itched where the skin was torn, his side pained when he moved too quickly.

The fighting was done for the moment. He would forget the details in time as they blended with other days and nights of battle. How does a man separate a corpse here and a sabre bloodied there, if most of his life has been filled with death and war? Don Antonio sighed. He was so far from home, so far from his youth.

He wished his wife were beside him now. He longed for the quiet comfort of her voice, the certain assurance she felt in his abilities to accomplish what he set out to do. She had been a part of him ever since that first night they had met at her father's hacienda, near Sevilla. He had been twenty-five then, young, ambitious, and confident that he knew the only way in which life must be lived. Only time could show him its infinite varieties. Only time showed him that there are moments in a man's life when he must make decisions which he will never be able to make again. Each man decides many times what life he lives and what life he abandons. Opportunity has a way of finding a man when he does not want it, is not ready for it, or no longer has the desire. There was so much Don Antonio had learned with his wife at his side. Now he felt he was the only one who knew the things they had known together. He had never discussed his thoughts with her. In his world women had a place—it involved children, a home, dignity, humour.Companionship was found with other men in a long night's talking. It was her presence he missed.

He reached again for some sand. It still held the heat of the sun. After a moment he tossed it into the slowly moving rio and heard the soft splash. He was alone and he wished for one desperate moment that he was not.

His wife had died in Cuba of the fever. There were so many other places she might have died and so many reasons why she should not have. He tried to recall her face in the darkness and found that he could not, because any face that a man has seen for years under every possible condition no longer has clear features, but is a blur of situation and memory and places and emotions that can never all be sifted away. Don Antonio realized there were fifty persons back at the camp on the rio whose faces he could see more clearly in his mind than that of the woman he had loved, and it was not because he loved her less, but because he knew her better.

His eyes closed and the taut body slowly began to rock back and forth. The ninth of August was only twelve days behind. The ninth, when first he heard, and then the fatal tenth, when everything fell away as the rio's bank fell away and washed downstream, never to be recovered.

He recalled the long discussion he had had with the Viceroy in the large room of the palacio in Ciudad Mexico only two weeks after he had been summoned from Cuba, only a month after he had buried his wife. The words became a drone and the only things he could separate from the encouragement and hopeful commands were the facts that the province was secure and that the Franciscans had done magnificent work and must be supported. Of course, every possible economy must be observed. After all, the province really does not pay its own way. It is in a sense one of the King's charities, one of the Crown's contributions to the Church. "But it will not be difficult to administer. In fact, it might well be considered a place for an old warrior to rest." These words, like the howl of the distant coyote, had an element of mockery in them.

The old warrior would have liked to rest. Would like to rest now under the stars and for a moment he thought of pulling off his boots and stretching out by the rio on the soft sands. But there was the camp back there and duty. He slipped on his tunica and rose sadly to his feet. He had avoided thinking of the reason for his walk. He had not been able to make the decision concerning the woman. He had not even been able to make himself think about her.

Turning back to the camp, he saw the small figure of Luis Quintana standing several paces behind him. The Alcalde Mayor came to attention with an apology.

"The Indians, Excellency. If anything should happen to Your Excellency none of us would ever get to Isleta. I hope Your Excellency understands." The words were fumbled, but Otermín understood and appreciated the warning. He should have known better than to expose himself alone at night. None knew what was behind them or ahead.

He clapped Quintana on the shoulder. "Gracias, amigo." Then, as they started to walk back to the camp, he saw the smoke across the rio, smoke in large white puffs exploding skyward. For a moment he held his place beside Quintana.

"They know where we are." Then he smiled. "We could not very well hide our tracks." Both were silent for a time. The smoke signals continued to climb in the darkness. "Well, if they will remain on that side, we will not bother them."

Quintana looked at his commander and grinned. "We will arrange to leave them alone, Excellency."

Together they walked back to the camp. Fires were beginning to die as more and more of the men and women stretched out on the ground and drew their blankets, coats, or dresses over themselves.

As they passed the two carretas with the wounded, Otermín smelled the stench of excrement. "Better get those people to a latrine tomorrow before we march out. Have a couple of women scrub down the carreta because no one will want to march behind it in the hot sun."

Luis Quintana smiled. "A certain sow-faced woman sleeping near the knoll over there would be a fine one to scrub it down, Excellency."

Otermín stared at the little man, at the black teeth in the broad grin. "Use your own judgment. What she said tonight she said in anger. Perhaps it should be forgotten."

They saw the guards come to an alert, and they waved them back into the shadows where Quintana had hidden them.

"The hides," Otermín asked, as they passed along the row of sleeping refugees. "The hides are staked out?"

"Yes, Excellency. We will put them under the wounded in the morning." Quintana paused beside the fire where Señora Isabella waited for him.

The Captain General understood. "I shall see you in the morning, amigo. We must be prepared to leave early, as we have far to travel."

Then he walked on and he was alone among the fires. A few heads turned his way. A few smiles and nods let him know there were those who understood his problems. But he was alone. For a time he stood in the middle of the area, listened to the cattle bawling because some strange animal had disturbed them, heard a bird boasting about its flight. Finally, he walked up the hillock to the place where María had spread their blankets. She was sitting up combing her hair. He looked down at her, saw the exposed top of her bosom where she had opened her dress, saw the shape of her knees pulled up under the circle of her skirt, and as he sank to the ground beside her, he knew that soon he would have to make up his mind about this woman. Now he was too weary to do so. He relaxed, and she knelt over his legs and pulled his boots off and set them beside his equipment. Several paces away he made out the small figure of Inez curled up and sleeping. There were no fires near by, and he was alone in the dark with María. As he reached out his left hand and passed it over her soft bosom, she moved closer to him.

6

JUAN OF TAOS lay on his stomach, nibbling the end of a long blade of grass and staring at the casas reales below. Behind him he heard the bustle of his camp. Across the open plaza mayor and the casas held by the People he saw the morning activities in the southern camp. He wondered who its new war chief would be now that Askon was dead.

Yesterday's defeat had been needless. Fay-yat blamed himself. But Juan knew it was his own fault. For a brief instant he had failed to appreciate his enemy. And in that brief instant the enemy had been bold. He had followed the path he always followed and which Juan knew he should have been able to predict. Instead, Juan had let himself be panicked. He, too, had caught the fear-fever spread by the Apache name. There was more, and he knew it. No one else did, but Juan felt no better for his secret. When Popé had suggested he explain to the Apaches how they had fought the Spaniards, instead of assuring his victory, he had leaped at the opportunity to display it like a young maid her bosom or a fool his ignorance. Juan was disgusted with himself. Now he had to create another plan, devise another means for defeating the Spanish; and as each day passed and he watched their courage, their boldness, their brilliant defence, he found it more difficult to face the task of destroying them.

He was thinking about this when he saw the first Spanish soldiers emerge from the palacio, blink in the morning light and ride across the open plaza. They were armed and prepared to fight.

In an instant Juan was on his feet. From the noise about him, he knew that others had also seen the enemy march out into the open. Then Juan saw a carreta enter the plaza pulled by an old horse, then another, and a third. There was a white canopy over the first, and he could not make out what was in it. The second revealed its contents—wounded sprawling on a green mattress. The third carried the same burden. Several war chiefs started calling for their men, and Juan felt a hand on his arm. Popé. Juan answered the question in the medicine man's eyes with a bewildered shake of his head.

The Spanish soldiers turned and crossed toward the rio. Then the women and children appeared. They walked behind the two-wheeled carretas, carrying their belongings. Juan could see that some of them were old. One black-haired girl caught his attention for a moment. Slight. Blue dress. Her weary figure moving with difficulty. Manuela. He looked closer and shook his head imperceptibly. Someone else. The sun reflected off an object and he recognized it as a clock. The blonde woman who carried it held a boy by the hand.

Then Juan saw the Governor. His horse was the best. His erect carriage, the authority of his bearing, the way he poured his orders over the heads of the others revealed him as the Governor. An Indian standing near Juan drew his bow, but the young war chief's hand went up. He saw that Popé was watching him. There was excitement along the entire hill behind the casas reales. The warriors, realizing at last what was happening, waited for their orders. Two junior war chiefs stood by to carry Juan's messages. But there were no messages.

The Spanish column stretched out across the plaza to the south. The women and children and aged comprised most of it, but soldados formed the rear guard.

Popé turned again to Juan and saw that there was pleasure on the youth's face as well as relief. "When will you attack?" he asked.

Juan did not seem to hear. Fay-yat of Tesuque joined them. His sabre was in his hand. His broad form hunched over as he set the point of the weapon in the earth between his feet and rested on it.

"They leave," he said. It was partly a question, partly disbelief of a sight he never expected to see.

Popé nodded. "We could destroy them down there." But he was less concerned about destroying them than he was about what Juan would do.

Without looking at the two elders beside him, the war chief spoke softly, half to himself, half-explaining. "The Spanish depart. They retreat. They are beaten."

He regretted that it was possible for these men to accept defeat. The Governor, whose back was growing smaller in the distance, reminded Juan of Don Jaime de Marcos, and he resented the smirch on his dead mentor's name.

Defeat.

The Spanish were defeated.

They had taken their women and their Blessing Men and their crosses and their food and they were seeking the Camino Real south. A hundred years. A thousand useless deaths. Two peoples left to find their separate ways to the place from which they had come.

Juan wondered how far a man could run backward. He watched the Spanish move out slowly, with deliberate care, prepared to fend off attack. He saw things which Popé and Fay-yat did not see. The Spaniards' lances rested on their boots. Their sabres were lying across the saddles. Their helmets were tightly pulled down over their heads. The fleeing enemy had the swipe of a bear and was prepared to turn as quickly on any who dared annoy it.

Finally, when only the dust of them could be seen, Juan knew that he must face Popé and Fay-yat. He closed his eyes against the sun and the future and turned to look at the elders who stood beside him.

"You could have destroyed them." Popé spoke quietly, but Juan saw the jaguar pelt was shaking.

"Now there is not a Blessing Man or a Man of Iron north of the Villa. Soon there will be none in the land of the pueblos," Juan explained.

Popé turned to Fay-yat and saw the old cacique look away. The days had taken their toll of his strength. They had drawn out the last of his hatred and all of his sympathies. He had seen the Spanish attack of the preceding day. He had seen Askon fall and the hundreds of others. It was he who had killed the Spaniard who had once been his friend. He could not understand what was to be gained by another death and another death. There were dead as yet unburied. There were men who desired to return to their homes and to their fields. He was aware that Popé continued to watch him. He stood as tall as he could and set the Spanish sabre in the sheath at his side.

"It is time for Popé to enter the palacio." In Fay-yat's mind was the picture of the giant medicine man standing in the church of the Immaculate Conception, laughing at the ceiling. It was to this vanity that he now appealed.

Juan spread out his arms and turned to the warriors who had gathered in great numbers behind him. He quickly selected a hundred men and a war chief with a great scar reaching from his right eye to his lip, to head them. Then he ordered him: "Follow the Spaniards. Ride close, but do not attack unless they attack you. They leave us now, and they will be gone," he paused, "we hope forever. See that they do not return. Empty the pueblos before them. Destroy any crops or cattle or stored meal they can use to feed themselves and recover their courage. Send us reports of everything they do." Then he turned to a cacique from a southern pueblo. "Where is a narrow place between two hills through which they must retreat?"

The cacique thought for a moment. "Above Sandia. Two sets of hills close together with heights to attack from. Near the hacienda of Captain Anaya."

"Where?" Juan half shouted the question to the surprise of those around him.

The puzzled cacique shouted his answer back. "The narrow pass above Sandia near the hacienda of Captain Anaya."

Juan nodded slowly as though thinking. Then to the war chief he had selected, "You had better take the best horses you can find and follow them now." Then he took the young war chief aside and talked with him alone. When the warriors had departed, he stood with Popé and Fay-yat again.

"We attack them at the Anaya Pass?" Popé was asking now.

Juan shook his head. "If they turn back. Or," he smiled, "if they move too slowly."

Fay-yat admitted his confusion. "If they move too slowly?"

Juan nodded. "Should they capture any of our men, the Spanish know how to make a man reveal secrets. It was Fay-yat who observed this so wisely when he changed the day of freedom to the Day of San Lorenzo. The Spanish know how to take the secret thoughts of a man, and our friend from Sandia shouted loudly enough so that all those who rode south just now know a fact which may not be a fact—that we might attack at Anaya Pass. The Governor is a wise man. He will race his people south and through that place. But we can wait to decide if we should attack."

Fay-yat nodded. He was impressed with the youth of Taos. But Popé slowly shook his head. He rubbed an open hand over his jaguar pelt as he spoke. "Our young friend thinks as deviously as a rio runs through hill country."

Juan was about to speak, thought better of it, felt his stomach tense with fear, and then let his shoulders fall back into place. He looked relaxed as he smiled at Popé, accepting the accusation as a compliment, knowing that it was not intended to be one. Juan feared Popé because the Spanish retreat had revealed clearly to both of them how different they were. Popé was willing to permit the Spanish exit because he wished to be rid of them. Juan regretted their departure because of what they took with them and the symbol that was struck down with their defeat. The difference could no longer be hidden.

Both men were silent. It was Fay-yat who finally spoke. "It is difficult to believe." Then, after a moment, "My father would like to have seen what we saw this morning." Then he knew what he said was what an old man would say. He tried to explain. "Once I had friends among them. My father never did." This was even less understood by Popé.

Juan placed a comforting hand on the old man's shoulder. "I believe the people of Tesuque will always be proud of Fay-yat, and I am certain his father is." Juan avoided the eyes of Popé who stood praying to the Sun Father high above them now. A soft breeze carried over the Villa de Santa Fe below. A willow whispered back to it. The high grass riffled. And the dried petals of a yucca flower drifted to the ground.

Popé spread out his long arms, palms up, and made an invocation to the day of victory.

When he was done, he brought his great palms together with a slap that could be heard across the fields. Then, without turning his head to the right or left, he strode directly down the hill toward the casas reales. He walked around the large compound to the empty plaza, followed by the curious warriors. The men of the southern pueblos were already entering the town, and as the two groups came together, Popé raised his hand.

There was a clear path between the two armies, and he stood looking down it. He opened his palm upward and the breeze scattered a handful of corn flour. His huge head went back. The long braids hung free behind him. He began to speak directly to the sun. "The People have fought. The People have carried out their pledge. The People have rejected the ways of their oppressors and with their own hands have removed their bonds. Upright they ask for the help of the gods. They are no longer suppliants to the false. They are no longer slaves—humble before the foreign. They seek only the ways of the quick who live in the fields and the skies."

His head came down as he looked at the eager faces about him, knew even he could hold them no longer. "They seek only the chance to rejoice." And he flung his arms wide.

This was signal enough for the warriors who had stared for days at the casas reales and dreamed of Spanish riches within, of wealth and weapons and cloth made in far places by unknown artisans. They burst past Popé with a yell. They rolled on the ground and they climbed in the windows, mad, happy, free.

They revelled in their victory. They ran through the buildings. They tore the tapestries off the walls and the windows and wrapped the brocade and linens about their waists. They grabbed at chairs and carried them out into the sunlight and set them on the bare earth. Then they walked around them and around them as they tried to decide what was the best thing to do. Finally, they took turns sitting down in the chairs. They opened the ovens and poked at the fat and the food scraps, put their fingers in their mouths expecting a foreign taste and were disappointed. They threw themselves down on the open slats of the Governor's four-poster bed and collapsed through to the floor and were angry and pulled the posts off the bed and swung them about like war clubs. They saw the mirror on the wall, and after an initial fear, they struck at the faces they saw and watched the polished metal bend and distort their images. They were frightened and so they struck again and again until there was no longer any reflection and they were free of the foreign thing. They found the supply of candles and set tapers up in a row on the tables and lit them all at one time and watched them burn down. They burst into the room that had been the Governor's office and they toppled over the vargueño and smashed open the front and spilled the documents on the floor and trampled on them and tore them to pieces and scattered the pieces. Then they went into the open area behind the palacio where they saw the graves where the Spanish had buried their own dead and the pile where the Spanish had stacked the Indian dead, and they were angry, and they dug up the Spanish bodies and hurled them out into the plaza and buried their own in the same holes and covered them up without waiting for prayers or ceremonials because they were more angry with the Spaniards at this moment than they were sympathetic with their own.

Fay-yat entered the buildings and watched the warriors desecrate the Spanish graves. He saw the hysterical youths hurl the large body of his dead friend, face down, into a corner of the compound, and he crossed over and stood looking at it. Since the first moment when the small tropa spilled into Tesuque weeks before demanding the two messengers of Taos, the conflict had resolved itself for Fay-yat into his relationship to Ismael Pando. He could not recall when he had first come to resent the difference between them or when he had first learned to love this huge man who had been his friend.

He looked about him at the screaming chaos and the mad confusion as two warriors ran into the open compound wearing purple velvet skirts that billowed like smoke about their legs. Naked to the waist, the two men rolled over and over on the ground, laughing and shouting about what they would do if they had the Spanish women with them in the skirts. They came to a halt at Fay-yat's feet and looked up into his sober face. Both of the men fell silent. Fay-yat was about to order them to bury the body that lay on the ground beside them. He hesitated and knew that he was afraid. He was afraid of the People, and he did not know why. This frightened him even more. There was no one he could ask to bury a Spaniard, no one who would understand his feelings. He nodded without smiling at the two young men who started pulling the boots off the Spanish corpse. Then he walked back through the building and out again into the open plaza. Popé was no longer in sight. Nor was the war chief of Taos. Fay-yat considered looking for them and changed his mind. He slowly walked around the large compound back to the hill where his horse was tethered, and he mounted it and rode down to the rio where he could be alone.

Inside the palacio of the Spanish, Popé wandered from room to room. This great capitol building of a province that was larger than kingdoms of Europe had been maintained for almost a century as though the King of Spain himself might arrive at any moment.

Five years before, Popé had been dragged in chains to this palacio. Here he had listened to Fray Pedro Duran accuse him and his companions of bewitching the Spaniards, of speaking with gods who were not the Spanish gods. And he had admitted it. He had not denied that he had power and that he had visions of a future for the People. He was proud of his powers, though he had not understood why he or any of his fellow priests would have used these powers to call down the spirits on any man as unimportant as the corpulent Fray Pedro Duran. Standing in the small chapel of La Hermita de Nuestra Señora, Popé looked about him. Here, where the governors of Spain had worshipped, he would have his kiva. He left the chapel and made his way down the small flight of stairs until he found the sleeping room of the Governor. It was empty now. An odour of sick flesh hung in the air. He wondered if the Governor had been wounded. He regretted that he had never met the man. He would like to have known him. There were those who had spoken kindly of him, but it had not been possible for Popé to listen to any talk that might have led to understanding with the Whitefaces. He had drawn that line beyond which his people could not be driven. He kept that line clean and sharp as the edge of a Spanish daga by listening to nothing good that anyone said to him about the Spaniards. Hatred and faith had carried him to victory. And though Popé was not rolling on the ground in the compound with a purple velvet skirt about his waist, he was revelling in his victory no less than the others. The sore on his foot made by the twisted moccasin thong pained him and he knelt down and removed the moccasins and flung them into a corner. This would be his sleeping room. He removed the heavy bull-horn headdress and looked about for a place to set it down. Finally, he crossed to the window and looked out across the plaza. The warriors were pulling the furniture out of a building near by. Several of the short, copper braves were stumbling over the black dresses they had found in the casa where the Whitefaces had kept their communal women. Three others were tugging a small cannon into the middle of the plaza. Its metal-bound wheels cut into the soft earth, leaving ruts that would turn to small streams when the rains came. Now the dust sifted over them. A group of curious warriors gathered about the weapon. They stood, erect and lean. The war paint had been washed off their faces. Their bandos were tight about their heads. Popé was proud of his army. He saw one youth from La Cañada empty the powder from his harquebus kit into the firing hole and then swing the small, heavy barrel around to point at the gutted church of the Immaculate Conception. A second warrior, a runner from Santa Clara, left the group and returned shortly with a lighted candle. While he was gone, the others stuffed rocks and rags and several iron balls into the open barrel of the cannon. When everything was ready, the warriors stepped away from the open barrel and stood at the rear of the gun. They ran their hands over the small, leaping dolphins they saw moulded there and scratched at the copper. Then the youth from Santa Clara touched the candle to the firing hole. There was a flash, a roar, and screams. When the heavy smoke cleared away, Popé saw four men rolling on the ground holding their faces or arms or legs. Two men lay still, and he knew they were dead. The heavy barrel of the cannon was split down its full length.

The Spaniards. Popé's hatred rose within him. He did not understand how a weapon was spiked, but he knew the explosion and catastrophe had to be blamed on the Spaniards. He wanted to walk out into the plaza and gather his warriors and chase after the Whitefaces who had left their blight on the land. He was considering this when he saw the old man with two young warriors at his side enter the plaza from the south. Popé recognized Ruaha of San Ysidro and his anger flushed his face. Now that the fighting was done, now that the enemy had departed, Ruaha appeared.

For days he had waited for the learned cacique to arrive with his warriors. For days he had known how the San Ysidrans had held back from killing their Blessing Man. Twice Popé had sent messengers urging the death of the padre. And then he had sent a third messenger with the warning that he would lead the puebleños south from the Villa de Santa Fe. Now he assumed the padre was dead. Now, when the fighting was over.

Still holding the heavy bull-horn headdress in his hand, Popé strode out of his sleeping room and the palacio across the plaza mayor. He did not pause to look at the wounded warriors who rolled on the ground clutching their torn limbs and blinded eyes. He stopped only when he stood before the cacique of San Ysidro. Fay-yat of Tesuque, returning from the rio, saw the two men together and, dismounting from his horse, walked over to join them.

Ruaha nodded his head in recognition of Popé. "We have killed the Blessing Man," he said. Then, as he watched the priest's face cloud, he added, "I wish now that my people had never seen him die. Though we burned him on his cross, he forgave us."

He had told Popé what he had travelled for two days to tell him. Now he was prepared to depart. His people were troubled and he was weary. There were mourning rites to be prepared for his wife Yad-wan and mourning rites for his daughter Poy-ye who had disappeared into the night.

He turned his back upon Popé, who had led the rebellion which had ended so disastrously for Ruaha, and he started to walk away.

Anger finally overflowed the medicine man who for five years had held anger within him and used it as a weapon. He swung out at the back of the departing cacique with the heavy horns in his hands, ripping open the skin of the small man's neck. Ruaha stumbled and collapsed at the feet of the young warriors who accompanied him. They whirled to face Popé, who stared down at the body of the cacique and then at the heavy headdress in his hands. The jaguar pelt at his waist hung limp. The long braids lying across his shoulders stretched even lower as he bent his head forward. Then, turning around, he walked sadly back to the palacio.

Fay-yat watched the two young men lift their cacique in their arms and walk out of the plaza towards the rio. When they were gone, he returned to his horse, mounted again and rode to the entrance of the palacio. This was what it was coming to—tyranny for tyranny.

Making his way through the warriors who clustered about the entrance, Fay-yat went in search of Popé. He wanted to withdraw the warriors of Tesuque and ride north. The rebellion was over; and as he thought of the gentle, learned man from San Ysidro, he could not bring himself to celebrate any longer. After walking from room to room, he finally found Popé seated on a high straight-backed chair behind the large table which Governor Otermín had used for his desk. The bull-horn headdress lay on a corner of that table and the giant priest was turning over a pile of documents which he had found stacked behind the desk. Fay-yat watched him from the doorway as he tried to decipher the language he had never learned from the writing he could not read.

Juan, standing by the window of the room, was also watching the medicine man. There was a smile on his face and Fay-yat tried to recall what he had heard concerning the youth. It had something to do with his being brought up in the house of the Silent Spaniard of Taos. Popé held up a large parchment so that the youth could see it. "What is this?" he asked.

Juan stared at it for a long time before he spoke. He could read the inscriptions across the bottom from where he stood. The sea serpents and the galleons, the bare-bosomed women with trays of fruit on their heads. He wondered which had caught the priest's angry eyes. At last he said, "It is a map. It shows this place, the location of each of the pueblos and the route of the rio." He could tell that Popé did not believe him. Then he saw the books set up in a row on a shelf behind the priest. He was about to say something and changed his mind. Both he and Fay-yat watched Popé as he tried to comprehend the meaning of the parchment. They saw his ignorance churn into anger and frustration as he tore the sheepskin in two pieces with several jerks of his large hands and threw it to the floor with the other documents before him.

Then he turned his attention to the books which Juan had seen. Gingerly, Popé picked up a book for the first time in his life. The tooled leather bindings impressed him. The gold lettering caught his eye, and he ran a heavy finger over it. Then he dropped the book on the desk as though it were a dangerous thing. It toppled over and fell open exposing a neat page of regular type. Popé shrank back. Here were foreign signs and symbols. Here was the strength of the Spanish enemy, and coming directly face to face with it, he feared all that it represented.

With a sweep of his broad arm, he knocked the book off the desk to fall among the documents. Then in haste he rose to his feet and turning from right to left he looked at Fay-yat and then Juan. "Tonight we will celebrate. Tomorrow night we will burn the messages of the foreign gods so they will not be an abomination in the sight of the Sun Father." He waved his hand unsteadily to encompass documents and books. "We will take all this and burn it." Then without waiting for comment, he reached for his head-dress and strode from the room, his huge figure shaking the floor as he left.

Juan watched him depart and then crossed over and picked up the volume from the floor. It was a heavy quarto, and as he flipped the title page open, he read: "The Ingenious Gentleman Don Quixote de la Mancha by Miguel de Cervantes Saavedra."

Fay-yat asked him quietly, "This is a dangerous thing?"

Juan shook his head. "It is the story of an old Spaniard who spent his last years looking for a way of life that was gone. He never found it, but he did not know that and so he was happy." He closed the book and set it on the table. Then he turned to see that Fay-yat was still watching him. For a time they stared sadly at each other. Then the cacique shook his head and walked out of the room. Juan believed he could understand this old man, and he felt sorry for him. He picked up the book again, settled down in a Savonarola chair and began to read.

7

IT was late in the morning of the twenty-second. The Spanish column had moved out of its first camp shortly before dawn and, despite two rests, the people were already beginning to show their fatigue. But Governor Otermín was not looking at them as much as at the pillars of smoke on the far side of the rio. The quickest courier system in the entire New World was telling the Indians to the south about the Spanish movements.

Late the night before, as he lay on his back, one arm under María's head, he had stared at the smoke in the sky and wished the old Nuevo Mexicano, Pando, were with him. Pando would have been able to read the signals. In the early morning Otermín sent the pock-faced sargento through the camp in search of another who might be able to interpret them. The only answer he received was that they frightened the women.

One elderly crone stalked over to where he stood beside his horse and demanded that he send out a column of soldiers to stop the Indians spreading word about their retreat. After a time Otermín understood she was embarrassed about the rout, about having to sleep on the ground, about what she would tell her daughter in Chihuahua concerning her jornada. The

Indians were merely a visible sign of her shame and somehow she thought it should be kept a secret. Otermín listened and found himself sympathetic, but he ignored her suggestion and started the column moving.

Afterward, each time he rode past the old woman, she looked at him with accusing eyes. It was he who was her tormentor now. The smoke on the horizon concerned Otermín, but so long as the Indians kept their distance, there was nothing he could do about it and he had no intention of stirring up any trouble. He could not afford to. He was short of food and even shorter of men and munitions. He had no idea what supplies remained with García at Isleta. But he had hopes, and behind his hopes were visions of reconquest. Supplies from Isleta. The column he had sent south under the command of Don Pedro de Leiva. Twenty-seven soldiers. Twenty-seven who rode as escort for the supply train. Men and munitions. By now that column should have reached . . . his mind trailed off. He had no idea when the column was due. The message from Ayeta was simple: "Departing Ciudad Mexico with a thousand horses and supplies to satisfy the needs of the province for a year." Otermín wondered now if those were supplies for an operating province, one with crops growing, ranchos with full, fat herds of grazing cattle and the best Basque sheep. He wondered if that thousand horses were to supply or supplement the needs of a colony that had numbered over twenty-five hundred. Twenty-five hundred. He had no accurate count of his own column, let alone the group gathered at Isleta. That small pueblo in the south had taken on special meaning for him.

The column drew to a halt less than a league from San Marcos pueblo. Quintana rode back to where Otermín waited on his horse. He suggested they turn east, stop at the pueblo of San Marcos and investigate the state of the mission there.

Don Antonio listened and shook his head slowly.

"We will camp here. The sargento, the youthful one with the pocked face —what is his name?"

"Barnabe Márquez, Excellency. He has never discovered what they did to his wife." The extra information was gratuitous.

Otermín frowned. "Send him to me."

Quintana saluted and rode back up the line to inform the refugees that they could drop their baggage and rest. Several minutes later the sargento approached the Captain General.

"You wanted to speak to me, Excellency?"

The Commander looked at the young man. "We will remain here for a time. Not too long. One hour, two. Do you feel able to undertake a recon-naissance?"

The silence of Márquez pleased Otermín. This was not an eager youth. He had seen too many of those in his years, and the eagerness of Quintana was enough for the moment.

Then, "I will go if that is what Your Excellency wishes."

Don Antonio looked over the man's weapons: a sword, a helmet, breast-plate, and what looked to be a daga sticking out of one boot. There was an easy manner and a poise that was comforting.

"I know I kept you out of the battles of the Villa de Sante Fe. It was necessary then. But, Márquez, should you meet any Indians now, fight and fight hard. I need you back here."

The sargento was pleased that his Captain General knew his name.

"Take eight men, mounted and ready to move in a hurry. Feel out the area about San Marcos. Feel it out. Do not stir it up. Seated out here in the middle of open country, we are too vulnerable to attack. But see what the strength is. Then get back just as quickly as you can."

"San Marcos. Yes, Excellency." The youth saluted, whirled off on his horse to the head of the column, selected his detachment and quickly disappeared to the east.

When he was gone, Otermín looked at the column about him. It rested in place as it had been instructed to do for the past two days. The women and children held their positions, their baggage beside them, the water bags out. Several had wandered down to the rio and he did not disapprove. Too much discipline did not set well with civilians. He knew that the Cabildo was already unhappy: unhappy with his plan of march, with the fact that they had been ordered to march, with the fact that he did not bother to consult them on details—how many cattle to kill? what guards where? Though, as far as he could determine, there was nothing at this moment he wanted to consult them about.

He slipped out of his saddle to the ground and walked his horse to the water's edge. As his horse drank, he looked at the sky. There were clouds there now. Probably rain soon. This would be cooling, but it would also be miserable. Mud. Mud to march across. Mud to sleep upon. He shuddered. The arroyos, they were problem enough empty. Filled, each would become its own small torrent fighting its way to the nearest rio, an additional obstacle, an added problem when it seemed one more would destroy them.

His horse satisfied, Otermín walked the beast back to the first clump of bushes he could find. Here he sprawled out in the sparse shade and closed his eyes. He was tired. His wounds continued to pain him. He had rested little through the night. There was no one else whom he trusted to check the guard, and so he rose each hour and walked the full perimeter of his camp before taking his place again beside María. She had been able to sleep, and most of the camp was able to find some rest, though the complaints grew that the camp sites might have been better selected, the pace more leisurely, the food better apportioned. But Don Antonio de Otermín was an old soldado and this was, he believed, a normal part of every military operation. Now that he had women along, he expected the same problems in greater degree.

He had not planned a siesta, but he saw no reason why he should not enjoy the halt. The sargento, the name kept slipping from his memory— Sargento Márquez, that was it—would be back soon enough, and then the work and the march could begin again.

Beside the rio below, the women saw that the Governor was resting. Dozens of them rose from their places in the long column and carried their bundles down to the high water. Here several slipped off their dresses and standing in thin cotton shifts began to cool themselves while washing the clothes they wore and any extra that they had been given by the soldiers. Soon there were over fifty women along the bank. They called to each other, pointed out a small water snake skating, head poised, along the rio, chatted about the heat of the sun, what clay does to a woman's clothes, how Doña Henares had lost a heel to one of her shoes and walked with a waddle that matched her weight. They talked, too, of the temper of the Governor, of his quarrel with the ranchero and how he had settled it with boldness. There was other talk, but this ceased as María made her way to the stream with her torn dress and the Governor's shirt thrown over her arm. Though she kicked off her shoes, she kept on her blue dress as she stepped into the stream. The dress that she washed along with the shirt was the same one she had worn the first day she had arived at the Villa, the brown dress with the torn bodice which had caught the Governor's eye. The women moved away from María, leaving her all of the room she wanted, and when Inez removed her shoes and stepped into the rio beside her mother, they allowed even more room. None of them spoke as they tried to ignore the Governor's woman. There were those who feared her, those who were willing to forget her, and those who resented her.

For a time there was silence, and then a heavy-throated voice could be heard above the noise of the stream and the slapping of clothes on rocks: "She does not wash his drawers because he has given up wearing them since meeting her."

María paid no attention to the comment. At first she was even willing to believe it was not intended for her ears.

Then the voice was heard again. "Too bad the Governor had to find him a whore when he should be tending to his affairs. And right after her husband was supposed to be killed, too."

It was the same throaty voice, but before María could turn to identify it, another was heard.

"Some men are willing to die for a woman. The Governor killed that poor little squint-eyed soldado for this one."

The thick voice again, "Too scrawny to satisfy even an old man like the Governor."

María froze as she was, bent over, laundry in hand, and she sought the eyes of Inez, who was walking out of the stream and away. Anger crawled over the widow Valdivia. She dropped the clothes she was holding and looked about for her tormentors. Several varas away, hands on hips, stood the sow-faced wife of the ranchero whom Otermín had kicked two nights before.

"Scrawny," the woman repeated. "Scrawny and unlucky. With all the men who have stretched her one would think she would have a brood of children."

María leapt through the water, fingers arched and tearing at the woman's full, fat face. There was a flurry of spray as she closed with the ponderous figure of the ranchero's señora. Then a scream as María's nails came down the length of the woman's face, tearing skin and flesh, trailed by a spurt of blood.

Before either could strike again, a strong hand grasped María from behind and propelled her toward the bank. She started to protest, wanted to turn again on her tormentor, but the hand held tightly to the back of her neck and slowly forced her out of the water. Only on the bank was she able to twist around enough to see who her captor was. She was stunned. Shoes soaked, skirt dripping, Señora Isabella Quintana had entered the water to break up the fray.

María tried to struggle with her, but Señora Isabella remained firm as she spoke softly. Only María heard her: "The Governor's woman does not brawl in public. The Governor's woman respects his name and lends it all the dignity she has." With these words Isabella dropped her hands. "Go to where he is resting. I will recover your laundry and your shoes."

The large woman placed her hands on her hips and waited until María slowly walked away. The widow had lost the quarrel with the ranchero's wife and she knew it. She lost because she had entered into it.

Señora Isabella Quintana slowly waded back into the stream. She held out her hand, and the woman who had caught the Governor's shirt and María's second dress handed them to her. Isabella looked at the dress and saw that it had been torn almost in two. She flipped it over her shoulder and stalked through the water until she stood before the sow-faced woman. They were two imposing bulks as they stared at each other. The ranchero's wife held her hands to her cheeks where the blood seeped through her fingers.

"The next time anyone says anything concerning the Governor and it comes to my ears, the column will depart without you and your husband. I would ask for your second dress to replace this one your friends just destroyed, but so big a sack is only for carrying dead cows."

She started to walk away when the other woman yelled after her, "Do you want to stretch out for the Governor, also?"

In a single gesture Isabella whirled about, swung one huge palm and smashed it against the side of the woman's head. The woman crumpled. Señora Quintana spoke softly to those about them, "See that she is laid out on the bank until she recovers her senses." Then she paused before she said, "Is it understood that there will be no more talk?"

No one answered and she waddled ashore, the torn dress and the Governor's embroidered shirt over her broad shoulder. On the rio's bank she picked up the shoes María had left there and made her way toward the clump of bushes where Don Antonio lay. Standing over María, she looked down at the younger woman.

"Luis tells me our lives depend upon him," pointing to the Governor, "and on the respect the people hold for him so that he can give his orders quickly and without anyone questioning them. I think Luis is right."

María nodded slowly. She had never met anyone like this woman before, and though she had laughed in the back of her own mind at the strange appearance the Quintanas made—the peppery, eager Luis and his heavy, shuffling Isabella, María knew that they had suddenly become important in her life.

8

DON ANTONIO lay, eyes closed, waiting for Isabella to leave. He had witnessed the scene in the water and was aware of the ludicrous picture it presented. Something inside him collapsed. Was this the route of failure, women scrambling and scratching over his name, his reputation? Half-naked, soaked to their navels, they had turned the weeks of combat—honour and dignity—into thin curses and small humiliations.

His fists closed painfully. He wanted to strike María, drown the sow-faced woman struggling onto the rio's bank, scream out his protests against the degradation they brought not only to him, but the others—those who had died, those who had fought bravely and were in honourable retreat.

Women. He had never commanded a column of them before, had never tried to hold their mercurial qualities to the firm mould necessary for a military operation.

Now for the first time, he did not know, he doubted. He questioned his own abilities to command, to lead, to bring these people to safety despite themselves. He was uncertain where he had always had confidence, where he had never before even questioned.

He opened his eyes and rolled over on the ground to look at María. Her wet dress clung tightly, her loose hair straggled thinly about her shoulders. Her eyes blinked back tears. Were they anger or humiliation? He could not comfort her. The desire was not there.

Slowly he sat up and faced her. The time was now. The decision had waited long enough.

Very softly he spoke. "María, you will hold your distance from me. I will hold mine from you. It is not right—you, me. There are too many others involved. We will eat apart. Sleep apart."

After a moment, he added, "I am sorry." And he was, because he wanted her. At first he did not think she had heard him. Then she spoke as softly as he had. "They are old women, jealous and afraid. Are you afraid, too?"

"They depend on me," he said. He rose to his feet and stood over her. "And they have the right to depend on me."

As he had not looked back at his dead, his palacio, or his capital, he did not look back now. His leather jerkin neatly laced, his black pantalones unwrinkled, the silver buttons shining, the boots clean, the Captain General walked over to where Quintana sat beside his wife.

"The sargento delays. We march now and hope he finds us."

The column was raised to its feet, the order given to march. Then in the distance, Otermín saw Sargento Barnabe Márquez riding slowly toward him from the east. Waving the column on, Otermín rode out to meet the small tropa. Among the horsemen, at the end of a long rope, ran an Indian. As Don Antonio joined them, the soldiers flung the stumbling native at their commander's feet.

"I found this, Excellency," Sargento Márquez picked at a scab on his face. "A Tewan. I know him."

The Captain General sat on his horse looking down at the Indian. His arms were bound behind his back. His clothes were ripped away. There was blood on his bared shoulders. As he stared up, Don Antonio saw that he was an old man, sixty years or more.

"You know him?"

"Yes, Excellency. He worked for me. A Christian. Called Antonio. Was with us in the casas reales a week ago. Then he joined the rebels."

The Commander turned to see the dust raised by the disappearing column. Then he watched the smoke signals flowing up from the far side of the rio.

"Bring him along. We will question him at the next halt."

Márquez signalled for his men to follow while he rode at his captain's side.

"San Marcos?" Otermín asked.

"Empty, Excellency. The people are in the hills."

"Or in the Villa."

The sargento nodded slowly. His brown eyes were set on the end of the column ahead.

The Governor looked at the youth as they rode, saw the bitter lines about his mouth, the half-shut eyes and the muscles moving nervously in the scarred and hollow cheeks.

"Could the Indian tell you of your family?"

Márquez shook his head. "I tried to learn."

"I know. The lash marks on his shoulders show you tried."

The pair rode silently together. When they reached the tail of the column, Otermín spurred his horse and joined Quintana at the head of the file.

"He took a long time," the Alcalde Mayor said.

Otermín nodded. "Stopped to interrogate an Indian."

"He is young and there is his wife."

"I know. I know." Cutting off further discussion.

There were rocks in the trail. Sometimes the carretas were hauled over them, shoulder to wheel and the spavined horses whipped. Sometimes the rocks were skirted as they cut a wandering path southward. Sometimes the men heaved the heavy boulders to the side of the trail, white grubs wriggling for shelter and shade, yellow scorpions swiping at leather-toed boots. And the wagons moved on. The long line moved on.

The red petticoat lay in a heap on the ground beside the white muslin breeches. The women moving past scarcely noticed the abandoned undergarments. The soldiers, however, snickered and made bad jokes as they tried to guess which of the women had given up the fight to preserve her shape against the August sun. One young man with a bandage across his head and a bright red scar across his cheek held the ruffled muslin breeches before him in jest. Soon he tired of the sport and dropped them into the dust near the flexible steel corset that was half hidden behind a juniper bush. Some of the women laughed and some blushed pink as two youths ripped the stays out of the stiff cloth and fought a mock duel to a mock death.

When the Captain General rode by, they dropped their intimate weapons, took their place again in the column and marched on, leaving the white and red undergarments to mark their passage.

Don Antonio did not interrogate the Indian captive at the next rest stop or the one after. He rode at the head of the column and, as they came to each halt, he ignored the others about him, the questioning glance of Luis Quintana and the puzzled expression on the face of Márquez. But the Captain General knew his own mind and he had made his decision to hold back his questions until he felt the prisoner was ready to talk. The rests themselves were difficult for Don Antonio. He had been in the habit of spending his spare moments with María and Inez. He had become accustomed to María's ready supply of food and drink, of clean clothes and all the small comforts which somehow she had brought into his otherwise disordered life.

Now the siestas were different. He rode to the farthest shade within sight of the column and stretched out under a tree. Sometimes he closed his eyes. Other times he watched the distant birds or attempted to recall what lay beyond the barren hills. Only when he closed his eyes did he allow himself to think of Isleta. Here was surcease. Here the end of his jornada.

Twice he had asked Luis to find water for him from the supply being carried. He had planned to join the Quintanas at the noon meal, but he held back. Partly because he did not want to intrude and partly because he did not want to give up his own privacy.

Long ago he had learned that the small actions of a commander were always under scrutiny, and he was convinced everyone was aware that he no longer joined María even though only four halts had passed. He was concerned for her. He wanted to ride back and rest beside her, wanted to take her strong hand in his lap and feel the strength of her. But he restrained himself. Night was worrying him. It was going to be difficult. The being alone. The being without her. He could almost reach out and lay a firm hand on a white breast. It was the thought of night that bothered him.

He rode the grey stallion hard. He did not care for the beast as most Spaniards cared for their horses. He had never seen this one before, knew only that it served him. He was aware of the concern most of his compatriots had for their horses. He did not, and that was all there was to it. If the beast wearied, he rested it. If the beast died, he would replace it. He assumed that his sargento saw that it was fed and watered.

Now as the sun began to reach the horizon to his left and the shadows of the small scrub trees grew longer, he knew he would have to find a camp site for the night. Without a word to Quintana, he spurred his horse and rode far ahead of the others. Soon even the dust of the column was no longer visible. A quarter of an hour later he found the site he wanted. It was broad, almost treeless, a slope to the rio, no cover for an Indian attack. He dismounted and threw the reins over a bush. Then he stretched his legs forward one at a time. He was stiff with riding. His age was bothering him. Not yet fifty, but no longer a youth. He should be resting somewhere, a cold drink in his hand, a hot wench at his side. He smiled to himself. Already he was retired again. The thoughts came so easily. Fell so quickly into place. Standing bareheaded in the late afternoon, he recalled the night—how long ago?—when he had been sprawled on his four-poster staring at the rain-stained ceiling, thinking about retirement. That was the night he had sought out the company of Pando and had spent the evening drinking and listening.

Pando. Ismael Pando. His thoughts came back to the old man more often than he would have believed. Unseen in the open land between the hills, Don Antonio de Otermín, Governor of Nuevo Mexico and Captain General of all the lands above el Paso del Norte, brought his wiry body to a stiff attention. Then with a carefully cupped hand he saluted the distant sun and the memory of Pando. He paid his lone respects to the ancient who had traded his life for that of the Governor, for an España he had never known. Pando. Otermín relaxed and, bending down, tore a leaf off a mesquite shrub.

He was still slowly tearing it into small pieces when the first dust of the column informed him that soon they would be encamped. Soon night would come and he would be alone again. He flung the pieces of leaf to the breeze-less air and watched them fall.

The interrogation would begin shortly. He would talk to the Indian and try to find the answer to a question he had day after day refrained from framing in his own weary mind. *Why? Why? Why?* There should have been peace and the quiet years. There should have been God and love. Now there were only the dead and the fleeing. And he was fleeing because he could not die.

He watched Quintana, the dark, vigorous figure swinging the long column into an arc about the camping ground. No need to give the small orders here. No need to tell the Alcalde Mayor where the women should camp and the men. No need to repeat the death sentence on four more of their cattle. A problem yesterday. A routine today.

When he had finished his evening meal, Don Antonio had the old Indian brought to him. An hour later the old man was led away. He had said only one thing of importance to his captors. "They plan to attack you, Excellency. They plan to attack in the Pass between the hills and the rio you call del Norte near the house of Don Cristóbal de Anaya."

When the Governor was alone with Luis Quintana, he shrugged. "It was the truth as he knew it. I am concerned about the ambush. But I am not convinced he would know the details. Double the guards. Rest well. I will check the camp through the night. We will move early in the morning."

Quintana started to speak and then hesitated. His natural eagerness was held back with difficulty. Otermín smiled. "I will remain here, Luis. See that the old man's report is recorded and that after he is fed he gets a chance to babble on about what he knows."

"You will remain here, Excellency?"

Don Antonio nodded. "Have one of the soldados bring my blankets. I will check the camp later when everyone is asleep."

The little man with the dark teeth stood, mouth open, curiosity crawling through him. Then he saluted the Captain General and slowly walked back to the camp. He was a simple man and ready to admit there were things he did not understand. Command was one, governors and their women another.

The last of the fat and waste of the cattle had been flung into the camp-fires where they sparked brightly. The evening meal was over. The guards were posted. The first fresh moment came at the day's end with the last of the sun and the breeze. Darkness claimed the outer edges of the camp, while in large circles about the mesquite and piñon fires the women and aged, the soldados and rancheros spoke softly and laughed loudly.

Farther back from the fires the children slept or listened to their elders. The cattle bawled and sought the burnt grass. Fireflies like small sparks crossed the night, and mosquitoes hummed hungrily near the rushes by the rio.

The girl rose to her feet and began to sway slowly back and forth. First the soldados picked up the rhythm and began to clap. Then the women slapped their thighs and the old men stamped the dark earth. The pace quickened as the lithe figure of the slight wench with the night-black hair began to stamp her feet and stretch her arms upward. Her sweated green dress shifted over her hips, and as her feet swung in greater and greater circles, the broad skirt took the shape of a disk about her browned thighs. The stomping and slapping became louder, the dance faster, and the bright face of the wench began to glisten.

Two young boys crawled out of their blankets toward the edge of the fire and one of them nudged the other as her skirt whirled higher and higher. The sharp rhythm disturbed the cattle and several began to bellow their protests. But the dance had caught the camp and none could see anything but the fine shape of the girl as she dipped her body forward and back, raised her feet in one great kick and landed, hands over, on her feet again. The clapping became a cross between the music of the dance and appreciation. Her bare feet flicked out and out again. The broad green skirt flapped upward and then fell between her legs. The sweat ran in great drops down her face, her shoulders, and between her breasts. The loose bodice clung about her and still she danced, still the slapping of thighs and the slap-slap of the open palms of the soldados and rancheros, still the ready stamp of feet on the hard earth.

The faces about the fires began to slacken, the women licked their lips, the tired, eager bodies began to tense. No one removed his eyes from the girl, and yet each sensed the man or the woman at his side. The stocky padre rose to his feet and for a moment the rhythm quickened. Then he turned his back and walked out into the darkness beyond the range of fires.

Don Antonio sat on his blanket looking down at the camp, felt himself grow tense, looked about the fires below for the face of María and saw her

as she sat swaying from side to side bumping shoulders with the two
rancheros beside her. He saw the sad face of Márquez and noticed when the
youth rose and joined the padre in the dark. Then he saw the others—men
and women—disappear into the darkness in pairs.

Still the dance continued. Still the girl whirled and her arms moved in
their slow patterns suggesting pleasure and release. Then one of the soldiers
—a youth of the criminal group who had ridden north with Fray Francisco
Ayeta two years before, a gambler from Durango who had killed his mistress—rose and joined the dance. His tight pantalones and heavy boots did
not stop his movements as he began to capture the pace and rhythm of the
mestiza dancer. There were fewer left to watch as men and women paired
off into the night. But the couple danced to their own rhythm now. It was
slower, more deliberate. The green skirt seemed to splash with greater control. The silver medallion of San Cristóbal—he of the buenas jornadas—
swung in a steady pattern across the open tunica of the youth.

Then the dancing stopped and the two young people were holding hands.
Only the aged and the wounded were paying attention to them. The two
children had crept back to their blankets. The other men and women were
looking at those about them, at the tense faces, the damp lips, the clinging
dresses.

Otermín rolled over in the darkness and stared up at the sky. He did not
want to see María Valdivia or the look on her face as she sought his eyes.

Later the campfires began to die. The refugees relaxed. The night sounds
were few. Men and women were rolled up in their blankets against the cool
evening. They were alone or they were not alone. The young whore slept
with one arm about the gambler from Durango and one hand clutching the
silver medallion that hung about her neck.

It was well past the midnight hour when Don Antonio roused himself
from his blankets and slipped into his boots. The night was dark. The
sounds were distant and unimportant. A few campfires still glowed. He
slipped his baldrick over his shoulder, drew his sword to see how easily it
came to hand, and began his rounds. A hundred paces to the south of where
he had slept, he found the first guards. There were two of them seated together. Neither heard his approach, and he stood for a time listening to their
lies.

"She was beautiful, I tell you. Real meat. Not like that woman from the
casa de puta in Durango. Not like the fat wench from the rancho south of
the Villa."

Both men chuckled.

"Fat but soft. Wonder how her husband found her."

"Never had a chance, what with one or the other of us climbing that
mountain."

"But this other one was beautiful, I tell you. Teats like a statue, and a
handful." The boaster sat with his harquebus leaning against his knee as he
whittled at a small branch with his daga. "Firm. Watched her bathing and
knew she was for me."

The listener snorted. "You will sleep alone tonight and tomorrow night for all she cares."

There was silence for a moment.

"It is a long jornada, amigo. Even women with beautiful teats get lonely and hungry and cold at night." He paused as he appreciated the possibilities of the situation. "Besides, no woman has bulbs like those without expecting them to be played with. It is part of being a woman."

Don Antonio listened to the philosophy and walked on in the darkness, leaving the guards alone. They were well occupied and fully awake, even if they were not alert.

He drifted to the east where two guards were resting, backs against the trunks of a pair of cottonwood trees. One of the men had taken off his boots and was rubbing the soles of his feet. The other sat sharpening his daga on a small stone he held firmly in his hand. They spoke softly but their voices carried far in the still night. Don Antonio listened.

"Marching backward I call it. A retreat before heathen savages. Lost a war and a kingdom and all because he was flattening a widow when he should have been out there fighting."

There was silence for a time. Then the man with the daga thrust it in the dirt at his feet.

"Women. We should have left them for the Indians. None of them ever gave out for me. But then, I am not a governor."

Silence again.

"That Hoz. He had the right idea, but something went wrong."

There was a laugh as the man seemed to be tickling the soles of his own feet. "Getting killed. That is what went wrong. All for a widow with the governor's seal on her bottom."

Silence.

"It is losing that bothers me. Losing to Indians. My father said any one Spaniard could lick any number of Indians. Matter of courage. Matter of knowing how. And we lost. We are running, and they have the palacio and a four-poster bed with a canopy over it."

A coyote complained in the distance.

"The old rooster is tough. Rides like he was born on a horse. Fights like he was born with a sword."

The man with the daga snorted. "Born in a bed like any other man. Should have got out of it more often."

The Captain General was satisfied with the guard to the east and moved quietly toward the west, near the rio, where one old ranchero sat with a youth from the Villa. They were trying to hit a floating branch with their spittle as they spoke.

"I recall when the padre came and fetched my wife and me and we followed him to church and were blessed with all of our children. The padres cared in those days." It was the old man remembering.

The youth spat and fell short of his target. "Me, I have had my fill of churches and preaching and God. A man lives and a man dies. I saw friends die back there and so did you. But I cannot say why some died and others lived."

The older man reached the target, smiled. "God could say. God knows who is going to die and who is going to live. Do not forget that, son."

The youth rose to his feet and stretched his arms. "If He knows, He is not telling, and I have had my belly full of blood and secrets." He puckered his lips and bent his body back, farther and farther. Then he jerked forward and watched the spittle fly right over the target now almost out of sight in the darkness.

Don Antonio moved on. In the next fifteen minutes he paused briefly at each of the guard posts. The men were awake, and after a hard day's march there was little more he could expect from them. When he had completed his rounds, he entered the camp itself. There were men and women sleeping singly or in pairs over the whole broad area he had selected for the night. None had removed their clothes. Privacy was one reason, the cold another. The temperature dropped at night, and there was a chill in the air.

Several men and women sat about the few fires which still glowed softly in the dark. They turned their heads to watch the Governor as he entered the circle of fires. One woman jerked her head toward the sleeping form of María Valdivia and whispered something to the man beside her. Otermín ignored the gesture, walked up to the group and stood looking down at them. There were five about this fire, knees up, backs against rocks or rolled jerkins. The men had sabres lying beside them. None wore shoes or boots and their toes flexed in the last heat of the fire.

The blonde woman with the clock beside her stared up at the Governor. At her side was a widowed ranchero whom Otermín recognized as part of the assault group that fought beside him through the siege of the Villa. He nodded to the pair.

"Does your clock keep good time, Señora?" He was making talk. He was also trying to point out how foolish it was to carry a clock which had ceased to function.

The tall blonde woman reached over and put an affectionate hand on the mother-of-pearl case. "It is the nicest clock I have ever seen, Excellency."

Otermín smiled. Maybe this was reason enough to haul the timepiece. "It is a beautiful clock, Señora. I am certain someday it will work again."

The blonde's face was puzzled. "What difference would that make, Excellency? I could not read the time anyway."

Don Antonio flushed in the firelight.

"Tomorrow we reach Santo Domingo. Should we arrive early and find food there, we might stop for the day." He was holding out hope.

"We will welcome the rest, Excellency. And a room with a roof." The ranchero was holding the hand of the blonde woman now.

The others remained silent. They did not know this Governor. From remote estancias, they only knew the tales of the Captain General and the widow from Acoma. They knew the story of Hoz as told by a certain sow-faced woman and her husband who had walked for the past day holding his neck as though it might snap. They feared as the old Indian had feared. But mostly they were uncomfortable because they did not know the man who was their Governor, and not knowing, they were doubly cautious. He might be short-tempered. He might be a tyrant. It is always better for the little man without authority to keep his mouth quiet and listen and evaluate. Then only he will ever know whether he might have said the proper words or the wrong ones.

Otermín waited for someone else to speak. Finally, he bade them *buenas noches* and walked out of the circle of the fire. Only when he stood alone in the darkness did he turn back to the camp and stare at the curled figure of María Valdivia, recognizable by the multicoloured blanket which covered her and the small mound of child at her side. The Captain General was lonely and he wanted someone to sit beside who by her very presence would tell him he was a part of more than himself. He shrugged and slowly walked back to the rock where his blanket was spread. He sat down to remove his boots and noticed that the blanket was more comfortable. With his left hand he jerked one corner aside and saw the bunch grass neatly spread beneath it. She had waited for him to check the guard. She must have spent the evening watching him, as alone in the darkness as he was alone. He felt better for the company of it, removed his boots, stretched out on the blanket and dreamed of a large villa near Ciudad Mexico. Several children ran toward him, and there was a woman at his side, but he could not quite make out who she was.

9

DON ANTONIO opened his eyes and stared at the bright sky above. It was morning already. Quintana was organizing the camp to move out. Someone had brought the Governor's grey stallion and tied it near by. He threw back his blanket and began to roll it up. Beside him the sun arched off a polished helmet. It was his own. María must have burnished it during the night and set it beside his gear where he would find it.

Taking the heavy headpiece in his hands, he turned it around and around. One finger traced a deep cut in the silver ornament where an English cutlass had tried for his head. Another gouge marked an Indian arrow the steel had fended off in the mountains of Chile. He thought for a moment of Chile, and the cold campaign in the high places, and compared it with the heat of Nuevo Mexico. Then his palm went flat over a dent no blacksmith had ever been able to obliterate—the ball of an English pistola. The broad palm shook as Otermín recalled the haze through which he had finished that encounter. Panama it was. Panama and defeat. Another retreat. A different loss.

He did not want to count the losses now, and he shifted his palm to cover the crest on the helmet. The smoothed edges fitted neatly under his fingers. After a time he held the helmet at arm's length and stared at the

silver crest—a small Moorish castle set against a battle-axe crossed with a
crucifix. His father's mark and his grandfather's. The years of Castile against
the Mohammedan. The years of Africa. The sure sun baking a man's brain,
the hot axe blade and the bright Cross. A world away; a different enemy,
but the same cause. And the same code in Latin beneath the crest, *Dum vita
manebit*—While Life Remains. The stubby fingers touched the silvered
crucifix. The Captain General prayed softly for a moment under his breath.
While Life Remains.

The helmet. He was tempted to slip it on, feel the leather bed of it rest
on his brow, pull the chin strap tight and know the comfort of it. Instead,
he reached down, scooped up a handful of red dust at his feet and rubbed
off the polish which had caught his eye. He was not going to wear the helmet
today unless he had to fight. A helmet is for fighting and not for the courage
that the weight and strength of it gives a man. He said the words to himself.
Then he looked about to be certain no one heard him. A helmet is for fighting, and Don Antonio had postponed his fighting. He was in full retreat. He
rose, tossed the helmet to the soldier nearest him.

"Tie it to my saddle. Not the day to bake one's brains out."

The soldier smiled.

The Spanish column moved out of their open camp.

The sun again.

Bright.

Clear skies and long vistas as they made their way toward Santo Domingo.
The caravan was organized as before. Soldiers in the fore and rear. Out-
guards to the east. The rio to the west. The women, the children, the aged,
and the two wagons of wounded between. Otermín rode at the head of the
column, Quintana at his side. The Governor had avoided letting the column
pass him since that pause the day before when he had separated himself
from María. He did not want to face her. He did not want the questioning
look or the upturned face staring at him. Don Antonio admitted he was being
a coward, but there were things about which he need not be brave, and still
not endanger his position or his command. This was obviously one of them.
And as he had learned a long time ago: no man is brave all the time and
about everything.

They had travelled almost a league when Quintana drew his horse to
a halt and pointed to the mesa and rocks about them. Don Antonio nodded,
reached one hand out for the bridle of the Alcalde Mayor's stallion and
pulled it on with him.

"We do not notice. We do not pause. We move and we move."

Quintana heard the voices raised behind him, heard the frightened cry as
others saw what he had seen—Indians lining the tops of the distant mesa.
Some were mounted. Most were afoot. They were still, frozen. Two columns,
one to the right and one to the left.

"Keep moving," Otermín ordered the small tropa behind him as he swung
and rode back down the column. "Keep moving. Do not stop. Do not hesitate.
Keep moving." He exhorted, he pleaded, he ordered. "We are almost to Santo

Domingo. We will find shelter there. We cannot be caught in the open. We must attain cover."

And as he rode the length of the long column, he wondered if Vegetius had ever known retreat with two lines of Goths waiting for him to falter; if Vegetius would have taken the time to write wise words.

He passed María and looked over her head at the women beyond. He forced himself not to see the expression on her face and he almost succeeded. It was a calm face. She had more faith in him than he had in himself at this moment. At the rear of the column he ordered the sargentos to permit no hesitation. "Drive them ahead if you have to use the side of your sabres. No man rests. No woman."

And he himself stopped and stared at the long lines of Indians who were watching him.

Was Popé there? Were his lieutenants? Was the information of the old captive correct? Would they wait to attack him below, where the pass was narrow and he had no choice but to move into their trap? That was not now. That was another time, a future battle, and he would worry about it then. Now he had to move these people to the shelter of the pueblo on the rise in the distance. And worse, he might have to fight to capture the cover he needed.

Spur to horse and back the length of the column. On a fast gallop past Márquez, he yelled, "Join me." The young sargento dug his knife-like spurs into the side of his bay and rode after the Captain General. Together they made their way to the head of the column and the side of Quintana. Here Otermín reined in and began to spill his orders.

"Márquez, take three men from this group and ride into Santo Domingo. Ride fast and come back. Do we fight for cover there or not? We must know."

As the sargento saluted and selected his three men, Otermín laid a hand on the youth's reins and smiled at him.

"I expect you to return. I need your help. We do not want to lose you. Ride fast and wisely." The words showed concern and faith. The younger man grinned back wryly. "I, too, want to return, Excellency."

And he was gone.

Half a league to go for the column. Half a league under Indian eyes. Half a league of broken country and with too much baggage. Half a league of fear inching down the length of the column, slowing the pace, faltering courage and edging towards panic. The small tropa which brought up the rear pushed the women and children before them. The aged were doubled and tripled on horses already sagging from the days of poor grazing and heavy loads.

Fifteen minutes later Márquez raced up the road toward them. He caracoled his horse and drew to a measured pace beside the Governor.

"An old pueblo. No ladders down. No entrances on the ground level. I did not check each house. The first few are empty. Others may be hiding rebels. I do not know."

"The church? The sacristy? The mission?"

"Doors closed. No one in sight."

Otermín nodded and, spinning his horse about, rode down the length of the column until he located the squat, chunky padre. "We may have to take cover in the church. I ask your understanding."

There was a long silence. The shaven head was bowed as Fray Pedro weighed the request. The Governor held step with him while the column moved as rapidly toward security as its clumsy character permitted.

Then Fray Pedro asked, "They saw no sign of the Fray Custodio or the others with him?"

Otermín sighed. He admitted to himself that the wiry old warrior of Christ had slipped from his mind. No time to concern himself now about his memory. There were a thousand people running and the Indians watching their flight.

"The men saw no one, Padre. We use the church as our first refuge?"

The cleric nodded slowly. "I am certain the Holy Majesty will understand granting shelter to the Secular Majesty."

Otermín bowed his head and rode back up the column, wondering what he would have done had he been refused, wondering, too, if the padre realized the mission might become an embattled fortress should the Indians descend the far mesas from which they watched.

The old man stumbled. The loose dirt gave way under his feet and his aged legs failed him. Soundlessly, he slid into the sharp cut of the arroyo. He lay dazed for a moment. Then he accepted the outstretched hand of the woman who walked beside him. It took all of his failing strength to gain his feet. He paused to look at his palms, torn on the jagged rocks of the arroyo bed.

The sun striking his head dizzied him and he almost fell again. The woman put her arm about his waist, drew one of his over her own shoulder and helped him cross the rocky bed. The heavy, worn boots on his spindly legs dragged as he measured each step. The warm air rising from the sun-baked stone welled through his shiny black, steel-buttoned pantalones and burned his withered skin.

A day's march would have been difficult for him; this race for Santo Domingo was impossible. Only an hour before, the Captain General had told him to take his turn on a horse. But he was a man; women and children were walking, and a man, even an old man, has his pride.

His years were not important. His failures no longer mattered, because all of those who walked beside him had also lost. The small defeats, the farms abandoned, the wife who deserted for a bigger bed, the sons who had ridden south for wealth and found only death. These things did not matter any more than the dreams he had conjured from a thousand emptied amphoras.

What mattered now was that he was a man. Not a woman, not a child, not a coward. His great-grandfather had been a Castilian; his grandmother the niece of a cacique. He was no less than they. He was no less.

Dragging his weary legs, step by painful step, he kept pace with the column. At the end of the march he could rest, for a short time or forever. But he would rest among the Spanish. Die among them. Be buried among them. The wayside grave with the piñon cross was not for the great-grandson of a Castilian.

And so the old man defied his years and marched on in his own way and for his own reasons.

The column dragged its way to the edge of the large pueblo that spread over three hundred varas from the shelf overlooking the rio. At the far side of the adobe village stood the mission church. Otermín posted his tropa to watch the small, irregular streets for an ambush and then led the refugees directly to the mission. For one brief instant he stared at the beautiful carvings that marked the broad doors—the escutcheon with the coat of arms surmounted by a crown. Then he shoved the doors open, stepped aside and let Fray Pedro lead in the flock. There were too many for the small mission, and the remainder clustered about the entrance as Otermín directed the sargentos to check each of the neighbouring buildings. The ladders leading to the second-storey entrances had been removed, and as there were no entrances from the ground level, the men pulled themselves up from their saddles. Fully armed, they broke into the grey adobe houses one by one. Each in its turn was found to be empty. There was not a single sign of life in the great pueblo, and as the Spaniards became certain of this, they began to relax.

The out-guard rode into the town and reported to Otermín, who stood in the middle of the bare plaza.

"The Indians on the hill, Excellency, they have gone. None to be seen."

The guard saluted and rode out to the edge of the town and his post again. Slowly, without saying a word to Quintana who sat mounted beside him, Otermín turned around and around.

Abandoned. As his capital had been abandoned. Why? Fear of him? Possibly, but he doubted it. There was not an Indian in the pueblo, not a stray dog or a lost sheep. Otermín shrugged and shook his head at no one in particular.

"Better get them out of the church," he ordered Quintana. The Alcalde Mayor dismounted and began to direct the refugees to spread out around the town square, while Otermín joined a ranchero who had called to him from behind the friary. The tall, helmeted ranchero stood with his sword tip resting on his boots, staring silently at the bodies of five Spaniards. Otermín crossed himself. The bodies were bareheaded and barefooted; all men. The Captain General walked from one to the other. Three stared with blank eyes at the blank sky. He knelt and turned the other two over. Strangers all. The wounds on their faces and arms and chests showed they had fought well. España would not know them, would not remember these foreign-born sons, but she could well be proud of them. Otermín stood quietly for a long time. One of the faces was all but covered with a full red beard. Another was too young to have raised one. Two generations, yet they had died together. *Por*

Rey y Santiago. Otermín crossed himself, and as he started to speak to the ranchero who still stood, sword tip to toe, Márquez strode up and looked at the bodies and crossed himself.

"Fray Pedro asks that Your Excellency join him in the mission."

The Governor nodded. To the ranchero: "Bury them, amigo. Bury them with honours."

And he followed Barnabe Márquez back to the mission and up the small set of stone steps. The building was empty now except for a few women kneeling in the pews. Looking around the large building, Otermín was pleased to see that the rebels had not disturbed it. Even the life-sized statue of Santo Domingo himself remained unharmed.

But there was something wrong. Fray Pedro stood before a large mound of earth in front of the altar and waited for the Governor to join him. Neither spoke, both fearing the same thing.

"If you will clear the church, Padre . . ."

The broad-shouldered priest pulled the sleeves of his cassock back and stood with his bared arms on his hips as though waiting to be proved wrong in his belief; hoping that he, who rarely made a mistake, had made one now.

"If you will clear the church, Padre, then between us we will discover what has happened."

Fray Pedro did not directly acknowledge the suggestion. Instead, he went to each of the communicants in turn and asked her please to use the small chapel in the friary.

When the mission was empty, Otermín himself slipped to his knees and began with his bare hands to scrape away the dirt piled before the altar. Crossing himself, Fray Pedro joined him. Ten minutes later they had uncovered the body of the Fray Custodio and those of two other Franciscan Brothers. Three martyrs. Three holy men buried before their altar. The Governor and the padre of Valladolid sat back on the earthen floor and rested from their labours. Neither sought to hide his tears from the other. For once they were in agreement, meeting for a moment on a mutual ground of misery and faith. Then Don Antonio reached over and brushed the dirt away from the face of the wiry old campaigner who had blessed him *only two weeks before.* There had been courage then as well as faith. Belief that he could reason with the Indians whom he had known since he was young and they were younger. Then he had slung one leg over his small, grey ass and ridden south. "To be with those of my parish, with my people," he had said.

"*My people. My people and God's.*" Otermín touched the cold, thin cheeks of the corpse. He did not see the rot or the insects that crawled away. He only recalled the soft eyes and the words—*my people and God's.*

Gone now. Gone. The old Nuevo Mexicano and the old padre. Gone the world he had been sent to govern and all of the symbols of that world. Now there was only the eternal glory of the eternal martyr and the dead bodies of those who had been his friends.

He looked at Pedro Martínez and did not see the padre, did not see the cold administrator who knew how things must be done. Instead, he saw a weary peasant coping with problems he had never believed could be brought to him. Sainthood and martyrdom were part of the old tales, part of the mysteries and paintings and lore of the Church which he had joined as a boy. Such were not of his time, not for him to cope with. They demanded more than he felt he could give, more than he felt even his vows had the right to expect. He was a simple man, a mortal man with all the weaknesses of any other. Otermín saw the peasant with the dark face and the square hands cross himself and clutch his cross and heard him pray.

Head bowed, Don Antonio's finger tips met beneath his beard. He, too, prayed. He prayed for the three padres lying dead before him. He prayed for the souls of those who had died within his province and he prayed for strength to save the thousand souls that waited outside the church wondering what was taking place between the padre and the Governor.

It was almost an hour later that the two men rose to their feet.

"If you do not mind, Padre, I would like to bury these here before the altar for which they died. The two of us bury them and close the church door. Then you would know and I would know. The others might only fear, and they have so far to travel."

The prerogative was the padre's, but the plea was clear.

"There is another buried here," Fray Pedro said. "And so I think it fitting."

Otermín cocked his head to one side and waited for the explanation.

"Almost sixty years now, Fray Juan de Escalona was buried within this church he built. It was his memorial. He would be proud to share it now."

He bowed his head for a time; then he began to cover the bodies of the three martyrs at his feet with the earth of the church floor. The Governor knelt and helped him. When they were done, Fray Pedro walked through the church, gathering the holy objects. There were six silver chalices and a wine basin, seven vessels for wine and water and a silver salver. The Governor removed the incense burner, the lamp, and several other silver objects. Then the two men walked out into the sunlight where the refugees waited for them.

Fray Pedro turned, crossed himself, and prayed as he closed the church door and said loudly so all could hear, "Mass will be said tonight in the chapel of the friary. We will not enter this church again."

There was a buzz of questions about the plaza as Otermín handed the holy objects to a soldier. "These belong to the padre. He will tell you what to do with them."

Then he strode off down an empty street, pausing only long enough to beckon Quintana to follow him.

Half an hour later the Commander and his aide walked back to join the others in the plaza. Most of the men and women were either sprawled out in the shade of the buildings or were seated in small groups eating their midday meal. They had ransacked every one of the empty houses and found nothing to eat except some dried corn and a small sack of meal. This was quickly cooked and devoured by the fortunate discoverers.

M

Quintana separated from the Captain General and checked his guards before joining the Señora Isabella in the shade of the mission building.

Most of the Spaniards were reluctant to remain in the Indian dwellings. The lack of windows and doors on the ground floor made them uncomfortable. They preferred the open sky and the freedom of the sunlight. Don Antonio looked about the plaza until he found María, saw that she and Inez were seated with a group of rancheros from Acoma. Then he entered the large friary, built almost a century before when it had first been decided that the padres of Santo Domingo would serve the smaller pueblos of San Felípe and Cochití. Inside the doorway, Otermín looked about him. The furniture was smashed and thrown in a heap in a corner of the room. Tapestries were strewn across the dirt floor, and there were patches of blood on the white walls and the floor itself. He knew now where the padres had been killed, and realized that they had been buried before the altar of the mission in jest, but a jest so fitting that it had brought honour to the dead rather than the defamation the rebels had intended. For this Don Antonio was thankful.

He found Fray Pedro seated alone in a corner of one of the cells, beads in hand, staring at a niche in the wall that had once held a crucifijo. It was clear that he, too, understood what had taken place. Otermín was about to speak to him, offer some consolation, some word of encouragement. Instead, he walked out of the building and crossed the small plaza to the first group of men and women he found seated together.

They had thrown their baggage on the ground and sat with their backs against the wall of an adobe house watching the shadows crawl like animals over the plaza. There were half a dozen in the group, and each looked up as the Governor approached. The old woman who had protested about the smoke signals frowned. The ranchero whose cattle had been killed to feed the camp the night before looked away. Only a young child smiled up at the Governor, and a brown-eyed mestiza with dimpled chin who brushed back her hair in anticipation and hope.

"The chapel," Otermín said. "Will the six of you try to straighten it up before the padre holds his services there?" The child rose to her feet and the young woman. The others hesitated.

"The chapel has to be cleaned," he said firmly. "Men fought there. Died."

There was general acquiescence then. Otermín watched them go and then found a place for himself in the shade just off the plaza where he could see the hills beyond the pueblo and the plaza itself. Soon Quintana joined him.

"You will eat, Excellency?" He offered food, and for the first time, Don Antonio realized he was hungry, that midday was long behind them.

"Thank you, amigo. Did you tell them they could rest?"

The black teeth showed with the thin-lipped grin. "I told them and they were pleased. Why do I always have the fortune to tell them what they want to hear and Your Excellency what they do not want to hear?"

It was not exactly a question, but it displayed a perception Otermín had not expected. He thought about the observation for a moment and then turned his attention to the food in front of him.

"When I finish this, Luis, we will plan the guard for the remainder of the day and the night before us."

Quintana waited for the Governor to say more. But seeing the conversation was ended, he wandered back to the place where his large wife sat waving the frond of a water lily as a fan.

"A strange man, that one," he commented.

Isabella knew her husband well enough to wait.

After taking off his helmet and removing his boots, Luis Quintana made his point. "I do not think he cares what these people think of him." The words, *these people,* were designated by a wide gesture that took in the entire plaza.

Isabella stopped fanning herself and looked at the refugees clustered in the limited shade.

"Do they really matter, Luis? Or is it the province that matters to a man like Don Antonio? Remember, little one, he is a grandee—the son of someone, a peninsular. Most of us here are Creoles and, yes, mestizos." She looked about her at the blank walls of the evacuated pueblo as she spoke. "I believe the province matters and his name matters. We do not matter."

Her husband nodded, proud that she understood the Governor, even if he did not.

"But the woman. She should matter?"

The rolls of fat which made up the bulky belly of Señora Quintana began to shake, slowly at first, and then faster.

"The woman matter? She is only a woman. She is only the wife of a ranchero who was not even faithful to the ranchero. How could she matter to the son of someone?"

Quintana stopped staring at the helmet in his hand and looked at his wife. There was the bitterness in her voice he had met before when she spoke of men in authority. She seemed to be unafraid of men who were important. She did not even fear to speak scornfully of Carlos II. It was she who called the King an idiot child, a bewitched fool. He saw to it that what she said was said quietly, but still she did not fear to say it.

"I shock you, little Luis." And the rolls of fat moved up and down her belly again under the black cotton dress. She reached out a large hand and placed it over her husband's. "Do not concern yourself about the Governor and his woman. He will be under her blanket again before this jornada is over." She paused. "Unless all of us are killed first."

The rolls of fat were still. She was not smiling. Her husband decided the Governor must be done with his meal and would want to discuss plans for the guards and the night. Coming to his feet, he looked down at his wife. "We will win, Isabella. I shall tell the Governor you are prepared to roll over the Indians, and that will stop their rebellion and there will be peace again."

She was laughing as he walked barefooted back to the Governor.

It was late in the night. The campfires were dead. The guards' heads bobbed. In the far distance an owl announced its hunger. Most of the camp slept soundly. Fray Pedro lay curled up on the ground, his cassock drawn close about him. His shaven head rested on the belly of the little donkey.

Only a few were awake. A lonely sargento lay on his back watching a cloud ride past the white castle of the moon. Don Antonio lay in his blanket wishing he were not alone. The blind woman among the wounded stared at the small world behind her eyes. And the middle-aged prostitute with the weeping sores rolled from side to side gasping for breath. The bare toes of her swollen feet seemed to reach out for the earth beyond and then relax. She retched as her tightened chest hungered for air. The pains in her abdomen would not leave her now. Her sides ached. If she could gather the air in her lungs, she would scream out her pain. But even breathing itself came hard. Her face paled. She groped at the sores on it. The skin was firm to the touch. And her belly was stretching. Her hands wandered down to the pain. She hurt. Her belly was growing like a nine-months thing. In minutes. In minutes. Her hands ripped at the tightening brown dress. All of her strength gathered as she sucked in her breath and her arms stiffened. Then the dress came away, leaving her distended belly a bloated blue like her lips. She coughed softly and the swollen skin rolled.

Then she lay still. The mestiza girl whose father had ridden off before her birth and whose mother had moved into the home of a distant ranchero weeks afterward had found her final lover. She gave herself up to the French pox as completely as she had to hundreds of men.

10

GREAT fires lighted the plaza of the Villa de Santa Fe. Thousands of Indian warriors, gathered since dusk with their booty, sat on the ground waiting for the arrival of Popé. There was happiness and peace on the faces of most of them. Though some few remembered their dead and the toll they had paid to sit in this plaza with the palacio before them and the gutted church to their right. They remembered the sabres swung, the lances drawn from pierced flesh, and the soft, reluctant whine of the dying. These few were silent. The others laughed and spoke of their women and the prizes they would carry home. They polished the pewter plates on their laps, brushed the dirt off the silk rebozos wrapped about their heads or waists, poked at the dirt at their feet with silver-handled dagas, and pushed the Spanish helmets back on their heads so that they could feel the early breezes of evening.

Juan of Taos stood looking at the only army the puebleños had ever had. And he thought of victory. What is victory? What does a man do with it? Is victory the defeat of the enemy? Or is it instead the removal of an obstacle in the path? Is victory the opportunity to do something better, or

merely something different from that which had been done? If victory was
the removal of evil, what assurance was there that good would follow? Or
was victory only the making of a great emptiness, the creation of a void into
which men must pour their futures if the costs were to have meaning? Juan
realized that victory was not the making of anything. Instead, it was a destruction of the past—and an opportunity to create something better. He
sighed softly to himself. Who was going to make the future here? Was it the
tall Popé whose heart was corroded with hate? Was it Popé, the only man
who had ever had the courage, strength, and faith to weld the People into a
weapon strong enough to be used? Popé had a greatness about him that Juan
respected. The priest with the angry eyes had, through the sheer force of his
own will, the energies of his hate and the belief in his cause, brought the
People to victory. Juan knew that he himself was only a tool for Popé's
purpose. He knew that the men who had died, as well as those who would
limp through their lives with the wounds of the siege of the Spanish capital,
had all been used to further Popé's cause. Juan respected the strength of the
man, and he could only hope that, the rebellion complete, Popé would be
able to fill the void he had created.

Carrion birds wheeled back and forth over the Villa. There were too many
men below for them to seek out the carnage they smelled. But they were
patient. One large black bird settled on the edge of the roof of the palacio
and stared with red-rimmed eyes at the faces of the warriors seated on the
ground. Its heavy wings were poised for flight. Its dirty beak opened as it
cawed its greeting to the night. Juan leaned against a post of the colonnade
and watched the hungry bird. Such were the symbols of victory. But for the
People the bird was important. The men seated in the plaza mayor knew
why the bird had come and hoped that it would come when they died so that
it would help them find their way to the dark earth and the Blue Lake.

The men in the plaza became silent and Juan turned to see that Popé had
stepped out of the palacio. The tall figure with the broad shoulders and the
leonine head stood as firmly as the posts of the colonnade. His dark eyes did
not waver, did not blink, as he stared beyond the men and the fires and the
town to that place in the distant hills where the sun was abandoning the
world to night. Even the black bird stopped cawing.

Just when his entire audience had reached the edge of their patience, the
medicine man strode to the entrance of the palacio and stood facing his
army. His long arms were limp at his sides. The bull-horn headdress did not
quiver. Even the jaguar pelt was still. Then Popé raised his right arm and
held it out toward the warriors. The fox fur that dangled from his wrist
rose in a great arc and came to rest in mid-air. Popé's arm remained steady,
the fox fur still.

Juan was conscious how precisely the older man moved, how completely
he held the attention of the puebleños. He had earned his leadership with his
own skills and his own strength. Juan would never dispute it. No one else
in the entire kingdom could have brought these men together or have held
them so completely. No one else would have had the foresight to abandon
the scalp dance and the victory celebration, in which the difference in status of

the various pueblos might come out into the open. Now there was no one who would be offended and no one who would have the opportunity to lay claims of superiority before his fellows. Now there was only Popé to be seen, to be heard, to be followed.

The medicine man of San Juan spoke out softly so that each warrior had to pay complete attention to his words.

"As I returned to the People from the land beyond the Blue Lake and the homes of the ancient ones where only the katchinas travel, I had a vision and I saw Montezuma and he told me the People would be free if they would free themselves and that the old gods whom their fathers had known would be waiting for them, to help them and ease their lives. He told me that the Sun Father who travelled the heaven with his two sons at his right hand and his left hand would be waiting for the People and that the Corn Mother and the Earth Mother would be waiting for the People and I returned and I told the People of my vision and the People listened to me and they raised their hands against the Whitefaces and the Blessing Men. The People drove the foreign ways out of their land. They killed the false god of the limp hands and his mother of the sad face and they washed away the false blessings and they rose as one great hand and smote the enemy and they are now free to live the way their fathers' fathers lived.

"The People fought like the sons of the gods who are now again their gods. The People fought with the courage of the mountain lion and the knowing way of the coyote. The People have taken the scalps which will please their gods. The Earth Mother is pleased and will bear, and the Woman Winds will bring the Woman Clouds and the Woman Clouds will bear rain.

"The People have fought and many of our brothers will travel to the holy places where they will undertake the far journey and will be as clouds and will be as lightning and will be as katchinas and they will not forget their brothers who remain for they will bring us rain.

"Our White Corn Mother and our White Corn Ice Mother will not forget their children who wandered to the east which was not the place and the west which was not the place and to the south which was not the place. But when they came to the north they found the place and they came out of the lake and their Mothers had not forgotten them then and they will not forget them now. We will know the good things and the laughing things and we will be happy.

"But we will only be happy if we believe as the fathers of the People believe and will live as the fathers of the People lived and will never turn again to the ways of the strangers who were an abomination to the ways of the fathers and the ways of the gods. We must drive from our midst all of the words of those who turned the People against their oneness with the whole sky above and the crawling ant below."

Popé's hand lowered and his head rose and he looked beyond the warriors who watched him and he did not look at the two men who walked into the centre of the plaza and began to feed the documents of the Spaniards to the flames of a great fire. Then the two men held up the leather-bound books of the Whitefaces and though he did not see what they were doing, Popé spoke out loudly for the first time so that none could fail to hear.

"We commit to the fires all sins which have been made against the People and the gods of the People and the ways of the People and the thoughts of the People."

As he spoke, the two men opened the books of the Spaniards and hurled them into the flames. Popé's arms went wide as he stretched out to take in the whole group who watched him in the plaza and he said loudly again, "And we must cast out those who have learned the twisted foreign thoughts of the Whitefaces, who think like the Whitefaces and yearn for what the Whitefaces yearned for. We must commit them to wandering forever with the coyote over the crooked paths to the lost ways which are not our ways but those of the Whitefaces. We must cleanse the land of the enemy that is within us as we washed away the false blessings with the roots of the amole."

Popé was silent. His arms fell to his sides and he swung his huge figure about and stood facing Juan of Taos.

"We must thrust from the land those who would abandon the People and flee the battles of the People and would talk to the enemy of the north and east and west who are the Apaches and the enemy of the south who are the Whitefaces and who, though honoured by the People and selected to lead the People against their enemy, would not turn upon the enemy and slay him when the enemy presented his throat for the knife and so permitted the enemy to walk out of the land of the People as though he had never sinned against the People. We must thrust from our midst the man who has learned to think like the crawling of the snake, who has learned the ways of the mole and the fish but not the ways of the eagle and the butterfly which are also the ways of the People. We must cleanse the land of those who are among us but who are not a part of the People."

Juan stared into the hard eyes of the older man. Popé became silent now. The entire plaza was silent now and the words came like a stone again at the mind of the youth. *"Who would abandon the People and flee the battles of the People and would talk to the Apache enemy. . . ."* Juan wanted to scream the truth to the faces that stared up at him and take the medicine man and make him tell the truth. It had been Popé who had asked Juan to travel north. It had been Popé who had wanted him to leave the battle-ground before the battle was over. Askon knew better. Askon had been there, but Askon was dead.

The betrayal. Always the betrayal. And always in the name of good or god or the People, be they one's own or the enemy's. But always the betrayal. The constant factor of man; his natural state. The total betrayal of self and friend, of state and enemy. The turning on one who has helped, felt compassion, and shared problems. Friendship is only a fool's dream, because a man's relationship to a man is as corrupt as a man's relationship to a woman. The routes are long, but they lead to the inevitable end—betrayal. The large act or the small but always the betrayal.

Juan realized Popé was speaking again, but he could no longer hear him.

Hate befogged the eyes of the warriors, and he realized the pueblenos believed that he, Juan, had betrayed them.

Then he heard the laughter. Cold, brutal laughter filled the plaza. At first he thought it was Don Jaime looking down from some celestial balcony and enjoying the scene. But when even Popé became silent, Juan realized who was laughing. He was. And he could not stop. *Betrayal upon betrayal upon betrayal.*

He strode through the crowd of warriors who hesitated and fell away before him. He walked around the palacio to where a messenger had tethered his horse, tightened the cinchas and pulled himself up on the great black stallion. Then he waved his hand to Popé, half in respect and half in scorn, because Popé was a man who had learned the fine art of betrayal, who could betray with fervour and full belief in the propriety of the world in which a prophet moves.

Before anyone could decide whether Juan should be stopped or not, he rode off to the north, out of the Villa de Santa Fe. Behind him lay the carnage and destruction. The laws of the Spaniards were suspended, but the People had not yet found—and perhaps never would find—their way back to the land of the past for which they had fought. They had destroyed the life they had lived for a century. And for what? A ghost? A vague legend spiraling back three generations into the tales of how the young world had been when their fathers' fathers had ruled it.

Juan knew it was naïve to believe they could shed the century-long contact with the Whitefaces—the stern rule, the harsh god of love, the innovations of steel, horses, new crops, recorded laws, and recorded history. For Juan, the erstwhile war chief of Taos, it was worse than naïve. It was the end of the People. The dying would be slow, generations of going down, generations of groping for some way to reconcile the worlds in which they lived. But it would always be a going down. He knew what the People did not know. Isolated and alone, theirs had not been a glorious past, only a quiet one, almost a sterile one. And even this they would never find again.

The hills of August were quiet. Juan of Taos was old now. In July he had been young. Betrayal and war had aged him.

The black stallion stumbled on a stone and almost slipped to its knees. The horse was leaner now than when Don Jaime had ridden it. The weeks had been difficult, the fighting hard. Two scars on its flanks testified to that. The coat that needed currying and the bones that showed through the slack hide told of the difference between July and August. Juan ran a hand over the Moorish filigree saddle.

Don Jaime. Don Jaime.

And yet Juan would not believe he had done wrong. His head cocked to one side as he seemed to be staring at the top of a spruce in the far distance. Loyalties and friendships were all confused in his mind. The People and Don Jaime. Each had had a claim upon him. But there was only one Juan— young, restless, educated but unknowing. And no way of learning. Whom could he have asked had he had the foresight to ask? The brimstone padre spouting the foreign Dante? The angry Popé demanding rebellion? Whom in the lonely world can a man ask other than himself about his loyalties and friendships?

Juan felt the weight of the sabre at his side. And as he rode toward the north among the tall aspen, quivering in the dark hills, he slipped the tooled-leather baldrick off his shoulder and for one unseeing moment held it in his hand. Then without looking, he flung it into a berry thicket and rode on.

He had fought well. Don Jaime would have conceded as much. But the old peninsular would have seen the irony of victory before achieving it. Juan saw it only afterwards.

The moon was high, the night cool. A long black snake slipped off a rock and fled the menace of the horse's hooves. Juan's square face set firm, his copper shoulders settled back. A moment later a jay rose from his path to a far limb. Once safe, it jabbered its complaints.

The Taoan ignored the animals on the trail, failed to see the insects or beasts he roused. He was not aware of the quick world about him. He looked the Indian warrior, and no one passing would have recognized the Spaniard in him, yet it was there. All confused, the Castilian mind with the Indian blood.

He wanted to slip to the ground from his saddle and pray. But to whom? What God listens? What God knows the pains inside a man? Popé's? Fray Vicente's? His lean body began to shake. He knew now whose victory it was. Now he was truly the son of Don Jaime. For Juan of Taos was just as dead as the former Conde de Iteo had been when he had received the last rites on the docks at Sevilla.

Juan was dead to the People who had spawned him. Juan was dead to the Spanish who had nurtured him. But at this moment he differed from Don Jaime in that he had hope. It lay with a young girl, white-faced, frightened, gentle, of fragile mind and haunted past.

He kicked his moccasined heels into the stallion's sides. The amble became a gallop. Juan's eyes shifted from the distant tree top to the trail ahead. He had been gone from Manuela longer than he had planned. If anything were to take on meaning for him again, he had to return to the high cave in the Sacred Place.

He rode north beyond Taos Mountain. Darkness deepened in the east. The night animals awakened to prowl. The distant hills were lost and then the tops of trees. Still Juan rode. He was weary, his stallion was sweated. But there was no pause, only desperation and the need for hope.

He was all Spaniard inside now: the romantic realist with a dream, and the dream was a woman. How Don Jaime would have scoffed at this frenzied ride. But he would have understood it. He would have ridden as hard himself, laughing scornfully every time his horse's hooves sparked the stones beneath. Finally, the horse began to quiver and slow its pace. Juan, knowing he could not afford to kill it, reined to a halt in a clearing between two imposing hills. He watered the animal at a small stream that flowed through the valley. Tethering the horse on a long riata, he stood and watched it graze. Then he turned his attention toward his own hunger.

He felt the night air cool across his bared chest. The pantalones he had worn south weeks before were dirty and ragged. He had cut them off just below the knees after he abandoned the heavy Spanish boots. His moccasins were still solid. The daga in the sash at his waist was the only weapon he carried, and with it he fashioned a spear from a young aspen. Then he lit a fire with the wood chips and a Spanish chispa. Once the fire was strong enough to sustain itself, he lit a piñon torch and walked back to the stream. Torch in one hand, spear in the other, he waded into the water and jammed the handle of the torch between two rocks. The flame flashed a hand's distance above the surface, reflecting a dozen paces in each direction into its shallow depth.

Juan stood quiet and patient. A few minutes later the trout appeared, eager and curious. Spear poised, he waited, selected his dinner, and struck. There was a flurry of tail, a flopping body dark in the stream, and quiet again. Leaving his torch to burn itself down to the water's level, Juan returned to his fire.

Without removing it from the spear, he cooked the trout. When it was done, he cut away the head and the tail and the guts and ate it. Most puebleños did not eat fish. There were beliefs concerning those who dwelt in the water, but Juan did not believe them.

Finally, he lay back on the ground and stared at the dark sky above him. The fire at his side wavered and died. Juan thought of himself in the night alone. He had not been raised in the mountains and the forests, had hunted seldom and then had returned at night to the hacienda. He could not remember sleeping alone in the fields. He was not certain he liked it. . . . Then he was asleep.

11

THE next morning the Spaniards marched out into the open country beyond the narrow streets of Santo Domingo. They were beginning their fourth day on the road. There were signs of progress. The baggage load was smaller. There was less grumbling when the column was formed and less time wasted forming it. There were also signs of fatigue. The cattle were visibly thinner. The horses were no longer fresh in the morning. More old persons were trying to ride in the two crowded carretas. And though the column took shape more quickly, it moved more slowly.

Don Antonio stood near the entrance to the friary and watched it pass him by. He saw the women grimace as they looked at the long road ahead. He watched one old man throw away his sabre as something he could no longer carry. He noticed also that the extra shoes that María had slung over her shoulder days before were gone. Someone was wearing them now—he did not know who. As she passed him, she turned her head toward him as the others did. But she did not smile. She did not seem to notice that he was standing there. It was as though nothing had ever passed between them, as though he had never known her. Inez smiled at him and waved. Most of the men nodded their heads in recognition. Some of the women smiled. One woman with loose blonde hair over her bare shoulders winked as she strode by. Another brushed back her hair expectantly. But María was already staring at the back of the head in front of her.

When the pueblo was emptied, the last soldier riding out and the donkey of Fray Pedro led beyond the last adobe building, Don Antonio de Otermín mounted his stallion, settled himself in the saddle and prayed quietly for a day without trouble.

The column threaded its way over the broken land. Though the obstacles were few for the moment, the pace was slow. The children who had frolicked the length of the line four days before remained with their parents. The spavined horses that had dragged the crude carretas now needed to be led and prodded. There was little noise from the carretas themselves, and when Don Antonio rode past the one which bore the two women, he saw only the blind one sitting up. The pregnant widow stared silently at the cotton canopy that hung loosely above her. The burial of the woman of the casa de puta left more space for others.

A slight breeze caught a tumbleweed and worried it over the open ground, bounced it off a rock and pushed it against a small yucca plant. Dried, white petals sprinkled over the sword-shaped leaves. Then the breeze shifted, picked up the rolling weed and tumbled it west across the path of the column.

The refugees were so weary they did not bother to turn their heads to watch the weed snag on the armoured mesquite. Sand began to gather about it. In time it fathered a small dune.

The sun again.

Clear skies and rising heat. The bunch grass browning. Red clay and shifting sands hot to the touch. Scarlet sky. Turquoise sky. Shadows sharp and few. Far buttes blocking farther horizons.

And always the smoke wispily climbing.

The wooden heel broke off the embroidered slipper. Madeira silk, styled in Madrid. The heel remained in the hard ground as the tall, blonde woman with the mole on her cheek stepped over a rock. She turned and stared at the torn blue silk still visible in the red clay behind her. The other women moved on without stopping.

Still she remained.

Still she stared.

The shoes had been a present from a friend who had gone to Madrid five years before. He had never returned. The shoes were more than a pair of blue party slippers. They were a world she had never known. A world where women wore dresses of fine embroidery and danced all night on marble floors.

A land without Indians and death and naked sun. A land where no smoke whispered to the sky of failure and retreat.

The sargento who brought up the rear waited patiently for the blonde with the mole on her cheek to move ahead and join the others. Finally, she slipped to her knees, and reaching into the clay, she retrieved the blue silk heel. When she got to her feet again, the hem of the coarse brown skirt was blotched with dirt. She hobbled after the others, carefully brushing the red clay off the high heel she clutched in her hand.

The cattle were lean. They had not been grazed since the siege began ten days before. Several had died in the confinement of the casas reales. Many would soon die from lack of food and the long droving. Many were un-branded, rounded up in the last hours between the uprising and the siege. A few were wild, almost uncontrollable, heads high, short, close-set horns ready for attack, bellows filling the air and tails switching nervously.

A few were black, Moorish, high-strung, better for breeding, and for fighting in the ring, than for food. But they were going to be food now, no matter how lean, tough-hided and shaggy-headed. One lava-black bull— a toro prieto—led the rest; slashed the young bulls with his needle horns, herded the cows. Most of the stock was mixed—brown, white, splotched. It was the milk of the black cows that went first to the children and the wounded. It was healthier than the milk of the others. The drovers were especially careful of the vacas prietas. The splotched cows—the striped, yellow, white, brown—were the first to be killed each night for food. Their hides were thinner, their bulk greater.

The ranchero who would make the kill in the evening looked at the long, wedged face of a brown, its long hairs, red-brown eyes, black muzzle, and knew this cow would not live through the day. It was slowing the herd, slowing the column.

Otermín was patient for a time. Then he signalled the drovers with a finger across his throat. The ranchero's whip flicked and the herd moved on. The bull hesitated a moment, but as two horsemen cut between it and the dying cow, the black head went up in assent. Unhurriedly, with a retention of dignity and a casual display of power, the broad, black shoulders shifted, and the bull turned to join the rest of the herd.

The lean ranchero, avoiding the half-closed eyes of the cow, drove the blade into the beast's throat. There was a flush of blood, a moan stifled as the flooded throat tried to bellow. Then there was a slow shudder and silence. Without waiting for the beast to die, the ranchero and his compañeros skinned the animal, hacked off the larger portions of beef and rejoined the column. Soon the flies came and two vultures. The birds left when a coyote sniffed the carrion and claimed the entrails.

The herd moved on with the column, smaller now than in the morning. When night came, it would diminish again.

They marched as quickly as both the countryside and their own fatigue would permit. The sun rose higher in the bright sky. There was no shade, no relief from the climbing heat. The old became dizzy. The young weakened. But the Captain General did not relax the relentless pace he set once he gained the head of the line. The sargentos who rode with Márquez shifted the lean buttocks of their stallions, forcing the laggards ahead of them. One old woman slipped to her knees and could not rise again. Those who walked beside her shouldered the package of floral silk she carried and two soldiers unceremoniously lifted her between them and laid her across the rump of a brown mare. They did not pause. They feared to lose even the time it took to scan the distant horizon.

The Spaniards had almost reached the pueblo of San Felípe when they realized they were not being followed, that the horizon silhouetted no Indians and, stranger still, no smoke wisped up the sky.

Quintana waited for the Governor to react to the disappearance of the enemy. But Don Antonio turned his head neither to the right nor the left. The dust raised by his grey half hid him from those behind. His helmet was hanging again from the saddle. The leather jerkin was open. Only the black polished baldrick and a bandage covered his bare chest. His boots were dusty now. Mud, from where he had approached the rio, clung to the high heels. The small beard had climbed up his chin and several days' growth darkened his cheeks. The scar on his cheek was red and he still rode with a limp right hand barely clutching the reins. Quintana saw that the Captain General was older now than when they had first met three years before at the official reception. Then there had been dancing, fine apple brandy and wine from España. The Governor, dressed in white linen and black velvet with silver buttons, had moved with the agility of youth. Now they drank from a dirty rio or the rank bladders of sheep. Now the Governor moved painfully, his legs wounded, his beard greying, his age consuming his energies. A grandee, yes, but a man in retreat. Quintana saw the erect form with the shoulders settled back and the head high. If they got through, it would be this man who got them through. If they lived, it was because he willed it, and not because of any failure or weakness of the enemy. Isabella might laugh at the Governor's being the son-of-someone, but she too recognized that he was the only person strong enough to will them life. And to will them life he had to desire it for himself.

Otermín made no mention of the Indians who no longer hugged their trail. He would not slacken his pace, and only when Quintana started to drop back to urge the line forward did he even bother to turn his head, nod agreement, and then ride on again. He was in flight, but with dignity and with honour and with the full knowledge that he and he alone controlled the movements of this column.

Finally, when they reached San Felípe, the refugees hoped for a rest. Several women threw down their baggage. Two soldiers dismounted. The youth who led the first carreta drew it to a halt. But the Governor still rode on. This small pueblo was as empty as Santo Domingo, but Otermín had made up his mind that they would not stop, not here, not now. There were leagues to travel before they paused. A league more today and a league closer to Isleta and the other half of the province—García, his people, his supplies, the strength of numbers, Spanish numbers for a change. Otermín could not afford to waste time in San Felípe and the soldiers wearily remounted. The women took up their baggage again and struggled on behind the carretas of the wounded.

Another hour and another. The sun had passed its zenith. The heat had climbed to a new high. The dust of the column flowed like a dirty rio above the long line, settled behind it as it moved, and rose again as it pushed on and on.

Those who were mounted shifted places with those who walked. Boots gave way and were abandoned. The trail became marked with the dropped rebozos, the soiled undergarments of the women and the heavy breastplates of the men. They were stripping down from fatigue and not through judgment. The Captain General slackened his pace only once. Turning, he saw a youth slip the baldric over his head and throw it into the dust. The sabre was heavy; the rough leather of the baldric had rubbed his shoulder sore. Twice he had tripped on the weapon, and he no longer carried it as proudly as he had when Maestre de Campo Pando had issued it to him ten days before. Waving Quintana to the lead, Otermín spun his horse about and cut the youth from the column like a ranchero separating a calf from a herd. He bumped the young man with the rump of his horse, edging him away from the line until they stood alone in a field beside the trail.

"Are you a man?" Otermín asked sharply.

The youth was disconcerted and frightened. "Yes, Excellency."

"Do you want to live?"

More fear now. "Yes, Excellency."

Then, very gently, "Pick up that sabre, son. My life depends on your being able to use it when the time comes."

A smile.

"And your life depends on it. Even the life of the blonde woman whose rump bounces in front of you as you walk, even her life depends on it."

The youth could not quite bring himself to grin.

"I understand, Excellency."

Otermín nodded and rode again to the head of the column.

Past San Felípe. On into the open fields beyond. Southward down the rio. The hills edged away. There was flat ground and a soft roll to the rio's edge. A cluster of cottonwoods. Finally, the Captain General swung up his hand and the long line fell apart. Women slipped to the ground where they stood. Horsemen reined in and merely sat. Only the children still had the energy to seek the shade. The guards swung out to the east, the north, and the south. None would cross to the west bank of the rio. None wanted to rouse the ire of their sullen Commander. After a time the women brought out the food and people began to eat. A few dragged themselves to their feet and sought the rio. Here they dropped on their bellies and let the cool water roll over their faces. The women splashed it down the front of their dresses, over their burnt bosoms, soaking their hair and their hands.

The men removed their tattered boots and stretched their feet out to the water.

Luis Quintana shoved back the heavy helmet that held the heat of the high sun and shook his dark head. The thin lips hung open, but his eyes were half-closed to the blinding glare of the day. He slowly dropped off his stallion and walked back to where Isabella sat heavily on the ground in the shade of the mare she had ridden. She saw through a blurred vision, and the gross weight she carried sagged as she rocked slowly back and forth with the pain of fatigue. Luis stood looking down at her as she set her arms, broad as tree trunks, behind her, and slowly eased her huge body flat to the ground. The small Alcalde Mayor dropped the reins of his stallion and walked down to the rio where he filled his helmet with water and brought it back to her. Only after he had washed her face with a cloth from his saddlebag, did he take the time to drink himself. After a while he crumpled to his knees and rested in the shade of the two horses.

"We covered much ground today," he said, almost as though he had to justify his fatigue.

Isabella rolled over and stared up at him. "We will hate that man before we are done, but we must try not to."

Half an hour later they moved on again.

There were three more pauses before dusk. Then, as he had each afternoon, the Captain General rode ahead and picked the camp site for the night. This time he and Quintana were not alone, for as they separated from the column, they saw the Indians again in the distance, watching, making no overt gesture yet seemingly following every move the Spaniards made.

That night the guard was doubled, the perimeter of the camp pulled in tight, fires lighted on the outer edges so that none could approach the camp unseen. Only the fatigue of the day's long march made it possible for any of the refugees to sleep.

Lying alone, rolled up in his blanket near the northern edge of the camp, the direction from which he anticipated attack, Don Antonio stared at the clouded sky above. He could hear the heavy breathing of several soldados snoring in the darkness near by and the crackling of the fire as fresh piñon and mesquite were added to keep it flaring bright.

It was over two days since he had removed his pantalones and looked at the wounds on his legs, three days since he had removed his long socks and changed his linen. There was a constant pain in his side where he had been wounded in the last day's fighting. The piece of undergarment wrapped about it was dirty now with the sweat and dust of the march, with the clay he had slept upon and the mud of the rio's banks when he had bellied down to drink. The shifting clouds caught his eye and he wondered when it would rain. Rain would cool off the days. Rain would keep down the dust and wash away some of the smell. The carts stank again. Excrement and sores. The green climbing up the leg of one of the rancheros gave off as sharp an odour as the excrement.

He closed his eyes against the night.

How long could he absorb the punishment he was giving the others? How long would he be able to drive the others and himself? The food was almost gone, the horses laming. The faces that stared up at him when he rode the length of the column were increasingly angry and hurt, bewildered and weary. How long could he keep them running as hard as they had run today? There was no denying his fear for the column. The Indians were following. They were strong and, only days before, had known blood and success.

12

THE first birds lazing through the morning sky saw Juan already mounted and riding north again by the small streams, the little valleys between the tree-coated mountains and the broken buttes. The hills were larger now. The mountains taller. The streams colder. The trees more naked as they reached through thicker darkness for the sun above.

When Juan found the trail he sought, he began to climb the mountain side on foot. Above him lay the dark shadow of the cave and the narrow ledge where he had left Manuela.

Twice he called her name. And as he pulled himself up on the shelf of rock on which he had last seen her, he rose to his feet and looked about. The waterfall which split the mountain silence fell flashing through the mountain morning. But there was no trace of Manuela. Juan stood for a moment looking over the precipice. Then he entered the shadowed mouth of the cave. She was not there.

He saw the empty food bag which he had left her, and he saw the bird, neck broken, eyes still wrathful, lying on the floor. He crossed through the darkness and stood over the bird.

After a time, he turned and walked back into the morning light, the waterfall beside him, the still sky above. At the base of a rock two red spiders battled with five black ants. Juan settled down on the ledge and stared into the dark purple distance where the mountains folded one upon the other.

It was long past noon when he rose to his feet, left the ledge and the cave of the Sacred Place and climbed down the trail to where the black stallion grazed. He approached the horse carefully, rubbed his hand over the scars on its flanks, recalled briefly the battles and drew himself up into his ornate saddle. Then he rode south. South alone. South no longer hoping. South without Manuela. He knew now that he no longer differed from Don Jaime. For hope was gone.

The sun settled again on the distant hills. The animals of the day sought shelter. The air cooled and breezes rose over the rios he rode beside. The head of the black stallion drooped. Its legs wearied. And at last Juan of Taos reined the beast to a halt before the broken walls that surrounded the hacienda of Don Jaime de Marcos.

The gate lay flat on the ground. The front of the great adobe house had collapsed in the explosion, and the portico, on which Juan had sat for so many evenings listening to the old Spaniard speak of España and the paths to empire, to decay, to destruction, and the belief that man was the least significant of all created beings, was now a ruin as Rome was a ruin and España was a ruin. Darkness had settled over the country. There were fires in Taos, and the peak of Taos mountain stook black against the night sky. And as he stood looking up at the shuttered balcony, head cocked to one side, Juan still saw the smile on Don Jaime's face just before he touched off the powder.

Loyalties and friendships. Betrayal upon betrayal.

Juan walked into the courtyard leading the great black stallion back to its own stable. The Indians had buried their dead, had plundered the remains of the hacienda, and then they had left the buildings and never went near them again, broken symbols of a broken power. As he stood in the darkness, Juan smelled the odour, strong and sweet and sickening. He dropped the horse's rein and stumbled through the darkness until he stood looking down at a body which could only be that of Don Jaime. The animals and birds had both had their way with it. A generation of flies had fed upon it. And the putrefaction created by sun and time and weather smelled like all of the places Fray Vicente had preached about.

But Juan was not thinking of this now as he ran into the part of the casa that stood beyond the ruins. The house had been well stripped by the pillaging Taoans, and as he fled from dark room to dark room, all the years of his life fled with him. At last he found a large piece of linen. A tablecloth? A curtain? In the darkness he did not know and he did not care. He staggered back into the night again and spread it as a shroud over the body of his mentor. Then he picked up that long-dead body and walked out into the fields beside the wall. Here, scraping a hole away with his hands under an unseeing sky, he buried his friend.

When he was done, Juan rose and stared at the stars that gathered above Taos mountain. But they did not know how to forgive. And so he walked back to the hacienda where the black stallion rested in the courtyard. Juan looked at the beast and wondered if he recalled his master. Turning, he entered the house again and climbed the stone steps that led to the rooms above. Only when he had reached the top of them did he see the dark figure of the girl standing there. He collapsed at her feet, and she knelt beside him and took his head in her hands and held it as she stared into his eyes.

"I was hoping you would come back. I wanted so much for you to come back. It is lonely here. The smell is strong. The flies are many. I have been very lonely, Juan."

Then she was silent. Her arms went about his shoulders, his head fell to her bosom and she comforted him. Night fled the haunted place and light crept in through the broken walls. At last they rose and stood facing each other.

"He never forgave me, Juan, never told me what I had done." Then she reflected for a moment. "I wonder what his sin was." But she was neither sad nor frightened now. She seemed stronger than he had ever seen her before. She had been assured when he had been uncertain. And as he heard the cynicism of her repeated "I wonder what his sin was," he realized that she was as much the daughter of Don Jaime as he was the son.

Somewhere she had found an old doeskin vestido with silver pins. Her feet were bare and Juan saw that the blanket he had left her in the cave covered the part of the floor where she had been sleeping. He looked at her face, burned by the sun to a near copper, framed by black hair pulled back behind her ears in the fashion of the girls of Taos, and he saw how much she was like an Indian in general appearance. But the shape of her face—the bright eyes, the long, thin nose, the fine eyebrows and the narrow chin— belied the fancy that she was anything but Spanish. Though sun and fortune had marked her, she was Manuela de Marcos and more a woman than she had been before.

"We will have to be careful," he said. "It would be dangerous if anyone should see you when we leave." And when she laughed, he realized he had never heard her laugh before.

"I have been inside Taos itself several times at night. The men are away somewhere and the only guard is an old man who sits at the entrance of a kiva." She whirled about, displaying the skin dress she wore. "I took this from a tree where a girl hung it when she went swimming." She paused and smiled again. "She must wonder what happened to it. I can see her now, accusing all her neighbours." She talked on: "I saw two women wearing my dresses. They looked funny in them, Juan."

He leaned back against the broken wall, bewildered at the change in her. "How did you find your way here?"

Silence, and then, "How did I find my way to the mountain cave where I awoke one morning with a great black bird attacking me? It was either Fray Vicente's hell or it was earth, and when I washed away the blood of my scars and felt the bright morning sun holding me, I knew this was earth and that I was alive."

Silence again for a time. "I never found out my sin, Juan, and then as I walked beside the cold streams and saw the bright-coloured jay and the small rabbits and the brown fawn and watched the cavorting of a coyote pup, I knew I had not sinned."

Silence again.

She brushed her hair back with the back of her hand. "If there was a sin, Juan, it was his sin. He was not a good man, my father. Though I think he loved you."

A pause.

"I have wondered. Did you betray him, Juan?"

She looked directly at the Indian youth. She was not accusing. He saw that she merely wanted to know what had happened.

He nodded his head. "I led the Taoans." And with as much pride as shame, "I also led the men of all the pueblo kingdom against the Villa de Santa Fe."

"All the pueblo kingdom?" She was trying to understand.

He nodded again. "There was a long battle first. Then the Governor took the Spaniards and walked south."

"And Juan commanded." He waited for her to say more, but she kicked the blanket into a corner at the top of the stairs.

Then, "I have been stealing food in Taos. There is some there if you want it." She pointed to a small platter of cooked corn meal.

She slipped to the floor beside him and watched as he ate.

"And Juan commanded." She was thinking about what he had told her. "Don Jaime would have appreciated that." The Indian youth started to rise. "Do not be frightened, Juan. I am almost pleased that you betrayed him in your way as he betrayed me in his."

She watched as he almost choked on his food. "Did you kill Fray Vicente, too?"

"He is dead."

When he was done eating, she said, "He was a foolish old man."

Juan rose, offered her his hand and helped her to stand beside him.

"Is the war chief of Taos going to kill me, too?" she asked.

He placed his hands on her shoulders. "We will ride south tonight. You will join your people."

She laughed softly in his face. "What would I want to do that for?" And he let his hands drop as he said again, "You will join your people."

He saw in that instant when she shied from his command that Manuela was not as confident as he had believed her to be. He walked slowly down the stairs and out of the house into the open courtyard. The grounds which had been tended with care in July were now a shambles. The grass was no longer trimmed. The bushes grew wildly up the walls. Weeds found refuge in the broken rubble. And the odour of corpses hung heavily in the dead air. Juan snaked in the reins of his horse before it could shy, tightened the cinchas, mounted quickly, and rode into Taos.

When he returned, Manuela sat waiting for him at the hacienda. He was leading a white horse and a bay laden with two large bags of food. She smiled as he handed her one of her own dresses.

"I remember when your father had this brought from Ciudad Mexico. The old padre told him you needed proper clothes."

She held the gown before her. "And you want me to be properly dressed when I join my people?"

He nodded. "Your father was a great man in his country. You are his daughter."

And he saw that she was laughing again. Then she stopped. "Would the Taoans kill me if we left now?"

He thought and then shook his head. "They respected Don Jaime."

Manuela looked at him. She saw that she was almost as tall as he and, knowing what the sun had done to her, believed she was as copper as he. "If you will wait for me outside . . ." He looked about him, closed his eyes for a time as though trying to remember something and then walked out through the break in the wall.

He was standing in the courtyard when she joined him soon afterward. She was still wearing the doeskin dress. The blue dress was still in her hands, and when she saw him staring at it, she explained.

"I wanted to be alone in there. I was looking for something. I never found it." She did not explain as he helped her into her own saddle which he had set on the bay. He took the silk dress from her, and folding it carefully, put it into a saddlebag. Mounting his black, he rode out of the courtyard leading the white. Manuela followed him, though she paused several times as he did to look back at the hacienda, the pueblo beyond, and Taos mountain looking over all.

The young Indian boy and the young Spanish girl rode south from Taos for hours. Sometimes they rode side by side. Sometimes when the trail narrowed one or the other dropped back and they rode single file. They did not talk. Juan kept his eyes on the trail ahead, and Manuela did not attempt to draw him into conversation. Several times Juan recalled the earlier journey they had made together to the high mountains. They had travelled at night then and she had sung much of the way. Now it seemed as though she had forgotten the lines of Dante which had poured forth from the darkness of her bewildered mind. He did not know what the change in her meant. He was aware that whatever he had felt for her father, he now felt for Manuela. And he knew now that he loved her, that she was the reason he had ridden north from the Villa and the reason he was riding south now. This thought jounced with him. If he were not with Manuela, where would he be going? Was there any other place or any other purpose for Juan of Taos? Where in all the world above or below the great Pass to the south which Don Jaime had told him about was there any use for an Indian who knew Castilian better than most of the Whitefaces, could read better than the padres, and had read more of the world's literature than any of them? Where was there anyone who could use the talents of a Juan? Could anyone use an Indian trained to think like a Whiteface? Juan pondered the questions as he rode through the high grass that lined the rio's edge. He was like the trained animals he had read about who performed for the royalty of Europe. He was an actor without a stage, a padre without a mission, a captain without an army. Where in the world above or beyond the great Pass was there a place for a man like Juan of Taos? He could not answer the question. He was not certain anyone could.

And so he rode south with the woman he loved, planning to give her up to her people, hoping that the Governor survived so that she might join him in his flight from the kingdom of the puebleños.

For her part, Manuela thought about very little as she rode. There was no memory of their earlier ride together, no recollection of the night spent in terror along the rio, of the lion and the hysteria which followed. The jornada back to the hacienda was almost the only thing she could recall, beyond the moment when she fled her father's house. And she had, as she travelled back to the hacienda, thought enough about Don Jaime, Fray Vicente, and the world of the past. She had arrived home in the early morning after days of wandering southward by the edge of large rios and small. She had eaten berries and a little bird which she had captured. And then she had come home. The hacienda had appeared undamaged in the distant morning sunlight. She did not see the destruction until she arrived at the gate, and at first she had not understood what it meant. Then she found her father's body and the pillaged house, and saw that Taos remained undamaged. She realized then it was the Indians' doing. She realized, too, this could not have happened if Juan had warned her father. And though she tried to blame Juan for his perfidy, she found that she could not. She knew enough about the Spanish who lived around Taos to know how the Indians were treated. She had heard often enough the hatred for the Indians which welled from Fray Vicente as he spoke of those who would people the special hell he shared with the dark Italian poet. The old padre had taught her sin better than he knew. He not only taught the girl the sins he preached but those he exhibited. On the long jornada back to the hacienda, she realized how much he had taught her and how fully. Then his own sins and those of her father became apparent to her. As she wandered lonely through the countryside, beauties which she had never seen before revealed their special quality and meaning to her, and she realized the extent of her innocence and the way she had, from childhood, been cruelly put aside.

Now, riding beside Juan, she saw the world about her as a beautiful place. It was she who noticed the scarlet bird break across a clearing and light upon a bright green tree. It was she who saw the wild shape of a distant butte above the horizon. It was she who noticed the small eyes of the opossum staring at them through a thicket as they passed, and the blue butterfly wavering with the wind and shifting its course in the breeze to pause above a rainbow flower.

Manuela had come to terms with the world in which she lived and was no longer concerned about any others, whether of heaven or hell. Dante was now a name to her, no longer a threat. She wondered as she rode if in some distant time she would recall his lines with pleasure and understanding. She did not know, and for the moment did not want to test herself. She was uncertain but she knew she was and so there was strength to draw upon.

It was late afternoon when Juan, calling for her to stop at the rio's edge near the clearing before them, started to ride ahead. Manuela kicked the sides of her horse and raced after him. They reached the clearing together and spilled off their horses at the same time. Juan was laughing as he removed the food bags and threw them to the ground.

"Can you cook a meal?"

She flushed as she wondered about the answer. "Will you make a fire?"

He set about gathering wood while she explored the two hide bags. Corn. Dried meat. Nothing else. She stared at the food she had spread out on the ground unable to decide what would be expected of her. Juan lit his fire and watched her out of the corner of his eye. When the blaze broke high and he knew it would burn without tending, he rose and stood beside her.

"This is corn," he said, "and this is meat, dried meat." She turned to see if he was serious. And only the corners of his dark eyes revealed the play.

"If you know what it is, then you should know what to do with it." And she settled back to watch him.

Soon he had mixed the corn meal and meat with water from the rio and had them cooking on a hot stone. Then he began to gather grass in handfuls which he dumped on the ground in a heap beside her. She stared up at him and he was aware of her eyes laughing at him. He turned away to add more piñon branches to his fire. Then he settled back against a rock and looked at her across the shifting firelight. The day was failing and the breezes blew cool breaths over the fire making it dance to strange rhythms.

Neither spoke for a time. He wondered what she was thinking as she stared at the light disappearing to the west.

"We have no blankets," he said at last. "You may have to take a hide bag and stretch it over your legs." He considered how this might meet her needs. "You had better put on the blue dress also."

Manuela made no sign that she had heard him. She rose to her feet and crossing over to the rocks where their meal was cooking, knelt and turned the food over. Juan watched her lean body as it bent down, saw her black hair come loose from behind her ears and the way she brushed it into place with the back of her hand. One lingering finger touched the edge of the hot stone and she dipped it into her mouth. He smiled and she wrinkled her nose at him. Shortly afterward they ate. Neither spoke through the meal and when they were done, Juan banked the fire with care, emptied one food bag into the other, spread it over the grass he had gathered, and handed Manuela the blue dress. She took it from him with the same disdain she had received it earlier in the day. It no longer mattered to her that the dress was fine silk off looms in Madrid. After a time Juan rose and mounted his horse. "You had better sleep now. We have a long way to travel tomorrow. I will be back soon." Then he disappeared into the darkness. Manuela stood watching as he went. After a time, she dropped the dress to the ground and sat beside it. It was dark. She stretched out and went to sleep. When he was certain that she was asleep, Juan of Taos stepped out of the bosque near by, stretched out on the ground and stared at her across the fading light of the fire.

13

FROM the moment the Spanish broke camp in the morning, they were followed by Indians. They could see the rebels on the far side of the broad stream, and after the camp was abandoned, they watched a small band of mounted puebleños cross to the east side to inspect the dead campfires. Márquez called this to the attention of the Captain General who merely shrugged and rode on.

There were going to be enough problems to survive this day without seeking to understand why the Indians were rummaging through cold fires. The Spanish had already abandoned most of the excess baggage with which they had begun the jornada. Their numbers could be counted from any hill. And any observant Indian could also determine the tragic state of their equipment, transportation, and supply.

No smoke was seen on the far side of the rio and after an hour of marching, the Spanish were no longer able to locate the Indians. Otermín never doubted that he was being followed, never doubted the wisdom of an ambush near the pass above Cristóbal de Anaya, and he felt increasingly nervous at having lost contact with the enemy. Twice he thought of sending out scouts to locate the main body of rebels, evaluate their strength, and perhaps test their temper. But as he looked back at the column trudging through the dust, he decided against even this small action. Hoz came to mind; Hoz and the fact that the Indians were watching, whether the Spaniards could see them or not, and if a rider should cut loose from the main body, he would be followed and destroyed.

Three times in the heat of the morning, Otermín broke his march, signalled the halt and watched the refugees take quick advantage of the moment off their feet. It was almost noon when he started the column moving after the last halt and rode off ahead with Quintana. Less than a quarter-league away lay the pass. They entered the thin strip of land between the high walls without hesitating and rode through, confident that the Indians would not reveal their plans of an ambush just to capture two men even if one of them was the Governor. There was better game moving up, and a sprung trap snares nothing.

Through the pass. On the far side lay a small estancia. The charred roof and the black streaks where fire had reached beyond the wooden windows told the story. But for Otermín this was cover if he had to have it. Back to the middle of the pass, he sat on his horse and stared at the heights about him. High enough for an ambuscade. A wiser enemy would have laid an abatis across the narrow area, slowed the column, and prevented the dash that he was contemplating. Otermín smiled to himself. *Dash*. The word was meaningless under these conditions. He could not move his people faster than the youngest child could walk or the oldest man. The spavined horses that dragged the two carretas of wounded controlled his destiny as much as all of his years of combat. *Dash*. He smiled at Quintana and that eager amateur soldado leaned forward expectantly.

"Those heights," Otermín's hand drew a large circle above his head. "I want every one of them. A few men here and a few there. The higher points. Control those, and we control the pass."

Quintana nodded. "But if they fight?"

"Then we fight. You take the highest, there," pointing. "Spread out ten men and no more. Those over there, Sargento-whatever-his-name-is-with-the-pocked-face-and-the-lost-wife. Give him ten men, no more."

The Alcalde Mayor stared at the two areas designated by the Commander. He shook his head slowly. "If they do not let us move up?"

"Move anyway. Once you are set, we will go through as fast as I can drive them."

Quintana was still sceptical. "And the remainder of the tropa?"

"With me. I will not commit them until I am certain where they will have to fight—with you or the sargento."

More satisfied now, Quintana started to ride back. But Otermín's hand went up and beckoned him again. "Luis, if they are wise, they might try blocking our exist, catch us in here and chop us up in small pieces."

The little man nodded. He was not certain where the Captain General was leading.

"If they do, I will hold the tropa here and fight through." After a minute, "You know where that leaves you?"

"Fighting up on that rise without support?"

Otermín smiled. "Ask the padre to pray for us, amigo," and he slapped the rump of Quintana's horse. The bay galloped out of the pass toward the advancing column of refugees.

Slowly riding his large grey stallion to the entrance of the pass, Don Antonio pulled his sabre loose in its sheath. Then he untied the helmet hanging from his saddle and slipped it onto his head. The strap came tight under his chin. The weight settled and the broad span began to hold the heat. For a moment he considered his heavy leather tunica and armour on the pack animals, shrugged off the idea and settled back to wait for the column. He saw the ten men ride off to the east with Quintana, dust behind, the lances set to boot. Several wore their steel breastplates and helmets. Some were bareheaded. A moment later the sargento's small tropa cut loose from the main body and rode for the rear of the buttes and hills.

The column approached him and Otermín assumed immediate command. He raised his hand and brought it to a halt. Then he sent two soldiers riding the length of the column.

"Do not rest. Do not drop baggage. We move and move fast through here."

From the expressions on the faces of the women and the rancheros, Otermín knew that the story told by the old Indian Antonio was known to all. Someone had talked too much and frightened the others. He was angry, but blamed himself for not cautioning those who had talked to the old man. Cautioning whom? The young and angry sargento all ready to curse the Indians, or the eager, talkative Quintana splashing his little knowledge and big fears to his wife?

Otermín selected fifty of the sixty soldiers who remained with the column. Twenty were gone, and as he scanned the heights above, he saw them emerge, silhouetted against the skyline.

The fifty rode to the head of the file. He faced them. "Column of fives, arms ready. We go through here. If they try to close off the end, we charge. If we get through, we keep on moving. Ride!"

His sabre came into his hand and he pointed the way. The men, mounted, ready to do battle, rode forward. Otermín trotted his horse to the end of the column where the remaining ten soldiers shepherded the line before them.

Minutes later Otermín realized just how slowly they were going. Too spread-out. Too frightened. Too weary. Too many people who were no longer fit to make the march. Time counted here and he saw that he was making none. He looked at the heights above him as he re-entered the pass. Nothing. His men and no others. No sign of battle. No sign of an Indian. No sign of even a column of smoke stretching upward with its message and portents.

How does a man measure retreat? The question kept bouncing back through his mind, as it had for days. If there were no signs of trouble, was this success? How could retreat be success? And why no signs of trouble? Why did not the Indians he had seen the past two days descend on his small bands of riders and knock them right off the heights with a single direct assault? Ten men and ten men. This was nonsense. Wars were not fought this way. Not against thousands. Not against men who know the terrain as well and even better than he.

The column moved on. The old were hurried by the soldados. The young gathered their endless energies, carried the extra baggage, set shoulder to wheel and urged the carretas along.

There were no signs of battle in the lead of the column. No signs of disturbance on the heights above. Otermín rubbed his beard with the back of his hand and shook his head. Another question to add to his list. Another *why* he could not answer. War without final victory. War without destruction of the enemy. This was as meaningless to the Spanish Captain General as the original cause of the uprising, that other *why*, that other gnawing question. The mind that had planned and organized the Indians for the revolt, the mind that had bound the pueblos together and brought them to a peak of wrath on a single morning, that mind would not miss this opportunity, could not miss it. Here was the final victory for the Indians: the Spaniards caught in an open trap and no one closing it. Otermín swung out and with the flat of his sabre caught a lagging wench on the rear. He watched as she hurried her step before reaching back to rub her bottom.

And then they were out of the pass. The land shelved wide, and in the distance lay the estancia he had seen earlier. Otermín ordered the tropa to keep the pace already set. No laggards. No resting now. He saw Quintana and his ten men turn and ride down from the heights. Moments later the other ten swung off the buttes. They had almost reached the estancia when the two patrols joined the main body.

Quintana trotted up to the Captain General and saluted with a smile. "None of them in sight, Excellency. None."

Márquez saluted. "We saw them in the distance, but not one moved in our direction." He, too, was smiling. The deep-set holes in his cheeks seemed to close.

Both men were surprised at the frown on Otermín's face, his hawk eyes dark, the lines about the edges of them running like furrows.

"Why?"

"I do not understand, Excellency. We are past them. They did not fight where they might have trapped us." Quintana did not comprehend this commander's reluctance to be thankful.

Don Antonio would like to have slapped both men on the shoulders,

thanked them for the fine job they had done, and declared a rest. But he did
not. The question he had asked still remained unanswered. The Indians had
been angry and they had been successful. Why stop? Why pause now? Why
did they hesitate to attack?

He rode silently for a time. Then he spoke so that both men riding beside
him could hear. "Keep the people moving. I understand there is another
house beyond this. We will rest there. We are too close to the pass. If they
should pour through. . . "

Quintana nodded, though he admitted to himself this was something he
would have to discuss with Isabella. Márquez fell back to the rear of the line
and both the Governor and Alcalde Mayor rode to the head of it.

"The house," Quintana said, "Márquez told me it would be here. It belonged to Pedro de Cuellar."

Otermín had never heard of the man. The fact showed on his face.

"A ranchero and silversmith. Made beautiful silver."

"The Anaya hacienda?"

"A little farther on, Excellency."

Otermín swung his horse off the trail and waved the refugees on.

The heat of the day seemed to raise a mist over the sluggish rio. The leaves
of a distant cottonwood barely stirred, and except for a small jay, even the
birds seemed to be avoiding the sun. A diamond-backed rattlesnake hissed
annoyance at the passing horse but did not bestir itself to move away from
the settling dust.

Reaching into the saddlebag that jounced behind him, the Captain General
pulled out the folded map he had prepared for the jornada. The sheepskin
parchment was yellow and the iron-gall ink already faded from the intense
brightness of the day. But this was not important because he could still make
out the simple landmarks he had drawn. The problems lay in the originals—
the Bleau and Colom maps which he had copied. Too sparsely marked, too
remotely conceived, too old. Distances recorded as "a day's ride," "a league,"
"five hundred varas." A hard day's ride on a good stallion, or a day's ride with
a thousand weary refugees on foot? Did a Dutchman drawing a map reckon
an English league or a Spanish league? A vara—the pace of a man. Quintana's
or the tall ranchero's who slept beside the blonde woman?

The terrain—mountains or merely decorations? And there had been decorations on the originals: bare-breasted Indian women passing out fruit, Greek
gods staring down from mountain tops oceans away, and fancy caravels—
sails blowing amidst imaginary sea beasts. Always the decorations precisely
drawn, but never the facts.

He had been over the country. Others had been over the country. But who
knew how to record it? Who was prepared to risk lives on these markings
or the fugitive recollections of someone who had ridden the route one or
three years before, seeing the mountains and the landmarks from the other
direction as they moved north? He would have to trust his judgment and that
of the men with him. Perhaps the map was more a soldier's habit than
a necessity.

In disgust, Otermín shoved the map into his belt and stared at the soft-moving rio. Here was much of the trouble and no denying it. In the broad valley between the mountains and buttes, purple-shadowed to the right, bright to the left, the Rio del Norte wandered from bed to bed like an eager whore. Each shift could mean an extra league, or five.

He shrugged again. There was no choice. The route had to remain the same: south by the rio.

The column was approaching a large hacienda when the Captain General caught up with it again. He scanned the horizon. There were only the hills, buttes, a few truncated mesas, and small clusters of cottonwood. Spurring his horse, he brought it to the side of Márquez, who trailed the column, lance resting on boot, reins lightly in hand.

"Sargento, send one of your men up ahead. Tell Quintana we will rest by this hacienda. My orders." He thought about this a moment as Márquez started to ride toward one of the soldados.

"Sargento."

The young soldier's bay came to a halt. "Excellency?"

"Tell Quintana no one is to enter the house. Post men to keep it empty until he and I have inspected it."

The strained face went to one side in question. No answer was forthcoming, and the sargento rode on to pass along the order.

A few minutes later the column came to a halt. Several women broke for the shelter of the rambling white adobe hacienda that stood on a small rise overlooking the rio. However, before they could reach the doorway, Quintana's men rode up and cordoned off the entrance. As Otermín approached, he heard the squabble between the soldiers and the angry women. Ignoring it, he dismounted, tossed his reins to one of the men, and looked for Quintana. A moment later the Alcalde Mayor joined him.

"You wanted me, Excellency?"

Otermín nodded, turned to the man who held his horse. "Tell the men to spread the word we will rest here for a while. Then we move. Anyone who wants to eat had better do it now."

The soldier saluted clumsily, bobbing his bearded face. Then he considered mounting the Governor's horse, saw he was being watched, and started to walk the length of the column instead.

Otermín smiled to himself. He clapped a hand on Quintana's shoulder as Márquez joined them. "This is the Anaya house?"

Quintana shrugged his ignorance, but the sargento knew. "No, Excellency. That lies beyond, to the south. This was the home of Captain Augustín de Carbajal." He said the name as though the others should recognize it. When he saw the Governor staring at him, he explained. "The captain was an old man, Excellency. A friend of my wife's family. An old peninsular who came here many years ago." He thought for a moment. "Before my time. He married a cousin of the man who was Governor before Treviño. A beautiful woman, Excellency." As though this explained everything. The youth appeared eager to enter the house.

Otermín ignored him and the staring, sullen faces of the women who had rushed to the entrance seeking shelter from the sun. He turned on his heel and walked into the hacienda. His two subordinates followed.

Inside the doorway, the three men stopped. Lying sprawled in the centre of the parlour, his dead hand clutching a broken sabre, lay a white-haired old man. His head rested against the broken leg of a chair. His eyes seemed to be focused on the wall just beside Don Antonio. Surprised at the expression on the man's face, Otermín looked at the wall. It was splashed with dried blood. On the floor beside the door, lying on her face, was a young girl. Her skirt was tangled around her stiff legs. One of her hands seemed to be reaching for something. Otermín stared for a moment and closed his eyes. Just beyond her finger tips her other hand lay on the stone floor in a pool of dried blood. Quintana knelt beside the woman and turned her head to one side so that they might see her face. She was fifteen, perhaps. The Alcalde Mayor crossed himself and rose to his feet. From the way he stroked the hilt of his sabre with an open palm, Otermín could see the man was angry. He turned to look at the sargento. His eyes were half shut, but even so, he was looking at the doorway beyond instead of at the girl. Otermín took the young man's arm and guided him through the room.

In the bedroom they found two naked women, lying, throats cut, across a large bed.

"The older one there is Doña Damiana Domínguez de Mendoza." Márquez made the identification in a slow, choked voice.

"The other?" Otermín asked as he stepped to the bed, picked a blanket up from the floor and spread it over the two bodies.

After a time, Márquez said, "The man," gesturing toward the parlour, "he is the captain. The girl is their daughter."

"And the other woman?" pointing to the younger of the two figures on the bed.

The sargento shook his head. "I do not know, Excellency."

"Send me the padre and four men for a burial detail."

Without answering, the youth turned and staggered out of the room and the hacienda. The older men watched him go.

"He is thinking of his wife, Excellency. No one knows what they did to her."

Otermín slumped against the wall, holding onto one of the bedposts to keep from slipping all the way to the stone floor. The wounds in his leg pained him. The one in his side ached as he bent over. His left hand touched the open slice on his cheek. Quintana saw that the wound was inflamed. Embarrassed, he did not know if he should offer his help or ignore what he saw. While he was making up his mind, Otermín pulled himself erect.

"See that the burial takes place at once. Behind the house so that the women cannot see it. They will know, but they do not need to see." His body tensed as he started to cross the small bedroom. Over his shoulder, he said, "Keep the young sargento busy. Have him check the guards while we are here. Anything, just so long as he does not come back into this house."

"Yes, Excellency, but. . . "

Don Antonio rested against the doorway. "Yes?"

"Should we try to find someone who can identify this other woman?"

Otermín shook his head slowly. "We already have. It is the sargento's wife. He would not identify her because he wanted no one to know what was done to her."

Then he left Quintana with the dead.

Outside, Don Antonio brushed past the guards and the women waiting to enter. He stumbled down the edge of the rio where he eased his aching body to the ground, retaining what dignity he could, forcing every muscle to keep from collapsing in front of the refugees who were staring at the strange expression on his face. With measured deliberateness he washed his fevered cheeks, forced himself to his feet again and looked about for his horse. The soldier was seated near by, the horse tethered to a hitching post. Don Antonio measured the distance to the horse, doubted if he could cross it, and signalled for the soldier, who rose slowly to his feet and brought the horse to him. As faces whirled dizzily before him, Don Antonio found himself counting every step the soldier took. He reached for the saddle as he felt his legs about to fold beneath him. Nodding his head to cover his feebleness, he dragged himself into the saddle and rode south out of sight of the hacienda and the staring faces. Once he rounded the bend of the rio, he let himself slip from the saddle to the ground. Breaking his fall with his good arm, he rolled under the shade of a small cottonwood. There he closed his eyes against the heat of the sun above and the fever within him.

Soon the thunder began.

It seemed to start in the north. Then it rolled south. The hills picked it up and bounced it back and forth between them. At first the noise was an isolated clap, loud and sharp, clearly defined. Then it shifted, became more frequent and began to roll, clap over clap, overlapping into one great roar, filling the skies and the far hills as well as the closer buttes and small cañons. Birds scattered to hide. A small toad leapt up on a rock and looked around, bewildered. The grey stallion that was grazing on bunch grass near where Don Antonio de Otermín lay, looked up in fear. Its ears fell back against its neck, its short tail brushed nervously from side to side. Then it bolted downstream for a short distance, only to whirl and return when thunder echoed in front of it from a near by hill.

The sky turned black. The bright sun of recent months was gone and a shadow fell over the land. It filled the crevasses of the valleys and climbed the hills. It hid the smaller insects and frightened the game. The sky became quick with the turbulent movement of growing clouds.

And the rain fell. Large drops. Single drops, heavy and sparse. Then more rain and the entire space between the dark heaven and the scorched earth was filled with water flowing downward.

The world was water again. And cool.

The frightened stallion bowed its head and stood shivering as its mane soaked up the wet and its eyes were filled with the running stream.

Don Antonio opened his eyes. Through the fog of his dizziness he tried to recall where he was. His tongue licked at his fevered lips. His hand brushed the wet grey beard and he tried to understand what had happened. Slowly, his mind crawled back to his departure from the rest area. But there was no sun now to tell him how long he had been gone, how long he had lain in the shade of the cottonwood before the rains started.

He was cooler now. The water had come. The sun was gone. His fever seemed to have subsided. He pulled himself into a sitting position. The frightened horse edged closer, and Otermín took advantage of this, reaching out to grab the reins before a thunderclap shied the animal again.

Holding firm to the reins, he stood up, tightened the cinchas of his saddle, and pulled himself into it. He sat for a moment trying to orientate himself. Then he swung the horse north and, spurring it, rode back the short distance to the hacienda.

The entire group was in chaos. Hundreds had taken cover in the house. The others stood outside trying to protect themselves and their meagre belongings from the overflowing sky. Otermín quickly saw that no guards were out now. Without pausing, he circled the house. The mounds behind it satisfied him that at least the burial had taken place before the rains began, and he rode again to the front of the white hacienda with the many porticos and simple solid walls. The refugees were in complete confusion. The water had soaked the dresses of the women. The children looked down at their feet and rain fell off their hair in small rivulets. Several of the men stood staring up at the dark sky, the water splashing over their faces.

Looking about, Don Antonio saw María watching him from the shelter of an arch by the gate. Inez, beside her, waved at him gingerly. He nodded in faint recognition and called out. "Quintana! Has anyone seen Quintana?"

There was a stir about the entrance of the house as the name was passed from one person to another and eventually made its way into the building. A few minutes later the Alcalde Mayor stepped out into the rain to stand beside the Governor.

"Excellency. We were concerned about your safety. There is certainly room for you within."

Don Antonio looked at the small man and shook his head. "We march. We march at once."

"But, Excellency, the rain."

The back of Otermín's hand rubbed against his wet beard as he spoke softly enough for Quintana to hear and no other.

"By the tears of the virgin we march now. Curse the rain. We get no fatter waiting for it to stop, and we gain not a vara toward our destination." His voice was hard. He was growing impatient.

The crushed look on the face of his subordinate was apparent. More gently, he explained. "The Indians are less likely to attack us marching in the rain. Besides, you know as I do that if we wait for this rain to cease we might wait until winter."

The Alcalde Mayor saluted. "We march, Excellency."

It was not a simple task to force the men and women out of the shelter of the hacienda and into the wet. It was difficult to make them understand, and the wounded groaned as much in disgust as in pain.

But Quintana did it. He cajoled, he threatened, and in some cases he had the soldiers lay their sabres across reluctant bottoms. The march began again.

Southward by rain. Southward with every step in mud and clay and puddles. Southward slithering, slipping, watching the Rio del Norte rise beside them, watching the arroyos fill suddenly, crashing down to dump their unexpected flows into the rio.

Southward in water and the loads growing heavier with wet weight. Hands fumbling to wipe away dripping hair, clear filled eyes; tongues lapping at lips. Southward slowly. And always the rain.

The sky dark. The thunderstrokes strong. A child falling to be picked up again. A horse stumbling, reined tightly to its feet and south again. Cattle bawling at the noise and the splash, the soaked eyes and uncertain footing.

Southward with chill. The carretas of wounded sticking and rutting in soft earth, bumbling over firm. The blank face of the blind woman searching the source of the water. The low moans of the pregnant woman appealing to God to stop the pain. The solid curses of the men. The bandages wet with green and water. Beds soggy, boots filled.

Southward along the rising rio in a long, wet straggle. The line stretching out with the faltering, the fears, and the sullen looks at the back of the Commander, the Captain General who had ordered the march. Mumbling fury and the sure dampening.

Southward by curses and a desire for sun.

Twice the Captain General dropped back to ride beside the sad-faced young sargento on whom he had begun to depend. The older man knew there was courage and satisfaction in numbers. He knew, too, that there were wounds and sorrows a man can only endure alone, and so they rode silently.

The way became muddier. The pools gathered in greater circles over the camino real. Southward by mud. Southward by misery. The wet hand wiping the wet face. The heavy tree dropping its load of water and the dripping branches. The dark hills echoing. The only other sound the slush of slogging feet.

And into the Anaya hacienda with the rain falling and the darkness early.

The Governor's hand went up. The column fell away, pressing for the cover of the low buildings—the house, the barns, the stables. But again the cordon of soldiers came first. Again the house was surrounded, and again the dead were buried. This time there were twelve. The haciendado, his wife, his children, and others. Twelve naked bodies strewn about the front entrance of the yellow building with the flagstone walks.

Then the soldiers relaxed. The women forced their way under the roofs, fought over the corners against the rain, and wearily made their toilet as best they could. The Governor allotted the stables to his soldiers and the barns to any who wanted them. He was making no ceremony for chastity. No woman was duenna on this jornada and he would be cursed if this was a problem he would even recognize as existing. There were women who protested, and the dour padre from Valladolid let his feelings be known. And when the talk was done, Otermín merely said, "If a woman protests that a man has bothered her, we will hang the man."

Then he rode out in the rain again to check his guard and returned to find a place for himself to rest under the portico that ran about the hacienda itself. His blankets under the hide covering behind his saddle were dry, and as the night fell quickly, he curled up early and was soon asleep. He did not eat with the others. He did not listen to the talk about Isleta and what the others hoped to find there. He did not notice that twice during the night Quintana himself went to check the guard. He assumed this would happen. He did not hear Sargento Barnabe Márquez, who lay near by, when he began to weep in the shelter of the darkness. But he knew that this, too, would happen.

Sometime during the night the rain stopped, and the morning was bright again.

The column trudged south along the rio. More haciendas. More bodies and so more burials. Two halts in the morning and then Sandia in the distance with the mountains rising above. Heavy cottonwoods along the rio forming a dense bosque, and fields between, the corn and the wheat, the melons and beans and chili. To the east the pueblo—the irregular plaza, the narrow streets running east to west. The houses low with two communals rising above the rest. The ovens scattered about the plaza, and the roofs, large, shaped like beehives, giving the appearance from the distance of old Moorish temples with faint memories for the peninsulars. And on a rise the mission buildings.

Otermín scanned the bosque and feared an ambush. But as he had decided before, there was only one route, and he would not lose the rio line. Swinging his horse about, he held his people in place until two scouts rode out and through the trees. When they returned, the column moved through the pueblo, guards forward, weapons ready, pausing only to search the mission. It was an empty shambles.

After they had travelled half a league, they saw the Indians following them. Otermín waved the column on and rode to the rear to watch the host, mostly mounted on unsaddled horses, riding just to his rear. They were above him and looking down. He was satisfied that he had withdrawn from the pueblo just in time, for to have been trapped there with the refugees could have meant a massacre.

Sargento Márquez rode at his side, head turned watching the end of the column and the approaching Indians.

Then the firing started. An harquebus in Indian hands sent a slug to the feet of the Captain General's grey. It was followed by another and another. The Indians kept drawing closer, closing the distance between them and the Spaniards. Their shouts could be heard now, and Otermín had fought natives long enough to recognize the signs. They were clearly working themselves up for an attack.

He shouted to a soldier: "Tell Quintana he is to keep the column moving regardless of what happens back here."

He watched the man ride the long length of the line. Then he turned to Márquez. "I kept you out of the fighting at the casas reales. Do you think you can stop this with fifty men?"

He saw a smile as the youth drew his sabre from its sheath.

"I will try, Excellency." Again the lack of eagerness and the sober understanding of the problem.

"Take your fifty men, mounted and armed. Charge and drive them back. But when they break, do not follow. That is an order. Scattered in the hills your men would be cut down separately. Do you understand?"

They had reined in their horses and the gap was closing quickly.

"I understand, Excellency."

"Then move, son. Move out."

The young sargento swung back to the line, singled out those who were going to ride with him. Some who were not mounted took the horses of others who were, of women and aged and those riding double. The Indians were close now. The harquebus fire continued. Seated on his grey without moving, Don Antonio watched their approach. Some few were armed with sabres. Others held Spanish lances. Many carried the macanas—the native swords with obsidian edges. None of them rode well, but all were mounted and they would outnumber his small tropa ten to one.

The Spanish detail galloped by the Governor, Márquez saluting as he passed.

"*Por Rey y Santiago.*"

The Indians drew their horses to a halt. The attack was unexpected, sudden, and brutal. Horse met horse and lances sought copper throats of the rebels or the thick necks of their horses. The shrieks rose over the battle and the yells continued. But the Indians had not worked themselves up to the hysterical peak they needed to fight and win. They had no plan for battle nor the stomach for it.

Otermín soon saw that something was missing. Was it the mind that had planned the strategy that had once defeated him in open battle, or was it the taste of victory over women that had carried rebels to their success behind the palacio? He did not know, but he could sense what was happening from where he sat. The Indians could not face the brutality, the viciousness of a direct attack, sabre against sabre, blood splashing freely, and the last cries of the dying. The rebels whirled, broke, and ran. For a moment he wondered if the sargento would remember his orders. Then he saw his men reassemble and ride back to where he waited for them. There were a half-dozen extra horses now, and smiles.

A victory in retreat removed some of the stain. He was about to wave them on to their places in the column when he saw the smoke billow up behind them. Raising his hand, he halted the tropa.

N

"It is the Mission of Saint Francis in Sandia," he called.

The soldiers sat in their saddles. Joy was gone now. Several crossed themselves. Two leaned over and spat their anger. The bearded faces were strained. The weapons swung freely in their hands as they turned back to their commander for orders.

Otermín watched them for a moment, recalled the hacked figure of the gentle Saint lying on the altar of the mission.

"You, with the wounded arm," he pointed to a ranchero who was clutching his bleeding wrist. "Take those extra horses back to the column and tell Quintana he is not to halt until he has my orders to do so." Then with a smile, "Ride, man." The ranchero nodded, took the reins from his fellows and galloped with the extra mounts after the main body.

Otermín's hand went up as he called to those about him. "We will ride in rows of ten. Stretch out," and he swung his arms to right and left, taking the centre lead position for himself. While he waited for those with him to find their places, he removed his helmet from his saddle and set it firmly on his head. The strap buckled, he drew his sabre.

"Into Sandia. The two men at the end of each line will peel off, find torches, light them at the church fire, and burn the pueblo. Not a piece of wood to stand. Not a house with a roof. Not a place for a rat or a roach to hide."

He set the pace, spurs to horse, and the red clay beneath. The half-league was covered in minutes and they swung into the plaza of the town to face the last Indians trying to flee. Otermín's hand went up, and the Spanish horses rose in their tracks. He signalled for Márquez to cut down the Indians before they could mount and for the torchmen to begin.

Márquez had completed his task even before the fire broke out in the first communal building. The Spanish tropa sat steady, ready for an attack, half-hoping they were provoking one. The next house caught fire and the next. The long poles that held the thatch roofs had collapsed in the first houses by the time the fourth and fifth were lit. The ten men ran wildly from building to building hurling their torches while their compañeros sat angrily watching the flames consume the roof of the mission. When the last building was aflame and the last torch thrown, Otermín called to his men to remount.

Then without haste, in complete contempt for the Indians they saw on the hills beyond, they rode in formation back to join their column.

When they halted it was only mid-afternoon. The day had already been long and difficult. The men who had fought were weary. Those who had not were tense and the long fatigue of the long days crawled over them. As he watched the women sink to the ground, Otermín rode down the length of the column to Quintana.

"We will rest here until morning. They have had their chance to attack. I do not believe they will now. Set out your guards. Kill the cattle for the evening meal. Rest the horses and graze them."

Without waiting to see how his orders were carried out, he slowly walked his horse past the faces of the men and women who watched everything he did. When he reached the side of Sargento Márquez, he congratulated him on his victory and promoted him to the rank of Teniente Alcalde Mayor—lieutenant alcalde mayor; a second to Quintana with civil, military, and judicial jurisdiction.

When Quintana joined him later, Otermín ordered the promotion recorded. The two men were seated in the open field, the camp lines drawn in close, the cattle and horses hobbled, the fires already climbing toward the darkening sky.

The camp had begun to take on a regular pattern. Those with responsibilities turned to them without being told. The butchering was done quickly, the spits raised, the wash tended. Women had taken on the preparation of food for certain men, widowers, soldiers, unattached rancheros. And as the days passed, the line between the soldier who had been brought north by Ayeta to help guard the province, and the ranchero who was half soldier in addition to his responsibilities as a settler, began to disappear. The men blended into a working group, as did the women. The children found their natural compañeros and those adults who willingly looked after them. Without a muster, Otermín did not know how many of the children were orphans and how many actually belonged to a family or the remnants of one. He did not know how many of the women had no formal relationships to rancheros or soldiers, and at this point he did not care. As he sat with Quintana and watched the orderly confusion about the camp, he was satisfied that they had survived. Now there was only Isleta before them. Isleta and the rest of the province. Isleta and food. Isleta and arms. Isleta and the strength to return.

Quintana watched the impassive face of the Governor, the dark eyes in the darker sockets; the grandee with the sudden flashes of brilliance, the abrupt temper, and the certain knowledge that his was the only way. Clean, quick, sure. No questions about this commander.

But as he stared at the camp before him, watching a tall ranchero help the blonde widow polish the rain-soaked case of the clock she carried, Don Antonio had questions, had doubts. The unexpected battle of the morning, the attack on Sandia with the torches thrown, the flames gutting. He had doubts. And then he knew why. He had exposed the whole column, left it without leadership, left it without guidance, left it for no purpose other than the satisfaction of his own anger and the need for revenge. This was less doubt than anger at his own mistake.

He wiped his face with a cloth from his saddlebag and pondered the stupidity of his action. No one else seemed to have been aware of it. This had its consolations, but at the same time, he knew that so long as no one else knew and recognized his error, there was no one in this camp capable of replacing him if something should happen.

Silently he watched Quintana scribble the record of the march as he had directed.

August 21 to August 26. Defeat and the long route downward.

How close they had come to losing him. He forced his mind to travel back the path of the past two days. The dizzy moments fleeing the carnage and his own fever down the trail to the cottonwood tree. Then the rain. And another lonely night. Long and dark and he was too ill and too weary even to miss the surcease María had given him in earlier days. *August 21 to August 26.* Was the time that brief? An instant even in a man's life, and nothing in a province's.

He looked about for María and saw her standing by the rio with Inez and a small group of women who were washing their clothes and their children's faces as best they could. Some laughter carried up from the water as well as a boisterous calling for the men to help them with the work. María was accepted now where she had been rejected before. She was not alone as he was, and for this he was glad. As for himself, he felt better. He could survive until Isleta. And after that he could rest and make his plans.

Quintana was done and laid the document, neatly written, before the Captain General. Otermín picked up the parchment and scanned it quickly. It told the bones of the story. Maybe the bones were all that were needed. Certainly any more would confuse the Viceroy's clerks. "Keep your dispatches brief and your excuses ready." He had first heard the words when a subaltern, still at the Academia. He took the feather quill from Quintana and signed the document with a flourish. "So long as it is on paper, it must be all right."

The Creole did not understand, though he smiled. He would have liked to talk to his commander, ask about the skirmish that had been fought only hours before and the full meaning of the smoke that covered the sky above Sandia. But the Governor was no longer paying any attention to him as he leaned against a tree and stared at the incline toward the rio where a young ranchero and a mestiza were playfully wrestling in the water. The boy won and the girl rose a moment later drenched and laughingly shouting curses. Her dirty blue dress clung to her shapely figure, half exposing her full breasts and the curve of her buttocks as she turned her back on the youth and walked farther into the rio.

Otermín smiled and Quintana abandoned the idea of asking serious questions now. They could wait. There were others who would be able to tell him. Márquez for one. The newly promoted lieutenant stood near by rubbing down the brown stallion he had ridden so hard through the day. If Otermín ignored his mount, Márquez paid almost too much attention to his. Quintana, not always so observant, saw this difference between the two men. He rolled the parchment and walked into the abandoned house where Isabella waited. Among the first to wash at the rio, she was cooler now and relaxed. Standing by the window looking north, she was smiling to herself as she watched the smoke hanging low over the pueblo in the far distance. "Was it wise to risk so much for that fire out there?" she asked her husband. Then she saw that he did not understand what she meant and that it was better forgotten.

"The men fought well today," Quintana commented meaninglessly.

His wife threw one large arm about his small shoulders and drew him to her. "And you wish you had been there?"

Luis Quintana nodded. "Yes. I found the fighting at the Villa different from what I believed a battle could be, but I wish I had been there this afternoon."

Squeezing him to her, Isabella chuckled softly. "You do not understand. He counted on you in the event of something happening to him. You were too important to fight today."

Then she stepped back and put her large hand affectionately on his cheek. "Little one, you have come a long way from the small farm with the hungry pigs. You have become an important person."

She knew him well enough to know his vanity, no more than that of any other small man, and no less. Later in the evening, when her Luis was checking the guard, Isabella carried a plateful of food to the place where the Governor lay on his blankets watching a beetle crawl up a rock.

He sat up as she approached and accepted the plate with thanks, recognizing it as part of the pewter service María had brought on the jornada. The company of the beetle did not meet his needs, and so he asked Isabella to sit with him while he ate. Settling her heavy bulk to the ground, she watched him strip down the meat with the daga he carried in his sash.

"Today meant great danger for all of us," she said at last.

Don Antonio stopped, the blade poised at his mouth as he stared at her. "The men fought well, Señora. They are of the old tradition."

She watched him as he ate with a neatness most of her compañeros would not appreciate. "The danger was not in the battle, Excellency, but to the rest of us when you returned to Sandia."

He ignored her comment, but she would not let it pass.

"What would happen to this rabble if you were not here to hold it tightly together, give it direction and, yes, courage?"

Chewing silently, Otermín stared at the huge woman before him. He had met others like this, with the trap minds of men, the perception of futures and larger values than a meal or a bed. He had not met many, and they always disturbed him.

"There is always Señor Quintana, your husband."

And he waited.

"Luis has never been so important in his life. He feels like a bigger man than he really is."

Otermín sliced off another piece of the hot beef and said the only thing he could: "He has done well." It annoyed him to be talking this way with a woman. It was a way he had spoken only rarely even to his wife, and this woman was gross and rough-spoken.

"Luis has never been taken seriously by most people," she said. "He is small. He is eager. He is willing to accept situations and not change them." There was a pause. Then: "Why did your Excellency select him from the other alcaldes mayores and junior officers?"

The Captain General resented being asked to explain his choices, his actions, to anyone, most of all a woman. But there was an intelligence here he had found nowhere else in the province, except, perhaps, in the devoted Pando. He hoped that he would find its equal in the Lieutenant Governor who would be waiting for him at Isleta tomorrow, or at worst the day after.

Then he saw the señora was waiting for an answer. "Señor Quintana has energy. More than most of us. And at this moment we need energy and someone who is willing to accept tragedy and not weep about it, not feel sad for himself and bemoan his losses; just accept the situation and live with it."

He saw that she continued to wait. "There is more to the man."

Otermín looked into her large eyes, brown against a skin surprisingly white for the sun that had baked it. "I have seen him show courage and anger when he needed courage and any sensible man would have been angry. Perhaps these are the qualities a good second-in-command should have."

He was done eating now and she reached for the plate. "I will wash it, Excellency." Then, before he could speak, "And when you join with the Lieutenant Governor?"

The woman was no fool. "There will be a need for everyone."

She rose now, her tall, broad figure standing above him. "And María Valdivia, will there be a need for her?"

Otermín came to his feet, spread them apart and rested his hands on his hips. Several persons passing paused at the expression on his face. He stared at them until, uncomfortable, they moved on.

"I will not ask what manner of woman you are, Señora. I will not ask what sort of woman speaks out on her husband's behalf. She may be in love, she may be a fool, she may only be meddlesome. But she has little faith in the man, because by speaking she belittles him."

A broad smile spread over the face of Isabella and she began to rock back and forth until her laughter burst out loudly.

"I have told Luis you are too proud to fail. Even hell would not dare face your wrath by dragging you down. You will bring us through, Excellency."

She started to walk away from the startled Commander. Then she hesitated and turned back. "Take care of yourself, Excellency. The fevers almost claimed you when you rode away from us yesterday. Take care. We cannot afford to lose you. You cannot afford to die. And when the time comes, you will not forget Luis Quintana."

For several minutes after she had left and made her clumsy way down to the rio to wash the plate, he kept hearing Pando. But he knew it was not Pando. The old Nuevo Mexicano would never have dared goad him. Nor would Pando have threatened him as she had in parting. It was with tremendous appreciation, however, that he settled back to consider what a great commander Señora Isabella Quintana would have made.

14

MANUELA and Juan had ridden south along the great rio for days. They were in no hurry, and though the food Juan had brought from Taos was gone, the Indian youth had no difficulty hunting game. Though Manuela's hands were stained and torn from berrying, she did not care. The days together made for an easy companionship and between them they shared the work that had to be done. For Manuela, whose only jornada beyond her father's lands had been to the cave and back, the one she was now making was part of a great revelation. She was seeing not only the angry countryside that is most of the province, the world that was quick with game and beauty, but she was seeing herself for the first time. Ever since she had mounted the horse Juan had brought her, she knew that she was changing. She was no longer a child. She was no longer afraid. She was no longer concerned about what she might have done or what others might have done. The day came and was enjoyed and the night was appreciated. Don Jaime would not have known his daughter and Fray Vicente would not have approved of his charge. Manuela thought often of these two men who had worked so hard to shape her life and who now appeared to have failed so completely. She sat on the bank of the rio and lifted her head to the heat of the sun and let the waters of the rio swirl about her bare feet. Ripples spread outward, and as she watched them, she wondered how long it would take Juan to bring back their food. He had shaped himself a bow and was proficient in its use, and only the night before they had made arrows together. She smiled as she thought of this now. She smiled as she thought of Juan. She had known him since he was a child. She remembered the first time her father had brought the thin, wild Indian youth to the manor house. They played together until the padre showed his disapproval. She realized now they had always been friends within the narrow limits permitted by their elders. She picked up a handful of dirt and let it sift through her fingers as she considered how much her elders had limited her life, and wondered what her life would have been if there had been a woman in it. She thought of her mother and was sorry there was no one who could tell her about that woman whom she had never known. Her hand was empty of dirt now, and she rose to her feet. The sun was beginning to fade in the distance. As though to embrace it, she stretched her arms about her head, smiled at her own foolishness, and slowly began to unpin her dress. Finally, she let it drop to the ground, hugged herself, and walked into the rio. The water rose to her waist and she placed her palms flat on the surface as though to hold the water down. She bent over, scooped up a handful of water and poured it over herself. Then she stepped farther into the water until it rose to cover her bosom. She laughed softly as she shook her head from side to side, freeing the hair pulled behind her ears. She had never been in the rio before. She had never learned to swim. Bending her knees, she let the water rise over her shoulders. She lifted her feet and felt herself light and free of the water. Twice she tried to stretch out on the rippling surface, and twice her head sank beneath. Spewing and laughing, she rose to her feet again. A small brown bird she had never seen before stalked to the water's edge, cocked its head at the strange sound of laughter and then quietly dipped its beak in to suck up a drop. Manuela did not move for fear of frightening the creature off. But the bird had no time for play. Its wings fluttered and it feathered into a near-by tree.

Manuela was still standing in the stream with the water to her waist when Juan came into the clearing where their horses grazed. He stood for a moment, a small deer on his shoulder, and watched her playing in the water, a white form set off by the shadows of the far bank. He dropped the deer to the ground, waved to her, and disappeared again into the trees that rimmed the clearing.

Finally, wearying of the wonderful sport she had found for herself, Manuela walked to the bank where her doeskin dress lay, spread it out on the ground and let the sun dry her. She closed her eyes and drowsed, thinking of Juan and how he smiled and how strong his hands were and how gentle his voice. After a time she rose and dressed again and began to prepare the evening fire as she had seen Juan do it on other evenings.

Sometime later he joined her by the fire and soon their meal was set on a small spit above it and they were seated with their backs against a rock watching the fat drip and listening to it crackle. Manuela reached for his daga that lay on the ground, sliced a corner off the meat, jabbed the point of the daga into it, and blew gently until the meat was cool enough to eat. Then she began to eat directly from the point of the weapon. Juan sat watching her, his eyes half closed. She was the old Spaniard's daughter all right. She would eat first without thinking of anyone else. She never questioned such prerogatives. He wondered for a moment what he would do about it. Then he rose to his feet and walked around the fire and knelt down before her. Manuela paused in her eating and smiled at him. His face was still. His eyes were gentle. Gentle, too, were his hands when he reached out and took the daga from hers. Then he swung himself about to sit beside her facing the fire. He was Juan of Taos who had been the war chief in the greatest war the puebleños had ever known. A woman did not eat before he did. Manuela stared at him in surprise, because she did not understand what he was doing as he slowly began to eat the piece of meat she had cut off for herself. After a few minutes, Juan turned to look at her. Then he looked at the daga and the meat on it. He hesitated before he held the meat out to her on the point of the knife. Manuela smiled at him and bit off a piece for herself. They ate the rest of their dinner taking turns with the daga. They never discussed this. They never needed to, because each understood the other.

When they were done eating, Manuela leaned back to stare at the failing sun.

"How did Fray Vicente die?" she asked him softly.

Juan looked at her for a moment. "I do not know. I was not there when they killed him. A war club. An arrow. A Spanish sabre. I do not know."

She saw his head go to one side as he seemed to be watching something above them. She did not know that he was already reacting to the question he knew would follow.

Then she asked it. "And Don Jaime? Were you there?"

Suddenly he relaxed. His head came down and he faced her directly for the first time since they had started talking.

"I was there. I planned the uprising in Taos. I had to be there. When Popé asked me to use my knowledge of the Spaniards to fight the Spaniards, I agreed. But there were doubts and questions concerning my loyalties. There were men who did not believe I would fight, and so I went with those who would kill your father." He hesitated a moment, and then he confessed. "Before I left the house the night before, I had made his armour and his weapons useless." He looked into her eyes and saw how much she looked like her father. "I had to do that," Juan explained. "He was a great soldado and I feared him."

She nodded. This much she could understand. "He was a very strong man in many ways," she said, and as she spoke she realized that in spite of everything, she was proud of her father.

"He won in the end," Juan said.

"But you killed him?"

Juan shook his head. "When we arrived, he was out on the balcony with two boxes of gunpowder I never knew he had. When we went to attack him, he killed one man with a small hand weapon I had never seen before, a weapon he had never showed me. Then he fired the gunpowder. He died with many others." Juan's voice showed his own wounds, his hurt at the distrust of the old grandee.

"He never trusted anyone after her," Manuela said, as she tried to help him. "And if he never fully trusted you, your betrayal was not really as complete as you think."

Juan showed his surprise. "Her?" he asked.

Manuela nodded. "Her. The girl from the villa north of Madrid." She smiled at his expression. "No, he never told me about her. He never spoke to me, but night after night I heard him talking to you on the portico below my window." There was a trace of envy in her voice. She was aware of it, and she shifted the subject herself. "If he did not show you the weapon, it was because he did not trust you, not really trust you. He held back. He believed you would betray him sometime."

Her logic was difficult for her and she groped after it with the little understanding she had of such things. Juan listened. The knowledge she had gained from the old brimstone padre and from her eavesdropping stood her well.

"If he withheld some of his love, he could not expect all of yours." She was still for a moment as she approached a problem that troubled her. "Perhaps," she finally said, "it is for us to forgive him."

Juan looked up at her. He felt relieved. He felt happier than he had at any time since the uprising. He waited for her to ask the next question.

But Manuela did not ask it. She had no reason to seek the cause of a rebellion. She did not need to ask why, because she would have rebelled in time herself. In fact, in her own small way she had, the night she walked down the stairs and out onto the portico to face her father. There were no more questions. As far as Manuela was concerned, this was a subject that would never again have to be discussed.

She reached out and placed one hand on Juan's as it rested on his knee. As he turned from the fire to look into her eyes, she leaned over and, pressing her bosom against his knee, looked up at him. Then one arm went about his neck as she clumsily pulled his face down to hers. She kissed him and his arms went about her. For a moment he held her tightly against him, crushing her breasts against his bare chest. He leaned forward farther and farther until she was flat on the ground and he was on top of her. Groping blindly with her eyes closed, it was Manuela who finally drew her skirt about her waist.

Later, when they lay in each other's arms, Juan kissed her again and told her that he loved her. And she kissed his ear and was happy. They stared at the great sky spreading above them. The sky was cloudless.

When morning came, they went down to the rio and bathed together. When they had dressed again, they sat down at their morning meal and faced their problem.

"I can take you south to your people," he said. "But I cannot join them. I was the war chief of Taos and for that they would kill me. You are of them, and I am an Indian, and if we were ever to be together, they would kill me."

She understood. "Could we stay right here? We could build a place to live and stay right here."

Juan thought about the idea before rejecting it. "We are in the kingdom of the pueblos and I am no longer welcome here. They believe I am of the Spaniards."

"And the Spaniards believe you are an Indian."

He nodded.

"If I joined my people, what would you do?" she asked.

He thought for a moment and then he said, "I know a place. It is not of the Whitefaces and it is not of the puebleños. In the great cañons to the west there are old cities built into the cliffs by the ancients." He pointed to the broad land that lay beyond the rio. "Men who have travelled far have seen them and spoken of them. They are held by some to be holy. No one lives there any longer."

Then Manuela rose and took his hand and said, "Let us cross the rio together."

Juan smiled and so it was agreed between them.

15

THE long Spanish column arrived in Isleta under the scorching sun of the early afternoon. The women were tired, the faces of the children blanched with fatigue. Around the carretas was the stench of wounds turning green and horses passing wind, while over the length of the column there was dust and there were flies.

They arrived in Isleta with hope, for this was a pueblo of legend. Here was buried Fray Juan Padilla, one of the first seekers to go north after the dream of Cibola, the Seven Cities of Gold in the far mountains; north as far as the rio called Kansas, where he had found dust devils and death. Here beyond this rio he was martyred. But legend returned the holy man's body to Isleta for burial, for an annual rising from his cottonwood coffin to pass through the streets, cassock intact over his bones and the natives awed by the holiness of it and the belief that they harboured a saint.

But when the Spanish arrived that afternoon, the pueblo was empty. The riders dismounted and stood with the others among the baggage in the empty streets. For a long time they were silent. Then the line broke and people scattered through the buildings, not quite believing that they had been abandoned. Finally, they accepted the emptiness of the pueblo as a fact, and turned to face their problem. There was some hesitation and some fear. But most of all there was despair. And the question: What next?

Governor Otermín scanned the plaza of the pueblo and read the question on their faces. He felt his stomach tighten as he turned his back on the thousand people who were waiting for him to make a decision, and he walked alone down a crooked street between the block communal houses. He remembered the orders he had written to Don Alonso García: "You will not depart Isleta without permission. Send military help and supplies." There had been no supplies and now he and the thousand were abandoned.

If he had withdrawn from the Villa de Santa Fe, it was to combine his forces and prepare for reconquest. But there was no such excuse for García to abandon Isleta.

He entered a large communal house and walked slowly through it. The rooms were dark. The furniture in every room was the same: a table and some benches and a pallet. There might be a broken bow in a corner or a piece of hide stretched on a wall, a torn blanket or a basket emptied of grain, a carved handle of a broken machette or a niche where an icon had been, a scalp souvenir of an ancient battle or a jug with black marks in semicircles calling for rain. But no people.

Don Antonio finally sat down on a wooden bench and stared at a clean spot on the wall where the outline of a crucifijo showed clear in the dust of the room. The table beside him was empty except for a small piece of hide— a greasy green bando. He touched it and then swept it to the floor. The

moment called for resolution and decision, and he did not feel able to meet
the moment. He rubbed his right arm with his left hand, more from habit
now than pain. The wound on his cheek itched and he wanted to scratch it.
Instead, his hand went to the dirty bandage that covered his chest and he
felt dizzy. His head fell forward, his breath came short, and he pitched to
the floor, breaking the fall with an arm before him.

He lay still.

Eventually he rolled over and looked about him. His shoulder hurt where
he had fallen on it. The dirt of the floor covered his face, arms, tunica, and
pantalones. He wiped them off with a shaking hand and then held the hand
before him. It continued to shake. His face was hot to the touch. Bobbing
back and forth to clear his vision, he rose unsteadily to his feet, holding on
to the table edge for support. There was a blanket hanging on the wall. The
greens and browns of it ran together before his eyes.

Fever now and dizziness.

Six days on the road. Slow days. Safe enough in the end. If this was the
end. But it was not. Six days to nowhere. The food dwindling, the wounded
dying, and women weary.

And no end.

He wiped his face again with his hand. The mist stayed before his eyes.
He remained standing where he was. There were noises outside: the children
playing, the horses' hooves on the stones, and the voices loud.

Nowhere. All of this, and nowhere. He wished he had his map even
though he knew he never needed it and could not focus on it. But to have
it in front of him, to be able to make a pretence at decision. He had neither
the map nor the will to find it now. His mind slipped back to the edge of
the rio and the shade of the tree where he had collapsed—was it yesterday
or the day before?

He removed his hand from the table, sought his balance, and unsteadily
made his way out of the communal house into the sun. Children were standing near by shying stones into a far window. A fire burned high in the centre
of the plaza, and men and women stood about watching it. Two rancheros
collected the horses from where they were tethered about the streets, and
drove them to a field outside the pueblo.

A line of women waited quietly before the mission where Fray Pedro was
hearing confession. Don Antonio looked at the sagging faces, the dirty and
torn dresses of the heavy figures and the old and wondered what they had
to confess.

Then two soldiers emerged from a hacienda and staggered by him down
the narrow street. Each clutched a jug by the neck as though to strangle the
life out of it. One of the men held his up to the Captain General:

"Brandy, Excellency? Excellent brandy, Excellency. Excellent, Excellency."
He was washed on by the flow of his own words.

Otermín made his way down the short street to the plaza. Quintana was
nowhere to be seen. After looking about for a few minutes, he called a
soldier to him.

"Find me the Alcalde Mayor of La Cañada and tell him to bring the

Valdivia woman with him. I will be there," he said, pointing to the empty hacienda from which the soldiers had come.

The messenger saluted and left on his search.

Don Antonio watched a rock skim into a window. Then he walked down the street past the mission and the line of women waiting there, and entered the hacienda. The rooms were large. Heavy piñon furniture was scattered about. Wandering through the empty building, he paused at a bedroom. There was a four-poster with a mattress but no bedding. He sat on the bed. It was soft. His thick tongue licked over his dried and fevered lips, and he rose to search the rest of the house. Finally he found the amphora in a small room across the piazza. Knocking the sealed top off the jar with the heavy butt of his daga, he sniffed. Brandy, native apple. Tilting his head back, he unsteadily tippled from the jug. It burned his raw mouth and his dried gullet. He spat a mouthful against a wall and drank again. His body shook. This was what he needed. His eyes cleared for the first time since he had fallen, as he focused them on a crack in the brandy-spattered wall. Then he drank again. When he was done, he picked up two more jugs and made his way back to the sitting room that overlooked the fields to the east on one side and the half-empty rock-rimmed pool of the piazza on the other. Carefully setting the extra jugs down on a long table, he relaxed and fell into the padded seat of a Savonarola chair. The amphora he clutched came to his lips. He tried to forget the lines down the map that rested in his saddlebag. The lines were too long. They extended from nowhere to nowhere. They ran maze-like through his mind and he drank again and again—to clear them up or wash them away. He did not know which; he did not care. His head hurt him and the fever mixed with the brandy and fatigue.

The messenger located Quintana beside the rio where he was seated in the shadow of a wall with his wife and several members of the Cabildo of the Villa de Santa Fe. They were eating cold meat and discussing the future. None of them had any suggestions, and fear seemed to be guiding their discussion. Señora Isabella Quintana snorted once or twice as a young ranchero expressed his hope that they could stay where they were because, to the south, he explained haltingly, "It is not too well known and there is the desert and nothing else for a long way." He thought for a moment and then added, as though it were news, "We are short of supplies."

Isabella looked up at the soldier who approached and nudged her husband with a large elbow.

Quintana pulled himself to his feet. His boots lay with his helmet, breastplate, and sabre on the ground beside him. His bare chest was damp with the heat of the day, and he stood scratching it as he listened to the report.

"His Excellency wants you to meet him at the hacienda. You are to bring the Valdivia woman."

The soldier, a shepherd, spoke slowly, unused to words and talking to officers.

Quintana stopped his scratching and looked down at his wife as though waiting for suggestions. There was a general snicker from the men and women.

"An alcalde mayor, an aide to a captain general, and a pimp," Señora Isabella laughed.

A hacendado who had lost one of the wealthiest properties in the province shook his head in disgust. "He should have moved faster, not diddled with women, not remained at the Villa trying to save his capital which was nothing. Then we would have found García here."

Another ranchero nodded. "If he had sent a real man, instead of trying to kill that fool Hoz, we . . ."

Quintana's hand went up. "We are here now and he is commander."

Señora Isabella held out her hand. Quintana braced his small figure and helped her to her feet. As she started to walk up the trail from the rio, she turned back to her neighbours. "Have you ever thought who could hold this rabble together if he died?" Then she shuffled on. Quintana followed with the soldado who did not know what was expected of him.

In the open plaza Isabella looked about her. Finally she found Inez. "Where is your mother, child?"

The large woman spoke softly, but the size of her always frightened the girl. She was slow to answer.

"Where is your mother, child? I need her now." The voice was more firm.

"She is in that house over there," the child pointed out a small building that Quintana recognized as the friary of Isleta, though the large cross which had once been raised over it was gone now.

"I will fetch her," he told his wife, and he walked down the short street. There were several soldiers standing in front of the building with the young woman whom he recognized as the dancer with the San Cristóbal medallion. Quintana nodded to them as he entered the building. The interior was dark. The doors of small cells off the long corridor were closed. He knocked on three before he received an answer. When he called her name, María Valdivia opened the door a crack and stood pulling her bodice closed as she waited for him to speak. Over her shoulder, Quintana saw a soldier rise from a cot and turn to stare out of the window.

After a moment, María said flatly, "You wanted something?"

The Alcalde Mayor was about to shake his head when he remembered Don Antonio. "His Excellency has sent for you."

María was silent as she thought about this. The man laughed softly. Then María nodded and without a word opened the door and walked down the corridor ahead of Quintana, straightening her dress as she went out into the afternoon sun. She looked for Inez, saw her and told Quintana, "See that she is taken care of tonight and that someone feeds her."

Quintana nodded.

"Well, where is he?" she asked impatiently.

"At the hacienda over there." He pointed to the long, low building in the far corner of the pueblo.

María shook her head as though the entire affair was ridiculous and departed.

"Señora," Quintana called after her, and she stopped and looked back at him, impatient with the interruption. "Señora, we thank you for anything you can do for His Excellency."

Her laughter trailed back to him as she walked on. He looked after her and then went back to the plaza, where Isabella stood watching the children throwing stones. The soldier was with her.

"Well?" she asked, as Quintana approached.

"She has gone to the hacienda." And to the soldier, "See that this child is fed and watched over until her mother returns."

Then to Isabella, "She was with one of the criminals they sent us from Ciudad Mexico." There was disgust in his voice.

But Isabella laughed softly. "This camp is no nunnery, and she took no holy vows."

Quintana looked up at his wife, smiled, and started for the hacienda.

María entered the building and waited. Don Antonio again. She had known it would come to this. He would send for her and they would be together again.

But did she want this? She was surviving without his condescensions, his small arrogance, his ready acceptance of her and his ready rejection. She thought of Hoz who was dead and she thought of the soldier who was not dead, who had come to her only the night before and crawled under her blanket. He was strong and as arrogant in his way as Otermín was in his.

She was a ranchero's daughter and had been a ranchero's wife. Where did she fit into the world of a governor? Why should she stand the accusations in his eyes, when it was himself he was accusing because he resented wanting her? And though she knew she was happy because he had sent for her, María rubbed away the dust clinging to her neck and bosom with an open palm, wiped the palm on her skirt, and prepared to leave the room. The column was a thousand people long. Let someone else take care of the Governor. Let someone else wash his clothes and warm his bed. Let someone else hear the mean voices and the vicious whispers.

Then she saw Don Antonio standing in the doorway looking at her. He held an amphora in one hand, while the other was set against the sill bracing his limp body. The sun had burned his face since she had seen him last. There seemed to be more grey in his hair, though less than a week had passed. His pantalones were dirty from the trail and bandages bulged under them. His tunica hung open and she could see the stained white shirt beneath.

"I wanted you again," he said softly.

María nodded. "Quintana told me."

He tried to understand this. "Quintana. The little man with the black teeth and the bad smell." The arrogance came out now that he had been drinking. He closed his eyes and asked, "Where are we?" It was the lines of the map in his head and he could not keep them clear.

"Isleta," she said. And she knew that he had been emptying the jug in his hand.

"That is right. I remember now. There was no one waiting for us with supplies and ammunition." A pause as he raised the jug to his lips and drank.

He looked over the top of it at her. "There were no men here to recapture the Villa."

She saw that he was feeling sorry for himself. She was not certain how sorry she felt for him. After all, he was the Governor. Who was she to feel sad for him? She struggled to keep her emotional distance.

He crossed over and took her hand. Together they walked back to the sitting room. She saw him stagger and knew that he was not well and wondered why he drank so heavily. Then he turned to face her.

"García is gone," he said. There was a trace of sadness in his voice she had not heard since he had made the decision to withdraw to the south. Now they were south and even she saw it was meaningless. And that was just what he was saying as he handed her the jug.

"We may as well have remained where we were for all the good the retreat did us."

He watched her tip her head back and drink deeply. He did not know that she, too, was trying to wash away a truth, and that he was that truth.

"If we had remained, we might have killed more Indians, gone down fighting for Carlos and Christ."

She did not know why he laughed or why he was suddenly quiet again. A fly buzzed through the room, lit on the bandage across his chest, and then flew away. His voice was softer now, though there was bitterness in it.

"The Indians. They did not even think we were worth attacking. They did not even bother to fight us when we left."

She set the jug down on the table and helped him onto the couch. He did not protest. She knew he had voiced the final insult. It hurt more than defeat, or battle wounds that he could touch. She felt sorry for him despite herself. When he reached up and pulled her down to the couch to sit beside him, she came easily into his arms.

"They were afraid of Your Excellency," she said. "It was only a week ago that you slaughtered them like beasts in a pen. You cut their throats and they bled. They did not attack because they feared you."

He rolled his head to look up at her. The dark eyes again and the thin face. The skin white with a trace of olive. His hand moved down and rested on her thigh. Both of them were silent. His fingers closed and she felt them tight upon her. He was staring at the ceiling. Then his hand relaxed and he drank again and offered her the jug. She stared at him. Why had she come here? He was a wounded man, beaten. He had rarely been gentle with her and never been kind. Her long fingers traced the lines of his beard and rested for an instant on the wounded cheek. He was not Valdivia, nor was he Hoz, he was unlike anyone else she had ever known, and though in the small corners of her mind she could laugh at him and say she did not want him, she knew there was something which set this man apart from others who had known her.

Now she sat on the couch and placed one hand over the wound on Don Antonio's chest, felt the warmth of it as he smiled at her. She knew what was happening to her. She was trapped as she was not supposed to be trapped, caught as she was not supposed to be caught. She wanted this Governor, this

Captain General, because he could give her something the Hozes of the world could never give her. She did not know if he would give it to her or, if he did, how long he would let her have it. But once in her life she wanted the security and position that came with being the woman of a man of importance. She wanted to be the Governor's lady. And she knew as she looked at the fine features with the thin brows and the thin nose, that she wanted him to want her not just because she was a woman but because she was María Valdivia—a particular woman.

Otermín opened his eyes and saw Quintana standing before him.

"Guards out?" he asked, not the least embarrassed by the woman at his side or the jug on the flagstone floor.

"Yes, Excellency." The black teeth again.

"Did we find any food?"

Quintana shook his head.

The Governor's hand opened and closed several times before he spoke. This time there was no mistaking the anger in his voice. "Not only did García leave Isleta against direct orders, but he stripped it of everything we could use." His toe touched the amphora at his feet, but he did not smile: Almost everything." His palm spread flat over María's back. "By the sweat of the martyrs I will have his rank and that false Don off his name, as well as his pension, if I ever find him."

María saw out of the corner of her eye that Quintana stood at attention. He was not a soldado, but like all men he came to attention when the Governor spoke. It was something in the Commander's manner. She wondered what that something was and why no one came to attention when Quintana spoke.

"I want an inventory of horses and cattle and food."

"Yes, Excellency."

"And see that a guard is stationed outside this hacienda. I do not want to be disturbed." He thought for a moment. "He will take his orders from Señora Valdivia, the Governor's lady." And he started to laugh as though he had discovered a private joke. Then he pressed his hand against her back firmly and brought her tightly against him.

Quintana saw the pained look on her drawn face. As he watched the drunken Governor nuzzle the widow's neck, he knew Otermín was done with him. He left quietly, and neither of them noticed him depart.

Otermín kissed María's neck and her throat and ran his hands down her warm body. All the while he was trying to banish a thought which kept crawling like an unwanted roach into the dark fringes of his brain. But he could not exile the idea. He pushed her aside and leaned over to take the amphora in his hand. It was empty. María thought he was going to cry, but instead he hurled the jug against a far wall and watched the shards fall to the floor with a crash.

"There is another," he said, pointing to the extra jugs he had set on the table.

She rose and opened one of them. He stared at her while the thought kept crawling back into the light.

When had he come to the conclusion that he had to have her, that he wanted her for himself, that despite his age and his fatigue and all the lies he had told himself for days, he was in love with this woman? He was in love with this woman. The thought crawled into the light and stood clearly in his mind. He raised a hand before his face as though to brush it away. It was a fool's idea. He was Don Antonio de Otermín, grandee and grandfather, Governor and Captain General of a great province. A graduate of the Academia Militar de Madrid. He could laugh at himself and deny the whole thing. But the thought stood there in the bright light of acceptance. He knew it was true. He knew he had to have her with him. His face went into his hands. Then he fumbled for the jug she offered him, took it and almost drained it before he looked up at her. Her face was white, her body full. He drank again and still the thought of her remained in his head all tangled up in the lines of the map which he could not banish either. He set the jug down on his knee and stared at her. The lines of her body showed through the dress as the light from the open door silhouetted her. "There is a bedroom there and a bed," he said at last. "Get undressed and I will be with you when I finish this."

Then he set about emptying the jug. He could not drown either his reluctance or his need. When the amphora was empty, he staggered to his feet and zigzagged into the bedroom and closed the door behind him.

The night sky was dark. Rain had fallen much of the day but now had stopped. The sentry who stood guard at the entrance of the hacienda which the Governor had commandeered for his own needs slumped to the stone step; his head began to nod, and he fell asleep.

Across the narrow street Márquez waited for his commander to emerge and issue the quick, brusque orders which would set everything moving again. Márquez did not expect any miracles. Ever since he had found his wife lying across the bed of the estancia to the north, he had hidden himself in the work Otermín had given him. Now the Governor was in the hacienda with the Valdivia woman, but no matter what rumours ran the course of the plaza of Isleta, Don Antonio could not disappoint him now, because Don Antonio was the man behind whom Márquez was hiding his own sorrows. The youthful subaltern stared at the sleeping soldado, thought of wakening him and changed his mind. Let the man sleep. Márquez wished that he, too, were asleep.

The pueblo was still. The only noise in the night was the rio. The only movements were the leaves as the wind brushed lazily over them. Men and women were scattered through the communal houses, the friary, and in the shelter of the eaves of buildings. Márquez was about to settle down on the step beside the sleeping soldier when he realized someone was standing in the archway of the hacienda. The figure almost blended with the darkness. Then it moved toward the top of the steps and he saw it was a woman, the widow Valdivia. She carried a small bundle under her arm. Not knowing what to do, he came to attention.

María was startled to see the tall figure draw up before her.

"Is there something I may do for you, Señora?" The rumours and vulgar jokes meant nothing to Barnabe Márquez. She was the Governor's lady.

María descended the stone steps and stood in the narrow street. She did not answer him, though she appreciated his offer, and, most of all, his courtesy.

"Is His Excellency better?"

She wondered what he meant by better. Did Don Antonio sleep? Had the fever fled? Was he sober? Was the last amphora emptied? Could she tell this young man how his commander drank himself unconscious again and again through a day and a night and another day and into another night? Could she tell him that the jugs all lay in smashed piles? Could she tell him that the wounds of the Governor required new bandages where he had torn them open in his passion? Could she tell him that less than an hour before, he had held her affectionately, the fever subsided, his head clear, as he stared at her and said, "I love you"?

"He sleeps," she said.

Márquez reached for the bundle she carried. "May I help you, Señora?"

She looked up at his face in the darkness, though even from the sound of his voice she knew he was not laughing at her. She nodded again. "Tomorrow he will rise and he will need clothes." She handed the bundle to the young officer. "If I wash these now, they will be ready for him to wear tomorrow."

"I can have someone wash them, Señora." Even though he was a very young man, he knew she had come out into the night to avoid the whispers and the harsh looks of those women who were moral, those who were jealous, and those who were both.

But "I will wash them," she said, as she made her way to the rio. Then he knew that she wanted to.

When the wash was done, María sat on a rock beside the rio. Márquez stood near by to protect her from the night. He could barely make out her figure in the darkness. He wanted to ask her about the Governor. He wanted to know about the man whom he needed. He knew that in spite of the talk and the grumbling, there were few in the pueblo who were not waiting for the Governor to save them from the starvation or worse that they knew lay before them.

María rested. She had had more brandy in the past two days than she had ever had before. She had been used more cruelly than she had ever been before, and by a man she believed was actually in love with her and whom she believed she loved, as much as she would ever love any man. For the first time since she was a child she was crying. She did not want to cry. She did not want to shed tears for herself or for the Governor lying alone back there in the large bed without sheets under him or blankets over him. But she wept.

The Lieutenant heard her and was confused. He said nothing as he took the bundle of clothes that lay beside her. He was patient. He could wait until she wanted to return to the hacienda. He would take her there and then try to sleep, though he knew he would not because he was troubled for both the Governor and his lady.

After a time María rose and made her way back in the dark. Márquez followed at a respectful distance, and when they reached the hacienda, he offered to hang the clothes. "There is a tree on the other side of the hacienda. They should be dry soon after dawn."

She nodded and disappeared again into the dark building.

It was almost dawn when Don Antonio rolled over, and reaching out for María, found that she was not lying beside him. He opened his eyes and looked about. With a sigh, he swung his feet over the side of the bed. His head hurt him, but his vision was clear. Fumbling in the darkness for his clothes, he found they were gone. He cursed softly under his breath and began to search for them in the darkness. Shards of the broken amphora caught his eye, and he kicked them with a bare foot. His chest felt tight and running his hand over it, he saw that his bandages had been changed. *María.* He crossed over to the window and stared out at the night. *María.* His hand slapped the sill of the window. *María.* The words he had whispered to her hours before returned to him. "I love you. I love you. I love you." *María.*

So now he was in love. Now, when it was late, when the lonely years were reaching an end, and age was overtaking him like a runner in the night. Now, when his authority and power were dwindled to nothing. Now he was in love. And in love with a nobody, a peasant wench good for flattening in the hay or the open fields. What had happened to him? He slapped the window sill again, saw his clothes hanging from the limb of the tree outside and snorted. He was Don Antonio de Otermín and he was in love with a nobody. He had been angry when the thought first came clear to him. He was angry now that it returned in a head no longer befogged with liquor and fever. This was not supposed to happen. Not to him. Not to Don Antonio. But he knew he was in love. He wanted María, wanted to hold her and feel the warmth of her and have her with him so that he could see her and be comforted with the idea that she was beside him.

Nonsense.

His hand touched the scar on his face. He was a wounded old bull fit for no more than rutting.

But he was in love.

Returning to the bed, he sat down and pulled on his heavy boots. He had to get out of this place that smelled of old brandy and soured vomit. He had to find his way out into the night. He wanted to mount a horse and ride until he was tired again. And until he knew he no longer wanted María. Leaving the bedroom with all the lack of dignity that nudeness can give a man, he entered the sitting room, where María was lying asleep on a padded piñon-plank couch. He settled down in a straight-back chair and looked at her. Then he knew that he could never ride so far that the desire he had for her would be left behind. She was beautiful now in the darkness of the room. The night covered the blemishes and left only her shape and his desires.

After the guard fetched him his clothes and his horse, the Governor slipped his baldric over his shoulder, felt the reassuring weight of the sabre at his side and walked out into the night. The sentry started to wander away from his post as he saw the Captain General mount to ride off, but Otermín called him back.

"You were sent to guard this place?" he asked brusquely.

"Yes, Excellency." The man was at attention.

"Then guard it. The widow Valdivia is asleep in there. She is not to be disturbed."

He swung his horse about and rode down to the rio. He passed groups of sleeping people in the pueblo, saw the dying fire, the bleary-eyed guards coming to attention as he rode by, and the heads of men and women lifted to see who was disturbing them in the darkness. He even saw Barnabe Márquez as he rose to his feet to look after his commander. But Don Antonio did not halt. He reached the bank of the rio and turned south again. He had work to do, decisions to make that he had put off for long, wasted days while he fled the prospect before him.

He could not flee any longer. There were two decisions he had to make. One concerned the column and the business of being a governor and captain general, and the other concerned María and the business of being a man. As he rode, he wished he could find the old Fray Custodio somewhere in the darkness ahead. He would like to talk to the old padre whom they had buried in the floor of his mission back at Santo Domingo. He would like to move among the words that led through logic to answers. There was no one in the pueblo he could talk to now. Quintana was a fool. Fray Pedro would not understand how a man could see the many sides of a problem when he himself knew there was only one. Márquez was a youth.

Out of sight of the pueblo, Don Antonio swung off his horse, tethered it to a small tree, and walked to the water's edge. He pulled his sword from the sheath and rested it on the ground as he knelt and drank from his cupped hands. There were streaks of light in the east now. The night would soon be gone. Returning to his horse, he pulled the tattered map out of his saddlebag and sat down on a rock. With his boot, he smoothed the ground in front of him and began to lay out his problem with the tip of his sword. The Villa de Santa Fe to Santo Domingo to Sandia to Isleta. And the time between and the fatigue, the animals galled, refractory, the boots worn and the feet bare. The cattle dying. The time between—eight days. And to the south, Socorro just as far. Then the abandonment of the province itself. If no relief in Socorro, then the Pass below. The long jornada beyond the border.

He tried to compute his resources, wished he had brought the inventory of stores from Quintana. Cattle. Eighty head when they had departed and five head for ten days. Leaves thirty cattle for six days' food, stretch it to seven or eight with the loud grumblings to follow. Horses. Two hundred. Shoes worn, bodies lean, and the load heavier as those who can walk become fewer. And the soldiers who must be mounted, the carretas that must be pulled. And the people: a thousand more or less. Decent people in a trap. The descendants of the conquistadores and those who had followed like scavengers to shear the land, those with the big dreams and the small acts who had dragged España down to this point where her people fled before natives. Don Antonio stared at the rio. The refugees. The men could fight and the women could walk. They could complete the jornada del muerto. The core was solid and Spanish, but the outside, the crust, the part open to the sun and daily living, was soft and rotten. Too many Indian servants, too many casual deaths, too many years scrambling for riches where there were no riches, too many quarrels between Church and State for either to hold its dignity, too many copper wenches and too few white women, too easy the conquest of the moment and no concept of the hardships that could come. Otermín sighed. The refugees. They had done well. They had complained and would continue to complain. They would pull against him and balk. They would quarrel among themselves, would snipe at each small act of authority, and spread rumour like manure down the length of the column. But he had to admit the men had fought well and the women had stood beside them. He shook his head. They were strong despite the weaknesses and flaws, despite the colonial morals that could sink lower the higher a man climbed up the back of a native.

What could he do with these people? Now where could he take them? And always that other question crowding him: *Why? Why? Why?* Why had Indians rebelled? Why had they turned from Christ? Why had they turned upon the Spaniards who had built with them and worked with them and shown them what civilization could mean? This he could not answer. He could not bring himself to think the way the natives did. He had tried. For days behind the walls of the palacio he had tried without avail to think into the head of Popé.

He shrugged. There was no understanding the primitive mind. A man could only try to hold it as he held a horse in check or strike it down as he struck down a wild animal that attacked.

The sky was brighter now. The birds could be heard in the trees overhead and the mist that rose from the rio began to disappear in the light of the sun. But Don Antonio knew he had not solved his problems yet. He had skirted the edge of them, had turned a few about so that he could see them better, but the decision as to what the refugees should do next he had not yet made. Nor had he made any concerning himself and María. That, too, could wait no longer.

Don Antonio rose and looked about for his horse. He was dissatisfied with the results of all his thinking and disgusted with his indecision. Then he saw a gaunt figure in a torn cassock on the far side of the rio quietly watching him. He remembered the legend of San Juan Padilla that Fray Pedro had told him as they journeyed south: the martyred saint who was supposed to be buried at Isleta though he had died in the north. Don Antonio feared his noisy hundreds had driven the Saint from his resting place. He crossed himself and slipped to his knees in prayer. When he looked up again, the large figure of the padre stood closer to the rio's edge. For a brief instant the Governor prepared to flee. He looked about for his horse so that he could ride away from this place. Then he heard the heavy voice carry across the water, "I would join you," and he prayed again as he watched the gaunt figure step into the stream and begin to swim across it.

Don Antonio did not know that Fray Julio had watched him for some time. He did not know that the padre of Santa Flora had spent two weeks in the wilderness hiding in the small valleys on the western side of the rio, praying and seeking absolution for the sins which he knew to be great. Only the week before when the padre had appeared by the rio, the Indians had fled before him in fear of the legend about which he had never heard. The crossing was difficult for the padre. His torn cassock was heavy in the water. His broken arm was thrown about by the strong current. But soon he was able to stand and walk ashore.

The Captain General stared at the lean, dripping giant with the aquiline face ravaged by pain and contrition who emerged from the water and walked toward him. Hesitantly, Otermín broached the question. "Juan Padilla?"

The shaggy head shook as the broken arm flapped in the direction of the rio. "Fray Julio. Santa Flora."

At first Don Antonio did not understand. He rubbed his beard with the back of his hand and rose to his feet to stand in the Franciscan's long shadow. "Have you been here long, Padre?"

There was a gentle smile on Fray Julio's face. "One week or two. I do not really know. Is it important?"

The Governor shook his head. He did not know himself.

"You were going somewhere. May I help you, my son?"

Otermín thought about this. "I have been riding south for a very long time." Then he knew that was where he was going to take the whole long column.

"Then we will travel together." The voice was soft, reassuring.

Don Antonio nodded. He had never seen this padre before. "You have lost your mission?"

At first the padre did not answer. It was a question he had not thought about. Yes, he had lost his mission, if by that the stranger meant he was away from it and that it was probably in the hands of the rebel and apostate Indians. Yet, in another sense and a greater one, he had found his mission, if by mission one meant purpose and aim. How could a padre explain such a thing to a stranger, a layman with an arrogant face who would never believe how lost this Brother had been in his life and how he was only now emerging from a wilderness. And as he stood thinking about the stranger's question, Fray Julio recalled the mission of San Ysidro and he wondered if the stranger would say that Fray Rafael had lost his mission or gained it. *Lost your mission?* It could mean so many things, and he did not think this stranger with the weary face and the deep-set eyes wanted to debate the theology of it. So he merely nodded his head and was aware that this satisfied the man.

Otermín smiled. He felt better now than he had felt in days. There was an assurance he had been lacking which seemed to be his again. They were going south. There was no question about it. He did not know why he had made this decision or why he was willing to credit this ragged padre with his new strength, but he was prepared to do it.

"If you will take my horse, Padre, we will return to Isleta."

"Isleta?"

Nodding, Don Antonio explained. "There are a thousand of my people waiting around the bend there. We have come down from the Villa de Santa Fe, and with your help, we will move on today." He thought for a moment. "Have you been to Isleta?"

Fray Julio shook his head. "I tried. I tried to reach Sandia also. That was days ago. There were Indians about then."

While Don Antonio gathered in the reins of his stallion, Fray Julio wondered who this man was who could speak of "my people" with such assurance. As Otermín offered him the horse, he saw the crested helmet hanging from the saddle and wondered who this grandee was.

"My son, I have walked farther than you and am more able to walk."

The Governor nodded and took his place in front of the horse with the padre and together they started walking toward the pueblo.

And as they went, Don Antonio found himself talking to the strange missionary with the figure of a giant and the face of a Holy Man. He told him about the uprising and what he had done. He told him about the battles and the refugees. He told him of the long march south and the disappointment. He expressed his anger at García and his confusion concerning María. The padre only listened. When Don Antonio was done, they stood for a moment looking at the pueblo before them.

Then Fray Julio counselled Don Antonio. "We have travelled a long way, my son. Should we burden ourselves with small problems and resentments? Until we know better, Don Alonso García is an honourable man. And the woman, you must decide if she is the one you want. We must not use people without giving of ourselves. Then we will not be using but sharing."

Otermín wondered what there was about this padre that reminded him so much of the Fray Custodio and so little of Fray Pedro. Then he realized he felt sorry for the poor padre from Valladolid who had failed so badly to meet the needs of those who travelled with him, and Otermín knew the compassion he felt at this moment was not his own but was drawn from the man who walked beside him.

Together they entered the pueblo and made their way to the plaza. As soon as the pair was seen, the refugees collected about the giant figure of the strange padre. Those who were close enough to see his face knelt as he passed, others asked in whispers who he was, while those who at one time or another had known the elegant and arrogant Franciscan of Santa Flora merely stared in stunned silence.

Quintana pushed through the crowd to the Governor's side. Without seeing the padre he spoke to the Commander. "We have been concerned about Your Excellency. And we were wondering . . ." He hesitated to ask the question.

Otermín answered quickly. "Assemble the column and start the march again."

"Yes, Excellency," and he turned to face the padre, who was looking intently at the man he now realized was the Governor and Captain General of Nuevo Mexico. "Fray Julio. It is Fray Julio?"

The padre acknowledged the greeting, not quite certain that it was one. He heard the scorn in the small man's voice, but he did not resent it; was not convinced that it did not belong there. He recognized Quintana and vaguely remembered the quarrels they had had in the past over the services of the Indians. The Throne. The Altar. There could be no quarrel now between Spaniards, believers, followers of God and Christ.

For a long time the two Creoles looked at each other. Then Quintana became aware of the change which others had seen, and that the padre standing before him was no longer the same man he had known for many years as the pastor of Santa Flora—the pueblo of the great mission. Quintana slowly sank to his knees and his head bent down. The padre softly blessed him. Then he reached down, and placing his good hand on the Alcalde Mayor's arm, helped him to rise. Others now knelt with those who had first gone to their knees and a quiet confidence spread over the entire group.

Otermín saw María standing with Inez on the edge of the crowd. He walked over and took her hand and held it so that others could see. When he asked a soldier to fetch a horse "for the Governor's lady," he saw the slight smile of approval on the padre's face.

Then he made out the figure of Fray Pedro coming through the crowd. The stocky peninsular had just completed his morning Mass. His surplice, always neat, always clean and flowing, still draped his broad shoulders. Otermín stood quietly by to watch these two men come together.

With a humility bred from a belief in his own unworthiness, Fray Julio was placing his hand on the heads of those about him and softly blessing them. As he passed the men and women, he reached down to help them to their feet. He was doing this when he looked up and saw Fray Pedro, feet apart, arms at his side, uncertainly watching.

Fray Julio began to weep. He placed his good arm on the shoulder of his Brother, and his head bent forward, and tears began to flow.

People watched in amazement. A small child tugged at his mother's skirt and asked what the tall man was crying about, and though the mother could not explain, she began to weep herself. In a few minutes most of those in the group were sobbing.

Otermín watched them and relaxed. Things were going to be better now. He knew he was not safe yet, knew that they were still short of food, shorter still of weapons and munitions, still in retreat and pursued, but he knew that things were going to be better. There was compassion in the column now, spirit and belief. From these would spring hope, and from hope would come new strength and even greater courage.

He waited for a time. Then he told the strange padre, "We must move on. Will you ride at the head of the column with me?"

Fray Julio shook his head slowly. "My Brother should ride with you."

Fray Pedro still had not spoken. He was visibly shaken, and those about saw the heavy cheek twitch as he looked from Fray Julio to the Governor. This was not supposed to happen. This appearance of a padre from one of the fallen pueblos should not have happened. It was unexpected, and more, this was Fray Julio. Julio. Julio. The giant could be no one else. But this man, this Brother was not what he had known him to be, nor what he or anyone else had ever believed him to be. Fray Pedro did not understand what had happened, and as always when he was confronted by the unexpected, his confusion approached anger.

"If Your Excellency needs a padre to head the column, I shall be pleased to ride with him." But after he had spoken, he knew how pompous and officious he sounded.

Fray Julio placed his good arm about the shorter Brother. "If we could walk together for a time, there is much you could tell me, and some things I believe you might like to know."

Quintana began to organize the column again. It took longer this time than at any other because of the number of persons who wanted to walk beside the tall padre. Otermín was patient. He could afford to be. He had gained a great deal, though he still could not fully define it. Perhaps when night came he could sit by a fire and talk to the strange padre. He, too, wanted to know the man's story. But more, he felt that he wanted to know the man.

Finally, when they started again, Don Antonio rode at the head of the column with María mounted on a bay at his side holding Inez before her on the saddle.

A young soldier began to sing, and as the deep voice of Fray Julio joined in, others began to pick up the song. For the first time since the Spaniards had evacuated the Villa, they were not frightened, though they had unknown leagues before them and hunger riding with them.

> My journeyings are long,
> My slumbers short and broken;
> From hill to hill I wander still,
> Seeking thy token.

16

AT that very hour, twenty-five leagues south of the pueblo of Isleta which he had been forced to abandon twelve days earlier, Don Alonso García, Lieutenant Governor and Lieutenant General of the Province of Nuevo Mexico, sat in the plaza of the pueblo of Socorro listening to a junta evaluate his plans.

When the two refugee rancheros from Taos joined his fleeing column with the news that ten days before they had heard cannon fire at the Villa de Santa Fe, García had presented his plan. It had been a simple proposal: fortify Socorro, garrison it with part of the tropa, and ride north with the remainder to determine if the Governor and his people were dead or alive. But as always in the way of war and peace, it was not to be that simple. For two whole days the junta had been talking.

The sky was grey over the plaza and clouds were gathering over the Sierra Magdalena to the west. García's shirt was open and he kept wiping his face with a huge palm as the talk droned on. It seemed as though each man in the Rio Abajo jurisdiction had something to say about the old warrior's proposal and each had to have his turn.

García winked at Nita, his mistress, as she emerged from a near-by communal house, a water jug in hand. She shook her head in disgust at the proceedings so that only he could see it, smiled at him, and disappeared toward the rio.

He wondered where his wife, Doña Josefa, was; hoped the talk was not disturbing her, and nodded slowly as Maestre de Campo Thomé Domínguez de Mendoza continued to speak. Mendoza, the Alcalde Mayor of Isleta, had been one of those who had initially pressured for the abandonment of Isleta itself. A middle-aged hidalgo, Mendoza spoke with all the assurance he felt belonged to him by both rank and birth. With the eloquence of a hard-drinking man, he tried to impress rather than persuade. However, García had discovered that he need not listen closely so long as he merely nodded his head.

"We have travelled twenty-five leagues. The sun has been hot upon us. The women have left the blood of their feet on the trail. Our bellies are empty. This is the end of no jornada. We must . . ."

Continue to retreat. García nodded. Twenty-five leagues of withdrawing and no word from Otermín in the north. And now that there was word— the eyewitness report of the two men from Taos that there was fighting at the casas reales—the junta wanted to continue the retreat.

"Excellency, we cannot agree with your plan. To split our force in half when we lack food and ammunition and . . ."

And courage. Why not go on? Why not admit that much? García was embarrassed before his sons who had been listening for two days.

"We cannot break up our forces and send men north to see if the Governor lives or not. We have only the word of these two men." Mendoza waved his hand in a wide flourish to indicate the Taoans.

"And these two only saw fighting and heard artillery. They were not inside the Villa. They do not know if any survived. But if we should part our forces . . ."

Half of them. That was all García was asking for. He had made it clear for two days. He was willing even to take less than half and his own sons and ride north. He was a soldier. He did not understand how a man abandoned his commander or a province of España. The Waif of Zacatecas had lost too much blood and borne too many wounds to give up a palm's

breadth of the King's land. He had worked too many years to establish
his own hacienda for his own family to ride away from it. But he had.
Twelve days out of Isleta and fourteen out of the hacienda.

"If we continue south, we will meet Fray Francisco from Ciudad Mexico
with food and supplies and then . . ."

There would be more excuses. More reasons for not riding north to
help the Commander or die. García nodded slowly. Ayeta. The hope and the
legend that had sprung up about the great stores of supplies which had
been moving up from the south for a year. The same caravan his old
compañero Don Pedro de Leiva had been sent with thirty men to escort
north from the pass of the Rio Del Norte. Thirty men. García would have
been willing to settle for thirty men.

"And Your Excellency knows we cannot leave the women here with a
reduced garrison. These Piros Indians of Socorro are not our friends. They
hid the messenger from the north for three days. They did not warn us. They
grow restless. You cannot trust . . ."

The Indians. Yes, the Piros had pledged friendship. They had been left
out of the invitation to rise and kill the Spanish and they were afraid of the
northern Indians now slashing across the countryside. But when had the
time been that a Spaniard could not hold down a pueblo?

"And Excellency, should you ride north now and we remain, it will mean
using up the food we have and being no closer to the supply train. If you should
ride north now . . ."

Mendoza would not ride with you. The train again. And the food.
Never the reason, never the flat statement—*We fear.* Never the admission
that there is no courage left in these men who are still thinking in terms
of ranchos lost and property left behind. And the dead. No mention of the
dead and what they might have died for. Only the going on, the extended
flight to the south with no thought of the continued warning that the
Manso Indians lived to the south and were ready to fight. Don Alonso
nodded. Wondered again where Doña Josefa was, wondered if the guards
were all posted, wondered if the messenger he had sent to the south to
meet with Ayeta had ever arrived, wondered if the talking would continue
forever. He scratched his cheek where a mosquito had bitten him, looked at
the blood on his broad, square fingernails, and nodded again.

"The Villa de Santa Fe being more than sixty leagues from this post
the men who go there would undoubtedly perish because of the great
numbers of the enemy, and those who remain here would inevitably perish
also, without human aid. We must . . ."

Perish in fear. Remain in retreat. García wished for ten men with the
courage of Spaniards. Retreat and the Camino Real again. Twenty-five
leagues in twelve days. The slow scraping feet under the scorching sun,
the crying of weary children, the burn on naked shoulders, the horses
few and the men quarrelling. Retreat again. Another twenty-five leagues.
Another twelve days. And where was he going?

"We must move towards our supplies. We must not risk the lives of our
women. We must . . ."

Hide behind the women. García tried to smile. The sun had cracked his lips and his cheeks had the feel of old leather. It was like coming home again—the dirty campaign in the dirty field. There was a familiar smell about it. But there was a difference now and he wondered if it was only his age. He did not think so. There was more to it than that. There were women now. There was cowardice. And for him there were the long speeches, the small responsibilities and the large ones. Command. How often he had told himself any fool could command where only certain kinds of fools could fight. Now he realized they were both special kinds and he was both of them. The "We musts" continued. García kept nodding.

Then Mendoza began listing his accomplishments in war and peace, all the reasons why he should be heard. Finally, he sat down in the shade of a building. García nodded his approval and at the same time his recognition of the next speaker. He took his daga from his boot and cut a notch in the arm of his chair as the speaker began. He was a middle-aged ranchero from the west who had fled without even pausing to bury his wife of a quarter-century. His spade beard bobbed as he wound his words about his thoughts.

"If Your Excellency should find that Governor Otermín survives, you would have little food and less ammunition to take him, and . . ."

Besides, we do not want to share it. García's fingers ran over the notches. Seventeen. Seventeen speakers and all saying the same thing.

The man from the west spoke on. "Ours is only a small camp composed of a handful of extremely poor and ill-equipped men without supplies or arms, munitions or provisions, and they, being burdened with their families, consisting of women and children and caught between the treasonable Christian Indians and the common enemy, the Apaches whom we have seen every day . . ."

"Enough!" García slammed down his hand on the arm of his chair. Curse the pride of words and the interwoven wrangling. "Enough. Put down what you have said, each of you. Then we will sign it and leave for the south."

To Luis Granillo, the talkative Alcalde Mayor of Jémez whom he had ridden out to rescue weeks before: "I hold you to the task. Draw up the documents and see that they are signed."

He resigned himself to further retreat. The shadows over the Sierra Magdalena had grown longer. Dust swirled to small breezes across the plaza as the men rose to their feet. No rain yet, but García had hopes. His sons gathered behind him as he rose from his chair and turned to them. "In España, it is the junta that decides, and so we must abide without reservation."

His hands dropped as his leonine head fell back, letting the sun fall full upon it. Those watching might have thought he was praying. They had no idea how difficult it was for the old warrior to endure retreat, even lead it.

The hidalgos could not sympathize. Each wished he were commanding the column. The two days would not have been wasted. They would be two days farther south, closer to supplies and safety for their families. The giant soldier from Mexico did not impress them. Most of the rancheros had very little respect for the professional warrior, and to them this great bully of a lieutenant general was only the slightest notch above the criminal soldiers who had been brought north by Fray Francisco Ayeta. A professional fighting for pesos and wine, a mercenary paid to guard the edges of the Empire. This brought no respect from the old men of the old families. The fact that García had brought his family with him, raised his sons, and fought like a wounded bear, made no difference. To the hidalgos, he was still the Waif of Zacatecas, an upstart with pretensions, a white wife, and a piece of land that had been handed to him for services rendered on a long-forgotten battlefield.

They congratulated each other on the victory that saved them from the dangers of a split camp. But they all knew they were still in danger, still must depend upon the giant with the tall sons and the strong hand.

Don Alonso heard the hidalgos, kicked a small rock out of his way and stalked off in fury down the path Nita had taken. Victory. A province lost. The rabble in rout and the soft-mouthed, gentle-handed fools stood about proudly. His great boots crushed a tarantula as he walked, punching fist to palm. Victory. He spat, rubbed his blouse sleeve across his beard and spat again.

He wondered whether, if one of the old men of the old families—the honourable and honorary Maestres de Campo—had argued in favour of a relief expedition, they would be riding north without having wasted two days. It was a tumbleweed speculation. These men would not argue that way. España was a name to them, a remote place where an imbecile king granted alms to worthy colonials and listened to the gibberish of the Council of the Indies. These men had never buried their compañeros on dark nights in unmarked graves. They had never fought for empire as symbol, had never raised a weapon in defence of any ground they did not own. How could they understand how retreat corroded the inside of a professional?

Nita waited for him by the rio. She had heard the angry crack of his fist against his palm and the heavy crunch of his boots on the trail. When he reached her side, he took the water jug she held out to him and emptied it without pausing. Then he turned to look wistfully up the rio.

She put a hand on his arm. "We march south?"

He nodded. "We run, my dear. We run. We turn our backs to battle and we run." His large arm went about her shoulder as they stood together watching the rio move quietly down from the north. The clouds gathered to the west. "It was difficult leaving the hacienda. Difficult leaving Isleta. Crown property. A royal province. But it was possible because we did not know the Captain General was alive and fighting. Now . . ." His fingers dug into her shoulder.

"And the boys," she said. "The boys."

"They can build as I built. I will show them how. We can conquer again."

Nita relaxed. He would swallow the gall of it, shake the mist of defeat from his dark eyes and rise again. She had seen him do it before when he had been overlooked for promotion or had lost a battle. For thirty years they had stood this way. Nita was as hard as the giant beside her. She had been bred in the back rooms and educated in the fields. She had met Alonso and followed him in the vans of the army. She had nursed his wounds and those of his compañeros. She had waited for him during battle. She had been with him in the time between. She was lean and hard with the years of living from small pay to small pay, with the years of bearing. And she did not know how to stop fighting any more than he did. If the smell was familiar to him, the dirty campaign on the dirty field with the lice scrabbling over the carcass, it was equally familiar to her. She had cooked more meals over an open fire beside a strange road than she had ever cooked over the fire of her kitchen.

She stood on her toes and kissed him on the cheek, recalling the cold night in the mountains of Chile where he had found her. The years between had been short, their sons tall, and their own fortunes high. He was right. There would be another hacienda, cattle again and horses.

But now their fortunes were in full retreat.

"Where is Doña Josefa?" he asked her.

Nita shook her head slowly: she did not know. She could have guessed. She could have told him how his wife looked at the Córdoban of the quick daga and the foul mouth. Instead, she only shook her head. Her resentment of Doña Josefa lay not in envy but rather in disgust with the woman, beautiful in a frail way, wise in a self-protective way. Nita had known for years that Alonso's wife held him at arm's length, had turned her cold back on him in the cold bed, had never understood him and never appreciated him.

To Nita, Don Alonso García was a particular and special man. She could recall the night she had told him their son was coming. He had lain in his bed and held her in his arms and spoken to her of the humiliations the son-of-a-nobody must live with, in a world ruled by the sons-of-somebody, the hardships and the ready boot. When morning came, he had trimmed his beard, polished his equipment, and started on the long route that led to his own hacienda, and the post of Lieutenant Governor and Lieutenant General.

He had learned the rules of leadership, supply, and tactics. He had pressed for an understanding of strategy, and those few old commanders who had been trained in the schools of Europe delighted in teaching the heavy-handed giant. They winked behind his back until they finally saw that he understood and appreciated all the implications of command. Then they promoted him again and again. Nita remembered the nights over the long table and Don Alonso learning the intricate ways of words on paper and the complex ways of computing gunpowder loads, rations per hundred and rations per thousand, and how many men can cover how much country in how many hours, and how to read a map the way a sailor reads a map, how to orientate himself on paper with the stars above him. And all the time the promotions, and the pesos saved. Don Alonso García was a special kind of man and the fact that his wife did not see it was shameful. And here lay the roots of Nita's anger and her resentment.

"You could ride north with the boys," she said changing the subject. The words did not come easily because this was casting a die that might never be redeemed.

He swung her about so that she faced him, and kissed her hair. "Thanks. But I am in command here. I cannot leave these fools to ride without me. I threw out the plan to the junta and the junta threw it back. I must live with that." He stared over her shoulder at the rio again. "Tell the boys to pack our gear before morning. I will find Doña Josefa."

He left her to fill the water jug again and strode back to the plaza of Socorro. The men of the junta stood beside the large table which had been dragged out of an abandoned hacienda. They were writing out their reasons why there must be a retreat. When they were done, they signed them. Granillo witnessed each deposition and put it aside. Don Alonso watched for a few minutes, then he approached the table, took a quill pen from the inkwell and read the first document aloud.

> Captain Antonio de Albizu said that he is of the opinion that this camp should march out until they meet the body of tropas with wagons, because their forces are small and because the enemy has the advantage of them. This is my opinion and I sign it with the lieutenant general and his assistant witnesses.

García penned his signature with an angry flourish and picked up the next document, reading aloud again so that all might hear and some, at least, know shame.

> Sargento Mayor Cristóbal Enriques. I state that I agree with the opinion of Maestre de Campo Thomé Domínguez de Mendoza because of everything he says therein being certain and true, under God; and I signed it with the lieutenant general and his assisting witnesses on the said post of El Socorro on 26 Agosto, 1680.

Another signature with a flourish. This was to anger the many who could not even sign their names but believed they knew better than an old warrior. Then García looked about him and began to laugh softly. "We continue our retreat in the morning." Then he paused and added: "Spaniards."

Embarrassed and ashamed, Doña Josefa stood by the window of an abandoned hacienda overlooking the plaza and listened to her husband's loud voice. Don Alonso was behaving like a peasant in front of the hidalgos, men of old wealth and old property who obviously knew what was best for all of them. She crushed the kerchief she carried and turned away from the window. She was angry with García, she could never forgive him. He had made her leave her heavy brocade gowns behind, insisting that she wear a cotton dress like his mistress. He had made her walk with the other women because his wife should set examples. He did not know the prerogatives of rank and position. He did not know how to rule or command. She blamed him that the Indians had risen against them because if he had held them down with a stronger hand the uprising would never have taken place.

She touched her white face and felt the dryness of it, hated what the sun was doing to her, wondered if her cheeks showed red and how many of the young hidalgos of the column had noticed that she was beautiful and if they knew that she had actually been born in Madre España.

Then she heard Don Alonso asking someone if he had seen her and she stepped away from the window into the darkness of the room. She did not want to see her husband now, did not want his crude hands upon her or his rough beard brushing her lips. She was waiting for someone, but it was not her husband.

She tried to ignore the voices outside. She was growing impatient for José Reyes to appear. They had been able to speak to each other only briefly in the past ten days. There were too many men and women eager to gossip, and Josefa knew that any tales would find their way to Nita. And the mestiza was not to be trusted. However, as they had sat about the campfire the evening before, Reyes had asked her to meet him at the hacienda. And so she was here and waiting. He had not appeared yet and she felt put upon. Her anger swelled, and she was about to walk out into the sunlight and face her husband when she heard footsteps entering the hacienda from the rear. She crossed through the empty rooms and found Reyes holding an harquebus in his hands.

"Guard," he explained. "Your husband selected the guard and set me out on a hill." His temper showed as he flung the heavy weapon into a corner.

"We are going south," she said, revealing to him what she had heard from the window.

He smiled thinly, his fingernails raking his beard. "That is where we want to travel."

Josefa nodded. "You have a plan?"

Reyes looked at her hungrily. He appreciated the full figure, the white skin, and the loose dress hanging over the swell of her breasts. He remembered that he had almost kissed her once, wondered what would happen if he tried to do it now.

She repeated her question.

"Yes," he said. "We go south with these people and then we continue south until we reach the first port that has ships sailing for España."

Josefa was quiet for a time. "That is your whole plan?"

He nodded. His thin lips opened and his tongue snaked out and wet them. "It does not take more. We will need horses. When we do, I will have them."

"We will need food."

Again the tongue wetting his lips. She made him nervous, and women were not supposed to do that. Reyes disliked the feeling. He had known wenches of class before, had killed for them and bedded them. But this one left him uncomfortable. For an instant he considered forgetting the entire project. But he remembered the child that had been his and the foot on the doorstep of immortality. This time he wanted a woman of quality to bear his child.

O

"We will have food when we need it," was all he said.

She pressed him further, uncertain now whether she should have committed herself to this stranger. "And money for passage?"

Reyes grinned his weak grin. He felt better now. He could relax. She was a woman and the basic aspects remained unchanged. "We will have all the money we need." And at that moment he made up his mind to know what he was buying before he risked the full anger of España and took a lieutenant governor's wife. He might as well take her out of the province with him and southwest to a port. There would be plenty of time on the way to decide whether or not she went all the way to España with him. He was already evaluating her sales value in the event that he should decide to leave her at some convenient casa de puta.

He crossed the room and placed one slim hand on her arm. "I will see you to España, Señora mia. We will leave this rabble as soon as it is safe enough to travel without them." He started to pull her to him. Then he heard heavy boots on the patio and sprang halfway across the room, his daga coming into his hand as he went.

Don Alonso García strode through the doorway. His brows came tight above his eyes as he stared without speaking from his wife to Reyes and back again. He noted the daga in the man's hand and Doña Josefa's strained gesture as she flicked a nonexistent bug from her sleeve. There was a long silence. The Córdoban felt himself growing stiff, tried to relax and found it difficult, because any overt action had to begin with the Lieutenant General. Don Alonso's heavy hand went to his chest where he wiped the black hair dry.

He could not conceive of Josefa meeting this man of her own volition. This was scum, the dirt of the gutters. This was a thief or a murderer or a fugitive from some greater crime. No. He shook his head slowly and began to cross the room toward the retreating Reyes. His hand came out in front of him, his palm open and up.

"The daga," he said softly.

Doña Josefa stepped out of his way. She saw the broad figure crowding Reyes toward a corner.

"The daga," he said again.

"No," Doña Josefa said.

He ignored her and continued to move in on the man.

"No," she said again. "I thought there was an Indian in here and I asked him to see if the hacienda was safe enough to enter."

García paused. Without turning his head he asked her: "You went to where he was on guard and asked him to come here?"

"Yes," she blurted out.

García saw the man's mouth twitch as he hurled his final question at his wife.

"Where was he stationed?"

There was a long silence and García's heavy boot swung into the man's groin before he could jump back, lash out with his daga, or shift his legs to protect himself.

There was a gulp and a gasp as Reyes dropped the daga and clutched himself. As he bent forward, García's huge hand smashed against the back of his head, felling him to the stone floor. The slight body twitched and lay still.

García swung toward his wife. "The next time a beast like this bothers you, do not try to protect him. It only dirties your name and mine."

Doña Josefa did not understand him at first. Then she realized he was holding only Reyes responsible for the assignation.

"If I hang him, my dear, I will have to tell why. It would befoul my wife before these . . ." he paused, "these cursed dons with the fancy names and the guts of rung chickens."

Josefa stared at him, her dark eyes barely visible in the shadows of the corner where she had hidden herself. "You want to keep your name clean? You want to keep your meaningless name polished? You can show yourself for a fool before them, but it is for me you want to keep your name clean." Her finger tips jabbed her breastbone as she spoke. "You lying fool. You ignorant savage. You make the column wait for two days to beat down your stupidities. You set yourself up as the judge of men whose names were España's before you were whelped in the gutters of Zacatecas. The Waif of Zacatecas."

She did not pause for breath or to see how he was reacting to her sudden attack. She yelled on, not even caring that those in the plaza could hear every word she said to her husband. "If you knew enough to be a lieutenant governor or a lieutenant general, your own wife would not have to walk or be dressed like the peasant bitch you stud. If you were a real don, an hidalgo you would know how your wife should be treated, and you—you want to keep my name clean."

She spat at him, and then she started to laugh.

Don Alonso wiped the spittle off his cheek with his hand, looked at it a moment and then lashed out at her with that palm, striking the side of her face so hard she recoiled against the wall on the far side of the room. Before she could slip to the floor, he caught her in his arms and carried her out of the building, across the plaza to the large, new communal house he had commandeered for his family.

Those men who were not yet done signing their depositions stood with their backs to him. When Don Alonso had disappeared into the darkness of the building, they turned to each other with a smile.

17

THE Indian war chief sat on his horse and watched the long column of Spaniards move out of Isleta to the south. He heard the voices rise and the singing echo across the fields and the distant hills. He noted the vigorous pace set by the Governor and the woman riding for the first time at the

Governor's side. His hand went up and he signalled his men to follow. They mounted and rode parallel to the Whiteface line of march just as they had been riding for days. Their horses were fresher now, their sabres and lances clean. Those few who possessed the captured harquebuses carried them loaded and were prepared to attack. They had waited through the long days of the Spanish halt in Isleta while they wondered how they could best prod the enemy retreat. Now that the enemy was moving again of his own accord, the Indians relaxed and rode easily.

In the days they had travelled since Juan of Taos had sent them out, they had clashed only once with the Spanish. They had lost many men. Sandía had been destroyed. They were not anxious to fight again. The bite of the foreign blade was still keen, the violence with which the enemy moved into battle unforgotten. The war chief rode with one hand on his reins and the other resting on his bare thigh. His square face was set like a block of butte stone. The scar down his cheek burning red on copper from his right eye to his lip reminded him how dangerous this enemy was and how much he hated him. The warriors riding behind the war chief would gladly have abandoned the march, would have been willing to accept the enemy's departure as a certainty and ride home. The day of freedom was long behind them and the weeks that had followed were the most difficult they had ever known. There was not a man riding there but had lost a brother, a father, or a friend. It was time to turn and ride north, time to accept the victory for a fact and turn back to the homes of their mothers or their women.

But the war chief rode on. His orders were clear. The tale had reached him of the defection of Juan of Taos, but it did not matter. That youthful warrior had known this enemy and he had said ride after them.

From a distant hill to the east a pillar of smoke built toward the sky. The war chief's hand went up as he paused to read it. A smile wrinkled the scar. The Spanish at Socorro had finished their talking and were on the road again. Now there were two Spanish columns in full retreat through the pueblo kingdom. His face set as he thought about the message. Then he signalled for one of his men to fall back and relay the details north to Popé who was waiting for word at the Villa. The hand went up waving the column on. They had a long way to travel yet and the enemy was setting the pace.

One day slipped by to the next. The two Spanish columns straggled on. The Indians followed both of them and sent their reports back to the waiting native priest who had turned the capital of the enemy into his own headquarters.

"The Whitefaces move slowly."

"The southern column has paused at the pueblo of Senecú."

"The northern column has tried to capture cattle on the west bank. We have turned them back. They continue to move on."

"Both columns move again."

"The northern column halts at the hacienda of Valencia." "The northern column sends four soldados and a Blessing Man south. We have permitted them to pass." "The southern column has stopped at Fray Cristóbal." "The northern column has stopped at the pueblo of El Alamillo."

18

DON ALONSO GARCÍA stood beside his great stallion and waved the column past him. His temper showed as he applied his heavy boot to a dawdling soldado's rear. He had the sour taste of withdrawal in his mouth and was choking on it. He had known the dour looks of his wife as she glared at him from her place in the column and he felt his patience had just about come to an end. Over the next rise was Fray Cristóbal. Here he would place his guard out to watch the Indians pressing his rear, bed down for the night and wait for morning to retreat again.

He saw the clipped head of Reyes as the soldier rode by him. Wiping a large hand across his face, García wondered where this thief had stolen a horse while better men walked. He shrugged. From the green look on the slim man's long face, he knew that the kick he had given him had caused injuries that would be felt a long time. He smiled to himself as he imagined how each jounce of the saddle must tear the man's innards. Then he spat after Reyes.

His eyes came to rest upon his wife walking with the other women. She turned away so that she would not have to look at him, and as she started to wander unseeing off the trail, Nita took her arm and guided her on. His head turned toward the rear of the column where Nita's tall sons rode. These were men, not dandies, not cowards. They were the only ones he trusted to protect the end of the long line from the sudden attack that could roll it up like a lady's ball of yarn.

Into Fray Cristóbal. The sun over it. The mountains beyond and south. Named according to tradition for Fray Cristóbal de Salazar, cousin of the settler, Oñate. A small camp site—two buildings, scattered trees, water—and directly to the south the thirty leagues of land named Jornada del Muerto.

García led his column in. He waved to the right and the left, motioning them to throw down their baggage, scatter, and rest. Then he went in search of water. Maestre de Campo Mendoza rode with him. The path to the rio was clear.

Neither of them spoke as they swung off their horses and bellied down to the ground. Mendoza cupped his hands and drank slowly while the Lieutenant General dipped his huge grey head full into the stream several times, to rise blubbering and spewing, but cooler. When they were done, they pulled themselves to their feet and faced each other as they had every night since they had left Isleta.

"Set the night guard," García ordered as he did each time, taking no chance that the hidalgo would forget to do it or forget to whom he was responsible.

Mendoza nodded. His anger was under control. His dislike for the bar-

barian had grown beyond his ability to hide it any longer, but he knew who
was in command.

Don Alonso led his horse back up the trail to the camp. Nita was waiting
for him with one of his sons. He threw the youth his reins and walked back
to the place she had selected for them.

"The buildings?" he asked.

"Both crawl with lice," she explained as she pointed to an open place
between the two small houses. "We will remain outside."

He nodded. "And Doña Josefa?"

"She sulks over there," pointing to a small group of women who sat
spreading goat fat over their sunburned hands.

García snorted. "And the soldado?"

Nita knew whom he meant. "He stands over there waiting to talk to her
as he has for days."

Mendoza watched after his commander. His hand came up as he picked
a crawling louse off his beard, crushed it between his nails and called to
several of his compañeros to help him set the guard.

The fifteen hundred men and women scattered over the area, quarrelling
over the small stores of grain they found in one of the buildings, over the
rooms with windows, over the abandoned benches and tables. Several large
fires were built from native furniture and newly felled trees. They glowed
hot in the crowded plaza and smelled of the spitted beeves. There was the
crackle of dripping fat and the constant noise of the horses going from guard
post to guard post. The sky clouded grey as evening approached, and García,
lying on his back between the buildings, stared at it hopefully. Rain would
make it cooler. The dust would settle again. The excrement would not smell
so strong. The Indians would be less likely to attack. He would welcome the
rain. His arm reached out and touched Nita's hair. She rolled over on the
spread blanket, placed one hand on his and held it tightly.

"We will get through," she said.

His fingers closed over hers.

They said nothing for a long time. Suddenly Don Alonso sat up and
stared straight ahead. A crowd was gathering about a strange rider who
stood talking to Mendoza. The Lieutenant General rose and, bootless, strode
over to them.

Mendoza was asking the stranger, "And they are all right to the north?"

"They were when I left them. But I must talk to Lieutenant General
García."

Mendoza did not notice the giant standing beside him as he spoke. "I will
hear your message."

The messenger hesitated.

"Tell him the message," García said softly, looking over the head of the
Maestre de Campo.

"I have left the column at El Alamillo," explaining to no one in particular.

García thought for a moment. "Above Socorro?"

The soldier nodded. "There are four of us here and a padre."

Relaxing his grip on Mendoza's arm, Don Alonso said loudly so that those gathered about could hear, "See that the others are fed and that the padre joins his brothers."

Then he reached an arm out, half encircled the courier and drew him into the narrow space between the two buildings where he had been resting. He called to a guard: "See that no one interrupts."

He waved the soldier to the ground. The man knelt beside the blanket where Nita sat. "Otermín lives?"

The soldier nodded. "He has been wounded many times, but he lives."

"How many others?"

"A thousand more or less."

"Supplies?"

"Almost none. We will be hungry in days."

García wiped the first drops of rain from his bared forehead. "And you carry orders?"

"Only one."

"And that?"

"Lieutenant Governor Don Alonso García is to join His Excellency as soon as possible."

García thought quickly. He was sixteen leagues south of Socorro now. Six leagues below the inhabited part of the province. Nine leagues below the pueblo of Senecú. Almost sixty leagues above the Pass of the Rio del Norte. If his messenger had reached Fray Francisco and his old compañero, Don Pedro de Leiva, supplies should be on the way.

He looked at Nita who sat smiling. This was the vindication of his plan. If they had stopped in Socorro, if the junta had agreed to his plan, given him the men and let him ride north, the gap between columns would be closed and everyone would be safer. He smiled back at her.

"Fetch Mendoza."

Nita took his hand as he helped her up, brushed off her skirt, and disappeared barefooted into the crowd.

"How many soldados does the Captain General have?" García asked.

The messenger thought for a time. "Less than you. Perhaps eighty."

García shook his head in disappointment. "The fighting was bad?"

The courier said nothing as he thought of the thirst and the deaths. Finally, he nodded. "It was bad, Excellency."

Then Mendoza joined them. García waved him to a seat on the edge of the blanket.

"You have your opportunity, amigo. You will be in command of the camp here. I will ride north with an escort and with Granillo of Jémez, who recorded the depositions explaining why we had to run away."

Mendoza shook his head in disbelief. "The Governor asks us to wait for him?" He was talking to the courier who, unused to hearing orders questioned, looked from the Maestre de Campo to the Lieutenant General. He decided not to answer.

García slapped him on the shoulder in approval. "You want to ride back with me?"

"If you wish, Excellency."

"No need. You have ridden enough." García stood up and called loudly so that he could be heard in the camp ground beyond, "Granillo."

The excitable Alcalde Mayor joined them, and García gave his orders quickly.

"We ride out in an hour, you and I and an escort. Select the best horses. See that the arms are in good condition. Take food enough for all of us for two days' hard riding, take extra horses for we will ride them dead. Pronto, amigo mio."

García was happy now. He could handle this situation. He knew how to think in these patterns. It was the talk and the bicker and the jealousy and the women that had bothered him ever since he had left the confines of his own hacienda. He knew his limitations and his strength. This was like campaigning again.

Then he gave his orders to Mendoza. They were brief and firm. "You will see that this place is fortified. You will see that there is an exact distribution of food. You will not permit the guard to be lax. You will not move one step farther south from this location until you hear either from me or from Governor Otermín. Should he order this column moved north again, you will move north with all possible dispatch."

"What if our stores are gone?"

"You will stay here and starve. But in no event will you move without orders."

Mendoza acknowledged the command with a surly bobbing of his head.

García smiled. "If supplies come from the south, you will see that they do not pause here, but are sent at once to the Governor. He and his people fought; we merely fled."

Then to Granillo who had joined him, "I want all of the documents which have been written and most especially those in which the junta demanded withdrawal from Isleta and Socorro." He thought a moment. "Be certain that copies of the messages we sent to the Governor informing him of our plans are also there."

His huge fist smashed into his palm with a loud noise. He grinned at his mistress with the joy of a young man. "They live. They live. God has blessed all, for they live. And we may not have to run any farther." She saw the dampness about the corners of his eyes and knew that he was as close to tears as she had ever seen him. Both of his huge palms spread over her arms as he pulled her to him.

"Take care." As his lips brushed her hair, he saw the grey that streaked it. "Take care."

Then he strode out of the area between the buildings into the street. Doña Josefa sat on a ledge, kicking her feet into the dampening ground. García looked up and felt a few small drops of rain on his face. Not yet. Soon. He crossed over to where his wife sat.

"I ride north now. The Governor has sent for me. You will be safe. You will remember that you are my wife. You will show the women here how the wife of a commander acts."

She did not look at him as he spoke. Instead she saw his stocking feet in the dust and the indignity of it.

"You are my wife, Josefa. Never forget that."

He turned away in anger. He had wanted to kiss her, at least hold her, tell her he regretted that he had to strike her. His fist smashed into his palm again as he stalked off in the approaching darkness to speak to his sons before leaving. His two oldest were posted as guards. He had never sought extra privileges for them, and the Maestre de Campo had taken advantage of this fact.

"You will listen as always to your mother and you will protect Doña Josefa from any trouble. And do not forget whatever your mother says you are to do is as though I had said it."

The boys nodded in the darkness.

"Watch over your younger brothers. They are too eager."

Again the nods. He placed a hand on a shoulder of each and squeezed tightly. Neither winced as they felt the pain of it. The game was an old one and passed as affection with their father.

"Good boys," he said as he walked back to the camp in the darkness. No rain yet but the evening was cooler. The ride would be long, and in rain. He shrugged. Granillo was waiting with the escort and the extra horses. García looked about at the crowd that was gathered to see him off. There were smiles on many of the faces. A thousand people to the north meant that husbands or wives, children or relatives or friends were still alive. Nita stood in the shelter of a doorway with his boots. He pulled them on, nodded to her, sought out the face of Josefa and raised his hand in a half-salute as he swung himself up into the saddle. The young man who had brought him the word that Jémez was under attack weeks before sat mounted beside him. A good youth, hard and willing. Granillo sat uncomfortably with the pouch slung from his saddle.

His two old campañeros were riding with them. One leaned over and kissed a wench with sad eyes and long lashes. García smiled. She was the one they had found with the others on the night of the uprising. He recalled her naked on the floor of the barracks with his foot on her rump and he was certain she would remain faithful to her soldier until the darkness swallowed him up on the edge of the camp. He held out his hand and took the lance someone placed in it.

"We will let you know the Governor's plans as soon as we learn them."

His hand went up and the lance pointed north. "We ride, amigos." His heavy spurs jutting out behind the wooden shoe stirrups dug into the side of the stallion and it leapt forward brushing several men and women aside. He smiled at Nita and disappeared into the night. The small detachment jabbed heel to horse and followed.

19

THE small tropa of Don Alonso García rode back through the night over the same route they had travelled through the day. Twice they paused to change horses. About midnight the rain began to fall, lightly at first and then more heavily. The Lieutenant Governor turned his face to the sky, felt the cool waters on his cheeks and his brow and prayed that the rain would deter the Indians he knew were watching him as he rode.

His old compañeros travelled at his side. The one he had seen kiss the mestiza wench was silent. The other only asked what would happen when they reached El Alamillo. García shrugged and spurred his horse. The youth from Jémez galloped beside Granillo, his Alcalde Mayor. The rain blinded him, and twice when he fell behind to wipe his face, Granillo did not hesitate to ride on without him. The petty official was creating wordy protests in his mind that he would make to the Governor about the arrogant and harsh way in which he and the others of the column had been treated by García. As he galloped on through the darkness, he had bright visions of himself being named lieutenant general of the province.

The pace was fast. The trail, difficult in the light of day, was almost impossible at night, but García never faltered as he pressed ahead.

The rain stopped and when the sun rose, it burnt away the low mists that had gathered over the ground. García's hand went up. He reined in his horse and dropped from his saddle to the ground beside the rio. Drinking quickly, he turned to the two soldiers who carried the food bag.

"We will eat now."

And they did, without talking. Then they watered their animals and rode on. Through the day they continued the hard pace and when night came again they did not stop.

It was almost morning of the next day when the fires ahead revealed the diminutive pueblo of El Alamillo. García's hand rose. The horsemen slowed pace, organized in twos, and trotted slowly to the edge of the town.

A sleepy guard stepped out from behind a tree, with an harquebus in his hand pointing directly at them. "Who is it?" in a half-frightened voice.

García identified himself and rode by without pausing, brushing the guard aside with the rump of his horse as he passed. Inside the town, he saw refugees sleeping in groups about the fires. Several men rose to see who had joined them, and a youth with a pocked face approached as García dismounted.

"I am Don Alonso García," the Lieutenant Governor announced loudly. His heavy head slowly turned to survey the plaza. Guards were posted on roofs. The fires were lighted on the edge of the pueblo to reveal any infiltration. Women, children, and wounded slept in the centre area of the plaza. García was satisfied that the Captain General knew his business.

He threw the reins of his horse to the small man with black teeth who officiously bustled through the crowd. Startled, the man caught the reins and seemed unable to decide whether he should keep them or not. Then Don Alonso saw a tall padre step out of the darkness and was puzzled. He thought he recognized this cleric from somewhere, but the face was different. And besides, Julio Malindez would not be here running south with a rabble army. Then he knew it *was* Julio, and asked, "Where is the Governor, Padre?" ignoring the small man holding his horse.

The padre nodded and smiled. "This is Luis Quintana, the Alcalde Mayor of La Cañada," introducing the small man with the black teeth.

García nodded. "The Governor?" he repeated, brushing by Quintana as the padre pointed to a small estancia at the edge of the pueblo. When Granillo started to follow, García whirled about and planted himself in the man's path.

"We will send for you when we need you."

To the others: "Rest, amigos mios. It has been a long ride." Then he pushed the crowd aside as the questions started spilling over the plaza. Who is alive? Who is dead? The exchange in choked voices, or casually, with bland curiosity. The exchange with fear and hesitation. The question about a brother, a father, a wife, a padre, a woman. García left the answers to those with him and walked up the two steps to the house the Governor had commandeered.

A guard at the entrance came to attention. His boots were dusty, his uniform wrinkled, but his salute indicated that he had once been taught how to greet an officer. García returned the salute and swept into the house without waiting to be announced. He found himself alone in the sitting room for a moment. Then a woman with a blanket pulled about her appeared in a doorway.

"I seek Governor Otermín," he snapped.

She disappeared, closing the door behind her. García touched a padded bench with his finger tips. He would have liked to stretch out and rest. The ride had been difficult, and he felt each one of his years now. Bending over, he wiped the dust from his boots with an open palm, buttoned his tunic carefully, wished it was not so dirty and waited on his feet for the Governor. He knew very little more about him than the fact that he was a professional soldier, a widower, and a grandee.

Then the door opened again and the Governor stepped out into the sitting room, his sabre at his side, his tunic buttoned, white cuffs and collar showing, the shiny boots reflecting the single candle in the room.

García saluted formally.

The smaller man drew himself up to his full height. His eyes were barely visible but the crows'-feet about them grew deeper as Otermín stared at his subordinate. He had waited a long time for this burly figure in the sloppy uniform before him. He noted the boots, the buttoned tunic, and appreciated the snap of the salute. Otermín relaxed: he knew this man, he had met the likes of him a hundred times on a hundred battlefields. This was the old professional risen through the ranks. Better perhaps than the highly trained youth without experience but no match in the long years for the educated man with experience.

"You are Lieutenant General Don Alonso García?"

"Yes, Excellency."

Otermín took one step forward so that he could see the man's face better when he told him, "You are under arrest. You have disobeyed direct orders to remain where you were and not withdraw unless you had specific permission to do so. You have abandoned Crown property and your own responsibilities. I shall see that this arrest is placed in writing. You will have an opportunity to be heard."

García stood rigid as he spoke. "I am thankful that Your Excellency is safe and that those with you still live. As for orders to remain in Isleta, they were never received. I sent four messengers north to inform you that my withdrawal was necessary."

Otermín half-closed his eyes. "There will be a formal study of the charges. Have you brought any supplies with you?"

García shook his head as he answered. "We approach starvation, Excellency. However, word was sent urging Don Pedro de Leiva to hurry north with supplies from the Pass. I left orders that those wagons were to be brought directly to you."

The Governor did not seem to hear what had been said. García had seen the reaction many times, and when the Commander walked past him, forcing him to turn about and face the candela, he had to hold back his annoyance. If Otermín knew him, he also knew the Captain General. He was the old officer who held himself aloof from his men, patted their heads or kicked their bottoms to get what he wanted, and if that did not bring results, he would hang a few men and promote a few. But always the right men because he had been taught the importance of being a good leader.

García stood without speaking. He had not been excused, and there were many things he wanted to tell this hard-faced peninsular who stood before him.

"What is the state of your column?" Otermín slipped into a chair though he did not offer one to his subordinate.

García held himself erect. "There are fifteen hundred more or less, half-naked, bad shoes, few horses. We have almost a hundred and fifty head of cattle. From the scattered reports I believe there are over two hundred dead in Rio Abajo, Jémez, and adjacent jurisdicciones. We had no warning other than the one you will find recorded in the documents."

Otermín thought for a long time as he stared at the giant before him. He wondered how close the southern jurisdicciones had been to siege. "They permitted you to withdraw without a fight?"

At first García did not know if this was a statement or a question.

"We have fewer than one hundred soldados, Excellency. Most of those are worthless—rancheros who can hold a weapon, criminals from the south, fugitives from justice in Mexico, and youths too young to be afraid."

The Captain General pressed his point: "But you were not attacked?"

"No, Excellency. Not after the first day. There were refugees. There was little food. The Indians in Isleta outnumbered us three to one. They became increasingly restless and we heard that those who were in the north would come south to burn us out."

Again the pressure. "But you were not attacked?"

García stiffened. "I have no excuse, Excellency. The circumstances forced us to withdraw." Then he threw his own opinion quietly between them. "The junta voted to withdraw."

"And you?" Otermín himself felt better now. His first opinion of the man was holding up, but there was more here than a clumsy giant with a glib tongue and a heavy hand.

"The papers will fully explain the situation and what has happened, Excellency. Included there you will find copies of the proposals which I sent to the Villa de Santa Fe for Your Excellency's approval."

Otermín rubbed his right arm with his left hand, noticed that María, dressed, stood in the doorway behind García. There was a slight smile on her face. He wondered how much of what was taking place she understood. He wanted to smile at her, but it would give the Mexicano the wrong opinion.

"You kept copies of each document that you prepared and each message that you sent?"

García wanted to laugh. He was certain this commander had done the same thing himself. It was part of their training. It was part of being an administrator in the Empire of Carlos run by all the small clerks behind the large tables in Ciudad Mexico and probably Madrid itself. "Yes, Excellency. I have full copies of every message that went forward."

The Commander closed his eyes and thought about all the thousands of cases of such documents that must be buried in the vaults and rooms where the Council of the Indies met.

"Where are your records?"

"The Alcalde Mayor Granillo of Jémez has brought them with him."

The nod again. The small man for the small task, the civil official serving the military man and the fact made clear so that none would miss it. He rose to his feet and went to the front entrance of the house. Quintana was there with a stranger who carried a pouch.

"Who is Granillo of Jémez?"

The stranger stepped forward and Otermín held his hand out for the pouch. Surprised, the stranger handed it to him. Then Otermín directed Quintana, "Prepare papers of notification to Lieutenant General Alonso García that he is formally placed under arrest for deserting his post without permission." He thought a moment. "I will sign them."

And when he turned back to the estancia, he felt a hand on his arm. It was the Alcalde Mayor of Jémez. Looking from the hand to the man's face, Otermín clearly showed his animosity: only a fool touched the Governor without permission. Granillo saw his mistake and dropped his hand.

"Apologies, Excellency. I merely wanted to tell you how right I think you are in arresting that man. He has shamed us all and mistreated us and endangered our lives and . . ." The words splashed nervously over the tense air.

The Governor cut him short. "You wish to testify against him?"

Granillo smiled, feeling important and hoping that those in the south would hear of this. "Yes, Excellency. I would gladly testify against this man. He is nothing but a common soldado who has travelled with a woman who would shame his good wife. He is the type who fights for pay and does not respect his betters, those who pay taxes and hire such as he and . . ."

The Governor cut him short again. "You will have an opportunity to be heard." To Quintana: "Prepare the papers at once. See that he receives them."

Otermín returned to the sitting room where García stood cursing Granillo. For himself he did not mind, but when a bantam rooster whose life he had saved spoke so of Nita. . .   The woman standing behind him had heard the strident voice of the Alcalde Mayor of Jémez and watched the large hands of the Lieutenant Governor and wondered what he thought as he opened and closed them.

Standing before his second-in-command, the Governor said flatly, "I see you have also engendered great loyalty in those who follow you."

García did not defend himself of the charge.

The Commander waited for an answer, and when it did not come, he merely shook his head slowly as though annoyed. "I will read the papers and listen to those who came with you. There is a room off the piazza where you may rest. Señora Valdivia will show you the place."

The woman stepped out of the doorway and García bowed clumsily. "Señora."

Otermín left the room and García knew the interview was over. The slim woman with the white face, the high, flat cheekbones, and the dark hair stood staring at him.

"The room, Señora?" he finally asked. His legs were weary. He had ridden to the end of his endurance only to be arrested for his efforts—for the long retreat over the bad ground with the Indians slashing at his heels and the hidalgos cutting into his authority with every step he took. His huge fist smashed into his palm as he released his anger against his own stupidities.

The woman took him to a large room where there was a bed with a straw mattress and a blanket spread over it. The basin was empty.

"I will see that someone brings Your Excellency water."

"Gracias, Señora." When she left the room, García slumped down on the bed. With great effort he pulled his heavy boots off and dropped them onto the stone floor, slipped his baldric over his head and with one hand quickly unbuttoned his tunica. He hung it over the bed and fell over onto his back. For a time he stared at the ceiling. He wished he had Nita beside him now. He wanted to ask her how he had misjudged the danger of fools like Granillo. How he had ever placed himself in a position where after thirty-five years of serving His Majesty he should find himself under arrest for crimes which could mean death. He closed his eyes against the light streaming in the window. When María Valdivia returned a few minutes later with the pitcher of water, Don Alonso was already asleep.

20

FOR two days José Reyes had lounged about the Fray Cristóbal Camp to the south waiting for an opportunity to meet privately with Doña Josefa. Their last meeting had cost him more pain and anguish than he had ever received in his life and had left much unresolved. He brooded on García's ready victory over him and believed he knew the quickest route to revenge. It was his good fortune that he shared a mutual enemy with the hidalgos of the column, for he no longer served as a guard or drew any of the other duties about the camp.

Reyes took advantage of Mendoza's small revenge upon the absent Lieutenant Governor and used his free time to wait for long hours outside the area where the García family bedded down for the night, and each time Doña Josefa emerged onto the street, he followed several paces behind her and García's two sons who accompanied her wherever she went.

This morning he waited for an opportunity to approach her. The sun was high. The camp bustled with its small business of survival and comfort-seeking. The women were washing clothes, the children playing, and the men sat around telling each other lies about the vast losses they had suffered at the hands of the Indians and how much recompense they would claim from the government in Madrid. They had long ago convinced themselves that the King would pay for their losses from the royal purse, and as none of them had any practical experience in dealing directly with the Throne and its representatives, they lived happily in their illusion.

Several sat under trees near the two small buildings watching Reyes as they talked. They had seen him sitting in the same place for days and they knew why he waited. Doña Josefa was a fine-looking woman. Several even hinted quietly what they would like to do to her if they had the opportunity. All agreed that she was much too good for the bear she had married.

One man winked at another when she emerged into the clearing, looking about her, nodded acknowledgement to Reyes and the men in the shade of the trees, and made her way toward the rio. The two youngest García boys followed her discreetly down the small path that led to the stream. One of them bent over to pick up a stone which he threw into the water and watched splash. The other knelt twice to polish the tip of his heavy boot. Each time, the distance between the boys and Doña Josefa grew longer and that between them and Reyes who followed, smaller. Finally one of them spun about and grasped Reyes by the collar before he could step back. But the

Córdoban had his daga in his hand and against the boy's side in an instant, the first pressure of the point bringing blood trickling through his shirt. The lad flung Reyes away from him, but not before the assassin had taken another swipe at him with his blade and this time the point cut deeper and the blood spurted across the white cotton. The surprised youth stared at the ever-enlarging pattern on his stomach and then grasped his hands over it in pain. And by the time his brother had torn away the bloody shirt, revealing the slightness of the wound, had washed off the blood and tied the remainder of the shirt tightly about the cut, both Reyes and Doña Josefa had disappeared.

It had been the boys' own idea to frighten away the Córdoban. They had not let their two older brothers into their plan and now they knew that they would have to face them as well as their mother unless they found Doña Josefa. Scrambling back up the rocky path, they looked about the crowded camp for some sign of the missing pair, but there was no sign though they walked the length of the area. Finally they made their way back to the space between the buildings where their mother napped on a large blanket, woke her up, and told her what had happened. She listened quietly, and when they were done, she thought for a while. Then she said they were to relieve their older brothers at guard and send them back to her.

She remembered Alonso's admonition: "Take care. Take care of yourself and the boys and her." She rose to her feet and watched the youths disappear. She was proud of the boys but she would not tell them so, because they had acted on their own and she knew Alonso would not approve of such a display of eagerness. As she went out into the sun, she recalled the nights he had spent talking to young soldiers all over the Indies, how he had warned them of the sin of eagerness and the stupidity of action without plan. Now her sons had fallen into that error and she would have to find a way out.

For a long time she looked at the men seated under the trees staring at her. She did not need to hear the whispers. García's mestiza mistress was going to make trouble for his peninsular wife. Shrugging, she walked away. Her figure was full but not fat. Her breasts filled out the loose cotton dress she wore, and her arms were gold in the bright sun where most of the women's were red with burn. Her black hair, straight and long, hanging in two tight braids, as well as her large nose and full upper cheeks, told of her Indian mother. However, Nita was different from most mestizas—the parent of whom she had been ashamed was her Whiteface father. He had rebelled against the King and died a coward, screaming for mercy with his hacienda burning about him while his Indian kitchen wench held his head and tried to comfort him. Nita, watching beyond the reach of the soldiers who had fired the house, knew that her mother had never whimpered as the flames burnt her into a sticky mass with the man she held in her arms. And Nita was proud of her mother and proud that she herself was partly Indian.

She watched her two youngest sons disappear in search of their brothers and started to walk through the camp that was Fray Cristóbal. Somewhere Doña Josefa was meeting José Reyes. She had to find them.

When her husband's son had grabbed at Reyes, Josefa had heard the surprised gasp behind her, had whirled about, and seen the quick daga draw blood. She fled, stumbled up a stony path, rose, and limped on. Then Reyes was beside her taking her hand. Together they paused to rest. His bloody weapon was stuck in the sash at his waist. His eyes were half shut from the brightness of the sun.

"They will be after us in a minute," he said softly, pulling her into the back of one of the buildings which proved to be empty. Urged on by her own needs and desires as well as by her long anger at her husband, she followed. Reyes pushed her into a room and looked about. They were alone. The light from a small window showed a straw pallet spread on the floor, a long bench beneath the window, and an Indian blanket hanging on the wall. He removed the heavy sabre and scabbard he carried, set them by the doorstep and reached out for Josefa.

She backed away across the small room. Reyes's long patience approached an end. He caught her arm and drew her to him, clumsily, trying to kiss her, as one hand pressed against the back of her head. She struggled at first, writhing in his arms and trying to push him away. But he slowly bent her head toward him, aware all the time that she was not shouting for help or fighting very vigorously to protect herself. He continued the pressure on the back of her head until their lips met. Then she relaxed and was limp in his arms returning his kiss. His nervous hand wandered over her bodice, caressed her breasts, and slowly began to rub her thighs. She no longer protested but pressed tightly against him. Once she sighed and shook her head. His hand grabbed at her hair and held her tightly while he kissed her again. Then her arms went about his neck as if to hold herself up. He let go of her hair and tore the laces of her dress. One hand sought the warm softness of her breasts while the other, flat upon her buttocks, pressed her close. His knees collapsed and they stumbled awkwardly to the floor. Reyes was fumbling with her skirt when all of his professional years came to his aid. He rolled over on his back and looked up to see Nita standing in the doorway. One of his arms was under Josefa who stared up at the middle-aged mestiza. Reyes's other hand reached for the daga in his sash.

Nita watched him as he stretched his hand over his head, flat on the floor, juggling the weapon. Only when he set the tip of the daga between his fingers did she realize that he was going to throw it. She jumped to one side, and when he shifted his arm to aim again, she saw the sabre. Grabbing the heavy cutlass which he had set beside the door, Nita jerked it toward the killer. The loose scabbard struck his face and spoiled his aim as the daga hit the wall behind her and fell to the floor with a clatter. Josefa whimpered. Nita looked down at the pair, the bared blade of Reyes's sabre in her hand. Pinned to the floor by the weight of Josefa on his left arm, the assassin half threw, half shoved her at the sabre, and as the two women came together, Nita jerked the blade aside, sparing Josefa's life. Both women tumbled to the floor, while Reyes plunged across it for his daga. Recovering the familiar weapon, he scrambled to his feet. He had to kill the intruder, and as all of his training had taught him that no man suffered a witness to live, he knew he also had to kill the other wench he had wanted so badly. Furious, he stepped forward to drive his daga into the older woman who looked up at him from the floor, and as he did so, she raised the sabre. His own momentum drove the point of it through his belly. There was a numbing pain and for an instant he was startled. Then he hurled his daga. It entered Nita's right breast. She dropped the sabre and clutched the hilt of the daga, tried for a moment to remove it as she rolled from side to side on the dusty floor. Then she stopped rolling and her hands relaxed and came away from the blade. Her mouth opened wide as though she were going to say something. Her eyes closed. There was a gasp of pain.

Reyes watched her die as he held his hand over his stomach. He had seen so many die, he wondered why he was watching this death with such fascination. The face of the old mestiza wench was not beautiful. Her nose was too large, her lips too full, her skin too dark. He was recording the details he did not like and wondering why he was doing it. In all his long intimacy with death, he had never before been wounded. And now that he was, now that the blood of the sabre thrust ran down the legs of his pantalones, he sought refuge in the face of a dead woman. He was trying desperately not to think of what had happened to him, not to believe that perhaps there was nothing he could do about it. He vaguely saw Josefa struggle to her feet beside him and back away against the wall, and all he could think of was how much he had wanted her and what she could have given him, and then as his hand came away from his belly and he stared at the blood on it, he thought of the Indian wench who had borne him a child. There had been a child and a future for Reyes, but now the child was dead and he was dead. Very slowly, as though he were reluctant, as though he had not quite made up his mind that he wanted to do it, José Reyes crumbled to the floor across Nita's feet. His bloody hand crossed his face as he sought to wipe away a mist that was gathering there. Suddenly, Josefa saw him smile. He was reminded of a foggy night in a dark alley of Córdoba. Then he was dead.

No one had heard them. No one came to discover what had happened in the small room of the empty house. Josefa remained in the corner where she had slunk. The two bodies on the floor in front of her bled for a time and then stopped bleeding. She knew both of them were dead.

The Córdoban had been killed trying to protect himself, hunger for her in his eyes to the end. But Josefa could not understand why the mestiza with the black braids and the large nose had died. She had made no attempt to kill Garcia's wife.

Then it slowly came to Josefa Garcia that Nita had died protecting Don Alonso's Spanish lady and that she was that lady.

Fumbling with nervous fingers, she tied the laces of her bodice together. Then she slipped past the two corpses on the floor, and out into the sunlight by a rear exit. Stumbling back over the trail she had used to escape from the García boys, she made her way to the rio. There she repaired the damage to her clothes and began the slow walk up to the plaza and back to the place where the García family slept. She was confident now that no one would be able to prove that she had ever been in the room where the bodies lay. No one would ever be able to say for sure that she knew why the man José and the woman Nita had died.

When Josefa reached the camp area, she was aware of the heads that turned in her direction and the puzzled stares. She drifted back to the blanket in the shadows between the houses and lay down. Later when the García boys asked her if she had seen their mother, she shook her head and pretended to sleep. And when the first shouts rose over the camp proclaiming the discovery of the bodies, she appeared as startled as those about her.

No one knew how terrified she was that night when she went to sleep or how much she hoped she would never hear again of the mestiza or Reyes. And when the bodies were interred in the dark earth and the prayers read over them, Doña Josefa remained in the place in the shade where she pretended to sleep and waited for the arrival of her husband. She could face the padres. She could face the day, and she could face the darkness. She could face García's sons, but she did not know if she could face García.

21

THEY buried the possessions of Askon and his followers at Galisteo.

When they were done they returned to the pueblo and killed the Spanish women for whom there was no longer any need.

And only an old man riding north from el Paso del Norte cared any longer what happened to the family of Don Pedro de Leiva.

Don Pedro de Leiva was galloping north with forty soldiers and four carts of supplies. He had been travelling over the hot countryside since the thirtieth day of August. Dust filled the air and fell away behind the small column. The small wooden wagons bounced along with a clatter of wheel on stone.

Don Pedro was a heavy man, fat with his years of wealth and power, quick-tempered and assured of his authority. He had been a junior officer in his youth, serving the King in Chile and Cuba. Then he had married and returned to his father's hacienda. In Galisteo he had been the only law and no one had ever questioned him. Now, as he guided his small tropa over the vague trail that was so loosely known as the Camino Real, he wondered what had happened in Galisteo.

The brief note he had received of the uprising had told him little. He, the wiry old Fray Francisco Ayeta, and the others had prayed for the salvation of the province. Then they elected him Acting Governor and prepared to rebuild the land above the Pass. García's letter finally arrived, telling them the extent of the troubles, the news that Spaniards survived, and that there was hope for survival in the north.

With this news he knew there was something he could do, and he had ridden northward into Fray Cristóbal only to hear García had departed to join the Governor and that García's Nita was dead.

Spurring his horse ruthlessly on, Leiva recalled the first time he had met García and his mistress. It had been long ago in Cuba after a small war that ravaged the Caribbean and left España weaker, always weaker. He cursed softly to himself. Now Nita was dead and he had to bring the news to his old friend.

And all the time as he rode, he wondered what had happened at Galisteo.

Don Pedro's horse stumbled. He had driven the beast hard. His corpulence sat heavy in the saddle. His years of campaigning seemed so far behind him, lost with his youth down the spillway of time. His cheeks filled as he blew the dust off his face with an upturned lower lip. His fat hands sweated in the dry heat. His eyes were half closed to the shimmer of sun off the rocks ahead and the dust about him. He knew the countryside he rode over, wished he had not been so highly honoured by the Governor with the office of escort for the caballada from Mexico, and angrily kicked the side of his horse with his heavy shoe stirrup. In his forty years in Nuevo Mexico, as a boy and then on his return as a Maestre de Campo, he had known other Indian uprisings. Quick, vicious fracas with the copper dead lying over the fields and the slaves trudging south to Mexico. But from everything he knew about this revolt, he could tell that it was different. It cut to the heart of things. It struck at the Church and destroyed the families. The families. Don Pedro cursed again. The family was Nuevo Mexico. The great families with many children such as his and Don Alonso's and . . . dozens of names poured through his mind. The men who rode with him. The men he had left behind at the Pass with the procurador. Names, and no one knowing who was widower or orphan, who was to mourn a child or a friend. When Leiva had heard that the Indians had struck at the families as well as the soldados, he knew that the blow was to the very gut of the Empire. When the tale drifted in to the Pass that Popé had been the inciting force behind it, he knew what almost no other Spaniard knew, that the giant native priest hated with a passion equalled by none in the province. Don Pedro remembered the soft curses he had heard five years before when Popé had been released from his shackles and permitted to leave the Villa, the scars of his exorcizing red across his back. Don Pedro had known enough to be frightened then. Now as he rode, he wondered how time had so completely obscured his memory of the incident and how the Spanish had allowed the devil from San Juan to set himself up in Taos to wreak his vengeance.

They were almost there now—El Alamillo where Thomé Mendoza had told him Otermín had been heard from and where he had ordered García to join him. Then the diminutive pueblo on the rise above, and the guards stepping from behind rocks and waving him on with cheers as they saw the strength of his column and the four wagons with supplies. And into the pueblo with a splash of dust and a clatter of horses' hooves.

Don Pedro dropped his heavy figure from the saddle and brought his right hand up to salute the Governor who appeared before him. The two men threw their arms about each other's necks and slapped each other's backs and kissed each other on the cheek. Then the shouting began and the harquebuses were fired.

Otermín stepped back as he heard the noise rise about him. He was smiling as he had not been able to smile for weeks. "Together. Together," he said repeating the word over and over. Now the province was a single force again. Now García's column was only days away, and the supplies were here. He sighed as he put one arm about Don Pedro and led him out of the crowded square to the small estancia he had commandeered for his headquarters. The two men were silent until they climbed the two small steps to the portico where María waited for them with two pewter mugs of aguardiente.

"The supply wagons?" were Don Antonio's first words.

Don Pedro drank deeply, wiped his beard with the back of his pudgy hand, and stared from Otermín to María.

"Any word of my family?" wondering as he asked where the Governor had found himself a mistress and why he had selected a farm wench.

The Captain General was slow in answering. Finally he said, "Nothing. Not a word of what happened at Galisteo."

Don Pedro nodded slowly. He was not surprised. He had expected nothing in the way of news.

"The supply wagons?" Otermín again.

"Four here. Mostly munitions and weapons."

"And food?" It was the woman, and Don Pedro ignored her.

Then they were joined by Barnabe Márquez, Luis Granillo, and Luis Quintana. They greeted Don Pedro, but none of them had any news of his family. The aguardiente still in his hand, he looked about and asked "García?"

Granillo snickered, but fell silent when Don Antonio stared at him.

"He is under arrest," Otermín explained simply.

Don Pedro shook his head and the fat about his jowls shivered. "The charges, Excellency?"

Otermín looked at him in surprise. "You have ridden a long way, you have just arrived, and we are happy to have you with us. Let us talk of García later." He believed the discussion was concluded as the firing of more harquebuses could be heard outside.

"I have ridden a long way, Excellency. But García is my friend. He served under me twenty years ago. He is a man of courage and honour."

Granillo snickered again. "He did not defend his own hacienda. He fled Isleta and he fled Socorro. He beat and he bullied the hidalgos who rode

with him. He did not protect the women and cared nothing about the
civilians. Only his own family came out of the uprising whole. All of his
sons and his wife and his mistress." Granillo was going to continue but he
became aware how silent the other men on the portico had become.

Leiva spat on the flagstone. "Granillo, you can do what no other swine
can do—whine."

The small man appealed to Otermín, "Excellency, I . . ."

Don Antonio had listened carefully. His hand went up. "Don Pedro, the
decision to make the arrest was mine. I have not yet heard the evidence
against García to be given by this man."

"There is an Indian from Galisteo among the prisoners." María offered
the information. She was changing the subject and shifting the tension.

Don Pedro turned his fat face questioningly toward his commander.

Otermín smiled. "For days we have been interrogating all the Christian
Indians we could find. There are some we have not yet talked with."

The Maestre de Campo nodded. "May I see this one?"

"Márquez, take Don Pedro to the compound. See that the Indian speaks
quickly. The Maestre de Campo is tired."

The young lieutenant saluted awkwardly. "Yes, Excellency."

The two men departed and Otermín stood looking at the others who remained. "See that those who rode north are fed."

"Yes, Excellency." And they, too, left.

Alone on the portico Don Antonio held out his hand and María crossed
over and took it. He kissed her gently and squeezed her hand.

"He never told you how much food he brought," she said.

The Captain General nodded absent-mindedly. He was thinking of something else and besides he did not care about what she had to say concerning
anything as important as the supplies of the column.

"Where is Inez?" he asked, changing the subject and letting her know the
limitations of her concerns.

María did not answer him because she knew that at this moment he did
not care about her daughter. She dropped his hand and stood beside him,
listening to the celebration still going on in the small pueblo outside. She
did not know what she could say to him. He had shut her out so many times
that she felt as restricted as the puebleños down in the small compound,
chained to the trees waiting to be asked only those questions Otermín
wanted answered. She wondered sometimes what he thought he could learn
from them with his insistent *Why rebellion?* and his ears closed to the small
reasons and their inability to find large ones.

The only difference was that from her he sought only the small things
and would not know of the large ones.

There was a noise on the steps outside and both turned. Don Pedro joined
them a moment later. His face recorded his sorrow. "I could only lose them
once," he said. "And somehow I knew they were all gone before I ever left
the Pass." Otermín did not know how to console the man. He waited for
María to say something, and when she said, "I am sorry, Don Pedro," he
realized how meaningless any words were.

For the first time since his arrival, Don Pedro openly recognized that the woman was there with them on the portico. "I thank you, Señora."

He knew that his commander and the woman were watching him and he did not want sympathy.

"García?" he said as he had asked earlier.

Don Antonio decided to be patient. "We will discuss him later."

Don Pedro shook his heavy head. "I must talk with him, Excellency."

Otermín thought for a moment. "It is important?"

The Maestre de Campo nodded. "It is his woman. She is dead."

"Which woman?" It was María asking.

Don Pedro wondered why this should make a difference. Then he saw that to the Governor's mistress it would. "The one who was the mother of his children. She was found dead with a soldado."

"With a soldado?" Otermín looked at María as he asked.

"It seems they killed each other, Excellency."

"I see." Though the Captain General did not. He shrugged. To María: "Will you show Don Pedro where García is?" *She was found dead with a soldado. With a soldado.* And he kept seeing María and not García's mestiza mistress whom he had never known.

Inside the small room where María Valdivia had led him, Don Pedro stood beside the bed where Alonso García sat, and he told him what little he knew of the two bodies found in the small room of the empty house in Fray Cristóbal.

Don Pedro's heavy hand rested on his old compañero's shoulder as he spoke. García, dressed only in his pantalones, swayed back and forth. "And they buried the two of them. The padres prayed for them. Your family stood beside the grave."

What the hidalgo was implying did not come through to the stunned García at first. Then he slowly raised his huge head and looked up at the Maestre de Campo. "The others, the dons and their women, did not attend her?"

Don Pedro shook his head. "I only tell you what your oldest son asked me to tell you."

Shrugging off his friend's hand, García rose to his feet. His large fist smashed into his palm in anger as he cursed the hidalgos, the well-bred bastardos. Don Pedro made no comment even though he was aware that the curses included him.

Then Garciá grabbed the two hands of his old friend. "Why would they do this?" he pleaded. He was taking refuge in the insult to Nita so that he would not have to think of the more important fact that she was dead.

Leiva felt sorry for the old warrior. "She was found with a soldado, amigo mio. They were together and they were dead." He tried to explain and he knew how bad it sounded.

García dropped Leiva's hands and with the back of his he struck the older man across the face. "She was a good woman," he shouted. "She was a good woman." Then he slumped down on the edge of the bed again and rocked back and forth as he kept repeating the words, "She was a good woman."

The fat Galisteon held his hand to his cheek, trying not to take offence at the blow. "I knew Nita a long time, amigo. I know she was a good woman. But the men of Rio Abajo did not know her as you knew her or even as I did."

Don Alonso shook off the words. "I will kill Mendoza," he said softly.

"You will kill no one."

Both men turned to see the Governor standing in the doorway. To Leiva, he said, "I have seen the inventory of supplies that you brought. There is little food there."

Don Pedro smiled. "I hoped we would be able to fight again."

"And so you brought weapons and munitions. I appreciate the thought but we have not the strength to fight." Then he said what the others knew was obviously difficult: "We will move to combine the two camps in the morning. Now we will have a trial." He was talking to García who rose from the bed, wavered, and reached for the bedpost to brace himself. "We will meet on the portico in five minutes. You will bring the prisoner," he ordered Leiva. Then he pivoted on his heel and left the two alone again.

García stood clasping the bedpost with both hands as he tried to understand what was happening to him. Nita, and a trial, and his honour, and the insult of the hidalgos.

Leiva held a blouse up and the old warrior slipped into it, buttoning it quickly with unsteady fingers. Then he accepted his tunica, brushed it smooth with his hand and put it on. His boots, his sabre, and he was ready.

Don Pedro held his hand out for the weapon and García drew it slowly from its sheath, held it for a time as he recalled the years he had carried it with honour, and then gave it up to his friend.

"I am sorry, Alonso," Don Pedro said as he accepted the weapon. Then they walked out of the room together.

22

"CAPTAIN JOSÉ TÉLLEZ JIRÓN said that he is of the opinion that this small camp should withdraw to a better place, because of our lack of munitions and horses. The rebellious Christian Indians have been conspiring for thirteen years to perpetuate the treason which is now being carried out, and the Christian Indians who are now in this said camp are part of the plot and conspiracy. Today I regard it as impossible for the said Lieutenant General Alonso García to give aid or assurance to the señor Governor and Captain General. . . ."

For two hours Don Pedro de Leiva had been reading slowly aloud from
the pouch of documents which Don Alonso García had brought with him
from Fray Cristóbal. His high-pitched voice droned on. García sat in the
straight-back chair staring at a dust spot on his boot. He had not moved
since the trial began. The young Lieutenant Márquez who stood behind
him fidgeted a few times, brushing the chair as he did so. García recognized
the man as a civilian and forgave him his restlessness.

Governor Otermín did not seem to be listening. His hands rested upon
the table which had been brought onto the portico. He did not move. His
eyes were half closed and he appeared to be thinking of something else and
far away. A small fly came to rest just beyond his finger tips. He watched
it walk slowly across the length of the table. The day was warm and he
wished he had not worn a shirt under his tunica. He saw the fly rise and
circle the room. His eyes came to rest on the dust spot on the defendant's
large boot. Without moving his head, he stared at the tall Mexicano who sat
so impassively while his career rested precariously in the hands of men he
did not know. Don Antonio saw the sad lines about the man's mouth and
remembered the news Leiva had brought from the south about the giant's
mistress being dead. Don Antonio wondered how he would react if he
heard María was dead. He felt sorry for the old warrior: like himself, García
had had both a Spanish wife and a mestiza mistress. He wondered if María
would bear him sons as the Mexicano's woman had borne them for García.
There was a trace of envy mingled with the pity he felt.

Don Pedro shuffled the documents and read from another:

"Captain Juan Luis, the younger, said that he is ready and willing to
serve God and the King on any and every occasion that may arise, and
that for the rest he concurs in the opinions of the Maestre de Campo,
sargentos mayores, and captains. This is his opinion and he signs it.

"Captain Pedro Varela Jaramillo says that he concurs. . . ."

Otermín saw that Márquez shifted his weight from one foot to another,
smiled to himself wondering how many formal affairs the youth had attended in his life, and wondered how many he himself had been a part of.

Inside the estancia beside a window where she could hear what was being
said, María Valdivia was impressed with the solemnity of the occasion. She
had never seen the government at work before, much less a formal court. She
could barely make out the figure of the defendant as he sat with his head
bowed, seemingly staring at his boot. She wondered about this large man
who seemed defeated by the loss of his mistress while he still had a wife.
She thought about Don Antonio and the possibility of his mourning her.

"Captain Pedro de Sedillo said that he concurs in the opinions of all
the rest, and . . ."

Outside the building Luis Quintana sat on the steps waiting to be called,
bewildered that the Governor had omitted him from the trial, wondered how
he had offended. He could not know that his exclusion had not been from

deliberate decision, but because Otermín had never thought about the small man's presence one way or another. Quintana picked at his nose and tried not to see the men who sat on the steps beside him. Luis Granillo of Jémez sat upright, feeling very important because he was certain his testimony would finish García once and for all. Because he was indebted to the man for his life, he hated him. Granillo was not admitting this to himself any more than he was admitting that his hatred was in part based upon the fact that García knew him for a bungler and a fool.

Isabella Quintana watched the numbers of refugees who had drifted into the area about the small estancia waiting for news of the trial. There was a carrion-bird quality about them, and though most of them did not know the Lieutenant General, they were in their small way eager to see him toppled as they were always eager to see men of authority shown up as human with the same faculties for error that they themselves possessed. It made them feel stronger to know that others were also weak.

She waddled up to Quintana and whispered into his ear. The voice was heavy and it carried in spite of her efforts to keep her secret.

"Did he ask you to wait?"

Quintana shook his head.

"Then come away, little one. He is among his own kind now."

Quintana shook his head in disbelief as she walked away.

"Will it be much longer?" Granillo asked no one in particular.

No one knew the answer to his question. The men standing about shrugged.

García himself hardly heard what Don Pedro was reading. He was far from the trial and back through the years with Nita as he tried to understand that she was dead and buried. And he tried to put together the pieces of the tale he had been told: Nita and Reyes, and both lying dead. The pieces did not come together.

Then Don Pedro set the last paper down before the Governor and stepped back. "That is all of them, Excellency."

Otermín pushed them to a corner of the table with his hand. "We will hear the Alcalde Mayor of Jémez."

While Márquez went outside to fetch the man, Otermín poured himself a drink from the amphora on the table, debated offering García or Leiva a drink, thought better of it and emptied his mug. From where he sat, he could barely make out the silhouette of María through the window behind García. He could not understand what could interest her in the proceedings, wished she were less meddlesome, and then looked up at the slight figure of Granillo of Jémez as the man approached the table, placed both hands on it and said:

"I am prepared to tell Your Excellency everything that you should know about this—" and he waved haughtily at García, "this soldado." He used the word as an epithet and failed to see the crows' feet spread about the Captain General's eyes.

Granillo waited for the Governor to acknowledge him. When he saw that nothing was being said, he mistook the silence for approval that he speak. He was about to do so when Maestre de Campo Leiva placed a heavy hand on his arm.

"You will stand over there," Leiva said, "and you will swear upon the Holy Book that you will certify to the truth." He half pushed Granillo to a place opposite García where the Lieutenant Governor could face the witness as he spoke.

Otermín did not smile. The procedure was correct. The fact that Don Pedro was making it difficult for the witness did not bother him for the moment. He had almost made up his mind what the outcome of this trial would have to be. The remainder was little more than a formality.

He heard the oath of Granillo, and then as though from a distant place he made out the flood of words that poured forth from the loquacious petty official feeling his own importance.

". . . and he broke into the small battle that I was having near Jémez, after I had notified him of the uprising, and frightened off the Indians before we could capture and destroy them. Then he rode south but did not stop to see what he could do for the people of Sandía, and that night instead of joining the people of Isleta and assuming his responsibilities, he tried to protect his own hacienda and risk the heads of the rest of us by riding about the countryside gathering in all the mestiza wenches he could find. And when he finally saw that he could not protect his own property, he marched south with his wife and his mestiza mistress, relying not on the advice of those of us experienced in affairs or even his wife, Doña Josefa, but talking all the time with that woman and . . ."

The incoherent flow paused and Otermín looked up to see that García had half risen from his chair, his huge shoulders bulging the uniform and his great palms gripping the arms of the chair until it seemed they must collapse. Slowly the Governor shook his head. And as he did so, he saw the face of María more clearly in the window. She had risen herself and was looking directly out onto the portico, the window framing the question in her eyes.

Then Don Antonio knew that García was not the only one on trial at this moment. He resented the position in which he found himself and was prepared to ignore it, but the dark eyes of the woman were on him and he found himself speaking out.

"Granillo. For your information, the lady of whom you speak is now dead. She is not, and has not been, placed on trial here. I will ask you a simple question: Have you any specific evidence that Lieutenant General Alonso García is guilty of neglect of duty or failing to meet his responsibilities as a civilian authority and soldado of His August Majesty Carlos of España?"

The Alcalde Mayor did not know what to make of the question. He saw García slip back into his chair and stare again at his boot. Then he began to repeat his accusations one by one, carefully omitting this time any reference to the mistress of García.

When he was done, Otermín thanked him and said, "We will consider what you have said." Then he waited for Granillo to leave. There was silence. Don Pedro waited. García did not seem to notice the delay. The dust on his boots appeared to claim his whole attention as his thoughts kept trying to build a whole of the pieces that would link Nita and Reyes. But the pieces would not come together. *Or even his wife, Doña Josefa.* Granillo's words kept coming back to him and he realized it was the first time he had thought of her since he had heard of Nita's death. Then he knew that somehow she was the catalyst which would hold the pieces together if he could only discover how she fitted into the tale of the two deaths.

García felt the tap on his shoulder and looked up. Márquez was bringing his attention to the Captain General who was speaking.

"Alonso García. You will rise and hear the verdict of this court."

García wanted to protest that he had not been heard, but he did not need to be reminded that he was a soldier. He came to his feet and stood erectly before the peninsular who was his commander and his judge.

Otermín nodded to Leiva. "You will record what is said and see that it is signed by me and that a formal copy is presented to Alonso García with witnesses present." He drew his breath and began to dictate slowly. The scratching of Leiva's pen and the inconstant buzzing of a fly were the only other sounds.

"I have seen the documents presented and the judicial proceedings drawn up by the said lieutenant and the rest that he submits for his justification, and the fact that all agreed in not stopping for the reasons expressed, all of which exonerate the said lieutenant, Alonso García, from the blame that might attach to him. Therefore in view of his loyalties and services I declare that I clear and acquit him of all charges or blame, and order that he be released from arrest under which he is held at present so that he may attend more diligently to the affairs of justice and war in which he is in charge as the lieutenant of the Governor and Captain General in the jurisdiction of Río Abajo."

García had difficulty following the legal language of the Governor as his mind kept drifting away to Nita and he became aware that he was cleared only when the last words were said. His huge frame relaxed as Don Antonio stepped around the table and placed a hand on his shoulder.

"We have much to do. I will leave the details to you. Tomorrow I believe we should travel south and combine the columns. South again with dignity until we turn to fight."

The Lieutenant General tried to smile his appreciation for the Governor's understanding.

"Yes, Excellency." Then Don Pedro was congratulating him. Together the three men started to walk out to meet the crowd that had gathered.

"My sympathies on your loss, Don Alonso," and García realized the Governor not only meant what he said but was accepting him as Don Alonso. Nita would have been happy about this. But Nita was dead.

The three men walked out onto the steps together and the crowd pressed forward. "You are in charge of plans, García," Otermín said softly so that no one else could hear. Then he saw Fray Julio standing at the edge of the portico with Fray Pedro. He walked over to them.

"I prayed for your wisdom and understanding, Excellency," Fray Julio said.

"I think you will be pleased," Don Antonio answered as he turned to hear the Lieutenant Governor.

García stood with his hands at his side and looked over the crowd. Granillo had risen from the steps and turned to face him. García felt he could afford to ignore the man. He nodded to the crowd. Leiva stood at his side. Luis Quintana of La Cañada stood in the crowd facing both of his commanders.

"We will move south at dawn tomorrow to join the column of Rio Abajo. Granillo of Jémez will be in charge of the cattle. Lieutenant Márquez will be responsible for the prisoners."

The lieutenant spoke up from where he stood in the crowd. "There were only three who were not interrogated. And Don Pedro has killed them." He did not state that the Maestre de Campo had sworn him to secrecy concerning what had happened to his family before he stabbed the Indians to death.

García turned to Don Pedro for an explanation.

"It was only a small satisfaction," Don Pedro said.

The Lieutenant Governor wondered if revenge was always only a small satisfaction as he thought about Mendoza, the insult to Nita, and the problem he could not solve as yet.

The Governor waved his hand before him as though he were waving something away. The assembly was concluded.

No one noticed Luis Quintana cease to smile as he made his way through the crowd in search of Isabella. She stood in the rear, aware that her fears had become fact and that the Governor among his own kind had forgotten his little aide. The refugees began to drift back to the fires.

23

THE Indian warrior leaned against the rock and scanned the small pueblo. Days before he had ridden into El Alamillo with his companions and relayed the orders of Juan of Taos that all pueblos were to be evacuated prior to the arrival of the Spanish. He had remained to see that the food was removed or destroyed. Then he had settled back in the hills to await the Spanish arrival. Now as he watched, he could make out the Whiteface guards lazily drowsing in the late evening. There were guards on the buildings and several stationed with the horses and cattle.

The lean war chief rubbed his hand gently over his cheek and considered as he had for days the advantages of attacking the fleeing Spanish column. However, he hesitated because he had no orders and because his men were eager to return home. Any more deaths and he would not be able to hold them. But the prospect was tempting.

The sky was dark now with night and clouds. The air was chill. A scorpion scurried away from his moccasined foot as he moved nearer to the Spanish camp. There were fires about the pueblo. When dusk first spread over the wide area between the hills, the war chief had watched the Whitefaces kill their cattle and skewer them. The fires flashed macabre forms against the small buildings and drew the attention of thousands of insects bred in the recent rains.

The Indian watched a tall giant whom he recognized as the leader of the southern column make his way alone down to the rio, saw the man's heavy sabre as he set it beside him before he drank, saw him rise again and walk back through the circle of fire to the low estancia that stood at the north of the pueblo.

The night would be long and cool. The war chief settled down to watch his enemy.

Inside the estancia the Governor and Captain General sat in a padded chair with a drink of brandy in his hand; and as he talked, María walked about the room pouring for each of their guests.

"It has not been the old families that have meant anything in the crisis. Too many of them have been here for too long. They have grown restless. They have not cared enough."

Don Alonso García nodded his agreement as María filled the heavy pewter mug he held in his hand. He smiled at her, half his attention on the Governor's words and the rest of it on the thin face of the woman who reminded him of someone.

"Too much pressure from families. Things did not work right. A governor comes here alone and every move he makes there is a cousin or a nephew or a sister of one of the large old families and someone is offended and they are all of them unhappy."

Don Pedro de Leiva pulled at his heavy jowls as he tried to remember if his large family might have been one of those the Governor was talking about. He held his mug out for the brandy as he wondered about this woman with the full breasts who apparently came from the south. She was not of the old Nuevo Mexicano families. He decided she must have been someone's servant; too healthy and strong for a doña. Only one child though, the little girl sleeping in one of the rooms off the patio. He cocked his head to one side before he sipped the brandy and pulled again at his jowls.

"Many of the families were talking about leaving when I first came," Otermín continued. "Wanted to flee to the south into Mexico. Not enough money to be made here. Too much trouble over the years. Forbade it then and they remained."

Fray Pedro, with his head resting against a high-backed chair, recalled the meetings between the Fray Custodio, the Governor, and the heads of the families. He shook his head when the woman approached him, thought about his own responsibility in having brought this man and woman together, and wondered what would come of it.

"Was Thomé Mendoza one of those who wanted to leave?" It was García breaking into the monologue as he thought he was on the trail of something that had long disturbed him.

Fray Julio watched as Otermín turned to Fray Pedro with the same question on his face. The Governor and the assistant of the late Fray Custodio shook their heads as they tried to recall. The young padre seemed disappointed that he did not have a ready answer, but the padre from the north saw that he was seeking it out of the back of his memory. He, too, shook his head when María approached him. He smiled at her; she was a lovely woman. He recalled the concern she had for her daughter and believed she was a fine mother. The mother and the child. He closed his eyes for a moment. He had not thought of Beatriz in many days. Perhaps in another time and another place there would be forgiveness for Beatriz and himself.

"Yes, Mendoza was one of them." The strong voice of the padre from Valladolid finally answered García's question.

The giant leaned forward in his chair that seemed barely to hold his weight and smiled wryly.

"I do not think your Thomé Mendoza was happy, Excellency. He used the rebellion as an excuse to run to the south." He thought a moment. "So did his neighbours."

Don Antonio nodded as he looked at his deputy over his mug. "There is a great deal that must be settled once we return to the Villa de Santa Fe."

Don Pedro was glad that he spoke as though assured of reconquest. He had scores to settle in Galisteo, and the three Indians he had killed earlier in the day left him unsatisfied.

"I would not presume to judge for those of you who represent His Majesty on how you will have to go about a resettlement, any more than I would speak for the Franciscans." The others turned to catch the soft voice of Fray Julio. "But ought we not all to take a very close look at why we have been here? I know now that I came for the wrong reasons, and what I did I am certain contributed to the rebellion."

Fray Pedro shook his head slowly. He did not approve of the Order being discussed with laymen. Nor did he approve of the padre from Santa Flora reminding anyone of the infamy of that mission.

But it was Otermín who spoke first. His eyes were on María who stood across the room from him, her back to the wall and her head resting on the wooden frame of the window. "You may be right, Padre, but I do not think we can evaluate another man's motives." He was silent for a moment. "For myself, I came for promotion and rank. I am no stripling and I wanted a quiet post."

Don Pedro smiled at the Governor. "My family came north with Oñate." This was a boast. "That was a long time ago. Home is home. We lived and lived well." He tugged at his lower chin. "And we will again."

García shook his head. Honesty was a rare quality in high places and he had long learned to suspect it. The Captain General's candour demanded the same from each of them. "My reasons were different." He turned to the Governor. "Do you recall the old song, Excellency, that went

They fought for the king of Spain.
They fought for the king of Spain.

They fought for the King and Santiago.
They fought for Christ and Santiago.

For pesos and wine,
For pesos and wine.

"Well, I fought for pesos and wine most of my life. Then when the children were growing older, I wanted more. More pesos to give the boys, a place to raise cattle and wine. I wanted more for them, and she wanted more."

It was Fray Julio who reached out and placed a comforting hand on the arm of the Lieutenant Governor.

"If our motives had been different, Excellency, would we have built better for the Two Majesties?"

Otermín flexed the fingers of his right hand as María crossed over and filled his mug again. He smiled at her as she bent over, her back to her guests. She touched the tip of her tongue to her lips so that only he could see it. Don Antonio was not used to having a woman about in the evening when he sat talking to his friends. It made him self-conscious and uncomfortable. His hand shook slightly as he held the mug and addressed himself to the padre's question.

"Different motives? Perhaps, but what were the motives that brought the puebleños to murder and pillage, and—yes—rape?" He wondered after he said it if he would have said the same thing had his wife been in the room with strangers. Then he remembered that she would not have been in the room.

Fray Julio's mind captured a far-off shriek and the flash of mastiffs swarming over a dancing man in a dusky compound barely a month gone by. He crossed himself.

Fray Pedro undertook to answer the question. "They had no motives. They were led by evil men, corrupted from the ways of God and Christ, and there is a flaw of sin through them which split wide open and violently revealed the corruption."

The other Franciscan did not say a word as he listened to the easy absolution of the Two Majesties.

Don Pedro shook his head. "Perhaps, but they were a long time planning it and we had no sign. That is what disturbs me. A small fight here. A small show of force there. But no warning of treason on such a scale." He tipped up his mug and drank as he thought about his own words, impressed with his understanding.

The Captain General smiled. "They fought us and threw us out. We can say what we want, but these Indians have beaten in battle the descendants of the conquistadores."

García sucked on his cheek. He did not know if the peninsular was giving praise to the enemy in order to lead the discussion to something in particular —the placing of certain blame or an absolution from it. He listened as the Commander went on.

"We were besieged. In military terms this is already a failure. We gave up the space we needed to fight and attack. We let ourselves be holed in, in an area where we had no room to move. It is usually a sign of ineptitude with famine and thirst given over to the enemy as an ally. We were left with only the courage of the snared animal. We were not like Spaniards hiding behind those walls, and only when we moved out to win were we honestly ourselves. But how did it happen? I cannot find a mistake in our defence."

María was impressed with his logic and his knowledge of his craft. But García felt differently. Did the Governor want an answer, or absolution? He had thought about the failures himself.

"I think, Excellency, we tend to forget that a siege is unlike an open battle in that it is made up of more parts and that it has the handicap of involving more than professional soldados working at their trade. A siege involves civilians—women and children, elders. The control is not in the commander's hand alone."

Now they were both absolved and Otermín nodded accepting the analysis. At the same time he wondered who the academician was who had taught this bear of a campaigner how to look at a battle as more than a sabre swung and an harquebus well fired.

Fray Pedro, bored with the discussion of military affairs, laughed softly. "Don Alonso would have preferred more pesos-and-wine men and fewer civilians and padres."

"That is right. I do not want to depend upon amateurs in a war."

The padre did not know if he liked the ready agreement he received from all three of the laymen. He rose to his feet. "I promised to hear confessions tonight. If you will excuse me . . ." He was annoyed with himself for having become involved in the details of the religious services since Fray Julio had arrived. But there was something about this sad-faced Brother that made him feel as though he ought to be doing more with the refugees than he had done in the earlier days of the retreat.

The others bade him good-bye and María walked with him through the sitting room to the door and out onto the steps before the estancia. As he was about to leave, he turned to her. "I hope my suggestion that you help His Excellency with his household has not compromised you."

María tried not to laugh at his innocence. She shook her head because there was nothing she could say. The change in the stocky padre in the neat cassock impressed her, and though she was not convinced she knew the cause, she laid much of this sudden interest in people to the example of the Franciscan from Santa Flora.

When she returned to the piazza where the men were sitting, Don Antonio and Don Pedro were preparing to inspect the weapons which had arrived from the south so that a formal transfer of papers could be made from the Maestre de Campo to the Captain General before the column began its march in the morning.

After the two men had left, María found herself alone with the Lieutenant General and the long-faced padre with the large hands and the worn cassock.

24

TWO men sitting in the open plaza staring at the estancia occupied by the Governor's household watched Don Antonio and the Maestre de Campo emerge from the building. Lieutenant Barnabe Márquez rose to his feet and approached his commander to see if there was anything he might do to help. The other man picked at his black teeth with his fingernail and tried not to show his watching wife how troubled he was by the fact that the Governor had overlooked inviting him to attend the evening dinner with the senior officers. The small Alcalde Mayor of La Cañada did not understand why the Governor had begun to depend upon the professionals with whom he felt comfortable and assured. And as Otermín and Leiva began to inspect the arms handed to them out of the carts by Márquez, Quintana drifted away from the fire where he believed everyone was watching him, and found a place in the shadows beside a building where he would be alone with his wounded pride.

The war chief watching from behind a large rock evaluated the strength added to his fleeing enemy and determined that the Governor lacked the men to use the arms. He relaxed and inspected the weapons from his place of hiding. There was nothing here he had not seen before. Armour and shields and swords and harquebuses and horse pistols. These were no added threat to the puebleños. He traced his finger down his cheek and settled back again to wait until one of his companions relieved him.

Inside the estancia, Fray Julio was relating the story of Fray Rafael to the Lieutenant Governor, who had not yet heard it. The old warrior sat in awed reverence at the wonder of it, and María, who had learned the details of the miracle by heart since the padre had joined them, turned her attention to the giant from Zacatecas.

"And he said, 'Let the lapsed equip themselves in order to regain what they have lost. May the uninjured be spurred on into the battle by honour.'"

The two Mexicanos represented the whole New World of the West, and though she was not conscious of this, somehow María was aware that the two tall men—one a priest and the other a soldier—were already a world away from that which had bred Don Antonio.

"And then he said, 'May you all be led into the light.'"

The padre finished his tale and crossed himself. Don Alonso was silent for a moment.

"It will always behove us to remember the padre from San Ysidro." Then Don Alonso turned to María, who had taken the chair opposite him in which Don Pedro had sat earlier in the evening.

"You remind me of someone of whom I was very fond, Señora." He was trying to be friendly to a person whom he knew must be as uncomfortable as himself in the company of governors and hidalgos, despite the fact that she was the mistress of none other than Otermín himself.

María accepted the gesture. "I am sorry to hear about your lady, Don Alonso."

García was puzzled. "My wife is fine," he explained. "It is my Nita who is dead, she who bore my sons."

The record was clear now. Even María had no difficulty understanding that García had drawn a line which he himself could not cross, between the woman he had married and the one with whom he had spent his life.

Fray Julio sympathized with the man who sat grinding his right fist nervously into his left palm. He wondered compassionately if Doña García, whom he had never met, understood the differences between wives and lovers.

Then García was explaining to María and the padre what had been troubling him all day.

"She was a good woman, my Nita." He stumbled on: "She loved me. She was found dead with this soldado, but she was a good woman. I had to marry someone else. She knew that."

It was María who finally rose and stood before him.

"If she knew you loved her, Don Alonso, and you did what you thought would make her proud of you and you did it for her sons and yours, I am certain that she understood and was everything you believed her to be."

The gaunt padre left them together. He would not dispute the widow's words, but he could not bring himself to condone them. A sin was no less a sin for all the intent.

García stared down at María. "Thank you, Señora. I think you would have liked her. She was of the stuff that grows. Soft and pliable before the winds, but back again and straight when they have passed. Rich and fertile like a handful of the dirt in which a man feels the growing. You would have liked her, Señora, for she was a woman."

Otermín appeared in the archway and stood quietly listening to his lieutenant.

"We used to talk through the night," García said. "We talked of battles and the English and the bad pay and how we wanted to build a place for our boys. She knew what I meant because she was as wise as any man, and . . ."

María nodded. She knew what he meant. She saw Don Antonio and she smiled at the puzzled expression on his face as he stood rubbing his beard with the back of his hand.

It was almost dawn when the Indian war chief withdrew from the immediate vicinity of the pueblo of El Alamillo where he had waited through the night.

25

ANOTHER day on the Camino Real and rain again.

The only thing worse than retreat under the glare of sun was retreat in the wet with the clay clinging to boots and the horses' hooves slipping.

The column marched as before. There were more wagons, more soldados. The Lieutenant General gave the orders. For the thousand nothing else was changed.

Only the southward direction of the column mattered to the Indians watching from the hills near by.

The thunder filled the valley of the Rio del Norte. The wounded turned from side to side to avoid the water swirling down in their faces, soaking their clothes, their bandages, the mattresses they rode upon.

Stumbling behind the carts the tall padre from Santa Flora led the blind woman who walked face upward toward the sky she could not see. With his injured arm he supported an ageing ranchero who no longer regained his strength after a halt of one day or three.

At the head of the column Otermín listened to the water strike the steel helmet on his head. He wiped his face with his hand and turned to watch María who rode beside him with Inez on the saddle before her. Water sleeked off the girl's hair and dripped from the small tip of her sunburned nose as she looked up. María smiled at him. He watched her wipe the rain from her lashes and pull her ribosa forward to shelter her face.

Don Antonio wondered what his children would think if they knew he had taken a woman again. He wondered what they thought of him, anyway. He hoped they remembered him kindly, hoped too that his failures would not reflect upon them. He wondered if his grandchildren looked like Inez and if they would ever ride the length of a province in rain and retreat. He hoped not.

He saw García spur his horse and ride ahead of the column and swing about on a small knoll so that he could see the length of it as it struggled by him.

A good man, García. A man Otermín felt he could understand. A man with handles one can hold and know what he is holding, can talk to and know he is being understood. There was no need to pursue details while García rode with him. The giant from Mexico knew how to hold a column tautly together and drive it on aware of its limitations as well as its astounding ability to move farther and faster than any one believed possible.

Don Antonio wished he knew more about the tale that Leiva had brought north with him concerning the two bodies found in Fray Cristóbal. He did not believe it was a matter of murder, and it was difficult for him to believe a mestiza woman was involved in a matter of honour. Four sons. He looked again at María. Somewhere riding in the van of the column on one of the rickety carretas was a pregnant widow. None of the other women seemed to know when her child was expected, and only Fray Julio was able to console her about the loss of her husband now that she was about to give birth to her first child.

Fray Julio. No one talked now about the padre's past. The gossip was stilled. All knew they owed much of their survival and most of their hope to the rugged padre with the long face who consoled and comforted and prayed, who urged and aided and led. Otermín shook a droplet of water from his nose.

How strong the Two Majesties were when they worked hand in hand, how much they could accomplish. He hoped the tall padre would be with him when he rode north again. It was going to require both faith and strength to bring the puebleños once again to the ways of God and España.

Don Antonio did not know where the energies were to come from. According to García, both columns were in desperate condition. A stream of water ran off his helmet and he shook his head again sharply. *España. España.* Too many things had gone wrong in recent years: the small wars with France and the bitter ones with England. The droves of ladrones—the petty thieves —pilfering the countryside from the Pyrenees to the great rock in the south. The casas del putas spewing their purveyors of filth and degradation and disease from one end of the Empire to the other. The large thieves who were grandees and titulos with position and property and the smaller ones who were hidalgos and caballeros, without fortunes or jurisdiction. All with sabres that could be purchased for pesos. And to what end?

The Lieutenant General assumed his position at the head of the column again beside his commander. "Too many women," was all he said. Otermín nodded. Both of them were used to seeing women in a Spanish column. Even the manuals of military affairs recommended eight women in common for every hundred soldados. But the women the manuals suggested did not matter—they were not wives and mothers, and their loss was mourned by none. No commander held up a column for them, shared his rations with them, or even paused to bury those who fell by the road. But as García said: "Too many women." Too many who mattered to someone, and not enough to spare for them.

"Leiva had better take his men and move directly south as fast as he can. He should meet Ayeta and get his permission to rush all of the food supplies north."

García saluted and guided his horse to the side of the column until Don Pedro de Leiva rode up to him. Then the pair conferred beside the Camino Real as the rest of the column passed them.

Ten minutes later, his detachment behind him, Don Pedro rode out to the right of the long column and galloped south, and García again resumed his position beside his commander.

Walking in the rain beside the weary stallion that bore the huge bulk of his wife, Luis Quintana watched the Maestre de Campo depart, wondered where he was going and why, felt himself left out of the activities of which only days before he had been a part, looked to his wife and then at the ground where the wet sand sloshed noisily under his small boots.

The rain continued through the day and into the evening. The column, huddled in the shelter of blankets and the small carretas, swore softly under their breath at the commander who had taken them from the shelter of El Alamillo. They were not concerned that there was only six days' supply of food, that they were still in Indian country, and that the land which lay about them would not feed them or their horses. They only knew the rain and their own discomfort.

There was no fire that night and the courier from Fray Francisco Ayeta far to the south almost passed them without even pausing. However, the line of guards heard the galloping horse and signalled the messenger to a halt. The young man swung off his horse and sought out the Captain General. Standing in the rain, he came to attention, saluted, and handed Don Antonio a folded pouch, wet with the rain and perspiration from the inside of his shirt. Half-smiling at the foolishness of the uncovered head with the rain pouring over it, Otermín opened the carta in the shelter of the blanket he shared with María and read it in the almost darkness of the night. When he was done, he handed the document to García who had joined him.

When the Lieutenant General read the paper, he laughed slowly. "It seems the good padre from Mexico wants to know if we really need supplies or not."

"In a great many words, that is what it comes to," Otermín agreed. To the courier: "Did you meet Don Pedro de Leiva on the Camino Real?"

Coming to attention again, the youth appeared to be thinking about a question that could only be answered yea or nay. Finally, he shook his head. "No, Excellency. I rode part way on the west bank. Perhaps he rode on the right."

Otermín nodded. Reasonable. He rubbed his beard with the back of his hand, felt the wetness of it and shook his head slowly. "Find Lieutenant Márquez somewhere and get yourself some food, young man." He waited until the youth had left before he looked up at García who towered over him.

"I had better ride south at once," he said softly. "Leiva will be given some supplies to rush north and I will try to discover what is available to us, will try to gather as much as possible for you when you arrive with the two columns." He felt María's hand on his arm and shook his head. This was no time for a woman to be involved. He wanted to tell her as much, saw García staring at her, and turned to face her himself. There was concern in her eyes as she counselled.

"Someone else who is not wounded, Excellency. Someone else can ride on your behalf."

Otermín shook her hand off his arm and rose to his feet. "Twelve men. I will not need any more." He thought a moment. "I dislike taking so many horses from you."

The Lieutenant Governor shook his head. "It is all right, Excellency." He was thinking of the problems he was going to have with the two columns together, his back exposed to the Mendozas and no Nita to warn him. He was looking again at the shape of the woman's head seated on the wet ground before him, saw the head shake in the darkness and knew her reluctance to see the Governor depart.

"Another can go in your stead, if you desire, Excellency." It was an offer, though he knew it would never be accepted.

The Governor brushed it aside. "I will ride tonight," he said, "if you will see that everything is ready."

García saluted and disappeared into the darkness. Otermín was alone now with María and the sleeping child. He knelt beside her and took her head between his hands and tipped it up so that he could see directly into her eyes. Then he said, in anger, "I never want to hear from you again when I am conducting my affairs. You will not make a fool of me again." His anger shook her. His hands which held her head trembled. In the darkness, María knew the dampness on her cheeks was more than the rain falling.

Through the darkness she heard him saying, "I will see that you are taken care of while I am gone and that you are treated as my lady." He snorted. "I am confident García will understand how a lady must be treated." She knew he was thinking of the grief the giant soldier had felt at the loss of his mistress, and how meaningless this very grief was to Don Antonio.

She nodded. She wanted to reach out and kiss him and tell him that she understood. But he was already gone. Minutes later she heard the horses ride off in the darkness, and she sat back against the carreta with the blanket spread as a shelter over her and the rain falling on her legs and the hem of her dress.

Later she made out the large silhouette of the Lieutenant General standing over her in the night. "It is all right, Señora," he comforted her. "I sent the eager young padre with him."

There was a scream in the night and she came to her feet beside the Zacatecan. Another scream. A woman's.

"She is having her baby," María said.

Somehow Don Alonso found the idea comforting.

And in the darkness not far away, the young war chief listened to the woman's screams and when he realized what they signified, was repulsed at the thought of another Whiteface.

26

THE thirteenth of September. Five days with the sun and the rain between, the rio swelling, the desert to the left and the mountains to the right, the horses weaker, the grazing poor, boots gone and bare feet torn.

And, finally, in the late afternoon—Fray Cristóbal and unity. The weary celebration, the consolations of sympathy, the finding of family, friends, neighbours, or the failure to find. The thorn-expression in the hurt eyes when no one knew about a missing wife, a lost child, a husband.

But unity at last. Twenty-five hundred now. The strength of numbers if numbers were strength. But the numbers were aged and women, the too weak to walk and the too young. Numbers were mouths to be fed, not wielders of weapons or guards.

The Lieutenant General rested on his horse, too tired to dismount, too fearful of what he faced when he stood again in Fray Cristóbal.

His older sons approached him, their heads high, the hurt look clear on their faces. He deferred the moment of dismounting as he smiled at them. "Señora," he said introducing María Valdivia who sat mounted beside him, "my sons." And to the youths, "This is the Governor's lady. I shall expect you to be at her side while she is with us." With the pride he felt as he looked at the boys, almost as tall as himself, almost as broad, he added, "They will help you, Señora, in any way you wish."

The young men acknowledged the greeting and went with María in search of a place where she and Inez might spend the night. García watched his sons lead her horse away and still he sat, alone now. He wondered if he was waiting for Josefa. He wondered where the camp commander was. His heavy hand swept the helmet off his head and for a moment he looked about for Nita. She had always taken his gear, cleaned it and kept it for him. Now he sat with his helmet in his hand and the heavy sabre at his side. There was no one to relieve him of it.

He swung one heavy boot over the saddle and stepped to the ground. Márquez approached him. "Is there anything that I can do, Excellency?"

García slapped the man on the back. Then he bent over and inspected the hooves of his stallion one at a time, shook his head. "Shoes going smooth and nothing to do about it here," partly to Márquez, partly to himself. "Get someone to feed him, water him, and then rest, amigo. You, too, have travelled far."

Márquez saluted. Returning the formality, García refrained from smiling. Willing, but not well trained, not one who would survive most battles. The youth led the horse away and the Lieutenant Governor found himself standing alone in the plaza. Some of the column were beginning to seek shelter while others stood about in small groups talking to old friends or family. He wondered where his younger sons were, his wife, his deputy.

Then he saw Josefa watching him from the space between the two buildings which Nita had taken days before to shelter his family. Her face was drawn, her dress dirty and wrinkled from rain and nights of sleeping on the ground. Her mouth twitched as she saw that he had found her.. Nervously, she knotted her hands beneath her bosom and waited for him. She had seen María Valdivia and was wondering who the woman was to whom her husband assigned his sons. She hoped the woman was his, that he had taken his interest to someone else.

García smiled at her and crossed the camp area to stand at her side. The refugees of the southern column who knew the tale of the two bodies had talked for days about the implications of the deaths, the part that Doña Josefa might have had in the tale, and how the old Bear of Zacatecas would react.

Standing among his neighbours and family, Thomé Mendoza watched

García approach his wife. He saw the giant take the woman by both shoulders, draw her to him for a brief affectionate moment and then lead her into the area between the buildings. Mendoza shooking his head slowly. "Poor woman." In the days since Nita's death he had talked to Doña Josefa many times. He had heard the tragic tale of her capture by the English and her equally tragic freeing by García who had forced marriage upon her. He had listened to her tell of her husband's excesses, of his drinking and his mistress, of how he had twice attacked the late soldier Reyes in moments of uncontrolled anger and of how he had even struck her. Mendoza had relayed her story to those about him and as he sympathized with her, others, too, shook their heads in pity.

Between the two buildings in the vague light of the late afternoon, Don Alonso stood with his wife. He placed one gentle hand on her white cheek as though it were a fragile thing. "I am sorry that I was not here. You would not have gone through this alone."

Josefa was bewildered at first, and then she realized that he believed she had mourned Nita, had missed her, had regrets or sorrows concerning the mestiza's death. It was difficult not to laugh, but feeling the strength behind the gentle hand on her cheek, she refrained.

"The younger boys," he asked, "where are they?"

Josefa smiled. His Nita would be alive now if they had not blundered with Reyes. "Guard," she explained.

Don Alonso dropped his hand to his side.

"I must settle with Mendoza," he said softly. Her face showed that she did not understand him. "Nita," he said as though the name was an explanation. Then with his broad hand on the back of her head, he pulled her to him and kissed her. She was his wife and despite their differences, he was proud of her because she was young and beautiful—a lady from España.

Josefa did not resist him, but when he walked out to the plaza, the back of her hand slowly rubbed over her bruised lips.

García planted his great boots in the mud, his hands on his hips, and surveyed the camp. No guards on the roofs of the two houses. No horses tethered at hand for ready mounting to repulse an attack. No messengers ready to alert the soldiers. Women wandering beyond the protection of the guards. His fist ground angrily into his open palm as he strode across the camp and whirled Mendoza around to face him.

"A deputy reports to his commander," he said quietly.

Those about Mendoza fell back. The hidalgo's hand came to rest on the hilt of his sword.

García goaded the man further. "You are relieved of all military and civilian authority." And to all, by way of explanation: "This camp is unprotected."

Then quickly to Mendoza's friends without regard to rank, "Four of you on the roofs to sound an alert in case of attack. Two of you bring a dozen horses and keep them ready for mounting." Finally, to Mendoza: "You will see that the women do not leave the periphery of the guard line. They may go down to the rio where you will be on guard."

The other men waited to see what Mendoza would do. His fingers whitened, tight on the hilt at his side, but he did not draw his weapon. García waited for a time. Then he shouted loudly, "At once!"

Startled, the other men scurried off to the tasks he had assigned to them. When Mendoza finally shrugged, García slapped him across the face with the back of his hand.

"As my deputy, you were responsible for the lives in this camp."

Humiliated and embarrassed before the hundreds who had turned at the sight of the two commanders quarrelling, Mendoza blurted, "She died with a man."

García's knee jerked up. Mendoza bent forward to protect himself. Then he crumpled to the ground as two quick blows struck each side of his neck. The camp was quiet. Doña Mendoza gasped and was silent. Don Alonso toed the hidalgo's limp body over onto its back and spat down into the gravel-torn face.

Then he looked up to see Luis Granillo watching him, Mendoza's body between them.

"They tell me your own Señora did not attend the funeral, Excellency." Granillo grinned.

García's shoulders sagged and his head shook from side to side in disbelief as he turned away from the garrulous Alcalde Mayor of Jémez and stumbled through the parting crowd to the place where he had left Josefa.

She had not been able to hear what had taken place between her husband and the men across the plaza, but she had seen Don Alonso strike the sympathetic Don Thomé and now as her husband approached her, she was afraid.

With a sweep of his hand, García pulled his wife to him and hurried her into the area between the buildings out of sight of the curious eyes in the plaza. Once they were alone he released her and stepped away. His great fists nervously opened and shut. The toe of one boot crunched pebbles as it twisted from side to side.

Josefa's arms hung loose at her side. Her lips parted, but she did not speak because she did not know what he wanted to hear.

At last his hands became still. He reached out and grabbed the loose hair on the back of her head and he shook her as he spoke, "You did not even attend her funeral."

Josefa wanted to deny the accusation, but she felt his fingers tighten in her hair and said nothing.

"You would shame me. You would not even pay her who was the mother of my sons a final respect."

"No," she said. "No."

He waited, his left hand drawn back, his huge palm open.

"She shamed you," Josefa said. "She and Reyes were found together."

García's hand holding her hair stiffened. Slowly he forced her down to her knees before him. Her hands, reaching back, tried to release his fingers as he shook her from side to side, no longer aware of what he was doing.

"She was a good woman, my Nita," he said. "She was a good woman." And then he said, "I loved her."

He let her go and she fell, face in the dirt, her arms swinging meaninglessly at his boots.

"I loved her," he said again as though the idea was a new one.

Doña Josefa turned her scratched face up and looked at her husband as he knelt before her trying to explain his madness. "She was a dirty mestiza whore," she said. "And she was killed minding someone else's business."

Then she felt his strong fingers close about her throat as he rose, pulling her from the ground. Her own fingers crazily raked at his cheek, missed, and fell away.

Then he relaxed and threw her away from him. She struck a wall and slipped to the ground and rolled over onto her back, gasping. Don Alonso stood over her, staring at a gaunt padre with a great head that was shaking from side to side as he said,

"Thou shalt not kill, my son. Thou shalt not kill."

The old warrior dropped to his knees before the padre and bowed his head as he sobbed. "This one speaks ill of my dead." He gestured with one hand wearily toward his wife.

There were bright spots growing and fading before Josefa's eyes. Her breath came more readily now. Her throat was sore where he had held her and she rubbed the white skin of it as she sat up and looked at the padre whose left hand rested on her husband's head. The two men were praying.

Josefa was angry and safer in anger with the padre present.

"I am going away," she said. "The old whore tried to stop me from lying with him and leaving with him. But it does not matter now. She is dead and he is dead." She reached for the side of the building and came slowly to her feet. "I do not belong to anyone, Padre."

"You are married to this man, child." Fray Julio tried to touch her with his limp right arm, but she backed against the wall. She pulled her skirt smooth and walked into the gathering shadows of the evening.

The padre from Santa Flora turned to the Lieutenant Governor. "Be patient, my son." Then he saw that the old soldado was smiling. "She died to protect what was mine, Padre. She died for me and the boys."

Fray Julio realized then how little the beautiful young lady from España really mattered.

27

TWENTY-FIVE hundred persons left Fray Cristóbal on the morning of the fourteenth of September. They were fifty-nine leagues from el Paso del Norte, and for the first time they retreated as a single column.

The Magdalena range lay to the west. The land underfoot was white with red patches and black burns. There were marshes along the rio to their right. A small black mesa lay directly before them. As they walked, they saw that the land beyond the marshes was covered with dead lava and the scattered cones of old volcanoes. There were hills to both the east and the west, and only the scattered shrubs and greasewood trees survived between.

In the early afternoon of the second day they held the last rites for a soldier wounded in the siege of the Villa. His compañeros stood bareheaded under the sky. The grave was quickly dug. The marker was makeshift—an old scabbard, a shepherd's crook, and the dead man's belt. Fray Julio performed the service. Then he walked among the wounded and told them of the bright future they would find in another place at another time. This did little to reduce the pain of the jouncing carreta, but they blessed him for it.

By the sixteenth of September they had travelled eight leagues and were fifty-one from the Pass. The Magdalena Mountains lay behind them. The hot sun swept the land. There were mesas and the tall yucca to their right.

On this day the Governor's lady shared her horse with Doña Josefa García. Lieutenant Barnabe Márquez carried the newborn child on his saddle as he rode at the rear of the column.

The earth was flat and the clouds cast dark shadows over the land. There were pebbles in greater numbers and the walking became more difficult.

On the morning of the seventeenth the hills almost closed in upon them. There were deep cañons to be seen across the rio. When the hills fell back again, dirty sand stretched from the base of them to the water. Behind all were the high, distant mountains. The country was naked of trees. The land was level for walking. They could see clearly the edge of the cliffs that marked the end of the hill line.

By the nineteenth of September they had travelled nineteen leagues and were still forty leagues from the Pass to the south. This was the day they arrived at the place of the dead horse. A universe of maggots lived under its sun-dried hide. Its smell followed them for hours. Where the clay land wedded the sand was the place of the Night without Fuel. They rested a cold rest on the hard ground and ate cold meat.

On the night of the twentieth of September they were twenty-four leagues from Fray Cristóbal to the north and thirty-five from the Pass to the south. They rested around the warm springs set in the hills near where the Cuchillo Creek joins the Rio del Norte from the west. The hidalgos remained sullen. Fray Pedro Martínez began to ration the food. The small factions grew with the small hatreds. The jealousies grew over food and shade and the need of the soldiers for women. The Lieutenant Governor rode at the head of the column by day and slept alone by night.

They passed the giant steps cut by erosion in the hills on their left. The rio wandered southerly around the base of the mountains west of the land between. There were high mesas in all directions. The trail was marked by the wedge-shaped skull of a cow and the skins shed by two rattlesnakes.

They passed Las Animas Creek on the twenty-second. The rio followed the edge of the hills on the east. There were cañons between. On the west the mountains were at a great distance.

The next afternoon the hills fell away three or four leagues between.

There was desert sand and then the walls of the hills closed upon the rio. Here they found three bodies the Manso Indians had mutilated. The mestiza wench with the long lashes identified the dead as the fugitives who had fled without fighting. The column moved on while two soldados and a padre buried the dead. This was the day the puebleños ceased to follow the column and turned back to the north.

By the twenty-fourth of September they were thirty-three leagues above the Pass. The San Andreas lay to their left with Sierra Los Caballos between. The mountains were gaunt and marked with their own shadows. The mornings were cloudless. There were sullen clouds in the afternoon. Underfoot were snakes among the broken rocks. This was the malpais—the bad country.

The next day was no better. They were more tired and moved more slowly. The cattle died on the trail and the horses lamed. The sand rose with the hot winds and cut the bare hands of the marchers. Their faces became sore to the touch. The ground was white dunes with red clay between. There were some scattered creosote bushes with a strong odour.

On the twenty-sixth the hills rose high on both sides of the rio. The trees were white with alkali. There were mouse tracks in the sand and shrikes overhead. The horizon remained serrated and blue. The woman with the newborn infant rode with Barnabe Márquez. The Lieutenant General's wife had her meals with the Mendozas and the Lieutenant General had his with his four sons and the Governor's lady. There was Mass each morning now before the march and the people came when Fray Julio presided.

They passed the Devil's Tower that stood tall and narrow. The rio widened at its base. The earth was white here and pebbled. They left the rio where its bed was marshy, and turned southeast. The wire-leafed popotillo grew here and the ground was crusted with alkali. The Guadelupe Mountains grew on the horizon before them. And then the outriders reported back to the Lieutenant General that there were huts scattered about the hills in the distance.

28

ON October 1, Don Antonio de Otermín stood in the middle of the field he had selected for his camp and waited for the column to arrive. This was the end of it—this empty field four leagues above el Paso del Norte and one hundred and twelve leagues below the Villa. This was all that España could claim now of what had once been the province of Nuevo Mexico. There were several small huts he had ordered to be constructed. There was some food and some equipment. And very little more.

He scanned the hills to the south and east of him. Beyond lay Mexico. He had discussed the problem of withdrawal with Fray Francisco Ayeta for days, and there was one point on which they were both agreed: no one would leave the province itself. There was to be no talk of giving up the land which lay to the north. Retreat was retreat, but neither of the Two Majesties would hear of defeat or concede that the province would not be retaken as soon as the column was rested, reorganized, and re-equipped.

Standing in his white shirt sleeves, his pantalones clean, his boots polished, his beard trimmed, Don Antonio felt as though he was ready to turn north again. But he had no illusions. The column whose dust he could see rising in the north was weary and demoralized. It would have to be fed and cared for and cajoled to move again. The women, the aged, the wounded were a liability. He rubbed his beard with the back of his hand. He wanted to mount his stallion and ride out to meet the approaching line, to welcome García and see María, but he held his ground. The aged padre from Mexico who stood near by was praying to himself. For Fray Francisco Ayeta the mere fact that the column lived at all was a miracle. He had stood at the side of Don Pedro de Leiva when the word of rebellion first came from the north, and both of them believed then that all was lost. But God had been with them and all had not been lost. Now the survivors were approaching and they were going to need him and his padres. He looked about to see that the fires were being lighted, that food was being prepared. Then he crossed himself and walked over to the Governor.

"Fray Julio will be with them?" he asked.

Don Antonio nodded. The story of the tall padre who had appeared at the río's bank and the tale he told of his martyred Brother were now legend.

A rabbit broke across the field, paused in its flight to stare at the two silent men watching the column as the outriders arrived and swung off their horses. Then the rabbit fled to quieter places. Otermín marked its course and smiled to himself. Not many days before he would have accounted it so much food lost. Now it could live. Though the days ahead would be difficult, there was going to be food here and rest and revival.

Then he saw García and beside him the smaller figure of María. With long strides he crossed the field and raised his hands to help her and Inez alight. He held her close for a moment, embarrassed, knowing that many eyes were upon him. They stood together as the whole column scattered over the fields. The mounted swung off their horses, felt the ground beneath their feet, and then joined the others in surveying the barren landscape that was for the moment the end of their jornada.

The padres of the column sought out Fray Francisco and knelt for his blessing. He placed one hand on the shoulder of Fray Julio and another on the shoulder of Fray Pedro. "We must pray together," he said. "We must give thanks that so many survive, and we must pray for those who did not survive."

Then he raised his hands high and those about began to kneel where they stood. The men bared their heads and the women slowly covered theirs and sank to their knees in the open field. It was the voice of Fray Julio that was heard.

When the prayers were said, the refugees rose and formed long lines where the food was being served.

The Lieutenant General turned his horse over to his sons, directed them to select one of the huts for the use of the family, and went in search of his commander. As he walked across the field, García saw the bustle of the camp and heard the loud cries as Márquez and the soldados assigned family areas. The cattle were set to grazing a distance away and paths were being cut to the rio. García noted that a guard had already been stationed against the Apaches who dwelled near this land.

He located Don Antonio with a cluster of officers about him. Mendoza and his friends were there. Don Pedro de Leiva joined the group. The Procurador stood among them, listening as Mendoza talked. Otermín looked up as his second-in-command approached, saluted and reported: there had been no difficulties en route. Don Antonio smiled his approval. Then his attention was again drawn to the arguments of Mendoza who began talking again as though he had been interrupted by the Lieutenant General's arrival.

"We must return to the north at once, Excellency. As loyal vassals of His Majesty, we cannot withdraw from his lands now that the women are safe. The procurador here offers to supply us with food and what equipment he can buy to the south. And I do not see how we can refuse. If we just capture some of the Christian rebels, treat them well and send them back to tell the others how we feel about them, then we will be able to reconquer the territory, and . . ."

His flow of words came to a stop as García snorted as loudly as he could before he began to chuckle. Mendoza looked from the Governor to his deputy, hoping that the Captain General would discipline the man. When he saw that Otermín was silent, he spoke out himself. "I am only proposing what the Lieutenant Governor himself proposed in Socorro."

García shook his huge head. "No. There I proposed we reconnoitre the area to the north to see if any lived, and perhaps help them. What you now propose is that we undertake a reconquest. It makes little sense. The circumstances are changed. We are far from the last Nuevo Mexicano pueblo. Our soldados are more weary, we are without arms or horses, we are burdened with families, and despite what the good padres can do for us, we are short of provisions. His Excellency will have to report to the Viceroy. We will have to request professional soldados who know how to fight. We will need every man who can ride to cover the neighbouring provinces for food. Then we will have to build shelter before winter reaches us. We are no longer talking about a rescue party. We are planning a reconquest."

Mendoza started to appeal to the Captain General, But Don Antonio's hand went up to stop him. "I will think about this and give you an answer. In the meantime," he looked about, saw Márquez and gave his orders directly, "notify the camp by the voice of the crier and the sound of the drum that there will be a muster beginning as soon as the noon meal is completed. Each man will pass before me accompanied by all the members of his family. He will carry with him his personal property, including arms, ammunition, and provisions." Then to the others he explained, "I have been thinking for days that we must plan for more than immediate necessities. We can only do this if we know our strength and our numbers."

He stared at Márquez until the young man, realizing he was excused, saluted and left to carry out his orders. Then Otermín placed one hand on García's shoulder and walked away with him, leaving the others behind.

Once they were where they could not be heard, the Captain General asked, "And why do you think Mendoza and his compañeros are so anxious to move north now when they pressed so hard to move south just weeks ago?"

García shook his head. "They are protesting their loyalty to His Majesty so completely that I do not understand it, Excellency."

Otermín was silent for a time as he listened to Márquez's crier in the distance. "Mendoza lost members of his family?"

Don Alonso nodded. "Many, Excellency. But that did not prevent his wanting to run earlier."

Rubbing his beard with the back of his hand, Otermín mused, "The man is no knave. I assume that the two of you do not work well together."

García did not know if this was a question or a statement. He did not know how he could explain his feelings about the arrogant hidalgo and the sons of the old families to someone so closely allied to them in background. He remained silent.

"Perhaps time will reveal what we need to know," Otermín finally said, closing the subject as he walked away in search of María.

29

HORSES and cattle milled about the plaza mayor of the Villa de Santa Fe while pigs rooted in the casas reales and the church of the Immaculate Conception. The puebleños lounged in the shadows of the buildings watching the women wash their clothes in the irrigation ditch which fed the palacio, and the stench of the uncleaned streets permeated the town.

Inside the palacio Popé stood at the window of the office that had been the Governor's. He no longer wore the jaguar pelt about his waist. The bull-horn headdress lay upon the table. His leggings were dirty from the bare floor where he slept. And as he looked at the swarms of Indians lazing about the plaza, the tall priest picked up a piece of wax from an old candela that he had found on the sill. For some reason he could not understand, Popé could not enter this room without thinking of the young war chief of Taos whom he had turned upon the night after the Spaniards abandoned the Villa. Only Popé knew why he had attacked Juan, and only Popé knew how much he feared the sound of Spanish voices and the flash of Spanish genius. If there was anything which still brought forth the passions of Popé, it was his dread of the departed enemy, and Juan had been the symbol of that enemy.

But why was he unable to relax and enjoy his victory? Of course, there were certain things which must yet be attended to: the Apaches and the final disposition of the column in the South. Perhaps when everything was done . . .

He crossed to the reception room where he knew the Apache chiefs waited to meet with him. Three of the barbarians had ridden in early that morning with their escort on his invitation, and Popé had let them wait. He believed they would be impressed with the puebleño capital which had been the Whiteface capital, that they would see the cannon and not know that they were useless, that they would notice the guards armed with Spanish sabres and Spanish harquebuses, and that as they waited, they would become aware of his confidence. Now he went to meet them in his own casa because he was afraid to insult their honour. The three Apache chiefs rose from the floor where they had seated themselves near the chairs and couch, and waited for the medicine man who was now the leader of the puebleños to speak. The invitation had been his and because of it, they had held back from attacking the pueblo kingdom.

Popé looked at the tall, lean warriors with the painted faces, the bows in their hands, the filled quivers slung over their shoulders, and the scalps hanging at their waists. His attention was held for a time by a black scalp with tightly kinked hair. The warrior who wore the scalp rubbed one hand over it as he boasted, "A great brown giant who killed six warriors before he died. His woman is now my third woman." Then he became silent and waited again as Popé in many words offered to buy the friendship of the Apaches with herds of Spanish cattle and Spanish horses. The three chiefs listened and agreed, knowing full well that when they wanted more, they would be able to return for it. Then Popé walked with them to the entrance of the palacio, and after pledging friendship, watched them walk into the plaza, select whatever horses they wanted from those that were tethered there, and ride out without a single protest being raised by the puebleñoes.

As Popé watched, he could see the small band of horsemen ride into the plaza mayor from the south. They were dusty, and their horses were sweated. They rode directly across the plaza to the palacio where their leader dismounted. Popé could see the bright red scar on the side of his face. He also saw his guards move out to block the warrior's passage. A brief discussion followed which he could not hear, and then as he returned to his room, he could hear the warrior enter.

So many runners had come and gone since the People had accepted the idea of rebellion, so many plans had been laid and so many men buried. Popé tried to shake off the lethargy which had held him since the first days in the Villa. He walked back to the large table behind which he greeted his visitors in much the same manner that his predecessors had. Here he took what he believed was a formal pose. His dark hands rested on the top of the table. His knees pressed against the edge of it as he sat rigidly upright in the hard, uncomfortable chair. Disciplined from youth to believe in symbols and signs, he did not move a muscle as the door opened and the two guards entered with the war chief from the south. When they stood before him, Popé nodded slowly as he had seen Treviño nod when he himself had stood before the Governor as a prisoner five years before. The war chief was nervous. His fingers traced the mark on his face as he stared at the foreign formalities of the room—the straight chairs, the large table, the torn tapestries. Finally his eyes came to rest on the bull-horn headdress. This was a familiar symbol.

Popé was patient. He had seen others confused, and he recalled how he had felt when he had stood in chains on the other side of this very table.

"We followed them to a place above the Pass where they have halted," the war chief said. He was angry, but he did not know why.

"Beyond the desert?" Popé asked.

The war chief nodded. The resentment was growing but he could not explain to himself what he was angry about. And when Popé asked, "Is there more?" he shook his head.

Only when the tall medicine man waved him off as though he were brushing something away did the youth realize that the priest of San Juan reminded him of the Spanish Governor he had seen conclude the assembly on the portico of an estancia weeks before. His lips set tightly as he strode from the room, out of the palacio to the place where his men waited for him. He paused to look back at what was now the capitol of the pueblo kingdom, shook his head in bewilderment, mounted his horse and led his men out of the Villa south and home.

Popé sat back in his chair and thought for a long time. Now there was no longer a Spaniard in the land of the pueblos. Now the People were rid of the enemy and the enemy was beyond the desert. It was over. His task was truly done. But he did not know what was expected of him beyond this point. He had planned for war and there had been war. He had never really planned the time beyond victory, and now there was victory. He wondered what Governor Otermín would do in his place. He tried to think as the absent Spaniard would think. But he could not. For a fleeting instant he wished he could consult with the youth of Taos, but that young man and his Spanish woman had journeyed across the rio to the place where the sun rests.

Popé slapped his large hands together as he had watched Treviño do that only time he had ever observed a governor in action. Two guards stepped into the room. The tall medicine man stood up behind the table that had replaced his jaguar pelt as a symbol of authority and spoke loudly as he believed a Spanish governor would speak.

"Notify the caciques of each pueblo that the enemy has departed our land. There will be a great dinner here in the palacio that was the Spaniards' and we will celebrate our success." Somehow the words did not flow as readily as they had before. There was hesitancy now and uncertainty. He knew he had celebrated this victory before, but the great priest who had bound the

People together and led them from their bondage no longer knew where he could take them, and so he followed the only precedent he knew—the Spanish. And he found himself fumbling with unfamiliar symbols.

He waited until the guards left. Then he sat down again and wondered what he would do after the dinner which he would hold at the great table of the Governor and if he could find still another excuse for not going to San Juan to see his daughter and explain to her why he had been forced to kill her husband, Nicolás Bua, who was the father of her children.

Seated alone in the room that had belonged to his enemy, Popé knew the same silence he had known when he had stood over the dead body of the padre of Taos. Suddenly, he crashed his fists down on the table top, and as the pain spread through his numbed hands, he was not conscious how meaningless was the sound he had made.

30

THE fields of La Salineta were the grey, dusty green of the desert's edge. The scraggy mesquite bushes spread their vicious leaves over the broken ground. There were no shadows. There was no shade. The furnace sun baked the red earth and split the dunes heaped by the hot winds and withered the leaves of the dwarf cedar trees.

The Rio del Norte trimmed the fields to the south as it flowed eastward. In the distance beyond, the mountains opened onto Mexico.

Near the rio a file of men and women and children waited to take their turns before the table where the Governor sat with Barnabe Márquez, drawing up a muster roll. The count was slow.

A husband. A wife. The number of their children dead. The number of horses they owned. And the weapons.

An old man. His wife dead. His children dead. On foot. Without arms.

A widow. Her husband killed by the Indians. With six children. Extremely poor.

A convict with a horse, a mule, a wife, and one small child. A daga belonging to His Majesty. Two female servants.

The Governor nodded as each signed the roll before him or made his mark because he could not sign it. He had seen these faces before. Not any one in particular. Not a face that he could remember. The first group drifting into the Villa de Santa Fe after the warning, the others running in without food or clothes, the ones needing shelter, the men who had ridden into battle with him on the first day when victory was almost theirs, and the second day when it belonged to the enemy, and that last sortie when they held it in their hands and it was as worthless as thistles.

Another set of faces before the table. Another name. He believed he recognized the face of the man who held open the gate of the compound of the casas reales as they marched out into the sun with the women and children and turned south. He signed the muster, no longer aware that he was doing it. Another set of faces and he no longer heard the names as he reached for a mug set on the table for his comfort and recalled another drink at another time so long ago that it might never have happened. But he remembered and knew that it had happened. *My mother, one of the first white women ever to make the jornada del muerto.* So many had made it now. And still he could hear the old man speaking as he had spoken that night when he could not bring himself to say where he thought trouble might begin. And the same voice drifted across his mind like a tumbleweed. *Some of us do not have the right to die, Excellency. Me, I can die for I am an old man.* And though he had died the words were still there, and Otermín responded to the touch on his shoulder as though he expected to see the old Maestre de Campo. It was García instead. The Governor bent forward to hear the words that were whispered in his ear.

"I know why Mendoza and his friends wanted to move out, Excellency." Otermín wondered for a moment what was being said. Then he looked up and waited for the explanation.

"Supplies, Excellency. They hoped you would issue what supplies we had before they left."

It was still just words. He nodded. The sun hurt his eyes. He squinted and the crow's-feet grew. "Before they left?" he asked.

"Several hundred have ridden south in the past few hours. Mendoza and his friends were among them."

"Mexico?"

"And Nueva Viscaya. From there anything south is safer and more comfortable than wintering here or riding north."

For García this was a vindication, and Otermín knew it. Then he was aware of what the flight really meant, and he snorted and turned his attention again to the faces before the table. García paused for a moment as though he expected something, saw the Governor wave his hand as though to close the discussion, then he drifted away.

Otermín watched him go and thought of the orders he would have to issue. Tried to focus on them: messages to the governors and alcaldes mayores of the neighbouring provinces. Every one who has left will be returned. Fines will be levied. No arrangements made by refugees beyond the border of their home province will be legal or binding.

He signed the muster set before him, watched the old hidalgo count his sons and grandsons and daughters and daughters-in-law on his fingers to check the count of Márquez who kept looking about for the young widow with the infant.

Otermín's thoughts did not stay with the counting. His eyes followed the retreating form of the Lieutenant Governor as that old warrior wandered about the fields as though he were looking for someone. He watched the already familiar gesture of the fist in the palm as García stopped before a pretty blonde woman seated on the ground combing her hair and he wished he could hear what they were saying.

For Don Alonso García the words came with greater ease than he thought they would. He had been postponing this decision ever since the column had marched out of Fray Cristóbal. During all the days of the march he had avoided his wife, but he knew he could avoid her no longer. Soon he would have to walk up to the table and sign the muster roll and list his family, his losses, and his possessions. And he knew he had to take into account this woman who sat on the ground looking up at him. She was one of the facts of his life. He knelt down before her so that their eyes could meet. She was still beautiful despite the sun and the long fatigue.

"You want to go home to España. I shall arrange for you to go," he said softly.

Her hand came down to her lap as she fumbled with the comb. Her husband was not asking her anything, and suddenly she tried to understand just what he had said, in terms of España so far away—a home that no longer existed, and the sullen face of the gambler who was her father. And all she could do was keep turning the comb in her lap over and over.

"I shall arrange for your travel to Vera Cruz. I shall give you money for passage."

Josefa waited to hear more.

"And that is all I have." The soft voice again. "You will be on your own. There is nothing more that I will be able to do for you."

He said what he had come to say. For his part there was nothing more.

She nodded slowly as she struggled to comprehend what all this meant to her, and found that she could not think at all.

"There is nothing left for me in España," she finally said.

He shook his head sadly. "I shall arrange for someone to take you south." He rose to his feet and looked beyond her. "I am sorry for you, Josefa, but there is nothing more that I can do."

As he walked away, the Governor, sitting at the long table across the field, saw the pretty woman begin to comb her hair again. He wondered who she was, but not for long. There were more faces before him again.

A bachelor with two lean and saddle-galled horses, an harquebus, and a sword. In addition, a mother, three grown sisters and a female servant. He did not know how to sign.

Another face. And while they were inspecting the weapons to see if they belonged to His Majesty, the Governor wondered what the small group of alcaldes mayores were discussing near the rio and why the Cabildo of the Villa de Santa Fe was joining them.

A family of eight, including brothers and small children. And another set of faces and the leathered face of a crone thrust into his asking why he did not do something about the poverty and the hunger and the Indians. Then the count. Four nieces. Spaniards, all on foot and extremely poor. More than thirty relatives dead. There was nothing he could say, and so he listened as the old woman reviled him. Then he signed the muster because she did not know how and looked up at the next set of faces, wondering all the time why he had not been consulted about the meeting that was taking place only a hundred varas away and who the fat woman was who was talking and what she was saying that interested all of them for so long. And then he recognized Señora Isabella Quintana and wondered why he had seen so little of her small husband since . . . he did not remember when.

More faces and he looked away as though to avoid them. The tall ranchero standing beside the blonde woman with the clock and a small boy. No horses. No arms. Otermín signed without thinking.

Beside the fires to the east of the field he could make out the Franciscan Brothers in their grey cassocks. Wondered what their meeting was about. Tried to recall how many of their number had died. Vaguely, twenty-one came to mind. But most of them were only names to him. He had not met them, and of those he had met, it was only the aged Fray Custodio who had made his mark on the Governor. He missed the old man now, missed the gentle air which he always appreciated in a man of God, and wished there were more like him.

Another face and hands fumbling for the table's edge. The blind woman from the Villa. Otermín watched Márquez reach out a hand to steady her, looked again at the youth who had refused to identify his wife and wondered how he would have reacted himself. He was glad Márquez had taken up with the woman whose son was born during the retreat.

The padres across the field were separating now, going their own ways. The Governor could make out the brisk walk of the hardened missionary from Valladolid and he recalled the night the efficient padre relaxed and talked of a farm that had been divided into too many pieces. He felt sorry for the young man, wondered what all the violence and tumult had done to his neat world, and wished that they had been able to understand each other better. He watched as the padre selected a horse out of the caballada and waited while a soldado saddled the beast. The padre was staring at the refugees trying to make themselves comfortable in the burnt fields. Otermín wondered what he was thinking.

Fray Pedro Martínez nodded across the distance that separated him from the Governor. He was going to ride out now, south again with a mission to accomplish, eighty leagues to travel. Fray Francisco was going to offer the Governor ten beeves and thirteen bushels of shelled maize daily and it would be the task of the rugged, well-organized padre to purchase those supplies and shepherd them north. He did not mind the task before him. He felt it suited him. He did not even mind that his Brothers, with the aid of the Fray Procurador, had selected another to serve as Fray Custodio when there were missions in the north again. He wondered where his ambitions had gone and if he were not a wiser man without them. Somewhere in the weeks which had passed, he had lost the desire to judge his fellows, and as he watched the lean figure of Fray Julio move among the women and children and saw how eagerly they turned to him, he wondered how one man judges another, how young he had been to pass judgment on a Brother like Fray Rafael, martyred, and how he had ever believed that he would have made a better Fray Custodio than another.

He had learned much about himself in the lonely days of the uprising and retreat—that he was not the only man who was mute, that each man is in his own way silent, that for each there is a gap of time or colour or sex or situation he cannot span with words and the horror is in the silence which lies between.

The horse was ready. The small escort the procurador had delegated to travel with Fray Pedro mounted. There was no longer any reason to delay. Fray Pedro pulled himself into the saddle, hoping that on this jornada he would be of greater help to the refugees than he had been on the one coming south, waved to the Custodio Elect and smiled across the fields at the Governor who nodded in recognition as he bent his head to sign another set of names onto the muster roll.

When the Governor looked up again, there were more faces and beyond them he could see the disappearing back of Fray Pedro as he forded the rio. Another face. The woman with the infant born on the jornada. He heard no questions as Márquez wrote quickly on the muster roll and turned it toward his commander. Otermín read this one before signing:

Teniente Barnabe Márquez. Twenty-three years. Wife and infant child. One horse, spavined, and a sword.

Otermín dipped his quill into the ink and signed. The tall padre's doing. He smiled, tried ignoring the conversation between the new husband and wife as he looked about the fields for Fray Julio. He made out the gaunt figure with the limp arm among the children near the stream. Otermín wondered if he would ever have had the courage to move out of Isleta if he had not met the padre on the bank that morning, wondered how many others had drawn their courage in these last weeks from the soft-spoken pastor with the compassionate eyes.

Across the fields, Fray Julio was telling the children who had gathered in a tight circle about him the story of Fray Rafael. Julio felt comfortable and at ease. Only once this day had he even thought of the years behind him and of Beatriz. He would pray for her when night came again, as he did every night, and as he would as long as he lived. He would never know that when the time came for her to bear her child, the Indians of Santa Flora staked her out in the empty mission compound with her legs tied together at the knees. He would never know that, dying, she cursed his desertion. But he would spend the rest of his years as Fray Custodio. And when he died, people would speak in wonder of the Years of Fray Julio.

The Governor turned his attention to the faces again. Don whatever-his-name-was. Three married sons. Wives killed by the Indians. Four horses, lean and useless. An harquebus belonging to His Majesty. He signed the roll. Looking across the fields as he signed, Otermín saw the Alcalde Mayor of Jémez and La Cañada leave the meeting that was breaking up and hurry over to the courier who was preparing to ride to Ciudad Mexico to carry the reports of the Governor and the procurador. He wondered what the two bantams wanted of the courier and what had taken place at the meeting. Then he saw the pretty woman whom the Lieutenant General had spoken to earlier cross the field to talk with the courier.

More faces. A ranchero. No weapons. Two female servants. The ranchero signed for himself.

And Otermín saw Don Alonso García standing near by with his sons.

García watched Josefa mount the horse that had been saddled for her and ride out of the camp behind the courier. She never took her eyes off the Pass that lay between the mountains to the south. She seemed small in the saddle of the last good horse he owned. He placed his arms about the shoulders of his two oldest sons and smiled at the younger ones. It had been Don Pedro de Leiva who had spoken of the small satisfaction of revenge. He knew now what the corpulent hidalgo had meant. He knew, too, that despite his own titles and his own hopes, he was still a pesos-and-wine man, still a scrabbler after enough to eat. His younger sons were leading the horses that were left to him. His own armour and weapons hung from the saddle of his stallion. His compañeros stood with him. They would register as part of his household. Several were accompanied by women, and he noticed that the sad-eyed wench with the long lashes was among them. Missing Nita now as he threw his shoulders back, he walked to the head of the long line that ended before the Governor's table.

Otermín watched him approach, wondered who the woman was who forded the stream behind the courier, and if he should protest another flight from the province. But he did not act. Whatever his reasons, there was pain enough on the face of the old Mexicano who stood before him. Slowly the Captain General began to dictate to Márquez:

"Lieutenant General Don Alonso García, Lieutenant of the Governor in the jurisdicciones of Rio Abajo, passed muster with . . ." He waited.

"Eight horses and five mules." It was García's youngest son who spoke. Otermín continued. "All lean, suffering from lockjaw and worn out." García nodded.

"His four sons. They have a complement of personal arms supplied by . . ." And he saw García tap his own chest. "Supplied by the said Lieutenant General. García is a native of . . ."

"Zacatecas." There was pride in the old warrior's voice as he admitted what he was. "And he is fifty-four years of age."

While Márquez copied this down, Otermín counted down the line. He recognized the hardened faces of old campaigners and the soft faces of the young men and women who had attached themselves for protection to the García household.

"Eighteen servants and an harquebus belonging to His Majesty."

He stared up at García who nodded his agreement.

Otermín reached for the document as Márquez signed it. He added his name and turned the paper about so that García could sign it. The old soldado signed with a flourish. Then he stepped back and saluted his commander. Otermín watched as García walked away across the open field with his retinue behind him. Then he turned his attention to the next person in the line.

Luis and Isabella Quintana. The Governor nodded his recognition as Márquez began to write. Neither the small man nor his obese wife smiled. They waited until they were recorded on the muster roll and the Governor had signed in his turn. Then Otermín saw the woman nudge her husband.

Hesitantly, Quintana drew a document from inside his shirt and held it out to Don Antonio. Surprised, Otermín accepted the paper and waited for an explanation before reading.

"It is the report of the Cabildo of the Villa and certain Alcaldes Mayores. We have just dispatched it with the courier to his Excellency, the Viceroy, in Ciudad Mexico."

The husband and wife waited for Otermín to read the document, and as he opened it, he saw Granillo of Jémez push up to the head of the line to stand beside Quintana.

Quickly Otermín scanned the statement. At the bottom were the signatures: Quintana's was there. Granillo's—a procurador—signing on behalf of another. Those men with whom he had met when the first warning of the uprising had reached the Villa de Santa Fe. The contents: complaints and accusations. Irresponsibility in leaving the main body to attack while in retreat. . . . Negligence of duty because of a woman. . . . Negligence of duty in alerting the colonists in time. . . . Irascibility with the clergy, namely one Fray Pedro Martínez who would not speak out on his own behalf. . . . Preference for professionals who were equally incompetent. . . . Failure to maintain proper communications between the Villa de Santa Fe and Isleta. . . . Error of judgment and personal involvement in the selection of a courier to Isleta. . . . Failure to consult with the Cabildo since the actual beginning of the uprising and forcing the Cabildo to demand a withdrawal. And so forth and so forth.

It was all there. Very little that could be misinterpreted was not misinterpreted. The Governor very carefully set the document on the table before him. The garrulous Alcalde Mayor of Jémez was smiling. The Quintanas were not. It was Señora Isabella who shook her head slowly as he stared at her.

"You brought us through it, Excellency. For this we are thankful. But for the other things. . . " Her voice trailed off as he rose to his feet and walked away from the line without a word.

For a time Otermín felt a numbness. He had difficulty seeing where he was walking and the refugees parted to let him pass. His deep-set eyes seemed to recede into his head. Once, as he stumbled across the field, he paused to rub his small grey beard with the back of his right hand, and when he took the hand away he stared at it, remembering the days when he had not even been able to feel pain. The days of battle with the Indians swarming about him and the vomit and sweat and the noise came up from the hot field and overwhelmed him again. He shook his head and wandered down toward the stream. Some children were playing there, but they moved away as they saw the Governor approach. There was something in his face that frightened them, something in his manner which bordered on fury, and they glanced back at him several times as they made their way back to the fields where their parents were standing in small groups talking about the Captain General. Everyone knew that the Cabildo had protested to the Viceroy. No one could have kept the action secret, and there were none who wanted to. For a long time Don Antonio stood staring at the slow-moving waters of the Rio del Norte. Then he realized that María was standing beside him. She placed a hand on his arm and they stood together looking up the rio down which they had travelled.

"You know?" he asked.

She nodded. "It was the Quintana woman."

He shook his head slowly. "She was the only one of them capable of making it sound so reasonable." Then without being aware that he was doing it, he began to lose his temper. All of the pent-up fury spilled over as he thought of what that document meant. "They waited, waited until I dragged them through the hell and hunger of it, waited until there were no more Indians eager to bury them, waited until there was no question that they were safe and their bellies full. They waited until they no longer needed someone to guide them and fight for them and get his gut slashed for them and lose his friends for them. They waited until they were here, seated on the safety of their big behinds to let their small brains suddenly decide that they could have done it better. What single one of them could have brought them through the siege, could have led them into the battles and brought them out of the Villa with only five men dead? What one of them could have driven them as a column and not a mob with a hundred heads?" He paused, and when he spoke again, his voice was soft. "Who else could have brought them here to be fed and cared for? No one. They knew it then and they know it now. But now they can grovel and spew out their excrement and dirty the names of their betters. Madre de Dios! And all because that Quintana woman wanted power for her black-toothed peon with the smelling mouth."

Otermín slipped down to sit on a rock, and María knelt on the ground at his feet and put her head in his lap as she listened to him, aware that he was talking to her and trying to understand all that he was saying and not certain at all that the understanding of it was as important as the fact that he was shedding his anger and his pain.

She looked up into his face and saw the wrinkles there, the burn of the months in the sun, and the pain about his eyes. And she reached up and touched his cheek. His hand went over her fingers, and he held still for a moment. Then he began to talk again.

"I can see some small clerk with a quill behind his ear and pesos for the evening bread in his pocket reading the complaint, horrified at the implications. I can see him bustle over to another clerk and together they will embroider the report into treason and rush it with stark faces to the deputies of the Viceroy who have never known the bite of a sabre or the heat of the sun braising their brains. All they will understand is that some other fools have written a document stating that they have been treated as fools and together they will scurry up a quiet corridor to bring the horror of it before the Viceroy. That idiot will read the document and all the appended notes and recommendations and wonder if he is supposed to do something about it or if he took the time to do something about it whether some good señora would be kept waiting for him to diddle her. I can see him sniffing twice and then calling for a council to act and meanwhile . . ."

He stopped as María's hand went over his mouth. "You must have friends in Ciudad Mexico."

He kissed her finger tips and pulled her hand down into his lap as he thought for a moment. "Yes, there are some there who will remember what I have done for thirty years, and even some who will bother to call it to the Viceroy's attention, if it does not mean he will associate them with my failures." He snorted. Then he was very still.

"I am not so certain now old Pando was right. Perhaps it would have been better to die back there. Pando said there were reasons why I should not die, could not. But now I am not convinced he was right. Now I have run, have taken everyone with me and the province is empty and the fault will always be mine, even if there was no other choice but to stay and go down there fighting as he and others did."

María saw that he was almost sobbing now that the anger had left him and the despair was taking over. She remembered how he had reacted after the decision to abandon his capital. She had wondered then why tears after victory as she wondered now why tears after a magnificent withdrawal that had saved the lives of all of them. She started to tell him as much and he brushed his eyes with the back of his hand and then squeezed her arm affectionately.

"It is a matter of . . ." He struggled with the word. *Honour* sounded almost correct, but he knew that it was more than this. He himself was under attack, his judgment, and then he realized that his relationship to María was under attack and in official places where no one would understand. He saw that he himself had never understood before and he lifted her face so that he could look at it. His stubby fingers tightened about her jaw as he knew that it had all been worth the effort. She was safe as were the others. "My decisions were right," he said, as he remembered thinking weeks before that survival might be victory. "I will have the hides of those who dispute my judgment."

María relaxed as he did. Everything was going to be all right now. He was not angry from pain and he was not sorry for himself. He was, as she believed a governor and captain general should be, convinced and sure and aware of the power he could wield. This image of him matched the one she had of authority, and in her simplicity she did not know that it was the image Don Antonio had himself. But the difference between them, and the one she was to learn, was that while everyone held the image, no one matched it all the time.

But Otermín was already thinking of something else as he rose to his feet and helped her to hers. "We are going to rest here for a time and then we are going to settle at the Pass where the food the padres have promised us will be more easily available. And as soon as possible, we are going back," and he gestured northward. "The land belongs to España and God."

María nodded, trying to understand why this was so important to him. "And then?"

He was smiling now as he turned her toward him. "And then I am going to find a villa somewhere in Mexico and we are going to live there. No one will have the right to expect anything of us, and I am going to rest and enjoy it to the end."

She saw that he was not asking anything of her and that she was not expected to give him any answers. But she did not mind. He was a governor, a grandee, and he took her hand as they went in search of Inez.

It was almost dusk when they returned to the table where Márquez was totalling the muster.

The lieutenant looked up at the Governor and his lady and the little girl who stood at their side.

Otermín picked up the muster roll and read the totals. Nineteen hundred and forty-three men, women, and children. One hundred and fifty-five able to bear arms, fewer than thirty-six of these fully equipped, while the rest were naked, on foot, and without arms.

And then the other total, the dead: twenty-one Brothers, three hundred and eighty men, women, and children. Don Antonio wondered how many had fled across the rio and how many of those who had lived would survive the hardships of the jornada they had just completed. But he had difficulty reconciling these figures of the dead with the people themselves— with Ismael Pando, the Fray Custodio, and all of the others, known to him and unknown. After a long time, he set the document on the table, picked up a pen and added himself, María, and Inez to the totals. Finally, he pushed the muster across the table to the lieutenant.

With one arm about María and the other about Inez he walked through the camp. His shoulders settled back. In the north he could see the rio disappear among the silent hills. He was already planning the route he would take when he returned to his capital.

AUTHOR'S NOTE

1

In the years that followed, Antonio de Otermín attempted to reconquer the lost province for España and God. Alonso García, Jr., rode beside him, as did certain members of the Mendoza family. But his support from the Viceroy was inadequate, and though his route north was marked by the fires which consumed the katchinas and kivas of the puebleños, he was forced to admit failure and return to el Paso del Norte. In 1683, another Governor was appointed, and Antonio de Otermín disappeared from history.

In the ensuing years, Popé was also to have his troubles. The year following the revolt brought one of the worst drouths in the history of the province as well as increased violence by the Apaches. For a time the medicine man from San Juan was removed as leader of his people, but after continued misfortune the puebleños turned to him once again. He died sometime before Captain General Don Pedro de Vargas marched north in 1692 and re-entered the Villa de Santa Fe. After the recapture of the palacio itself, Vargas executed the seventy puebleños who had fought to hold the building, and sold four hundred of their women and children into slavery.

2

In the telling of this story I have taken certain liberties with history. They have been fewer than those not familiar with the details might imagine. In some instances I have combined the office and activities of actual characters and given them fictional names. The two pueblos of Santa Flora and San Ysidro are fictional, as are all of their inhabitants. Antonio de Otermín, Popé, Alonso Garcia, Fray Francisco de Ayeta, Pedro de Leiva, Dorotea de Leiva, Luis Quintana, Luis Granillo, and many others were actual participants in the tragedy. The complaint of the Cabildo against the Governor was not prepared until a later date than that given, and the actual muster itself required several days to complete. There was a small mission and a cluster of huts on the south bank of the Rio del Norte in the autumn of 1680, but the arrival of the refugees from the north established the town of El Paso, which has since been renamed Juarez.

3

Of the many volumes consulted, the following were the most valuable. *Revolt of the Pueblo Indians of New Mexico and Otermín's Attempted Reconquest 1680-82,* prepared by Charles Wilson Hackett and Charmion Clair Shelby, contains an excellent historical summary of the revolt and translations of the documents prepared by the participants. The articles of Francis V. Scholes on seventeenth-century New Mexico in the *New Mexico Historical Review* were indispensable, as were the *Pueblo Indian Religion* by Elsie Clews Parons; *The Spanish Empire in America by* C. H. Haring; and *A Documented History of the Franciscan Order* by Father Raphael M. Huber. Other volumes which were of special value were *Historical Documents Relating to New Mexico, etc.,* collected by Adolph F. A. Bandelier and Fanny R. Bandelier and edited by Charles Wilson Hackett, *Sky Determines* by Ross Calvin, *The Romanticism of St. Francis* by Father Cuthbert, *Benavides' Memorial of 1630* as translated by Peter P. Forrestal, *The Concept of Martyrdom According to St. Cyprian of Carthage* by Edelhard L. Hummel, *New Mexico's Royal Road* by Max L. Moorhead, *Spanish Churches in New Mexico* by L. Bradford Prince, and *Masked Gods* by Frank Waters.